Red
Journe

By Michael Reuel Teller

In Memoriam

To my father, may his memory be a blessing – I carry
him with me always;
To my uncle, who did not live to see the completion of
this quest;
To the Beckers' beloved daughter, cut down in her
youth – may G-d avenge her blood;
To the friends I lost along the way.

Copyright © 2021, 2022 Bradford J. Hauser
Second Edition © 2023
All rights reserved.

Edited by Joshua B. Hauser

Cover art by Yehonatan E. Hauser

Chapter Artwork Credit: NASA
(United States National Aeronautics and Space Administration)

This is a work of fiction. Names, characters, places and incidents either are the products of the author's imagination or are used fictitiously. Any resemblance to actual persons, living or dead, businesses, companies, events or locales is entirely coincidental.

ISBN-13: 978-965-93055-3-7

Contents

MiniHab	5
Providence	22
Electricity	36
Water	51
Orbit	66
Gravity	84
Autumn	101
Departure	122
Thanksgiving	144
Falling	168
Spinning	187
Trial	208
Air	231
Misgiving	252
Sun	266
Meital	282
Spring	303
Loss	318
Doriel	335
Missive	353
Dana	364
Breech	382
Adele	396
Simeon	422
Return	443
Moon	461
Mars	476

Dramatis Personae

Michael Reuel Teller..........the narrator
Dana Teller......................physicist, chemist, engineer; Michael's mother
Meital, and
    Shirel............................his younger sisters
Denver Günter König........his best friend

Dietrich Becker..................dentist, electrical engineer; captain of the ship
Cecylia Becker....................biologist, agronomist; Dietrich's wife
Helga, and
    Marcelina (Celina)......their young adult daughters

Jhonathan Meyer................physician, radiation engineer; first officer
Esther Meyer.....................metallurgist, geologist; Jhonathan's wife
Samuel David...................their teenage son
Rebecca (Ruby), and
    Susan (Susy)................their young teenage daughters

Louis Bouchet....................physician, life-support systems engineer
Claudine Bouchet...............surgeon, biologist; Louis's wife
Jasmine, and
    Sophie..........................their young daughters

Omar Sidda......................agronomist, mycologist
Boris Radechov..................systems engineer
Simeon Radechov...............electrical engineer; Boris's younger brother

MiniHab

Sunday, September 24th, 2028 16:30

It wasn't supposed to be this way! I was not supposed to be so sickeningly anxious, and my sister Meital should not have been digging her fingernails into my arm on the armrest, and poor Ruby's vomiting was completely unplanned. I was not supposed to be feeling fear, trepidation, and uncertainty. One does not train for the mission of a lifetime, to fulfill a dream of humanity, and then, when the quest finally begins, feel anything but excitement. Especially when one has spent his entire adolescence training and preparing. True, this was our first time in actual spaceflight. The liftoff's roaring noise and terrifying shaking and lurching was new to us – we had experienced no such thing during our microgravity training. We had now been weightless for fifteen minutes, far more than the forty-five seconds spent in each parabolic peak during those training flights. My pride was injured: I had imagined that we were ready for the undertaking. The anxiousness and vomiting belied the hubris.

Here we were – finally, after so many years of preparation! – lying in a row of flight couches, on the lower deck of a Murke Industries MiniHab capsule. To my left were Meital and our younger sister Shirel; to my right was Ruby. According to the flight clock in the ceiling display, we had launched twenty-three minutes and forty-five seconds earlier, which meant that my friends and I had joined the rarefied ranks of adolescent astronauts. I was the second-oldest young man on this shuttle; of the youth, only my best friend

Denver, soon to be eighteen, was older. He was riding on the upper deck with Captain Becker, Dr. Claudine Bouchet and Dr. Claudine's little girl Sophie. Ruby's mother, Dr. Esther Meyer, was right below us, on the lower half of the lower deck, holding hands with Susan, Ruby's little sister, and Jasmine Bouchet, Sophie's older sister. Ruby joked that her mother was the chaperone for the field trip. But field trips last a few days at most, do not require seven years of preparation, and rarely involve leaving home permanently.

Probably permanently. My parents had made a twenty-five-year commitment, anticipating that technology for returning to Earth would be invented by then. Sadly, returning to Earth was no longer relevant for my father; his participation in this adventure had become permanent. I hoped that he would still be alive when we reached him ten months later. I prayed for a miracle, even just to hug him again. That hope, and the notion that we might someday be able to return, somehow made leaving easier.

I eagerly watched the ceiling above me. It was a continuous, wide nano-LED display: in the latest MiniHab update, every centimeter displayed data, or animations, or pictures from outside. This was the spaceship version of the NLED wallpaper that had become ubiquitous in houses around the world. That is, the old world, the world we had just left, the world that now appeared on the screen in brilliant blues and greens. Nineteen minutes after first-stage separation, the computer displayed the red-striped second stage and our MiniHab over the Caribbean, at an elevation of 243 kilometers, traveling more than twenty-eight thousand kilometers per hour. The second-stage engine had completed its first burn, but we could not yet release our straps and buckles, as there was still one more rocket burn to go.

"Ruby, take another vomit bag," I said, reaching to hand her the pouch from my launch-pack. The couches were oriented in opposite directions, so I could see that her face was pale. She forced a smile as she took the bag. Holding it over her mouth, she heaved, spit up more of her last pre-flight meal, and quickly sealed it before the contents could float back out.

"Thanks, Michael," she said. "I hope that's all that's left. I'm glad I barely had any lunch before launch." She giggled at her own pun.

"I wish there were something more I could do for you," I said, feeling helpless. I pulled my hand from under Meital's and turned in her direction. "Meital and Shirel, how are you feeling? What's it like being in space for the first time?"

Shirel, at thirteen the baby in our family, had long brown hair, which she had bound in a knot for launch. She grinned at me. "This is awesome – like an endless drop on a roller coaster! I can't wait to unbuckle and float around the cabin."

Dark-haired Meital looked at her dubiously, wrinkling her freckled brow. "Interesting comparison, Shirel. I didn't think we signed up for an amusement park ride." She sighed. "We'll have gravity by the end of the week. That's what I'm most looking forward to."

"Me, too," I agreed, pressing my hand to my belly to calm the butterflies. "I hope this space-sickness doesn't last the whole time until then."

I tilted my head back to face the open hatch to the upper level, and called out, "Denver, how are you grown-ups doing up there?" There was no answer, which was not surprising, given the constant whirring noise of the atmosphere control systems.

Then Captain Becker's voice came over the intercom. "Everybody, prepare for the second burn for rendezvous orbit insertion, coming up in one minute. Make sure you are all still buckled in place. This burn will be only one gravity of thrust, and we will not feel the crushing weight we felt during launch, but I do not want to risk any injuries."

We braced for the sudden lurch of acceleration. Captain Becker counted down, "four, three, two, one, burn!" Although, in terms of physics, it was the flight couch that pushed up against me, it felt like I had fallen hard against the couch. I had my Earth weight back again, perhaps for the last time. The captain was right: the second stage's burns were easier to bear than the first stage's, though the shaking and vibration were not less intense.

Ruby groaned. "I'm not sure which is worse for my stomach, the weightlessness or this insufferable shuddering and vibration." At least she did not vomit again.

We followed the display as it counted down the time remaining. "Thirty seconds left," Meital called out. When the timer reached zero, the shuddering stopped as abruptly as it had begun and we were weightless again.

Captain Becker's voice came again. "Good news, fliers. It appears that all systems performed optimally, and we are perfectly on course. We will arrive, seventeen hours and forty-six minutes from now, at the spaceship habitat that will be our home during our upcoming journey. Lots to do now! Unbuckle and stow the straps. Everyone will meet on the upper deck in exactly twenty minutes, for a review of the atmosphere-conversion process. Use the bathroom if you need to. Go in order of age, youngest first. Remember, weightless protocol: make sure the vacuum fan stays engaged until everybody finishes."

We unbuckled, pushed ourselves out of our couches, and stretched. I clumsily banged my head against the ceiling before managing to grab one of the handholds. Meital and Ruby fared better: though Ruby's face was still pale, she glided out gracefully, frizzy hair floating freely. Neither of them looked happy, though both wore stoic expressions. Shirel, on the other hand, laughed ecstatically, performing somersaults in the weightlessness.

Dr. Esther called to us. "Michael and Ruby, while you are waiting for the bathroom, please unpack the fowl corrals and the egg incubator. We need to unharness the birds and pack their corrals into airtents. There's also the vermiculture carton – Meital, I want you to be responsible. Shirel and Susan, please help her. I'll get the airtents out."

I pulled myself from handhold to handhold across the flight couches, then across the packed piles of duffels. It was almost like swimming, but without any water resistance. I reached the bright blue wall of the bathroom, where the corrals and the incubator had been latched for launch. Apprehensively, I released the first corral and disconnected its power supply, while Ruby did the same for the second one. I pulled mine away from the wall and examined the two-week-old chicks through the plastic mesh. Sedated during launch, they were now beginning to stir. I removed them gently, one by one, from their harnesses. "Good news!" I called out. "All sixteen of the chicks are alive."

Ruby was less enthusiastic. "I'm not sure about these canaries and parakeets. Some of them aren't moving."

Dr. Esther brought us airtents. She glided over easily, barely touching any of the handholds. She was the only one to have flown in space before and seemed to need no time to adjust. "It's too early to tell," she said, resting her hand on her daughter's shoulder. "The duration of the tranquilizer's effect is very individualized. For now, Ruby, unharness only the ones that have awakened."

She handed out the airtents, one to me for the chicks and a smaller one to Meital for the worms. She demonstrated on the third tent, inserting the corral with the parakeets and canaries. "Unzip here and pull the sides over the cage. For now, leave the birds exposed. Tomorrow, before the atmosphere test, we'll cover the netting and seal the tents."

Ruby groaned as she took the airtent from her mother. "We know how to do this, Mom. We're not children: we've practiced this dozens of times!"

"You guys are astronauts now – I'll grant that – but whether you are no longer children – we'll see." She spoke sternly, but she was grinning.

We managed to finish packing the corrals and the vermiculture carton into airtents, and then re-latch them to the blue wall. I put the incubator with the eggs into a fourth airtent. There were slots for sixteen eggs, and I counted to make sure they all were full. The plan was for them to hatch in eight or ten days. In gravity, I hoped.

Dr. Esther handed out oxypack units for the airtents. They would supply oxygen to the birds and worms after we sealed them the following day. We all carried similar two-liter units on our utility belts, for personal use in case of emergency decompression. It was easy to attach the soda-bottle-sized oxypacks to the airtents' Velcro patches, but we needed Dr. Esther's help to make sure the oxygen seals were airtight. If we lost cabin pressure, the oxypack units would maintain air pressure and temperature in the tent, circulate the air, and filter out carbon dioxide, but only if they were sealed correctly.

Waiting our turns to use the bathroom, my sisters and I observed the stirring chicks and canaries through the airtents' netting. Susan joined us, cheeks pink with excitement. We were happy to see that most of the birds were moving, though a few were flapping their wings agitatedly, maybe because they felt like they were falling. Research had shown that chicks would calm down after fifteen or twenty minutes, and the smaller birds after thirty or forty, though stress would kill a percentage of them. Echoing my thoughts, Susan said, "I hope none of the birds die. It seems so unfair!"

"Michael, your turn for the bathroom," Ruby said, floating out of the doorway. "Don't forget: weightless protocol." She exaggerated her smile.

My first time in a weightless bathroom! We had drilled with habitat toilets, but only in Earth's gravity. This was my first time without it. The constant whirring of the air systems was a sound I could get used to, but the air rushing into the systems' vacuum pump, running loudly at full power, was disconcerting. And I was about to sit directly above that vacuum. The toilet, besides its regular function, also served as the main air intake for the ship's atmosphere control and water reclamation systems. That was good, because it meant we would not have to worry if we lost control of water droplets when washing in weightlessness: they would be sucked into the toilet. Also, having the toilet be the main air intake solved a bunch of problems with odor control.

I pulled myself onto the toilet and buckled the belt over my lap. Besides the feeling of the rushing air, the operation was quite regular, as these things go. Following "weightless protocol," I loosened the straps to clean myself up. The experience was quite exotic, except for the toilet paper, which was just regular toilet paper. It was the only paper we had on board, and, we were told, the only paper we would have with us in our new home. We had electronic datapads for reading and writing, but paper was necessary for hygiene. And for our artificial ecosystem: the toilet paper was the main vermiculture feedstock. The worms would eat our garbage and turn it into high-quality soil, which in turn would grow our food in our future home.

The vacuum toilet technology was amazing! A pump pulled air, liquid and solids through a centrifuge to separate them. The air passed through a filter to remove dust, then through the air conditioning unit to remove moisture, and finally through a zeolite molecular sieve to adsorb carbon dioxide. The condensed moisture passed into the water recycling system. The solid waste was stored, eventually to be baked at several hundred degrees to kill bacteria. Then would come the manual work: we would periodically remove and pack the denatured solids, for use, someday, as fertilizer. Also, since no technology was perfect, the toilets would break, and somebody would have to stick his hands inside to fix them. That somebody might be me, because I had trained to be one of the water-systems specialists in our ZubHab group. I was a minor expert in the toilet's engineering.

I remembered not to put the toilet paper into the toilet – it would clog the centrifuge. Instead, all paper went into a small cloth bag hooked underneath. Finishing, I did not flush the toilet, because, in "weightless protocol," the vacuum had already done all the work.

To prepare for washing my hands, I anchored myself to the floor by the sink, using the Velcro patches there that matched similar ones on my socks. I placed one hand under the water faucet and pressed the dispenser button with the other. A single large drop of water oozed onto my palm. I rubbed the water over my hands, then pulled the soap bar out of its clips and scrubbed a bit before putting it back. I rinsed several times with additional large drops, each of which I shook off toward the toilet. Washing may have been unusual, but I dried my hands the normal way with a white cloth towel that was Velcroed to the wall.

The sink and toilet were designed for both gravity and weightless use. We would not have gravity during the one-day ride in our MiniHab, but, if all went well, we would have artificial gravity for most of the ten-month journey in the ZubHab, the spaceship we would meet up with the following morning. Its bathrooms were identical to the one in the MiniHab. With gravity, we would be able to open the faucet and wash normally under a stream of water, and even take almost-standard showers. For now, however, rubbing our hands with water droplets was the closest approximation.

Denver had come down from the upper level and was hovering outside the bathroom door as I opened it. Thick dark eyebrows overshadowed pale blue eyes that glared at me. "Hurry up, lazy boy!" he admonished in his German-accented English, but his broad smile gave him away. "Captain Becker wants to start the meeting, and I'm last in line for the bathroom. I'm going to remember that I had to wait for you." He flashed his faux angry face one more time, playfully punched my shoulder, and pushed me out of the way.

Ladder rungs to the upper level were mounted on the bathroom's front wall, which was painted bright yellow. Climbing in weightlessness was so easy, I could do it with my fingertips! I propelled myself off the top rung and flew up through the meter-wide hatch. The smaller upper deck was crowded, with nearly everyone else already gathered there. The floor was a circle more than three meters in diameter, but the room tapered inwards to less than two and a half meters at the base of the domed ceiling. The girls crouched on the flight couches that hugged the hull, making room for Captain Becker, Dr. Esther and me to stand, so to speak, in the open area. Dr. Claudine hovered by the kitchenette counter, her wiry hair tied tightly in a bun, her Ivorian complexion contrasting beautifully with her white mundies suit. She clutched five-year-old Sophie to her chest, in weightlessness as easy as carrying a newborn.

Sophie was indeed the baby among us, perhaps the youngest astronaut in history. I wondered at the ethics of bringing such a young child on this journey. Earth-bound pundits had expressed similar doubts about all of us underage participants. That amused me: I considered myself most definitely mature enough to have agreed to come along.

Denver emerged through the hatch just as Captain Becker began speaking. "Attention, everyone," the captain said. "As you know, we are going to live our lives in an gaseous environment very different from that on Earth. Earth's air is one-fifth oxygen. By contrast, the air systems in the habitat, which will be our new home, maintain a mix of forty-five percent oxygen. This higher percentage is necessary because the overall air pressure will be very low, only one-third the air pressure on Earth at sea level."

"Excuse me, Captain Becker," Meital interrupted, "but didn't our bodies adjust to low oxygen levels over the last year while we lived at the Altiplano Mexicano spaceport?"

The captain looked down at her. "Yes, Meital, and it was important that they did. But even the spaceport, high on the slopes of Pico de Orizaba, has twice the air pressure of the spaceship. Lower pressure means lower stress on the habitat. More importantly, it reduces the quantity of buffer gas – the gasses in the air other than oxygen – that we will need to carry with us, or to collect from the atmosphere once we have reached our destination. But because we will have only half the air pressure, we need twice the proportion of oxygen – forty-five percent instead of twenty-one percent. Though you probably did not notice, the flight computer already began the process of changing the air in our MiniHab, so that we be ready, tomorrow, for our spacewalk, and for the air in our ZubHab."

He paused and looked around, making sure we were paying attention, his ruddy face conveying a commanding demeanor.

"This process will continue slowly and will finish only twelve hours from now. By tomorrow morning, after we have slept, we will have our ZubHab atmosphere. Then we will execute a breach-simulation exercise."

He looked around again, locking eyes with each of us, the weight of responsibility in his expression.

"Tomorrow's test will be the most dangerous part of our short MiniHab ride. For the rest of our lives, our dwellings will be surrounded by extreme low-pressure environments, both during our journey and after we settle at our destination. The danger of an atmosphere breach will be ever-present. Each one of us must be ready, at a moment's warning, to don his or her fleximet helmet. You have all practiced the procedure multiple times, including short stints in the spaceport hypobaric chamber. Now, the danger is real for the first time."

Captain Becker paused and took a breath; then his face relaxed and the stern expression disappeared.

"Esther will disperse rations for supper. Denver, please help her. We have two hours until lights-out. Then no talking: I want everyone to sleep well. We have a lot to do tomorrow, starting with the atmosphere test, followed by unpacking the duffels in preparation for docking. Meanwhile, follow the safety procedures you trained for: make sure your fleximets and oxypacks are near you at all times."

*　　*　　*

Monday, September 25th, 2028 07:00

One does not toss and turn when sleeping weightlessly, but whatever the equivalent is, that is how I slept. When Dr. Esther's voice came over the intercom, I was not sleeping deeply.

"Wake up, everybody! Wash and meet upstairs in thirty minutes for breakfast. We have four hours to docking, and have a lot to do before then."

Meital, opening her eyes in her flight couch next to mine, faced me. "Michael, you are my beloved brother, but I hope never to have to sleep near you again. You snore, you groan, you were restless all night long!"

"Don't blame me if you had trouble sleeping," I chided. "Obviously, you're no expert at weightless sleep, either. And stop complaining. Tonight, you and Shirel will have your own bedroom, and you'll never need to suffer me again."

"More than the private bedroom, I'm looking forward to a hot shower and a change of clothes," Shirel said as she unbuckled her thin frame from the couch on the other side of Meital. We've been wearing the same clothes for a whole day now."

"I just want to be able to eat something without throwing up," Ruby said, pushing herself off the couch to my right.

"You don't look as pale this morning," I said. She smiled feebly.

After we washed up – again, weightless protocol – Dr. Esther handed out breakfast. "Don't get used to these rations," she said. "We'll start cooking fresh food in a couple of days." She paused to look sympathetically at Ruby, judging her daughter's appearance. "And I'm sure you'll feel better once we've spun up for gravity."

Susan appeared out of the bathroom, her shoulder-length hair secured by a rainbow-colored headband. "Mom, 'don't get used to the rations?'" She laughed. "You've got to be kidding. This stuff is barely food. How could we get used to it?"

We had just finished eating when Captain Becker's voice sounded from the ceiling speakers, calling us to meet upstairs to prepare for the atmosphere purge test. Not five minutes later we were crowded together again.

"I hope you slept well. Overnight the computers adjusted the atmosphere, which is now at three hundred and fifty millibars pressure and forty-seven percent oxygen. Perhaps you noticed the change?"

Nobody had.

"You should all have your fleximets and oxypacks attached to your belts. In a few minutes I will initiate a purge of our vessel's atmosphere. The air pressure will drop rapidly. You will have forty-five seconds to don your fleximets, close the neck seals, activate the oxypacks, pressurize the fleximets, don your gloves, and check your buddies."

I looked around the room. The girls, even Shirel, looked anxious. Denver, by contrast, appeared eager for the challenge. Dr. Esther and Dr. Claudine reassured us, acting – I smiled at the thought – in their roles as field-trip chaperones. Dr. Claudine again held Sophie in her arms.

The captain continued. "We will pause the purge twice. First, at three hundred and twenty-five millibars, we will stop to check the seals on the fleximets. Then, at two hundred and seventy-five millibars, we will examine the mundies suits you are all wearing. Just as when we tested at Altiplano, the suits' smart fabric should compress automatically as the pressure drops. Each of you will carefully examine your buddy's suit for bulges. I remind you that bulges indicate failures in the smart fabric's electroelasticity, and will need to be patched promptly. From the gloves, move up the arms and check around the neck seal. Then check the trunk, back and sides. Complete the examination by looking over the mundies trousers, down to the bottoms of the legs, then the socks. Please bring any bulge to my attention or Esther's."

"It will be like when we trained, yes?" Jasmine asked. She was a precocious and enthusiastic nine-year-old.

"Yes, Jasmine, that is right." Captain Becker looked at her, then drew his attention to each of us in turn. We had tested our mundies many times and were used to the buddy system of examining each other's suits.

He asked, "Who is responsible for each corral?"

"I have the canaries and parakeets," said Ruby. She had more color in her face now.

"I have the worms," Meital declared, her voice serious.

"I'm in charge of the chicks and the incubator," I answered.

"You'll need help with one of them. Denver, can you take the incubator?"

"Yes, Captain."

"Do you remember the pressurization details? As soon as the pressure begins to drop, and you have donned your own fleximets, you must close and seal the tents. If not, the animals will suffocate."

I recalled the airtent rules: first seal the tent, then activate its oxypack.

He continued. "The timing is critical. As the pressure drops, oxygen levels will dip below the level we, and the birds and worms, need to live. You will have thirty seconds to activate your own oxypacks. Your fleximets and marsmitts must be sealed before then. Next you'll seal the airtents and activate the animals' oxypacks. Do not forget: first your own oxygen, then the animals'."

I froze as he held my eye, his gaze inquiring. Then he looked at Meital and Ruby, and finally to Denver.

"Are you all ready? The lives of the animals will be in your hands."

"Yes," we muttered. I felt sweat on my forehead.

"Okay. The four of you head back down to the lower deck. Esther, please accompany them. Jasmine, you are Esther's buddy; go with her. I will announce the start of depressurization in two minutes."

Sophie, still in her mother's arms, burst into tears. "*Maman,* he is scaring me!" she cried. "Why can't Jasmine stay with us? And what will happen to the animals?"

Dr. Claudine hugged Sophie tightly against her chest. "Jasmine will be with Esther, Sophie," she comforted her, her English spoken in a French accent. "And nothing will happen to the animals. *C'est bon.* Don't worry, *mon bébé.*"

"*J'ai peur!* My stomach feels funny. I do not like it here." She squeezed her eyes closed, and tears wet her cheeks.

Captain Becker tried to comfort her, though perhaps he should not have. "Sophie, your stomach will adjust soon. We are just practicing, and there's nothing to cry about." Sophie looked up at him, but did not stop sobbing.

Denver grabbed my arm. "Michael, let's get going."

We pulled ourselves headfirst through the hatch, then down the ladder to the lower deck. The moment I positioned myself by the fowl corral, a loud alarm began screeching, indicating that cabin air pressure was dropping. The pressure alarm blared even though the flight computer had initiated the atmosphere purge intentionally. My ears popped. I pulled my fleximet – a flexible helmet – out of my utility belt's emergency pack and unfolded it as quickly as I could. My ears ached, and I swallowed, trying to free the pressure. I pulled the fleximet over my head and rotated it until the transparent part was in front. Three fasteners protruded from my mundies' shoulders and neck, matching three buttonholes in the fleximet's hem. Blindly, I used my fingers to find each hole and slide it over the corresponding fastener. Then I started pressing the fleximet's fabric into my mundies shirt's neck and shoulders. Each had hundreds of matching micro-ziplock grooves that would join together to create an airtight seal. I massaged my neck and shoulders to create the seal. Next, I grabbed the oxypack off my belt, slid it into the fleximet's air valve until it clicked, and Velcroed it to the side of my neck. My hand found the oxypack's activation screw, which I rotated to open the flow. The oxypack's computer released a burst of air to fill the fleximet, and a rush of cool wind blew against my cheek. The circulation fans started up and the ache in my ears subsided. I took a deep breath of cool, clean air. I remembered to twist the three fasteners, to lock the fleximet in place and reinforce the seal. They would prevent the fleximet from popping off my head in the rare event of a seal breach.

Reacting to the low air pressure, my mundies began constricting around my torso, arms, legs and feet. The human body requires a pressurized environment: without it, one's limbs and skin would bloat with blood, and – even if one wore a pressurized helmet – breathing would be nearly impossible. Under normal conditions, the mundies were comfortable, tight but flexible. But in a vacuum environment, they compensated for the lack of air by tightly squeezing the body that wore them. Computerized sensors, embedded in the fabric, detected drops in ambient pressure. In response, they activated the fabric's electroelastic fibers, causing them to contract like artificial muscles. The fibers were very strong: working together in a woven garment, they could simulate more than twenty-five percent of Earth's sea-level air pressure, enough to keep the body safe and healthy.

The mundies were designed to be worn all the time, as a safety precaution, covering most of our bodies, but leaving our hands exposed. I felt my fingers begin to swell. I pulled my marsmitts off my belt, unfolded them, and pulled them over my fingers and wrists. Like the mundies suits and socks, they compressed automatically in vacuum, but they were designed to be more flexible, to make it easier to use our fingers, even in complete vacuum. I made sure each finger was secure inside its sheath, and that the cuffs overlapped the sleeves of my mundies shirt. The marsmitts sensed that I had put them on, waited fifteen seconds while I adjusted them, then started contracting automatically.

"Forty-five seconds," announced Captain Becker over the screech of the alarm. "Three hundred and thirty-five millibars."

I looked over at Denver, to make sure he also had finished in time. The fleximet's transparent faceplate did not hide his cocky grin. "What always takes you so long?" he taunted, before turning toward the incubator. I ignored him to attend to the chicks, while Meital and Ruby reached for their own corrals.

"Sixty seconds. Three hundred and thirty millibars." The captain's voice was clear over the fleximet radio.

I folded the airtent's transparent plastic cover over my corral, covering the netting. Like the fleximets, the tent had micro-ziplock bands, which I massaged shut using the tips of my marsmitted fingers. I closed the zipper to reduce the stress on the ziplock bond, then double-checked the corral's seal and activated its oxypack, starting the circulation of high-oxygen-content air. The tent's walls puffed outwards, indicating that the oxypack was pumping the tent's air pressure back to the requisite 350 millibars.

The sudden quiet as the low-pressure alarm ceased was almost as jarring as the alarm itself had been. Captain Becker announced, "Seventy-five seconds. Three hundred and twenty-five millibars. The purge is paused. Check your own fleximet seals and your buddies'."

Denver, who had been watching me finish sealing the chicks' tent, turned his attention to my fleximet and oxypack. He pressed my oxypack's test button to initiate a seal test. My ears popped again, as the oxypack's computer temporarily raised the air pressure, then released it.

"Okay – your light is green," he said.

I performed the same test on Denver's oxypack, watched as his fleximet ballooned slightly, and confirmed that his oxypack's green "okay" light also lit up. Meital and Ruby were doing the same to each other.

"Ruby, you have a leak," came Meital's voice on the radio. "The red LED is blinking. Can your mother help us with this?"

Dr. Esther floated over to Ruby and Meital. She held her daughter by the shoulders and rotated her around, examining the fleximet. She massaged the ziplock seals at the base of her neck. "Let's try again," she said, and pressed the test button.

We were all happy to see the green LED light up.

"Ruby, your seal was not fully closed. You'll need to practice donning your fleximet once we have settled into the habitat."

The girls and I floated back to the corrals, and Denver to the incubator. I ran the test on my own fowl corral – the green LED lit up – while the others tested theirs. As we were finishing, Captain Becker called to each of us in turn, over the radio. "Denver!"

"Okay," his voice answered, loudly and clearly.

"Michael!"

"Okay," I said.

Captain Becker continued down the list, calling each name, finishing with "Sophie!"

Dr. Claudine answered, "Sophie and I are okay, and I've confirmed that her radio is working."

"I remind you all," Captain Becker said, "that you check the oxypack's status by pressing the button at its back end. Please do so now."

I reached behind my right ear and pressed the button. In response, a computer-generated voice announced, "Ninety-nine percent full; one hundred and seventeen minutes estimated supply." It amused me that the oxypack was the only thing that could speak to me directly, not via radio, in vacuum.

The pressure alarm screeched again over our radios as the flight computer resumed the atmosphere purge. As the air pressure dropped, the electroelastic fabric in my mundies tightened considerably, pressing tautly against my skin. Nevertheless, I marveled, I could still move my body almost normally, with just a bit more effort than usual – something I expected to get used to. With the mundies, we would be able to function in vacuum environments as long as we also wore our pressurized fleximets.

"Two hundred and seventy-five millibars," announced Captain Becker on our radios as the screeching stopped again. Denver and I examined each other's suits for malfunctioning bulges, checking each centimeter both visually and by touch. Meital and Ruby did the same, and Dr. Esther checked Jasmine's suit.

"I can check your mundies for you, Dr. Esther," Jasmine said over the radio. "I know how to do it."

Dr. Esther had been examining her own suit. She nodded to Jasmine, but held a vertical finger to her faceplate, quietly shushing her. The fleximet radio system, when tuned to the shared channel, permitted no private conversations. Everyone could hear everything.

"I found a bulge in Denver's suit," I called out. Just above his left hip, on his side near the back, six centimeters of his mundies swelled out nearly a centimeter. "Denver, can you feel that?" I asked, as I poked the bulge.

"I feel it now," he said. "It's like something is sucking on my side. *Pfui*! That is a strange feeling."

My sister Shirel's voice sounded on the radio. "I found a bulge on Susy's sleeve."

"I'll patch that," Dr. Esther's voice answered, "and Captain Becker can fix Denver's suit."

Captain Becker's head appeared through the hatch. "Does anyone else see any bulges?" he asked. Nobody did.

He appeared by our sides with a mundies repair kit in his glove. He pulled out a circular patch a bit bigger than his hand, then two small epoxy bottles. After applying epoxy from one of the bottles onto the patch, and contents from the other bottle directly onto Denver's suit, he pressed the patch firmly over the bulge.

"Michael, wait for my signal, then activate the patch." He handed me the activation transmitter, a green box a bit larger than my thumb. Then he headed back to the upper deck.

Two minutes later his voice came again on the radio. "Activate the patches."

I held the activation transmitter over the patch and pressed the button. The microprocessors in the patch fabric recognized the code and set themselves to active mode. Immediately, the fabric contracted, and the bulge disappeared.

"Whoa!" Denver exclaimed. "That tickles."

Captain Becker polled us about the integrity of our buddies' suits. Everybody confirmed that their mundies were performing as required. Then the screeching alarm began again, as the flight computer purged the remaining atmosphere from the MiniHab cabin. My suit stiffened and each movement required more effort. I flexed my hands and pulled my fingers to my thumbs: it felt like squeezing dough. Air was definitely more convenient than mundies, but the mundies were an excellent backup. Vacuum was no longer something to fear.

"Repressurization beginning," Captain Becker finally said, and the alarm's screeching stopped. "Wait for confirmation." My mundies steadily loosened their grip on my fingers, hands, legs and trunk. A few minutes passed and Captain Becker announced the conclusion of the emergency simulation exercise. "Repressurization is complete, to three hundred and fifty millibars, with oxygen now at forty-seven percent. You may remove and fold your fleximets. Michael, Ruby, Meital, and Denver, please open the corral and incubator airtents. Free time for half an hour; then we begin unpacking."

Having experienced a vacuum environment, we were now officially-certified astronauts, ready to set off for planet Mars.

Providence

Monday, September 25th, 2028 09:30

Even in weightlessness, moving heavy bags requires muscle. I was sweating. The MiniHab's lower deck was divided vertically in two, with most of the lower half packed solid with equipment for our journey: vacuum-packed foodstuffs, kitchen utensils, sleeping bags, blankets and towels, and our personal satchels, which contained all the belongings that would accompany us to our new home. Which was not much: small mementos, washcloths, some favorite light clothes that could be worn over our mundies, and, for each of us, one individually selected artifact. My artifact was a set of sourdough cultures, so that we and future settlers would have a variety of tasty bread. Everything was crammed into duffel bags, all of which had been latched tightly in place for launch. Only a few hours later we would be transferring them to the spaceship habitat, so the bags needed to be unlatched and extracted. This took nearly two hours. We stopped to celebrate Susan Meyer's birthday: she was turning thirteen the day of our docking.

"I'm so sorry we don't have a cake for you!" Dr. Esther told her daughter.

"Mom, what fun is a cake if I can't have candles to blow out?" Susan giggled. "No open flames in high-oxygen environments!" she recited. "But anyway, I'm getting the best birthday present ever. Who gets a trip to space for their thirteenth birthday?"

"Forty-five minutes to docking," came Captain Becker's voice over the intercom. "We are now three kilometers from our target. I'm putting the bottom camera view up on the displays."

"Let's get into our seats so we can watch the approach," Ruby suggested.

I buckled myself into my couch, again sitting between Ruby and my sisters, facing the ceiling-mounted display. I tried to imagine that I was looking out a window. The MiniHab capsule had no windows, but dozens of digital cameras installed throughout its hull offered almost the same experience. The habitat, too, had no windows, but hundreds of cameras were distributed throughout the PlyShield, its outer skin. We would need to get used to imagining that our NLED screens were windows to the outside.

"I see a sliver of Earth," Susan declared from her couch below us. "Look at the very bottom of the display."

Shirel answered her friend. "I think that was Madagascar." The whitish halo of Earth's beautiful atmosphere lingered briefly as the blue and green sliver scrolled off the screen.

"Our ship is rotating," Captain Becker's voice announced. "Watch as more stars appear."

Susan called out, "There's the moon coming into view."

As the half-moon passed across the screen, I looked for signs of the habitat ship and its rocket stack. Reflecting light from the day side of Earth, it would appear as a bright white object on the display, but what would a sixty-meter-long cylinder look like from nearly three kilometers away?

"There it is!" Susan exclaimed, and the ship came into view. It appeared as a two-centimeter white column at the top of the display. I could just barely make out the three boosters that would lift us into our high Earth orbit a couple of days later.

Ruby's striking green eyes caught mine. "I see it entering from the bottom of the screen." Her view was upside-down compared to my own, because our couches were oriented in opposite directions, but that made it easy to talk face-to-face.

Meital, by contrast, was lying in the same orientation as me, so she, like me, saw the ship sliding down the screen she shared with Shirel. "Why do we see the ship from the side?" she asked. "If we are approaching from behind, shouldn't we see just the bottom of the rockets?"

Dr. Esther answered. "Great question, Meital. We are approaching from below the ship, from the point of view of Earth. The habitat is oriented tangentially to earth, slowly rotating as Earth rotates, so that it will be in the ideal orientation when we fire the rockets to boost our orbit on Thursday. Coming from below, we see the whole ship as if we are approaching from its side."

I asked, "Will we also dock from below, or will we have to maneuver around the ship?"

"We'll dock from below to avoid complex navigation. You can't see it from here, but the water tanker is docked on the starfield side, exactly opposite from where we will attach. If you look carefully, you may be able to see the first group's MiniHab, docked to one side."

The habitat's stack slowly reached the center of our display. We felt a shudder as our own navigation thruster fired briefly to stop our rotation, and the starfield and habitat ship stopped moving across the display. We spent the next half hour watching in awe as our new home appeared increasingly larger.

"It's like moving into a new house, but in a completely empty neighborhood," Shirel commented. "Standing all by itself in an empty field."

"But in a field of stars, not a field of grass," said Susan.

The quiet approach was interrupted by the sound of a phone ringing on the intercom. "I'm calling the ship," Captain Becker announced, "and you can all listen in as we discuss the docking procedure."

A very familiar voice answered, "*Providence* here. Welcome to our neighborhood!"

"Hi Mom!" Shirel called out.

"I don't think she can hear us," said Meital. "She hears only Captain Becker."

"Maybe, but I'm excited we're going to see her soon."

"Dana, is everything set on your end for our docking?" Captain Becker asked.

"We're double-checking the position of the tanker's pipe," my mother answered, "but other than that, your docking position is clear."

"By the way, I have you on the intercom here."

"Lovely! Susan, your father wishes you a very happy birthday, as do I and everyone here."

While Captain Becker and my mother went over details for the docking, I examined the rocket stack, which now filled the display. At the top, from my point of view, was the habitat itself. In meetings during our year-long stay at the Altiplano Mexicano spaceport, we had discussed names for all six of the habitats that would be setting out together. Our group had settled on the name "Providence" for ours. The more religiously inclined among us intended the name as a prayer that Divine Providence protect us and help us with our adventure. But we also intended to honor the city of Providence, where my parents met while earning advanced degrees at Brown University.

The habitat was a narrow dome-topped cylinder. At sixteen meters, it was twice the height of an average house. Inside, it had four stories of living space, plus an attic above for storage and a large airlock at the bottom. Outside it was nearly featureless. Its PlyShield skin – a twenty-five-centimeter-thick shield against micrometeoroids and space debris – was a uniform off-white color throughout. Four folded landing legs hugged the hull. Columns of handhold rungs rose up between them, for spacewalkers to use to traverse from airlock to apex. The landing rockets' nozzles were visible where the rounded bottom met the sides, and the smaller nozzles of the maneuvering rockets encircled the top. The only decorations were the logo of the Murke-Berger Foundation and the flags of the participants' nations, the United States flag most prominent.

At the bottom, a set of titanium beams linked the habitat to the Mars-Entry rocket stage, which was nearly as tall but only three fifths as wide. We would fire its rockets at the end of our trip to slow us down in preparation for landing. Below the Mars-Entry stage were three huge identical boosters, two of them "High Earth Orbit Insertion" stages, the third the "Mars-Transit Injection" stage. We would use those – and discard them – in the coming days and weeks, first to boost ourselves to a much higher orbit, and then, later, to depart Earth and set out on our interplanetary expedition. If everything went as planned, they would return to Earth and be reused for future missions. All in all, the rocket stack measured sixty meters from the bottom of the booster rockets to the tip of the dome, as high as a twenty-story building.

"We will attach below *Providence* where it connects to the Mars-Entry stage," Captain Becker announced. "Remember that there will not be a direct connection. We will need to go outside to climb across to the habitat's airlock. You will all experience your first spacewalk, as we transfer ourselves and our equipment between the vehicles."

"I see the second MiniHab, the one that launched the other group," Shirel said. "But what is the huge blue thing shaped like a plate on the right side of the habitat?"

"That's the heat shield," answered Dr. Esther. "The first group installed it a couple of days ago. It will protect us and slow us down, in ten months, as we enter the Martian atmosphere."

The heat shield looked like a large flattened bowl, twice as wide as the ship. "Shouldn't it be below the ship," I asked, "and not on the side, since we will be entering the atmosphere bottom-first?"

"Yes, when we land. Until then, it serves a secondary purpose as a radiator, to shed excess heat. To radiate heat effectively, it needs to be on the ship's side, where it won't be exposed to the sun when we're in tethered rotation. We'll swivel it and lock it into place, underneath the habitat, just before we enter Mars's atmosphere."

The rocket stack grew steadily to fill the display until we made contact. We felt, more than heard, the click-clack of our docking bar latching onto one of the titanium beams.

"Are we here?" Shirel asked.

"Yes, I think we've docked," said Meital. "Are you ready to step outside?" The two of them looked at each other and giggled.

Captain Becker announced, "Everybody, please prepare for the transfer. Don your fleximets and marsmitts, activate oxypacks and check your buddies. Seal the corral airtents. I want to purge the atmosphere in fifteen minutes so we can open the hatch and prepare the tether."

Because the ships had no docking adaptors – it made no sense to carry equipment we would never use again – we would spacewalk over to the other ship. Again, as we had done earlier in the morning, we donned our fleximets and marsmitts, and I activated my oxypack. Denver, fully suited up, floated through the hatch from the upper deck. He checked my seals and suit, and I checked his.

"My oxypack reports two hours of air," Denver confirmed.

"Michael, Ruby, let's get the corrals sealed," Meital said. We pulled ourselves over to the blue bathroom wall and repeated the procedure we had tested earlier. Like us, the birds would pass through outer space on the way to the habitat.

"Claudine, confirm the integrity of your suit and Sophie's," Captain Becker requested over the radio, as he began polling each of us in turn. Before long he got to me. "Michael?"

"Denver's suit is fine," I answered, "as are the chicks."

Last was Denver, who confirmed the integrity of my suit and its neck seal, and of the incubator.

"You are an excellent team," the captain complimented. "We just completed that whole procedure in six and a half minutes. I'm initiating the atmosphere purge now."

The low-pressure alarm screeched and I felt my mundies stiffen as before. I caught Denver's eye behind his visor and watched his fleximet balloon slightly as the air pressure changed. By then I could no longer hear the alarm from outside. The screeching continued a few more seconds, much more quietly, from my fleximet's radio speakers, until someone finally deactivated it. Then Captain Becker appeared through the hatch from the upper deck, his eyes on the datapad in his gloved hand.

"Another minute or two until the purge completes. Then we'll open the hatches."

"Let's make room," Meital said. "Squeeze into the upper couches."

Susan and Ruby, Shirel and Meital, and Denver and I pushed back onto the couches. I leaned out to watch. A moment later, Dr. Esther braced herself and grabbed and twisted the hatch's handle. Then she swung the hatch up in the direction of the bathroom. Captain Becker was ready with a short nylon strap to secure it; then he pulled himself down into the airlock.

Curious, I pushed myself headfirst off the couch.

"Michael, you're blocking my view," Shirel said, shoving me to the side.

We jostled for positions from which to watch Captain Becker through the airlock's inner hatchway. He braced against the airlock walls, pulled back the outer hatch's handle to retract its bolts, and pushed it open. Normally, the two airlock hatches could not both be open at the same time: either the inner hatch would be open and the airlock pressurized, or the outer hatch would be open and the airlock empty of air. But since the entire MiniHab had been purged of atmosphere, we had no need for an airlock, and both hatches could be open at once, exposing the interior to the vacuum of space.

"I can't see outside from here," Meital murmured, but we all heard her clearly on our fleximet speakers. "Do any of you see something?"

"Not yet," I answered. "But we'll all be outside in a few minutes. I'm hoping for awesome views of Earth and the stars."

Captain Becker stuck his head outside and was talking to somebody over the radio. "I see your feet, Simeon."

Simeon Radechov answered in his Russian-accented English. "I am bringing you the end of the tether. I have latched it inside our airlock, and will float over."

A few minutes passed before Captain Becker spoke to us. "The tether is set up, suspended between our MiniHab's airlock and the habitat's airlock. We are eleven people and we have more than thirty duffels and packages. Each adult and teenager will be responsible for taking three or four duffels. You will need to pull yourselves along the tether across five meters. Does anyone have any concerns?"

I was not surprised that little Jasmine was the first to respond. "Why only the teenagers? I am able also to help."

"Jasmine, I agree; you can be responsible for your own duffel."

"I'm nauseous and a little nervous," Ruby said. I wondered if admitting her weakness over the open circuit embarrassed her.

"Everyone, remember that you will be latched to the tether. If you feel any discomfort, just close your eyes. You can continue pulling yourselves across even with your eyes closed. To avoid –"

Dr. Esther interrupted. "Ruby, I'll accompany you if you want. That goes for anyone else who is uncomfortable with their first spacewalk. I don't mind going back and forth a few times."

Captain Becker resumed his speech. "To avoid argument, we'll go over by age, starting with the youngest. Claudine, please take Sophie across. The habitat airlock has room for only half of us and half the duffels, so Chief Officer Meyer will pressurize it twice during the operation. Those who go over first will wait in the airlock until pressurization, then help move the first set of duffels up into the living areas."

Chief Officer Meyer was Dr. Esther's husband. Dr. Jhonathan had arrived at the habitat with the first group and had been in charge of the mission temporarily, but Captain Becker would take over once we were all across.

"After the first group is safely inside, Jhonathan will purge the airlock and the second group will transfer. Then I will perform the final checkout of the MiniHab and seal its hatch before joining you."

The work began. Over the next forty-five minutes, while the younger children made the transfer, Denver and I worked with Dr. Esther to pass the duffels, one by one, into the airlock. Jasmine was second to go, after her mother had taken Sophie across. She was quite the young champion and negotiated the tether, while pulling her duffel along, with no trouble at all. *"Je vois tant d'étoiles!"* she exclaimed exuberantly. Shirel and Susan followed; then it was Meital's turn.

She turned and showed me her smile. "Wish me luck, Michael!"

"You don't need luck. Just have fun! See you on the other side."

After she crossed over, Simeon Radechov pulled himself into our airlock, holding the far end of the tether. He poked his head into the cabin. "Hello, all of you! Captain, I closed and secured the habitat hatch."

We waited another forty-five minutes while they pressurized the airlock on the other side and brought all the duffels upstairs. We used the time to recharge our oxypacks from the air dispenser in the kitchenette in the upper deck. Finally, my mother announced over the radio that the ZubHab airlock had again been purged of air, and Simeon went across to open the hatch and reattach the tether.

"You're next, Ruby," said Captain Becker.

"I'm not feeling well, Captain. Can someone else go before me?"

"Let's go over together," I suggested.

"I need to vomit again," she moaned. "I was so hoping not to have to vomit inside the mask."

Dr. Esther put her arm around her daughter. "Don't worry; you won't be the first. Just aim for the absorbent pad."

Captain Becker turned to me. "Michael, go now instead of Ruby. Into the airlock, please."

"Okay," I said, my heart racing with anticipation. I pulled myself in headfirst. Outer space was just a couple of meters away! I could see stars, though the water tanker, docked directly across from our MiniHab, blocked some of the view.

The airlock itself was not cramped. Shaped like a funnel, it was wider at the top, where the inner hatch was offset to one side. At the bottom, it narrowed to a circle a meter and a half in diameter, all of which was open to space. The tether Simeon had set up extended from a hook in the ceiling above me, out the hatch and across to *Providence's* airlock. Several carabiners hung from it.

Captain Becker stuck his head into the airlock. "Michael, grab your spacesuit pack and get dressed up. Activate the light on your fleximet just before exiting."

I pulled myself over to where the packs were stowed and found the one with my name. The spacesuits were light Mylar pants and hooded pullovers, with reflective aluminum coatings inside and out. There was also a pair of heavily insulated Mylar gloves. We would wear the suits over our mundies during spacewalks, to help with temperature control and reduce radiation exposure, even if only by a little. The gloves would prevent us from burning or freezing our hands if we touched any outside surface. I unpacked the pants and pulled them on, pushing my feet into the attached insulated boots. I unfolded the top and pulled it over my fleximet, pushed my arms through the sleeves, and donned the gloves. Though fitted to my size, the suit, other than the boots and gloves, was roomy by design, to allow empty space between it and the mundies.

Captain Becker handed me a harness and the end of a nylon cord that he held coiled in his gloved hand. We had drilled this procedure, so I knew how to pull the harness up and secure it at my waist. As Captain Becker began to uncoil the cord, I grabbed a carabiner and latched myself to the tether. Captain Becker disappeared up through the inner hatch; then one of the duffels appeared.

"Michael, take the duffel and latch it to the second carabiner."

I pulled at the cord, latched it to the duffel's handle, then pulled out more cord and latched a third carabiner to the tether. I repeated the process three more times. By then my harness was linked to a chain of duffels, and they and I were latched at multiple points to the tether. Four duffels would follow me as I pulled myself across to the ZubHab airlock, and none would float away by accident.

"Okay, go!" Captain Becker instructed over the radio.

I switched on my fleximet's forehead lamp. My heart raced with excitement. I pulled myself hand-over-hand out the hatch. Grabbing the tether required extra effort, as the marsmitts's stiffness resisted my fingers. Other than that small inconvenience, it was not difficult to pull myself along in weightlessness, even with the four duffels trailing behind. As I left the MiniHab below me, I found myself in an open garage-sized area bounded by several spacecraft. In front of me was the bottom of the habitat, the rough outer surface of its PlyShield skin clearly visible. It was oriented perpendicularly to the MiniHab, which was now at my feet. The tether I was following ended in the habitat's airlock, a room's length diagonally above and ahead. Twelve columns of handhold rungs spread out from the airlock hatch, along the bottom of the habitat ship's hull, like numbers on an old-fashioned clock. The rungs continued up and around the sides. Every meter or so small black spots, which I knew to be cameras, dotted the way.

I tilted my neck up toward the stars. The water tanker was there, directly across from our MiniHab, but not close: it was at the far end of a long boom. The boom's near end was attached to one of the titanium beams that connected the habitat ship to the Mars-Entry stage. Two pipes, each a few centimeters in diameter, connected from the bottom of the boom to two valve fittings that protruded from the habitat hull a meter beyond the airlock hatch.

I paused to look around. Above to my right was the MiniHab that had delivered the first group of travelers several days earlier, docked bottom-first, like our own MiniHab. Its hatch was closed. To my left, the bottom of the heat shield blocked most of the view, even though it was more distant than the spacecraft, almost two car-lengths away. I was not looking at its light blue convex side; instead, its inner concave side was visible, though very dark.

The fleximet's visor afforded a wide viewing angle, but to look at the Mars-Entry stage behind me, I had to rotate my whole body. The Mars-Entry stage's skin was an off-white color like the habitat's, but did not have cameras or handhold rungs. Instead, there were hatches to several closed compartments.

I pulled myself farther from the MiniHab and gazed at the part of the sky I could see. My eyes adjusted to the darkness, then widened in wonder. What a glorious sight lay before me! More stars shone than I had ever seen. I was surprised to see that they shone in many different colors. Most were bright yellow or sparkling white. Some were reddish, others faintly blue.

The most glorious view was Earth below. I looked around at an astonishing work of art, a painting by the Creator. It was a variegated image: blue seas, white swirling clouds, green-brown continents covered by a shimmering airy blanket. Having exited head-first from the bottom of the upside-down MiniHab, I was oriented vertically, as if standing on top of the world. The MiniHab blocked much of my view downward, but I knew that I would see much more if I were just a bit higher. So, closing my hands on the tether, I pulled myself up, hand over hand, then stopped and looked around again. Our orbiting ships were crossing into Earth's night side and I found myself looking back into a cosmic sunset. I recognized southern Africa below, its mountains silhouetted in shadow. There was the island country of Madagascar again, this time visible directly, not just on a display screen.

"Have we really completed a whole orbit since we first saw Madagascar?"

Captain Becker's voice on the radio startled me. "Two whole orbits, Michael, not one," he corrected. "Are you almost across?"

"The view is so beautiful out here!" "*Ma rabu ma'asecha Hashem,*" I recited from Psalm 104 in the original Hebrew. "How numerous are your creations, O L-rd! In wisdom you have made them all; the earth is full of your possessions."

Then I remembered the Jewish blessing one recites when seeing the ocean for the first time after thirty days, to express awe at G-d's creation. We had been on a Mexican mountain for nearly a year, so I qualified. "You are the Source of blessing, O L-rd, our G-d, King of the Universe, who made the great sea."

What a beautiful world! A life-sustaining world, with an atmosphere custom-designed for life. Or perhaps life designed for the atmosphere: air for free, requiring no effort. Plentiful water; comfortable temperatures. Were we really choosing to leave this all behind, and settle on a frozen world with barely an atmosphere, no free oxygen, no bodies of water? A world where we would need to engineer even the air we breathe?

My stomach tightened and I felt queasy. Gazing at the atmosphere below, my heart filled with misgiving. Sweat gathered on my brow and my breathing must have quickened, because the fleximet fan increased its speed and a stronger current of cool air began blowing against my cheek. The louder whirring broke me out of my anxious reverie. I tried to encourage myself. *Yes, we had chosen* to leave Earth, and we would create a lovely new environment, with lots of healthy air, in our new home.

"Michael, please hurry up. This is no time for reciting blessings! We need to finish the transfer!"

I strongly disagreed with Captain Becker about the blessings, but it certainly was no time for a panic attack. I resumed pulling myself and the duffels along the tether.

Though nothing more than my mundies and the Mylar suit separated me from the void, I felt neither hot nor cold. For the first sixty years of manned spaceflight, spacewalkers had worn bulky pressurized suits with built-in air conditioning systems. Then, with the invention of the electroelastic self-tightening fabric used in mundies, research determined that, since the fabric was porous and could breathe, the human body would regulate its temperature even in vacuum environments. Keeping warm was not difficult: there being no air, no heat was lost to convection. The human body did lose some heat by radiating it as infrared light, but the Mylar suit reflected most of that heat back onto the wearer. Keeping cool during strenuous activity was also not difficult: sweating worked in the normal way. The hotter molecules of moisture evaporated quickly, through the fabric, in vacuum, leaving behind only the colder molecules. Sunlight might have been uncomfortably hot had it shone directly on my body, but the Mylar suit also reflected away most sunlight, so I barely felt the setting sun's warmth.

I neared the ZubHab airlock and saw Simeon, who reached through the open airlock hatch and grabbed my hand. He pulled me in.

"Let's remove you and the duffels from the buckles, and send the harness back."

The habitat's airlock was much larger than the MiniHab's. It was the size of a small living room, though completely round and with a low ceiling. It would serve as an extra room, a basement to our interplanetary apartment building, during most of our journey. Now, however, it was empty of air, and nearly empty of anything else other than hooks and straps latched to the wall, and, roped to one side, a bunch of meter-long cylindrical canisters. The canisters were turquoise blue, labeled in bright green lettering.

I doffed the harness and handed it to Simeon. It was still attached to the rope, the duffels and the tether. Simeon hauled in the duffels and bunched the rope at the end of the tether as he did so. Meanwhile, I removed my Mylar pants and pullover and began folding them.

"Michael, release the duffels' carabiners and latch them to the wall. We do not want them to float back out!"

I folded and stowed the Mylar suit, then helped with the duffels. After we had latched all four to the wall, Simeon spoke to Captain Becker on the radio. "We are ready. Pull the rope back."

Simeon waited by the open hatch. Five minutes passed before he reached out again, this time helping Ruby and Dr. Esther come through. Ruby removed her Mylar suit, drew close to me, and pressed her mask into mine. She peered into my eyes and smiled wanly. She looked terrible: her face was pale. Her green eyes sparkled, but this time it was due to tears; she had been crying. She had also vomited, attested by stains on her mask. Unfortunately, the fleximet's absorbent pad was not foolproof, so vomiting in the mask was rarely a spotless affair.

"Ruby, you need to drink some water." Simeon retrieved a pouch from a box on the wall and handed it to her, and she screwed it onto the outer part of the fleximet's straw accessory. This caused the straw's vacuum valve to open. She tilted her mouth to the straw and squeezed the bottle, forcing the contents through.

Ruby's mother finished latching the duffels the two of them had brought over, then gracefully flipped over, pushed off a wall, and floated back to the hatch. Reattaching her harness to the tether, she said, "Ruby, wait here with Michael. I'll be back with more duffels in a few minutes." We watched her exit head-first and depart down the tether.

I wanted to ask Ruby how she was feeling. But I kept silent, as we were still broadcasting on the general band, and I did not want to embarrass her.

Denver arrived with more duffels a few minutes later. "Michael, that was awesome. Did you see the volcanoes?"

"Stop bragging. There's no way you got a better view than I did. We're on the night side. It's too dark to see volcanoes."

"Not true! There is a lot to see in the moon's light."

Dr. Esther returned with more duffels; then, while the four of us waited in the ZubHab airlock, Simeon exited again to help Captain Becker retrieve the tether and close the MiniHab's hatch.

Ten long minutes later, after Simeon reentered the airlock with the coiled tether in his hand, Captain Becker's head appeared through the hatch. "I have sealed the MiniHab's hatch. It's ready for its trip back to Earth." Then, in an official-sounding voice: "Chief Officer Meyer, I request permission to come aboard."

Dr. Jhonathan answered over the radio. "Permission granted. Please assume command of ZubHab *Providence*."

Captain Becker pulled himself into the airlock. He folded and stowed his Mylar suit while Simeon closed and sealed the outer hatch. Then he announced, in the same official voice, "I am assuming command of ZubHab *Providence*." With that, he became responsible for the ship and our mission, a responsibility he would carry until our arrival on Mars.

Electricity

Monday, September 25th, 2028 19:00

Denver and I were sitting, so to speak, in our bedroom on the second floor of our new home, the ZubHab habitat *Providence*. After a brief sponge-bath, I had changed into a fresh set of mundies and left the dirty set in the laundry bin in the bathroom. The privacy of the small bedroom was comforting after the close communal experience of a day in the MiniHab. Bunk beds were mounted on the ZubHab's curved outer hull and stretched the whole two-meter length of what was the room's widest wall. From there the room tapered to less than a meter wide at its doorway. That was the general architectural theme: because the habitat was round and the apartment's rooms were placed around the circumference, most of them were wider at the hull and narrower inside. An off-white floor-to-ceiling closet took up much of one of the bedroom's side walls. Six folded dining room chairs were latched against the other wall, leaving just enough room for a couple of people to comfortably stand, or float, in the space between the beds and the doorway.

"I didn't think my muscles would ache so much in weightlessness," I said.

Denver laughed. "We just spent four hours moving and unpacking. You braced yourself against walls and floors with muscles you're not used to using, and pushed and pulled large duffels and airtents around. The duffels do not weigh anything in microgravity, but remember our physics classes: they still have plenty of mass."

"I'm sure glad it's the Beckers who are responsible for packing the storeroom." The storeroom was a large attic – almost thirty cubic meters of space – above the fourth floor, under the habitat's domed roof. "Cataloging and stocking a year and a half's supply of food for twenty-one people is not something I feel like doing at the moment."

"You're aware, aren't you, that the adults spent several days setting up before we arrived? Stop complaining." He smiled again. "We kids had the easy part."

I changed the subject. "Did you call your mother before we left?"

His smile disappeared. "No, and I don't want to talk about it."

"Denver, you're going to have to at least say goodbye eventually."

The room's folding door opened, saving Denver from having to answer. Samuel Meyer, Ruby's older brother, appeared in the doorway.

"How are you guys feeling?" he called out.

"Not as exuberant as you, apparently! Can you tell me why my armpits are aching?" I asked.

"Sure. You spent a couple of hours in vacuum. The mundies are not a perfect replacement for air pressure, and the underarm padding is notorious for not putting quite enough pressure on the skin. Some capillaries always rupture. You'll feel better in a day or two."

He glanced at my midsection, then looked back up with raised eyebrows. "What about the other part of your body where it's hard to supply pressure evenly?"

"I feel it there too, but not as bad as my underarms."

Denver shook his head at me. "You're just full of complaints this evening!" Then to Sam: "I was surprised by how huge the heat shield looked from close up. How big is it actually?"

"Seventeen meters."

"What was it like installing it?"

Sam's eyes widened. "It was amazing! When we got up here Thursday the water tanker had already docked. It was attached to the habitat by its long boom, but the heat shield was still in its launch position, next to the boom, folded up in four sections. That's the only way it would fit inside the seven-meter fairing."

"What did you do with the fairing?" I asked.

"We didn't have to do anything. The fairing was jettisoned right after the water tanker launched last week. It was long gone by the time we got here."

Meital appeared in the doorway. "These walls are really thin. Even with the noise of the air conditioning I could hear you talking about setting up the heat shield. What did I miss?"

I caught Denver's eye. "We'll have to get used to keeping our voices down when we want to talk privately."

Meital responded with a nasty look. She settled herself against the closet.

Sam turned to her. "Hi, Meital. I was just explaining that the heat shield was exposed but still folded up when we got here. Four of us went outside to set it up. My father oversaw the mission from inside the MiniHab."

"Why the MiniHab?" Meital asked. "Why not from the habitat?"

"We opened up this ship only yesterday. We had to spend three days cooped up in the launch vehicle!"

Denver laughed and elbowed me. "I told you we had the easy part."

Sam continued. "We can't live in here without the Air Management System up and running, and the Air Management System can't start up before the radiator is functioning. The ship would overheat really quickly. Our radiator is the heat shield. It's the only mechanism for releasing the heat that the machinery generates, so we had to get it installed first."

"Then why don't we call it a 'radiator' instead of a 'heat shield?'"

"I wonder about that, too, Meital. It will be a radiator for ten months and a heat shield for only fifteen minutes, when we finally hit the Martian atmosphere before landing, so 'radiator' makes more sense. But Dr. Louis – Dr. Claudine's husband – says that all the specs call it a 'heat shield.'"

"Okay. So, you took a spacewalk and unfolded the heat shield?"

"You make it sound simple, Michael, but actually it was a complex operation. Helga Becker and I joined Simeon and his brother Boris outside. First, Simeon and Boris climbed out along the boom, released the shield's arm, and rotated the whole thing up alongside the ZubHab."

"I'd be afraid it would float away," Meital said.

"That's why it was connected by tethers the whole time. After the brothers finished rotating it into position, they connected the arm's base joint to the Air-Management System stud."

"What that?"

"It's a twenty-centimeter structure that sticks out of the ship's bottom edge, just inside the ring of landing rockets. The stud holds the heat shield to the habitat structurally, and also circulates compressed ammonia gas between the radiator and the Air Management System. Boris secured the bolts and Simeon connected and sealed the pipes and the electrical system. Then we all waited in the airlock while my father ran a partial test of the arm's rotation system by remote control."

"Rotation system?"

"To move the shield below the interstage beams for when we reach Mars. It has to be under our craft when we hit the atmosphere bottom-first, but it needs to be positioned to the side the whole time before that. We'll have a very hot landing next August if the arm doesn't rotate the shield into the correct position."

I laughed. "You're the master of understatement. I hope the test succeeded."

"We got everything working. Then the four of us spread out along the height of the shield to get it unfolded. I got top position, farthest from the airlock."

"So you got to do an open-free spacewalk, not holding on to any structure?" Denver asked.

"Almost. I climbed out to the end of the arm and latched my tether to one of its hooks. But then, yes, I did push off, and floated freely, to the shield's farthest handhold."

"Were you scared?"

"No, we were too busy to be scared. I had to circle around to reach a cable that would unfold the sections. Once the four of us were in position, we pulled the cables to rotate the sections into taut contact with each other. Then there were fifty bolts to be secured at each joint. All in all, it took almost four hours. We had to stop in the middle to recharge our oxypacks."

"You said the whole huge heat shield is connected to the ZubHab only at one point? Isn't that a dangerous single point of failure?"

"At the moment, yes. But during tomorrow's spacewalk to roll out the flexible solar panels over the hull, we'll attach a bunch more tethers. They'll stabilize the shield during rocket burns, and also later, after the ships start rotating for artificial gravity."

Shirel appeared upside-down in the doorway, her unbound hair floating wildly. "Michael, Mom says we're having a family dinner, and that you should set up the dining-room table. Denver, you are part of our family now, so you're also expected." Noticing Sam, she added, "Sam, you can join us too, if you want."

"Thanks, but my parents are expecting me upstairs."

"Why are you upside-down, Shirel?" Meital asked. "You're giving me vertigo. Please turn over."

"I hope you're not being serious," Shirel pouted. "Until we get gravity, there's no up or down. And, anyway, I won't be able to do this after next week. I'm going to have fun while I can."

We pushed ourselves out the bedroom door into the living room. The living room, at the center of the apartment, was a wonder of spacecraft architectural design. Though the ship was round, the living room was rectangular; though the apartment was tiny, the room was large enough to seat six, comfortably, around a dining table, with space left over for a sofa on one end. In the bedroom, with its trapezoidal shape and prominently curved outside wall, it was hard to forget that we were in a spacecraft. By contrast, the living room was designed to make us feel at home. Three walls met at right angles. The room's only curved wall was obscured by the sofa, which hid much of the outer hull. The apartment had no windows, but two of the living room's walls were floor-to-ceiling nano-LED displays that could transmit outside views from any direction. At the moment, the displays were blank, and the room was lit only dimly. And it was empty, except for the sofa.

The dining table, a simple fold-up model with two hinged plastic sections that closed like a book, was stowed in the girls' bedroom. As the bedroom doors were next to each other, I needed only to turn around and catch the table as Meital pushed it out to me. I made sure to press my feet into a Velcro patch on the floor;

otherwise, the table would have caught me, instead of me catching it. We unfolded it together and extended its legs.

My mother appeared in her bedroom's doorway, wearing a floral-patterned summer dress over her mundies. "Do you see those holes in the floor?" she asked. "You can snap the legs into them." I caught her eye and she smiled at me. "I missed you guys. I know we were apart for only four days, but a mother worries when all her kids are going into orbit for the first time, and on a different spaceship."

She brought rations from the kitchen, an alcove that opened from the living room, across from the bedrooms. But we did not sit down to eat. We did not even take out the folding chairs. Instead, we hovered weightlessly. We did put our food trays on the table, though; it had Velcro patches to keep them from floating away. My mother perched herself at the narrow end, and Denver and I floated next to each other on one side, facing the girls.

Shirel glanced at the empty space across from my mother. "I wish Dad were here. Have you heard from him?"

My mother nodded. "A short message came in earlier today. He said that the water mining continues to progress according to schedule, and they already have one hundred and sixty cubic meters of water stored. They've also completed two hundred and eighty meters of trenches."

"Mom, that's good, but it's not what I meant. How is Dad feeling?"

"Shirel, he's sick, but he's still working and is feeling okay. That's the best we can hope for. He'll be waiting for us when we arrive, and we're bringing better medical facilities. All we can do now is keep praying."

Nobody said anything for an awkward moment.

I broke the pause in the conversation. "Well, I think it's exciting for the four of us to be together, actually beginning our trip."

Shirel corrected me. "The five of us. Denver is now officially our brother!"

Denver, suppressing a smile, announced in a deep voice, "Dr. Dana, I'm proud to have you as my stepmother."

"May this be the first of many happy family dinners on board *Providence*," I declared, holding up my covered cup of water. "And may Dad have a complete recovery."

There was a general chorus of "Amen."

Meital spoke up. "Why is it so dark in here? Can't we turn up the lights? The dimness is depressing."

My mother answered. "We're running on less than half power at the moment. Until we install the habitat's solar panels tomorrow, we have only the Mars-Entry stage's panels. Almost everything we're generating is being used for basic life support. I think you'll be pleasantly surprised tomorrow, though: the living room lights, when turned on fully, are actually quite bright. Besides, I don't know if you noticed, but two of the walls are virtual windows, and we have thousands of scenery videos available. How would you like to have dinner tomorrow night by the beach?"

"That sounds weird in zero-gravity," Meital laughed. "How about just a view of outside?"

"We can have that too. The displays can show views from any of the hull cameras and can even combine multiple streams. But don't you think you'll get bored just watching starfields?"

"No, Mom, I don't think so, not after seeing the stars for real this morning!"

"Hi, everyone," Dr. Jhonathan interrupted, appearing at the bottom of the staircase at the living room's corner. His dark trimmed beard contrasted with the sky-blue longshirt he wore loosely over his mundies. "Can I join you? Did I hear you discussing electricity?"

"Yes, we had a complaint about the lights being too dim," my mother jested.

"We had complaining upstairs, too. That's why I'm here, to talk about tomorrow's operation to get the full power system up and running. We have twenty solar sheets to roll out. If we can get ten people to join the spacewalk, we should be able to finish in under two hours. So far, we have Boris and Simeon Radechov, Dr. Bouchet, Helga and Celina Becker, Sam and me, and Omar Sidda. I need two more volunteers."

"Rabbi Meyer, which Dr. Bouchet?" I asked. With all the doctorate degrees and medical doctors on board, it was hard to keep track of husbands and wives. Making things more complicated, both the Bouchets were experienced surgeons.

"Louis." He looked at me and raised his eyebrows. "But does it make a difference as to whether you volunteer?"

"No, that's not what I meant." Dr. Claudine was very pretty, and I felt awkward around her. I felt myself blushing and rushed to change the subject. "Yes, I want to take part in the operation."

"I also volunteer," Denver said.

"Excellent – that completes the roster. Please meet us in the airlock tomorrow at ten o'clock prompt. And, Michael, I remind you again: I am not a rabbi."

"You've been teaching me Torah, Dr. Jhonathan, so you're a rabbi to me."

Denver asked, "Ten o'clock Mexico time, right? And can you guys stop already with your silly argument?"

"Yes, we will maintain our launch-location clock until we leave Earth orbit. All times are Mexico time." Dr. Jhonathan caught my eye and grinned. "And no, I don't expect that Michael and I will resolve our argument." He turned, grasped the railing, and zipped back upstairs.

"I wonder why Ruby isn't participating in the spacewalk," I said.

"Are you kidding?" Meital answered. "She still hasn't recovered from her queasiness. There's no way she's going on any spacewalk anytime soon."

It was late by the time we finished our dinner rations. We washed up and retired to our rooms. I took the lower bunk; Denver had preferred the upper one. Our mattresses were superfluous in microgravity, but we needed to sleep in the beds anyway, because they had clasps to secure our sleeping bags. I preferred knowing that I would wake up in the same place I went to sleep instead of floating away while dreaming. Still in my mundies – always in our mundies, in case of an emergency loss of air pressure! – I pulled myself into my sleeping bag. After such an eventful day I had lots to think about, but exhaustion overwhelmed my thoughts and I fell asleep immediately.

* * *

Tuesday, September 26th, 2028 07:15

I opened my eyes seven hours later, momentarily surprised to find myself in the dimly lit bedroom. A couple of foggy moments passed before I recalled that this was my new home, the spacecraft we had been anticipating for years. We were here! I thanked G-d for the new day and reached for my datapad to check what time it was. The datapad, one of the few personal items I had gotten around to unpacking, was fastened to the wedge-shaped night table at the head of my bed. It read 07:15 Mexico City time.

I pulled myself out of the sleeping bag, quietly, so as to not wake Denver. I did not have to try hard: the fans were loud enough to drown out any noise I could make pushing myself off the bed and floating across the room. I braced myself to slide the folding door aside, then exited into the living room. That's when the shock of being enclosed in a windowless apartment hit me. There were no hints of morning: no light streaming through cracks in window blinds, no birds chirping, no roosters crowing, no morning breeze; nothing at all different from how the room had looked or felt at dinnertime the night before. In any case, windows would not have helped: in low Earth orbit the sun rose and set every ninety minutes. If the bedroom had a window, I would have missed, or, more likely, been disturbed by, five sunrises while I slept.

The bathroom was on the other side of the small living room. I glided over the dining table. That was something I had never done before in any other house. I used the toilet (weightless protocol!), washed my hands and face (five drops of water), and brushed my teeth. My mother had unpacked toothbrushes for all of us; mine was red. For most heavy-use consumables – bread, for example – we had only raw materials and would need to produce the final product. But toothpaste was different. We had a two-year supply, which, for twenty-one people, would fit inside a couple of bathroom drawers, so it was more efficient to bring the full supply with us and have more sent along in later cargo deliveries.

Back in the bedroom, Denver was yawning and stretching, pulling himself out of his bedroll.

"How did you sleep?" I asked.

"Not too bad. But I'm really looking forward to gravity."

"Careful when you get to the living room. You might be a bit shocked."

He turned to me, eyebrows raised. "What happened?"

"Nothing. That's the problem. It looks just like it did last night. Not a hint of morning."

"What did you expect? We're sealed inside a large tin can."

"It just kind of surprised me."

"I'm going to get something for breakfast. What about you? Are you going to pray this morning with those black boxes you wear? I haven't seen you pray in a few days."

"I think I will. By the way, the boxes are called 'phylacteries.' But I have a problem. I'm not sure what direction to face when I pray."

"Go ask Dr. Jhonathan."

"You could pray, too, Denver."

"Yeah, sure, ... but I doubt it. You know I haven't prayed since my family stopped going to church when I was little. I doubt anyone's listening upstairs. But you keep praying just in case. We have a dangerous spacewalk today. Maybe you'll get us some extra help."

Taking Denver's advice, I headed upstairs to the Meyers' apartment to find Dr. Jhonathan. The Meyers' living room was empty; they had stowed their table after dinner. The door to the room Sam and Omar Sidda shared was open, and Omar was folding his prayer mat.

"Omar, good morning. Have you been praying? Do you mind if I asked what direction you faced?"

"Good morning, Michael. I directed my heart and thoughts toward G-d and Mecca, as I concentrated on my prayers. But if you are asking for yourself, I cannot help you with Jewish recommendations. Jhonathan is awake; why not ask him?"

Dr. Jhonathan emerged from the bathroom. "Ask me what, Michael?"

"Rabbi Meyer, can I pray now? If so, which direction do I face?"

"From the point of view of Jewish Law, either our point of departure, or our last hometown, determines all times, at least while we are in Earth orbit. Mexico was both, so our Jewish schedule is the same as the on-board clock, which Captain Becker has fixed based on Mexico time. So, yes, you can pray the morning prayer now. Regarding direction, since the direction to Jerusalem is changing all the time, there is not much you can do other than focus your heart. Imagine that you are standing in the Holy of Holies in the rebuilt Temple in Jerusalem. And don't forget to concentrate on the words."

"Thanks," I said, as I turned back to the staircase. "How's Ruby this morning?"

"She's still sleeping. I hope she feels better. And Michael, I am not a rabbi."

*   *   *

Tuesday, September 26th, 2028 10:00

I prayed and joined my sisters for breakfast rations, then headed downstairs to the Bouchets' first-floor apartment. The open hatchway down to the airlock, a gaping hole, took up a third of their living room floor. I bent over, grabbed the edge with my hands, and pulled myself in headfirst. Apparently, the others had done the same, as everyone else was also upside-down, relative to the orientation of the furniture in the living spaces above. I pulled myself over to one side and settled next to Denver against the airlock's round white wall. The egress hatch to outer space was in the center of the hull above us, still sealed closed.

Boris Radechov was perched in the center of the circle. He was stout and muscular, with pale green eyes and a receding hairline. He acknowledged my arrival with a nod. "We are waiting just for Helga and Celina," he said, his Russian accent subtle but noticeable. "Then we can start."

The Becker sisters floated up through the hatch. Helga's hands were behind her head, busy gathering her curly blonde hair into an elastic band. "Sorry we're late," she said. "The airlock is so very far from the top floor!" Her eyes twinkled, but she managed to keep a straight face.

Boris cleared his throat. "Today will be our last group spacewalk preparing our new home. Our job is more complicated and difficult than what we have done until now. On Friday, when we opened the heat shield, we could see each other the whole time. Also, Sunday, when we transferred food supplies from the water tanker ship, the operation was all line-of-sight. But today we will be climbing up and around the outside of the ship. We will not be able to see each other."

"What about our buddies?" Celina asked. Her auburn hair was braided in pigtails. "Don't we need to see our buddies all the time?"

"Yes, you must see your buddy, who will be on an adjacent ladder, close by. But most everyone else will be hidden by the curve of the hull."

He took a breath and gathered his thoughts.

"Okay. We will divide into two groups. Simeon's group will roll out ten panels on one side of the habitat while my group rolls out ten panels on the other side. Each of you will take two canisters" – he pointed to the meter-long turquoise cylinders stored against the airlock wall – "and latch them to your harness. Then you will exit the airlock and climb along your ladder to the edge where the wall starts curving upward. Wait there for everyone else to arrive at their positions. Then, at the same time, everyone will pull a panel out of a canister and fasten it to hooks on the left side of the ladder."

"Just one of the panels?" I asked.

"You will unroll one panel on the way up and the other on the way back down. When we reach the top, everyone will fasten their first panel to its upper hooks, then start the same procedure with the second panel. We will come back down together. When we return to the bottom edge, we'll fasten the ends of the second panels. After you all reenter the airlock, Simeon and I will attach the electric system and Jhonathan and Louis will install tethers to stabilize the heat shield. Any questions?"

He paused but nobody asked anything.

"Okay. The safety procedures. Your harness will have two cords, each ending in a carabiner, which you will hook to the ladder rungs. You must be attached to at least one rung all the time. Always, always! – this is the part where you all make me nervous – attach yourself to the next rung before you detach the previous carabiner. Does everyone understand? You must never be free from the ship at any time. If you float away, we have no way to save you!"

Dr. Jhonathan spoke up. "Protocol is to latch and unlatch only while your buddy watches. That means only one of a pair moves at a time."

"You'll tell your buddy when it is okay for them to move. Do not move until your buddy tells you that they are watching."

Denver turned to me and spoke quietly. "You look like you are worried. You're not having second thoughts, are you?"

I felt myself sweating. "Actually, I am having second thoughts," I whispered. "Denver, psych me up. Remind me that there's no problem."

"Obviously there's no problem. We trained to climb the habitat, and you did great."

"I know, but it's more than ten meters, and we won't be able to see the airlock, and –"

"Fleximets and marsmitts on, everybody!" Boris announced. "Check your buddies. We'll begin purging the airlock, but will stop the decompression halfway through to check the mundies. Here are the buddies: on my team: Helga with Celina, Michael with Denver. Simeon's team: Louis – you are with Jhonathan; Sam with Omar. Let's go."

For the third time in two days, I pulled my fleximet over my head, sealed the neck, and pulled on my marsmitts. Denver checked my seals and I checked his. Dr. Louis closed the hatch that led to his living room, making it possible for Dr. Jhonathan to begin the airlock purge. When we stopped halfway through to check the mundies, a couple of us found bulges on our buddies' suits and Simeon patched them. Other than that everything went smoothly. Only a few minutes later we had all donned our Mylar suits and insulated gloves, and had attached our harnesses to our waists and thighs.

I heard Boris's voice in the fleximet's speakers. "Michael, latch these to your belt." He handed me two canisters and I examined them closely through my visor. Bright green printed lettering read "Advanced Solar Technologies." A second line of text, in smaller letters, said, "Rolled thin-film 1 mm solar panel: 10 meters by 80 cm." The ends of both canisters had metal rings, which I latched to my harness.

"Michael, you've put that one upside-down."

I hoped that my blushing was not visible through my mask as I released the canister and reattached it in the right orientation.

Simeon announced, "My team: switch to channel two. Each team will have a separate conversation during the procedure."

Dr. Jhonathan released the airlock's outer hatch and pushed it open. It was much larger than the inner hatch, wide enough for two or three people to pass through together. Simeon's team exited first. Once they were all out, our team prepared to follow.

"Denver and Michael, with me," Boris said over the speakers. "Denver, you take ladder seven; Michael ladder eight." He pointed to the first rung of each. I reached out and latched one of my carabiners. Denver did the same.

"Denver, I'm watching you," I said. "You can progress to the next rung." I kept my eyes on him as he reached forward and latched his second carabiner. Then he reached back and unhooked the first one.

"Michael, your turn. I'm watching."

I pulled myself ahead and latched my second cord. I knew that, in the direct sunlight, the ladder rungs were blisteringly hot – hundreds of degrees – but I felt no heat when I grabbed them with my insulated Mylar gloves. Denver and I continued forward, watching each other as we radiated outward from the open hatch, slowly moving apart. We reached the edge where the habitat's bottom curved up to meet its side, and passed the very large nozzle of one of the landing engines. Most of it was embedded in the hull, but the edge protruded twenty or twenty-five centimeters. I reached over and peered inside.

"Denver, take a look at this."

"You should be glad the engine is not firing at the moment!"

"Pardon the cliché, but cut the chatter," Boris said. "Everyone: take out your first panel and latch it to the hooks."

I located both hooks at the base of the hull, pulled out the panel, and latched it to them. We resumed our careful trek upward, following the safety protocol while slowly unrolling the panels. Progress was more difficult now: two hands were barely enough. Each time I reached out with one hand to latch myself to the next ladder rung, I clutched the panel tightly with the other, praying it would not get free and float away. Then I used both hands to unroll the next part of the panel, bracing myself by hooking my feet into the ladder rungs. It took fifteen minutes to reach the top edge. Finally I latched the panel to the two hooks I found there, jutting out from the PlyShield.

"Confirm that the first panel is attached!" said Boris. "Denver?"

"Yes, both hooks are secure."

"Michael?"

"Yes, secure." I answered.

Helga and Celina also affirmed that they had affixed their panels.

"Take out your second panels. Same procedure!"

I hoped it would be easier the second time. I turned myself over, took out the second panel, fastened it to the hooks on the other side of my ladder, and began my trek back down. After another fifteen minutes, Denver and I found ourselves at the ship's bottom edge, and we attached the unrolled ends of our second panels.

Boris queried us, again, one by one, and we confirmed that all the panels were successfully installed. "Nice work," he said. "Take a couple of minutes to rest and enjoy the view."

I looked around. Only then did I notice that our team was on the ship's upper side, the side that was facing out to space, not down toward Earth. The Radechovs had timed the procedure perfectly: we had exited just as the sun was rising, and were back down at the base before sunset forty-five minutes later, having done the whole job in daylight. Now, as the sun was setting, we could gaze into a gorgeous starfield. I found myself quoting again, in wonderment, from Psalm 104, "How numerous are your creations, O L-rd!" And, from Psalm 147, "He counts the number of the stars; to all of them He assigns names."

"That's a lot of names," I thought out loud.

I saw Denver turn in my direction. "What's a lot of names?"

"The stars! Every one has a name."

I could not see his face, but I knew him well enough to picture his sardonic grin.

Water

Tuesday, September 26th, 2028 15:30

    I had my ebook open and was leafing through the pages of Isaac Asimov's science fiction classic, *Foundation*, which I had loaded into the blank one-hundred-page book's flexible liquid-crystal pages before launch. Focusing was surprisingly difficult. I closed the book. I myself had been spacewalking that very morning. How can science fiction, even space science fiction, compete with that? I tried again, opening the ebook and leafing through its pages, back to page six. I read a sentence, and my mind wandered to my experience exiting the airlock. Another sentence; then I was seeing the starfield in my mind's eye. Another sentence; then the confusion of changing perspective between up and down.

    Fiction had been a rare diversion during the years of training. My mother had told us "You'll have lots of time to read on the journey, to keep yourselves busy. I don't want to hear 'are we there yet?'" We had nearly all of humanity's literature available on our datapads – if not in local storage, then uploadable from Earth – but getting it into our brains took concentration and effort just as in the olden days of handwritten manuscripts. Perhaps I expected too much of myself, two days into our trip, while we were still busy getting the habitat up and running. Perhaps it was too early to sit and relax over a book. I gave up and closed it.

    Ruby appeared at the bottom of the staircase. "Michael, how was your second spacewalk?" Her frizzy brown hair was tied back, but still floated like a halo above her head. She wore a striped yellow overall-skirt over her mundies.

"It went well. We got all the panels installed and nobody floated away." I smiled. Her face lit up.

"Can I join you on the sofa?"

"You look like you're feeling much better. But no, we can't really sit on the sofa. We can hover above it, though!"

She pushed herself off the wall, grabbed the armrest and swiveled down. "I'm feeling much better. Dr. Claudine said my space sickness was one of the worst cases she'd heard of, so she prescribed Dimenphillax. I finally got some really good sleep." She nodded at the closed ebook in my hand. "What are you reading?"

"I'm trying to start the *Foundation* series. It's one of my father's favorites, and he's been pushing me to read it. But I can't concentrate." I Velcroed the ebook to the sofa armrest.

"I know what you mean. Now that I'm not on the verge of vomiting all the time, I'm feeling really excited about being here and starting the trip and everything. But one thing I am looking forward to is a bit more light."

"Let's check on that." I pulled my datapad from my thigh, opened the videophone application, and tapped Boris's picture. He answered immediately.

"You know you can come downstairs to talk to me."

"Yeah, but we have technology. Ruby and I were wondering what's with the electric system."

His image nodded. "Patience, Michael. I am in the middle of checking the battery status. We might have enough charge to start up some systems. Would you like me to launch the daylight program?"

"That would be great. Thanks!"

His picture cut off and I Velcroed the datapad back to my thigh.

The lights began brightening a few minutes later, and the living room's details slowly came into view. To our left were the stairways up to the Meyers' apartment and down to the Bouchets'. A narrow wall, painted bright green, concealed them. Beyond, the living room opened into the kitchen alcove, its white counter and light blue cupboards now clearly visible. In the far corner was the door to the bathroom. Across from where we were sitting, the floor-to-ceiling nano-LED screen – currently blank – occupied the whole wall. Next to it were three sliding doors into the three bedrooms. A second floor-to-ceiling NLED screen, on the wall to our right, was similarly dark, as was the small greenhouse that opened off the living room.

"Let's put on some scenery," Ruby said.

"Not yet," said my mother, arriving from downstairs. "We have work to do. Boris and I confirmed that we have just enough power for the water pump. I want to begin filling the tanks. Ruby, can you go get your brother?"

Ruby nodded, pushed off the couch and floated upstairs. Sam and I had trained together on the water systems, so he and I would help oversee the procedure. "Mom, how long do you think it will take?"

"We have fifty cubic meters to transfer. We should be able to finish in four or five hours. But it's the first time the tubes are being filled, so we'll need to check every one."

Ruby reappeared with Sam. "I haven't been helping with much of anything," she said. "Would another pair of eyes be useful?"

"Sure. Why don't you stick with your brother or Michael? They'll show you what to check. Let's start downstairs."

The Bouchets' first-floor apartment was nearly identical to ours, and to the apartments on the habitat's top two floors. To differentiate them, the stairwell walls were painted different colors. Ours was green while the Bouchets' was a deep mauve. The Bouchets shared their apartment with Boris and Simeon Radechov, who had moved into the third bedroom. We found Boris with Dr. Louis Bouchet at the dining table, examining a datapad. Dr. Louis pointed at the screen. "We'll start at the bottom floor and progress upwards."

"Where are the tanks physically located?" Ruby asked.

"They surround the ship, against the outer hull. You might have noticed them in your bedroom wall."

"I didn't see any tanks."

Sam brushed sandy blonde hair across his forehead and faced his sister. "That's because they're still empty. Picture a very large bicycle tire tube, twenty centimeters wide, but currently deflated. Now picture forty-eight such tubes, each divided into nine sections, stacked one on top of another. They would form a cylindrical shape, four stories high. We're inside that cylinder. Once the tubes are filled, we'll be enclosed and surrounded by water."

"I like that analogy," Dr. Louis said. "Ruby, the tubes are fastened flat against the outer wall for launch, so you might not recognize them as tubes. But you probably noticed the black shelves sticking out from the wall. The shelves will hold the tubes in place when they are filled, especially when we have gravity."

"Why so complicated? Why not just have one tank with all the water in one place?"

Sam answered. "Because of cosmic radiation. On Earth there's a magnetic field that protects us by deflecting it. Without the field, radiation would shower down and endanger all life on the planet. The magnetic field is one of the Creator's greatest gifts, and we should be very grateful for it! But we don't have that protection in interplanetary space, so we need something artificial to absorb as much radiation as possible. Water is as good a material as any, and it turns out that a thickness of just twenty centimeters reduces our exposure by half. The water encircles us to protect us."

Ruby turned to me, a sympathetic look on her face. "In my medical classes we learned that radiation exposure increases the risk of cancer and other illnesses. Is that why your dad is sick? Not enough water protection on the MiniHab?"

My mother looked up at the mention of my father. "The MiniHabs did have a similar water tube system." She sighed. "We knew from the start that radiation would be a risk. The Vanguard group's ships were equipped with the Murke-Berger Foundation's first design. Our own spacecraft is safer. We made improvements to the design based on what Doriel and his team learned."

She changed the subject. "We've started the pumps. Boris has set the computer to open valves to fill three sections at a time. We need to watch every section as it fills up, so split up. Michael, start in the master bedroom, behind the closet. You'll continue into the bathroom. Sam, to the kitchen, where the first tube will fill up behind the kitchen cupboard; then you'll continue to the living room. I'll take the greenhouse and the bedrooms.

Ruby followed me into the Bouchets' master bedroom, which was just big enough to contain a king-sized bed and a medium-sized closet. The fowl corrals and the egg incubator were latched to the wall, as were a couple of duffels; they had not finished unpacking. While Ruby stopped to check the birds, I kicked across the room toward the far-right corner. I peered at the lowest section of tubing where the hull met the floor. It was jet-black and rubbery. This particular tube began behind the closet, where we could not see it, and continued behind the double bed, where we also could not see it, but its middle part was exposed.

Ruby squeezed in by my side. She reached out and touched the tube, and exclaimed, "It's cold!"

"The tanker's power system heats the water minimally, keeping it just above freezing." I also pressed my hand against it. The rubber was stiffer than I'd expected. The thick casing would protect the tank from rupturing accidentally.

The tube stopped expanding. "This one has filled up as expected. Let's get ready for the next one." I floated over to the other side of the bed; Ruby followed close behind. Only a small part of the second tank was exposed – it stretched from behind the bed and continued behind the bathroom wall – but we could see its middle section filling up, expanding as expected. It reached full capacity within two minutes.

A folding door led into the bathroom, where the next tank would fill up. We headed through. The narrow space between the solids processor and the toilet was just big enough for us to reach into and feel the tube. Less than a minute later it was completely full.

"Back to the bedroom?" Ruby asked.

"I'm not sure. Wait a few seconds."

The tube directly above the first started filling up. "See that? The computer alternates the order, so we don't need to run back and forth quite as much."

But we did float back and forth between the bathroom and bedroom repeatedly, over the next hour, as the first floor's twelve levels of tubes filled up.

"Mom, can we take a break? This is getting tedious."

"We'll take a short break, but we do have three more floors to go. Let's swap positions to make it a bit more interesting."

On the second floor, Ruby and I took the kitchen and living room position. We opened the kitchen cabinet and reached our hands inside to check that the first tube was filling. When it finished, we exited to the living room to look for the next tube, which was mostly hidden by the air-processing equipment behind the stairwell. The third tube began at the edge of the stairs and stretched all the way behind the sofa.

"So that's how they fill up," Ruby said, pointing to the wall where a vertical pipe came out of the floor and passed up through the shelves that held the tubes. Valve assemblies branched out to the tanks on either side. Electric cables connected to the assemblies. "It looks like the computer opens and closes the valves to direct the water to each tube."

Ruby and I continued back and forth between the living room and the kitchen, as level after level of tubes filled up with near-freezing water. More than half had filled when Sam called from my sisters' bedroom, "Stop the pump! There's a problem here."

We followed my mother into the bedroom. Meital, Shirel and Sam were examining a tube in the wall between the bunk beds. It was about a third full.

"It was filling up slowly, then stopped. I think the valve is blocked."

Dr. Louis was in the living room, monitoring the operation from his datapad. My mother called to him. "Louis, check valve 157."

"I'm instructing the computer to skip that tank and continue with the next one."

"Let me see if I can fix the valve," I said. "Ruby, can you continue observing the tubes in the kitchen and living room alone?"

"I think I'm capable of the task," she answered drolly.

It took me fifteen minutes to remove the assembly casing, take apart the valve, find the blockage – some metal shavings, apparently left over when the part was manufactured – and clean and reassemble the valve's ball. Happily, there was no need to replace anything. We did have a small stock of replacement parts, and the ability to print more if necessary, but it was better not to have to replace anything on day two of our journey. I rejoined Ruby just before we finished the second floor.

We continued for almost three more hours in much the same way, examining tube after tube after tube, but taking short breaks between floors. We found and repaired two other problematic valves (numbers 308 and 394). Finally, when our datapads showed 20:05 Mexico time, we reached the last row of tanks, which encircled the Beckers' apartment on the top floor. Ruby and I had taken the greenhouse room and Helga's and Celina's bedrooms.

Water

"Well, this sure is different from my bedroom," Ruby said as we checked the last tank. "Is it fair that Helga and Celina get single rooms, when everyone else has to have a roommate?"

Because the habitat's top was a dome, the fourth-floor walls curved inwards toward the ceiling, somewhat like the walls of a small jetliner. "You see that there's no room for a second bunk here, don't you?" I asked. "Besides, do you mind sharing a room with Susan?"

"No, of course not. I love my sister. Still, the Becker girls do seem lucky."

"Maybe, but the rooms on this floor feel cramped to me."

Back in the living room, where Dr. Louis was examining his datapad with my mother, the Beckers had gathered around their table for dinner. "Pardon our intrusion," I said. Then, whispering to Ruby, "Even the living room feels smaller because of the wall curving over the sofa."

Dr. Louis read from the screen. "The computer reports that the water-tanker ship is almost completely empty. I'll head down and close the master intake valve." He disappeared into the stairwell. My mother waved to us to follow.

Dr. Cecylia Becker, Helga's and Celina's mother, turned from the table to face us. "Michael, while you and your mother were busy with the water tanks, I made sure to bake extra bread. Take a loaf from the breadbox. And take the pot of bean stew: there is plenty extra and we have finished eating. Just don't forget to return the pot – we have only three."

"Dr. Becker, thank you; that is sweet and thoughtful! My mom and sisters will also be really happy."

"Ruby, I would offer you some too, but I think your mother prepared dinner."

I noticed that the Beckers had put scenery up on the NLED wall. They were eating their dinner, virtually, by a lush green garden, tall trees towering over a bed of tulips, pink, maroon and cream-colored. A light breeze rustled the highest leaves. Three young girls were running around playing tag. A pale green bird swooped down from one of the trees.

Ruby asked, "Where is that beautiful garden?"

Dr. Cecylia smiled. With wide cheeks and a flat chin, she looked proud and aristocratic, but her brown eyes were soft and friendly.

"That is the backyard of our old house in Amersfoort," she said. "We recorded years of scenery, in all four seasons, before we moved to Arizona." Gesturing toward the wall, she said, "This one is from the wrong month: it's a springtime video. If you come back tomorrow, I promise we'll put up a timelier autumn scene. We have some beautiful scenery of leaves changing color along Amsterdam canals."

The question of whether Northern Hemisphere seasons mattered to us anymore briefly crossed my mind, but we had our own dinner to prepare. Ruby took a large loaf from the breadbox while I approached the induction stovetop, where a pot, inserted in a pot-sized socket, was turning rapidly. Like everything in the habitat, the stove was designed for both weightless and gravity use. In weightless mode, a magnetic disk under the socket rotated the pot and an induction coil surrounding the socket caused the pot's outer edge to heat up. The rotation created enough artificial gravity for convection currents to form, starting at the outer edge and rising, from the inside-pot point of view, toward the pot's center. This allowed the pot's contents to cook evenly.

I turned off the stove and stopped the rotation, then braced myself and grabbed the pot's handles to pull it out. Thanking the Beckers again, Ruby and I pushed off the wall and headed downstairs.

*   *   *

Tuesday, September 26th, 2028 20:30

"This is so much better than the rations!" Shirel said, taking another spoonful of bean stew from her bowl, which was Velcroed to the tabletop. "I like the hot-pepper spice." She snapped the bowl's top closed again.

"I didn't think the rations were all that bad," Meital said. "But freshly cooked food is great. And Dr. Cecylia's bread is really tasty. What did she add to the dough?"

"I think it's the freshly milled whole wheat that makes it taste so good," I said. "It has so much more taste than industrial flour. But wait for the bread I want to bake tomorrow. I'm planning on using some of my sourdough culture, which should make it taste great."

"It will taste interesting, Michael," Denver said, glancing at me and brushing hair out of his eyes. "But let's wait on the 'great' part.

We've had experience with your sourdough cultures." The corners of his lips hinted at a smile.

"Michael, you've let some breadcrumbs loose," my mother said. "Please try to avoid crumbs. We don't want to overload the filters unnecessarily."

I tried to scoop the crumbs out of the air, but they were already following the air currents toward the kitchen vent.

My mother's datapad, fastened to her thigh, vibrated loudly. She pulled it off and looked at the screen. Her face brightened. "Kids, we have a treat! It's a video message from Dad. Let me put it up on the wall." She tapped the datapad screen and my father's face appeared on the NLED wall behind her. He was sitting in the upper deck of his group's MiniHab spacecraft, which had remained their home after its successful landing on the Mars surface more than a year earlier. The kitchenette was visible behind him.

"Hi everybody! Mom told me that you have successfully arrived at the habitat, and are preparing for the boost to high orbit. Congratulations, new astronauts! I'm excited for you. Now I can start counting down the days until you get here.

"We continue to make progress. The robotic mining machines produce more and more water every day. We're outside with them most days now, as they need continual maintenance. They almost never break down, but they need to be cleaned, and the wheels sometimes get stuck. Stephen and I in particular have gotten used to being outside. We've been taking regular exercise hikes to the nearby hills.

"You all have a long journey ahead of you. It will be important to keep yourselves busy. Keep up with your schoolwork, and do everything your mother tells you. And obey Captain Becker. He's a good man. If he seems strict, remember that your safety depends on discipline."

Denver groaned.

My father continued. "Most of all, have fun. You are doing something that no children have ever done before in the history of mankind! Every day when you wake up, remind yourselves that you are pioneers. Seize the adventure!" He paused and smiled at the camera. "But don't do anything dangerous."

"The whole trip is dangerous," Shirel said. "How does he expect us not to do anything dangerous?"

My father wrapped up his message. "I send my love and miss you all. Please record a video and send it back. Oh – all of you, and especially Michael – start writing now. Don't wait to begin recording your thoughts and experiences. You'll be happy to have a personal record. All of humanity will benefit, too, someday. Love you all!"

The video cut off and the beach scenery we had put up earlier resumed. A wave broke, exactly where my father had been sitting a moment before.

"Mom, should we record an answer now?" Meital asked.

"Yes, let's do that. I'll activate the wall camera. Look toward it as you talk." She clicked her datapad screen. "Okay, start now."

I faced the wall. "Hi Dad! We filled the water tubes today. Ruby and Sam and I spent four hours with Mom examining what felt like every centimeter of the ship. Tomorrow, I want to use the kitchen for the first time and bake some bread. I'll start writing – thanks for the reminder!"

Meital spoke next. "Dad, how are you feeling? You looked great in the video message. We're doing well adjusting to our new home. The chicks survived launch; I hope nothing changes. I promise you a fresh omelet when we get there. Take care of yourself."

She turned to Shirel. "Your turn."

"Dad, I miss you. I'm having fun in zero gravity. I'm doing lots of somersaults, like you said I'd be able to. And you'd be proud of me: I've been helping Mom with unpacking and getting the kitchen in order. By the way, did you know that Susy and I are in charge of the worms? I love you! Bye."

Denver turned toward the camera. "Dr. Dana, Michael and Meital have officially made me part of the family, so that means I'm now your adopted son. I hope you don't mind! And I hope you are feeling okay."

"Doriel, be strong," my mother said. "We'll be there before you know it. Hang in there for us. I love you!"

She tapped her datapad. "I've sent the message. If he hasn't gone to sleep, he should have it in seventeen minutes."

Meital spoke. "He said they're outside most days. Wow! He makes it sound like a simple thing to do, to go hiking on Mars."

Water

"It must be so cramped inside their little ship," Shirel said. "They don't even have a ZubHab! Imagine spending years inside such a small space. It makes sense that they'd want to go outside."

My mother went to the kitchen and retrieved a plastic container from the small refrigerator. "Here's a bit of dessert – I reconstituted some applesauce. I hope I didn't add too much water." She opened the container and scooped a sticky tablespoonful into my bowl, making sure no drops got loose. After I closed the lid, she served Denver, then passed the container to the girls.

Back in the kitchen, she found a white bottle of pink pills. "Vitamins, everyone! Everybody must take one every day. Even the best, most balanced space diet we can prepare here will be lacking." After she handed them out, she pulled her datapad off her thigh and tapped the screen. "We'll keep track of vitamin intake in the nutrition app. Each day, when you take a tablet, either record it yourself or let me know and I'll put it in."

The NLED screen on the side wall lit up and Captain Becker's face appeared.

"I'm sorry to bother you all if you are still eating," he said.

"Mom, can he also see us?" Shirel asked.

"Yes, Shirel, I see all of you. Captain's prerogative: I have control over all the screens and their cameras. But don't worry. I do not plan to spy on you." He smiled stiffly.

"I am interrupting because I want all the youth to join me for a short meeting in twenty minutes, at 21:25. We will meet on Level Three in the Meyers' sitting room. You must all start your regular tasks tomorrow. I want to make sure you all know what you are responsible for. Okay?"

"We'll be there," Meital said. We all nodded.

The wall screen went blank.

"Clear the table, everyone," my mother said. "Wash the bowls before you go upstairs. Who volunteers?"

"Me," I said. "I want to see if I can figure out how you wash dishes in weightlessness."

It turned out to be easier than I expected. A nylon netting stretched over the sink to keep the dirty dishes from floating out. I put a few drops of water on a sponge and added a drop of soap. I slid the netting to the side and pulled out a dirty bowl, let the netting snap back into place, and washed the bowl with the sponge. Then I pulled the netting back a second time and slid the soapy bowl underneath.

"Michael, you forgot to turn on the water vacuum!" my mother yelled, startling me.

I switched it on and, whirring very loudly, it began sucking air toward the sink. A few drops of water that had escaped from the sponge began moving back toward the intake.

While I washed the bowls and spoons, Meital wet a second sponge and started rinsing.

"Thanks for helping, Meital, but you are being very liberal with the water," I said. She was squeezing out the sponge and refilling it with each bowl.

"How else can I rinse the dishes? This is how you're supposed to do it. All the water is getting sucked into the sink – I'm making sure of it."

*   *   *

Tuesday, September 26th, 2028 21:25

"Girls, let's start with you," Captain Becker said, addressing Susan and Shirel. His sparse brown hair was combed back neatly, somehow staying in place despite the weightlessness. "You need to go to bed soon."

We were gathered in the Meyers' living room, one level above ours, where the stairwell wall was painted pink. I braced myself at the edge of the couch. Turning to observe the water tanks we had filled earlier, I was happy to see they were still full.

"Vermiculture is one of the most important jobs to be done during our journey. You will create the soil we will use to farm on Mars. You also will create soil to help fertilize the vegetables we will grow during the trip. And perhaps most important, the worms will dispose of much of our rubbish and food leftovers. You will need to be very responsible, as the worms need to be checked and fed every day. The two of you will do most of the work, but my wife, Cecylia, will teach you and help you. Please come up to the top floor here tomorrow morning at ten o'clock to begin. Okay?"

"Okay," Susan answered. Shirel nodded.

"Good. Then off to bed. Good night, girls!" He looked around at us, considering who would be next. "By age," he said to himself.

Water

"Meital and Ruby! You will be responsible for the poultry. Over the next few weeks the surviving chicks will require daily care, as will the new chicks when the eggs hatch. You'll set up their coops in the airlock. The chickens will also need to be fed every day, and the coops cleaned. When they start laying eggs in several months, you'll be responsible for collecting the eggs. You both studied poultry farming. Are you ready for the task?"

Ruby answered before he even finished asking. "Of course we're ready for the task!"

"Don't forget the parakeets and canaries," Meital added. "We'll take care of them too."

"My wife will oversee your work, too." He turned to Dr. Cecylia, who was standing by the kitchen. "Should they come up at eleven?"

She nodded.

"Eleven o'clock prompt. Okay?"

"Okay," they said.

"Next, water and air. These are the most critical life-support systems." Captain Becker turned to face me. "I cannot overstate how much we will all rely on you, on your diligence and responsibility. The water equipment, especially the toilets, needs to be cleaned and inspected every day." He turned to Sam, who hovered by the door to his bedroom. "Michael and Sam, the two of you will also be responsible for overseeing the compost system, running the kilns when the toilets fill up, and packing the resulting soil."

"We know; we're all set to go," Sam said.

"Louis and Dana will oversee your work. Please meet with them tomorrow at ten o'clock, in your apartment, Michael. I expect a full inspection already tomorrow."

"We're all set," I said. "We started working with Dr. Louis and my mom today, when we filled the tanks."

Captain Becker actually smiled. "Fair enough. Next, air systems. Remind me who is responsible?"

Denver and Boris raised their hands. "We're all set," Denver said.

"You know that the air filtering, purification and conditioning systems need to be inspected and tested every day. Filters need to be cleaned or changed as necessary."

"We know," Denver answered impatiently.

Captain Becker glared at him before continuing. "Air quality and composition also need to be checked daily, and you'll collect adsorbed carbon dioxide for the laundry."

Denver started to say something, but Captain Becker cut him off. "Meet with Claudine upstairs in our apartment at ten o'clock tomorrow morning."

"Upstairs?" Boris asked. "Not in our apartment on the first level?"

"Yes, upstairs. I think that will be our general practice throughout the journey, for the married women to work upstairs and the married men downstairs."

He glanced at his datapad. "That leaves my daughters and Omar and Simeon. Celina and Omar, we won't begin planting until we have artificial gravity, but please meet with Mam – my wife, Omar – tomorrow afternoon to work out a crop schedule. I'd like to see a detailed plan for what you want to grow on each level, and when you expect to harvest. Both vegetables and fungi."

Omar answered. "It will take a few days."

"You have a few days. I doubt you'll be able to plant anything before Sunday."

He looked back down at his datapad, then up at his older daughter. "Helga, you are responsible for structural analysis and ultraviolet and chemical surface sterilization. You'll inspect a complete level each day. You'll run a bacteriological surface sample analysis each day, too. Good?"

"I'm ready to start. I've already discussed it with Dr. Esther."

"Fine. Please start with the first level tomorrow morning." He turned toward Simeon. "Simeon, you and I will inspect all electrical and communication systems, and run the standard diagnostic tests, every day. I won't have time until Thursday, but let's meet then at ten o'clock, downstairs in your bedroom, and we can get started."

Simeon stroked his short goatee beard. "I'll run the diagnostics tomorrow morning."

The captain nodded at him and looked around at all of us. "I think that's everything. Thanks for attending the meeting at such short notice. Ruby, I'm happy to see you looking much better."

"Thanks, Captain Becker."

"On a different topic. First Officer Meyer – that's Dr. Jhonathan – and I are releasing the MiniHabs and the water tanker tomorrow morning. If all goes well, we will boost to high orbit in the evening. I will want us all to meet together, sometime in the afternoon, to discuss preparations. I'll call the meeting fifteen minutes before we start.

"Also, I believe that Jhonathan will want to meet with you all on Thursday to discuss school schedules. I remind you that summer vacation is over and spaceflight will not be an excuse for skipping school!" He smiled, more warmly this time. "All of us, from our youngest, Sophie and Jasmine, to our most elderly, Cecylia and myself" – his eyes twinkled – "will learn throughout the trip. Those of you still in school, whether elementary or university, must study diligently. Dr. Jhonathan will track your progress, review test results, and assign grades! Plan to be busy."

With that, he ended the meeting.

Red Valley

Orbit

Wednesday, September 27th, 2028 07:15

A knock on the wall interrupted a fast-action dream, which faded away as I opened my eyes. I thanked G-d for the new day, then looked around the spaceship bedroom and remembered where I was.

"Boys, we have a big day ahead! Time to get up."

It had been years since my mother woke me with a kiss, but the look in her eyes as she smiled from the doorway was almost as sweet.

"Denver and Michael, we're having breakfast at eight o'clock. It's seven fifteen now, so get yourselves started."

"Thanks, Dr. Dana," Denver murmured.

"I've unpacked the wall covers. I want you to pick out hangings to cover the wall and pipes next to your beds. Do you want a solid color or a pattern? The girls chose lovely bright floral designs."

"Mom, thanks. Let us get up and get ready; then we'll choose."

Forty-five minutes later we were again gathered around our family dining table. We had dressed and I had prayed, and Denver and I had even managed to pick out and install wall hangings. I chose a paisley design in pastel blues, reds and yellows, while Denver took a dark navy cover for his wall by the upper bunk. My mother assured us that there were plenty of extras and we would be able to change the hangings from time to time. The variety of hangings made possible a bit of interior decorating in what was otherwise a simple, bland spacecraft environment. If Dad had been with us, he would have cited a study that showed improved psychological health when astronauts had even just a bit of control over their visual environment. For me, the main benefit was that the water tanks, which looked completely out-of-place in a bedroom, would be covered. Still, we would be able to access the tanks whenever necessary, to sterilize surfaces or fix faults, just by unsnapping the covers.

My mother waved her hand toward my sister. "You should all thank Meital, who prepared breakfast this morning."

"Thanks. When did you have time to make the oatmeal?" I asked.

"I crushed half a bag of kernels in the mill last night and let them soak until morning. Cooking didn't take long. I left the other half in the refrigerator, so we can make more tomorrow."

"It's really good," Shirel said. "Did you use milk? Where did you get it?"

"You know we have no real milk aboard. I added a little of the powdered soy milk."

"Meital, did you log the ingredients in the Foodstock application?" my mother asked. "The computer needs to keep track of everything we use."

"I found the powdered soya in our cabinet. Everything in our cabinets is already logged, right? I got the oats from Dr. Cecylia, and she was very strict about updating the application."

"Okay. I'm just making sure."

Meital changed the subject. "Mom, Captain Becker said that we are releasing the MiniHabs this morning. That means that we're going ahead with the mission and can't turn back, right?"

"In a way, but not exactly. Are you having second thoughts about what we are doing? Any of you?"

"No, I made my decision and am excited about the trip," Meital said. "But it does seem like a final commitment. Now we'll have to go."

I caught her eye. "We're still going to be in orbit around Earth for the next month." "It's not quite final."

"Let's discuss this," my mother said. "The mission plan calls for the MiniHabs to remain docked only until we get the habitat up and running, just before the boost to high Earth orbit. If we discovered a major problem with the spacecraft's structure, or with the electrical systems, or with the water tanks, we would abort the mission and use the capsules to return to Earth. Thank G-d we've had no major problems: everything so far has been within specifications."

Denver asked, "Doesn't the mission plan also require that everybody agree to go, before we release the MiniHabs? Aren't we supposed to take a poll?"

"Technically, yes, anybody can decide to quit, but no, we do not have to take a poll. As far as I know, nobody has asked Captain Becker to abort the mission." My mother paused and looked around. "But okay, let's take a poll. Who wants to go to Mars?"

I raised my hand. Denver waved. Meital gestured, tilted her head, and smiled.

"Shirel, what about you?"

"Mom, don't be ridiculous. I've spent half my life preparing for this."

My mother smiled too. "Then I won't tell Captain Becker to abort." She glanced at her datapad. "It's almost nine o'clock. I need to go. We're releasing the water tanker and Jhonathan needs me to oversee the pipes. Michael, if we're not finished by ten, you and Sam go ahead and meet with Louis without me."

She headed upstairs. Shirel followed with Meital, who announced, "I'll make sure Shirel and Susan get to their meeting with Dr. Cecylia on time. Ruby and I can chat a bit until it's our turn."

Denver and I remained behind to clean up. Denver Velcroed his feet to the floor by the kitchen sink and began washing the breakfast dishes.

"You're being very quiet," I said. "What are you thinking?"

He rinsed a bowl and clipped it to the drying rack, then spoke, softly at first. "I didn't think it would affect me. But I am feeling like today is the final break. It is like, when the MiniHabs are released, there's no going back, and my past ends. Then my future – our future – begins."

"Denver, you know we can still abort from high Earth orbit. The Murke-Berger Foundation can launch MiniHab capsules to an intercept orbit to pick us up. We can land safely after a couple of aerobraking orbits."

"Michael, that's not the point. I'm talking about a feeling: I'm talking about the symbolism of ejecting the MiniHab capsules. They represent the way back. Once they are gone, we can go only forward." He took a breath. "And besides, you know an intercept is not going to happen. Everything will go as planned, we'll leave Earth orbit as scheduled, and we'll head off toward Mars."

"You're thinking it's like throwing away the keys, or burning a bridge behind us. Up 'til now, returning to Earth was in our power. Now it's not something we can do anymore."

"Yes, but it's more than that for me. You are only moving from one place to another, but you're staying with the same people, the same family." There was a hint of sadness in his eyes. "I'm leaving my old family and can only hope to find a new family at the other end."

"Denver, first of all, you already have your new family. Us!" I forced a serious expression onto my face. "We made that decision, officially, the day before yesterday. Second, you have been avoiding contact with your family for more than a year now. What changed your mind?"

He examined his fingernails. "I did not change my mind." He paused, considering. "There is truly no point in contact. They don't deserve it."

"You don't seem so sure."

"No, I'm sure. But somehow, I always hoped that something would change. That my mother would reach out. Apologize. Or just try for some contact. That my father would send a heartfelt letter. Not just another attempt at justification, but a real attempt to make a connection. Something that would make a reason to see them again."

He paused again, and took a deep breath. "But that's finished now. I'm really never going back."

That was followed by several minutes of silence, during which we dried the dishes and put them away, snapping them into place in the upper cabinets. I did not know what to say. Perhaps it was enough that I was by his side, because when he finally turned to me, he had a genuine smile. "It is almost time for our meetings, to start our new jobs."

Sam appeared in the kitchen doorway, wearing a white buttoned longshirt over his mundies. "It's ten to ten, Michael. Let's head down and find Dr. Bouchet. Denver, are you meeting the other Dr. Bouchet – all these doctors are so confusing! – downstairs too?"

"No, Captain Becker told Boris and me to meet her at the top level."

"Oh, on 'Yellow Level?'" Sam said.

"What's 'Yellow Level?'" I asked.

"I thought we could identify the levels by color. You noticed that the stairwell wall is a different color on each level, didn't you? We can call the Beckers' apartment 'Yellow Level.'"

Denver said, "Okay, I'm heading up to Yellow Level. See you later." He pushed out of the kitchen and headed upstairs. Sam and I followed him to the stairwell, but propelled ourselves downward.

"Mauve Level!" Sam announced, as we entered the Bouchets' living room.

Dr. Louis Bouchet was just exiting the master bedroom. His curly brown hair framed a narrow, tanned face, and small lines met at the edges of his eyes as he smiled, happy to see us. "Sam, Michael, I was just coming up to meet you. But since you've come down, we may start here." He pointed toward the bathroom. "Are you excited like I am to be finally starting our journey?" His eyes narrowed, but his smile remained as he regarded us. "Or are you nervous about the whole thing?"

"I am excited," I said. "I would not say that I am nervous, but I certainly feel some trepidation. We are venturing into the unknown, and face lots of new dangers."

"Oh, it is not so unknown," Dr. Louis said in his slight French accent. "We know a lot about what we are doing and where we are going. In particular – let's get to our business this morning – we are all experts at water recycling technology. And its less pleasant side" – he smiled broadly and winked – "sewage treatment."

Sam spoke. "Are we going to go over the solids processing procedure? We've done it multiple times, but I'm wondering if we'll have special problems in weightlessness. I'd like you to take us through it again, please."

"Yes, I want to review the procedure with you. But first let us discuss general procedures." His expression became serious. "We have twenty-one souls on *Providence*. The four of us, we three together with your mother, Michael, will be responsible for the lives of these people. Drinking, cooking, and bathing all depend on functioning pumps and valves, which we will examine and test on a daily basis. Even more critically: you know that improper treatment of waste can cause disease which, in our enclosed space, could, G-d forbid, wipe us out quickly. And even more dangerous are waste gases, which must be strictly controlled. Methane, ammonia, and sulfur dioxide are poisonous even in small concentrations, and the waste processors must not inadvertently release them."

"We studied all of this," I said.

Dr. Louis tilted his head down and looked up at me as a professor might regard a slow student. "In Altiplano, it was theoretical. Now it is real. I want you to understand how important this is here."

"Yes, we understand."

"This is why we will spend so much time inspecting the systems. Every day we will do visual inspections, and we will run automated diagnostics. We will keep track of parts that show signs of potential failure and will promptly repair anything that actually breaks. This is besides regular waste treatment work, which will also be our responsibility.

"Dana – your mother – and I will run the diagnostics. Most days, I want the two of you to do the visual inspections. Occasionally we'll give you a day off and do the inspections ourselves. But this will be your regular work most mornings.

"We have four redundant water systems on board, one on each deck. Each of you will be responsible for two of the systems, inspecting them every day."

Sam cut in. "I have an idea. Does it make sense for us to alternate? For example, one day I'll examine Mauve and Green, and Michael will examine Pink and Yellow. The next day we'll switch, with Michael doing Mauve and Green, and me doing Pink and Yellow. Then even if I miss something, Michael will notice it, and vice versa."

"Mauve and Green, uh, what?" Dr. Louis looked perplexed.

"He means the different floors of the habitat," I explained. "Sam has an idea to refer to the different floors by the colors of their stairwell walls."

"Oh." Dr. Louis raised his eyebrows and wrinkled his forehead. "I like both ideas, Sam. Switching each day gives us human-factor redundancy." He pushed off the wall and floated toward the bathroom. "Let's get started."

In the bathroom we inspected the pipes and valves, and Dr. Louis explained how the computer's diagnostics program tested them. He showed us how to access the holding tank behind the shower wall at the room's far right. We examined the toilet in the middle of the room and, finally, the waste-processing unit, which was situated between the toilet and the shower.

He pointed toward the floor. "Note the window on the side of the kiln. The toilet's vacuum pump directs solid waste into its main chamber. You will need to inspect visually. If the chamber appears more than two-thirds full, you will activate the processor. The chamber holds six liters, so we will need to run a cycle every two or three days."

Sam flipped himself upside-down to look into the kiln's window. "It's pretty full now. Shall we run a cycle?" He pulled his datapad off his thigh and tapped the screen. "I'm opening the waste processing application."

I lifted my own datapad and found the same application. After it launched, I tapped to open the Mauve-Level data view. Apparently, the toilet's electronics kept track of usage, because the computer displayed an estimate of how full the solids chamber was: eighty-three percent.

"Do you want to initiate the cycle, or should I?"

"You can start it if you want, Michael," Sam answered.

I clicked the "Process Solids" icon. A diode lit up on the front of the kiln and the machinery came to life. A whirring sound started, then increased in frequency until it reached a high pitch.

"That's the macerator," Dr. Louis explained. "Two very strong knives rotate at high speed to break up solids."

Within moments, the high-pitched whirring noise subsided.

"You see that the first part does not take long. Now the kiln will start."

On my datapad, the application displayed a message: "Checking power utilization. Please wait."

"What's it doing?" I asked.

"The kiln uses lots of electricity, so the computer first checks that other high-power applications, such as waste-processing units on the other floors, or the washing machines, or kitchen ovens, are not running. If necessary, it will wait until power becomes available."

"That's pretty cool," I said. "I wonder who wrote the habitat management software. Managing power for all the equipment sounds like an interesting programming challenge." Glancing at the datapad, I noted that it had switched to "Dehydration Phase." A second diode lit up on the front of the kiln.

"The kiln now heats to one hundred and fifty degrees to boil off fluids," Dr. Louis explained. "A fan pushes the resulting steam into the small still." He pointed to a set of transparent tubes behind a large window above the kiln. "After the steam condenses, the water enters the wastewater tank, joining liquid waste from the toilet, sink, and shower. This phase takes thirty minutes, and you do not need to observe it. But nobody can use the toilet while it runs, so you might want to use the time to perform your visual inspection. Halfway through, after fifteen minutes, make sure to check that water has begun condensing."

While the dehydration phase ran, Dr. Louis took us into the kitchen to point out the pipes and valves we would need to inspect each day. Then we circled around the apartment, checking for leaks in the valves that fed the rubbery tube-tanks. We returned to the bathroom just as my datapad's display message switched from "Dehydration Phase" to "Sterilization Phase." The kiln's third diode lit up.

"Now the computer will heat the kiln to three hundred degrees, to sterilize the waste, killing bacteria and other growth. During this phase the kiln is sealed, so no steam exits into the still. Sterilization lasts another half hour. You do not need to monitor the kiln during this phase, but do check that the computer reports that the proper temperature is reached."

While the sterilization phase ran, Dr. Louis demonstrated the diagnostics application. He showed us how the wall-tank valve test worked. The computer pumped small amounts of water from tank to tank and reported any anomalies in flow levels. The datapad's screen displayed a rotating schematic that indicated which valve was being tested at any given time.

Eventually, my laptop chimed, informing us that the kiln's sterilization phase had finished, and we headed back to the bathroom. The toilet's vacuum pump was running, blowing cold air through the solids chamber to cool the waste product and flush out dangerous gases.

"Remind me what happens to the gas products?" asked Sam.

"They go to the air processor." Dr. Louis pointed to a pipe that exited the waste-processing unit and entered the ceiling. "This pipe passes over the kitchen and enters the air processor behind the stairwell. It also needs to be examined every day, but that is not your responsibility. I think Boris, and your friend Denver, are meeting with my wife right now to go over procedures."

"Yes, Denver headed upstairs when we came down here," I said.

"Sam, grab that black bag." Dr. Louis pointed to a sealed container latched just above the waste processor. Sam reached over and handed him the bag, which was not quite empty. "See the lights on the kiln, that they have turned off? That means that the kiln is cool enough to open." He reached down and rotated a handle above the kiln's window, then pulled the small door open. "You need to be careful in weightlessness. Put your hand inside and grab the waste, but gently. You do not want it to crumble. Take it and put it into the bag."

Sam did so with a disgusted look on his face.

Dr. Louis noticed his expression. "There is nothing to be bothered about. This material is sterile now and will become an important fertilizer on Mars. Seal the bag and latch it back on top of the processor."

"What if it fills up?"

"It will definitely fill up," Dr. Louis said, smiling. "We will pack the full bags into the ZubHab's outer wall. As we slowly use up the ship's water supply, some tanks will empty and the fertilizer bags will take their place. The waste product is organic material, so it is good protection against radiation, no worse than the water."

He showed us how to reseal the kiln and how to use the datapad application to reactivate the chamber's regular function, which was to collect solid waste each time the toilet was used. Then, after we scrubbed our hands and took a short break in the kitchen (his wife, Dr. Claudine, had baked cookies), he showed us how to inspect the large still, which filtered, boiled, and then condensed liquid waste from the toilet, sink, and shower.

"The condensed water is of potable quality," he explained, "but we will not actually drink it. We will use it for washing and for cooking, and for watering the plants. We do not need to drink it, because we have enough fresh water on board to supply all our drinking needs for the entire journey. The water management software keeps track of which wall tanks have fresh water and which have recycled water. It draws only fresh water to the drinking faucets."

"Remind us how to tell when it's time to activate the large still?" Sam asked.

"The computer runs the wastewater distillation process automatically when the collection tank fills up. There's nothing manual to do there except for the regular visual inspection and cleaning and sometimes replacing the filters. Distillation will usually run at night when more power is available. Dana and I will check our datapads each morning to make sure none of the systems reported any faults. You can check, too." Tapping his datapad screen, he showed us how to access the daily reports.

"I think that's it, then, young men. It's now 11:35, and there are three more levels to inspect. Today I expect you to finish by 13:00. Starting tomorrow, and each day going forward, please start at 09:30. Once you get used to it, I think you will complete the inspection, including running the solids processor, by 11:00."

"I do have one more question," Sam said. "On Saturdays, the Jewish Sabbath, Michael and I would prefer not to use the datapad or run the solids processor. Will that be a problem?"

"Why don't you run the processor every Friday? You can do so even if the chamber is less than two-thirds full. That way it will not need to run on Saturday. But you will inspect the chamber on Saturdays, too, will you not? Inform me in the rare case that a chamber has filled up again.

Sam and I thanked Dr. Louis and headed upstairs to do our first independent inspections. It took longer than he had expected, but I was able to join my mother, sisters, and Denver for lunch at half past one.

"I'm sorry the meal is so simple," my mother said, scooping boiled rice and lentils into my lidded bowl. "We finally released the water tanker only half an hour ago, so I had to choose ingredients that would not take long to prepare."

"Mom, it's very tasty," Meital said kindly.

"How did all your meetings go?"

"The worms were *disgusting*!" Shirel exclaimed. "I loved it. Dr. Cecylia has been taking care of the worms by herself since launch, and is happy to have help now. She showed Susy and me how to prepare the vermiculture drawers. We set up eight drawers and spread the worms among them. We installed two in each level's greenhouse. Then we fed the worms all the dirty toilet paper and food leftovers. Dr. Cecylia checked our work and said we did a good job. It will be our responsibility to feed the worms the same way every day from now on."

"That sounds so appetizing," Meital said sarcastically as she scooped a handful of rice and closed the lid on her bowl.

My mother turned to Meital with a smile. "I can't imagine that your morning was more appetizing, Meital."

"It was not as repulsive but probably just as dirty. Ruby and I helped Dr. Cecylia set up the birdcages in the airlock. The poor chicks – they were still in their corrals up to now, and the corrals were quite dirty. We moved all the birds into the cages and filled their food bins and water bottles. Then we scrubbed and stowed the corrals."

"How are the birds handling weightlessness?" I asked.

"The ones that survived seem to have adjusted quite well, but only nine of the chicks survived; seven died. Most of the canaries and parakeets are still alive and doing well. Their flying isn't great, but they seem to have mastered jumping from place to place in their cages."

"So that's it, only nine chicks?" Denver asked.

"Remember that the incubator has sixteen eggs. So far they all seem to be okay."

"Michael, how was working with Louis? I apologize that I wasn't able to join you."

"Mom, stop apologizing; it was fine," I answered. "But maybe Denver should tell us about the air-processing systems first, since we're still eating. Let's save the sewage for after we finish."

Meital and Shirel giggled.

Denver looked up. "Boris and I reviewed procedures with Dr. Claudine and she showed us how to run diagnostics on the vacuum pumps and the compressors. Then we examined the piping and HEPA filters on all levels. No filters needed to be cleaned, so we could not yet learn the procedure. But we did get to purge the carbon dioxide scrubbers."

"Is there enough carbon dioxide for doing laundry?" Meital asked.

"Not yet. We purged twenty kilograms on each level, but we need twice that to run each washing machine. It will be a few days before we can do any laundry.

He changed the subject. "Dr. Dana, please tell us about releasing the other ships. Are the tanker and MiniHabs gone now?"

"My part was only with the tanker. Most of the procedure went smoothly. All the pipes disconnected automatically, and Dietrich – Captain Becker – was able to release the tanker's boom from the habitat's interstage beams. When I left him and Jhonathan, though, they were having trouble getting the boom to disconnect on the other end, from the tanker."

"Why does the boom need to disconnect from the tanker?" asked Meital.

"The boom is disposable, and will burn up in the atmosphere. But the tanker is reusable and needs to return to the Altiplano Mexicano spaceport."

At that moment Captain Becker's face appeared on the side NLED wall, replacing the windswept-field scenery the girls had selected for the afternoon. "General meeting in fifteen minutes, at 14:20, on level three. Everybody is required to attend. Please do not be late. It will be crowded, so we'll keep it short." He disappeared, and the nature scenery – it looked like a Kansas wheat field – reappeared.

"Let's clean up," my mother said. "Michael will have to tell us about the sewage another time."

*   *   *

Wednesday, September 27th, 2028 14:20

Everybody gathered in the Meyers' living room on Pink Level. Captain Becker floated behind the Drs. Meyer, who were seated, so to speak, at the head of their table. Sam and Omar, and Ruby and Susan, hung back in their bedrooms' doorways. My sisters and I crowded into the kitchen; the Bouchets hovered over the couch, and everybody else squeezed around the table. This was the first time we had all met together, and there was barely room to move.

"Thank you all for joining me so promptly," Captain Becker began. "I'm happy to announce that everything is going according to plan. We released the water tanker this morning, the first MiniHab soon after, and have just finished releasing the second. We were having a minor problem with the tanker when we handed it off to ground staff, but I'm confident they will resolve it and that all three ships will land safely.

"The computer has scheduled our first high orbit boost burn for 16:14 this afternoon. It will last fifteen minutes. During the burn, while the rocket stack accelerates, we will experience slight gravity. The simulated gravity will slowly increase during the burn, reaching just above one-seventh Earth gravity. If you weigh seventy-five kilos, you'll feel like you weigh eleven. The feeling will stop as soon as the burn ends and we return to weightlessness.

"Please make sure everything is secured before the burn: anything that is floating will fall. In particular, please check that everything is fastened in the kitchen cabinets and drawers. Also, I would like someone to observe the fowl during the procedure."

Ruby called out, "I'll head down to the airlock and watch the birds."

"Thank you, Ruby. Now, the first burn will boost our apogee to seven thousand and forty-nine kilometers above Earth. A second burn will occur when we return to perigee."

Shirel whispered, "What is he saying?"

Denver answered, also whispering. "We will rise to seven thousand kilometers above Earth after the burn, but will still be orbiting, and the orbit will take us back down close to Earth. Then there will be a second burn."

Captain Becker continued talking. "The second burn is scheduled to occur at 19:07 this evening. It will be similar: fifteen minutes, during which we will have simulated gravity that will reach more than one-sixth Earth gravity. Apogee will be nearly sixty-two thousand kilometers. A third, two-minute burn is scheduled for 15:17 tomorrow afternoon to put us into our parking orbit, with an apogee of one hundred and twenty thousand and ninety-five kilometers. Jhonathan or I will make an announcement ten minutes before each burn." He paused to look around. "Any questions?"

Celina spoke up. "Pa, why will the gravity be stronger during the second burn?"

Captain Becker turned to his daughter. "Good question. As we burn off fuel, the rocket stack loses mass, but the engines continue to deliver the same thrust, and the same change to our momentum. With less mass we'll accelerate more quickly and feel heavier. Any other questions?"

I raised my hand. "Yes, sorry. I was planning to bake bread this afternoon. Does this mean I cannot use the kitchen?"

"Not at all. Everyone, please continue with your regular activities. Just make sure, as I said, that everything is secure. And that someone is observing the birds at each burn."

The meeting ended and we dispersed. Back on my family's Green Level, I headed for the kitchen. After checking the cabinets to make sure nothing would bounce around when the engines fired, I began my first attempt at baking bread in weightlessness. I took out the hand mill and affixed it to the countertop. I found a one-kilo container of wheat kernels that my mother had stocked in our cabinet. I unzipped the bag but held it closed while I fastened it to the intake tube on the mill's left side. I remembered to turn on the water vacuum in the sink, in case any kernels got loose. Pushing the bag of kernels against the intake tube with my left hand, I turned the crank with my right, and watched the flour receptacle slowly fill.

The next task was to mix the ingredients for the dough. I Velcroed a mixing bowl to the countertop and attached a cover. The cover was made of a soft rubber material and included built-in gloves for kneading the dough while the container remained sealed. I removed the flour bag from the mill, opened one side of the cover, and squeezed the flour into the bowl. I then filled a water packet and squirted its contents into the flour. I closed the cover quickly before anything could escape. Then I inserted my hands into the gloves and started to knead. It took a few minutes to gather all the water droplets into the flour and to knead the mixture into a dough. At that point I did not need the cover any more, because the dough had become a sticky solid. I removed the cover and clipped it to the drying rack.

The fun part: I selected one of my sourdough-culture jars from the closet in my bedroom. I extracted half a handful of sourdough and kneaded it into the bread dough, and added some sugar and a little salt. Weightlessness was not a problem for the ingredients themselves, because the dough stuck to the inside of the bowl, but kneading was possible only while my feet were Velcroed to the floor. I discovered this the hard way: the first time I tried pressing the sourdough into the dough, nothing happened to the dough, but my body shot up toward the ceiling! After I Velcroed my feet to the patch on the floor, though, I was able to knead effectively. I continued for ten minutes, adding water along the way by wetting my hands with drops from the water dispenser. When I felt the dough beginning to rise, I reaffixed the bowl's cover but left it unsealed so the dough could breathe. I set a timer on my datapad for forty-five minutes. The clock read 15:25.

The girls were talking with Denver in our bedroom. I poked my head in to check what they were up to.

Meital saw me. "You never told us about the sewage treatment. Was it foul?"

"Yes, but not quite as much as I expected."

I described the solid waste processor and the girls talked about fowl care in spaceflight, and Denver talked about what he had learned about the air-processing systems.

Dr. Jhonathan's voice sounded on the public address system. "Ten minutes to burn."

The girls went to their room to check one more time that everything was secure. Denver and I did the same in our room. Then my datapad's alarm sounded, reminding me to check the dough. As I headed back to the kitchen, the image on the NLED wall changed. Snow-covered peaks were replaced by an outside view projected from one of the hull's embedded cameras. We were looking down from the edge of the habitat toward the booster-stage stack. The Mars-Entry stage was clearly visible in Earth-reflected sunlight, and Earth, in all its beauty, filled the top of the screen. Swirls of white clouds over blue ocean curved back across the horizon. The sun was behind us, below the boosters, illuminating the planet. I was able to make out the silhouettes of all three booster stages, below and beyond the Mars-Entry stage.

Denver joined me in the living room just as Dr. Jhonathan's voice sounded from the speakers. "I'm putting the countdown up on the screens, along with a couple of the camera views Captain Becker and I will monitor during the burn. Feel free to stop whatever you are doing and watch."

A timer appeared at the wall's upper corner: four minutes and fifty seconds and counting!

I remembered my dough. Four minutes would be enough to pound it down for a second rising. Once in the kitchen, I saw that it had risen nicely. I again anchored my feet to the floor, pounded it a few times, and resumed kneading.

"Michael, get back out here."

Denver was pointing to the second NLED wall on the side of the living room. It showed something dark, but I could not make out what it was. Meital and Shirel had joined us and were examining the display.

"Are those the engines?" Meital asked.

"We'll know in a minute," Denver answered.

Shirel announced the final countdown. "Four, three, two, one …"

The burn started quite suddenly. The walls around us began vibrating gently and the floor came up to meet us. I straightened my knees to support my very slight weight. Nothing changed at first in the mystery picture. Then, slowly, something began to glow vaguely red: an engine nozzle. We were watching a close-up view of one complete engine nozzle, and the edges of two others, all now glowing a brilliant orange-red.

The view on the other NLED screen did not seem to have changed: we could still see the entire height of the Mars-Entry stage and the three boosters below it, but the glowing nozzles at the very bottom were hidden from view.

We were now standing on the floor, which, I knew, was pushing up at our feet.

"This is awesome. Fathom the power of the boosters!" Denver stared at the screen. "We studied the rockets in theory. But actually feeling them in action … all three at the same time … astounding …"

"The silence is disconcerting," Meital said. "So many rockets firing and no sound."

Shirel, her eyes still on the screen, said, "If you listen very carefully you can hear the vibration." Then she pointed at the screen. "Why is there no fire coming out of the engines?"

"There sure is fire coming out." Denver said. "The hot gases now burning from the engines would roast us all in a second! But it's not like watching a launch from Earth. The gases that glow so beautifully in the atmosphere are nearly invisible in vacuum."

We watched the screens in silence until the sound of laughing caught our attention. Susan emerged from the staircase, a wide smile stretching her rosy cheeks. "That was the first time I've actually walked down the stairs," she said. "Now I understand why each staircase has only seven steps, and each step is so big. Since we fall so slowly, we can practically just jump down the whole staircase."

She walked across the room delicately. "Let's dance! Put on some music."

Meital obliged. She tapped her datapad and a popular early twenties neo-swing tune began playing, in stereo, from the NLED walls' speakers. She grabbed hands with Shirel and Susan and the three of them started dancing around the table. Meital tapped the datapad again to raise the volume.

"This is great!" Shirel exclaimed, as she leaped upward and fell back down in slow motion. "It's like the moonwalk ride at the amusement park."

"I've missed having my feet on the floor," I said, joining them. I jumped a bit too high and bumped my head on the ceiling. Everybody giggled.

We were still dancing around the living room, to the fifth or sixth song, when the burn ended as suddenly as it had begun. We found ourselves floating in random directions, and we all bumped our heads on the ceiling.

The live rocket images disappeared from the screens, replaced by tranquil golden meadows rippling in a summer breeze. Meital stopped the music just as Dr. Jhonathan's voice announced, "Good news, fliers. The burn was nominal, and all data indicate that we are in the expected orbit. I'll stop bothering you now, but stay tuned for our next announcement at 18:57, ten minutes before the second orbit-boosting burn."

I waited another hour for my bread dough to finish rising, then went back to the kitchen. There was no oven on board, only the single induction stovetop in each kitchen. It would do: I would bake my bread in a sealed pot. I took the deepest one from the cabinet and inserted it into the stovetop socket, where a magnet held it in place. I divided the dough into two equal parts. Reaching through the pot's narrow opening, I stuck one-half against the left side, the other against the right, making sure they were balanced so the pot would not wobble. Then I locked the lid in place to create an airtight seal. I activated the stove and set its timer for thirty minutes. As the pot heated up, it spun in place to create artificial gravity, which in turn created convection currents, which baked the dough evenly. I watched the pot with satisfaction: my first space-baked sourdough bread would be ready by dinnertime.

*   *   *

Wednesday, September 27th, 2028 18:30

"I'm sorry supper is the same as lunch," my mother said, as she dished out leftover rice and lentils.

"Stop apologizing, Mom," Meital said. "Anyway, we have Michael's bread now. Michael, it's really good."

"Thanks, Meital." I turned to Denver. "What's your verdict: interesting or tasty?"

Denver smiled broadly. "Definitely interesting." He paused. "But I admit: it's the best bread I've had in days."

"I'll take your ambiguity as a compliment."

The conversation had moved on to our experience of minimal artificial gravity during the first burn, when Captain Becker's voice announced, on our datapads: "Ten minutes to the second burn. Please check that everything is fastened."

"Mom, should we get the chairs out?" Meital asked. "We might actually sit for a few minutes of dinner while we accelerate."

My mother considered the idea. "No. We don't need the chairs. I think we should dance instead. That was a great idea this afternoon, and I'll join you this time."

We followed the countdown on the wall screen, then watched the rocket nozzles glow as they heated up. Meital put on another dance tune, we all joined hands, and, laughing at our unusual circumstance, we danced around the table for the duration of the burn.

Gravity

Thursday, September 28th, 2028 10:55

By Thursday morning I was almost used to waking up in my orbiting bedroom. After a brief family breakfast – oatmeal sprinkled with chia seeds – Sam and I met to divide the day's water-management tasks. I took Yellow and Pink, the top two floors, and he took Green and Mauve downstairs. I examined the systems and ran computerized diagnostics, but found it unnecessary to cycle either of the bathrooms' waste processors. I finished quickly and found myself back in our living room before eleven o'clock.

"You know, we're supposed to be exercising every day," Denver said. He and Boris had finished inspecting the air-processing systems and running the daily diagnostics. "But nobody's talked about setting up a schedule. I really need a workout."

"Dr. Jhonathan has been developing our education plans," I said. "Maybe he's been too busy to deal with exercise schedules. Or maybe he decided to wait for when we have gravity tomorrow."

"The exercise equipment works just as well in weightlessness as in gravity. What do you say we set up the cycles and work up a sweat? Let's fold away the table to make room."

We bent down – actually flipping ourselves over – to unsnap all four legs from the floor. Denver folded the table and pushed it into my hands. "I'll get the cycles out," he said, and went into my mother's bedroom to retrieve them. After I stowed the table in the girls' bedroom, he emerged holding what appeared to be two metallic-blue meter-high posts, each with a seat at the top and pedals sticking out from the sides. Velcro straps hung from each seat.

"Take this one and attach it there," Denver instructed, handing me a cycle and pointing at one of the holes in the floor. I snapped it into position, turned it on its axis so that it faced the NLED wall at the bedroom end of the living room, and tightened the locking screw. Denver snapped his own cycle into the adjacent hole. We mounted, strapped our hips onto the seats, and pushed our feet into the pedals.

"What movie should we watch?" I asked, browsing on my datapad through a list of recently released drama films. "How about *All Along the Crime Train*?" I tapped the datapad to project the movie onto the NLED wall.

"Fine with me." Denver began pedaling.

I latched my datapad to the Velcro patch under my seat as the opening credits rolled.

"Let's race!" Denver panted, pedaling vigorously. He still held his own datapad in his hands. As he tapped the screen, both his and my pedaling speeds, calculated in kilometers per hour, appeared on one side of the wall screen. We cycled for the next forty-five minutes, almost maintaining our initial racing pace. The film helped pass the time, though neither of us paid much attention to the weak plot. As regards the competition, Denver clearly won, racking up more kilometers than I, though we did not pay much attention to that, either.

Sweat on his forehead and sweat patches visible on his mundies tunic, Denver asked, "Should we do an upper-body workout?"

"I think so, since we're already exercising."

We unstrapped ourselves from the cycles. Before we could unlatch them from the floor, Shirel emerged from the stairwell. "We finished feeding the worms." Noticing the cycles, she said, "Nice idea! Are you starting or finishing?"

"We just finished. We're putting these back and taking out the sprowers," I answered, referring to the spring-based rowing machines we would use to exercise our arms, chests and bellies.

"Leave the cycles out, so Meital and I can exercise. There's room for both them and the sprowers."

"Okay." Denver and I retrieved the sprowers, also stowed in my mother's bedroom, and snapped them into four other slots in the floor. Each sprower was a bright blue bar a meter and a half long, with a sliding seat on top and heavy steel springs underneath. A Kevlar cord, wrapped around a pulley, connected the seat to one of the springs. Additional cords linked handgrips to other springs. The springs created resistance as we sat, strapped in the seat, pushing with our legs and pulling with our arms. We could also turn the seats around and push forward with our arms to work a different set of muscles.

Denver and I had been working out on the sprowers for fifteen minutes when my mother came down from the upper levels wearing a bright yellow dress over her mundies. Shirel, sweat visible on her neck, was cycling energetically. She had been joined by Meital, who was maintaining a more relaxed pace on her own cycle.

"I see you all remembered how important it is to exercise in low gravity," my mother said, and paused to watch us. "Perhaps you forgot that the plan was to start only next week?"

"Yes, Mom," I said, "but we figured that we don't need to wait for Dr. Jhonathan to prepare the schedule before we start informally. We want to stay healthy."

"I can't say I'm not happy about that." She smiled at me, then raised an eyebrow. "And do you also want to stay clean and wear clean clothes?"

"Of course ... we'll shower after we finish."

My mother continued to look at me, her lips pressed together in a tight smile, eyebrows raised, waiting.

Meital was first to realize what she was hinting at. "But we won't have clean mundies." She stopped cycling and looked up at our mother. "We can't use the washing machine until we have collected enough carbon dioxide, and we're wearing our last sets." She smiled embarrassedly. "*Oops!*"

"Yes, dear; that's why the plan was to wait." She laughed and turned to the kitchen to prepare lunch.

An hour later, we had finished our workout and showered (sponged, actually). We wore dirty mundies pulled from the laundry bin. Even though we had worn them earlier in the week, they were still fresher than our sweaty workout clothes. Putting them on had not been fun, but it was better than the alternative.

We gathered around the dining table for lunch – we had stowed the exercise equipment and reinstalled the table – and were eating a chickpea and lentil stew my mother had cooked.

"How are you all feeling, five days into our journey?" she asked casually.

For a long moment nobody answered. Then Meital spoke. "I feel overwhelmed." She took a breath and squeezed her brow in concentration. "Living on a spaceship, doing something no family has done before, pretending that it's all routine. My feelings are all confused: excitement and trepidation, exhilaration, fear of boredom, hope that my chicks don't die, doubt that I can handle all the responsibility, happiness that I am with all of you, sadness that we won't see Grandma again."

She looked around, took another breath, and blushed. After a few moments of self-conscious silence, she added, "Well, you asked."

Denver's mouth was agape. He appeared to be working through all the emotions Meital had described. He opened his mouth as if to speak, then closed it, then opened it again. "I feel exactly the same. Couldn't have said it better."

Saving Denver from his awkward moment, I said, "Meital, I think you described all of our feelings excellently. At the risk of sounding shallow, I would add 'vertigo' and 'nausea' to the list of feelings."

She laughed. "Yes, at least until we get gravity. Mom, when will we tether and spin up?"

"Our final high-orbit burn is scheduled for a couple of hours from now. If all goes well, we will meet up with our sister ship, *Mars Hope*, entering the same orbit. Then we can install the tether. We might have gravity by tomorrow night."

"Tomorrow night is Yom Kippur," Shirel pointed out. She looked at Denver and added, "That's the Jewish holiday of repentance and atonement, the holiest day of the year."

"Yes, I know," he answered. "I have been observing the Teller family's religious customs for several years now." Looking at my mother, he added, "Does that mean you will skip eating and drinking for a day? Isn't that dangerous to the mission?"

"I don't think so. If there were an emergency, we would break the fast. That's the same rule as on Earth. The Sabbath, too: all restrictions would be suspended for any life-threatening emergency. But as long as there's no emergency, I think it's safe to fast."

"Sorry to interrupt your meal again." We turned toward the sound of Dr. Jhonathan's voice as he entered the living room from the stairwell. "I've been working on educational programs for everyone and I'd like to meet individually with all the youth this afternoon." Looking around at us, he asked, "Can the four of you please come upstairs, one at a time, between 15:00 and 16:00?"

"Yes," we answered.

"Denver, you come first. Can I assume you and Michael will be happy to study most subjects together?"

"Yes," we answered again.

"Excellent." Dr. Jhonathan departed down the stairwell, murmuring "Last stop: the Bouchet girls."

After we washed and put away the dishes, we lingered to wait for our turns with Dr. Jhonathan. Shortly after two o'clock, Susan and Ruby came down.

"Dad kicked us out," Susan said, looking affronted, "so that he can talk privately with everyone." She had a game of magnetic Scrabble – an actual physical game, not a computer version – in her hand. She held it up. "Anyone want a challenge while we wait?"

The girls started playing and Denver and I watched. At half past two, Ruby went upstairs to meet with her father, leaving me to stand in for her until she got back fifteen minutes later. I managed to place some words and score some points before she returned.

"What courses have you been assigned?" I asked her.

"Mostly the same subjects as at Altiplano. My dad wants me to start Electrical Engineering, but I told him I'm not ready. I want to continue focusing on biology. It will be more important for becoming a doctor, right?"

Denver's turn was after Susan's. He returned with a dazed look on his face. "I sure won't have to worry about being bored! Dr. Jhonathan has me listed for a dozen courses. All the sciences, including Advanced Chemical Engineering and Introduction to Agriculture. And humanities: English Composition, German Literature and Theory of Government. Michael, be prepared to be overwhelmed."

I headed upstairs and found Dr. Jhonathan poised at the side of the table, stroking his short beard. The NLED screen behind him showed a real-time outside view looking down at the booster rocket stages. A bright silver sliver of Earth loomed large at the top of the screen. All three booster stages were clearly visible in Earth's reflected light. Dr. Jhonathan motioned for me to settle across from him.

"Michael, I've been reviewing your latest test scores, and am impressed by how well you've been doing." He examined the screen of his datapad, which was Velcroed to the table. "Given your grasp of the courses you've been taking, I think we can introduce additional subjects for the winter semester."

"'Winter semester?' Rabbi Meyer, we need to think of a different name. I don't think it's winter in the interplanetary regions we'll be navigating."

"Yes, well, until we think of something else, let's just agree on your course load. And Michael, I am not a rabbi. As for the coursework, these are the courses I'm recommending, though I'd like to add one or two more." He tapped his datapad and the list appeared on my own datapad's screen. "Continuing your chemistry curriculum, you'll see that I've signed you up for Materials Synthesis. That's one of the courses Denver is also taking, and you'll be able to study together. I've also assigned both of you to –"

Captain Becker's voice interrupted from the wall speakers behind Dr. Jhonathan. "The third high orbit burn will commence in two minutes. Please prepare." A countdown appeared on the side of the NLED wall.

Dr. Jhonathan gestured toward my datapad. "Michael, secure that to the table." He looked back at his own. "As I was saying, I would like you and Denver to take the college-level introductory biology and physics classes together."

"Don't we already know much of the material, from our agriculture and spacecraft systems training?"

"Some of it, on a practical level, but I want you to get a strong theoretical foundation in the sciences. If you can get through the material quickly, great – you can start Living Systems and Electrical Engineering and perhaps even complete them during the trip."

The NLED screen's countdown reached fifteen seconds.

"Rabbi Meyer, can we watch the burn?" He nodded and I joined the countdown. "Five, four, three, two, one, –"

As before, the rockets ignited, though, again, in the vacuum, their exhaust was not visible. The floor came up to meet my feet and I stood. I felt the ship's deep vibration through the floor and the table, but the silence was disconcerting. The screen switched to a view of rocket nozzles that turned brown, then orange, as they heated up.

The wall again emitted Captain Becker's voice. "I'm putting up a second view, from one of the habitat's side cameras. If you look at the bottom left of the screen, you may be able to spot *Mars Hope*."

We turned toward the NLED wall to my left and found our sister ship. Though only a small dot, it was not hard to identify against the dark backdrop.

His face still turned toward the screen, Dr. Jhonathan said, "Back to your education plan," but Captain Becker's voice interrupted again. "Releasing the Orbit Insertion stages in five seconds."

On the NLED wall, the booster stages on the left and right ended their burn. They separated from the middle stage as if pushed off by a hidden hand, and began falling away. I immediately felt much lighter on my feet.

A few moments later the middle stage ceased firing and weightlessness returned. Dr. Jhonathan turned back to face me. "You and Denver can take Linear Algebra together."

"Okay," I answered.

"You told me you want to continue studying computer science. Can I sign you up for Distributed Software Systems? Nobody else will be taking it, so you'll need to study on your own. Is that okay?"

I nodded. "Computer Science is a field I can learn by myself." I glanced at my datapad screen, which listed the courses Dr. Jhonathan was recommending. "Distributed Software Systems" appeared at the end of the list. Besides the science and mathematics courses, I saw Writing and Composition, English Literature, Hebrew Literature, Earth History and Mycology. "Who else is taking Mycology?"

"You'll study with Celina Becker, and Omar will oversee your progress. Is that okay?"

"Sure, if I can participate in growing actual mushrooms."

"That you'll need to discuss with Omar." He looked down at his datapad. "Regarding the other courses. You expressed an interest in starting Talmud studies. Sam told me he would like to learn with you. I can oversee your progress and perhaps give a class from time to time. Would you like that?"

"Definitely. I was hoping Sam would agree to be my learning partner." I felt the edges of my lips curl into a smile. "In Talmud class, can I call you 'Rabbi Meyer?'"

"Yes," Dr. Jhonathan said, suppressing his own grin. "But only in Talmud class." He again glanced at the datapad. "That makes eleven courses, but I think you can handle more. How about an art course? Denver signed up for Three-Dimensional Printing Design. Does that interest you?"

"I'm sorry, Rabbi Meyer" – he glared at me and cleared his throat admonishingly – "but I'm wary. I think I can handle what you've listed, but not more than that right now."

"Let's see how you do, and revisit the discussion in two or three months. I wish you success in your studies, and you know my door is always open to talk about anything."

"Thanks," I said, and headed downstairs to call Meital for her turn with Dr. Jhonathan.

Captain Becker's voice again echoed from the living room wall. "I'm happy to announce," he said, "that the third high-orbit-insertion burn was successful. We are in the correct orbit, apoapsis at one hundred and twenty thousand and ninety-five kilometers, periapsis four hundred and five kilometers. We will orbit Earth each forty-seven and a half hours or so. *Mars Hope* also had a successful burn, and shares our orbit. We'll be maneuvering now to prepare for our rendezvous."

The others had gathered around the table to watch the wall screen, and I joined them. "How many courses are you signed up for?" Denver asked.

"Not as many as you. Only eleven."

Shirel pointed at the screen. "Look: the booster is separating!"

On the display, the two Orbit Insertion stages were still visible in Earth's reflected light, but just barely; they had become very distant in the minutes since their release. Shirel was right about the third stage: it had also separated, and was itself moving slowly away.

"Isn't that the Mars-Transit Injection stage that we need to send us on our way?" Ruby asked.

"Yes, but it can't be attached when we are spinning with *Mars Hope*," Susan answered. She turned to face her older sister. "The ship would be too heavy and the tethers would break. Boris explained it to me. The stage will park near us for the next month. We'll attach to it again when the time comes to leave."

"What about the other rocket stages? They'll return to Earth, won't they?"

I answered. "It will take a few weeks." I glanced at the receding dots on the wall display. "They'll dip into Earth's atmosphere over several orbits, using air friction each time to slow their speed. Eventually they'll fire their engines briefly and begin a controlled descent. If all goes well, they'll land softly at the Altiplano spaceport, ready to be used again."

While we were still watching the screen a few minutes later, discussing the mission and our course schedules, the starfield began to move. Earth, which had barely been visible at the top of the screen, slowly came into view.

"We're rotating!" exclaimed Meital, who had returned from her meeting with Dr. Jhonathan.

Susan said, "I think we're turning to line up with *Mars Hope*. Let's put a top view up on the screen. Maybe we'll be able to see them."

Denver said "I'll do it" and tapped his datapad. "I'm selecting one of the dome cameras." The view on the wall changed and Earth disappeared. Before long, we spotted our sister ship. It took half an hour to reach the center of the display, at which point it was positioned directly above the top of our habitat, though quite a distance away. That is when the starfield stopped moving, indicating that our own ship had completed its slow rotation.

Captain Becker made one more happy announcement late Thursday afternoon. "Our maneuvers were successful and we are in position to rendezvous with *Mars Hope* tomorrow morning. We can congratulate ourselves! Though we are still in Earth orbit, we are well on our way to Mars. Our ships have more than ninety percent of the velocity, relative to Earth, required to get there. One more small burn, scheduled for November tenth, will send us on our way."

* * *

Friday, September 29th, 2028 09:45

It was hard to concentrate on my daily chores Friday morning. I had started downstairs in the Mauve-Level living room with my datapad, examining the results of the overnight distillation and diagnostics processes. Unfortunately, the view on the NLED wall was hugely distracting. A live outside feed from a camera mounted at the top of the habitat showed *Mars Hope* in the distance. It was still several hundred meters away, but the gap between the two ships was closing steadily as the ships approached tether distance. I looked back at my datapad. The overnight water management processes had completed without incident, so I went into the bathroom to begin my visual inspection of the plumbing and waste-processing systems. I struggled to focus – the display in the living room was so much more interesting! I stole a glance at the screen through the bathroom door, reminded myself of my responsibilities, and turned back to the machinery. Then I stole another glance. Focusing again on my datapad, I saw that the waste processing application reported that the solids chamber was sixty-three percent full. I initiated a waste-processing cycle.

Crossing through the living room to head up to Green Level, I paused again to look at the screen. *Mars Hope* was discernibly closer than before. As I turned back toward the stairwell, my datapad unexpectedly buzzed and vibrated in my hand, indicating an incoming call.

A familiar voice purred "Hi, Michael!" as my friend Hannah's face appeared on the datapad screen. Her black hair was tied behind her head in a tight bun. Hazel eyes contrasted with a pale round face and full red lips, which curled into a very pretty smile as, I surmised, my picture appeared on her screen. Hannah Gordon and I had become close during our year at Altiplano. Her family's group had launched a week before us, which meant that they had been resident in their habitat, *Mars Hope*, for more than ten days. We had not spoken since before they launched.

"Captain Ravel announced that the ships' communications networks have been joined. I couldn't wait to talk to you!" Her cheeks turned pink. "There's so much to tell. My father has been keeping us busy with maintenance tasks. Dr. Tavera has been pushing us all week to start our studies. But with so much going on –"

"Hannah," I interrupted, "you look great, really pretty even in weightlessness." I made sure to smile back. "I'm glad you called. But I'm right in the middle of my maintenance chores, and Dr. Louis expects me to finish by eleven o'clock. I'm sorry, but can I call you back later?"

She ignored the question. "What time is it in your ship? Here it's ten fifteen. We're on Mexican time."

Unnecessarily, I checked my datapad's clock. "It's ten fifteen here, too; Captain Becker also has us on Mexican time. But I'll be in trouble if I don't finish my inspection. Can I call you back when I finish?"

"Yes," she pouted. "But don't forget. My mom will have us eating all afternoon before Yom Kippur tonight. Okay?" She raised her eyebrows; then the screen went blank.

By the time the waste processing procedure had completed on Mauve Level, *Mars Hope's* domed top loomed large on the wall display. I bagged the disgusting desiccated detritus, then joined my sisters and Denver in the Green-Level living room.

"Look," Shirel exclaimed, pointing at the screen. "You can see the maneuvering rockets firing." Indeed, brief flashes alternated among the other ship's nozzles, as its computer made final adjustments to its position and orientation relative to ours.

Denver pulled up next to me and pointed at the edge of the screen. "I think these flashes are from our own maneuvering rockets. Our computer is positioning our ship, too."

"If so," I answered, "the movements must be minimal. I don't feel us moving at all."

"If we float perfectly still, perhaps we can see the habitat moving around us."

"Kids," my mother called from the kitchen, "please help me make lunch."

Over the next hour we worked in the kitchen, preparing a bean-and-barley stew and a pea-and-chickpea salad (my mother had soaked the freeze-dried peas and chickpeas overnight). Susan came down to join us, and Meital went upstairs, with some of the bread I had baked the night before, to join Ruby and her family. At a quarter past twelve we settled down for an enormous pre-holiday meal.

"My father says that eating the day before Yom Kippur is considered like fasting on Yom Kippur," Susan said, an earnest look in her brown eyes. "'Eat 'til you're full,' he says. It's like fasting two days in a row."

We were still eating nearly an hour later when Jhonathan Meyer and Captain Becker passed through on their way down to Mauve Level.

"We're going to do the tethering today," Dr. Jhonathan said. "We're on our way to prep Simeon, who will do the spacewalk from our end."

"We'll put Simeon's camera view up on the NLED screen," Captain Becker added, and they disappeared downstairs.

Twenty minutes later the view from Simeon's fleximet camera appeared on the wall at the end of the table, replacing the blues and greens of the coral reef video Denver had selected. Once Simeon had exited the airlock, the view rotated each time he turned his head. Earth, half lit by the sun, passed back and forth several times. It looked surprisingly small.

"We must be almost a third the distance to the moon by now," Denver commented.

"I thought we were still orbiting Earth," Shirel said, a slice of bread in her hand. "Aren't we supposed to stay at Earth until November?"

"Yes, we're still orbiting Earth." I pointed to the screen as the home planet appeared briefly. "But the orbit takes us quite far out. That's why it looks so small."

Simeon turned to the top of the Mars-Entry stage, a couple of meters away, opposite the habitat's airlock hatch. Its rounded hull came into sharper focus, and we could see several embedded handles. His hand reached out and grabbed one. His voice sounded from the wall speakers. "I'm taking out the MMU."

We saw him turn the handle, open a hatch, and unlatch something inside the compartment. He pulled out a soccer-ball-sized gadget and attached it to a carabiner on his waist harness.

"What's the MMU?" Shirel asked.

My mother answered. "Our mini-maneuvering unit. It has a bunch of thrusters that can be controlled remotely. Simeon will use it to send the tether cords across the gap to the other ship."

I took a few more bites of stew as Simeon turned around and pushed himself back to the airlock hatch, where someone, face hidden behind a fleximet visor, handed him a large spool. It was twice as wide as Simeon, but only half his height.

"Are those the tethers?" Denver asked.

"Yes." My mother's eyes did not leave the screen. "There are four tethers, each one wrapped around a section of the spool."

Simeon secured the spool to two long cords, both of which he latched to the carabiner on his harness. His camera's view turned toward rungs that extended from the hatch, and he began pulling himself across the bottom of the habitat. The next twenty minutes were not as interesting, as he slowly made his way around and up the hull. During his climb he flashed us amazing views of the starfield and even of Earth a few times. Each time he reached a rung, he stopped to latch one of his waist cords, then turned around to unlatch himself from the prior rung. He kept pausing to adjust the MMU and the spool, trying to keep them from banging against the solar panels and PlyShield.

We finished eating. Susan and Shirel went to the kitchen to reconstitute freeze-dried applesauce for dessert, and my mother handed out vitamin tablets.

"I've reached the pinnacle," Simeon announced over his radio. "I'm securing the spool." We watched as he unlatched one of the cords from his waist harness and linked it to a horseshoe-shaped hook that protruded from the very top of the ship's hull. He left the spool's other cord attached to his harness.

The spool had a crank on the unharnessed end. Simeon began turning the crank with one hand while steadying the spool with his other. After few rotations, the ends of the tethers stuck out far enough for Simeon to latch them to the MMU. Then he released the maneuvering unit and pushed it toward the other ship with the tethers trailing behind. He resumed cranking, releasing more and more of the length of the tethers, as the MMU continued onward in the inertia of weightlessness.

"This is Arjan," said a gruff, Punjabi-accented voice over the radio. "I'm taking control of the maneuvering unit."

Simeon turned his head in the direction of the other ship, which came into view on our screen. We could just barely make out Arjan Ravel's form. Arjan, whose father was *Mars Hope*'s captain, was perched at the pinnacle of his own habitat, one hundred meters away. The MMU was no longer visible on our screen, but apparently Arjan could see it.

"I have it under control. I'm directing it my way."

"The tethers are fully unwound," Simeon announced, and stopped turning the crank.

Eight minutes later, we heard Arjan's voice again. "I've grabbed the MMU. I am fastening it to the hook."

"Is that it? Are the ships tethered?" Shirel asked.

"Not yet," my mother said. "The tethers need to attach at the base of the habitat's dome, on different sides. Simeon and Arjan will carry the ends of the tethers to their correct positions."

We watched from Simeon's camera as he unlatched the first tether from the spool. The tether cord was about as thick as Simeon's gloved thumb. It ended in a loop around a red metal ring, which he latched to a carabiner on his waist harness.

He announced, "Arjan, I'm starting with the red tether." He turned toward one of the lines of ladder rungs and began climbing down toward the edge, more than four meters away.

Shirel turned to Denver. "How can such a small rope hold the two ships together?" she asked. "Won't it tear when we start spinning?"

"That's one of the strongest ropes in the world. One twenty-five-and-a-half-millimeter aramid cord can carry two hundred tonnes, enough to hold the ships together by itself when they spin for Mars-level gravity. But we have four, a wide margin of safety."

"Simeon!" Captain Becker called out.

"I'm inserting the red tether now," Simeon announced, as he reached the edge of the dome. We watched him push the ring into a small cavity in the hull. "Please close the clasp now."

Jhonathan Meyer's voice answered from the speakers, "Closing the clasp." A thick, red metal clasp, embedded in the cavity, rotated through the ring and locked it into place.

Simeon turned and began climbing back toward the spool. We heard Arjan announce, "I've inserted the red tether at my end. Please close the clasp."

"I'm closing the clasp," said a surprisingly soft woman's voice. Jean Gordon, Hannah's mother, was *Mars Hope's* first officer.

"Simeon!" Captain Becker yelled again. "Follow protocol!"

"I am following protocol!" Simeon answered, as he climbed back up the ladder. "I am taking the green tether now."

"Follow the safety protocol! Latch yourself to each rung as you climb!" He sounded angry.

"Captain Becker, I am attached by a rope to the spool. I am not free-floating."

Captain Becker spoke slowly and clearly, but his voice was shaking. "I command you to stop and latch yourself to the nearest rung. You will follow the full safety protocol on my ship. I will permit no risk-taking."

Simeon stopped moving. One hundred meters away, at the top of the other ship, Arjan had stopped moving, too. He and his shipmates shared the same circuit and would hear the argument just as clearly over the radio.

"Captain Becker, with all respect," Simeon said, trying to speak calmly. "I am taking no risks. I am attached to the spool, which is attached to the pinnacle ring." He took a sharp breath, loud enough to be picked up by the microphone. "Latching and unlatching at each rung is a redundant waste of time."

Susan and Shirel, who had been clearing the dinner table, froze in place behind me, dishes in their hands, as they stared at the screen.

"Simeon: safety measures, even when redundant, are not a waste of time! Please do as ordered."

"Captain Becker!" Simeon said, too loudly this time, "My oxypack registers just over forty-five minutes of air. That is not enough time if I follow your protocol!"

My mother said, "They need to stop arguing and get on with the procedure."

"Simeon, follow the protocol. I have nothing more to say on the matter."

Over the next fifteen minutes, Simeon and Arjan installed the green, blue and yellow tethers on the two ships' corresponding clasps. Simeon climbed to *Providence's* pinnacle one last time to retrieve the empty spool, then made his way back down the hull. After unlatching the spool, which had been his only connection to the ship, he was careful to follow the safety protocol, latching himself to each rung ahead before unlatching the rung behind. As such, it took him longer to traverse the twenty meters to the airlock entrance than it had to traverse back and forth eight times between the pinnacle and the edges of the dome, a total distance of more than thirty meters.

We had cleared the table and Meital had returned from her meal with the Meyers, when Simeon emerged from the airlock into the Mauve-Level apartment he and his brother shared with the Bouchets. We knew this because of the brief but loud argument that reverberated up the stairwell, between him and Captain Becker. We could not hear exactly what they were saying, and neither an angry Captain Becker, nor a somewhat unsettled Dr. Jhonathan, were willing to share details when they passed through our level on the way up to their families. Dr. Jhonathan did stop, however, to fill us in on plans for the afternoon.

"Now that Simeon and Arjan are back inside, the spin-up process will start. The computers on the ships are communicating with each other, and will soon commence brief coordinated firings of the maneuvering thrusters."

Shirel floated over. "So that means gravity will start?"

"You won't feel anything at first, though if you pay attention, you might notice the habitat begin moving sideways. The process is very slow, because spinning tethered ships is inherently unstable. Each time the computers add a bit of angular momentum, they need to stop to measure any twisting or wobbling. Then they'll fire the exact combination of thrusters needed to correct the errors while adding momentum to the spin."

"It sounds like a lot of wasted fuel," Denver commented.

Dr. Jhonathan tilted his head as he looked at Denver. "It depends on what you call 'wasted.' If we want artificial gravity, we'll need to use fuel both to spin up and to maintain a stable spin along the way. The Mars-Entry stages and habitats have enough maneuvering fuel to spin up and back down four or five times, depending on how much error correction is required."

He and Susan left and went upstairs. Meital joined my mother in the kitchen to prepare another meal that we would eat before the fast. Denver had retreated to the living room sofa to read a book; he had his datapad floating in front of him, half an arm's length from his eyes. Remembering Hannah, I went to call her from the privacy of my bedroom.

Hannah's face appeared on my datapad. "Well, that was exciting. Do you think your captain will punish Simeon?"

"I hope not! I don't think we need extra stress at the start of our journey."

We spoke for half an hour. Hannah filled me in on everything their group had experienced since launch. Most of their chicks had survived and were thriving, despite the weightlessness. She was excited finally to be traveling, but complained about the limited food offerings. "I'm getting tired of eating stew for breakfast, lunch and dinner!"

"Once we have gravity, it will be easier to cook a wider variety of dishes," I said. "I'm looking forward to making pasta."

"How about pancakes with reconstituted maple syrup?"

She described her chores and the responsibilities she had been assigned. "Captain Ravel set up a rotation system so that everyone will get to do every job. I've been doing air systems this week, and have structural analysis and surface sterilization assigned for next week."

"Captain Becker has a different philosophy. He wants us to be experts in our particular fields. Sam Meyer and I are in charge of water and waste systems, and I don't expect that to change anytime soon."

We compared our course listings. "I'll miss having you in my math and literature classes," Hannah said. "I thought our classes in Altiplano were small, with only eight or ten students per class. Most of my classes this semester will have only two students – including me!" – she threw her hands up in mock shock – "and I'll be studying the rest of my subjects by myself."

"Didn't Dr. Tavera assign you teachers and advisors?"

"An adult is assigned to oversee each class. But I'm doubtful that they'll actually take the time. I'll believe it when I see it."

"I'm sure everybody will take their educational roles seriously," I answered, nodding slowly. "Statistics show that, in interplanetary high school study programs, course advisors take an active role in ninety-five percent of cases."

Hannah's round face stared incredulously at me from the datapad screen. "Considering that never before, in the entire history of humanity, has there been an interplanetary high school study program, I question your statistics!"

We both laughed.

We talked a few more minutes about how we were settling into our new homes, and wondered about our friends who were launching to our expedition's other four habitats. I wished Hannah a meaningful Yom Kippur and an easy fast.

"Michael, you too. I can't believe I won't be able to hug you for ten more months, even though you're only a hundred meters away!" Blowing a kiss, she shut the connection.

Autumn

Saturday, September 30th, 2028 08:00

As expected, Yom Kippur was stranger than any I had experienced. By the time we woke up Saturday morning we had gravity – simulated – the ships having completed the slow spin-up overnight. The gravity itself was doubly surprising. First, after we had gotten used to living in an apartment where up and down were no more than convention, now we found the floor to be the floor and the ceiling the ceiling. Which meant that Denver had to jump from the upper bunk, instead of just floating off.

"Watch out – I'm coming down!" he called out, as I stretched and sat up in my sleeping bag. He landed softly on the floor next to my bed. "That felt weird. I fell so slowly."

That was the second surprising thing: we had spun up to Mars's gravity, not Earth's. Besides weighing only forty percent of our Earth weight (I weighed thirty kilos and not seventy-five), we fell more slowly. On Earth it would have taken only half a second to drop from the upper bunk, but, in our ship, it took more than a second. Denver's drop looked like a slow-motion replay of a sports broadcast.

The noise was disconcerting – I had to remind myself it was Yom Kippur. On Earth, our Sabbaths had always been quiet, Yom Kippurs more so, as we avoided the use of most electrical appliances. But all systems were "go" on *Providence*. The sound of the air-processing units was constant; the whooshing of circulating air ever-present. Behind the paisley hanging to my right, valves clicked and clacked as the ship's computer completed the automated water systems diagnostics. I got up and walked – for the first time on *Providence* – to the bathroom, where LED lights blinked on the distiller, indicating that wastewater distillation was in process. Only the kitchen was quiet, though we could hear the cranking of the Bouchets' mill, on the floor below, as they prepared flour for bread-baking.

"Shoes, shoes everybody!" Captain Becker called out, as he exited the stairwell into our living room. "You know the drill: now that we have gravity, you must wear shoes at all times to protect your mundies socks." The shoes were simple plastic sandals, with hard toes and low sides, to keep the mundies from wearing down or weakening as we walked. "Let me know if you have any problems with them, and we can print new ones," he said, turning and continuing downstairs. "Shoes, shoes!" echoed up from the Bouchets' apartment as he made the same announcement there.

Wearing shoes was forbidden on Yom Kippur, but the religious prohibition covered only leather shoes. We had no leather on board, shoes or otherwise. Denver and I rummaged through the drawers under our beds to find our sandals, and pulled them on over our mundies socks.

Dr. Jhonathan led an informal holiday prayer service in his living room for his family and ours. We sat on chairs for the first time. Sitting in a makeshift synagogue is not usually thrilling, but after a week of floating, it was nice to be able to stay in place without Velcro. I prayed with unusual clarity, perhaps because we were truly in the heavens, though maybe it was just the novelty of worshipping in a spaceship.

Taking a break in the early afternoon, we found ourselves in the Beckers' living room on the top floor, Yellow Level, where a sequence of autumn scenes from somewhere in Holland played out on the NLED walls. Ruby and Meital had been climbing up and down the staircases, just for the fun of it, and I joined them.

Helga was sitting on the sofa reading her datapad. She looked up at us and shook a blonde curl out of her eyes. "How is your holiday going?" Her hair was untied for the first time since we had come aboard, and it fell to her shoulders. "Isn't this supposed to be a

Autumn

solemn day for you?" She glanced at the stairwell where we had been playing.

"It's very solemn and introspective," Meital said. "But we're allowed to take a break. Fasting is hard for me and I need a distraction."

Celina turned her chair around to face us. "Why are you fasting? We need to be eating healthful food every day. It is irresponsible to weaken yourselves and put everyone at risk."

Ruby, shocked by the accusing tone, stared at her.

Dr. Cecylia, at the far end of the table, looked up from her datapad. "Marcelina! It is rude to criticize people's religious beliefs."

"I think it's a fair question," I said quickly so that Celina not be embarrassed. "Fasting is not risky. People have been doing it safely for thousands of years, with no ill health effects."

Celina shook her head. "I don't buy it. What's the point? Okay, primitive people thought they had to appease the gods. If they didn't do various rituals, or fast, or something, there would be natural disasters or no rain or people would die. But we're living in the twenty-first century! We have technology. We have medicine. We know better."

"We even have spaceships," Helga contributed, giggling.

"I'm serious. It doesn't make sense here, where we control everything – air, water, food – that superstitions should concern us." She looked from me to Ruby, waiting for an answer.

"Celina, we look at it differently," Ruby answered. "The fast is not about G-d as much as it is about us. Yom Kippur is a day of reflection, repentance, self-examination. Fasting weakens our physical bodies –"

"But not enough to be dangerous to the mission!" I interjected.

"– suppressing base urges and desires –" she flashed me an "I'm talking" look and continued "– allowing us to be more aware of our spiritual part. Technology may have developed, but human psychology remains the same. Humans are not perfect; we still need to grow. I for one think it is still necessary to dedicate a day each year to thinking about where we have gone wrong and plan concrete steps to take so that we can grow and make ourselves better in the coming year."

"Wow ... you really thought this out. I agree everybody should grow and become better. But I still think it is ridiculous to turn it into a set of rituals."

I said, "Sometimes people, busy with day-to-day lives, forget to engage in life's most important things, and need a ritual to keep them on the right track."

"Maybe something simple. But fasting seems like a dangerous exaggeration."

Diplomatically, Meital changed the subject. "What do you think about the gravity?"

"I think it is not fair," Helga answered, smirking curiously.

"What's not fair?" Meital looked puzzled.

"It's totally not fair that you get more than us, and the French and Russians get most of all!"

Helga's mother gasped. "Helga, we're not in Europe anymore, and I don't think it is helpful to encourage nationalistic rivalries."

At that, I laughed, momentarily feeling very un-Yom Kippur-ish. "Dr. Cecylia, don't take your daughter too seriously. If I'm not mistaken" – I flashed Helga an understanding grin – "she's referring to the fact that the lower levels of the habitat, being farther from the center of the ships' spin, have stronger artificial gravity." I recalled that everything weighed nearly fifteen percent more on the Bouchets' Mauve Level, three floors below the Beckers' apartment, due to the greater angular momentum. Just as the outside of a spinning wheel moves more quickly than the hub, so too the parts of our tethered spaceships farthest from the midpoint of the tethers moved most quickly, generating the strongest centripetal force.

"You are very funny, Helga," Ruby exhaled. Looking across at the clock display on the upper corner of the far NLED wall, she added, "It's time to head down for the *Ne'ila* service that marks the end of Yom Kippur. We'll break the fast afterwards. My mom says you're all welcome to join."

*　　*　　*

Sunday, October 1st, 2028 11:00

My school semester started full-throttle our second Sunday in space, the morning after Yom Kippur. It was hard to believe that only one week had gone by since our launch on the MiniHab. Time seems to pass more slowly when one has new, memorable experiences; by that measure, it felt as if we had been in space for months already, preparing our habitat, learning new tasks, getting to know our home, cooking, exercising, tethering, spinning up gravity, and even celebrating our first holiday. So, when I sat down with Sam and Rabbi Meyer for our first Talmud class at eleven o'clock Sunday morning, it was like returning to school after a long summer break, though we had taken our last lessons in Altiplano only a week and a half earlier. Truth be told, since we had never actually taken summer breaks during our years of training, I had no experience to which to compare, and could only assume that it was like returning after a summer break. We had taken holiday breaks, each family according to its own religious or cultural tradition, but never for more than a week at a time. There was simply too much to learn, if you were part of the founding team of a new branch of human civilization.

Talmud study required intense focus. "Let's delve in," Rabbi Meyer said, and we opened the text of the Talmudic tractate "Bava Kama" on our datapad screens. "Bava Kama, the first tractate of the Mishnaic order of 'Damages,' teaches and analyzes the details of one's obligation to refrain from damaging another's body or property, and the remedies if one does indeed do damage."

Sam and I delved in. After Rabbi Meyer gave an overview of the introductory section – the excerpt from the Mishna – he left the two of us alone to break our heads together on the Talmudic discussion that questioned, explained, elucidated and expanded on the Mishna's topic. Within minutes we were analyzing Jewish tradition's breakdown of the different ways one person or his property could damage another person or another's property. The hour and a half passed quickly, and before we knew it, Rabbi Meyer was with us again.

"How did your first session go, my young men?"

"The Aramaic text is difficult for me," I said, "but Sam knows most of the words and has been a big help."

Sam returned the compliment. "Michael's really quick with the logic. I have a feeling we're going to be great learning partners."

"Then I'm going to leave the two of you on your own for most of the week. For Friday, if you want, I'll prepare a review session, and try to tie together everything you'll be learning. Would you like that?"

"Sure," we answered together.

"Let me leave you with some general questions that I'd like you to keep in the back of your minds as you learn. As the founders of a new branch of human civilization, how will the general concept of damages – refraining from damaging others, and paying for damages you inflict – be relevant to yourselves and to the civilization you establish? What relevance will the ancient Jewish legal tradition have to the modern Martian community? And how will you reconcile Jewish law, which sees itself as divinely mandated and absolute, with other legal traditions that our fellow founders will bring along and introduce?"

I stared at Rabbi Meyer, my mouth agape, absorbing what he had just asked. "Rabbi, I'm only seventeen – those are big questions –"

"I'm not asking for answers now," he interrupted, smiling wisely. But you do need to keep in mind the magnitude of your undertaking and the responsibility you'll bear in the years to come. The growth you'll experience from Talmud study will be crucial, I think, in helping the two of you become great leaders." As we got up to prepare for lunch, he added, "Don't worry: I have similarly high expectations from every one of our expedition's youths. You two may be the only ones studying Talmud, but everybody is going to have to contend with big philosophical questions!"

After lunch, I had my first Mycology class with Omar Sidda, who was teaching Celina and me. He wore a simple white longshirt, in the traditional thawb style, over his mundies. We had studied agriculture before: an introductory course had been mandatory in our spacefaring preparatory high school. The study of mushrooms and fungi would become one of my favorite courses, and I found myself looking forward to the sessions with Celina and Omar each Sunday and Wednesday. Perhaps it was Omar's teaching style, or perhaps it was the hands-on nature of the subject: Omar had our hands in the dirt in his Pink Level's greenhouse room from the first session. Though the three of us started each class in the bedroom he shared with Sam Meyer (Sam's schedule had him studying metallurgy upstairs with his mother during those periods, so the room was free), we invariably ended up on our hands and knees, two at a time, in the tiny greenhouse room. We prepared and analyzed our initial compost, which we kept in a dark, closed box to the right of the vermiculture drawers. We would not spawn for several weeks, but there was a lot to learn in the meantime about the requirements for the medium in which our mushrooms would grow: microbe culture, ammonia levels, organic substrate, and more. Mushrooms were an excellent source of protein, required little light, and thrived on our refuse, so mission planners had selected them as an important component of the soon-to-be-nascent Martian agricultural industry. During our journey, a tiny mushroom crop would add a bit of variety to our diet, though our work would mainly be educational.

Mushrooms were not the only crop we would grow in the habitat's four greenhouse rooms. During those first few weeks in high Earth orbit, Denver, Sam and Celina planted a variety of vegetables as part of their Grains and Vegetables Farming course. Celina's mother, Dr. Cecylia, instructed them in the planting and cultivation of tomatoes, cucumbers, zucchini, peppers, radishes, and carrots. They also planted beets, turnips, kale, lettuce, and parsley, and even a couple of potato plants that the course required. Later in our flight, several months down the road, we would enjoy an occasional fresh salad.

*   *   *

Tuesday, October 3rd, 2028 21:40

We began to settle into a routine over the following days. Everyone was busy, we youth perhaps most of all. Our in-flight school's winter semester began, and our daily schedules were full and strict, from early wake-up until lights-out at 23:00. My days began at 06:00, Mexico time, for prayer. Except when I overslept. Promptly at 07:00, Denver, Meital, Shirel and I met in the living room for exercise. Mars-strength gravity was not sufficient to prevent loss of bone and muscle mass through regular activity, so Dr. Jhonathan (outside of Talmud class he did not want to be called "Rabbi," and I was trying to comply) required everyone to engage in two hours of strenuous activity every day, an hour in the morning and an hour in the evening.

Shirel pointed out that we would not need Earth quantities of bone and muscle, since we would have no more than Mars gravity even at our destination, but my mother was not impressed. "First, nobody knows how much bone and muscle mass is required for long-term survival on Mars. What if there are medical effects beyond strength and stamina for day-to-day activities? Second, as long as we are still in Earth orbit, there is still the possibility of aborting the mission." She paused and sighed. "We will diligently follow the exercise schedule Jhonathan and Louis have worked out."

She set a good example, usually completing her sprower workout before we even started. Then she would prepare breakfast and sometimes also lunch, while we took turns on the two cycles and the two sprowers. When we finished at eight o'clock to take our short showers (everyone had exactly six minutes, girls first), she would put some nineties soft rock and a nature video on the NLED wall and cycle for another thirty minutes, until we met for breakfast at 08:30. She often joined us for the meal, but sometimes she showered first and ate only after we had begun our chores.

By the middle of our second week, the air-processing units had collected enough carbon dioxide for laundry. There was even some extra left over for the soda machines in the kitchens. Clean mundies – what a relief! We had been wearing the same set of sweaty mundies for every exercise session, changing back into our other less-sweaty dirty clothes after showering. That ended, finally, Tuesday before dinner. After we finished our evening exercise session – the same hour every day, except Friday and Saturday, from 18:00 to 19:00 – again alternating cycles and sprowers, my mother handed out clean sets of mundies.

At dinner, after we had showered and changed, Shirel expressed feelings we all shared. "I almost forgot how fresh clothes feel! Mom, I like my mundies again. Thanks! Now that we can do laundry, we can wear pretty clothes and look almost like normal people." She herself looked almost normal: she was wearing a lavender floral-patterned overall-skirt over her mundies.

Our weekday schedules included a period of free time at night before bedtime. One evening, looking for a change of scenery, Meital and I headed downstairs to Mauve Level, and that is how we came to learn how the laundry machines worked. As we entered the living room the Bouchets shared with the Radechov brothers, we found

Boris, Simeon, and Dr. Louis sitting around their table chatting. An Impressionist painting of a field of poppies hung, virtually, on the NLED wall.

"Dr. Louis, I didn't know you spoke Russian," Meital said, as he motioned for us to join them.

He switched to English. "I do not really, not yet, but I am learning from my apartment-mates. We were discussing an issue with the laundry machine on this level. The computer alerted us to check the radiator cycler."

"What's that? Is it broken?"

"It is the part of the laundry machine that removes heat as the pressure pump fills the laundry drum with carbon dioxide. Because of the high pressure, the gas would get much too hot without the cycler. It is not broken yet, but the computer detected an anomaly in its functioning."

"How high is the pressure?" I asked.

"Sixty-five bars."

Meital squinted her eyes in thought. "Is that the same as the Mars atmosphere?"

Boris laughed, mirth in his pale green eyes. "Sixty-five bars is sixty-five *thousand* millibars. Mars's atmosphere is six millibars. It is ten thousand times more pressure than the Mars atmosphere! That is a lot of pressure. If you dive six hundred meters deep into an ocean on Earth, the water pressure will be about what the pressure is in the laundry machine."

Simeon interjected, "Maybe you've mixed up your planets. Sixty-five bars is closer to Venus's surface atmosphere pressure."

"Why is the laundry machine's pressure so high?"

Boris answered, "At that pressure, the carbon dioxide is a supercritical fluid." He sounded like he did when lecturing Denver and me in physics class (he had been assigned as our teacher).

"What's a 'supercritical fluid?'" I asked. "And what does it matter to the laundry machine?"

Boris looked at me. "That's a question for class. Are you sure you want the answer now?"

"Yes, please," Meital said. "I'm not in your physics class."

"Okay." He took a breath. "A 'supercritical fluid' is a state of matter. A gas becomes 'supercritical' when it exceeds a particular pressure and temperature, called the 'critical point.' Supercritical carbon dioxide is great for cleaning mundies because it acts both like a gas and a liquid. It reaches everywhere in the clothes like a gas would, and dissolves dirt and organic materials, such as sweat, like a liquid would. But the mundies don't actually get wet, so the embedded microprocessors and batteries do not get damaged. Best of all, carbon dioxide can clean without any detergent, so we can do laundry without using consumables."

"What happens to the dirty supercritical fluid?"

"The carbon dioxide gets flushed out of the drum with the dissolved dirt, then evaporates as the pressure is reduced, leaving the dirt behind. Most of the gas gets collected for reuse. A small amount escapes into our air and gets filtered again by the air processor."

"Can't it explode if it has such high pressure?" Meital asked.

Boris shook his head. "The laundry drum will not explode. It is built to withstand the pressure. Sixty-five bars is not considered particularly high. For example, the habitat's air tanks hold much higher pressures and do not explode."

Dr. Louis cut in. "The bigger problem is the high temperature of the pressurized gas. Gases heat up when their pressure increases, so the laundry machine has to remove heat from the gas as the carbon dioxide is pumped in. Later, when the gas is released from the tank and drops back to ambient pressure, it cools off and can even freeze. That is where the radiator cycler comes in. It must maintain a constant temperature of thirty degrees Celsius for the laundry cycle, cooling off the pressurized gas and reheating it when the pressure is released. That's why the computer's alert about the radiator cycler concerns us. If the cycler fails, we can't do laundry."

Boris nodded, then stood. "Louis, I'll check the radiator cycler tomorrow, but I'm heading to sleep now. Good night, everybody!"

* * *

Thursday, October 5th, 2028 21:30

Having clean laundry was great, but having gravity – even our weak, Mars-strength gravity, was even better. For one, it made it possible to prepare a wide variety of meals, including dishes prepared with boiled water. My mother was especially creative, cooking up rice and soups, and pastas, which quickly became a favorite for our family. Once or twice a week, Meital or I would stay up late and prepare pasta dough – non-dairy, and no eggs yet – and pound it flat. We cut it into narrow strips, which we left in a bowl overnight in our small refrigerator. One of us – usually my mother – would boil the strips in a sealed pressure pot before lunch the following day. She developed a tomato sauce recipe we all liked, combining reconstituted freeze-dried tomato powder with garlic, pepper and hot pepper spices. Sometimes Meital would add soybeans, ground almonds or ground hazelnuts for variety.

We usually prepared boiled dishes in the pressure pot, but occasionally used an open pot for low-temperature recipes. At habitat air pressure, water boiled at only seventy degrees Celsius, which was good for rice stews, but only when one of us had time to stand in the kitchen to oversee the process. Watched pots *did* boil, quite promptly, aboard our vessel! An unwatched open pot was not an option, due to the possibility, however remote, that the tethers might fail and cast us into instant weightlessness. The kitchen protocol for sudden loss of gravity was to activate the water vacuum first, then try to cover and seal any open pots and bowls. But open-pot cooking was a rare occurrence: it was just easier to keep everything covered and sealed.

Kneading dough and baking bread was my favorite hobby for relaxation. It was definitely easier with gravity than without. No need to use a sealed bowl and the rubber-gloves top to mix the ingredients! More importantly, gravity made it possible to sprout wheat kernels before grinding them into flour. Sprouting enriched the bread's nutritional value, adding essential vitamins. Though we had a variety of long-storage grains and legumes on board, our diet was still limited, and anything we could do to enhance nutrition was beneficial. Also, the bread tasted better.

I kept two liter-sized jars in one of the kitchen cabinets, each full of grain, and each covered with a loose netting. At any given time, one stood upright, filled with water, while the other was upside-down, draining into a bowl. Twice a day, usually before breakfast and after supper, I swapped the jars: I flipped over the full one and drained its water, then added water to the second. The wheat sprouted in three or four days, at which point I would lightly roast it, in a pot on the stove, to dry it. Then I would grind it, prepare dough, and bake enough bread for several days.

The other place where gravity noticeably improved our lives was the bathroom. We had gotten good at "weightless protocol," but everyone preferred gravity, especially the men. I don't think any man would get used to sitting when standing would otherwise do. Furthermore, at least for me, standing was interesting from a scientific-inquiry point of view. Rotational gravity had a couple of side effects, one being that streams of liquid fell in what appeared to be curved trajectories. In other words, a challenging aiming requirement. No more need be said, other than to mention that, since the toilet seat was fixed in place, our women needed extra patience whenever our men were lazy.

*   *   *

Wednesday, October 18th, 2028 21:45

Even our weekday nights were busy. We had a study period after dinner – for me a different class each night – but after that we had an hour and a half of free time where we could visit, talk, read, watch films, or just relax. Or bake bread, when I wanted an activity that did not require much concentration. I baked once or twice a week, often preparing extra loaves for our neighbors upstairs or down.

One Wednesday night I found myself in the kitchen next to my mother, who was kneading pasta dough on the counter while I kneaded my own bread sourdough in a bowl. Her hands were busy, repeatedly folding, pressing, and rotating her dough, but she had a distracted look on her face.

"Mom, what are you thinking about?"

"Oh – just making pasta," she said absentmindedly.

"No, I can see there's something else. Is it Dad? I'm worried about him; you must be, too."

"I don't want you to worry, but, yes, I am a bit worried. He was noticeably thinner in his last video message."

"He sounded so encouraging, though," I commented, looking up at her.

"He's not giving up. The work mining water motivates him. As I know your father, he is singularly focused on making sure we'll be taken care of when we arrive." She pounded the pasta dough.

"Shouldn't he be focused on himself? Maybe he should rest more. We need him to be healthy when we arrive."

"I'm not sure he considers his own health as his top priority." She turned to look at me. "Michael, we knew the risks when we joined this project. When we said goodbye to Dad two years ago, I prepared myself for the possibility that we might not see him again. The first people ever to set out for Mars ... we knew his team's chances for success were far from certain. When *Armstrong* was lost with your uncle's squad, we accepted it stoically, and continued our own preparations; when Dad's *Goshna* landed successfully, followed by *Eternum* and *Eagle,* we rejoiced!"

"We accepted the good and the bad. That is part of being a pioneering family, isn't it?"

"Yes, that's the choice your father and I made." She sighed. Gazing blankly at the cupboards, she squeezed her dough, then paused.

"Mom, are we going to be okay? Are you okay?"

"Everything will be fine. Maybe I did let myself become too hopeful. I'm struggling with that. But don't you worry about me." She smiled warmly as she turned to face me. "It's my job to worry about you guys."

"Too hopeful? What's wrong with that?"

"For the past year and a half, I've imagined our family being together again. I think about your father all the time; I picture our reunion. But now I can't help losing hope. Each time I see him, weaker than before – I can tell; he can't hide it from me – my heart aches a bit more. My hope diminishes day by day."

"Mom, we'll be there before we know it –"

"Stop. Pray for your father's health, and stay encouraged and happy, but don't try to comfort me."

* * *

Sunday, October 29th, 2028 10:25

The weeks in Earth orbit passed increasingly quickly. The Succoth holiday came and went, and we shared festive meals with the Meyers. Obviously, we lacked a Sukkah, the holiday's requisite temporary dwelling. It would have felt more like a normal Succoth had we eaten under a patchy ceiling of palm branches covered only by starry sky, but palm branches, not to mention open sky, were in short supply. We made do with the holiday-themed images Shirel and Susan found for the NLED walls.

Denver and I spent a lot of time studying together, since we shared a bunch of science and mathematics courses. I also had English and Earth History classes with Ruby and Meital, Mycology with Celina, and daily Talmud study with Sam, so I was rarely alone. My computer science class (Distributed Software Systems) was the one exception, as I was the only one studying programming, and none of the adults had been assigned to teach me. I admit I enjoyed the rare time by myself each Sunday and Tuesday, sitting on my bed with my datapad on my lap. But alone-time was the exception, and that was intentional. The mission designers considered social interaction critical for psychological health during the long journey. Nevertheless, everyone needed some private time, and Denver and I made sure to give each other space, particularly after our evening class session, before bedtime each night. Denver would leave me alone in the bedroom to video-chat with Hannah, to write in my journal, or just to sit and think. He spent even more time alone, while I baked bread, or visited with Helga and Celina, or with Sam and Ruby, in their living rooms upstairs.

Our weekdays were full, but weekends were more relaxed, and we tried to make them special. Every family had two lightly scheduled days each week, but the particular two days depended on personal cultural or religious choice. For the Meyers and us, Friday and Saturday were special each week: Saturday for the Jewish Sabbath and Friday to prepare Sabbath meals. Denver, having no religious preference of his own, joined us, both in our schedule and in our festive meals. Omar, who shared the Meyers' apartment, also shared our schedule, dedicating time each Friday for Muslim prayer and study. The others – the Beckers, Bouchets and Radechovs – took Saturday and Sunday off. The Bouchets religiously observed Sunday as a day of rest, but all three families used both days for rest and recreation. Back in Altiplano we had discussed adopting a common weekend for the Martian week, regardless of Earthly religion and culture, but had reached no conclusion, so we retained our differences.

Monday morning, I finished my examination of the Green-Level and Mauve-Level water systems more quickly than usual. The computer reported that all valve and flow diagnostics had succeeded, and neither waste chamber was full enough to require a processor cycle, so by ten o'clock I found myself free in the Bouchets' living room. The hatch to the airlock, in the floor at the end of the room, was open. Meital had been urging me to come down to see the chicks in their cages in the airlock, so I knelt down with my back to the opening, gingerly placed a leg through the hatch, and climbed down the red rope ladder. I dropped the last half-meter to the floor.

I could not get used to the airlock's low ceiling. Upstairs the ceilings were nearly two-and-a-third meters high, and I could barely touch them standing on my toes, though we could all bump our heads just by jumping. By contrast, the airlock ceiling was only a hand-span above my head, and felt constricting.

"Wow," I exclaimed, overwhelmed by the birdcages' aroma. "They sure smell more than they did last time I was here!"

Meital, a dirty red apron covering her mundies, turned to face me, eyes wide, her forehead creased. "Of course the smell is stronger! You haven't been down here in a couple of weeks. Look how the birds have grown! Bigger birds, more to clean up, more smell." She handed me the chick she had been examining. It was as large as my hand.

"Michael, I think it's funny you're complaining about the smell," Ruby said, catching my eye as I turned to her. She was wearing a yellow apron, just as dirty, and her frizzy hair was tied back. "The airlock is the best ventilated room in the whole habitat."

"The rest of the habitat has no smell to it, just a dull antiseptic feel. I guess I've gotten used to not smelling anything most of the time. I'll try to get used to the birds, too. Can I see the others? How many are there?"

Ruby pointed to the chicken coop, a large floor-to-ceiling cage on one side of the round space. Chicks of various sizes sat on a series of shelves. "The larger chicks, like the one in your hand, are from the batch that launched with us. Eight have survived. The smaller ones are those that hatched the first week we had gravity. All sixteen hatched, and thirteen have survived. If half turn out to be female, then, after the culling in a few months, we'll have ten eggs to eat every day."

"Culling?" I asked.

"We don't have room to raise twenty-one chickens here," Meital answered. "Maybe thirteen or fourteen total. As soon as we can figure out which are males, we'll start slaughtering them. Chicken dinners!"

"The canaries and parakeets are doing great," Ruby said, directing me to a smaller cage to the right. The birds were all various shades of yellow. "In the cage are a dozen from the first group. We moved them out of the incubator a couple of weeks ago. The second group are still there, until they grow their feathers."

"Michael, put that chick in here," Meital said, opening a door in the middle of the large cage. I stepped over and gently set the chick down on one of the shelves, pulling my hands out before Meital latched the door shut. "Since you've apparently finished your work early, do you mind helping us?" She stepped across the room, pulled a green woven polyester bag off a Velcro patch, and brusquely pushed it into my hands. "Can you clean out the incubator?"

"I guess I don't mind...."

"Scoop up the droppings and seed shells and put them in the trash bag. When you finish, I'll close and latch the incubator, and you can take the bag up to Shirel for the worms."

I started cleaning as my sister had instructed.

"Michael," Ruby chuckled, "I'm sure it's not as unpleasant as cleaning the toilets." She bumped me with her shoulder as she crossed behind me to the smaller cage, which she proceeded to clean in the same way. "You should come down more often."

I gathered a handful of detritus and put it in my bag, then reached in again to gather some more. We continued this way for several minutes.

Ruby spoke without looking up. "My father mentioned that our laser communications satellite launched successfully this morning. It's great news, because the satellite is the last prerequisite for our departure to Mars next week. Did you hear about it?"

"I didn't hear, but that is great news. In fact, thinking about it, I'm getting quite excited!" I scooped out more dirt. "How about you? Are you guys ready, psychologically, to leave Earth behind?"

"I'm counting down the days – twelve to go!" said Meital. "I'm feeling the adventure of it all."

"That's easy for you to say, Meital," said Ruby. "You don't have a problem with weightlessness. I'm terrified that I'll be sick again when we spin down next week."

I tied the bag shut and Meital closed the now-clean incubator. I turned to Ruby. "Did your father say how long it will take for the new satellite to match our orbit?"

"He didn't say much other than mentioning the successful launch."

Meital said, "Remind me why the satellite is necessary for our departure?"

"It's the basis for all communication with Earth and Mars during our journey," I answered. "It has to leave Earth orbit with us on the same trajectory, so we can't depart until it reaches our orbit."

"Why do we need a satellite to communicate with Earth? Don't the ships have antennas? We've had no trouble communicating up to now."

Ruby closed the door on the smaller cage. "We covered this in the unit on radio communications I took last year. While we've been in Earth orbit, we've used our low-gain antenna, which is strong enough to reach Earth even when we're at our farthest point. That all changes once we leave. Within a few days of departure, we'll be so distant that only a high-gain antenna, directed straight at Earth, will be strong enough to send and receive signals."

Meital asked, "Don't the habitats have strong antennas?"

"Actually, no. Since we'll be spinning most of the time for gravity – I'm so happy about that! – it's impossible to keep an antenna pointed toward Earth. Instead, the satellite will travel along with us, never more than a few kilometers away. Our low-gain antenna will communicate with the satellite, which will relay signals by laser to and from Earth."

Meital tied her own trash bag shut. "I'm sure glad the Murke-Berger Foundation has money to spend on a satellite for the expedition."

"Actually, Meital," I said, "there are three satellites. Each pair of habitats has to have its own."

"That sounds like a waste. Why not share a single satellite?"

"*Pioneer Alpha* and *Beta* are scheduled to leave for Mars this week, seven days ahead of us. By the time we depart, they'll be a million and a half kilometers away. That's way too far to share a satellite."

Ruby pulled her datapad off the wall opposite the big cage and checked its screen. "It's a quarter to eleven. We need to get ready for our classes." She and Meital circled the room, checking the latches on the cages and the incubator. "You go up first, Michael."

I climbed the rope ladder with the bag in my hand and pulled myself into the Mauve-Level living room. Meital followed, with Ruby coming up last, each carrying her own trash bag. "Michael, can you get these up to Shirel or Susan? We need to freshen up before class."

Taking all three bags, I poked my head into the Mauve-Level greenhouse, on a mission to find Shirel or Susan. Their job was to care for the worms and both were studying vermiculture during winter semester. I did not find them in the greenhouse, but Omar and Celina were there, down on their knees, peering into an open mushroom cabinet.

"The compost looks excellent," Omar was saying. "We should be able to inoculate this cabinet within a few days."

Having spent the month studying mycology with Omar, I knew that he was referring to the planting stage of mushroom growth. They had spent several weeks preparing the compost in which the mycelium would grow. Celina was in class with me, but while I had been assigned responsibility for water systems, Celina's job on board was to assist Omar with the actual farming, so she was getting hands-on experience.

"Have you seen Shirel or Susan? I need to get this bag of chicken droppings to them."

"They were working upstairs on our level today," answered Celina, wiping her hands on a dirty cloth. "If you don't find them there, ask my mother. I imagine she's preparing lunch."

Celina's mother, Dr. Cecylia Becker, was our vermiculture expert, and directed Shirel's and Susan's work with the worms.

"We'll see you in class after lunch," Omar said. "Today we'll discuss the spawning process."

I climbed three flights of stairs – twenty-one steps in total. At Mars-strength gravity, thirty-five-centimeter risers were easy to climb, allowing steeper staircases that took little space. Shirel was just emerging from the greenhouse room, Susan behind her, as I exited the stairwell.

"Shirel, Meital and Ruby gave me these bags of droppings for the worms."

"Oh, did you visit the birdcages in the airlock? I've been checking the parakeets every few days, but none of them have begun growing colored plumage."

"Yes, I finally had a chance to go visit."

Shirel took the bag and darted back into the greenhouse room, leaving Susan standing by the couch. She looked excited about something. She caught my eye and said, "Dr. Claudine and Dr. Cecylia were here a few minutes ago. They harvested the first vegetables!"

"Dr. Claudine and Dr. Cecylia harvested already?"

"Yes. Aren't you excited? Our first fresh vegetables!"

Shirel emerged from the greenhouse room, wiping her hands on the thighs of her mundies. "Captain Becker called a celebratory dinner tonight. Some lettuce is ready, so they came in and selected some of the largest leaves while we were working."

Captain Becker, who was sitting at the far end of his table, only two meters away, looked up from his datapad at the sound of his name. "Yes, that is right. I will inform everybody at lunchtime. We will all eat together this evening, so we can discuss our plans and preparations for the next week." He returned to his reading.

"Where is there room in the ship for all of us?" Shirel asked.

"I guess we'll find out at lunchtime," I said. "Susy, I'm also excited about the vegetables, and wondering how anything we planted just four weeks ago can be ready to be eaten. But we'd better get going – it's almost time for class."

I headed back down to Green Level to freshen up. My mother was in the kitchen chopping radishes. She smiled when she saw me, and gestured at the cutting board. "Special dinner tonight! These are the first radishes that ripened."

"That's amazing – only four weeks!" I kissed her on the cheek and turned toward the bathroom to wash up. At that very moment, Denver opened the bathroom door and stepped out. "Morning!" he waved, as he rushed off to his Moral Philosophy class.

The chicken dirt on my hands required more scrubbing than usual. I had already spent quite a bit of time in our bathroom earlier, checking the water systems, so I was surprised to detect a faint, unfamiliar smell. It was not the smell of the toilet. The air actually smelled a bit sweet, but with a slightly smoky odor. Denver had checked the Green-Level air systems an hour before, so I made a mental note to ask him about it at lunchtime.

"Michael, you're five minutes late," Rabbi Meyer said, glaring at me while he stroked his beard, as I sat down at his Pink-Level table. The NLED wall showed an image of Jerusalem's Western Wall.

"I'm sorry. I got held up helping with the fowl. It's difficult for us: there aren't enough minutes in a day for schedules as full as ours!"

"I'm not looking for excuses. You should be punctual for all classes, but especially for Talmud class. Talmud learning is a meeting with the King – the King of Kings." He looked at me sternly, a look I would experience many times during our journey. "I doubt you'd arrive late to a meeting with an important human politician. All the more so, to a meeting with the Creator."

His expression lightened. "As to not having enough minutes in a day, we'll start addressing that next week. Once we've departed Earth orbit, the computer will gradually lengthen our days to match the Martian sol by the time we arrive. They'll grow by about a minute each week. Before long, you'll have five extra minutes every day." He smiled broadly as he raised his eyebrows. "You'll never again have to be five minutes late!"

After four weeks of daily Talmud sessions, Sam and I were starting folio four of tractate Bava Kama. Since Talmudic tractates start on page two, we had actually covered only two folios, but each folio had two sides (virtually, on the datapad), so that meant four pages. We had gone into great depth analyzing different categories of torts in Jewish Law, and Rabbi Meyer assured us that we were progressing well. "Look at what you've accomplished, not how far you have to go," he said, when he caught me scrolling to the end of the tractate (folio 119). Happily, Sam and I enjoyed learning, especially when we found the material difficult to understand and we managed to overcome the difficulty. Rabbi Meyer told us that that was most important.

He sat with us as we delved into a question raised in the Tosafot, the brilliant, deep medieval commentaries that were printed (also virtually, on the datapad) around the edges of the Talmudic text.

The question concerned the Talmud's comparison of damage done by a slave to damage done by one's animal. "No, Michael, we will never have slaves on Mars," Rabbi Meyer said, in response to a comment I made, "but you can see how the discussion is relevant to an analysis of one's intentions when he damages another's property." Indeed, I did see the relevance, though it took the full ninety-minute session to understand both what the author of the Tosafot was asking, and how his proposed resolution answered the question.

Departure

Sunday, October 29th, 2028 19:35

A few hours later, Denver and I were sitting on the Mauve-Level couch in the Bouchets' living room, plates on our laps. My mother's fresh radish and lettuce salad, dressed with olive oil and reconstituted vinegar, tasted amazing. It was not sweet – the vegetables were only barely ripe, the radishes sharp, the leaves slightly bitter. Even so, the first fresh food we'd eaten since launching five weeks earlier awakened taste buds that had become used to a limited variety of grains and legumes. I raised another forkful, feeling festive.

The festive feeling was due mainly to our having joined the Bouchets and the Radechov brothers for dinner, downstairs in the living room they shared. Sophie sat on Dr. Claudine's lap and Jasmine shared a chair with her father. My mother and sisters also crowded around the table. Captain Becker had called for a communal dinner, and he and his family appeared on the NLED wall behind Claudine, though they were actually gathered around the Meyers' table, two flights up on Pink Level. The effect was that of two tables joined lengthwise in a long, narrow room, though the other room's inhabitants appeared in miniature. Captain Becker himself sat sideways, visible to all of us, both in-person and on-screen.

"Can you all hear me?" he asked. "This is the first time we've used the NLED walls and cameras in this way. Is it working?"

Departure

Louis, similarly positioned in our (real) room, turned to face Captain Becker's image. "Yes, we hear you clearly."

"Good. I asked that we all dine together because we have happy news to share and many preparations to make. The expedition's plans have proceeded on schedule, with few mishaps, and we are set to depart for Mars a week Friday."

Several of the youth cheered, "Yes! Awesome!"

Captain Becker ignored them. "Many things need to happen by then, and Jhonathan and I have been working with the Foundation on final coordination and planning. We'll discuss details shortly, but first let us eat." He raised his fork. "By the way, I understand that Boris has worked out a small surprise."

Boris stood so all would see him, from both tables. "Actually, it was Laura, on *Mars Hope*, who had the idea. Setting it up was not difficult. He spoke into his datapad, apparently to Laura Tavera, then tapped the screen a couple of times. A moment later, the second NLED wall lit up. Side views of two crowded living rooms appeared, one in the top third of the wall, the other in the middle third. The inhabitants of our sister ship turned toward us as we turned toward them. Everybody waved and called out greetings. I found Hannah in the top third, sitting with her back toward us, but she turned around to look for me. She wore a light brown dress that matched her hazel eyes. I smiled and waved.

"As you can see, Captain Ravel and I scheduled similar events for this evening," Captain Becker resumed. "Eat, mingle and celebrate!"

Dr. Claudine brought over her own salad, also with radishes and lettuce, but she had added chickpeas and quinoa. "See," she said, dishing salad onto our plates, "human creativity is a function of limitations. The fewer materials you have to work with, the more ideas you will have!" She continued on to the girls at the table.

I turned to Denver, speaking over the din of more than forty people conversing. "Did you discuss the funny odor in the air system with anyone?" I had mentioned the strange bathroom smell to him at lunchtime; he had brushed me off, indicating he would check into it.

"It's nothing to worry about. All the air system tests passed this morning."

"I thought you said you needed to check into it."

"Yes, I checked; everything's fine. What do you think about fifty consecutive successful launches?" he asked, changing the subject. "Will the Murke-Berger Foundation's luck hold for the fifty-first?"

Meital turned her chair around to face us. "Don't even joke about that. It's not luck: the inspections are very thorough."

"Is it really that many launches?" I had never made the calculation, and the large number surprised me.

"Think about it," Denver said. "Six habitats. Each habitat requires two launches, one for the habitat itself, the second for water, the heat shield and other supplies."

"That's twelve," Meital counted.

"Three launches for the three boosters, and one for the Mars-Entry stage."

Meital calculated out loud. "Four launches for each of six ships is twenty-four more, so thirty-six total."

"Three communications satellites."

"Okay, thirty-nine," I summarized. "How did you get to fifty-one?"

Denver stared at me as a patient teacher might stare at a particularly slow student. He gave up waiting after a few seconds. "I'll give you a hint. How did you get here?"

"Of course! Twelve MiniHab launches to populate the fleet."

Meital looked at Denver. "That's a lot of rockets to pay for. The Foundation is investing a lot in this mission."

"The Foundation is rich," Denver agreed. "But remember that they reuse the same rockets. After each launch, both stages land back on Earth. Even the High Earth Orbit Insertion stages land after a few weeks of aerobraking. The Foundation saves money by not having to buy more equipment."

Meital nodded.

Some minutes later, Captain Becker spoke again, his voice emanating from speakers embedded in the NLED wall. "I need the attention of everyone on *Providence*. Boris, please cut the connection with *Mars Hope*."

The room became much quieter.

"We have a busy schedule this week and next, and everyone will be involved. We are set to depart Earth orbit for Mars in twelve days. You are all to be congratulated: because the mission has been successful so far, the Murke-Berger Foundation has approved the departure of all six ships. All equipment is functioning nominally. Just as important, we all have passed our final psychological evaluations. You might not have known that Jhonathan and I have been busy communicating with Dr. Goldsmith and his team, down in Altiplano, about each and every one of you.

"Here's the plan. Our communications satellite launched successfully this morning and was boosted into its transfer orbit. It is on schedule to match our own orbit by the end of this week. That will give us time to test all communications channels. By the end of next week, we and *Mars Hope* need to be in boost configuration. Not only will we spin down and detether, but each ship must successfully dock with its Mars-Transit Injection stage, and the stages must be reheated and checked out. Any questions?"

Helga, visible on the screen behind her father, spoke. "Who will do the spacewalk to gather the tethers onto the spool? Will Simeon go out again?"

Captain Becker turned to her. "That has not been decided yet. Perhaps we'll ask Boris this time."

Boris was sitting near the end of the table on our side, diagonally across – virtually – from Captain Becker. "Simeon is best for the job. I do not need to fill in for him."

The captain turned toward us, apparently facing Boris's image on his NLED wall screen. "We'll discuss this later." Then, after a pause, "Any other questions?"

Ruby lounged on the sofa at the far end of her family's living room. I could barely see her on the screen, but I heard her clearly. "After spin-down, how many days will we be weightless?"

"If all goes according to schedule, we'll start spinning down Friday afternoon and detether on Saturday night. That gives us nearly a week to maneuver the ships and test all systems. After Mars-Transit Injection the following Friday, we should be in position to tether and spin up within two days."

Ruby groaned. "Can't we shorten the weightless time?"

"Not really," Captain Becker answered. "I understand that you find weightlessness difficult, but we must have buffer time in case we run into problems with the complex maneuvers that will be required."

Jasmine whispered something to her father. I heard Dr. Louis encourage her with something like "*C'est une bonne question.*"

She stood hesitantly and faced the screen. "Pardon, Captain. If we will not have gravity for a whole week, will we still need to attend classes?"

"Yes, Jasmine. The plan is to continue our regular schedules as much as possible. You are all astronauts, you all have experience now with microgravity, and you are all expected to function normally with or without gravity. The only scheduling change will be on Thursday to prepare the habitat for spin-down. Everybody will participate; everybody will be responsible for locking down equipment. This includes personal belongings, furniture, and all kitchen implements. Also, the fowl and everything in the greenhouse rooms." He smiled and raised a finger. "I am officially canceling all classes Thursday!"

Jasmine smiled and clapped her hands. Surprisingly, none of the other youth reacted. Nobody else seemed interested in a day off from studies.

"Jhonathan, do you have anything to add?"

Dr. Jhonathan, sitting across from Captain Becker, was visible on the left side of the NLED wall.

"Perhaps I'll fill in details about the overall mission; I'm not sure what everyone knows at this point. Assuming the Mars-transit injection executes as planned, we'll spend the next nine months traveling to Mars, tethered to our sister ship, *Mars Hope*. As you may recall, we will not be the first to depart. *Providence* – our own vessel – and *Mars Hope* are the second set of ships to set out. *Pioneer Alpha* and *Beta* will be first, later this week, and I understand that they are completing their final preparations. *Fearless* and *Audacious* are to leave last, a week after us."

He took a sip of water. "Once we depart Earth orbit, we will become quite distant over the following weeks, and before long, direct video calls will no longer be possible with family and friends on Earth. As we set out on our journey, every day of travel will add half a second to the time taken for signals to reach Earth from us or us from Earth."

My sister Shirel spoke. "So that means that after two weeks of travel, if I talk to my grandmother, I need to wait seven seconds for her to answer everything I say?"

"That's the idea, Shirel, but it's more like fourteen seconds – seven seconds in each direction – though these are just general

Departure

estimates." He looked around at everyone sitting in his own living room, then gazed from the NLED wall at us. "The upshot is that you should spend this week and next talking to everyone you love back on Earth. We'll have email, and will always be able to send and receive video logs, but we'll never again have face-to-face conversations with earthlings."

"Will we be able to talk with the other ships?"

"With *Mars Hope*, yes; you'll be able to call any time from your datapad. With the other ships, no. Throughout our journey, they'll be too far away for direct conversations, but even if they were not, it would not help. We'll have no direct connection to them. Our communications satellite will focus on Earth alone, so anything we send has to be routed through the home planet.

"One more thing. According to Murke-Berger Foundation rules, we need agreement from every individual to continue the mission. We are not permitted to leave Earth orbit without your explicit assent. We'll do this informally: Captain Becker and I will speak with each of you over the next couple of days."

Nobody else asked a question, so we set about cleaning up. My mother directed Meital, Shirel, Denver and me in gathering our own dishes and leftovers, and scooting them up the stairs to our kitchen. Meital volunteered to wash the dishes, and Shirel joined her with a towel to dry them and put them away.

On normal evenings we had a study session after dinner, but the communal festivity had lasted well beyond the half hour normally allotted for dinner. By the time we finished cleaning up, the evening period was more than half over. Meital and I suggested to Dr. Louis that we skip the scheduled Earth History class, and he agreed. I was planning to get in bed with a book, but when I entered our room, Denver had his guitar out, the first time since we had launched five weeks earlier. The guitar was a small model that he had brought along as his individually selected artifact. He looked particularly happy, sitting there up on his bunk, tuning the strings. He began strumming the opening chords to "Flying High" by the Little Rocks, then launched into the song's neo-swing beat and began singing. I clapped my hands and sang along, elated by the tune.

Denver's guitar playing did not go unnoticed. Meital and Shirel, their room separated from ours by only a narrow spacecraft bulkhead, burst in to join us. Meital used her datapad to call upstairs to Ruby, and within minutes she, Susan, Sam and Celina had crowded into the room to listen in and sing along. Helga soon arrived with her clarinet. As Denver began a twentieth-century song called "Stairway to Heaven" – my grandparents had enjoyed it back when they were kids – I noticed that there were more people in our bedroom than ever before. Meital, Shirel, and Susan squeezed onto my bunk next to me; Celina and Helga hopped up onto Denver's bunk; and Sam and Ruby dragged chairs in from the living room. For the next song, Helga thought it appropriate to suggest "Martian Rap" by the Olympians, prompting Sam to step out and return a few minutes later with Dr. Claudine's djembe, the traditional West African drum that she had brought as her own personal artifact. Simeon followed Sam into the room and leaned against the wall. Sam, it turned out, was a surprisingly adequate hand-drummer, and Simeon's singing added a Russian timbre to the mix of English and Dutch accents.

Later that night I lay in bed awake, listening to Denver's steady breathing. The singing had been genuinely fun, raising our spirits even beyond the excitement of the communal dinner and the fresh vegetables. I had not realized that my spirits needed raising. For weeks I had been following my busy schedule aboard my orbiting home, constantly aware of my awesome mission. Awaken, pray, exercise, eat, work, study, exercise, prepare food, relax, sleep, awaken, and do it again. And again. Day after day, all the time animated by the novelty of spaceship life, excited about the impending departure, driven by the awareness of awesome historic responsibility, the responsibility of those soon to become the pioneering architects of humanity's new branch. Now, however, I wondered. Had I really agreed to leave Earth? To endanger my life on a ridiculously difficult venture? Was mine a conscious, measured decision? Had I considered all alternatives, and only thereafter freely made my choice? Or was my participation determined from the moment my father had left for Mars two years earlier? Were all my subsequent thoughts no more than an exercise in self-justification? Perhaps my destiny was fixed far earlier, when, at age ten, I had joined my family in the intensive preparatory training program. Had I essentially no choice in the matter, only imagining that in some way I had influenced my life's extraordinary vector?

Departure

No choice in the matter – that was a surprisingly comforting thought. If I, Michael Teller, age seventeen, had chosen to join this wild excursion, then I was responsible for the outcome, guilty of any tragedy that ensued. But if it was all my parents' doing, I held no responsibility. Children everywhere moved, willingly or not, with their parents, to a new neighborhood, or a new city, or a new country. Or a new world. No choice, no authority, no culpability.

What if I said no when Dr. Jhonathan spoke with me? As he had explained, technically, by Foundation rules, any participant could decline to join the Mars-transit injection, refuse to leave Earth orbit, and thereby prevent his ship's departure. I had already passed the psychological evaluation. Would they take me seriously? Did I have an obligation to try to go back home?

With these confused thoughts bouncing around my brain, I settled into fitful sleep.

*   *   *

Tuesday, October 31st, 2028 10:35

I called my grandmother Tuesday morning after completing my waste-management chores. She lived near Jerusalem, eight hours ahead of our Mexico-based clock, so it was early evening for her. She smiled when she saw me.

"Michael, you look a little pale. You need to get more sun."

"Grandma," I said, "you know we don't get any sun here. But I am getting plenty of exercise, two hours every day. How are you doing?"

It was the wrong question to ask.

"How do you think I'm doing? Three of my grandchildren are leaving and I'll never see them again. I've already lost my younger son to this cursed mission, and my older son is sick in a place with no medical care."

"Grandma, I don't know what to say, other than that I love you."

"Michael, I've spoken with Shirel and Meital, and with your mother, and I know all of you are enthusiastic about the journey. I won't discourage you. But I'm not going to hide my feelings. I wish you success and pray that you all have long, happy, healthy lives. But I am not happy."

That was just about the whole conversation. We ended with small talk about the autumn weather in Jerusalem, we kissed each other remotely, and we blessed each other with good health. That was it. Though we could still call earthbound relatives for another week, I wondered if I would call her again.

*   *   *

Wednesday, November 1st, 2028 10:20

"Simeon, can you take a look at something here?" I called from the Mauve-Level bathroom door. It was midmorning and I was trying to run a waste-processing cycle in the bathroom the Bouchets shared with the Radechov brothers. Everything had gone smoothly upstairs in the Green-Level bathroom, but now, just as I was hoping to finish my daily chores a bit early, a light on the kiln's front panel was blinking red. I had initiated the cycle, and it seemed to start out okay, but a minute later the fan's whirring stopped abruptly, the light started blinking, and my datapad indicated an "electrical fault." Sam and I had experienced minor problems while running waste-processing cycles over the preceding weeks, but in each case the machinery recovered by itself. At most it had been necessary to reinitiate a cycle after an automated self-cleaning procedure. This time, however, the computer seemed not to want to solve the problem by itself.

"Just wait one minute, please, Michael," Simeon called out from his living room sofa without looking up. He was scrutinizing his datapad, reviewing, I assumed, results from habitat-wide electrical self-tests that ran continuously. I was lucky to have found him there. A moment later, I heard him mutter "level-one bathroom waste processor." His gaze did not leave his datapad's screen. He was using his finger, apparently scrolling through data, and sat concentrating a few more seconds. "Ah, I see, Michael. It looks like you blew a fuse on the macerator motor." Only then did he stand and come over. "This should be easy to fix."

For the next twenty minutes Simeon knelt on the bathroom floor, carefully opening the cover above the kiln, then removing several layers of electronics, until he finally exposed the motor.

"Did you make any last calls to relatives?" I asked while he worked, recalling the uncomfortable call with my grandmother.

Departure

"Boris and I have spoken with our parents every day this week."

"That must be difficult. How are they taking it?"

He looked up at me without removing his hands from the cabinet. "Well, obviously, having both of their sons move to Mars is not something they planned." He turned back to look at whatever it was in his hands. "But they are very supportive. They know this is our dream and always encouraged us." He grimaced as he struggled for a moment with something deep in the cabinet. "My father actually helped me a lot getting on the mission." He placed a circuit board on the floor next to me. "Boris and I watched an interview Papa and Mama did with a St. Petersburg news group. They spoke very proudly."

"But they'll never see you again. Aren't they upset about that?"

"You grew up in America, right?" He reached for a screwdriver. "But I think your family came from Europe, yes?"

"I grew up partly in America and partly in Israel. But yes, some of my great-great-grandparents came from Europe to the United States a long time ago. Around the year 1900."

"What did their parents think when they left Europe for America? They probably never saw them again." He placed the screwdriver on the floor and reached back into the cabinet.

"Yes, but they must have sent letters. It's not like they were leaving the whole planet."

Simeon looked up at me dubiously. "You are joking, right?" He turned back to the cabinet and carefully removed the motor he had been detaching. "In those days, leaving for a different continent was like leaving the planet today. Except that we can send voice and video messages to our loved ones every day for the rest of our lives. Even when Earth is most distant from Mars, we can send messages in less than twenty-five minutes. When your ancestors went to America, they waited months for a letter. What we are doing is nothing like that."

"So, you are one-hundred-percent comfortable about leaving? No second thoughts?"

He stood up and placed the motor on the counter by the sink. "I told Captain Becker that I am one hundred percent with the mission. I miss hugging my parents, and I think Boris feels the same. But we expect to make them proud grandparents someday, and that is more important than hugging. I'm comfortable knowing that my papa and

131

mama will be able to watch their grandchildren grow up, even if they will be on a different planet."

"I also agreed to depart, when Dr. Jhonathan spoke with me yesterday."

"It would have been strange if you did not. Now let me get a replacement fuse and we'll have this working right away."

I followed Simeon to a small storage locker behind the staircase, where he found a fuse. While he worked to install it, I opened the inventory application on my datapad and registered that we had taken it. Five minutes later, Simeon snapped the motor and circuit board back into place, then walked out to the sofa to retrieve his datapad. "That was a simple repair," he said, pleased with himself. "Let's test the motor." He tapped the screen as he stepped back into the bathroom.

For a moment nothing happened. Then there was a bright flash from within the cabinet and a very loud "pop!" that made both of us jump. Simeon yelled out something in Russian that is best left untranslated.

"What happened?" I asked.

"I don't know how to fix this," he said, flustered. He ran his hand through his hair, clutched his goatee, and looked back at the datapad. "Uh, I don't think you'll be able to run the cycle today." He peered back into the open cabinet and shook his head. "Not good. I'm going to have to get Captain Becker – he's the master electrician." He looked extremely perturbed. "This is exactly what I did not want to happen," he murmured. "Now he's going to make even more trouble about the spacewalk Friday." He turned and walked out, calling back to me, "Do not let anyone use the toilet for now."

Normally, one would put up an "out of order" sign in such a case, but I knew of no pencils or paper anywhere in the habitat. We did have lots of duct tape, though. I found a roll in a kitchen drawer, tore off a strip, taped it over the top of the toilet, and washed my hands. Having nothing more to do in the bathroom, I headed upstairs for Talmud class. The conversation with Simeon had left me feeling uncomfortable. Certainly I felt bad for him that his attempt at repairing the macerator motor had failed, and even more so at his tension with Captain Becker. But that was not what primarily bothered me. It was what he said about his parents being happy and supportive. What a contrast with my grandmother!

*   *   *

Thursday, November 2nd, 2028 13:00

    Thursday started out like a regular day, but there was extra excitement in the air. It was the day that classes had been canceled so that we could spend the afternoon securing everything aboard the ship, in preparation for impending weightlessness. We were supposed to be prepared for weightlessness at all times in case of a tether failure, but in practice we had become lazy. We left dishes out to dry, clothes on our beds – bright-colored longshirts that we wore over our mundies and floral-patterned overall-skirts that the girls wore – and silverware, pots and pans, unsecured in their kitchen drawers. There were soap and toothbrushes and toothpaste to put away in the bathrooms. We had stashed open food containers in the kitchen cupboards and leftovers in the small refrigerators. Less noticed, dust that had accumulated on all surfaces needed to be vacuumed before spin-down.

    We finished our regular chores and gathered on our respective levels. Sam happily informed me, as he passed me on the staircase, that the Mauve-Level waste processor was functional again. Evidently, Captain Becker had spent five minutes air-cleaning the circuit boards, then identified and fixed a short circuit. I wondered if Simeon was embarrassed. Perhaps not: for an engineer, booms and flashes were the kinds of challenges that made the profession interesting. But perhaps so: Simeon had been visibly troubled the previous morning, having failed at his own attempt to fix the fault.

    I really did not know how he felt. Of everyone on the ship, I knew Simeon and his brother Boris the least. They had been late additions to the expedition, joining *Providence* only a year earlier, toward the end of the summer of '27. It was after my uncle's spacecraft *Armstrong*, one of the four MiniHabs in my father's Vanguard mission, had failed to make its Mars-insertion burn. The Foundation decided to replace my uncle and the other three lost astronauts with candidates from the waitlist. Simeon and Boris were accepted into our group, joining the Bouchets. Boris had been an engineer at a Russian air systems manufacturer, and Simeon came straight from university. We did not grow close during the year at Altiplano. The brothers spent most of their time together, generally ignoring the youth of our group. Maybe it was a language thing: Simeon did not seem to get comfortable speaking English until the final months before launch. Only then did he become more friendly toward us.

"Michael," my mother called from her bedroom's doorway, "can you help me in my room? I'm going upstairs to examine the water processors. Can you vacuum the floor and bed?" She handed me a handheld electric vacuum cleaner, one of two on board. I kissed her cheek and set to work. A handheld was the wrong tool for the job, but since we had nothing bigger, several of us spent more time on our hands and knees that afternoon than we would have preferred. We vacuumed dust from the composite floor, paying particular attention to the Velcro patches spaced every few centimeters. After I finished my mother's room, I passed the vacuum to Meital. She cleaned my room, then handed it off to Shirel, who cleaned the girls' room. When she finished, she gave the vacuum to Denver, who had volunteered to do the bathroom and kitchen. That left the living room, which we divided among ourselves.

"Michael, what about your sprouts?" Meital reminded me helpfully. "Don't forget your jars full of wheat kernels."

I would have remembered to secure the sprouts for weightlessness, I told myself, as I had been attending to the jars twice a day, adding and draining water. Meital seemed to read my thoughts, because she laughed as she watched me. "You would have forgotten. You would have emptied the full jar and filled the empty jar tonight, then obliviously put them back on their shelf."

"Thanks for your confidence, my dear sister." Lest I forget and prove her right, I went straight to the kitchen to secure the sprouting grain. I sealed the open food packages, too.

Sometime later, Omar and Celina came bounding down the stairs and popped into our living room. Shirel was vacuuming under the table while Meital and I took a break on the couch. A documentary about the early American space program played on the opposite NLED wall. "Who will help us in the Green and Mauve Levels' greenhouses?" Omar called out, his eyes settling on Meital and me. "Lots of plants to secure."

I groaned. "We just sat down for a break."

Departure

On the screen, the Apollo 8 countdown was approaching zero.

Meital punched me in the shoulder as she rose. "We're astronauts and pioneers, Michael. We don't take breaks. Get up." Apollo 8 rose from its pad and I rose from the couch.

Celina laughed, "Nice, Meital, you keep your brother motivated. Come with me." She and my beloved sister headed downstairs. I followed Omar into our own deck's greenhouse room.

"We need to make sure no soil covers are missing and that they are taped," he said. "Also, that none of the planters are loose."

The triangular room was quite small, barely large enough for us to stand together shoulder to shoulder. The brilliant light compensated for the lack of space. LED lights covered the entire ceiling – the four identical greenhouses were by far the brightest rooms in the habitat. We entered through a folding door in the middle of the longest wall. The second wall, to our right, was part of the spacecraft's circular hull, so it curved inward. The third wall began at a right angle two meters in front of us and extended back, diagonally, in the direction of the center of the habitat. The curved wall held two vertically-stacked racks of plantings, behind which we could see the black tubes we had filled with water weeks before. More LED lights, installed on the upper rack's underside, shone onto the lower rack. The diagonal wall in front of us held only one rack, but it had deeper soil. The walls converged to our left in a sharp-angled corner that contained a small cabinet. Such was life in a circular home: many walls converged in the direction of the circle's center.

"Examine the covers, starting from this side," Omar instructed, pointing.

I examined the soil covers in front of me. A series of ten-centimeter-wide strips, each half a meter long, snapped onto the near and far edges of the rack's planter, to cover the soil and secure it during times of weightlessness. The plants rose through notches cut into the edges of the strips. Each pair of adjacent strips was taped together, between the stems, sealing off the soil. The plants had grown impressively in the weeks since planting and reached more than twenty centimeters into the air.

"Is it normal for these to grow so quickly?" I asked.

"Yes, especially with the extra help we give them. Hand me a roll of duct tape from the cabinet."

I found rolls of tape secured to a hook on the cabinet's middle shelf. Like the room, the cabinet was triangular, filling the whole corner. No space could be wasted in our compact home. I retrieved two rolls of tape and handed one to Omar. In exchange, he handed me a bottle of water that had a spray top.

"What extra help?"

"High carbon dioxide levels and lots of light. We keep the greenhouse rooms lit fourteen hours each day. Did you know that more than seven percent of all our electricity goes to the greenhouse lights?"

"I remember something about that," I answered, while I snapped off the leftmost plastic strip and checked the soil. It was moist, so I snapped the strip back on. I removed the second one and found the soil moist there too, so I reattached it. I continued along the same way, checking all sixteen, spraying water onto the soil where necessary. Omar did the same with the curved wall's racks. Having two racks instead of one, he had twice the work to do, but he worked more quickly. He was, after all, our group's lead agronomist, the expert at interplanetary agriculture.

"Why is there only one rack on this side?" I asked. "If there is room for two racks on the curved wall, there could be two racks here, too."

"It is for different types of plants, Michael." Omar turned and leaned back to make space between us. "The plants you are inspecting are tomatoes. Specifically, 'indeterminate' tomato plants, which will grow quite high, *in sha'All-h*. Perhaps almost two and a half meters."

"Then there's not enough room here. Certainly not two and a half meters."

"Actually, the ceiling is less than one and a half meters above that rack. The vermiculture cabinet is fifty centimeters and the rack above it, with its soil, is forty. That leaves one hundred and forty centimeters to the ceiling."

"What happens when the plants get higher than that?"

"See the strings?" Omar pointed toward the tomato rack. I'd ignored them before, but indeed, at each plant, a string stretched from a small stake in the soil next to the stem all the way to a wire strung along the ceiling. There were two such wires, parallel to each other, matching the two rows of plantings. "As the plants grow, we'll drag the strings along the wires, stretching the bottoms of the vines along the soil. Those on the left will grow toward the right, and the ones on the right will grow to the left. They will keep growing, and, if all goes well, will continue yielding tomatoes throughout our journey."

"That's cool. If these plants are tomatoes, what's growing in the smaller racks?"

"It is not 'cool,' Michael. It is a well-tested method of greenhouse tomato cultivation." He shook his head scornfully. His distaste for youthful slang was curious, given that he himself was only twenty-five years old. "In the small racks on this level we've planted beets, radishes, turnips and carrots. Upstairs we are growing celery, lettuce, kale, and some cabbage. Also, a bit of mustard and cress. Downstairs we have onions and even some potatoes for the agriculture class."

"And the big racks upstairs and downstairs? Are they only for tomatoes?"

"Upstairs on Pink Level we are growing cucumber vines; on Yellow Level some tomatoes and some zucchini; and downstairs on Mauve Level we've planted several types of peppers. Why don't you go examine them? You might enjoy watching them grow."

After we finished inspecting the soil and its coverings, we crouched down to check the mushroom cabinets, which were below the curved wall's racks. The compost, covered by a burlap sheet, was moist and firm, so nothing was needed to prepare it for microgravity.

Omar went downstairs to see how Celina and Meital were progressing, and I joined Shirel and Denver back in the living room. Soon it was time for afternoon exercise. Meital came back to join us.

"What about the birds?" asked Shirel, in the middle of her sprower session. Did anyone remember to secure them?"

"There wasn't much to do," Meital answered. "Ruby and I checked the cages' latches with Dr. Cecylia this morning. We're all set for spin-down tomorrow afternoon."

*　　*　　*

Friday, November 3rd, 2028 18:15

We were seated at the table for our weekly Sabbath dinner. A beautiful Sabbath candelabrum, candles glimmering, appeared on the NLED screen behind my mother. Real candles were forbidden in our high-oxygen environment, so Shirel had taken to finding a new video of pretty candles or elegant candelabra each week. The virtual candles burned slowly, and Shirel programmed the NLED wall to turn off when they expired. The image provided an appropriate ambiance. Also, by increasing the light in the room, Shirel fulfilled the Sabbath obligation to prepare abundant light before the start of the holy day.

A white tablecloth covered the table, and a traditional embroidered challah cover cloaked the two braided loaves I had baked earlier that afternoon. The table was set with covered bowls of special dishes. Meital had prepared a chickpea-and-carrot salad – mostly chickpeas – with some of the very first baby carrots to have been harvested, from our greenhouse room, only hours before. Shirel had prepared pasta with reconstituted tomato sauce, and my mother had cooked a spicy bean and rice stew. For the first time since launch meat was also served. From the small reserve of kosher beef kabanos on board, my mother had taken two, cut them into six small pieces, and set them at the center of the table as the core of the main course.

On *Providence* we drank mostly water – often carbonated – but for our Sabbath meal we reconstituted half a liter of grape juice. I had gone upstairs to withdraw a parcel from the storage attic's small reserve of juice powders. Following regulations, I had meticulously logged the withdrawal in the Foodstock application. I now stood, holding a silver ceremonial Kiddush cup, one of two on board, full of the juice. Jewish tradition is to recite Kiddush, the Jewish blessing to mark the start of the Sabbath day, over a glass of wine. I recited the benediction over the closest available analog.

"… and G-d completed, on the seventh day, His handiwork He had made …." I quoted the traditional verses from Genesis in the original Hebrew. "… G-d blessed the seventh day and sanctified it, because on that day He ceased all his handiwork that G-d had created to completion." Then I recited the blessings over the grape juice and the Sabbath, concluding with "The source of all blessing are You, my L-rd, the Sanctifier of the Sabbath."

As my mother and sisters, and my best friend Denver, said "Amen," I drank most of the cup of juice, then passed around the remainder. We washed our hands ceremonially, according to Jewish custom, and blessed G-d for the bread and everything we would eat with it. Then it was time to enjoy the meal, and the final hours of gravity.

"By morning, will we be weightless again?" Shirel asked.

"We are already losing our gravity," Denver said. "Spin-down started a few hours ago. We can float out of our beds when we wake up tomorrow!" Looking at me with a grin, he dropped a piece of bread onto his plate to demonstrate. As usual, it fell more slowly than it would have on Earth, but it was hard to detect any difference from the ship's normal gravity.

"Do you think anyone will be spacesick?" Meital asked. "Since we're all used to Mars-level gravity, which is so low anyway, is it possible to feel sick from weightlessness?"

"I guess we'll know in a few days," my mother said. "Oh – I shouldn't forget. I received a note from your father just before sundown. He is quite excited that we're preparing to set out. He wished everybody a good Sabbath."

"How is he feeling today?" Meital asked.

"He wrote that he has some of his strength back and spent the week out and about with the water miners. They've made good progress."

"That's good news."

"It is. Both the progress and that Dad is feeling stronger." She gazed wistfully across the table.

Shirel filled the silence. "This is our last Earth Sabbath. By next Friday night we will have completed Mars-transit injection."

"I was thinking about that," Denver said. "When you said that blessing for the grape juice, you were quoting from the Bible, right? G-d created the world in six days and stopped on the seventh?"

"Yes. From the beginning of Genesis."

"Well, that makes sense, in some sort of way, in reference to Earth. A day is the twenty-four hours it takes for Earth to rotate. I don't know why it would take an omnipotent G-d so long to make the Universe, but at least on Earth you can talk about days."

I smiled, always amused by Denver's unreligious views. "Okay. So?"

He tilted his head and smirked. "You can even talk about sundown on an orbiting spacecraft. We're still on Altiplano time, and I'm pretty sure there was sundown there today."

The girls giggled.

Elbow on the table, he held up his fork. "Even if we are now one hundred and twenty thousand kilometers above Earth, we are still in orbit, so we can pretend we have Earth days. But what about next week, when we have left Earth behind? What seven 'days' will you count for your G-d? How will you know when to celebrate your Sabbath?"

"That would be a good question to ask Dr. Jhonathan," I said.

"Michael, I want your answer, not Dr. Jhonathan's. You are the one who quotes Genesis each week at our table!"

"Maybe the Torah's intention is that G-d created the concept of 'day,' not just a unit of time, but a stage of a creative process. The Earth's rotation is a physical manifestation of the concept, but the concept itself does not depend on a particular planet. We don't have to be at Earth to appreciate the creative process that resulted in the existence of the Universe. And in the existence of us!"

"Nice explanation. But you didn't answer my question. Try again."

"Denver, be nice to my brother," Meital said, shaking her finger.

"What I mean is that, after we leave Earth orbit, you will have no way to count seven days." He leaned back in his seat. "The computer will start stretching our days, making the clocks run a bit more slowly, so that we will be used to Martian sols when we arrive. Soon there will be no correlation between our daily schedule and Earth days. Does your G-d allow you to count the seven days to each Sabbath using days of whatever length the computer chooses?"

When I hesitated to answer, Shirel looked at me with a twinkle in her eye, and mimicked me, nodding, "That would be a good question to ask Dr. Jhonathan."

* * *

Saturday, November 4th, 2028 20:00

Saturday evening, Simeon, Boris and Captain Becker donned their fleximets and entered the airlock. Captain Becker had grudgingly agreed that Simeon perform the detethering spacewalk, but only after publicly admonishing him to adhere to all safety procedures. This happened in the Bouchets' Mauve-Level living room, where many of us had gathered to help transfer the birdcages from the airlock. The airlock served as our aviary most of the time,

Departure

as it was the habitat's only extra room. But sometimes we needed the airlock to be an airlock. During these times all the birds had to be moved elsewhere so that the airlock's atmosphere could be purged.

We put the parakeets and canaries in the Bouchets' master bedroom. Since cycles and sprowers were also stowed there, there was little room left over for chickens. The other bedrooms, too, had no room – in order for the airlock hatch to open, in the middle of the living-room floor, the dining table and chairs needed to be folded and packed away – so we carried the chicken coop up to my family's Green-Level living room. This was easier than it sounded, as by Saturday evening we had become completely weightless. I would not have wanted to lug seventeen one-month-old chicks and their cages up two flights even in Mars-level gravity. The birds seemed agitated in the freefall environment, but there was little we could do about that.

"Simeon, you will latch yourself to every rung."

"Yes, Captain."

"You will never, even for a moment, not be latched to at least one rung."

"Yes, Captain."

"If you do not follow protocol, this will be your last spacewalk."

"Yes, Captain."

After that uncomfortable exchange the operation proceeded smoothly. They closed and secured the airlock hatch to the Mauve-Level living room. The airlock purge was without incident; then Boris opened the outer hatch. Everybody watched on the NLED walls, which showed Simeon's fleximet camera view. He exited the ship, latched himself to one of the nearest rungs on the habitat's underside, then turned back to face the open hatch. Captain Becker handed him the empty tether spool.

Outside, Simeon progressed from rung to rung quite quickly, latching and unlatching every forty-five seconds or so. Most of the time he – and we – focused on the rungs on the ZubHab's hull, but occasionally he – and we – looked up at the starfield. We had reached periapsis some twelve hours before, and had passed beyond the little that remained of the outer Van Allen radiation belt, but Earth still loomed large off to the side. Would this be our last time seeing it?

Red Valley

Simeon held the empty spool. Even though it was tethered to the belt of his harness, he could not let it out of his left hand, because it might bump the solar panels that stretched alongside the ladder. Only his right hand was available for latching and unlatching. Nevertheless, he reached the pinnacle in only twenty minutes. We watched on our screens as he latched the spool to the horseshoe hook at the tip of the ship, unlatched it from his belt, and finally released it from his hand.

After some delay, Arjan Ravel's gruff voice sounded from the NLED wall's speakers. "I've released all four tethers on our end." No longer attached to *Mars Hope*, the tethers would float in space until Simeon reeled them in.

We watched from Simeon's fleximet camera as he climbed down to each tether hook, successively releasing the red, green, blue and yellow tethers, carrying each in turn back to the pinnacle to link it to the spool. After the final one was secured, he grabbed the spool's crank. He held the spool in one hand and began rotating the crank to gather in all four tethers. It reminded me of my father, years earlier, winding up a garden hose in our yard at the Murke-Berger Foundation's Red Rock facility in Arizona. But that took only a minute or so, whereas Simeon spent fifteen minutes rolling up all four tethers, each one hundred and five meters long. He stopped from time to time to check that they were rolling up smoothly.

"How's your air level?" Captain Becker asked, as Simeon began his rung-by-rung journey back to *Providence's* bottom hull.

"Enough for twenty minutes. I need to rush."

"That's enough time for you to follow protocol. Please continue as you have been doing."

"Simeon, I will meet you at the bottom edge," Boris announced. "I'll take the spool from you there, so you can rush into the airlock."

Simeon, knowing that Captain Becker was scrutinizing every move, was careful to latch himself to every successive rung before unlatching from each previous one. Happily, the captain found nothing to complain about. Simeon reached the bottom and handed the spool to Boris, then rushed across to the airlock's entrance. Perhaps forgetting for a moment that he was still broadcasting on his fleximet radio, he addressed his brother. "Boris, thanks for the help. Just two minutes of air left. No way I could have gotten back in time following the captain's protocol if I had to bring the spool in myself."

Departure

But once he was safely back inside the airlock, he seemed to realize that his fleximet camera's view was still visible on our NLED walls. He kept his focus on the action while he refilled his oxypack. We watched through the hatch as Boris, still outside, passed the full spool into the airlock. Captain Becker stowed the spool in its proper place on the airlock bulkhead, while Boris entered and closed the outer hatch.

Twenty minutes later, after the airlock had been repressurized, we began passing the birdcages back downstairs. Everything was back in place within an hour. Sam, Denver, and I stayed behind to help Meital and Ruby clean the airlock and feed the fowl; then it was bedtime.

Thanksgiving

Sunday, November 5th, 2028 13:30

    We were supposed to be back to our regular schedules Sunday morning, everything as usual, other than the weightlessness. But with so much happening in preparation for our expedition's departure, it was hard to concentrate on our studies. After lunch Sunday, Celina and I headed downstairs to meet Omar for Mycology class. As we hovered by the entrance to the Mauve-Level greenhouse room, Omar crouched inside the room to open the mycelium compost cabinet under the outer wall's planting racks. The living room NLED wall to our left unexpectedly lit up. I was surprised to identify the Altiplano Spaceport launchpad, on which stood a Harrier 6 rocket, about to launch. "Professor Sidda, we have been interrupted! Take a look."

    "Michael, I appreciate the respect – if you are not mocking me – but you can call me 'Omar' even in class." He pushed off the floor and floated into the living room to watch with us.

    Not unexpectedly, Captain Becker's voice came over the intercom. "Listen, all fliers. The third communications satellite is ready to launch. As this is our expedition's final launch before our departure, we thought it would be fun to see it live."

    Everybody stopped to watch. Dr. Claudine had been tutoring Sophie and Jasmine at the other end of the table; her husband was working on his datapad in the kitchen; and Boris emerged from his bedroom, his own datapad Velcroed to his sleeve. We gathered around the table for the final countdown.

"Three, two, one ... launch!" we recited in unison.

The rocket surged upward, a fiery plume gleaming below, and Dr. Claudine explained the launch to her girls. My French was good enough to understand the gist, something like "this is the satellite that will be the telephone for *Fearless* and *Audacious*, the last two habitats in our group, so that they can talk to Earth and to us while we travel to Mars."

The wall went blank after the successful launch and we returned to our class activities. We examined the compost for the mushrooms and reviewed the spawning process with Omar. "It will be easier to spawn after we've restored gravity," he said. That was disappointing: we had been preparing the compost for weeks, and now, when it was finally ready, we would need to wait another seven days.

Sam and I might have focused all the way through Hebrew Literature class with my mother later that afternoon, but it was not to be. Just as we started class in the Meyers' Pink-Level living room, the NLED wall's mountain scenery disappeared, replaced by a starfield view. The starfield was rotating very slowly around a central point. This, I knew, meant that the view was from either the very top of our vessel, looking up, or the very bottom, looking down. When not in tethered spin, the habitat rotated on its vertical axis once each thirty minutes, to expose the entire circumference of our hull to the same amount of sunlight, to maintain uniform surface temperature. In a side-camera view the stars would all seem to move in one direction, but from a top or bottom view the starscape appeared to rotate like a wheel.

Compounding our growing attention deficit, the second NLED wall lit up. More starry space appeared. Those stars were all moving in the same direction; hence, a side view.

Captain Becker's voice again emerged from the wall's speakers. "We are starting the maneuvers that will position us for departure on Friday. I thought you might all like to watch."

Sam's mother, who was listening from the kitchen, turned toward us and said, enigmatically, "It's time to get our engines back." Without explaining, she turned back to the food she was preparing. Her hair, gathered under a brown kerchief, swung behind her head.

"Mom, please don't do that!" Sam protested, rising from his perch beside the table. "What are the maneuvers?"

"Sam, my dear astronaut son, figure it out with your friend."

I examined the first wall. The top of *Mars Hope* – half visible in sunlight – was right in the middle. I knew the two habitats would need to be facing precisely the same direction when we lit our rockets for Mars-transit injection, but if we were seeing the other ship's pinnacle, the two ships were still facing each other. "We or *Mars Hope* need to flip, to align in parallel before the end of the week. That is one of the maneuvers."

Sam, also having accepted his mother's challenge, examined the other screen. He pointed. "Here ... and here. Those are the two Mars-Transit Injection stages." I followed his hand. It was hard to make anything out, but when I approached the screen, I could see the vague white streaks he indicated, one at the top of the screen, the other near the bottom. "Those are the 'engines' we need to get back: they will propel us toward Mars. We need to dock with them."

"They look very far away."

Dr. Esther faced us again. "Very good. Each is about two kilometers from us and two kilometers from the other. We parked them in parallel orbits after high Earth orbit insertion." In a lilting voice, she added, "Far enough away so we wouldn't crash into them as we spun."

My own mother explained, "We will move very slowly toward our Mars-Transit Injection stage over the next twenty-four hours. Or perhaps the stage will move toward us. It's hard to say. Tomorrow we will attempt docking." Then she pointed at her datapad. "Let's get back to the text we're supposed to be studying."

The NLED walls continued to show their respective camera views into the evening. As we studied, as we exercised, as we ate, and especially as we tarried in preparing for bed, we kept examining the screens regularly, trying to discern movement. *Mars Hope* slowly grew more distant and our Mars-Transit Injection stage slowly approached. This continued through most of the following day, too. We managed to maintain our regular schedule, more or less, despite the distraction. Later, as the stage approached the bottom of our Mars-Entry stage, which had remained attached even while we rotated with *Mars Hope* for gravity, the computer swapped cameras to keep it in view. Just after dinner we felt a slight bump, and Captain Becker announced that we had successfully joined to our Mars-Transit Injection stage.

*   *   *

Friday, November 10th, 2028 15:00

We returned to our regular schedule for the rest of the weightless week. Ruby did suffer minor space sickness, as did Helga, and, unexpectedly, Helga's father, the captain. It seemed that the adjustment to Mars-level gravity had mitigated the effects somewhat, because nobody needed to skip chores or classes. I was surprised, Tuesday night, to realize that I had not thought about weightlessness all day, as I exercised, maintained the toilets, studied, and baked. "I've mastered spaceflight," I said to Meital, who was reading something on her datapad next to me at the living room couch.

"Oh, yes, I'm sure my seventeen-year-old brother is a master of spaceflight," she said without looking up. "Master, I'll come to you if I have any questions."

Mars-transit-injection burn was scheduled for 15:14 Friday afternoon. Mid-afternoon, Ruby, Susan and Sam joined me and my sisters, and Denver, in our Green-Level living room. "It's time to dance again," Susan announced. She projected a video, in which an obscure orchestra played Strauss's *The Blue Danube*, onto the NLED wall. She apparently considered classical music to be funny and had selected *The Blue Danube* in jest, but to my thinking a waltz was a great thing to dance to – if only we had known how to waltz.

"Are you guys ready?" Shirel asked, visibly thrilled, brown eyes wide, her hands moving to the music. "This is it: we are about to be the first families to leave Earth orbit!"

"Not the first," Denver corrected. "There are nine families on *Pioneer Alpha* and *Beta*, and they left a week ago."

Susan interjected, "She meant, we are about to be *among* the first families to leave. Don't be a buzzkill."

The other NLED wall lit up. A cloud-covered Earth filled the bottom half and a clock in the corner read 15:00. The clouds moved below us. We were approaching periapsis, 405 kilometers above Earth's surface, the closest we would ever again be.

"It's so beautiful," Ruby murmured to herself, her hand clenching her belly.

"How quickly are we moving relative to Earth?" I asked, as we all watched the wall.

"I'll check," said Sam, pulling his datapad off his sleeve. After a few seconds, he read off its display. "At closest approach we reach thirty-eight thousand and sixty-six kilometers per hour."

"We are fifteen minutes from periapsis," Dr. Jhonathan announced from the wall's speakers, barely louder than the music. "The burn will commence in nine minutes, then continue for twelve."

"Dad took over announcements from Captain Becker today," Ruby explained. "He said the coordination with the other ships requires the captain's full attention."

"We have to accelerate at the exact same rate, in the exact direction, with both *Mars Hope* and the communications satellite," Susan added. "Otherwise, we won't end up traveling together and we'll have no gravity and no way to talk with Earth."

"It's funny how close we are to Earth," Shirel said. "You would think that we would officially leave for Mars when we are as far away as possible."

Denver answered. "It's because of how orbital mechanics works. The same acceleration close to Earth gives our ship much more energy. Think about it. To accelerate, we have to push against the hot gases of our burnt fuel. If we leave the gases in high Earth orbit, they'll have much more potential energy, because things high up have more potential energy than things low down, and that leaves us with less kinetic energy. Whereas by leaving the gases close to the planet, they'll have less potential energy. We get the extra energy in the form of much more speed as we fly away from Earth."

"I kind of understand," Shirel answered, but her expression was confused. "For some reason the same amount of fuel is much more effective when we are close to Earth moving quickly."

"Can we see the other ships?" I asked.

Everyone crowded next to the side NLED wall to look. Meital pointed at a small but clear spaceship stack visible in Earth's reflected blue light. "There ... that's *Mars Hope*, I think."

"And that's the communication satellite booster," Sam said, his finger on a point a few centimeters below. Ocean now appeared as Earth rotated below us – at least it appeared that way – while we sped across the surface at our parking orbit's greatest speed. That parking orbit was about to come to an end.

"Three, two, one," said Dr. Jhonathan's voice. We heard a slight vibration as the floor came up to meet us. Unexpectedly, someone grabbed my hands, and I found myself face-to-face with Shirel, who tried to direct me in what she thought was a waltz step. We bounced higher than expected, as did everyone else.

"What kind of gravity is this?" Susan exclaimed disapprovingly. "I can barely keep my feet on the ground."

As if in response to his daughter's question, Dr. Jhonathan declared, "You'll note that acceleration is minimal: only about one point one meters-per-second per second. That's eleven percent Earth gravity and thirty percent Mars gravity. Those of you who are dancing will need to have a very light step."

Twelve minutes later even that minimal gravity stopped. The dancing had not been graceful, but we did have fun. Dr. Jhonathan announced that all three craft had had successful burns. "We've added eight hundred and three meters per second. The additional speed, almost two thousand and nine hundred kilometers per hour, will be sufficient for us to escape Earth's gravity. All three craft are now in close parallel trajectories and we are on our way to Mars. In the next few minutes, we will release the Mars-Transit Injection stage. You might feel a slight jolt."

"Well, that was a disappointment," Meital said. "That was it? Twelve minutes of almost imperceptible acceleration, and we've left Earth permanently?"

"We haven't even left Earth," Shirel said, pointing. "Look at the screen – it's still there!"

We kept the NLED wall showing the camera view of Earth for the rest of the afternoon. Slowly the planet receded below us. Eventually, before our Friday night Sabbath dinner, we waved goodbye to the planet, and Shirel swapped the display of Earth with a festive, shimmering candelabrum.

* * *

Sunday, November 12th, 2028 01:15

"Lost forever! Never going back! No escape ... never to return!" My heart pounded. The words echoed in my head. "Never see them again! Trapped forever! No escape!"

I was drenched in sweat. "Lost forever ... no way back!" It was a dream ... I was waking from a fitful sleep, from a nightmare. Who had been saying the words? "Never going back ..." I muttered to myself, trembling. "No way home!" Was it me? Or was someone talking to me? My hand found the handkerchief at the head of the bed. I tore it from the Velcro and wiped the sweat from my brow. I tried to move my legs, but they were stuck! Something was blocking them, tangling them. "I'm trapped ... I can't move!" My heart banged against my chest and I gasped for breath. It was my sleeping bag that was trapping me. I had to get free. I wanted to vomit. Frantically, I struggled against the bag, trying to disentangle my legs. "No way out!" I pushed and pushed and finally my feet cleared the opening. I swung myself around, shoved off the bed, glided across the small room, and bumped into the folding door. I pushed it aside. My stomach felt queasy. "Escape!" I panted. "Anywhere but my cramped bedroom!"

In the living room I stopped to catch my breath. The room was nearly empty – the table and chairs were stowed for the night – but the walls seemed to close in on me. Our largest room was too small! I kicked at the wall and soared across the room, then pushed off the sofa and crossed back again. I was doing laps in a tiny, cramped swimming pool, but with no water to cool me. There was nowhere to go, no way out, and I was never going home. What stupidity! How could I have agreed to such a thing! Mars-transit injection, just a day before, I now realized, was the beginning of the end. Too late to stop! Did the others realize what we had done? If I screamed and woke everybody up, would anybody understand? My heart pounded; my whole body trembled. No more earth, no more wide-open spaces, fresh air, grassy knolls, vibrant bustling city parks. Never another ocean sunset, no autumn breezes, no rainstorms, not even an open window! I felt hot and my mundies were soaked with sweat.

I should cry out, I thought, but I held back. They would brand me a psychotic, add "panic attacks" to my medical record. They would label me, medicate me, ignore me, and go on with the mission regardless. I was doomed to spend my life in cramped, claustrophobic, enclosed spaces, and there was nothing I could do. "We're never going back," I repeated.

"Panic attacks" in my medical record … I'm having an anxiety attack, I thought to myself, as lessons from seven years of training kicked in. I recalled the stress ordeals, the anxiety analyses, the claustrophobia trials. Sitting, locked, in a tiny, cramped room for more than an hour. Without warning they began vacuuming out the air. I had managed to remain calm, time after time, while donning my fleximet and starting the oxypack airflow. We were trained for this. We were the "fliers." They drilled that into us: "F-L-I-E-R-S," a mnemonic for getting control over ourselves even in the most stressful situations. "Freeze, Listen, Inhale, Exhale, Redirect thoughts, Seek help."

Recall the training. *Freeze*: I grabbed at the sofa and stopped propelling myself back and forth across the room. *Listen*: I listened to my body, noticing my symptoms, my pounding heart, my panicked breathing, my sweating: all just typical adrenaline responses. *Inhale, Exhale* – I took a deep breath and released it slowly. *Redirect*: I tried to think calming thoughts. We were pioneers, we were excited about our adventure, we were going to meet Dad. But we were stuck, I was cramped, there was nowhere to go! No – wrong thoughts. I tried again: we were together, we were healthy, we were trained, we were going to build a new, beautiful world.

Finally, *Seek help*. I looked across at my mother's bedroom door. There was no one better than a mother for reassurance and calm. How fortunate was I to be here with her, just a push away! I knocked softly on the door, then quietly slid it open. "Mom, are you awake? I'm sorry to bother you, but I need help." I floated to her bedside and touched her shoulder.

She stirred. "Michael, is everything okay?"

"Mom, I'm feeling anxious about the mission. About our departure from Earth. I can't sleep."

"Come here for a hug." Rising up in her sleeping bag, she extracted her arms and reached out and embraced me. "A mother's hug can fix anything," she soothed.

Unexpectedly, I felt self-conscious. "But I'm seventeen."

"As long as I'm alive, you'll never be too old for a hug. Especially when you are anxious. What happened?"

"I woke up from a panicky dream. It all became so real to me: now that we've left Earth orbit, it's permanent. I'll never see the world again."

"That may or may not be true. But it's nothing you don't already know. You are having normal feelings, and it would be surprising not to feel apprehension about our mission. If any of us did not feel apprehension. It does not mean that you've changed your mind, and it does not mean that we've made a mistake."

"But the feelings were so strong. Like it is really a big mistake."

She tightened her hug. "That's how feelings are. It's good you can feel so strongly, and even better that you're able to express your feelings so articulately."

Gradually, my heart slowed and my breathing calmed.

"Mom, is this not all a mistake? Shouldn't we have quit the mission? Shouldn't Dad and Uncle Aviel have quit? We'd still have Uncle Aviel, and Dad would still be healthy."

"We made a choice, Michael. It was not an easy choice. No real choice is: there are always arguments for and against. Your father and I took a long time to decide. You know that; you were part of the discussions."

I separated myself from my mother and looked at her face, lit only by dim nightlight. "Isn't it obvious now, from a logical point of view, that we made the wrong choice?"

She looked back at me without letting me go.

"No, it is not obvious. And even if it were, major life choices are not always made logically. Often, I think, people make the most important choices based on emotions. Perhaps even you."

"Sorry, Mom, but that sounds dumb to me. Intelligent people should make decisions intelligently, weighing all the factors logically!" My anxiety had passed; I was now feeling indignant.

"Michael, do you remember when we decided to move to Arizona to join the Murke-Berger Foundation's training program? When you agreed to start the seven-year program, you exclaimed, 'Yes, I want to be a pioneer!' and danced around the room with your sisters, chanting 'we're going to outer space!' That was hardly a logical decision."

"We were children! We trusted you and Dad to decide logically."

"We decided intelligently. Not necessarily logically, but we weighed all factors, including emotional ones. For your father and me, most important was the desire for a greater challenge. Israel's desert agriculture was so advanced, it was becoming too easy. We wanted to develop technologies for more difficult environments. That was an emotional choice."

I considered that for a moment, then thought out loud, "That is how I feel, too. I want to be a pioneer. I'm excited to face real challenges. I would not want to turn back, even if we could."

She hugged me close again.

"Isn't it foolhardy, though, Mom? Aren't we being irresponsible?"

"No, neither irresponsible nor foolhardy, Michael." She patted my back and gave me a squeeze. "Well-considered and well-planned."

We floated there, above her bed, for some time, my mother hugging me and uttering calming thoughts, and I began to feel drowsy again. "We're going to build a great life for ourselves," she whispered. "We'll have towns, and parks and farms and trees, and wide-open spaces under huge airtents. We'll have beautiful sunsets and swimming pools."

"Dad is waiting for us," I murmured.

"Dad is waiting for us," my mother repeated quietly.

I kissed her on the cheek and tasted her salty tear on my lips.

*   *   *

Tuesday, November 14th, 2028 08:20

There was that sweet smell again. I noticed it as I entered the bathroom for my sponge-bath after morning exercise. It was not a bad smell; there was something pleasant about it, a bit smokey, but it certainly did not belong. It was not the smell of plastic burning – thank G-d for that – and was also not a normal bathroom smell. I tried to place it while I toweled myself off and brushed my teeth. I gave up the effort as I spit toward the airflow into the toilet. The vacuum sucked down the remnants of the unidentified aroma along with the toothpaste. I knew it reminded me of something but I could not recall what.

As I was the last of the four of us to shower on Tuesdays, my sisters and roommate had already gathered for breakfast when I floated out of the bathroom.

"Denver, I think I smelled that funny smell again. Can you see if everything's okay with the air system in the bathroom?"

"Michael, I'll do my full inspection after breakfast," he said. He chuckled to himself as he looked away from me, and added, "I think you're imagining things again."

"Retethering is scheduled for this afternoon," my mother said. "Dietrich – Captain Becker – confirmed the timing of the procedure with Captain Ravel."

"Susy said she heard Dr. Claudine saying that Boris is doing the spacewalk this time. Captain Becker is angry with Simeon."

"Shirel," my mother admonished, "avoid gossip. It's *loshon hora*," she added, using the Hebrew term for forbidden, evil speech. "I will not tolerate it."

"But, why is –"

"Is Captain Becker upset?" I interrupted. "I thought Simeon obeyed all procedures correctly last time."

Meital cleared her throat. "More interesting," she said, "is that we did not notice while we flipped around and reoriented since the departure burn. Didn't the ships have to be exactly parallel to set off into identical trajectories? Which of us flipped over into tethering configuration?"

Denver looked up. "I was tracking the maneuvers on my datapad on Saturday. Both ships rotated ninety degrees over the day. Then Sunday and Monday we slowly closed the gap. From a distance of around a kilometer, we have approached to –" he glanced at his datapad, Velcroed to his sleeve - "exactly one hundred meters from each other. Our pinnacles seem to be aligned perfectly."

"And yet I haven't felt a thing," Shirel mused, as she rose and detached her plate from the table.

Later in the morning, finishing my inspection of the Pink-Level water system after running a waste-processing cycle, I found Simeon by the stairwell. A panel of the atmosphere processor was open and he was examining something inside.

"Is it Boris or you who's doing the spacewalk today?"

Simeon closed the panel and snapped it shut. "Boris, not me. We both think it's a mistake. I have more experience. I'm familiar with the details of the procedure, of attaching the tethers to the clasps." He turned toward me and shrugged, apparently resigned to the decision.

"What happened? I thought you did a good job last time."

"Captain's decision. That's why he's the captain. Apparently, he thought my 'attitude was uncooperative.'"

I felt bad for Simeon, but it was not my place to argue. Captain Becker was the ultimate authority on our craft.

After lunch, Denver and I had chemistry class – Materials Synthesis – with my mother. That was the end of school for the day, though. Meital had come upstairs from Mauve Level to inform us that Dr. Claudine had canceled Linear Algebra. "Everybody needs to help Ruby and me to clear out the airlock again. We need to start now."

Nobody argued. We gathered downstairs and cleaned the cages, then began carrying them upstairs. At some point I found myself alone with Meital in the airlock, working on the last parakeet and canary cages. The others had pushed the chicken coops up through the hatch.

"Did Mom mention my little panic attack the other night?" I asked, feeling my face flush.

Meital stopped and looked at me, concerned. "No, she didn't. Is everything okay?"

"I'm okay now, but the finality of it all really hit me. Meital, have you had second thoughts about the expedition? About leaving Earth?"

"Well, yes, of course I think about it. About what we've given up, about the opportunities before us, about the challenges. About saying goodbye to Grandma forever. That was hardest for me."

"Any trepidation? Anxiety? Or is it just me?"

"Honestly, maybe some trepidation. Isn't that normal? But no, I've had no panic attacks. Not yet, at least." She touched my hand. "But it's not just you. Definitely don't be embarrassed. What we are doing is unprecedented. And scary."

She grabbed the parakeet cage and pushed it into my hands, then paused to look at me. "Michael, my dear brother, you know I'm always here for you, if you need to talk, or be calmed. And I know that you'll be there for me if – no, when – I need support or calming."

How good was it to be doing an unprecedented, dangerous, scary and crazy mission with those I loved!

My self-taught Distributed Software Systems class was canceled, too, as we gathered in our living room at 16:30 to watch the spacewalk on the NLED walls. Boris's departure was delayed a few minutes as Dr. Esther Meyer, also dressed for space, patched several electroelasticity failures in his mundies. They opened the video feed from his fleximet after she had fixed all the bulges and he had donned his Mylar suit.

The habitat's hull appeared as he exited the airlock, and proceeded, rung by rung, across the bottom. He paused at the edge and looked around, broadcasting a fantastic view of our surroundings. Very empty surroundings: space appeared so much darker, so far from the background glow of Earth. In fact, it was completely empty, other than the thousands of stars apparent on the screen. Where was the planet?

As Boris turned, planet Earth finally passed into view. It looked so small, a moon-sized bluish-white shrinking circle. Only four days out and the difference, even compared to how it looked when we had been at our former orbit's apoapsis, was striking. Everything we had known was receding inexorably.

Simeon exited the stairwell and joined us. "My brother has an easy job. Nothing to carry up the hull."

"Why not?" asked Ruby, who had come downstairs with Susan to join us for the spectacle.

"This time we will use *Mars Hope's* tethers, not ours, so Boris does not have to carry the spool to the pinnacle."

"Why not use ours again?"

"We used our MMU to send the tethers across the gap last time. We need *Mars Hope* to send it back, which they will do now with their tethers."

The pinnacle appeared on the NLED wall and Boris began pulling himself along the curve of the dome. He looked up and *Mars Hope* appeared in our view. A few minutes later we spotted the mini-maneuvering unit approaching from the distance. Boris snatched it from space not long afterwards. The four tethers Arjan had attached stretched into the distant blackness, toward the pinnacle of *Mars*

Hope, which passed in and out of view as Boris looked from side to side. He began his four treks down to the base of the dome, each in a different direction, to attach each tether to its clasp. We watched as he reached the red clasp and attached the red tether; then climbed back up to the pinnacle to get the green tether and take it down to attach it to the green clasp; then back up for the blue tether; then finally to yellow.

He inserted the tether's thimble, a yellow steel ring that the end of the tether looped around, into its cavity in the hull. He rotated it into the correct orientation and called out, "Close the yellow clasp now."

Dr. Jhonathan confirmed, "Closing the clasp now."

We did not hear any scratch or scrape in the vacuum of space, but something was wrong, because Boris called out again. "Jhonathan, the clasp caught on the thimble. Open it again, please."

It took two more tries, opening the clasp, repositioning the thimble, and trying to close it, before Boris confirmed that the yellow tether was properly secured.

"It looks like something broke in the yellow clasp," Susan exclaimed, her eyes glued to Boris's view.

"I don't think so," Sam said. "He did get the tether locked in place."

"But it should have been easier, like the first three. I don't want to think about what could happen if anything happens to any of the clasps."

"Captain Becker would have said something, Susy," I said, "if there were any danger."

Having secured all four tethers, Boris began his trek back to the pinnacle to retrieve the MMU, which needed to be put away in its compartment in the top of the Mars-Entry stage. "This is the hard part for Boris," Simeon said. "Now he has to carry the MMU all the way back down and stow it. I doubt his oxypack will last long enough."

We watched as Boris pulled the MMU slowly down the hull. He was mindful, as Simeon had been, not to bump it into the PlyShield or the solar panels.

"My oxygen is running low."

Simeon nodded in an "I told you so" manner.

"My oxygen is not going to make it. I apologize, but I'm going to need someone else to stow the MMU."

"No problem. I'm on my way out," said Dr. Esther.

Boris focused his camera on her as she exited the airlock. We watched her approach and grab hold of the MMU. Boris then scooted for the airlock to swap oxypacks. Ten minutes later, after Dr. Esther had stored the mini-maneuvering unit in its Mars-Entry-stage compartment, she followed him though the hatch. They repressurized the airlock, and we and *Mars Hope* were ready to begin spin-up.

*   *   *

Sunday, November 19th, 2028 21:40

"Mount Fuji?" Meital squinted her eyes at the NLED wall's indistinct mesh of colors. In response, a computerized voice announced "Wrong!"

We watched as a blurred image slowly resolved. "But there is something mountainous there," Sam mused.

He had invited us to spend evening free time together in his family's Pink-Level living room. Some of us pulled up chairs; others sat on the couch. We had our Mars-level gravity back, having spun up over the twenty-four hours following Boris's and Arjan's operation to retether the two ships.

At first we chatted, but then Celina suggested that we play "Name that Location," a video game she had asked the Foundation to purchase. "Let us see if we can remember places on Earth," she said, "now that we've left orbit and started our voyage!" Remembering places on Earth did not particularly concern me, but I did share her nostalgia.

"Are those giraffes?" Ruby asked, looking up from the scarf she was knitting. Knitting needles and balls of yarn in multiple colors were her personal artifacts for the journey. "And those blobs – they might be zebras." She pointed at the screen.

"So, Africa?" I suggested. "A mountain in Africa?"

"Mount Kilimanjaro," Celina said. The image sharpened, and the computer confirmed, "Correct!" Celina raised her arms in victory.

A mix of white and blue appeared on the wall. As the picture began to clarify, most of the whiteness congealed toward the center.

"A boat on the ocean," suggested Helga.

"Could be an airplane in the sky," Sam said.

The image sharpened. The middle part was definitely a building; it appeared to have a domed roof. But whitish streaks remained on the sides.

"The Taj Mahal," Meital said, stroking her freckled cheeks. "Definitely the Taj Mahal."

The computer agreed.

The wall blurred again. The top became lightly reddish, the bottom a deeper crimson. "It looks like Mars," I said.

My friends nodded. But as the picture became less fuzzy, Helga said, "I think it's on Earth. A desert somewhere."

Ruby's needles clicked and clacked. "Funny that we can't tell the difference. You wouldn't think different planets could look so similar."

The image sharpened. Sam guessed, "New Mexico? Those look like bushes, so it can't be Mars."

"Correct," announced the computer.

"Mars," Meital said. "It's really happening! We've left Earth behind. After so long preparing and waiting, we are actually flying to Mars."

*   *   *

Thursday, November 23rd, 2028 19:30

Once again we had crowded together for a festive meal. This time we had joined the Beckers in their Yellow-Level living room on the habitat's top floor. The Bouchets and Meyers, and Omar, Simeon and Boris, were visible on the NLED wall at the end of the table, packed into the Mauve-Level living room. Our colleagues on *Mars Hope* appeared, for the second time, on the side wall. It was, more or less, Thanksgiving in the United States on Earth, enough of an excuse for a celebration as far as our international crowd was concerned. We had lots to be thankful about, having succeeded in all the complex activities required to reach our Mars-transit trajectory.

I relished Dr. Cecylia's crisp radish and lettuce salad, garnished with cress leaves, all newly harvested for the festival. My mother's staple chickpea-and-lentil salad was also delectable, though less novel.

At the other end of the room, Captain Becker raised a glass of soda water and faced the NLED screen and its cameras. "A toast to all of you. Our success is due to your diligence in your tasks, your responsibility and your efforts. I thank you all. Also, in their latest message, Leon Murke and Jake Berger of the Murke-Berger Foundation asked me to thank the whole team."

Two weeks after departure from Earth orbit, we were too far away for two-way video calls: the delay sending and receiving laser transmissions made such calls impractical. Nevertheless, the complex communication link – from the habitats to our communications satellite and from the satellite to Earth – was working as expected, and we continually sent and received email and video messages.

Dr. Jhonathan, visible in the end-wall NLED screen, stood and turned to face us. "And, of course, we thank G-d, who has blessed our entire project thus far. May He continue to do so. G-d, bless us that our tribulations be in our studies and not in our health or habitats."

Some of us answered "Amen."

We had indeed been blessed. Life was largely back to normal as we rolled along toward Mars. I had been spending my time praying, exercising, maintaining the water processing systems, and, mostly, studying.

Celina, sitting between me and her sister on the sofa, turned to face me. "Where's Denver? Does he not want to join us?"

"He said he'll come up in a few minutes." My plate was empty, but Celina had started her second course. "How's the tofu?" I asked.

"Actually, quite good."

Helga called out, a bit too loudly, "Michael's plate is empty. Somebody get him tofu, quickly!"

Meital and Ruby had spent a couple of evenings processing soybeans in lieu of a turkey. The chickens, at two months, were too young to slaughter, and we had decided to save the remaining beef kabanos, so our Thanksgiving meal was vegetarian. Shirel reached over from the table and handed me the serving bowl, and I scooped fried tofu onto my plate. It was surprisingly delicious. Much more, I assumed, than the final course would be. From the leftover soybean

Thanksgiving

pulp I had made okara patties, fried in oil. I knew they would be nearly tasteless, but on board nothing could go to waste; hence my attempt at a dessert.

"Michael, do you want to serve your patties?" my mother asked. "With some sugar, they'll be a tasty last course."

I thought she was overstating the case, but did not argue. Realizing that my friend still had not appeared and dinner was almost finished, I said, "I'll go get them and see what's with Denver."

Two Mars-staircase flights down – in only four steps, as I skipped five of each seven stairs – I found our living room empty. The folding door to the bedroom Denver and I shared was open and I stepped in. Denver was lying on his top bunk, facing the wall.

"Denver, everyone's enjoying themselves, and only you are missing. Won't you come up? We're almost finished eating our Thanksgiving feast."

"Thanksgiving is an American holiday. Not for me."

"It's not a Russian, or French, or even a Jewish or Muslim holiday, but that's not stopping anyone else from having a good time. Please come up."

"Sorry, not interested." He turned over and looked at me. Dark hair covered his eyes but did not hide the shadowy patches under them. "I'm not in the mood. I'd ruin the meal for the others."

"Denver, what's going on? If you're feeling down, confide in me. I'm your best friend."

"Not your problem, Michael. I do not mean to be rude, but please leave me alone."

That was unexpected. "Denver, I don't care whether you 'mean to be rude' – snubbing me is not called for. I'm trying to be your friend." I suppressed the rest of what I was about to say, turned, and left the room.

Back upstairs, my mother had been right: the okara patties were reasonably good with a bit of sugar. But my mind was no longer on Thanksgiving. Why had Denver talked to me like that? Had I annoyed him? Was he regretting the mission? Were my own misgivings subconsciously influencing him? "You are not always to blame for someone else's feelings," my father would have said, but I felt responsible for Denver. Perhaps I would try to get him to open up with me. Or maybe I would just ignore him.

* * *

Monday, December 11th, 2028 13:45

As the days passed, I managed to remain cordial, even warm, with Denver. He did not open up, but he was friendly in his rebuffs. Like it or not, we spent a lot of time together, not only as roommates but also in school. We shared eight science and mathematics class sessions every week, studying together at least three hours most days. That is when he seemed happiest, which made sense, as science and math were his favorite subjects.

"What's with your mother and the bathroom?" he asked, in the middle of our Introduction to Biology class one Monday after lunch. Dr. Jhonathan taught the class, but had left us alone for a few minutes while he went to check on a navigation issue with Captain Becker. We were reading about the alternation of generations in plants between haploid and diploid phases.

"I don't know. What are you referring to?"

"She never leaves us alone in the mornings. She pushes her way into the bathroom between our showers. It's like she thinks she needs to clean up after each of us."

"I didn't really notice, but now that you've pointed it out, I'll pay attention. But what's so bad about Mom tidying up?"

"It's intrusive."

Maybe it bothered him that a mother could be helpfully involved in her children's lives, something I suspected he had never experienced.

We had a ten-minute break between biology and physics ("Mechanics, Electromagnetism and Optics"). While we waited for Boris, who taught the course, my mother emerged from the stairwell. I glanced briefly at Denver, wondering if he was going to say something to her, but his eyes were focused on his datapad.

She tapped me on the shoulder. "We have a treat: we received a video message from Dad. We'll watch it together at dinner."

I looked forward to my father's message all afternoon. After evening exercise and showers, we set up the table and chairs and sat down together. Freshly grown vegetables were still too rare except for special occasions, so dinner was standard fare, a grain stew and a legume salad, but we did not mind: my father was the main feature.

My mother tapped her datapad and his image appeared on the NLED wall behind her. He wore a blue cotton shirt over his mundies.

"Hello, my dear fliers! We are so excited that you are all finally truly on your journey here. Twelve people on an entire planet are not enough. It is heartening to know that one hundred and twenty-seven more humans are coming to populate this world."

The background was different. My father was in his bedroom on the lower deck of their MiniHab spacecraft, not in the common upper deck.

"We're making better and better progress on the water mining. We have two hundred cubic meters of water stored now, and have dug three hundred and forty-five meters of trenches. We hope to be able to start walling them soon."

He was on his bed, leaning against the wall. His face was pale, but his brown eyes were bright.

"We heard about the successful departures of the two supply ships. They should arrive here just a few weeks after you.

"Shirel, Meital, and Michael: I send all my love. Keep strong. And Denver, too, keep up the good work and study. Michael, have you been writing your journal?

"Dana, my beloved, I love you. Get here quickly and watch over our precious ones."

The transmission ended, replaced by an underwater fish scene. Sea bass and flounder swam across the screen. It looked like something from an aquarium, not a real ocean.

"What did he say about supply ships?" Shirel asked.

My mother answered, "The two supply habitats that the Foundation launched after we left Earth orbit. Food, equipment, spare parts." She glanced at the wall as a gray-blue manta ray swam by. "They launched the last week of November and set out for Mars at the beginning of December."

"Mom, Dad looked like he was slumped on his bed. Is he okay?"

"Michael, he's doing the best he can. Keep praying. And, each of you, send a video response tonight. He'll be very happy."

*   *   *

Sunday, December 17th, 2028 10:30

Only rarely did I smell the funny smell when I went for my morning shower; most days I did not. I wondered if my mother smelled it, too. Denver had been right: she did seem to be checking the bathroom quite a bit each morning. But she also checked in on us during classes, and appeared while we exercised, and cooked with us, and gave us hugs at unexpected times. I guessed that was normal for teenagers who traveled in space with their mothers.

Sunday was a weekend day for the Bouchets. The girls, Sophie and Jasmine, had no school, and often followed us around while we performed our chores. One typical Sunday morning I was checking water-system diagnostics in our Green-Level bathroom while the two of them watched. They both looked adorable, wearing, over their mundies, orange and red flowery dresses that complemented their mocha complexions.

"If something breaks, what do you do?" Jasmine asked.

"Usually, I call your father to help. I do the regular things, but he's the expert at fixing problems."

"*Mon papa* knows to fix everything," Sophie said. I did not argue; I had great respect for Dr. Louis, and considered him a sensible choice of hero for a five-year-old.

There was nothing left to do, so I stepped into the living room. The girls trailed close behind.

"Read us a story, Michael!"

Anticipating this, I had already picked out something appropriate.

As we settled on the couch, Helga came bounding down the staircase. "Good morning, Michael. I hope your bedroom is free."

I knew what she meant, but played along with her. "I beg your pardon – what exactly do you want with my bedroom, my dear Helga?"

"Your sample failed analysis yesterday. It's time to disinfect you!"

"I'm hoping that you mean my room and not my body," I chuckled. The spacecraft's atmosphere was a closed system and biofilms tended to grow on all surfaces. Even though the air-processing systems' HEPA filters removed the vast majority of organisms from the air, plenty remained, and it was not uncommon for Helga to need to disinfect the walls. "I actually keep myself quite disinfected."

"You are so full of bacteria, Michael," she said, shaking blonde hair out of her eyes, "that I would not be able to disinfect you if I tried." She stepped into my room, then turned back to flash me an exaggerated grin. "But it's not your fault; you are only human." She obviously had no interest in tact, but one could not find fault with her smile.

As she went to work, I opened the story on my datapad and the girls nestled in, one on each side. I enjoyed reading to them. Besides doing my part to babysit our youngest fliers, it was an excellent opportunity to practice reading French. Jasmine always laughed at my poor pronunciation, but that did not bother me. My pride suffered only when the older girls were present to join the mocking.

Meital and Ruby exited the stairwell just as I started.

"The chicks have grown so much," Ruby was saying.

"Some of them are getting quite large," Meital answered.

Sophie looked up and blurted, "*ma maman* is getting fat, too!"

"Sophie," Jasmine chastised in a loud whisper, "you don't say things like that!"

I caught Meital's eye and raised my eyebrows. Looking back at me sternly, she declared, "It's okay, Jasmine; we all eat well. Michael, get back to your story."

Actually, given our limited diet and strict exercise regime, it was difficult to maintain our launch weights, let alone gain weight. Nevertheless, lest I suffer my sister's wrath, I resumed reading. Meital and Ruby pulled up chairs. Ruby said, "Let's listen to Michael's French."

"No mocking!" I protested. But, of course, they laughed, even more so after Helga finished her disinfecting and sat down on the armrest to join our little group.

I was just concluding the story with extra words of my own, in English, "… and they lived happily ever after …"

BOOM! A sound like an explosion ripped through the ship, the floor shook violently, and Jasmine screamed. My datapad flew off my lap as I jumped up involuntarily in an instant rush of panic, my heart beating wildly. Sophie burst into tears.

"What was that?" Ruby cried out. "What happened?" She, too, had jumped to her feet.

I recognized the signs of an adrenaline rush and took a deep breath. The shaking had stopped – the floor's shaking, not that of my arms and legs – so perhaps whatever had happened had passed.

"Check your datapad for alarms," Meital yelled to me over Sophie's shrieking. I picked my datapad up from the floor, while she pulled Sophie to her chest and gathered in Jasmine and comforted them both.

Helga reached for Ruby, who had blanched.

"A pressure breach would have triggered an alarm," I said. But I tapped my datapad and launched the systems diagnostics program to check the ambient pressure, just to make sure.

My mother came bounding down the stairs. Seeing us all standing there, she glanced around to see who was missing. "Where's Shirel?"

"We saw her and Susy downstairs, tending the worms," Ruby said, color returning to her face. "She's with Dr. Cecylia."

Denver exited the stairwell next. "Did you hear that? I was up on Yellow Level when it happened." Panting, his face flushed with excitement, he continued, "Captain Becker was there with me." He caught his breath and spoke more calmly. "Captain Becker told me to tell you that it was a micrometeoroid hit, and that he's checking the diagnostics." He spun toward the staircase. "I'm going downstairs to inform everyone else." He grabbed the banister and jumped halfway down.

"Air pressure is holding steady," I said, reading from my datapad.

We had not yet calmed completely – Sophie was still sobbing in Meital's arms – when Captain Becker's voice sounded from the wall speakers. In a composed, authoritative voice, he said, "We suffered a micrometeoroid hit. This is not unexpected, and there is no need for concern. The ship's PlyShield skin functioned as expected, absorbing the kinetic energy. We appear to have lost one surface camera; from this it seems that the hit was outside Yellow Level, on the fore side as we rotate, behind the rear of the living room."

"That's why it was so loud," Meital said, turning to point to where the wall behind the sofa met the ceiling above us. "It would have been just a few meters above where we were sitting."

Captain Becker's voice continued. "I have calculations from the computer's vibration and sound analysis." His tone was relaxed.

"The computer estimates that the micrometeoroid was between two and three millimeters across, traveling seven kilometers per second relative to us. As expected, based on statistics, it impacted at an angle. The PlyShield functioned with maximum effectiveness. All system metrics are now within expected limits."

"I hope the next hit is also diagonal," I said.

Looking alarmed again, Ruby said, "I hope there is no next hit!"

Falling

Wednesday, December 20th, 2028 21:15

Linear Algebra with Dr. Claudine was Wednesday's last class, evening period after dinner; she would join us after putting Sophie to bed. Denver and I were solving the fifth equation of the day's exercise, multiplying matrices by hand on our datapads. We sat next to each other in our Green-Level living room. Sam and Celina sat on the other side of the table, eyes and hands on their own datapads, working on a different set of exercises. Though they were a year ahead of us in math – their course was Applied Differential Equations – Dr. Claudine had no trouble instructing them: she could teach two classes at once.

Having sketched the matrices on the screen, I might simply have declared, "solve these matrices," and my computer would have done the rest of the work instantly and automatically. I dared not do so. Dr. Claudine would, no doubt, assign us additional pages of work, which we would invariably fail to complete during class. In that case, she would check in on us during evening free time to make sure we were doing the work by hand. I set my mind on completing the whole assignment before the end of class.

Denver thought differently. He looked up and pushed away his datapad. "I think that's enough – I've got it." This was typical: Denver would solve four or five equations, then protest having to do another twenty.

Falling

Also typical was Dr. Claudine's response. "Complete the exercise," she said, "so that you will understand the whole cycle." Then, usually, she would declaim her philosophy of mathematical education, reciting "from the concept to its representation, the representation to its notation, notation to its transformations, transformations to applications, and applications back to concepts." Then she would stare at us until we resumed working.

Today, however, she relented, but only after we had completed several more equations, and I commented, "That meteoroid that hit us Sunday was scary. It still has me on edge."

"Really, Michael? You seem relaxed to me. What about you, Denver?"

"Oh, it's nothing. The ship is built to withstand minor collisions."

"Yes, but what if it had been a major collision?" I asked. "What if the rock had been the size of a baseball?"

Sam looked up from his datapad. "There's a novel thought, Michael: perhaps there's somebody outside playing interplanetary baseball!"

"I am not sure how big a baseball is, but I understand that particles larger than dust are very rare," Dr. Claudine reassured, "and the chance of one hitting a ship of our size is negligible."

"Yeah, logically I know that. But the big bang keeps reverberating in my mind."

"If we are talking about meteors causing damage," she said, "in my opinion, we really do need to be concerned about being destroyed by a large meteor."

I straightened, slightly startled.

She raised her eyebrows at my reaction. "Not for us in *Providence*, or even for the settlement we will build on Mars. For Earth, however, I have always been concerned."

"Meteorites crash into Earth all the time," Denver said.

"Yes, and very large ones, too, from time to time. Historically, whole species have been wiped out by asteroid collisions. Earthquakes, climate change, mass extinctions – all written into Earth's evolutionary record. The next one could destroy humanity! That is why we need to act."

Her concern was surprising; her incongruently calm demeanor even more so, as she described humanity-erasing disasters.

"Isn't that ridiculous?" Celina asked, stretching out a pigtail and readjusting its band. "I'm sorry, but how urgent, really, is something that happens only once in tens of millions of years?"

"And, anyway," Denver added, "how can we act? What is there that we can do?"

"What can we do?" She raised her hands and her wiry hair bounced in its bun. "Exactly what we *are* doing. Spreading humanity to different planets!"

"Different planets" was perhaps an exaggeration, but our destination, Mars, was indeed one "different planet."

"So, if humanity is destroyed on one planet," I thought out loud, "it will continue on another. That's a depressing thought!"

"Yes, but it underlies everything we are doing here. Have you not read Leon Murke's treatise on the Survival of Humanity? Where he explains why he founded the Murke-Berger Foundation? That is why our mission is so important: it is our job to settle Mars and create a large, viable population, as quickly as possible."

She smiled as she stood from the table: it was time to put Jasmine to bed. As she turned toward the stairwell and appeared in profile, I noticed her prominent belly and recalled Sophie's outburst Sunday morning.

* * *

Monday, December 25th, 2028 10:45

Six weeks after we had departed Earth orbit, the computer's adjustments to our clock had added six minutes, in Earth time, to each of our days. We barely noticed the difference, but it was simple to calculate that our clock was now more than two hours behind Mexico time. The difference was growing by a greater and greater amount each day, as the computer continued to lengthen our hours, minutes and seconds. Nevertheless, the clock was close enough to Earth's that our dates still overlapped. Thus, it was our December 25, as well as Earth's, when the Bouchets celebrated Christmas. The occasion was sacred for Drs. Claudine and Louis, and they had spent days preparing. They invited the Beckers, who would share the celebration, if not the religious faith, and, of course, Simeon and Boris, their Mauve-Level apartment mates. Though the two brothers planned to celebrate their own Russian Orthodox Christmas two weeks later, they would not skip an opportunity for a holiday feast.

On the morning of the twenty-fifth, coming up from a visit to Meital and Ruby and the fowl, I poked my head out of the airlock's hatch into the Mauve-Level living room.

"Look, Michael, see what we have for *Noël* feast!" Jasmine exclaimed, bright brown eyes flashing with excitement.

I crawled out onto the floor, dragging behind me the trash bag of droppings Meital had shoved into my hands, and stood.

"Yes, I'd like to see. Just a minute." I crossed over to the doorway to the greenhouse room and found Shirel there, as I had expected.

"Oh, thank you so much for this worm-food!"

Jasmine avoided my hand, which was black with birdcage filth, and instead grabbed my wrist to pull me toward the kitchen. Her excitement was warranted: never had I seen a habitat kitchen's counters so full. Dishes covered every centimeter, some stacked two or three high. There were salads of many types. There were local standards like chickpea and lentil, chickpea and green pea, chickpea and kidney bean, and chickpea and peanut. Others, however, contained small amounts of freshly harvested vegetables, such as pale green lettuce and bright orange baby carrots. There was also a plate of beef kabanos, the ship's last remaining ones.

Ruby emerged from the airlock. "Dr. Louis, you can close the hatch. The birds are all set for the day." She peered into the kitchen.

"Beets – you harvested beets!" she exclaimed, pointing. One of the bowls contained deep purple slices mixed with dark green leaves and several small, round slices of an unidentified pale vegetable.

Dr. Claudine looked up as she extracted her pot of stew from the induction stovetop's socket. "Yes, the very first baby beets! We dug them out this morning. Also, Cecylia agreed that the first kale – those green leaves there – and the first zucchini squash could be used for our celebration. The new vegetables remind us how much we have to thank G-d."

"What are those pastries?" I asked, pointing to a plate of puffy, light brown, sugared pancakes.

"They are supposed to be *'poffertjes,'*" Claudine answered, pronouncing the Dutch word slowly and deliberately. "At least that is what I hope. I researched recipes for Dutch desserts, a gift for the Beckers, to make them feel at home."

Gift-giving was difficult in an environment where we had everything we needed and nothing else was available. However, as Dr. Claudine often said, creativity grows out of limitation. Within our severe limitations, she had found a way to give a holiday gift to the Beckers.

At that moment, Dr. Cecylia appeared by the mauve wall at the bottom of the stairwell, holding a plate stacked with her own concoctions. "Claudine," she said, concentrating on balancing the plate's contents, "I hope these are recognizable as crêpes and chickpea pancakes." She set them down gently on top of a stack of bowls.

I guessed that Dr. Cecylia was as new at French cuisine as Dr. Claudine was at Dutch baking.

"Michael, you are blocking us," Simeon said, and pushed me aside. He and Boris had emerged from the Bouchets' bedroom carrying the dining table. Shoving me farther into the corner with his shoulder, he unfolded the table with his brother. They secured its legs in the sockets in the floor.

"Michael, you and your family are welcome to join our banquet," Dr. Claudine offered kindly.

"Thank you, but I have a regular day of studies scheduled, and anyway you'll barely have room for the ten of you."

"I'm expecting eleven, if Denver will join us."

I hoped Dr. Claudine was right. Denver had exhibited a tendency to skip communal feasts.

"If we have leftovers, we will send them up to you," she called behind me, as I headed upstairs to wash up before Talmud class. A few minutes later, hands scrubbed, I emerged into the Meyers' Pink-Level living room and joined Sam and Rabbi Meyer at the table. Sam held his baseball in his hand. The baseball, along with a bat and two gloves, were the personal artifacts he had chosen to take to Mars. He had been bringing the ball to Talmud class each day to keep his hands busy.

"Eleven o'clock exactly," Rabbi Meyer said, checking his datapad. "I'm glad to see you being punctual." He looked at me with a hint of a smile and added, "Especially since you now have less

Falling

and less of an excuse as our days get longer and longer. Punctuality is a sign of reverence."

"A requirement for a meeting with G-d, Rabbi Meyer," I said. "You taught us that the Talmud can be learned properly only if we understand that it is all divine wisdom, the very wisdom that G-d imparted to Moses."

"Yes. Let's delve into that wisdom." He turned to his datapad, which displayed folio nine of the Talmud tractate Bava Kama. "We are starting the new Mishna today. Michael, please read."

I recited the introductory passage, first in the original Hebrew, then translated, "If anything I am obligated to guard causes damage, it is considered as if I facilitated that damage."

"Is that the only translation?" asked Rabbi Meyer. "Examine Rashi's commentary carefully, and compare his two proposals." He stood. "I'll leave the two of you to work on the page. Call out if you have questions."

Such was the typical start of our daily Talmud session. Rabbi Meyer would move to the far end of the table and sit, studying whatever tractate of Talmud he was working on at the time. Sometimes, instead, he scrutinized an esoteric text. Regardless, he would stop whenever we asked a question.

Sam and I read, discussed, and endeavored to understand. "The Talmud implies that a smoldering coal's potential for causing damage is comparable to that of a bull that is properly secured or to a pit that is safely covered," Sam said, tossing the baseball into the air and catching it with his other hand. "What's the comparison?"

I ignored the baseball. Sam could concentrate fantastically on any Talmudic discussion, but he could not stop fidgeting. I responded, "The next line of text contrasts those cases with a burning flame, an unsecured bull, and an uncovered pit in a public space. What's the difference?"

Peering into the text displayed on his datapad, Sam rolled the baseball between his hands. "A burning flame is already in a state where it can do damage," he ventured, "like the bull and pit." He tossed the ball again. "Whereas the smoldering coal needs to be blown into a flame before it can set something on fire."

Thus we launched into a typical Talmudic discussion, working to discern the concepts underlying the statements of the Talmud's myriad rabbis. I would propose an explanation. Sam would listen carefully, then prove – often from the next line of the text – that my explanation could not be correct. He would propose an alternative. Once I was sure I understood him properly, I would point out why, in my eyes, his idea was incomplete. As we sharpened our ideas, we consulted the commentary of the brilliant eleventh-century European luminary, Rabbi Shlomo Itshaki, universally known as "Rashi." His terse commentary was displayed on the inner edge of nearly every page of the Talmud, even on our electronic datapad edition. Rashi directed us toward proper understanding. Being able to say "our idea fits Rashi's explanation" meant that we were on the right track. More commonly, however, it was "our idea seems wildly incompatible with Rashi," and we would have to go back and revise our understanding. Rashi, nine hundred years after his passing, and millions of kilometers from Earth, was teaching us Talmud class every day.

As was Rabbi Meyer. "Tell me what you've learned," he said, as he came over and put his hands on our shoulders. Sam and I would recite the text, explaining each of the Talmud's questions and answers. Rabbi Meyer pushed back. "Why is that a valid answer? How does the fact that "a smoldering ember tends to burn itself out" explain the difference in one's culpability for damages, compared to damage by a bull that was properly secured or a pit that was properly covered?" I would venture an explanation, Sam would add to it, Rabbi Meyer would push back, and we would try again. Such was class most days. Sometimes our explanations satisfied the rabbi in the end, and he would conclude class with a compliment and a smile. More often, he would say, "Enough for today, but I'll want a sharper explanation tomorrow." Thus we continued, day after day, six days a week. Sam fiddled with his baseball and we discussed, proposed ideas, examined the text, argued, revised our ideas, and articulated our conclusions to Rabbi Meyer.

A week later we began folio ten of the tractate, still following the Talmud's analysis of cases where one bore responsibility for damage resulting from insufficiently guarding one's property. I thought about the meteoroid hit and how fortunate we were that no damage had been done. "I have my own case to compare, Rabbi Meyer."

He looked up and turned to face me.

"Here's my question. What if the meteoroid that hit us a couple of weeks ago had breached the ship? According to the principle of responsibility for damage when one did not guard sufficiently, since Iron Planetics built the habitat, would they be responsible because they did not build enough protection into the outer skin?"

Sam looked to his father and back to me. "That's the wrong comparison, Michael. The principle is about preventing your property from damaging others, not guarding your property from being damaged."

Rabbi Meyer said, "That's correct, Sam. But Michael asks an interesting question. Jewish Law obligates both the one who damages and the one who is damaged. It obligates you to prevent your property from damaging, but at the same time obligates others to guard their own property. There is always a careful balance between the two obligations, and the balance changes in different circumstances."

"So, is Michael right? Would Iron Planetics be held responsible for damages if we were injured because the ship cannot protect against large meteoroids?"

"Perhaps, if we had not signed our rights away when we agreed to travel in the ZubHab habitat," he answered. "Once we knowingly accepted the risks, we lost any claim against the Murke-Berger Foundation or the manufacturers. The responsibility for injuries is all our own. Besides, even if they were liable for damages, in what currency could they compensate us? What use have we for terrestrial money?"

"They would have to provide medical care to treat our injuries," I said.

"Which they do anyway," Sam answered. "They stocked us with medications and provided us with medical equipment. And," he added, gesturing at his father and grinning, "they pay our doctors' salaries."

Among his many areas of expertise, Rabbi Dr. Jhonathan Meyer was a Doctor of General Medicine, and our resident hypobaropathy expert.

"In sum," the rabbi concluded, "we would have nobody else to blame but ourselves. Which raises the moral question: in G-d's eyes, were we permitted to put ourselves in danger by joining this mission?"

"That's a heavy question," I said. "I know the Torah forbids us from endangering ourselves needlessly: it commands us to guard our souls and bodies."

"But Jewish Law permits normal jobs," Sam said, "even if they are dangerous, like repairing roofs on high buildings, despite the danger of falling. Is space travel a normal job? People crossed oceans to create new settlements, and that was dangerous."

"And there is no way to settle new planets without danger," I added. "What is the answer, Rabbi Meyer? According to Judaism, does G-d permit us to go to Mars?"

"I don't know, Michael; I don't know. The question concerns me very much, perhaps even as much as the danger itself."

That surprised me. "Then why are we here? Why are you here?"

He sighed. "That's a discussion for another time, not for today. G-d willing, we'll have an opportunity at some point."

Getting up to prepare for lunch, I wondered if Rabbi Meyer regretted being on the mission. I would need to remember to have that discussion with him.

* * *

Wednesday, January 10th, 2029 21:40

Wednesday night, after finishing our evening class in Materials Synthesis with Dr. Esther, Denver and I stowed our Green-Level dining table and prepared to relax in the living room. I lounged on the couch. Denver went to the bedroom for a moment, then crossed to the bathroom. He wore navy overalls over his mundies, and something was stuffed in their pockets. Mundies had no pockets, but our overalls did; that was an advantage. The other advantage was modesty: the tight-fitting mundies by themselves left little to the imagination.

A few minutes later Denver emerged from the bathroom and joined me on the couch. We began debating which movie to put up on the NLED wall. I wanted science fiction; Denver wanted drama. Then Sam came downstairs to join us and changed the subject, and we forgot about watching a film.

"What's the latest on the water mining? Do you think they'll finish by the time we arrive?"

I answered. "My dad sent a video log yesterday. He said they're making progress, with nearly two hundred and ten cubic meters already mined."

"They are supposed to have three hundred cubic meters when we get there," Sam said. "We're going to burn almost all of our water before landing. They have to mine at least enough to replace it all."

"The mining robots have six more months to work before we arrive. That should be enough time."

"What about covering the trenches?" Denver asked. "They also need to do that before we arrive, and that needs human labor, not robots."

"My dad mentioned that they've started and have already walled the first ten meters."

"It's not all manual work," Sam pointed out. "You know they have a brick-making machine, right?"

"But they lay the bricks by hand," Denver said. "They'll be busy outside for months to come."

"I'm looking forward to getting outside," I said, standing and stretching. "When we arrive, we'll have been cooped up in the ship for more than ten months. I'm looking forward to going for a run under the open sky."

Denver tilted his head as he looked at me and dark hair fell into his eyes. He had been avoiding a haircut. "You do realize that they are not going to let us outside, don't you? They're going to move us straight from the habitats into the tunnels, and keep us there until the tents are built."

"I don't believe that. We'll get to go out whenever we want."

"Don't be so sure. They'll want to protect us from the radiation. Since your father is sick, Michael, they'll be extra-strict with you." Glancing upward, Denver chuckled uncharacteristically. "I'm imagining you fighting with Captain Becker about it. That'll be funny."

"I think you're exaggerating. We'll be careful to limit our exposure, but nobody will stop us from donning our fleximets and going out for a walk."

"Maybe nobody will stop the rest of us, but your father might lock you and your sisters inside." He giggled again. "He did look better in his message yesterday, don't you think?"

"My father? Yes, maybe. He was smiling. And standing in the kitchen. I think Stephen filmed him cooking dinner."

"That's an improvement, isn't it?" Denver looked at me. His eyes were unusually red.

"Yes. He filmed his other recent messages in his downstairs quarters."

Sam looked from me to Denver, and back again. "Then we should be happy, if Doriel is having a remission. Denver, maybe get your guitar and play something for us?"

Denver smiled and nodded, and went to retrieve the instrument. Consequently, we found ourselves, a few minutes later, clapping our hands to a German rock song I did not recognize. Our days were too busy for music, being filled with studies, chores and exercise, but late evening was designated for relaxing pursuits. We discovered that Denver's repertoire was broader than he had let on. At Altiplano he had rarely played, but he had practiced continually in the years preceding our arrival there. His skill was an unexpected blessing.

It did not take long for Meital and Ruby to land at the bottom of the stairwell. Both wore overall-skirts, Meital's bright yellow and Ruby's bright green, matching her eyes.

"We heard you playing," Meital said. "Can I get my flute and join you?"

At such moments I regretted never having mastered a musical instrument. Meital returned with her flute and challenged Denver to play a classical piece. "Do you know 'Ode to Joy' from Beethoven's Ninth Symphony?"

Denver began playing immediately, and my sister scrambled to catch up. Their playing together was surprisingly beautiful: the flute's high-pitched notes were a perfect complement to Denver's mid-range strumming. We were not the only ones to think so: not three minutes passed before Celina and Helga came downstairs and joined us. They knew the words to the original German poem.

"Play '*An die Freude*' again," Helga said. "We can sing along."

That was followed by an excerpt from Mozart's Fortieth Symphony; then Ruby asked Denver to play "Fantastic Flight," by her favorite neo-swing band, The Good Man. Denver knew that one, too. Helga ran upstairs to get her clarinet, and she and Meital performed a reasonable accompaniment. The minutes passed in song and laughter.

Falling

During a pause, while we debated what to sing next, Celina looked at Denver. She narrowed her eyes in concern. "Denver, your eyes look very red. Are you okay?"

"I'm fine, Celina. My eyes are fine."

"No, they really are bloodshot. Maybe you should have Dr. Claudine look at them."

"I can take a look," Ruby said. Aspiring to become a medical doctor, Ruby had trained in nursing before and during our year at Altiplano. She stepped over to Denver and crouched to peer into his eyes."

"Leave me alone," he said, suddenly annoyed. He turned away from her. "I said I'm fine!"

"Okay, Denver," Celina tried again, "but we're concerned. We care about you."

Inexplicably, Denver got up, took his guitar, and, not looking back, strode across into our bedroom and slid the door closed behind him.

The rest of us looked back and forth at each other incredulously, asking, "What just happened?"

*   *   *

Tuesday, January 23rd, 2029 18:00

The Muslim month of Ramadan began, on Earth, on January 15 at sunset. Our computer-adjusted days were now ten minutes longer than Earth days. The computer accomplished this by stretching each second, minute and hour by approximately 0.7 percent, compared to their earthly counterparts. This meant that our January 16 began six hours after Altiplano Mexicano time and fourteen hours later than Egypt time, but that was close enough for Omar to begin observing the holy month. He had been rising early each day to eat what, on Earth, would have been his pre-dawn meal; then he would fast twelve computer-adjusted hours, and eat his *iftar* meal just after what our clocks registered as 18:00, after he finished praying. That was earlier than we usually ate – dinner was normally at 19:30 each evening, after afternoon exercise sessions. We rearranged our schedules in order that Omar not be alone during his *iftar* meals. Each family hosted him once or twice a week, eating an hour and a half early, rescheduling exercise or a class for after dinner.

Other than Omar, everybody on board had a religious community with whom to commemorate their respective holidays. Two weeks after the Bouchets' Christmas celebration, they had repeated the whole event on January 7, for Simeon and Boris. It was Orthodox Christmas, and the first cabbages were ready for harvest. Boris showed Dr. Claudine how to prepare *golubtsi*, Russian cabbage rolls filled with rice, and they celebrated with a fitting feast.

It was our turn, for the second time, to host Omar in his observance, on the second Tuesday of Ramadan. We invited him to join us for an early dinner, and I rescheduled my Distributed Software Systems class for the evening. My sisters, and Denver and I, exercised and showered early, then joined my mother in preparing the very special meal we had been planning for several days: falafel sandwiches! The key ingredients were on board: dried chickpeas, wheat for pita bread, sesame seeds, and a tiny amount of parsley waiting to be harvested.

Preparations had begun the night before, starting with the chickpeas, which needed to soak overnight. We put a kilo in a bowl, filled it with water, sealed its cover, and Velcroed the bowl to a corner of the countertop. Next, Denver and I cooked a second batch of chickpeas, with which to make hummus, and after that roasted a half-kilo of sesame seeds. For the flatbread, I selected enough of my best sourdough culture for a dozen pitas. Each took only a few minutes to bake, but, overall, it was a lot of work, as only two at a time would fit in the deep pot that substituted for an oven. We ended up getting to bed later than usual Monday night.

"We'll strain and save the oil after we finish frying today," my mother said, as she poured an entire liter of the precious liquid into a pot she had inserted in the induction stovetop's socket. "Start preparing the falafel balls. The oil will heat up quickly." She pressed the pot's lid into position, then twisted it to lock it in place and seal it.

Next to us, at the living room end of the kitchen counter, Meital and Shirel mashed soaked chickpeas in a bowl. They added freshly harvested parsley leaves and ground onion, and mixed them together. Then came garlic, cumin and coriander spices. "I think that's enough for now," Meital said. "I'll start making the balls." She grabbed a handful of chickpea mash and began rolling it between her palms. She reached across the sink to place the first bite-sized piece on a plate near my mother.

Shirel continued mashing chickpeas. "Tell me when to stop, Meital."

Meanwhile, at the dining room table, Denver and I prepared hummus to smear on the pita flatbread. We used the food processor (there was one on board, shared by all families) to grind the chickpeas that we had cooked the night before. We added the toasted sesame seeds for the tahini component, a tablespoon and a half of olive oil, and a tablespoon of water. Lemon juice was lacking, but we put in other basic spices, including garlic powder and pepper, a pinch of lemon salt, and, of course, table salt.

"Never take gravity for granted," my mother said. "Boiling oil would be extremely dangerous in weightlessness." She turned to Meital. "Hand me the plate with the falafel balls, so I can drop them in." She unsealed the pot's lid, poured the contents of the plate into the pot, and promptly resealed it.

"Dr. Dana," Denver said, "I think you worry too much. We have a stable spin. The oil is safe in the pot."

"That's right, Denver," my mother answered, watching the timer application on her datapad, which she had Velcroed to the wall above the stovetop. "We have stable gravity. But we have to be super-careful with boiling oil. Don't take gravity for granted." Again, she unsealed and opened the lid. Acting quickly, she used a strainer ladle to remove the fried falafel balls. She dropped them into a plastic bowl, then took the next plateful from Meital and dunked them into the boiling oil. Again she closed and sealed the lid. Meital began rolling the third batch while Shirel mixed more chickpea mash.

Denver and I scraped the finished hummus out of the food processor and spread it on a serving dish. House rules were to clean up as we went along, so we meticulously washed out the food processor and put it away before we set the table.

The smell of fresh falafel filled the air. With growing excitement, we laid out the ingredients for a make-your-own-sandwich meal: a plate with a stack of whole-wheat pitas; a bowl with dozens of brown falafel balls, and the dish of creamy hummus. A true falafel sandwich required fresh salad, which we lacked, but we had done the best we could.

But even that problem got solved, at least partially. "Look what I've brought you," exclaimed Omar, coming down the stairs.

"Cucumbers, our first!" He laid three medium-sized, freshly picked cucumbers on a plate on the table, and dumped several small carrots next to them. "We had planned to start harvesting the cucumbers next week, but when Shirel told me what you were preparing, I checked and found these, ready today."

Meital shot Shirel a disappointed look. "You revealed our secret!"

"Omar was working on the plants downstairs when Susy and I were packing new soil," Shirel answered defensively. "He saw me and asked what was for dinner. What was I supposed to say?"

"Oh, so it's Omar's fault."

"Yes, it's my fault." Omar smiled. "But don't worry: it was a pleasant surprise, and very considerate of you."

"Cucumbers," I mused, picking one up. It had been only four months since I had held a cucumber, but the year back in Altiplano, on Earth, seemed like another lifetime. I held it before my eyes. "It's awesome! What a beautiful deep green." I examined its skin. "It's smooth, but here and there are ridges of small bumps. They give it an interesting shape."

"It's just a cucumber, Michael," Denver said, but I barely heard him.

I looked more closely. One end of the cucumber had a series of pale green stripes that started at the tip and spread out around the sides. "Like the ladder rungs around the habitat," I thought out loud, picturing the tip of the cucumber as the bottom of the habitat, the dot on its end the airlock hatch. "It's not 'just a cucumber,' Denver. It's an incredible divine invention, carefully designed and even decorated!"

"Let me see one," Shirel said, picking up the second cucumber. Omar was now examining the third.

"Every vegetable is a miracle. Shape, color, texture, –"

"Taste, Michael?" Meital interjected. "Can we get on with supper?"

"Yes, and taste. I think I'll never take a cucumber for granted again." I put it back on the plate. "G-d's world is so amazing."

"Yes, it is." Omar gathered the other cucumbers. "If each of us eats one and a half pita sandwiches, that is nine sandwiches." He looked at me, eyebrows raised. "Is it okay with you if I slice them now?"

I nodded.

He took a knife from the kitchen drawer and began cutting. "So, a third of a cucumber per sandwich. At the best stands back home in Madaba they would scoff at so little! But the chefs don't have to grow their own vegetables."

"I've never been so happy to eat a third of a cucumber," I said.

The six of us sat down and began filling our pitas. After we finished spreading the hummus and packing in falafel balls, cucumbers and carrots, I recited the traditional Jewish blessing on a bread-based meal: "The source of all blessing are You, our L-rd, King of the Universe, who extracts bread from the Earth." We began to eat. I realized that my blessing had been said with more fervor and concentration than usual. Ironically, that disappointed me. All the Jewish blessings of gratitude – all the blessings I recited every day – ought to be said with such fervor and concentration! Our debt of gratitude to G-d was endless. Paying attention when thanking Him was the least I could do. I needed to remember how excited and appreciative I had felt when seeing the new cucumbers.

"I grew up eating falafel," Omar said, picking up his sandwich and taking a bite. "Madaba falafel is always served with tomatoes, not just cucumbers and carrots. I checked the tomatoes this afternoon to see if I could find a couple ready for tonight."

"I think none are ripe yet," Denver said.

"That is correct. Unfortunately, as I expected, not a single one. Maybe in two or three more weeks."

"Our mushrooms are almost ready," I said. During Mycology class with Omar on Sunday, we had examined the mushroom buttons, which were by now growing quite quickly. "In Madaba, would they put mushrooms in falafel?"

"I expect we will harvest the first mushrooms next week," he answered. "But we would not put them in falafel. At least not back home in Madaba. Maybe in hummus, though." He tore off a bit of pita and dipped it in our hummus. "You did a great job, guys, given the limitations."

"Where do you get cucumbers and tomatoes and carrots in Jordan?" Shirel asked. "Isn't the country mostly desert?"

"Shirel, don't be dumb," Meital said. "Jordan is like Israel: there are forests and fields and farms."

Omar looked at her. "It is not a dumb question. A large part of Jordan is desert. But Madaba is surrounded by farms. And the Jordan Valley is especially lush. There is no lack of fresh tomatoes, cucumbers and carrots."

"But it is basically desert agriculture, isn't it?" I asked. "Isn't that why you joined the Murke-Berger Foundation, because of your expertise in desert agriculture?"

"Well, yes and no, Michael. I grew up in a city, not on a farm. I did not know anything about plants before taking a botany class in high school. But then I started growing vegetables in a garden in our yard, and before long was experimenting with different amounts of water. That made the idea of growing food in dry climates a fascinating challenge." He took a bite of his sandwich.

"How did the Foundation find you?"

"I found the Foundation. I started visiting local farms and was disappointed that nobody seemed concerned with developing new water-saving techniques. Most of the farms there rely on winter rainfall. Some use Israeli irrigation pipes, which provide good results. I wanted a bigger challenge. I thought of applying to study at an Israeli research institute –"

"Hebrew University School of Agriculture in Rehovot?" Meital asked.

"That and several others. When I suggested the idea to my parents, they were shocked!" He laughed as he looked around at us. "They adamantly refused to let their son have anything to do with Israel. So, instead, here I am, on my way to Mars, with a group of Israelis."

"You skipped part of your story. How did you get from Israeli Universities to the Murke-Berger Foundation?"

"I investigated, to figure out who was researching the most difficult agriculture problems. Murke-Berger was it."

"And they hired you, just like that?" Denver asked.

"I applied for a chance to join a research group. I had no serious research experience, so of course they were not going to accept me at age seventeen. But I guess they were impressed with my interest and high school achievements, because they provided a scholarship to study at King Abdulaziz University in Jeddah, in Saudi Arabia. When I graduated, I got my original wish: they hired me and brought me to Arizona."

"Were your parents upset with that?"

"No, no, they tell me they are proud of me, and they are happy I'm fulfilling my dreams. Mostly they want me to get married." He took another bite. "I hope they miss me. I think they do."

"So, how is the falafel, Omar?" my mother asked. "Were our efforts successful?"

"Oh, yes, definitely. It's been a while since I ate genuine Madaba falafel." He paused to savor the food in his mouth. "Maybe I'm not remembering perfectly, but I think it is exactly the same." He exaggerated his nod. Then, more seriously, "Yes, actually, it is very good."

Everyone agreed. Despite lacking several Earth-standard ingredients, our interplanetary falafels did taste amazing. Especially the cucumbers: I had never truly appreciated the taste, and the crunchiness, of a juicy cucumber.

My mother turned to my sister. "Shirel, did you mention something about packing new soil? Tell us about it. Was today the first time?"

"We started Sunday. Some of the vermiculture drawers are nearly full. Dr. Cecylia showed us how to separate the worms and identify the healthiest ones. We moved those to other drawers. The rest of them, those that are smaller or don't seem to be thriving, go into jars. They'll be food for the chickens."

Denver interrupted. "Can we skip the details on the worms while we're eating?"

Shirel narrowed her eyes at him censoriously and continued.

"After we removed the worms, we put the soil into a polyurethane bag. That was hard work: Dr. Cecylia made us punch the soil over and over, to pack it as hard as possible. She says that when the bag is full, we'll need to store it until we reach Mars, and it needs to take as little space as possible."

"That's right," my mother said, "the bags are packed against the hull, in spaces where the water tanks have been emptied. You know that we slowly use up our water, extracting oxygen via electrolysis –"

The whole room lurched suddenly, tilting violently. Meital screamed, "Mom!" and Shirel gasped. The floor and walls shook violently. Omar shouted, "Grab hold!"

"What's happening?" I cried out. The food slid off our plates. An alarm sounded, a high-pitched shrieking buzzer. My mother, a petrified look on her face, dove to her left to grab Shirel.

Then the whole world fell out from under us. Everything went flying, gravity disappeared, and the room spun out of control. I banged into the ceiling. Denver, shouting, knocked into me and flailed, grabbing at anything he could reach. Somebody was screaming, and I felt dizzy, and everything whirled around me, and I wanted to vomit, and the screams filled my ears, and I realized they were my own.

Spinning

Spinning

Tuesday, January 23rd, 2029 18:33

Somebody smashed into me and pinned me to the ceiling. A moment later I rolled over Omar, and both of us bounced toward the sofa end of the living room. "Grab the table!" he yelled. I crashed into the ceiling again and my wrist erupted in searing pain. I shrieked in agony. Out of the corner of my eye, I saw Meital clinging with all her strength to the wall by the kitchen; then, a moment later, she tumbled toward Omar and me, crying in terror, the leg of her mundies stained red. I found myself pressed into the edge of the ceiling above the sofa, although – in those frightful moments, with the whole world spinning out of control – it was hard to tell what was up and what was down. I caught a brief glimpse of my mother, crouched between the floor and the table, pinning Shirel against one of the legs.

Twelve seconds. The twelve longest seconds ever! The flight computer waited twelve full seconds before firing the reaction control rockets to counter the terrifying spin. For twelve seconds we bounced across the ceiling and walls, banged against each other, knocked our arms and legs against furniture and doorposts, and frantically tried to grab onto something, anything! Finally, the rockets fired and the frenzied spinning diminished. Gradually the room steadied around us. Our screams subsided, replaced with shocked, adrenaline-fueled sobbing. I grabbed the sofa arm and pulled myself down. I waited, my left wrist throbbing in pain, for twenty more seconds. The room still spun, partially in actuality, but much more in my dizzied head. Finally, everything stopped moving. We were weightless again.

I was woozy. The pain in my left wrist was excruciating. My head throbbed. My heart raced. Partially eaten falafel sandwiches floated overhead.

My mother noticed the blood on Meital's mundies. "Meital, your leg!" She extricated herself from under the table and kicked off in our direction. Floating above me, she grabbed my sister's foot, pulled off her mundies sock, and rolled the pant leg up over her knee.

"I need something to stop the bleeding. Michael – give me your overalls!"

Using my good hand, I unsnapped the straps of the checkered green garment and pushed it down off my legs. My mother grabbed it from my hand, folded it several times, and wrapped it tightly around the bleeding leg.

"Meital, hold this and apply pressure." Then she glanced around the room. "Shirel, are you hurt?"

Shirel was pulling herself from under the table, breathing heavily but not quite crying. "I think I'm okay, Mom. I don't see any blood."

"Mom, Denver!" I said, pointing to my roommate, who was floating by the stairwell, covering his face with bloodied hands. Omar was holding his shoulders.

"Dana, Denver may have broken his nose. We need tissues."

"I'll get paper from the bathroom," I said, pushing myself in that direction with both hands. A jolt shot through my left arm. "Ah!" I cried in pain.

"Michael, I'll go," Shirel said, her voice quavering. My mother turned to examine me.

"Triage, triage," called a voice, and Ruby appeared in the stairwell, datapad in her hand. "Oh, no!" she called, seeing the blood. She blanched noticeably, but spoke professionally.

"Denver: bloodied face. Meital: bleeding calf."

"Denver may have a broken nose," Omar said. "I'm working on the bleeding." He took the pile of toilet paper Shirel handed him.

"I'm okay," Shirel said, voice still shaking.

Spinning

Ruby continued taking notes. She examined me. "Michael, your hand – it's purple and swelling." For the first time I stopped to look. No wonder it was throbbing in pain. My nausea returned.

"Anything else?" Ruby asked, catching my eye. Color returned to her face.

"My head hurts," I answered, using my good hand to feel the top of my skull. I felt quite a bump and it stung when I touched it.

"Possible broken wrist, possible concussion," Ruby murmured, making notes. "Dr. Dana and Omar, anything else to list?" They shook their heads, so Ruby turned to depart down the stairwell. "I'll be back, but I need to check on everyone downstairs."

Dr. Claudine came up a few minutes later, wearing white overalls over her mundies. Her pockets were stuffed full. "Shirel, if you are feeling well, can you go and comfort Jasmine and Sophie? Sophie is all right – she was secure in bed when we lost the tether – but Jasmine is not yet calm. Ruby is with her now, but she needs to finish the triage."

Shirel wiped her eyes, nodded silently, and left.

Omar, having stabilized Denver, gathered the floating chairs. He folded each and stowed them all in the bedroom.

Dr. Claudine looked around the room. "Who needs a painkiller?" She pulled a yellow medicine container from one of her stuffed pockets and handed out pills to Denver, Meital and me.

An alarm sounded from the NLED wall, followed immediately by an automated announcement. "Sixty seconds to emergency burn. Brace yourselves and secure all free items." The voice began counting down.

"Who can help me gather the floating food?" my mother asked. She pushed herself around the room and began grabbing and bagging the floating remnants of our meal.

The automated voice said, "Fifteen seconds: brace yourselves!" Then: "Five – four – three – two – one – fire!" A barely perceptible vibration echoed through the walls and the floor rose to meet us. Or, in my case, the couch rose to meet me and I found myself sitting in almost imperceptible gravity.

Meital moved to help my mother, but Dr. Claudine caught her wrist and pulled her down to the couch next to me. "Let's look at your leg." She extracted a pair of surgical gloves from another pocket and put them on. Kneeling on the floor, she began unwrapping my now green-and-blotched-red overalls from Meital's leg. While Meital gripped the couch to hold herself steady, Dr. Claudine examined her wound, manipulating it gently with her hands. "You will need stitches, but they can wait a bit."

The engine burn stopped as abruptly as it had begun and even the very mild gravity was gone. The engines had burned for less than half a minute; now we were floating again. A moment later there was another slight vibration, which I knew to be the reaction control rockets firing. They would adjust the habitat's orientation relative to the sun, starting a slow rotation, to control temperature by exposing all sides equally to sunlight.

Dr. Claudine wrapped Meital's leg back up in my overalls and turned to examine Denver's nose. Narrowing her eyes, she said, "We will need an ultrasound CT. Denver, come upstairs with me. You, too, Michael."

Murke-Berger Foundation rules required at least two surgeons on each spacecraft, besides additional fliers trained in medicine and dentistry. Dr. Claudine and her husband Dr. Louis were our two resident surgeons. Both would be busy all evening.

Upstairs on Yellow Level, Sam joined us in the Beckers' living room. While Helga and Celina floated around stowing exercise equipment and setting up the dining table, Dr. Claudine disappeared into Helga's bedroom to retrieve medical supplies. Cabinets above the young women's beds – there being no top bunks in the habitat's domed top floor – contained most of our medical diagnostics equipment.

"Michael, you are first. Please lie down on the table."

I did so, amused that I was turning a dining table into a surgical bed, which seemed very silly to me at the time. Clearly the painkiller had started working. Dr. Claudine secured me with several straps that she pulled out of a medical supply bag. She was very gentle as she secured my injured arm; I was grateful. "Lie still," she said, activating the ultrasound scanner. Starting with the top of my forehead, she pressed the sensor to my skin. She rocked it back and forth, rolling it around its point of contact until a green LED lit up. She moved the sensor to a second point a couple of centimeters to the side and repeated the procedure. She continued this way around the circumference of my head. It took a minute or so to complete the circuit, though, given my woozy state, I am not sure I was sensing time accurately. She scanned a second circuit a centimeter down my forehead. She reached the base of my skull after a few more circuits, and then moved on to my arm, beginning by positioning the probe at the elbow and finishing at the palm of my hand.

"That's all, Michael," she announced, opening the straps. "Wait on the sofa while I check the results. Denver, to the table."

Latching the scanner to the side of the table, she pulled her datapad from its Velcro patch on the kitchen counter. "The complete three-dimensional images of your head and arm will be ready in a few seconds. Hmmm ...," she muttered, examining the screen intently, "let us see if you have any bleeding."

Denver, meanwhile, positioned himself on the table, waiting to be secured.

"Michael, you do have a minor concussion," she said a minute later, pointing to the image on the datapad. "We will need to check you in a few hours and make sure the bleeding has stopped. The happy news is that your wrist is not broken. Sprained, but no fracture."

Her diagnosis did not relieve the pain in my sprained wrist, which throbbed, despite the painkiller.

"So, no operation for now," she continued. "I'll bandage your wrist for you as soon as I finish with Denver." Dr. Claudine was an expert in orthopedic surgery of the extremities, though, like all surgeons, she had also trained in general surgery. I imagined, in my foggy state, that she was disappointed that she would have no opportunity to exercise her expertise.

She strapped Denver to the table and probed his nose, face and head. Celina perched next to him, watching the examination, looking concerned.

The abundance of surgeons notwithstanding, there were no cardiac or oncological experts on board any of our expedition's six ships. The Murke-Berger Foundation was very practical: high-risk surgery, even when successful, would have limited utility on Mars, but low-risk surgery that kept us productive would be beneficial to the expedition. An operation to restore use to a hand was the textbook example of high-utility, low-risk surgery.

Over by the sofa, Sam grasped my elbow and Helga inspected my now quite swollen wrist. "You guys got banged up terribly," he said.

"What, none of you were hurt?" I asked.

"No, not really," he answered. "We were lucky to be in the middle of afternoon exercise. Susy and I were buckled tightly to the cycles, and Ruby and my mom were strapped to the sprowers. I know Ruby bumped herself while we were tumbling – her knee was hurting quite severely – but there was nothing more serious than that."

"She showed no signs of any problem when she came to triage us."

"My sister takes her nursing responsibility quite seriously. She's very professional, especially in times of stress. But she was definitely in pain."

My wrist throbbed and my headache was getting worse, but I tried to follow Ruby's example of stoically ignoring pain. I failed. Grimacing, I asked, "What about you, Helga? Anyone hurt in your family?"

"Celina and I were also on the bikes, and they saved us from injury." Her lips curled as she fought a smile. "This is very funny: the safest activity in outer space is bicycling!" Then she smiled broadly and laughed briefly, before forcing a serious expression back onto her face. "But my father did get hurt. He was in the kitchen preparing dinner and got thrown about." She furrowed her brow. "That was the worst for me: watching Pa struggle to brace himself, and not being able to help him."

"Where is he now?"

She pointed at the bedroom. "Being examined by Dr. Jhonathan."

Denver, having been probed, treated, and unstrapped from the table, joined our discussion. He looked terrible. Dr. Claudine had bandaged his face: his nose and cheeks were completely covered with bright white gauze. "She said I do dot have a codcussion," he said, struggling to pronounce the words despite his blocked nose. "But by face hurts awfully."

While Dr. Claudine bandaged my sprained wrist, Dr. Jhonathan emerged from Captain Becker's bedroom. "Dietrich bruised his back quite severely. He will need two or three weeks of bedrest and supervised physical therapy. He's not happy about it."

Dr. Claudine prescribed more painkillers for Denver and me, then sent the two of us downstairs with instructions to rest but not yet sleep. We rejoined my mother and sisters. Dr. Louis was just finishing stitching up Meital's leg, and my mother was in the kitchen still cleaning up the remnants of our falafel dinner. I thought about how fortunate we were that the pot with the boiling oil had been sealed shut when the tumbling started.

"I think it was the side of the table that ripped into my leg," Meital said giddily, also heavily medicated. "I did not know that mundies could tear so easily."

Shirel, to her credit, was much calmer now. Perhaps the responsibility for comforting Jasmine had fortified her. Smiling tentatively, she said, "Meital, you have ruined a perfectly good set of mundies pants. I'm sure G-d will fix your skin automatically, but how will you bind the torn mundies?"

My mother, whose forehead was bandaged, scolded Shirel without looking up. "It's not Meital's fault; any of us could have torn our clothes. It is not a reason for concern. We have sufficient replacement mundies, and, if necessary, we have kits for patching even large tears."

"Mom, I'm not taking her seriously," Meital said, chuckling. "In fact, at the moment, I don't think I can take anything seriously!"

I glanced at my sisters and mother. All wounds now dressed, and most nerves calmed, I stopped to consider what had befallen our ship. "What happened? Did we lose our tethers? What malfunctioned?"

My mother said, "I'll check the status as soon as I finish getting the kitchen in order."

"Mom, I'm sorry." I was startled to realize that nobody was helping her. "Do you want me to help clean up?"

She looked across the room, considering us and our injuries. She shook her head. "No, Michael; I've got this. Each of you obviously needs to sit tight and rest for now."

Then Boris and Simeon appeared from downstairs, datapads in their hands. "Did I hear you asking about the tethers, Michael?" Simeon called out. "We lost them. We had a breakage."

"We are going to review the details with Dietrich and Jhonathan," Boris said, "but the diagnostics program reports that one tether failed at 18:33." He noticed my mother tidying up the kitchen and turned to inspect the room. "Dana, I see food stains on the ceiling." He glanced at the four of us gathered indolently at the couch. He lowered his eyebrows disapprovingly, turned back to my mother, cleared his throat, and said, loudly, "Would you like Simeon and me to help clean up?"

"Yes, if you don't mind. Here are a couple of towels you can use as rags."

The brothers fastened their datapads to Velcro patches on the walls and got to work.

After a few minutes of silent scrubbing, Simeon commented, "It was the yellow tether that snapped. That is why the habitat suddenly lurched."

"Yes, we felt that lurch, just before we lost gravity completely," Meital said. "But there are supposed to be four tethers. Did we lose all of them?"

"Oh, no, we lost only one, but the computer will not allow the ships to spin with fewer than four tethers," Boris said. "The spin-management software unlatched all of them, freeing both ships and sending us flying apart."

"That was on purpose?" Shirel exclaimed, her indignant voice fully recovered. "The computer made us twist and twirl like that on purpose? So that everybody would get injured? Who would write such a stupid program?"

"Shirel, believe me," Simeon said, "the controlled spin was nowhere near as violent as it would have been from an uncontrolled loss of multiple tethers."

Boris explained. "Rotation on three tethers becomes unstable very quickly. Both ships would rock and wobble, more and more out of control with each revolution. The tethers might tear under those conditions. To prevent loss of control, the spin management software intentionally releases all the tethers within three seconds of detecting the loss of any one."

Simeon added, "Anyway, in a controlled release, as I am sure you noticed, the software stops the spin and stabilizes the habitats right away."

"That was 'right away?'" Meital asked. "It seemed like we were bouncing around forever!"

"True, not exactly right away." Boris said, scrubbing the ceiling, not looking down this time. "A twelve-second delay is programmed intentionally. But no more than that. After twelve seconds the computer activates the reaction control rockets to stabilize the ship.

In emergency mode, the reaction control system needs only twenty more seconds to stop our rotation completely."

"If the whole thing was only thirty-two seconds, then those were the longest thirty-two seconds ever," Shirel said, shaking her head and thinking. "But why wait twelve seconds? That sounds stupid. Why not stop the spinning right away?"

"The computers avoid engaging the reaction control system while the two ships are in close proximity. The exhaust gases can damage the solar panels and other equipment. They wait until the habitats are a few hundred meters away from each other."

"What?" Meital asked. "Are you saying that we moved away from *Mars Hope* after the tether broke?"

"'Moved away?'" Denver repeated. "We were flung away from each other at high speed! Like two rocks slung from a slingshot. We could be hundreds of kilometers away from the other ship by now."

"No, Denver," Boris said, "that is an exaggeration. Recall the calculations we made in physics class early in the semester." He floated down. "We rotate, for artificial gravity, two and a half times a minute. That makes our angular velocity, at the ship stack's center of mass, about seventeen meters per second. Accordingly, we traveled ten kilometers, relative to our initial inertial position, in the ten minutes or so before the stabilization burn began."

Meital looked up. "Oh, so that's why the rocket fired when Dr. Claudine was examining me? To bring us back to *Mars Hope*?"

"No," my mother called from the kitchen, "to stop us from moving farther apart, for now. It will take a few days before we rejoin *Mars Hope*. We should get a status update soon, but protocol is for the computers to set us on a very slow course toward each other, to minimize fuel use."

"That means we're ten kilometers from *Mars Hope* at the moment," I said, thinking of Hannah.

"No, Michael, twenty, not ten," Boris said, taking a deep breath and shaking his head at me disapprovingly, a teacher disappointed in his student. "They were flung away from us, just as we were flung from them, so we both moved away from each other at the same speed. Perhaps we'll need to review that physics lesson?"

I shook my head, afraid of extra homework.

"What happened to the tethers?" Denver asked from behind his bandages. "I assume we lost them, yes?"

"Yes," Boris said. "When the spin control software releases the tethers in an emergency, they are essentially jettisoned."

My mother commented, "the tethers will continue to Mars, but they are kilometers away from us and we have no way of retrieving them."

Shirel looked up in realization, her eyes wide. "So we cannot spin up again for the rest of the trip? No more gravity?" Her expression was not one of disappointment. If anyone on board would be happy without gravity for the next six and a half months, it would be Shirel.

"No, Shirel, we will have gravity. The lost tethers were *Mars Hope's*. We still have *Providence's* set, the set we were using when we were orbiting Earth."

Shirel nodded silently, seemingly not thrilled by the idea.

I was still thinking about what went wrong. "I'd like to know why the tether broke in the first place," I said. "I thought the aramid cords are unbreakable."

"No material is unbreakable," my mother said. "Every material has its limits, and something evidently caused the tethers' to be reached. I know Captain Becker well, and I have no doubt that he will not rest – even if his doctor orders him to! – until he and Captain Ravel have figured out exactly what happened, to make sure it does not happen again."

*   *   *

Tuesday, January 23rd, 2029 21:20

An angry, frightening shriek sounded from our bedroom, followed by a string of German words I was happy not to understand. Clearly, Denver was not happy.

We had rested for a couple of hours; then Dr. Claudine had probed Denver and me a second time to make sure there was no internal bleeding. Given a clean bill of health, other than his bandaged fractured nose, Denver had finally ventured into our bedroom to check that there was nothing to clean up.

"Denver, what happened?" I called out.

He appeared in the room's doorway, tears in his eyes. In his hand was his guitar, the only guitar within millions of kilometers, and it was severely smashed. He turned it over in his hands and held it up, showing the body's underside. The damage looked bad: two long cracks led to a jagged hole, a few centimeters across, just below the guitar's waist.

"Denver, that's horrible," I cried. "How did it happen?"

He glided over slowly, his face looking even worse than before. His eyes, just barely not hidden by bandages, were bloodshot, but that was nothing compared to the heartbreaking anguish they conveyed.

"I forgot to secure the guitar," he moaned. "It came loose, and banged into something, maybe into a closet or drawer handle."

Dr. Claudine looked at him compassionately. "Denver, I am so sorry." She put a hand on his shoulder, but he brushed it off. Reluctantly she turned toward the stairwell, saying something about needing to check on Jasmine and Sophie.

"Just one artifact," Denver sobbed. "Only one artifact allowed! My only real possession, gone." He shook his head in grief.

My mother reached out with both arms to hug him, but he recoiled.

"It's terrible," Meital said sympathetically. "You were starting to really enjoy playing." She turned to our mother, then to Simeon and Boris. "We can fix it, can't we?"

My mother shook her head. "It looks like it needs a professional repair shop. Unfortunately, we are very, very far from any."

"I have an idea, Denver," I said, trying to be encouraging. "We can download plans and print a new back panel for the guitar."

He lifted his eyes toward me, nodding slowly, though his expression remained anguished.

"Let's ask Dr. Esther. It could be a project for the Three-Dimensional Printing Design course she is teaching you."

Perhaps there was a flicker of hope in his eyes, before his head drooped and his gaze returned to the floor.

*　　*　　*

Tuesday, January 23rd, 2029 22:00

We were fortunate that nothing else in the habitat was seriously damaged, but we did lose a number of not-quite-ripe cucumbers, zucchini and tomatoes that flew off their vines during the seconds of wild spinning. Omar and Celina gathered everything up, darting from greenhouse room to greenhouse room over the course of the evening. On our Green Level we watched them snatch floating vegetables from the air. They replanted everything that had become uprooted and checked that all the soil covers were securely in place. Happily, they reported that the mushrooms and the worms, secure in their cabinets, had not been damaged. They gave the unripe vegetables to Ruby for the chickens.

Ruby also reported good news: none of the fowl seemed hurt, "though from the mess in the cages," she said, "I can only imagine how panicked the poor birds must have been!"

Unsurprisingly, Dr. Jhonathan canceled all night classes. There was a lot of movement up and down the stairwell that evening, as friends checked on each other and everybody discussed what it was like to experience a "rapid unscheduled gravity loss." As bedtime neared, I found myself on Mauve Level, musing with Simeon and Dr. Louis, then with Sam, Ruby and Helga, who had also meandered downstairs.

The NLED wall was showing a beautiful sunset over white-capped Mediterranean waves, somewhere on the Côte d'Azur. Exactly at 22:15, the view disappeared, replaced, after a brief blank moment, by an image of Dr. Jhonathan perched in his Pink-Level living room. He appeared to be facing us. Dr. Esther and Susan floated next to him. Omar was also visible behind them.

"I'm sorry to interrupt," he began. "Because some of you are recovering from minor injuries, we thought it best to update everybody on our status by video, instead of gathering for a general meeting. The video is two-way: I can also see and hear you, so feel free to ask questions." He glanced up and down, apparently looking at images from the other levels. "Captain Becker and I, with Boris's help, together with Captain Ravel of *Mars Hope*, have been examining all the data available from the ships' sensors and computers, to try to determine the unfortunate sequence of events. As you may know, Captain Becker injured his back. He is resting now. He asked me to lead this meeting in his stead.

"What we know is that the yellow tether failed, at our end, and broke free of its clasp at the top of *Providence*. If you felt the ship tilt momentarily before the complete loss of gravity, it was that break that you felt. According to protocol for such a situation, both ships' computers immediately released all the tethers, ending artificial gravity and allowing both ships to speed off in opposite directions."

"He makes it sound so much calmer that it was in reality," Ruby whispered to Helga, who was floating behind me.

"From that point on, the ships behaved nominally to recover from the situation." He smiled as he looked around again at the screens we could not see. "It may have felt to you like the habitat was out of control, behaving haphazardly, but in actuality the computer was in complete control, executing an exact sequence of events programmed for the situation."

Pausing, he held his hands up, lightly clenched, about ten centimeters apart, and rotated them slowly around each other, as if he were turning a steering wheel.

"Picture the two habitats rotating. At the moment of a tether break" – he stopped rotating his fists and let each continue outward in the direction it had been moving – "both habitats fly off straight in whatever trajectories they happened to have been traveling, at the speed they were traveling. But the different parts of each ship stack were moving at different speeds: the Mars Entry Stages, farthest from the center of rotation, were moving faster than the habitats. This caused a new rotation in each ship stack. Unfortunately, from the point of view of all of us inside, this meant that our ship started spinning, slowly, around its own center of mass." He rotated his hands around each other a second time, and again showed them moving apart as if released from each other, but this time he also rotated his wrists back and forth to simulate the ships spinning head over heel.

"Dad, spinning 'slowly?'" Susan interrupted from behind him. Dr. Jhonathan twisted to face his daughter. "During the *disaster*" – she emphasized the word, dramatically widening her eyes – "there was nothing 'slow' about how we were spinning!"

"Yes, Susy, from our point of view, the spin was certainly disconcerting." He turned back toward the camera. "And it's possible that the spin was unstable, because of the tilt introduced when the first tether broke, before the computer released the other three. When you learn physics in a couple of years, you'll learn equations that relate radius of rotation to angular velocity, and you'll also learn about chaotic systems. Because weight is not distributed evenly within the habitat, and even more because the fuel in the Mars

Entry Stage's tanks is liquid, it's possible that the new spin was not stable."

"Possibly not stable? That's an understatement." Susan shook her head and laughed. "Everything was whirling wildly for the longest time! Until the reaction control rockets finally fired and stabilized the ship."

Dr. Jhonathan glanced upward for a moment, then turned back to the camera. "Marcelina asked why it took so long before the computer fired the reaction control rockets. That's a good question. Flight rules require a distance of at least four hundred meters between the ships before the rockets fire at full thrust. The computers on both ships waited until the ships reached this distance."

Ruby asked, loudly, "Dad, when will we have gravity again?"

He smiled sympathetically. "Ruby, that is also a good question. We're currently around twenty kilometers from our sister ship, now approaching each other at the breathtaking velocity of six centimeters per second. At this rate we should meet up within four days."

"Only six centimeters a second? We cannot tether and spin up for four more days?"

"Possibly even more than that, Ruby. Dietrich and I have yet to finalize plans, and we'll want to discuss the details with Foundation officials back on Earth, but we may use this opportunity to perform a course correction. Since we can't adjust our trajectory while in tethered spin, we were going to have to spin down anyway, sometime in the next month or two, to execute a burn. We might as well utilize the current situation. A course correction, if we make one, may delay retethering by a day or two."

"Sorry to belabor the point, Dad," Ruby said, "but why are we so far from the other ship in the first place, and why are we moving back so slowly? Can't we go faster?"

"No need to apologize. I know that you prefer gravity to weightlessness." He shrugged and sighed. "As do we all. After the tether break, as I explained, the ships were flying in opposite directions until each fired its main rocket to stop the relative motion. Why so much time before this happened? The Mars-Entry stage's rocket cannot just fire up instantly. After being dormant for months, its fuel tanks needed to be pressurized and its engines primed. That took several minutes. Also, a series of diagnostic tests had to execute – and pass – before any rocket firing."

Simeon, behind me, said loudly, "I think we were lucky that everything went well and both ships were able to fire within only ten minutes."

"I agree, Simeon. We were fortunate."

Sam, hovering next to me, cleared his throat. "Dad, to Ruby's point: if the rocket was firing anyway to stop our movement relative to *Mars Hope*, why not have it fire another few seconds, create more acceleration, and get back to *Mars Hope* more quickly? Why stop at six centimeters per second?"

Simeon answered before Dr. Jhonathan could respond. "To save fuel, Sam. Think. When we get back to the other ship, the reaction control rockets will need to stop our relative movement. Having to remove more than six centimeters per second of inertial movement would be a really stupid waste of reaction control fuel."

"Oh," Sam said, turning, apparently startled at Simeon's tone. "That makes sense."

On the screen, Dr. Jhonathan nodded, though he was frowning.

"I think I understand our plans," I said, tentatively, getting his attention. "But something is still bothering me."

"Yes, Michael?"

"Um, you said that the yellow tether 'failed.' But you also said that it 'broke free of its clasp.' Those are two different things. What exactly happened? Did the clasp break or did the tether break?" I glanced around at the others. Simeon looked at me, then turned back to stare at the NLED wall. His expression was tense, angry.

Dr. Jhonathan answered. "We're not sure yet, Michael; perhaps we'll never know for sure. Our best guess, based on data the computer recorded leading up to the break, is that there was a crack in the tether's thimble. The thimble normally protects the tether from rubbing against the clasp. Even a microscopic crack could have spread during the two months we have been spinning, slowly exposing the tether's edge. Over time, as more and more of the tether came into contact with the clasp, the continuous rubbing would have frayed it to the breaking point."

"It is Captain Becker's fault!" Simeon exclaimed, startling me. "He is such an idiot!" I turned around to look at him. His face was flushed and his shoulders rose and fell as he breathed.

Dr. Louis, hovering by my side, glared at Simeon. "That language is not called for." He grabbed his elbow and spun him so they faced each other. Simeon tried to shake off his grip. Dr. Louis raised his voice and said, "The Captain does not permit such insubordination! Calm down."

On the screen, Dr. Jhonathan looked down, watching, I presumed, his view of us on Mauve Level. He spoke calmly. "Simeon, what I just explained is our current theory as to what happened. Please do not consider it as established fact. At this point we still don't have enough information to definitively determine the cause of the break. And certainly not to assign blame." He narrowed his eyes. "Why do you think this has to do with Captain Becker?"

Simeon's pale face flushed a light pink and he turned back to face the NLED wall. He seemed surprised, perhaps because he had not expected Dr. Jhonathan to ask his opinion.

"Because ... because it was Captain Becker who sent Boris to do the spacewalk to attach the tethers. Instead of me."

"So your brother was responsible for the break? How?"

"No, not Boris – it is not his fault. But do you not remember that he had a difficulty, when attaching the yellow tether? When you tried to close the clasp, Dr. Jhonathan, it closed onto the ring, not inside it. Twice. That is when the ring cracked."

"That is an interesting theory, Simeon, but do you have evidence that it was the clasp that caused a crack, and at that particular moment?"

"Evidence? What evidence? It is obvious! The clasp caught on the yellow tether, and the yellow tether broke. All because Boris did not have enough experience."

As he said this, his eyes were on the NLED wall display, so he did not notice that Boris had entered the room from the stairwell and now hovered right behind him.

"I trained the most for the tethering. It should have been me out there. With all respect to Captain Becker" – Simeon's sneering expression was anything but respectful – "he made a stupid decision sending Boris out. Dietrich deserves the injury he got."

Ruby and Helga gasped. Dr. Jhonathan's expression turned sour. Boris, still unnoticed by Simeon, floated silently behind us with his mouth open and eyes narrowed, looking hurt.

Dr. Jhonathan declared, "Simeon, G-d forbid that anybody on this mission ever 'deserve' any injury! We will not be vindictive, neither here en route nor when we arrive and build our community on Mars. Please apologize for your cruel statement."

"Okay, I apologize." Huffing, he pushed against the wall and propelled himself toward his bedroom. As he turned, his eye caught his brother's. Startled and embarrassed, he averted his gaze, pulled himself into the bedroom, and slid the door shut.

* * *

Thursday, January 25th, 2029 12:25

Studies resumed the following morning, despite our injuries and the missing gravity, and by Thursday I almost would have forgotten our little adventure, if not for my bandaged, aching wrist. Sam and I had progressed through our Talmudic tractate, nearly completing folio twelve, preparing to start on thirteen. We were analyzing the Talmudic Rabbis' opinions on whether, and under what conditions, one who is responsible for watching another's property is permitted to delegate that responsibility to a third party.

"Michael, you articulated your questions, and your explanations, very well today," Rabbi Meyer said. "I'm seeing good progress."

"Thank you, Rabbi Meyer." He was right; I did feel that my analytic capabilities and my ability to express my thoughts were becoming sharper.

"We struggled with that Tosafot today, though," Sam added, baseball still in his hands, as he followed me downstairs after class. He was referring to an intricate discussion by brilliant medieval French rabbis, about reasons a property owner might refuse to let a guard that he appointed independently delegate responsibility to someone else. We had struggled to understand the details of their argument. "Don't let my father's compliment go to your head."

"Thanks a lot, Sam," I answered, gently punching his shoulder with my uninjured hand, pushing him back up the stairwell. "Nice of you to let me feel good about something."

I had invited Sam to join us for lunch, so he followed me back down. We joined Denver and Shirel at the dining table. As was normal during periods without artificial gravity, the chairs remained stowed in my bedroom, but we took our regular places around the table. Sam perched at the far end.

"Thanks, Mom, for preparing lunch," Meital said, as she helped dish out and cover bowls of stew.

"It's nothing fancy, just leftovers from last night. I've spiced it up, though. Let me know if it's too hot. Also, everyone, take a vitamin if you did not do so this morning."

We fastened our bowls to the table's Velcro patches, all of us other than Shirel, who insisted on eating upside-down. "Only a few more days and we'll be on chairs again," she said, rebuffing my protests with a giggle from above.

My mother joined us at the table, holding several large lettuce leaves in her hands. She tore each leaf in half and handed out the pieces. "The lettuce continues to grow nicely. If we ration carefully, we can have some every day or two."

"What are the plans for spinning up for gravity?" Meital asked.

"I heard Captain Becker talking to Dr. Louis this morning," Denver said from behind his bandaged nose. Dr. Claudine had replaced his wrappings; now, the rest of his face was exposed, and it looked dreadful. Dark bruising had spread in both directions, below his eyes, into his cheeks. It was clear from his speech that his nasal cavities were still blocked. "The captain said the Foundation approved a course correction burn. They have scheduled it for Monday."

"So," I thought out loud, "if we are back together with *Mars Hope* by Saturday, make calculations for the burn Sunday, and complete the correction Monday, does that mean we will attach the tethers Tuesday and spin up?"

"I don't know if the computer needs a whole day to calculate burn coordinates," my mother answered. "The computer tracks our position continually."

"I wonder if we can delay spinning up for a day or two," Sam said.

From above, Shirel squealed, "great idea!"

"It's not healthy to be weightless so long, Sam," Meital said. "Why would we delay? And your sister hates it."

"Maybe it isn't such a good idea." He looked at Meital. "But I kind of want to go outside. We've been cramped up in the habitat for four months. I need a breath of fresh air and open skies."

"Fresh air!" My mother laughed.

"Obviously not literally. But seriously, why can't we go out a bit? Once we've spun up, we can't do a spacewalk."

"I like the idea," I said. "I'll join you. Who else wants to come? Denver?"

"Me? No thanks." He frowned and shook his head. "Things are dangerous enough inside."

"You guys are crazy," Meital said, a smile on her lips and incredulity in her eyes.

"So what? Sam, what do you say you take your baseball outside and we toss it around a bit?"

"Cool idea, Michael. We may be the first in history to play ball in outer space."

Both Meital and Shirel started giggling.

"Certainly we'll be the first to play in this particular part of interplanetary space."

"But Michael, there's a problem: what about your wrist? My second glove won't fit over your bandages. How will you catch the ball?"

"Oh yeah, that's your problem," Meital said, playfully derisive. "That the glove won't fit." She laughed out loud.

Shirel laughed, too. "Meital, wait, let's see if they can figure it out."

"What's the problem?" I looked across at Meital and up at Shirel. "I can catch a baseball with my right hand, even without a glove."

"And what if you don't, my silly brother?" Meital was now having trouble controlling her laughter. "Will you go running after the ball to retrieve it?"

Imagining myself haplessly watching a ball I failed to catch fly off into space, inertia carrying it away forever, I started laughing, too.

"Okay, no baseball," Sam smiled. "But I still want to go out."

"Me, too," I said. "Let's talk to Captain Becker and see if we can get him to agree.

*   *   *

Friday, January 26th, 2029 13:30

Surprisingly, Captain Becker approved our request, though reluctantly and with reservations, when Sam and I approached him the following afternoon.

"You want to do what?" He was strapped to a sprower in his Yellow-Level living room, arms and legs stretched out in front of him. Dr. Jhonathan was overseeing physical therapy for his back injury.

"We have been holed up in the ship for four months," Sam said. "While the ships are still untethered, we would like to have a few minutes outside. Michael and I will go together; we'll be buddies."

The captain leaned forward, stretching slowly, Dr. Jhonathan's hands gently on his back. He winced in pain. "It seems like an unnecessary risk. We generally approve spacewalks only for essential maintenance purposes."

"Captain Becker," I said, "on Mars we expect to go out often, to work outside on construction and manufacturing projects, right? Isn't that the point of the mundies, to make being outside routine?"

"Yes, Michael, that is part of the vision of the Murke-Berger Foundation. Normal life outside on Mars. Though with precautions to limit radiation exposure."

"What's the difference? The Martian atmosphere is effectively vacuum, from a life-support point of view. So why not go outside now?"

"Well, your arm, for one thing," Dr. Jhonathan said, gesturing at my bandaged left wrist. The bandages extended down my hand past the knuckles. "Your marsmitt won't fit."

"We have emergency fingerless mittens, though," I argued. "I can borrow one of those."

"You would have only one hand with which to grab rungs and propel yourself."

"We don't have to go far: we don't need to climb around the ship or anything. We can remain in the area of the airlock hatch. And anyway, we'll be tethered at all times."

"That is obvious," Captain Becker said. "Nevertheless, it is risky." He leaned backward, gradually, as Dr. Jhonathan again guided his posture. "And we do not want to add unnecessary airlock depressurization and pressurization." Then he leaned forward again, groaning almost inaudibly. Then back again, then forward again. "But your request is reasonable and mature." He turned to face Dr. Jhonathan. "Jhonathan, what do you think? Could we permit Michael and Sam to go outside briefly during the spacewalk Wednesday, after Boris installs the tethers?"

Dr. Jhonathan did not answer immediately. After considering for a moment, he said, "Assuming everything goes as planned in the next few days, then perhaps yes. But only after Boris completes the installation and is safely back in the airlock. We might delay repressurization for fifteen minutes. Esther will be in the airlock, so she'd be able to help in case the boys have any problem."

Dr. Jhonathan had meant no disrespect when he said "boys," but I still needed to bite my tongue and not protest.

Captain Becker looked up, trying not to wince as he stretched. "You understand that you will need to wait in the airlock during the whole tethering procedure. You will need to recharge your oxypacks before venturing outside. You will have fifteen minutes, no more. You will follow all safety procedures, including confirming that your buddy is latched to the habitat at all times. That means you must be extra attentive, Sam, given Michael's injury. If you agree to these conditions, then my answer is 'yes.'"

"We agree," Sam and I said without hesitation.

Trial

Sunday, January 28th, 2029 10:40

I had finished running waste-processing cycles on Pink and Yellow Levels, and was packing Pink Level's processed fertilizer into the half-full bag that had been latched to the top of the waste processor, when Captain Becker's voice sounded from a speaker in the bathroom ceiling.

"Six minutes to burn."

My left wrist was still tightly bandaged and I barely managed to grip the edge of the bag with my fingers. I used my good hand to push the processed waste deep into it. My wrist ached. I ignored it. Sam had taken pity on me and offered to do the inspections on all four levels' water systems while I recuperated, but I had refused. Shirking responsibility was no way to build a new branch of human civilization.

I managed to seal the bag and latch it back in place above the machinery.

Sam peered into the bathroom and looked at my bandages. "Michael, is your hand hurting? You really should let me help you. You're going to miss the burn!"

"I'm just finishing up. Thanks again for your offer, but I'm managing."

We joined our sisters, who had gathered in the Meyers' living room. All eyes were on the NLED wall, which was not showing much of anything. The sun was not in view, but some stars were visible.

Susan pointed to a speck in the center. "That's *Mars Hope* – you can see the sunlight reflecting off its Mars-Entry stage."

"How far away are they?" I asked.

Dr. Jhonathan, preparing lunch in the kitchen, answered, "two kilometers." He latched the lid on the pot and placed it into the stovetop, then turned to join us. "We reached *Mars Hope* last night. The flight computers spent most of the night maneuvering both ship stacks to the orientation required for the course-correction burn."

"I didn't feel anything moving last night," Meital said. "Shouldn't we have felt the ship rotating and starting and stopping?"

"Not necessarily. The reaction control rockets produce only negligible acceleration."

"Dad, what about our communications satellite?" Sam asked. "Doesn't it also need to make the same course correction?"

"Yes; it will fire too, though its burn will be shorter than the habitats'. The satellite's rocket accelerates it much more quickly."

"Isn't our rocket engine much bigger than the satellite's?" Shirel asked, adjusting her ponytail, but without removing her eyes from the screen.

"Yes, but the satellite is tiny compared to our rocket stack. Its engine is more powerful, relative to its mass."

"But we'll end up on the same trajectory," Sam said, "right?"

"That's what we're hoping for," his father answered with a smile.

Meital tapped her datapad. "I'm starting the music." The second movement of Beethoven's Fifth Symphony started playing. "Get ready to dance!"

"Four, three, two, one, burn ..." the captain's voice announced from the NLED wall, barely audible over the music.

After a moment of waiting, Shirel complained, "Nothing's happening."

But that was not quite accurate. The walls vibrated, just barely perceptibly, and the floor came up to meet us, very slowly. I stretched out my legs to stand.

Laughing, Dr. Jhonathan explained. "The Mars-Entry stage has much lower thrust than the rockets that launched us out of Earth orbit." He put a hand on the kitchen counter to steady himself. "It's designed for long burns in transit, not short gravity-escaping burns. It does not have to be powerful, just very reliable."

"Well, I'm officially lodging a complaint with its designers," Shirel said with mock indignation. "How can we dance in this gravity?"

"Very gently," he answered with a grin.

Sam asked, "How long will the burn last?"

As if in response, the vibration ceased and the floor stopped pressing against our feet.

Meital turned off the music, mumbling "What a disappointment!"

Captain Becker's voice sounded from the NLED wall. "This is your captain speaking. Both habitats are now synchronized in identical trajectories. We added fourteen point six meters per second of delta-v, exactly as the computers calculated."

He continued. "The computers report that both ships' rockets burned the exact required time, just over twenty-two seconds." He paused again, perhaps to check status reports. "The course correction succeeded for both ships. This means that we should arrive at the correct position in the Martian atmosphere, traveling in the correct direction, seven months and one week from now."

"G-d willing," Dr. Jhonathan whispered.

Sam was gazing at the ceiling, mumbling what sounded like a calculation. "It took twenty-two seconds to accelerate us by fourteen point six meters per second ... divide fourteen point six by twenty-two ... so around sixty-six centimeters per second squared acceleration." He looked at me. "No wonder we barely felt the burn: it was less than seven percent of Earth gravity."

"So, I weighed what?" I thought out loud, "Like five kilos?"

"No wonder we couldn't dance," Shirel said, shaking her head.

"You can all dance tomorrow, after we retether and spin back up."

* * *

Monday, January 29th, 2029 15:30

"This is the last one," Meital announced, and pushed a cage of canaries up through the hatch in the Bouchets' living room floor. I grabbed it and sent it toward Sam, who perched in the master-bedroom doorway. He caught the cage and passed it to Ruby, who had already latched the parakeet cages to the bedroom's walls. Shirel and Helga had taken the larger chicken coop upstairs to my mother's bedroom. "The airlock is clear."

"All set to go, Michael?" Celina asked, her face glowing with excitement. "What do you think we will see?"

For three days since getting permission for the spacewalk, Sam and I had barely stopped talking about it. Despite our continual appeals to everybody to join us, only Helga and Celina had chosen to come along. Perhaps that was fortunate. Surely Captain Becker would have rescinded his permission if eight or ten of us had wanted to go out, if only because the airlock had limited capacity.

"I wonder if we'll see anything, here in the middle of nowhere. But we can try." I floated through the hatch into the airlock, Celina behind me.

Dr. Esther, already down there with Sam and Boris, had overheard our exchange. "What you see depends on which direction you go. The ships are stable and unmoving for the tethering operation, so the sun will be on one side the whole time. The other side will be in shadow."

After the course correction the day before, the computers had fired the reaction control rockets to align *Providence* and *Mars Hope* for tethering. The process was exceedingly slow; it had taken nearly six hours. The two spaceship stacks were now perfectly positioned, pinnacle facing pinnacle, exactly one hundred meters apart. At first, the computers had set both ship stacks rotating, very slowly, to balance exposure to the sun on all sides. But even slow rotation would make it difficult to send the tethers across the gap – the MMU might veer off sideways – so the rotation had stopped over the past hour.

"Which side should we go to, Dr. Esther?" Helga asked, as she followed her sister into the airlock.

I flipped upside-down to match everyone's orientation, feet toward the hatch to the Bouchets' living room, heads toward the doorway to outer space.

"I recommend the shadow side," Dr. Esther answered. "Your eyes might have time to adjust to see the stars. Everybody set?"

We nodded.

"Who is whose buddy?"

"Michael and I are buddies," Sam said.

Helga grabbed her sister's hand. "Celina and me."

"Boris, I'll be in the airlock hatch waiting for you, just like last time," Dr. Esther said.

"Okay."

Dr. Jhonathan's voice sounded from wall speakers. "The reaction control system has us in position. The computers confirm that both ships are stable and the four corners are aligned by color. You may seal the inner hatch and prepare for atmosphere evacuation. Laura and Arjan are doing the same now on *Mars Hope*."

Boris closed the hatch and we donned and sealed our fleximets. I wore my regular marsmitt on my good hand, but for the injured one, I used an emergency fingerless mitten. I waited for Sam to fasten his fleximet, then pressed his oxypack's test button. His fleximet ballooned and the oxypack's green "okay" light flashed. He then tested my seal.

"Vacuuming the airlock," Dr. Esther announced. *Mars Hope's* spacewalk team was connected on the same radio band, so we heard Laura Tavera saying the same thing. I felt my mundies contract around my body, and especially around my fingers, as the air pressure dropped. Then Dr. Esther announced a pause in the vacuuming so that we could check our mundies for failures. Boris found a couple of bulges in her suit and patched them; then she proceeded to finish emptying the airlock's air. Finally, at 16:45, Boris donned his Mylar pants, hooded pullover and insulated gloves, and Dr. Esther opened the hatch to outer space.

"I am going to retrieve the MMU," Boris said, and pulled himself out the hatch. Dr. Esther also donned a Mylar spacesuit and positioned herself in the hatchway, head outside, feet dangling into the airlock. The four of us waited below her, off to the sides. We could barely see outside because her body blocked much of the opening.

"I just realized that we are the only ones who cannot watch the spacewalk," Helga said. "Everybody else can see Boris's camera view on the walls."

"That's ironic," Sam said. "We'll miss the outside events because we are going outside."

Dr. Jhonathan's voice sounded from the radio. "Please, no chatter. This channel is for spacewalk status only."

We were able to listen in, though, as Boris described his activities. "I have the MMU. I'm ready for the spool, Esther."

"Michael, hand me the tethers," Dr. Esther requested. I was happy to have something to do. Sam and I retrieved the spool with the tethers, from its stowage location against the airlock wall, and passed it to her. She pushed it through the hatch into Boris's hands.

"I've latched the spool to my waist harness and also to the MMU," Boris announced. But then he was mostly silent, only occasionally announcing his status.

Having watched both Simeon and Boris perform the tethering procedure, I could picture his progress in my mind. I imagined him balancing the MMU and the spool, careful not to bang either of them against the habitat's PlyShield skin.

Minutes passed. "I'm about one-third up the side." More minutes. Then, "I'm about halfway." Finally, after twenty minutes, Boris announced, "I'm at the pinnacle. The spool is latched. I'm attaching the tethers to the MMU."

I pictured the MMU carrying the tethers across the gap, Arjan retrieving them, and then Boris and Arjan beginning the process of climbing down to each of the clasps.

"Close red, please."

"Closed," answered Dr. Jhonathan.

I pictured Boris making his way up to the pinnacle to retrieve the next tether.

"Close green."

In my mind's eye, Boris was climbing back to the pinnacle again, then back down another side with the next tether.

"Blue tether secure."

Sam and I caught each other's eyes through our masks. He looked as impatient as I felt.

"Yellow tether secured. I'm heading back up to retrieve the spool. I have fifteen minutes of air."

We waited as Boris began his trek down the side of the habitat.

"Kids, now is the time to recharge your oxypacks and don your Mylar suits," Dr. Jhonathan told us over the radio. "You'll have fifteen minutes outside from the moment that Boris returns."

I moved to one of the recharging stations on the airlock wall, and Sam helped me attach its hose to my oxypack's receptor. I pushed the recharger's button to begin the flow. Three minutes later the oxypack beeped in my ear and announced, "One hundred percent full; one hundred eighteen minutes estimated supply."

Sam and the girls also filled up on air. Then we retrieved our Mylar pullovers and pants and dressed for the spacewalk. We donned our gloves and attached the harnesses that would latch us to the habitat's ladder rungs.

Dr. Esther exited the airlock. "Give me the spool, Boris."

She followed Boris in a moment later, the empty spool in tow. I took it from her and passed it to Sam, who replaced it against the wall.

"Okay, fliers, you're up," Dr. Esther said. "First Helga and Celina, then Sam and Michael."

As I climbed out the hatch, I activated my fleximet's forehead lamp and looked around. The girls had set out on two adjacent columns of handhold rungs to my left. Sam was waiting on a third behind me. Off to my right, a sliver of sun shone very brightly, though most of it was hidden behind the curve of the ship. I turned in the opposite direction and moved out.

"I'm latching to my next rung and unlatching from this one," Sam announced. I watched and made sure he followed the security protocol. Then I made a similar announcement and pulled myself forward.

Sam made faster progress. "Sam, wait up," I called on the radio. "I'm not supposed to use my bandaged wrist. I have to do everything one-handedly."

It took a few minutes to reach the edge where the hull started curving upward. Helga and Celina, off to our right, had already rounded the bend.

"Just a bit farther and we'll be in complete shadow," I heard Celina say.

She was right. Three rungs later Sam and I paused and looked around. Other than the bit of hull lit by my forehead lamp, I saw nothing. Only darkness. Not even stars. "The sky is completely black!" I exclaimed.

"Wait a couple of minutes and let your eyes adjust," Dr. Esther suggested.

I turned off my lamp and saw Sam and the girls do the same. The bit of hull I had been watching disappeared. Nothing but pure cold darkness remained. We waited in pitch-black emptiness, holding ladder rungs we could not see. I knew the rungs were freezing cold when shielded from sunlight, but I felt nothing through the insulated gloves and boots. We passed a minute in eerie, lonely silence. I listened to my own rhythmic breathing. "This is a little scary," I whispered. I heard Helga giggle and whisper back, "Just a bit more waiting." Another minute passed, and another. Then, gradually, the blackness started changing. A spark appeared above, then a pinpoint of light, then a dozen pinpoints, then hundreds. I watched in wonderment as the starfield opened up before me.

"Look at those stars!" Celina exclaimed.

"It is amazing! *Ik ben sprakeloos*," her sister added.

Sam said, "This is disconcerting. When we were last outside, Earth was nearby. Now there's nothing. Really nothing. We are *so* in the middle of nowhere!"

Nowhere was becoming very interesting, though, as my eyes continued to adjust to the darkness. I could see thousands of stars and galaxies and nebulae. Nothing sparkled, there being no atmosphere to scatter light, but a palette of colors appeared: red, crimson, yellow, gold, orange, even some bluishness. Psalm 104 came to mind, as it had four months earlier, when we had been spacewalking in low Earth orbit. "*Ma rabu ma'asecha Hashem*," I recited in Hebrew, "How numerous are your creations, O L-rd!" At a loss for any other words, I repeated the same verse over and over. But then I was speechless again, as I beheld the amazing, exquisite, still-expanding view.

A voice on the radio interrupted my reverie. "Time to come back in!"

"Dr. Esther, can't we have just a few more minutes?" I asked. "My eyes have only begun adjusting."

"And we haven't even started playing catch with the baseball!" Sam added. I imagined a twinkle in his eye.

"Cute, Sam. No, guys, head back immediately; we need to follow the captain's rules. Otherwise he'll never agree to another spacewalk."

"You make Pa sound so strict," Helga said, chuckling. "Maybe he will not agree to another spacewalk, but maybe he will; who knows?" But she was first to switch on her forehead lamp and turn to head back in.

Ten minutes later, all four of us having carefully followed the security protocol, we were safely back in the airlock, followed closely by Dr. Esther, who had waited outside for us the whole time. Boris floated over and sealed the hatch. As the airlock began to fill with air, we doffed, folded and stowed our Mylar suits. Then we hovered in our fleximets until the room fully pressurized.

"Thank you for waiting so patiently, Mom," Sam said as soon as he had removed and folded his fleximet.

"And you, too, Boris," I added, folding my own helmet. Boris was busy opening the inner hatch, but he turned to me and nodded.

The bottom of the hatch had barely cleared the floor above, when the alarming sound of screaming voices rent the airlock's tranquility. I took a startled breath.

"On my ship? You insolent fool! You dare, on my ship!" It was the captain, and he was livid.

"Leave me alone! Let go of me! What did I do to you?"

I looked at Dr. Esther questioningly, but her face showed the same bewilderment I was feeling. I pushed myself up through the hatch and followed the voices.

"You lit a fire – an open flame! You endangered our lives! You threatened the mission!"

Another shout, something in German. Then, hissing, "there was no danger! Get out of my way!" It was Denver, quarreling with Captain Becker. My stomach twisted; I was afraid for my friend. Never, since joining the Murke-Berger program, had I heard shouts like these. The voices were upstairs, so I launched myself across the room toward the stairwell. Sam followed close behind.

"You will not tell *me* there was no danger!"

As I emerged from the stairwell onto my own Green Level, I saw Captain Becker, by our bathroom door, seize Denver's arms and lean into his face. The captain's neck and cheeks were red with fury as he yelled at my roommate. My heart pounded. What if it had been me there in his place? "You lit a flame," the captain said, more quietly but more furiously. "You nearly murdered all of us – every one of us on my ship! My ship! And for what? To smoke a forbidden drug!" He shook Denver roughly. "You are a mortal danger to us all!" He took a breath and lowered his voice, but did not release my friend. "You ought to be punished for attempted murder!"

Dr. Jhonathan appeared, having rushed downstairs. The captain noticed him and caught his eye. They nodded to each other; then the captain turned back to glare at Denver.

Dr. Jhonathan spoke. "Dietrich, please, wait." He took Denver's hand and pulled him away. "Let's deal with this calmly."

Denver looked at Dr. Jhonathan imploringly. Poor Denver: his bandages had come off, revealing a streaked and red-scabbed nose. Black and blue bruise marks spread under his eyes and across both cheeks. He must have been in great pain.

"Denver will indeed need to be punished," Dr. Jhonathan continued, coolly concurring. "He has endangered our lives." Denver's jaw dropped and his eyes widened with shock as he stared at his new accuser; I think he had been expecting support. "But being screamed at is not the punishment he deserves."

Captain Becker released his grip and pushed Denver away. He took another deep breath. Releasing the air slowly through pursed lips, anger still in his eyes, he said "you are correct." He looked around the room. Following his gaze, I noticed that nearly everybody had gathered. Meital and my mother perched behind Dr. Jhonathan; Ruby and the other girls hovered above the couch at the end of the room; Dr. Esther and the Bouchets had squeezed in by the kitchen. But Omar and the Radechov brothers were absent. Wisely, it seemed, they had avoided getting involved.

The captain winced in pain and reached back to rub his lower spine. He caught Dr. Jhonathan's eye again before addressing Denver. Teeth clenched, he spoke coldly. "The accepted punishment for endangering our lives and the mission is the airlock." He raised his eyes to meet Denver's, and his fury melted to sadness. "Disembarking the ship permanently."

There were gasps from around the room. Denver's face – the parts that were not black, blue or red – turned white with dread. "What?" he howled, his expression incredulous. "You cannot do that to me!"

"You would have one full oxypack, with two hours of air."

"No! It is against the Murke-Berger Foundation's rules," Denver protested, eyes filling with tears.

I myself ought to have screamed an objection, but I froze in shock as I watched my friend beg for his life.

"There is no Foundation out here. There is only my ship, and I am captain." He looked around the room at stunned, silent faces. "Day-to-day, living our routines, we forget that we have embarked on an exceedingly dangerous journey. Ultimately, I alone hold overall responsibility for the lives of everyone on board. That makes me the Law here. I alone must determine what is necessary to protect our lives and the mission."

He was not saying anything we did not already know, but my perspective of the mission's structure shifted subtly. Aside from G-d, it was Captain Becker who held the keys to our lives, and to our deaths, like an absolute monarch of ancient times. On *Providence* he was king.

Denver stood, frozen with trepidation, tears streaming from his eyes.

The captain again looked to Dr. Jhonathan and waited for him to speak.

"Dietrich, in my role as Chief Officer, I request that you defer your decision. Let's hold a trial. Denver deserves a chance to defend himself."

"I can assure you," he answered coolly, "that even in a trial I would reach the same judgment."

"Then you should not be the judge," Dr. Louis interrupted, pushing past me to hover opposite the captain and Dr. Jhonathan. "Appoint one of us as judge."

Denver looked at him gratefully. He blinked away tears.

"And let us appoint a defense attorney. Who would defend Denver?"

Meital spoke loudly. "I volunteer to defend Denver." She pushed up toward the ceiling so that everyone would see her. "I don't want anything to happen to him. We adopted him as our brother!"

My mother smiled sadly. "Meital, you are sweet to volunteer, but it should be an adult. I'll defend him." Then she added, "– as his adoptive mother."

Dr. Jhonathan turned to her. "Dana, you would do a fine job, I am sure. But I suspect there's more to Denver's situation than just the drugs, and I want to work with him to see if we can reach some understanding. I've become close to him, teaching him several courses over the past months, and may have insight. Would you agree that I defend him?"

She nodded.

"Jhonathan will be the defense advocate," Captain Becker announced. "Louis, since you suggested the trial, you shall be judge."

"Who will play the role of prosecutor?"

"That will be me, of course," the captain said. "If I am not decreeing Denver's guilt, I will at least be responsible for arguing it, lest one of you have to."

"We will decide nothing in haste tonight," Dr. Louis said. "We will hold the trial tomorrow afternoon. We will convene at 15:00."

"On Yellow Level," Captain Becker added. "In my living room."

"Please, everyone, back to your apartments and rooms. Jhonathan, work with Denver to prepare a defense. Dietrich, please gather and organize your evidence."

"I am sure that Denver will hand over all of the marijuana that he apparently has stashed somewhere. But I will search his room now anyway."

"No!" Denver yelled. "You cannot do that!"

"I certainly can," the captain said, eyes narrowed as he stared at Denver and rubbed his back again. "Michael, stay outside here with your friend until I have finished."

*   *   *

Tuesday, January 30th, 2029 15:00

Butterflies tingled in my stomach as I waited on the Yellow-Level living room couch. Gravity had returned overnight as *Providence* and *Mars Hope* slowly spun back up to two and a half revolutions per minute. Still, I felt light, possibly because Yellow Level, at the top of the habitat, had the least gravity of all the levels, but more likely because of my nervousness. I had been called as a witness in Denver's trial. Captain Becker suspected that I knew more about Denver's illicit activities than I let on. Dr. Jhonathan, by contrast, thought I could offer exculpatory testimony, and they both had informed me that they would call me to the witness chair. The other witnesses, Boris and Celina, sat next to me on the couch. Boris was to be called to testify against Denver. Celina would be a witness for the defense.

Dr. Louis – now Judge Louis – sat at the head of the table at the far end of the room. Captain Becker sat to his left, sitting twisted in his chair, suffering from his injury. Denver and Dr. Jhonathan had their backs to us at the near end of the table.

Judge Louis looked to the captain and nodded, "you may begin."

Captain Becker spoke. "I hereby accuse Denver König of three crimes. First, he lit an open flame on board the ship, endangering the lives of all on board. Second, he ingested marijuana, which is a drug forbidden by the Murke-Berger Foundation. Marijuana is doubly forbidden: the Foundation forbids the substance on board its ships and habitats, and forbids the substance to participants in its programs."

"That is two counts, or three?"

"Three: endangering the mission and the lives of the fliers, ingesting marijuana on board a Murke-Berger vessel, and ingesting marijuana as a Murke-Berger employee and mission participant."

"Okay. Please call your first witness."

"I'll be the first witness."

"Objection," Dr. Jhonathan said, rising from his seat. "The prosecutor cannot be a witness."

Captain Becker looked at him. "I'm sorry, Jhonathan, but I shall speak. I grant myself the prerogative."

He turned back to Judge Louis and leaned forward. But he winced in pain, and leaned back again. "Yesterday afternoon, at approximately 17:30, I found Denver in the Green-Level bathroom, smoking a cigarette. There was an open flame – I saw it. Later we examined the cigarette and found it to be composed of marijuana."

"Isn't the bathroom a private space?"

"There had been suspicions that Denver was behaving illicitly in there. When he entered the bathroom yesterday afternoon, I was informed, and went down to check. I knocked on the door and entered, and discovered that the suspicions were correct."

"Ignoring for the moment the question of illegal searches –"

"There is no such thing as an illegal search aboard my ship. I may search anywhere at any time."

"Okay," Judge Louis said. "But you said there were suspicions. Who suspected, who informed you, and what did they suspect?"

"I would prefer not to identify my informant. Several weeks ago, one of our participants – an adult – told me that they suspected someone was smoking in the bathroom. They were perplexed, because the signs appeared only occasionally. Days would go by with nothing suspicious, then the signs would appear again."

"What type of signs? What exactly caused the suspicions?"

"Certain fleeting smells. Also, patterns of bathroom usage, such as too much time – slightly too much – spent there. Nothing definitive, but, my informant said, enough to trigger intuitive suspicion. Normally I would have told them to ignore the signs. In my experience, trusting teenagers, sometimes even naïvely, encourages them to work to earn that trust. But in this case the allegations of open flames on board were too serious to ignore."

My butterflies pounded against the walls of my stomach. I had a strong suspicion about who the informant was, and the idea made me nauseous.

"And yet you accused nobody until yesterday."

"As I said, the signs were only occasional until this past week. But in the days since the tether broke, my informant told me, the smells became more frequent. Ultimately, suspicions rested on Denver. We agreed that I would check on him when he next entered the bathroom, if he stayed longer than expected."

Now I was sure: my mother was the informant. For weeks she had been paying a bit too much attention to our bathroom use. My poor mother! First to suspect Denver, whom she had undertaken to love as her own son, and then to have to report him to the captain. How could she face him again?

"I was called downstairs, I entered the bathroom, I saw the lit cigarette in his hand."

And yet, I thought, Denver had eluded her for weeks. I felt a pang of pride for my friend, in a strange, rebellious way. To get away with something so forbidden, for so long, even while under suspicion!

"Michael, please take the witness stand," Judge Louis said, interrupting my thoughts. The butterflies went wild. Now was the very wrong time to take pride in insubordination. I stood, shaking slightly, and approached the far end of the table. I sat down next to

Judge Louis, facing Denver and Dr. Jhonathan across the length of the table. Denver caught my eye and stared, but I looked away, uncomfortable about what I might have to say.

Captain Becker waved to get my attention, then spoke gently, without leaning forward. "Michael, I imagine it may be unpleasant to talk about your friend, but the alleged infraction is too grave to ignore. Please tell us anything suspicious you have noticed in Denver's behavior, or in your bedroom, or in the bathroom, over the past weeks."

"Uh, I don't know what to say." The question was not fair. Lots of things could be suspicious – anything, really – if you considered them from a suspicious point of view.

Captain Becker watched me intently.

"There was this smell. In the bathroom. Sometimes."

"Go on, please."

"I first noticed it, I don't know when exactly, a couple of months ago. A sweet, smoky smell. I guess now, in retrospect, it could have been marijuana. I'm not sure." I frowned embarrassedly. "I'm not an expert."

"I'm glad to hear that," he said drolly. "Did you tell anyone about the smell?"

"Yes. I mentioned it to Denver, because he is responsible for the air systems. He said he would check on it. Later, he told me that the air systems were fine and there was nothing to be worried about."

"Denver checked the air systems." He stroked his chin. "Very interesting. I will call Boris next, to testify about the air filters. Michael, did you mention the smell to any adults? To your mother?"

"No, not that I recall. I didn't think it was that serious."

The captain went on to probe me about Denver's behavior in our room and in classes, but I had little more to add and he relented. Then Judge Louis called Dr. Jhonathan to cross-examine me.

"Michael, please describe Denver's relationship with you over the past months. Have you noticed any changes?"

I studied the ceiling. My bandaged wrist was aching. "Yes, now that you mention it, there has been a change." I looked down toward Denver. "All last year at Altiplano, and at the beginning of the flight, we talked a lot, laughed a lot, and spent a lot of time together. But less, recently. He spends more time alone. Like he lost interest in the friendship."

Denver's eyes widened, over his awful bruised cheeks, as he looked at me quizzically and protested. "Michael, that is not true. You are my best friend."

I forced a smile. "I'm glad you say so. But you don't seem to participate as much. Like at Thanksgiving. You didn't want to join the festive meal."

"That was months ago. What does that have to do with anything?"

"Denver, please let Michael speak."

"But it's been the same since, Denver." I shrugged. "Besides class, you barely hang out with us, except for a couple of times you played the guitar."

His eyes drooped in misery at the mention of his guitar.

I turned back to Dr. Jhonathan. "That's all. I love Denver. It just seems that he is more withdrawn recently."

"Withdrawn because he is under the influence of drugs?"

"No, that's not what I mean. Withdrawn emotionally. Like he is not happy. Like he is struggling with personal feelings."

"And do you have any insights into what he might be struggling with?"

I shifted uncomfortably. "Those are questions for Denver, please. I do not want to speak for his feelings."

"Thank you, Michael," Dr. Jhonathan said. "No more questions."

Boris was called to the witness chair and I returned to the couch. Captain Becker began his questioning.

"Boris, would you consider yourself an expert on spacecraft air-processing systems?"

"Yes, Captain, though of course many on board are more expert than I. As you know, my main work experience was designing carbon dioxide filtration systems. After I received my Aerospace Engineering degree, I worked at *Voronezhskiy Kislorod* for three years."

"Please describe the dangers of open flames on board."

"Flames, of course, can be dangerous in any environment. In *Providence's* atmosphere, flames are especially dangerous, due to the low buffer-to-oxygen ratio."

"Please explain."

"The air processors maintain forty-five percent oxygen against fifty-five percent buffer gases, nitrogen and argon. That is a one point two ratio, compared to the Earth's three point seven five ratio between buffer gases and oxygen. Due to the high proportion of oxygen, flash fires are more likely than on Earth."

"There were never any flash fires!" Denver exclaimed. "That is ridiculous."

"Denver," Judge Louis said patiently, "please control your outbursts."

"One risk," Boris continued, "is that an air system malfunction could cause the ratio to drop. In other words, if the proportion of oxygen increased unexpectedly, even a spark could cause a flash fire. But besides that, we all know" – he stared at Denver for a moment – "that there are flammable materials on board, and even the remotest chance of a fire must be avoided. Life-support systems could be destroyed." He paused, perhaps imagining the disaster he was describing. "I do not think anybody would notice, though, because toxic fumes would kill us first."

"Thank you for that graphic explanation. Now I would like to establish that Denver has been smoking for quite a while, and did not start just yesterday. Boris, you are responsible for the daily inspections of the air-processing systems, is that right?"

"Yes," Boris answered, a neutral expression on his face. "Denver and I were assigned responsibility, under Claudine's supervision."

"If something burns on the ship – and does not cause a fire – are the air filters capable of filtering out the smoke?"

"Yes, of course. The HEPA filters can filter out even microscopic dust particles. Large particles, like tar and ash from burning organics, certainly get filtered."

"When you inspect the filters, are pollutants like tar and ash noticeable?"

"Very much so. Smoke, tar, ash, pollen from the greenhouses, skin and hair shedding, all of these are not only apparent; they can clog the filters. This is why we clean them regularly."

"Can you tell the difference between substances? Specifically, would you notice that something had burnt?"

"I think so. Different types of contaminants appear differently in the filters. Tar and ash are so unusual that we would notice them immediately. We would probably smell them when checking the filters."

Captain Becker nodded. "I thought so. So, when did you first notice them?"

My eyes darted back and forth between prosecutor and witness. The question was incriminating, not just to Denver, but to Boris, too, if he had failed to report evidence.

Unexpectedly, Boris shook his head. "I never noticed any tar, ash, or any other evidence of smoke or burning."

"Never noticed?" The captain raised his eyebrows. "But you just said that one would notice immediately. How is that possible? Was there another way for Denver to clean the air before it reached the filters?"

"No." Boris narrowed his eyes as he considered his words, "I am guessing that Denver smoked directly above the toilet, always on Green Level. The toilet is the main air intake to the Green-Level air processor. Its vacuum fan is always running."

"So, the smoke should have been apparent on the filters."

"Yes, but only on Green Level. Unless the computer diverts the air pipes, which it would do only in case of a failure, that air goes only to the Green-Level system."

Dr. Louis suppressed a smile as he stared at Denver, his expression one of amazement. *"Brillant. Diabolique!"* He turned to Boris. "Denver was responsible for Green-Level air systems inspections, was he not?"

"Yes. From the beginning of the trip, we divided the levels: I took Yellow and Pink; Denver the bottom two floors."

Captain Becker, astonished, asked, "So you have never inspected the Green-Level filters?"

"Not for several months, Captain. I trusted Denver's work." Face still neutral, he looked across at Denver. "Perhaps I was mistaken."

"Perhaps you were. It seems, however, that I have erred, allowing, on my ship, a situation where a single person can endanger the mission while hiding all evidence. It was a mistake to assign Denver to the air systems. Jhonathan, please remind me to rearrange those assignments as soon as we finish here."

Dr. Jhonathan nodded, then began Boris's cross-examination. It was short: everything interesting had already been said. He then called Celina to the stand to ask about her friendship with Denver. Apparently the two had become close – had I not noticed? – because she was able to describe Denver's conflicted feelings.

"Pa, please give Denver a break," she said, facing her father. "You know his family situation. But did you know that he has received only one message from his mother since departure? And nothing from his father. Not even a birthday card – his birthday is Saturday – at least not yet. Is it surprising that he is conflicted?"

Captain Becker skipped cross-examining his daughter. All witnesses having testified, Judge Louis called for closing arguments, prosecution first. Boris headed downstairs, but Celina and I stayed, anxious to hear the verdict.

"We have demonstrated that Denver König is guilty of three crimes," the captain summarized. "First and second, he smuggled on board and consumed a substance that is explicitly banned by Murke-Berger Foundation rules. This is forbidden twice, first because Denver is a Murke-Berger employee and participant, and second, because he did this on board a Murke-Berger vessel. We have presented the evidence to the court: fifteen grams of marijuana confiscated from a drawer under Denver's bunk.

"Third, in consuming the forbidden substance, Denver created an open flame aboard the ship. I witnessed the flame myself. Although we have presented evidence, at least circumstantial, that Denver committed this same life-threatening violation multiple times, even just one open flame would warrant the severest of punishments.

"Denver has demonstrated a wanton disregard for his own safety and for that of the entire crew on board. As a graduate of the Murke-Berger preparatory program, Denver is well aware of the dangers of spaceflight on board Murke-Berger craft, and well aware of his own responsibilities as a participant. He cannot claim he did not know the severity of his actions. Furthermore, we have demonstrated a general pattern of antisocial behavior. Denver has withdrawn from social activities, has taken less interest in the well-being of his companions, and has let personal problems affect his behavior in critical and dangerous ways. His transgression was not the result of a one-time uncontrolled compulsion, but rather a planned, intentional act, performed in full awareness of, and complete lack of concern for, its inherent hazards."

He concluded, "The severest punishment is warranted."

"Thank you, Dietrich," Judge Louis said. "Jhonathan, please summarize your defense."

Dr. Jhonathan rose and rested his hand on Denver's shoulder. "Denver is a troubled youth. He is suffering emotionally, lonely and distressed. We ought to have noticed the severity of his misery. I myself should have noticed. Here we have a young man who separated from his family to join a pioneering mission on his own. At Altiplano, he adequately demonstrated that he has the intellectual maturity required for the journey. But did we in the Foundation endeavor to determine that he has the requisite emotional maturity? Is it realistic to expect that any adolescent be emotionally prepared for the stresses of such a mission?

"Dietrich, you described Denver's social withdrawal as antisocial. I disagree: his withdrawal is an obvious sign of depression. His drug use was an ill-advised attempt at self-medication – something that is, tragically, common among depressed Earth-dwelling youth. Should we be surprised to find it here, too? Look at the bruises on his face: it is obvious that he is in physical pain and has been since the tether loss. Is it surprising he started using his stash of drugs more frequently, to dull the pain?"

Denver sat up straight in his chair and looked around, a hopeful expression on his face for the first time since the beginning of the trial.

"Smuggling marijuana aboard the ship was a gravely poor decision, and Denver will need to suffer the consequences. Smoking, however, was a result of distress, and we ought to consider that in determining the gravity of his offense. And in selecting a punishment."

"Thank you, Jhonathan," Judge Louis said, turning to face the accused. "Denver, we will, in a moment, step out, to consider our decision. Before we do so, would you like to say anything? To admit your guilt, perhaps?"

Denver looked back and forth from Dr. Louis to Dr. Jhonathan and nodded. "Okay. Do I have to stand up?"

"If you want, you may."

Denver stood and again looked uneasily at Dr. Louis, the captain, and Dr. Jhonathan, in turn, before beginning to speak. "You all do not understand. Other than Dr. Jhonathan; maybe he understands a little. I did not do anything –" He stopped mid-sentence and looked around again, reconsidering his words.

The butterflies were active again in my stomach: I felt my friend's nervousness.

"Dr. Louis," he began again, "there was never any danger. Boris talked about very scary scenarios, but the reality was nothing like he described. I took every safety precaution. I always held the cigarettes directly above the toilet air intake. All ashes went straight into a non-flammable apparatus, and the vacuum airstream extinguished them instantly."

I felt queasy. I wanted to grab Denver's arm and tell him to stop talking, that he was only hurting his case.

"Boris talked about flash fires, but that was impossible! I am not stupid: I never used my 'organics' without first making sure oxygen levels were normal. You can blame me for behaving in a non-standard way, not exactly according to Murke-Berger rules, but I resent that you all are exaggerating to make it sound worse than it was."

Celina buried her face in her hands and shook her head silently.

"I'm sorry," Denver said, "that this has turned into such a big deal. I promise I will not smoke again on board. The captain took away everything I had, so you do not have to worry." He paused and looked around again. "That is enough punishment. Please do not punish me more than that. It would not be fair." He sat down.

Judge Louis, staring at Denver, sighed. "I will return in a few minutes with a decision." He stood up. "Dietrich and Jhonathan, will you join me?"

The three retired to the Beckers' master bedroom, while Celina and I waited nervously with Denver. None of us spoke. There was no way they were not going to punish Denver, and I was afraid. What would I do without my friend and roommate? If they gave him the airlock – a horrible euphemism for pushing someone out into space to die – how could I ever face Captain Becker again? How would I face any of the adults? How would I face myself, always wondering whether I could have saved my friend by protesting more vehemently?

And what about me? What if I lost control at some point and did something wrong? Would they kill me, too? We all knew all the Foundation's rules, having studied them in Civics classes during our year at Altiplano Mexicano, but there and then it was all theoretical. The Foundation had a lot of rules. What if I inadvertently forgot one or two? In real life, would they go ahead and execute us, one by one?

My increasingly panicked reverie was interrupted when Dr. Louis entered the room, accompanied by the others. Donning his judgelike demeanor, he sat again at his place.

He faced Denver with a stern expression. "Denver, you have shown exceptionally poor judgment. You knew that marijuana was forbidden, yet you smuggled it on board. You knew it was exceedingly dangerous, yet you smoked it, apparently repeatedly. I grant that you took care to smoke in the safest way, but I disagree that doing so made it safe. I grudgingly admit that your ingenuity impresses me, misguided as it was. It was similarly ingenious of you to select the particular air system whose filters you yourself would clean."

Denver's lips curled ever so slightly.

"Do not misunderstand me. I am not praising your poor, illicit, dangerous choices. Rather, I am recognizing that you have a special ability to solve complex problems. I entreat you to put your skills to productive, safe use as we continue our journey, and, more so, as we build our settlement on Mars. I implore you to do so: please, Denver, direct your efforts toward building, not endangering."

Realizing I had been holding my breath, I exhaled in relief: thank G-d they were not going to kill my friend.

"I find you guilty on all three counts. You ingested a forbidden substance on board a Murke-Berger vessel, doing so as a Murke-Berger employee; furthermore, you created an open flame in the vessel's high-oxygen environment. Thus, I find that Captain Becker's initial judgment was correct."

Denver's smile disappeared. He froze in his seat and stared at Dr. Louis. Judge Louis stared back.

"Breathe easy, Denver. The captain's suggestion notwithstanding, I will not sentence you to the airlock. You are too important to the mission. You are too important to your friends, to your family here – we are your family – to our future society. You will go on to build great things on Mars, G-d willing: a family, children, grandchildren; buildings, farms, towns, factories; new solutions to problems that arise. Choose well, and you are set to be a crucial pioneer in the establishment of humanity's new branch. Choose well, and you will be a blessing for us.

"Denver, you did indeed put all of us, including my own little girls, in mortal danger. Nevertheless, I have a hundred reasons to reject severe punishment. We do not want to establish a regime of fear. We do not want to traumatize your friends. We do not want to diminish our numbers: the journey itself threatens to take our lives, and does not need our own foolhardy contribution. Most important, whether or not you agree with the phrasing, you are a creation in G-d's image, and we will not take away the life that He has given you.

"Nevertheless, your punishment will be harsh. For endangering our lives and the mission by lighting an open flame, I sentence you to four hours in the stockade. You will stand, immobile, in your Green-Level living room, your wrists latched to the wall. This will happen by the end of this week, but we will let you choose the day. I sentence you with a heavy heart, and wish it were not necessary. But it is necessary, given your defiant attitude and the need to deter future dangerous behavior. In addition, you will begin regular psychological counseling. I recommend Jhonathan for the task, but you may pick the adult with whom you feel most comfortable."

Air

Wednesday, January 31st, 2029 09:00

"Michael, how is your arm? Let us take a look." Dr. Claudine lifted my bandaged wrist and poked at it. "Does this hurt? What about here?"

I had been instructed to come downstairs to meet Dr. Claudine right after breakfast Wednesday morning. Captain Becker had wasted no time after the trial in rescinding Denver's responsibility for the air systems. Pulling me aside, he informed me that, henceforth, I would work with Boris to maintain and oversee the habitat's air systems, while Denver would take over my daily inspections of the water and waste-processing systems. "You will meet with Claudine tomorrow morning on Mauve level, promptly at 09:00, to learn everything about your new task."

Dr. Claudine seemed more interested in how I was healing. "Can you bend your hand up? Does that hurt?"

Only after she was convinced that everything was healing as expected did she scratch her forehead and say, "Why are you here? Oh yes, to learn about the air filters. Come over here."

I followed her to a niche behind the stairwell. On the upper three levels this same space was the entrance to the staircase going down, but the Bouchets' Mauve level was the bottom of the habitat, above only the airlock, and there was no staircase to the airlock. A small closet occupied the bottom of the stairwell. To its right, behind the niche, was a stack of complex machinery. This, I knew, was the same on all four levels; we saw the machinery every time we went up or down a staircase.

"The air-processing systems," Dr. Claudine said, pointing. I knew that, too, though I had never taken a closer look. "Most of the machinery is behind the stairwell; here all you can see are the controls and the filter slots." She pointed to a row of hand-sized vertical handles, just below eye level. "Each handle pulls out one of the filters. Your main job, besides monitoring the results of continual diagnostics tests, will be to examine every filter each day. We will show you how to clean the filters, and we will discuss how you will know if a filter needs to be replaced. But first" – she turned around and pushed me out of the niche – "some theory."

On any of the upstairs levels we would have sat at the dining table, but the Mauve-Level table was folded and stowed. The hatch to the airlock, in the floor at the end of the living room, was open, its round door hinged upward. Meital and Ruby always left the hatch open while they tended to the birds that lived in the airlock. They were down there now, I knew, because I could hear their voices, mingled with the chickens' clucking and the parakeets' chirping.

Dr. Claudine sat me down on the couch. "Look here," she said, as she settled next to me and shifted into a comfortable position. She pulled up a schematic on her datapad. Pointing to three arrows in the upper-left corner, she said, "This shows the path of the air through the filtration systems. These represent the dirty air – that is, all the air in the habitat. There are three intakes. One is in the bathroom, in the toilet; the second, a smaller one, is in the kitchen ceiling. The third takes gases released during the bathroom waste-processing cycle. All lead here" – she pointed to a series of connected rectangles – "to the filters."

"Why are there so many filters?" This was going to be more complicated than the water systems.

"Each HEPA filter – a 'High Efficiency Particulate Arrestor' – is designed for particles of a different size. The first filter traps large particles such as skin cells and pollen from the plants. The second traps large dust particles; the third smaller particles such as spores and mycotoxins, and so on through all five. The finest filter traps large organic molecules."

"And I need to check all these filters?"

"Yes, and clean them regularly." She pointed back to the schematic. "After it passes through the HEPA filters, the air continues through an activated carbon filter."

"How do we clean that?"

"You do not have to. The computer executes a process that heats the carbon until trapped pollutant molecules are released and vented."

"Vented to space?"

"Yes. Where else could they go?" She looked at me with narrowed eyes. "Then, after the activated carbon" – she was again pointing to the schematic – "the air passes through a series of zeolite scrubbers."

"Zeolites? I remember learning something about that last year, but I forget the details."

Dr. Claudine turned to me again. I looked away, avoiding those dark brown eyes and the inevitable blushing that eye contact with her would cause me. "Zeolites are porous materials that adsorb various gases. The most important ones adsorb carbon dioxide, but we have others for removing methane, sulfur dioxide, ammonia and other poisonous gases."

"How do we clean those?" I concentrated my gaze on the diagram.

"That is also automatic: when necessary, you will initiate heating processes that will flush out the gases."

"Are they vented, too?"

"Most. But let us talk about the carbon dioxide process." She pointed to the screen. "Carbon dioxide contains oxygen, lots of it, and we do not want to waste it."

"Don't the plants in the greenhouses solve that for us? Extracting oxygen from carbon dioxide?"

"Yes, the plants help a bit," she said, looking up from the datapad, "but they convert only a tiny percentage of the carbon dioxide the twenty-one of us exhale. We would need a hundred times more plants to replace our machinery."

She looked back down. "The computer executes a complex process each night. First, it heats the carbon dioxide zeolites to release the gas." She pointed to a box on the diagram. "Some of the carbon dioxide is saved, pumped into small tanks." Arrows pointed from the box to several small cylinders. "You will exchange tanks, when necessary, to recharge the laundry machines."

That made sense, because we used supercritical pressurized carbon dioxide instead of water to launder our clothes, and the gas that escaped during each cycle would need to be replaced. "We also use carbon dioxide in the kitchens to make soda water," I pointed out. "Will I need to recharge the soda machines, too?"

"Yes, swap canisters when necessary." Pointing to a large circle in the center of the screen, she continued, "Next, the rest of the carbon dioxide is processed to extract oxygen, using the reverse water-gas shift reaction." She tapped the circle and a document opened, describing a chemical reaction:

$$H_2 + CO_2 \rightarrow CO + H_2O$$

She looked at me again. "Is it clear?"

"We learned about this in chemistry last year. We add hydrogen gas to carbon dioxide in the presence of a copper-based catalyst and it converts to water and carbon monoxide."

"It is a bit more complicated than that. We are fortunate to have quite advanced equipment on board, including the most advanced self-renewing catalysts. But essentially you are correct."

"Do I remember correctly that the reaction is exothermic?"

"No, you do not. The water-gas shift reaction releases energy, but this is the *reverse* water-gas reaction, which is endothermic: it requires heat. Our reactor heats the gases to seven hundred degrees. You'll oversee the process to make sure it runs as required."

I looked back at the datapad, where an arrow showed the carbon monoxide being sent overboard, and pointed at that part of the diagram. "Isn't this a waste? Carbon monoxide is half oxygen. Why do we waste half the oxygen?"

Dr. Claudine smiled at me approvingly. I looked away. "Very good observation, Michael. We do recover only half of the used oxygen and expel the other half. It seems like a waste, but the energy cost of separating the second oxygen atom, from carbon monoxide, is so much more than the cost of separating the first atom from carbon dioxide, that it is just not worth the effort."

"Will we run out of oxygen?"

"No, because we replace the lost oxygen from our water supply. We use electrolysis to separate the water into oxygen and hydrogen."

"So we'll run out of water?"

"No." Dr. Claudine laughed. "Over the course of ten months, we convert around seven cubic meters of water to oxygen. That will leave us forty-three cubic meters, most of which we will burn anyway as we prepare for Mars entry."

"What about the water's hydrogen?" I began to ask, but Boris emerged from the stairwell at that moment, adjusting hair he did not have.

"Claudine, I have finished inspections and procedures on all four levels."

"Excellent, Boris," she answered. "Would you mind taking over with Michael, so I can prepare my lessons? We have reviewed the process. Please show him how to examine the filters." She gathered her datapad and stood to leave.

As she crossed the room, I watched her gait, which seemed unusual. Her belly was more rounded than before. Was Dr. Claudine indeed pregnant? That made no sense, I thought, because Foundation rules absolutely forbade in-transit pregnancies, not only because we had no facilities for neonatal care, but also because nobody knew how interplanetary radiation would affect fetal development.

"Come over here, Michael," Boris was saying. "I will show you how to clean the filters."

Back in the niche behind the stairwell, Boris pressed a switch labeled "Disengage," and a series of green LEDs went out. "I've temporarily stopped air processing on this level. You can do it on your datapad, in the Air Systems program, but I think this is easier." He reached for the first filter handle and pulled at it firmly. The thin metal plate that the handle attached to disengaged from the air-processing unit. Behind it trailed the filter, a long, flexible, whitish plastic rectangle that encased what looked like a very fine sieve. He held it up and stretched it flat, delicately clutching the far end between his left thumb and index finger. It was as high as his hand, perhaps nine or ten centimeters, and twice as wide. "By the way," he was saying, "never try to pull out a filter before you turn off air processing. That would not be good. Make sure the green lights are off."

I nodded and leaned in to look more closely. "Wow, it looks clean. I was expecting it to be covered with dust or lint or grease or something."

"I cleaned this filter not half an hour ago. Too little time has passed for it to be noticeably dirty again. Look closely: this is an example of a clean filter. I will show you a dirty one in a moment." Turning back to the equipment, he said "Watch closely how to put it back." He meticulously inserted the filter's flexible end into the slot, then slowly fed the filter inward until the metal plate contacted the machinery wall. I heard a quiet snap.

"Now, the second filter," Boris said, looking at me. "I skipped it earlier, leaving it for you to practice. Grab the handle and pull it out. Gently."

I tentatively reached for the handle and tugged. Nothing happened.

Boris laughed. "Not quite so gently. Pull harder."

"It's my first time!" I protested, and tried again. I heard and felt a snap; then the filter came out easily.

"Hold it up so we can examine it."

As Boris had done, I clutched the end of the filter in my left hand, very gently, not just for the filter's sake, but because my hand was still bandaged and feeling weak. I stretched it out. This one was not white: a dark gray mat of fine lint covered it, end-to-end. "This needs to be cleaned, right? Can I just blow on it to get the dust off?"

Boris laughed again and shook his head incredulously. "What good would that do?"

"The filter would be clean, wouldn't it?"

"Think, Michael, think. Where would the dust go after you blew it off?"

"Back to the air processor ... and the same filter again. It was a stupid idea. That's why you are laughing at me."

"No," Boris said, "I laugh at the idea, not at you. Everyone makes the same mistake the first time. We are too used to Earth, which has excellent automatic air-processing systems. On Earth you can blow dust into the air, where it will blow away in the wind, and eventually settle, or be washed out by rain."

"Earth is amazing," I agreed. "Sometimes you have to leave to appreciate what you have."

"Now I have you talking in clichés. Great." He bent over and pointed to an open slot below the row of filters. "Look here. This is where the machinery 'blows on' the filter and removes its dust."

I knelt down, still comparing, in my mind, earth's automated systems to the ship's. "I hope it never rains inside the habitat," I mused.

"The chamber, Michael, the chamber." The horizontal opening Boris was pointing to, at knee level under the row of filters, was slightly wider than the filter slots above. Just inside the opening, two cylindrical brushes protruded from top and bottom. The bristles appeared very fine. "You will insert the filter gently, until the handle snaps shut against the panel." He waited while I did so. "Now, press that switch."

Letting go of the filter, I pressed the switch Boris indicated. A red LED lit. Nothing else happened for a moment – the computer was checking the pressure seal, I found out later – then a new whirring noise began, just barely audible over the blustering of the upstairs fans. The brushes had started spinning.

"The brushes you saw will move slowly down the length of the filter, freeing the dirt from the filter."

"Into the air?" I imagined a miniature dust-storm raging inside the chamber.

"Yes, into the air in the chamber. Then, when the brushes reach the end of the filter, the computer will open an aperture in the hull and the dusty air will flush out to space."

"Does that mean that we'll run out of air if we clean the filters too much?"

Boris shook his head, curled lips hinting at a smile. "I actually ran the calculations once. If we clean each filter every three or four days, then over the course of the trip, based on the size of the filter-brushing chamber, we will flush a quarter of a cubic meter of air, at ship standard pressure. That is a tiny part of the habitat's volume, easily replenished from the water and from the nitrogen tanks. I think we do not need to worry."

After thirty seconds the whirring stopped. A few moments later the red LED went out.

"That is all. Now, replace the filter and reengage the air systems."

Red Valley

I examined the filter as I pulled it from the chamber. It was clean and white. "That was easy," I thought out loud, as I stood and carefully reinserted the filter into its original slot, feeling for the snap.

"I am happy you think so, because you will be responsible for two levels' systems every day. Meet me on Mauve Level tomorrow – and every day – at nine o'clock. We will review the automated test results, execute zeolite purges, then split up to check and clean filters and gather carbon dioxide canisters. Everything is finished for today. Tomorrow, I'll walk you through the other processes."

* * *

Wednesday, January 31st, 2029 12:30

After my Talmud class with Sam and Rabbi Meyer, I joined my family for a typical lunch. Today's meal was simple: bread I had baked after yesterday's trial, together with a chickpea and barley salad my sisters had prepared. The salad was special because Shirel had added slices of a fresh carrot and pieces of a cucumber. Though the greenhouse fare was minimal, the variety it added made a big difference. Otherwise, eating would have become a tediously boring chore.

Denver sat down next to me without saying a word. He did not even look at me. At breakfast, too, he had ignored me. Turning to face him, I asked, "What's up? Denver, how are you feeling?"

He ignored me again.

"Denver," I tried once more, "talk to me, my friend. Did you decide which day to take the punishment?"

He turned and glared at me. "'Friend?' A friend would not betray me like you did. You could have helped me, but instead, because of you I am going to be punished." He appeared quite furious.

Stunned, I sputtered, "I betrayed you?" I looked around the table for support. "What are you talking about? I came to testify to help you, to try to get you off the hook!"

Denver looked like he was going to spit at me, but he turned back to stare at his food. Then, in a snide imitation of my voice, he muttered, "'He lost interest.' 'He is withdrawn.' 'Antisocial behavior.'"

"I never said anything about 'antisocial behavior!'" I protested angrily. "Captain Becker said that, not me."

Denver glared at me again, teeth clenched. "Based on what you told him." He poked at his salad. "To answer your question, yes, I decided which day to take the punishment you helped to cause. Tomorrow. Now please stop talking to me, Michael."

"That's not fair. My testimony did not hurt you – it helped you."

He ignored me.

My mother and sisters looked back and forth between us, shaking their heads, everybody at a loss for words. Shirel's eyes glistened with tears she held back. Nobody said another word until the time came to clear the table and wash the dishes.

* * *

Thursday, February 1st, 2029 11:00

"I can stand here without shackles!" Denver shouted, holding his hands behind his back. He stood just outside the door to the bedroom we shared.

"I am not going to argue with you," Captain Becker said in a strained voice. He stood face-to-face with Denver, but he was hunched slightly, leaning to his left, rubbing his back again. He clenched his teeth and squinted in pain. "Hold out your hands, because I am going to cuff them."

"No, please!" Denver protested. "I will stand still the whole time, without moving. Trust me; I promise!"

"That, Denver, is the problem. I do not trust you. You have lost my trust. Accepting the consequences of your choices will be the first step in regaining it."

"I accept the consequences, except for the shackles part. I will stand here until three o'clock, but I refuse to have you cuff me."

The captain turned to face the crowd that had gathered in our living room. "Everybody, please go back to your activities. This is difficult for all of us, and there is no need to embarrass Denver further."

"We're supposed to have Hebrew Literature class here now," Shirel said. "And I'm not here to embarrass Denver. I'm here to support him!"

"That is very kind of you, Shirel," Captain Becker said. She looked stunned by his harsh expression. "Even so, we will leave Denver alone for the duration of his punishment. Dana," he addressed my mother, "please find an alternate location for today's class."

Shirel reluctantly followed my mother to the stairwell, as did the others. I hung back. Denver's resentment notwithstanding, I was determined not to leave my friend alone this morning.

"Hands, Denver! I'm not going to ask again." The captain's face was turning red, his chest heaving with building rage.

"And if I refuse? What will you do?" Denver taunted defiantly.

"You bastard," Captain Becker spat. "Are you trying to force me to threaten you physically?"

"Yeah, threaten me. I have agreed to your punishment. I am standing here waiting to begin. Who is the bastard?"

Denver, not again! My heart beat heavily and I was sweating. I was watching my friend dig himself into a rut, yet again, and there was nothing I could do to save him from himself.

"Denver, listen carefully. I will say this just once," hissed the captain. "There is one lethal weapon on board *Providence*, a twenty-two-caliber air pistol that is programmed to recognize only my fingerprint, locked in a chest that only I can open. I endeavor to lead this mission by spoken instructions always; never by violence. But if you force me, I will engage physical force. You have a choice. Either allow me to cuff your hands because I command you to do so, or I will hold the pistol to your thigh, and then, I have no doubt, you will hold out your wrists eagerly."

"I do not believe you. You would never shoot me."

"Son, you err, and severely so. Given the choice of mutiny or physical force to prevent it, I will follow Foundation directives and choose force."

Denver finally did the smart thing. Reluctantly, he held out his hands. The captain, wincing again in pain, secured Denver's wrists in the handcuffs and snapped them shut.

A chain, attached to the cuffs, ended in a large, open ring. The captain grabbed this ring and reached up, dragging Denver's hands and spinning him around to face the doorpost. He secured the ring to a small hole through the edge of the wall that separated our bedroom from the girls'. The wall's edge was the doorpost for both

Air

rooms' sliding doors; it was also, it turned out, a stockade for corporal punishment. I wondered if that was by design. Did the Foundation's spacecraft architects plan for this situation? A macabre image appeared in my mind: a group of engineers seated at a round table, calmly sipping water as they discussed various ways fliers could punish each other.

Denver sobbed, interrupting my reverie. He now stood with his back to me, facing the edge of the wall between the doorways, hands shackled above his drooping head. Captain Becker had departed the room, leaving just the two of us. Though Denver was supposed to be alone during the punishment, the captain had ignored me on his way out. I walked, slowly, tentatively, around the table, and put my arm around Denver's shoulders.

"I'm sorry, Denver. I never wanted this to happen." I hugged him.

For a moment he stood still and did not resist. Then he turned his head and said softly, his voice a broken whisper, "Go to your class, Michael."

Talmud class, always challenging, was more difficult than usual. Today's text discussed whether a person may claim payment for injuries his animal sustained when in somebody else's property without permission. I mouthed the words, but my heart was elsewhere. How could I study enthusiastically on Pink Level while Denver stood shackled just below me on Green Level, almost directly under where I was sitting? I rubbed my wrist, which was hurting again, perhaps from my own injury, but perhaps in sympathy with Denver, whose wrists, I imagined, were chafing against his cuffs. I tried to focus on the gored bull the Talmud discussed, but all I felt was an emptiness in my own gut.

"He's going to be okay," Sam said, guessing my thoughts. "He's just standing still for a couple of hours."

"It bothers you, too, doesn't it?"

"Yes, of course it does. It could happen to any of us. I don't like the idea of punishment, but I understand the need. Don't you?"

"In my mind, yes. In my heart, I'm not sure Denver has the emotional strength at this point."

"You'd be surprised," Rabbi Meyer said. "Denver is extraordinarily strong. The fact that he chose to join us, even after his parents left the program, is proof. And the way he made the choice – I won't go into details, but I can tell you he is very special. I am confident that he will tap his emotional strength."

Shirel appeared unexpectedly, exiting the stairwell, followed closely by Susan. Anguish on her face, Shirel sobbed, "He's crying! It's awful! Denver won't stop weeping! Dr. Jhonathan, you have to stop the punishment now. It's not right!" Her eyes glistened.

"Shirel, please calm down. Denver crying is not a bad thing. It shows that the punishment is effective."

But tears rolled down her cheeks and she sobbed again. "Then it's enough already. Let him go."

Susan watched her friend silently, her expression neutral, unreadable.

"Introspection is a good thing," Rabbi Meyer continued. "Crying can be an important part of it. Let Denver go through the process. Let's just leave him alone, so he not be embarrassed."

"Dad, I agree with Shirel," Susan said. "Denver's been standing for more than an hour. If that's enough time for him to cry, then it's enough time for him to be punished. Let him out for lunch."

Susan's dispassionate plea was even more convincing than my sister's emotional outburst. I wanted to agree.

"Susan and Shirel, your concern for your friend encourages me so! The love you have for each other will help us succeed in building our new home in the years to come. But for Denver, today, I'm the wrong address. The captain delegated judicial authority to Louis. Louis sentenced Denver; only he can commute the sentence."

"Let's look for Dr. Louis downstairs," Susan said, and the two girls were gone in an instant.

Our next interruption was my mother, who emerged from the stairwell carrying a couple of loaves of bread. "We'll eat lunch here with the Meyers," she said. "We won't make Denver watch us eat."

Half an hour later, the table was stacked with hummus sandwiches, and we crowded around it with the Meyers. Omar was there too, though, in observance of Ramadan, he was not eating. Meital and Ruby had stayed up late Wednesday night preparing the hummus in a large vat, and I had kneaded a tasty sourdough. My mother garnished each sandwich with a couple of thin slices of fresh cucumber. Nutritionally, the meal was almost balanced.

Celina appeared from upstairs, and we invited her to join us. Taking a sandwich from the pile, she asked, "How is Denver doing?"

"Not well," Shirel answered. "I feel really bad for him. Susy and I asked Dr. Louis to release him, but he said it's still too early."

"I thought you would be sitting with him, Celina," Meital said.

"He asked me not to come down, that he would be embarrassed if I saw him today. I'm being careful to wait until the time is up."

I nibbled at my sandwich, but had no appetite. "Denver must be hungry," I said, looking at the half-eaten sandwich in my hand. "Did the punishment coincide with lunchtime on purpose?"

"Yes, Michael, I think so." Dr. Jhonathan said. "I think Louis intended for him to miss a meal."

"That's too much," Meital said. "It's not fair." She grabbed two sandwiches and stood. "And nobody told me I can't bring Denver something to eat." Before anyone could protest – nobody did – she had gone downstairs.

"You know," Shirel said, "Denver's birthday is Saturday. Let's throw him a big birthday party. Maybe it'll make him happy."

"I think that is a lovely idea," my mother said. "Let's make it Saturday night after the Sabbath."

"It can be a '*melave malka*,'" Ruby said. Turning to Omar, she explained, "that's the Hebrew term for a traditional post-Sabbath meal."

"It can be a festive *iftar*, too," Omar said, referring to the nightly Ramadan break-fast meal. "That is three excuses for something special." He thought for a moment. "I have an idea. The first mushrooms are ready. We can harvest twenty or thirty for the party. Everybody, think of recipes that we can use mushrooms in!"

* * *

Friday, February 2nd, 2029 04:00

After hours of tossing and turning in bed, I finally gave up. Feelings of distress prevented deep sleep. The bit of dozing I had done was quite unpleasant, half-dreams filled with people quarrelling, shackled children crying, alarms screeching, and a general feeling of claustrophobia. I thought I heard Denver sobbing above me, on and off through the night, but it was hard to distinguish reality from figments of semi-consciousness.

I sat up in the darkness. What was bothering me so? Denver had survived his punishment. In the end, Dr. Louis had acquiesced to the girls' entreaties and Denver was freed an hour early. That did not make him a happy man: he immediately closed himself off in the bedroom and stayed there the rest of the day, other than briefly visiting the kitchen to grab leftover sandwiches for dinner. It made sense that he was annoyed. But standing still for a few hours would do no worse than strain one's muscles and injure one's pride. Ultimately, my friend would be fine. So why was I so miserable?

I stood and paced to the doorway. Was it that Denver refused to talk to me? I had given him space all afternoon, avoiding the bedroom until it was time to sleep. When I finally came in for bed and asked how he was feeling, he ignored me and turned to face the wall. That was insulting, but not a reason to keep me from sleeping.

The dark living room was empty, table and chairs stowed in the bedrooms for the night. I paced back and forth. Tears welled in my eyes. Why? What was the crisis? What was I missing? I glanced at the door in the living room's far wall, and thought of waking my mother, asleep behind it. Her hug would be comforting. I paced across the room.

Disturbing her sleep – was that really necessary? She could hug me in the morning. That was not what I needed now, overcome by emotion in the predawn darkness. At seventeen and a half, I should at least try to make sense of my own feelings. I would need to become calm, I told myself, slow my heart, untangle the knot in my stomach, quiet the rushing waves of words crashing through my mind. Not here, though. Not in the living room, the place we spent our crowded days, where Denver had been tethered to the wall just hours before. I needed to go someplace else, a place to introspect, to talk to myself. Where did people go where there was no place to go?

A vision appeared in my mind, an image from a story I had once read about a Hasidic master, a rabbi of that Jewish Eastern-European Movement, who would wander into the forest to spend time alone, in contemplation and communion with G-d. Away from civilization's distractions, among G-d's living creations, he prayed, poured out his heart, clarified his motivations, goals and purpose, and made himself aware of G-d's immanent presence.

I was no rabbi and we had no forest, but I did need to pour out my heart, and we had a greenhouse full of plants adjacent to where I was standing. I slid open the door, stepped into the dusky room, and closed the door behind me. It would have been pitch-black if not for a couple of nightlight LEDs. Barely-illuminated silhouettes of tomato vines climbed high before me. Leafy shadows filled the shelves to my right. Branches rustled in the airstream blowing from vents in the ceiling, though perhaps the sound I heard was just blood rushing in my ears.

I took several slow breaths to calm my racing heart.

What was I doing here? Why was I cramped in a closet-sized greenhouse instead of wandering through lush woods? How did I get myself into a place where a friend could be shackled to a wall, like in a medieval dungeon? A miniscule world without grass lawns or verdant gardens, just some greenhouse rooms, each a simulacrum? Even solitary-confinement inmates had an hour of fresh yard air and sunshine every day, but we were denied even that, here in the tiniest of prisons! What insanity drove me to give up a youth's normal life, abandon cousins and grandparents, and set out for a world where even air – the freest of commodities – needed artificial filtering and scrubbing? Any teen would crave a bit of danger and excitement, but this was madness. What foolishness drove me to a life of ever-present life-threatening peril?

Not really peril, a voice whispered from a corner of my mind. Our systems were safe and we maintained them responsibly; even the young among us knew how. Learning to shoulder responsibility was part of growing up; the more responsibility, the better. Faithfully fulfilling our tasks each day made us more capable, just as exercising each day made our muscles stronger.

Too much responsibility! another voice yelled. Growth ought to be gradual, yet the demands of spaceship life precluded a proper pace. I, a teenager, was now responsible for the air filters, the very air everyone breathed, everyone's lives in my hands. One small mistake and, at best, I myself would be shackled to a wall; at worst, I could kill them all. Was I capable enough, reliable enough? What seventeen-year-old bore such a burden?

My heart beat uncomfortably and I was sweating. I recognized the signs of anxiety, as I had been trained to. "This is not why you secluded yourself here," a rational voice interjected into my agitated contemplations. "Deep, slow breaths," it said. "Calm yourself."

But I was too upset for deep breaths to suffice. It was time to pray.

"G-d, are you here?"

That was a dumb question, I thought to myself. The Creator of the Universe contained the Universe. The rabbis taught that one of G-d's Hebrew names is *"HaMakom,"* "the place." Even empty space between Earth and Mars was part of G-d's creation.

"G-d, did I abandon you by leaving the world you created for mankind?"

That was a better question; actually, quite a scary question, and I shuddered. Life on Earth was His greatest gift to us. Earth itself, with its natural systems for filtering air, converting carbon dioxide to oxygen, purifying water, recycling waste, growing food, and even shielding against radiation, was a gift, perfectly engineered to provide all of our needs. And gravity! All the time, everywhere, effortlessly. What greater insult could there be, to the Giver of all, than to reject His loving gifts? We built our own systems and abandoned G-d's, brazenly pretending that we did not need Him or His world. That was the sin of the Tower of Babel, repeated.

"G-d, if we offended you, forgive us; it was not our intention."

I took another deep breath. "We need you. I need you! Please don't let me make any critical mistakes. Don't let any of us make mistakes. Don't let our systems fail."

System failure, I admitted apprehensively, was more likely than not. Any physical machine part could break, but an even scarier prospect underlay everything. Computers controlled all our systems, billions of transistor state changes every second, each relying on extremely precise quantum behavior predicted by physics. We were utterly dependent on G-d maintaining that exact behavior, and any thought otherwise was ridiculously arrogant. "G-d, please don't change the laws of physics!"

The loud, contrary, agitated voice in my head said, "You had no right to put yourself in such danger. Jewish Law forbids relying on miracles."

Were we relying on miracles? That, I thought, was a question for Rabbi Meyer, and would need to wait for daytime. Here and now, in the middle of the night, though tears were drying on my cheeks, a knot remained in my stomach and I was still distraught. How long could I walk this tightrope, always being responsible, always acting maturely, always performing perfectly, lest I find myself in shackles? Who was I to think I was up to the task? And my friendship with Denver? How could I ever mend it? Perhaps he was right: did I make his punishment more severe by implying that his behavior was antisocial?

"G-d, help me fix my relationship with Denver; help me be friends with him and everyone."

I felt I would explode from agitation and distress. I wanted to scream and shout, jump up and down, break into a run, sprint across a rolling, grassy field! Like any normal person, to use simple physical activity to release pent-up emotion. But we were no longer normal people. How long could I continue in confinement, my physical activity limited to bicycling to nowhere and rowing pointlessly on a dry, stationary beam?

"G-d, help us keep healthy, both physically and mentally, using our limited tools."

How long could I continue in this dry, sterile, artificial environment and remain cheerful, encouraged and encouraging? How long could we eat the same monotonous meals: grains and legumes, bread, legumes and grains, more bread?

"G-d, help me appreciate the abundance we have here on *Providence*."

A few LEDs lit up. That would make it five o'clock, ship time, the time the computer began to simulate sunrise in the greenhouse rooms. Over the next hour, the light would increase gradually, fooling the plants into thinking a new day had begun. Simulated sunlight would continue all day until 19:00, when the computer would begin the sunset sequence.

How long could I endure? The whispering voice answered that thought, saying, "Endure? So melodramatic! What an easy life you have. You are healthy, with family, and all your needs are provided."

All our needs were indeed provided – the Murke-Berger Foundation had seen to that. Perhaps the whispering voice was right, more than the obnoxious yelling voice. I had much to be thankful for, to appreciate, here in this ridiculous, artificial environment.

"G-d, thank you for my health. Thank you for Mom and Dad, for Meital and Shirel, for Denver and Hannah and Sam and all my friends. Thank you for protecting our ship, nonstop, all the time."

I thought about the food we had, which required no toil or worry on our part. We had more than a year's supply on board, with more provisions waiting on the surface of Mars.

"G-d, thank you for the Murke-Berger Foundation, through which You have provided everything we need."

More LEDs turned on. Colors appeared: mature dark-green leaves, young light-green leaves, orange rims of carrot tops poking through holes in the soil covers. Bushy tops of turnips and beets spilled out from the shelves to my right, and the leafy vines of tomato plants rose before me. Verdant, lush, growing life!

"G-d, thank you for this life."

Feelings of gratitude grew within me, contending with the distressed emotions. It took little effort to see I had far more to be grateful for than to be distressed about. Punishment might come and go, but friendship would ultimately persist. Loneliness might strike, but family and friends remained together here with me. Fear and anxiety were real and justified, but I knew my mother's reassuring hugs would dull those feelings. The rational part of my mind reminded me that the adults, at least, maintained our systems well. Boris and Dr. Claudine would oversee my work and protect me from myself.

What was I doing here? How could I not be here, I reminded myself, on the way to Mars? My father was on Mars, and the only way to reunite our family was to go there. That was reason enough to quash my doubts and fears. Ridiculous or not, this journey, and the dependency it created on manmade physical systems, was the only way to see him again. I missed my father and yearned to hug him, talk with him, feel his pride in me.

More lights lit and I found myself looking at several reddish orbs hanging before me. Our first ripe tomatoes! As the light slowly increased, they turned a deep, intense red. A dark green star-shaped leaf capped each one, connecting it to its stem. I reached out and held a tomato gently in my hand. Firm, yet soft to the touch, this thing had come to be from nothing, aboard our ship as we flew through space. That was a miracle: Earth's vitality accompanied us. G-d was here, and I was holding His new handiwork in my hand.

Gratitude, trepidation, awe, self-doubt, excitement, anxiety, yearning, fear; a mix of feelings gushed through me. Confused, I had run out of my own words, but my urge to talk to G-d had not abated.

Fortunately, King David had solved my problem three thousand years earlier, when he composed the Book of Psalms. I ran quietly to my room, retrieved my datapad and one of the folding chairs, and returned to my little forest. I sat down and began reading Psalm 40, a favorite. "To the Conductor, a psalm of David. My hope was always to the L-rd; He leaned toward me and heard my cry." The simulated sun slowly rose, while I alternated between reading psalms and examining the greenery around me. I felt myself relaxing, finally, and before I knew it, the lights had lit completely and it was nearly six, time for me to rise.

As for the tomatoes, I counted seven ripe ones. I refrained from picking any: that would be for Omar and Celina. Perhaps they would agree to harvest them for Denver's party. We could have our first tomatoes together with our first mushrooms. Tomatoes and mushrooms: that sounded to me like pizza. Pizza for Denver's birthday party!

*   *   *

Saturday, February 3rd, 2029 18:30

Having no seasons, and no actual sunrise and sunset, we had taken to observing the Jewish Sabbath from 17:30 ship time Friday afternoon through 18:30 Saturday night. The Sabbath was a relaxing, holy day even aboard *Providence*, just as it was everywhere, when properly observed. Fresh-baked challah bread; a stew of beans, chickpeas, and barley; creative, if limited, salads; soda water; and a cup of reconstituted grape juice for the Kiddush benediction – all combined to make the meals special. Even more important was the camaraderie, as we sat around the table, talking and singing for hours. I had used the opportunity to try to repair my friendship with Denver.

"Denver," I had said, turning to face him, "maybe you were right." Trying to meet his eye, I continued. "Maybe what I said at the trial did make your punishment worse. If so, I sincerely apologize. It was not my intention."

He looked at me silently for a few seconds before turning away. Perhaps that was progress.

"We're throwing you a big party tomorrow night," Shirel said. "You're turning eighteen and we're going to celebrate."

The corners of Denver's mouth curved upward, his first smile in days. "Thank you, Shirel. I appreciate that. I am not used to having birthday parties."

"In our family," Meital said, "we celebrate every birthday. Now that you are part of the family, get used to it."

"That's right," my mother said. "No way to avoid it. No son of mine" – she looked meaningfully into Denver's eyes – "skips a birthday party."

Hearing that, Denver laughed, finally.

Now, Saturday night, I held the silver Kiddush cup in my hand, again full of reconstituted grape juice, and finished reciting the short Havdalah blessings that officially ended the Sabbath day.

Shirel announced, "Time to get to work on Michael's tomato and mushroom pizza. Party starts in two hours."

We had no milk and no cheese, but we had olive oil, powdered tomato paste, and spices: oregano, basil, pepper, and ground onion. Most importantly, we had our first fresh tomatoes and our first harvested portobello mushrooms. There were only a few of each, so we sliced them very thinly, spreading them among twelve pot-sized pizzas. We calculated that there was time to bake them all before the party, but only if we borrowed all four habitat kitchens. We baked the pizzas in pots on the induction stoves, just like we baked our bread, but the thin pizza dough cooked more quickly.

Everyone attended the birthday party, even Sophie and Jasmine, whose parents gave them special permission to stay up late. There was just enough room for all twenty-one of us to gather, briefly, on Green Level, to sing together, but only because a bunch of us squeezed into the bedrooms.

"Happy birthday to you, dear Denver," twenty voices sang, while Denver blushed and giggled embarrassedly.

We divided up the pizzas: everyone got at least half a pie. After the adults retreated to their respective levels and Sophie and Jasmine went to bed, the rest of us, the youth on board, remained behind. It was a happy party, with singing and drumming. Meital played her flute and Helga her clarinet. Denver's broken guitar was conspicuously absent, but, I thought, now that his spirits were returning, he would be motivated to start the work to print new parts and repair it.

Air

*   *   *

Monday, February 5th, 2029 12:30

"Michael, I need a favor." Sam grabbed my arm as we got up from our daily Talmud session. We had dealt with a question on Bava Kama folio fourteen about circumstances in which a person is responsible for his animal's damage and circumstances in which he is not.

"Sure, Sam, anything."

"I'm glad you said that," he replied, an uncharacteristically devious smirk on his face. He pulled me into his bedroom and whispered. "Purim is coming in a few weeks. We need something to get drunk on. I need some yeast to make beer."

"What, are you out of your mind? The Foundation bans alcoholic beverages." An unpleasant image flashed before my eyes: my pious friend, Samuel David Meyer, handcuffed to the living room wall.

"You and I will keep it a secret, and it's only for the one day. And, anyway, it probably won't work."

"Still, you'll be breaking the rules. What would your father say?"

"I'm not going to tell him, at least not until I can hand him a glassful at the Purim party." He peered at me, a serious look in his eyes. "Michael, I need a side project to break the monotony. This will be something to get excited about. What do you say, are you in?"

"Okay, I'll give you some sourdough. But after that I have no part in this. I'm not risking getting in trouble! Or getting your dad angry at me."

"Fine with me. I've already malted the barley, so I need the yeast as soon as you can give it to me."

"Sam, it's not exactly yeast – all I have is bread sourdough. Do you know if that works for beer?"

Sam shrugged his shoulders, but he looked relieved. "I don't know. I guess we'll find out on Purim!"

Misgiving

Thursday, February 8th, 2029 19:00

"Mom, why are we here?"

My mother put down the knife she was using to dice two small carrots and looked at me quizzically. "Because you're baking challah bread for the Sabbath and I'm making dinner?"

I kneaded my dough on the kitchen counter. "No, I mean, why are we here on a spaceship going to Mars? Why did we decide to leave Earth?"

Her eyes widened. "That's a big question for a young man who is already a third of the way to Mars. You were there in all the family discussions. You voted unanimously with us. So, tell me: why did *you* decide to come?" She lifted up the cutting board to dump the carrot pieces into the pot, which was full of brown rice and lentils.

"Why did I agree to join the rest of the family? I'm not sure I know anymore. I've been thinking about it a lot lately." I flipped the dough, folded it twice and pounded it again. "Can you remind me?"

"I know you're upset about our recent difficulties," she said sympathetically. "Not only your injury when the tether broke, but also Denver's trial and punishment." Shaking ground onion into the pot, she added, "It makes sense if you are having second thoughts or even doubts."

"It does?" I squeezed the dough between my fingers and folded it again. "What about you, Mom? Are you having second thoughts?"

Misgiving

She inserted the pot into its stovetop niche. "Of course I have second thoughts sometimes. Doesn't everybody? But my 'first thoughts' always win out. Your father and I joined the Murke-Berger mission because we want to be pioneers."

My dough seemed ready, so I stuck it into its proofing bowl, snapped on the cover, and Velcroed it to a spot near the edge of the counter. I turned to face my mother. "But why? Why did you want to be pioneers? Tell me. Please."

She poured half a cup of water into her pot, added a tablespoon of olive oil, and closed and sealed the lid. After tapping the stovetop's controls to start the induction heater, she turned around, nodded, and said, "Okay." Her eyes lost focus while she thought.

"Your father and I wanted a greater challenge," she said, facing me. "We did love living in Israel. We loved the Negev Desert, especially the pioneering spirit of the farmers there. But at a certain point we wanted a greater challenge. The Negev is very developed; most of its problems are solved. I think your father was getting bored. Engineering agricultural solutions for the Martian desert was a more interesting challenge." Her gaze wandered, unfocused again, a wistful expression on her face.

"And you, Mom? Were you bored too?"

She shook her head. "Not really, no. I wasn't bored in Israel. I loved being chief engineer at Lehavim Advanced Irrigation. We were working on cutting-edge recycling technologies."

"Then why did you leave? Because Dad and Uncle Aviel were recruited by the Foundation?"

She shook her head again, smiling this time. "No, it was me that the Murke-Berger Foundation originally recruited, not your father. They were looking for recycling experts to develop the one-hundred-percent water recyclers. Dad didn't even want to go at first. But the technical challenge captured my heart, and eventually Dad came around. So we all moved to Arizona."

"So you wanted to go to Mars, but Dad didn't?" I raised my eyebrows.

"Neither of us wanted to go to Mars, at least not at first. We were recruited as experts, not as participants."

"Then why didn't we go back to Israel after you finished your work on the recyclers? The whole thing is sounding like a mistake, Mom."

"No, there's no mistake. It just worked out differently," she answered, shrugging her shoulders. "One project led to the next: after the recyclers came the MarsTent project, which was even more challenging. That involved some of the most advanced Materials Synthesis research in the world. The Foundation really roped me in, taking me back to my Brown University Ph.D. days."

"But you finished the MarsTent project, too, didn't you?"

My mother checked how her rice and lentil stew was cooking. "Not really," she said, resealing the pot's lid. "We completed the design, but until we successfully manufacture MarsTent in situ and build our first habitat, we won't truly have finished the project." Turning back to me, she continued, "Anyway, by that time the Foundation had recruited your father and Aviel for the Vanguard mission. Your father was deep into his Psychology doctorate, working on his dissertation on the effects of long-term isolation. That's when we voted, all of us as a family – you included! – to join the first colony group. Now Dad's on Mars, and we're going to join him."

*   *   *

Tuesday, February 13th, 2029 21:30

I had been feeling melancholic again late Monday night. After tossing and turning in bed for a while, I got up and decided to use the insomniac opportunity to shoot an email off to my father. I asked him the same question I had asked my mother: Why did we join the mission to Mars? I tried to phrase the question analytically, but did not fool myself that my father would miss the anxious subtext.

He had not delayed in answering, and I scanned his response immediately upon its arrival Tuesday morning. Now, Tuesday evening, after Sam and I had finished our Hebrew Literature class – taught by my mother – I retired to my bedroom to read his response again, and maybe even respond.

First, I reread my own email:

> *Dad, I've been thinking about the Mars mission, wondering why we are doing this. Can you share your ideas about why we, as a family, chose to participate in the excursion?*

Misgiving

An uncomfortable feeling fluttered through my stomach. What had seemed analytic in my late-night disquiet now sounded accusatory, perhaps panicky. Never send an email written while overwhelmed with emotion! At least not without first reviewing its text after the emotions have passed. Tonight, I was feeling happier, more relaxed, having spent much of the afternoon programming an assignment for my Distributed Software Systems course. I enjoyed computer programming; I found the effort strangely comforting. What folly, to take feelings so seriously, when a couple of hours of enjoyable activity reverses them so thoroughly! I took solace knowing that my father alone had read the email and he knew me well enough to interpret it fairly.

My dear son Michael,

We've been enjoying bright sunny days. Summer starts in a few weeks here, and the temperatures outside have been almost moderate. We've been working on the trench walls. The robots help, but there's physical work for us, too, and I've been enjoying the exercise, at least until I get tired each afternoon. Knowing I am helping to build the first abode for humans on a new planet is exhilarating. I retire each night feeling that I fully utilized the day, that I am using well the time I have been given on this world.

Your question is a good one, though I sense a maelstrom of underlying emotion. My first reaction, written with a loving smile, is that it's a bit late now for you to be asking the question! At this point, deep into the mission, you have no choice in the matter. There's no station to get off at, no train to go home on.

But that's not a fair answer to what is a fair question. From a logical point of view, you of course know exactly why we – and you – chose to join the mission. I remember our discussions, and I remember your enthusiasm to be part of a pioneering family. Now you are a few years older and have spent months confined on your ship. It makes sense – it is proper and expected – for you to question your decisions. The seventeen-and-a-half-year-old Michael must find meaning in his current circumstance. Unfortunately, I don't think I can help much with that. What I can do is share my own reasons for joining the mission, the same reasons that fortify my resolve every day here as I await your arrival. Perhaps my reasons will encourage you.

Simply put, your mother and I found ourselves with an opportunity that was too awesome to ignore. We started out with the Murke-Berger Foundation as employees, research scientists, no more than that. But that mere 'employment' turned into so much more. It was hard not to be swept up in the Foundation's vision, and Leon Murke in particular made us feel like part of a big family. He and Jake Berger offered your mother and me the opportunity to help found a new branch of human civilization! How could I turn that down? In moments of doubt – yes, I have them too – when I wonder if I made the right choice, especially given my predicament, I think about the alternative. What if we had refused? How would I have lived with that choice? My life would have been filled with far more self-doubt, far more regret, had I passed up the opportunity to be part of this. Some opportunities are too important to miss, even if they require great personal sacrifice.

Michael, questioning your motives is a good thing. Never stop examining yourself: it is a requirement for growth. But do not second-guess yourself either. The choices you made in the past stand; you cannot undo them. I apologize for the bluntness, but you have no choice now but to live out your earlier decision to come to Mars. Make the best of it: be the awesome pioneer, on an awesome venture, that I know you will be.

Perhaps you can turn your questioning into a writing opportunity. (I do hope you are still writing!) Why not take upon yourself to research and document why everyone in the expedition chose to join? I imagine you'll find an interesting variety of reasons and motivations.

I wait excitedly for you and your mother and sisters to arrive. I am counting down the days (literally: you are arriving in 169 sols).

Love,

Dad

Yes, Dad, I thought, *I am still writing.* I would mention that in my response. Meanwhile, his suggestion was a great idea, an intriguing project. I would push through my anxiety and questioning, and get to work documenting everyone's reasons for leaving Earth to go try to create human civilization on a cold, dry, empty, radiation-burned planet.

*   *   *

Wednesday, February 14th, 2029 14:45

"So, to summarize, many European weaving families lost their livelihoods due to the eighteenth-century technological advances in thread spinning and textile weaving. This was an early example of the Hozian thesis that technological advances displace second-tier workers into the third tier."

Dr. Louis Bouchet was leading my twice-weekly Earth History class. The current segment, which he had named "The Impact of Technology on Western Social Development," was remarkably interesting, at least compared to other History classes.

"Hozian thesis?" Meital asked. "Can you explain what you mean?"

"Meital, that was part of your reading assignment last week. Did you not complete the article on the Hozian approach to labor market development?"

She and Ruby exchanged a look. "Yes, we read the article, but I'm not sure we fully understood."

Ruby nodded in agreement. "Dr. Louis, would you mind summarizing the thesis again for us?"

"Okay, I will try in brief," he said, stroking his chin. "The Hozian thesis divides the labor pool into four tiers. The second tier is the subset of society that is busy in productive work, to provide for the needs of everybody. In other words, the employed workers, whether in farming, industry, or services. The third tier are those who have nothing to offer that anybody requires. Since everybody already has everything they need, there is nothing left for the third-tier people to do. It is not that these people are incapable of doing work; it is that any work they do would be superfluous. Hence they are unemployed."

"So you are saying," Meital asked, "that when weaving became automated, nobody needed the hand-made textiles that weaving families produced? So they lost their jobs?"

"That is an accurate synopsis, Meital. A smaller number of people produced more material, of higher quality, more quickly, using the new technologies. Society requires a limited quantity of woven material each year. The mechanized mills supplied the required amount less expensively, so nobody needed weaving families to weave anymore."

"But that's not the whole story," Ruby said, raising her hand. "Eventually people become employed at other jobs. Can you remind us about the other two tiers?"

Dr. Louis glanced at his datapad. "We have just a few more minutes until your next class. So, quickly. You should go back and read the article again to make sure you have it clear.

"The first tier, according to the Hozian thesis, consists of 'need creators.' These are people who create new needs, or at least the perception that new things are needed. For example, before the washing machine was invented, nobody thought they needed washing machines. Now, of course, everybody needs washing machines. Nobody does laundry by hand."

"So," I asked, "any technological advance creates a new need?"

"No, Michael, but that is a good question. Lots of people invent new things that nobody uses and nobody needs. Technology by itself is insufficient. 'Need creators' need to be good marketers. They need to persuade people that the service a new technology provides is useful – so useful, sometimes, that they cannot live without it."

"How do 'need creators' relate to the second and third tiers?" Meital asked, a doubtful expression on her freckled face. "These are employed, those are not; what do perceived needs have to do with it?"

Dr. Louis again checked his datapad, then looked up at Meital. "The second tier looks to create technology to improve efficiency. That tends to push people down into the third tier by making their labor unnecessary. Meanwhile, first-tier people develop ideas for using new technology in new ways. Society perceives new needs. This creates new opportunities for third-tier people, who can join the second-tier effort to provide the new needs. For example, when weaving families lost their jobs weaving textiles, new opportunities arose to fulfill needs created by the new technologies. Factories required workers to manufacture automated looms and to produce machines for spinning thread. Textile mills needed mechanics to maintain and repair the machinery."

"I think I understand the first three tiers," Ruby said. "What about the fourth?"

"The fourth tier is what Hozian Economics calls 'technology blockers.'"

"That sounds bad."

"No judgment is implied. It is not that anyone intends to block technological development. Fourth-tier workers are those who are willing to work at menial jobs for long hours, under poor conditions, for very low pay. Because it would be more expensive to develop technologies to automate the work, they effectively delay technological advancement."

"Then it sounds like a good thing," Meital said, "because it keeps people employed."

"Except that it's hard to survive with very low pay," Ruby said. "Why would anyone agree to work long hours for a low salary?"

"Fourth-tier people often come from poor societies where they live in terrible poverty. In many cases, they are illegal migrants, working unofficially, unprotected by local labor laws. Despite all this, they prefer a poor job to no job at all."

"It's heartbreaking to think about such hardship," said Meital.

"Doesn't Hozian Economics consider the third tier the worst?" I asked, recalling details from the article we had been assigned. "Having nothing to offer others – not being needed by anyone – sounds devastating. At least fourth-tier people provide something for other people."

"From that perspective, yes," Dr. Louis answered. With another glance at his datapad, he added, "Off you all go. Time for next class."

"Just one more question," Meital asked, halfheartedly raising her hand. "I think I understand about the weavers. But can you give a modern example of the Hozian thesis?"

He half smiled, shaking his head vaguely in a resigned sort of way. "Yes, here's an example," he said, gesturing to the wall in front of us, "nano-LED wallpaper." The wall displayed a calming mountainside scene, evergreens swaying gently in the wind. "Ten years ago nobody needed walls to change their appearance. Now it is hard to find a living room in the United States – that's a country back on Earth" – he winked at us – "that does not have continually changing scenes, patterns or colors. Think of all the people involved in manufacturing huge quantities of NLED wallpaper. The Korean 'need creators' who produced and marketed the technology shifted the tier-two boundary downwards into tier three, effectively moving thousands of people back up into the employment tier.

"Now," Dr. Louis said, distracted by his datapad, "class time is finished for today. Please, all three of you, read the labor market article again."

Getting up, I remembered my father's idea to research everyone's reasons for being on the expedition. I grasped Dr. Louis's wrist. "Do you have a few minutes when I could talk to you about our journey to Mars? About why you think we are going? My father suggested I write about everyone's motivations. What you are seeking on Mars, why you chose to leave Earth?"

Dr. Louis examined me, considering the request. "Okay, I can do that. I will have time tonight after the girls are asleep. Do you want to come by after nine?"

"Is nine-thirty okay? My math class with Dr. Claudine finishes then."

He nodded "okay" as he got up from the table. I rushed upstairs, already several minutes late for Mycology class.

*   *   *

Wednesday, February 14th, 2029 21:35

"*Bon soir*, Michael." Drs. Louis and Claudine sat on their Mauve-Level living room couch, Claudine looking a bit heavy. "Michael wanted to discuss motivations for the mission to Mars," Dr. Louis explained to his wife. "Please, sit down," he gestured.

I pulled over a chair and sat facing them, unexpectedly feeling awkward. Reluctantly, I started, "My father suggested documenting the various reasons people chose to join the expedition. I'm hoping to interview everybody aboard." I shifted in my seat. "I'm starting with you, but now I wonder if the idea is silly."

"Silly? *Pas du tout!*" Dr. Claudine exclaimed. "I think it is a marvelous idea. The ideas behind the journey should be documented. Your journal will be more authentic, I think, than anything written by historians on Earth." She glanced at her husband. "Louis agrees, do you not?"

"Doriel – your father – would himself have written about all of us," Dr. Louis answered, "if he had stayed behind and not joined the Vanguard mission."

Misgiving

"Yes," said Dr. Claudine, laughing airily, "but he would have included a full psychological analysis. Better that you write it, Michael."

"Okay. Well, thanks for all the encouragement. So, can you tell me why you chose to leave Earth to come to Mars?" I directed the question to Dr. Louis first.

"Michael, it is not easy to answer, because there are lots of different motivations, all mixed together." Narrowing his eyes and tilting his head, he continued. "I have been thinking about it since you asked me earlier. I would say that, for me, the main motivation was fear."

"Fear?" his wife repeated, surprised. "What have you ever feared, *mon mari chéri?*"

"Yes, fear. Fear of not being able to contribute. Fear of not being needed. Fear, perhaps, of idleness."

"I cannot imagine you having nothing to contribute." Dr. Claudine looked fondly at her husband. "And you are needed. I will always need you."

"Michael, make sure you marry a great girl," he said, looking back and forth between me and his wife. Raising his eyebrows merrily, he added with a wink, "I have some suggestions – let me know if you want ideas."

"Thanks," I said, faintly discomfited. "Dr. Louis, you are an expert at so many fields, among them medicine – you are a medical doctor, a surgeon, right? I think that guarantees that you would always have lots to contribute, wherever you are, even at home on Earth."

"Well, Michael, that is the question, is it not? Think back to what we discussed in class today, about what Hozian Economics predicts. I have felt rattled more than you might imagine ever since I studied the thesis. Technology has been advancing rapidly toward the day when everything I might do can be done by computers and robots. Or, in Hozian terms, when the boundary between the third and second tiers rises so high that neither I – nor barely anyone – remain in the second tier, the productive group."

"There are many jobs that can be replaced, but a surgeon and engineer like you?" I shook my head. "I don't see it."

"*Au contraire*, Michael." He shook his head. "Surgeons are rapidly being replaced by machines. Microsurgery is already completely robotic and increasingly automated. A surgeon's hand, unlike a machine appendage, is not always steady."

"A doctor is more than a surgeon. You can diagnose illnesses and prescribe medicines."

"Computers are already better than doctors at diagnosis. Neural networks can recognize tens of thousands of illnesses and conditions. No human knows that much. That doctors on Earth still diagnose their patients – that is an illusion, maintained because some people are still more comfortable with human doctors. That will change, I am sure, within a few years."

"So, you see yourself becoming obsolete?" I shook my head disbelievingly. "I don't see it. But let's say you are right. How does going to Mars help?"

"Going to Mars helps, Michael, because Mars is empty. We will need to build everything from the start. For many years there will be new problems, still unforeseen, that only humans will be able to solve. Mars is a perfect example of the Hozian first tier. Settling there is the greatest 'need creator.' There is no better opportunity for people to be able to fulfill each other's needs than by going to an empty planet where there is no infrastructure to provide human necessities."

I thought about that for a moment, but something seemed wrong with the idea. "Dr. Louis, we already have automation on Mars. My father and his team use robots to mine water and machines to create bricks. Won't the result be exactly the opposite, that we will need even more automation and robots than on Earth, because we'll have so little manpower?"

"Oh, do not misunderstand me. Mars is not a permanent solution to the Hozian dilemma. Even on Mars, eventually, none of us will be needed by anybody else. Mars for me is a temporary solution. By joining the mission I have delayed my own displacement from tier two to tier three. Sadly, I doubt I can fix the problem for Jasmine and Sophie, but at least Claudine and I will have the opportunity to provide useful services for the whole community for some years to come."

"Louis is a pessimist," Dr. Claudine said, looking from him to me. "He makes going to Mars sound like escaping from an objectionable situation, instead of progressing toward a fantastic challenge!"

"*Vraiment*, Claudine." He sighed. "I feel like we are escaping a life of forced self-indulgence, a meaningless life where nobody gives anything to anybody else and nobody is concerned with anybody else, because nobody needs them for anything. That is the unfortunate conclusion of the process described by Hozian economics."

"Dr. Louis," I objected, "doesn't life offer more choices than either giving to others or being completely self-indulgent? Aren't there other sources of meaning in life?"

"I do not think so. To me, the purpose of living is to give to others. In religious terms, if you do not mind, we are enjoined to emulate my religion's founder, whose life and death were filled with concern for others and their needs. If there is nothing other people need from me, I see no reason to live."

"That is so depressing."

"No, Michael, be happy for me! I am going to Mars to live a life where there will always be something for me to do to help others. And for you, too. This expedition is for us the greatest opportunity to live full lives. That should make us extraordinarily happy."

I sat quietly for a few moments, absorbing what Dr. Louis had said. Then I turned to Dr. Claudine. "I think your husband might have said something very inspiring." My brow furrowed as my eyes darted around the room. "I'm not sure. I need to think it through."

"Yes, 'e can be very inspirational," she said in her Ivorian French accent, gazing at her husband with a warm smile. Then, to me, she said, "But I am not sure I agree with him. Perhaps you would like a different perspective."

"Yes, please. I'm supposed to document all the different motivations everybody has."

She looked at me intently. I averted my eyes. "For me, Michael, to join the Foundation's project was an easy decision. Nothing so philosophical, I am afraid, as for my husband. I simply love the challenge of the new frontier. Putting humanity in a new place, building a new family of humans, building new technologies to sustain us in a new place, *c'est irrésistible*! I cannot contain my excitement, the excitement of doing something so important. Humanity will spread to the stars, and I am part of it!"

"Because you helped develop the air-processing systems?"

"Yes," she said, surprised, "that is part of it. But only a small part. The important part is being there, building a family, building a community, that is what will be most important." Shrugging, she concluded, "That, Michael, is my motivation."

I thanked both Bouchets and stood. After sliding the chair back to their table, I headed upstairs for bedtime.

* * *

Wednesday, February 14th, 2029 22:55

I was getting ready for lights-out when my datapad buzzed. I tapped it and Hannah's round, pretty face appeared.

"Did I get you before you got in bed?" she purred, playfulness in her eyes.

"Yes, you did. How is everything on *Mars Hope* tonight?"

"Very exciting. I need your advice. I got a job offer today!"

"A job offer? I thought you had a job. Aren't you responsible for waste processing this week?"

She glared at me from the datapad screen. "I mean a real job, a paying job. You remember the job I had the summer before last?"

"Where you designed user interfaces for marketing sites?"

"Yes, at Kokebi Studios. They sent me an email asking me to update one of the sites I programmed. They've already sent all the files. It's work that can be done remotely."

"I should hope so!" I exclaimed. "You're certainly not going to visit their offices in Phoenix."

"I should remind them about that." She smiled. "They're paying well: they've offered me fifty dollars an hour."

"That sounds reasonable. How big is the project?"

"They estimate thirty or forty hours. I won't have a lot of time to put into it, but it's a low-pressure project. If I work a few hours each week, I should finish by May. I figure I need the intellectual challenge to keep me sane."

"I empathize. My writing serves the same purpose. Sure, take the job, if you'll enjoy the opportunity to do some coding." I paused to calculate. "So, a couple thousand dollars earned. That sounds nice. Except ..."

"Except what?" Hannah raised her eyebrows.

"Except that you have no need for the money. Where will they deposit it, First Bank of Mars? What will you spend it on?"

"That's cute," she feigned a smile. "You're right that we don't need money as long as the Foundation pays for everything. But it won't hurt having some money invested on Earth. In case I ever go back."

"Or in case someone sets up a mail-order business," I added gleefully.

"You joke, but it will happen." She paused to glare at me again, narrowing her eyes in a fair imitation of an irate expression. "You'll be able to order flowers for your girlfriend on Valentine's Day."

"We Israelis don't observe Valentine's Day."

"That may be the case, but it seems you need an excuse to think of me. I'm a hundred and twenty meters away from you, Michael. You could have made an effort."

"What do you want me to do, climb a tether and come over to visit?"

She struggled and failed to maintain her stern expression. A warm smile broke across her face. "That actually would be very nice."

Sun

Thursday, February 15th, 2029 10:30

Harvesting vegetables had become common. On days that Sam, Denver, and I managed to finish our chores well before first class, we would search upstairs or down for Dr. Cecylia or Omar. Those two would go from greenhouse room to greenhouse room each morning, examining plant growth and deciding which vegetables were ripe for picking. They were careful to pace the harvest, always leaving some for later. On a typical day they would pick a vegetable or two per person on board. For me, the best mornings were those when Omar pointed to a tomato and said, "Michael, pick that one," or Dr. Cecylia, kneeling on the floor with her head in a mushroom cabinet, showed us a ready group of mushrooms and asked Denver or Sam to gather them in a bowl.

Thursday morning, having finished our chores, we found Dr. Cecylia and her daughters at their Yellow-Level greenhouse. Helga stood outside the door holding a couple of zucchini squashes. Her mother stepped out and pushed a romaine lettuce head into Celina's hands. Seeing us, she said, "Special day today; we are helping Omar celebrate! Lots of vegetables to pick, to prepare an *Eid al-Fitr* feast." Pointing to the stairwell, she commanded "downstairs!" Helga and Celina deposited their pickings in the kitchen and ran after their mother. Exchanging brief glances, Sam, Denver and I followed.

We waited outside the Pink-Level greenhouse while Dr. Cecylia and Omar examined the cucumber, kale, and cabbage plants.

Shaking sandy hair out of his eyes, Sam asked Denver, "How is your guitar repair coming? My mother said you've printed a series of test plates. What are you testing?"

Denver's face lit up as if he had been hoping someone would ask. Most of the bruising from his tether-loss injury was gone. His normal pale color was returning and his nose was noticeably less swollen. "Dr. Esther is helping me try to invent a material with good acoustic characteristics. The first test patch, simple solid plastic, did not resonate the way I wanted. We've been experimenting with meshes and foams, different ways of creating small holes in the material."

"Do the holes make the plastic more flexible?"

"They change how the plastic vibrates. It changes the sound in different ways."

I asked, "In what ways?"

Denver looked at me for a moment, considering whether to answer. He decided not to ignore me. "It is difficult for me to find words to describe the different sounds. You have to listen to the guitar being played with each patch attached."

"Maybe you could keep a set and swap them for different effects?"

"If we can print one plate that I like, it will be enough. We will glue the plate to the guitar body, so you would have to break the guitar again to swap on a different plate.

Dr. Cecylia handed me a cabbage. "Michael, can you take this up to our kitchen? Add it to the pile."

It took me no more than forty-five seconds to race upstairs and back, but by then the group had already descended another level. Dr. Cecylia stood in our Green-Level greenhouse room, inspecting several bright red tomatoes, before turning to examine the root vegetables growing on the shelves to the right. The others waited in my family's living room.

"Maybe you'll end up with a better guitar than before," Sam was saying. "You're doing something no earthly guitar manufacturer has ever done."

Denver nodded, thinking. "Maybe, if I can get away with printing a few more examples –"

Dr. Cecylia stepped out and pushed two dirty beets, three medium-sized carrots and a turnip into his hands. "Upstairs you go, if you want to help!"

Sam followed Denver a moment later, carrying three red tomatoes. The captain's wife was careful to employ each of us equally.

"What are you going to cook with all these vegetables?" I asked the Becker sisters, as we headed down to Mauve Level at the bottom of the habitat.

"We have a recipe for Turkish *borek* pastries," Celina said. "If all goes well, Omar will enjoy something approaching home-country food."

"She means," Helga cut in, "we will try to bake vegetable pastries, and hope they do not come out disgusting."

"Certainly, they will not be disgusting," Celina protested, playfully punching her sister's arm. "I, at least, know how to bake."

Dr. Cecylia crawled out of the greenhouse room and stood, cupping a pile of small button mushrooms in her hands. "Girls, grab the red peppers I cut – they are sitting on the soil covers." Walking toward the stairwell, she added, "I also pulled out one potato, so you can try to bake some" – she twisted her smile as if smelling something putrid – "*disgusting* potato *boreks*."

*   *   *

Friday, February 16th, 2029 12:45

"What a feast the Beckers made for Omar last night," Shirel said, her mouth full of a purple beet pastry. "I haven't tasted such tastes since, well, before we launched."

We knew that Omar had enjoyed the celebration and had eaten to his heart's content. Nevertheless, abundant leftovers remained, evidenced by the overflowing plate that Helga had brought down to us and Velcroed to our table. Grabbing another *borek*, I bit into it, and the sharp, bitter taste of turnip filled my mouth. For more than five months I had tasted nothing like it.

We scooped more pastries onto our plates and chewed them, one by one. Shirel squinted, focusing her attention on the novel taste of what she had selected.

"Here's some interesting news," I said, breaking the silence. "Hannah told me she got a job offer. They want her to update a marketing site she developed a couple of summers ago."

"A job, like work for a salary?" Denver asked, skeptically.

"Yes, and they are paying quite well."

"That sounds imbecilic," he said. "How on earth are they going to pay her?"

"I asked the same question. She said she has a bank account – on Earth – and they'll deposit her salary there."

"That will be really useful where we are going. Who on Mars will accept Earth credit?"

"Why not?" Shirel asked through a mouthful of food.

"Say I open a factory someday to manufacture something. Like Mars shoes. Why would I accept payment in Earth money? What would I do with it?"

"You could pay to import raw materials from Earth," my mother suggested.

"My factory would use local materials to print the shoes," declared Denver. "I won't need anything from Earth." Before I could protest that he would need to import the three-dimensional printer, he added, less antagonistically, "Anyway, the Foundation provides everything we need. How can Hannah benefit?"

"She anticipates that there will be mail-order from Earth someday. She'll order flowers online."

Everyone else laughed, but Denver continued. "She's wasting her time. And did she get permission from our slave masters to take another job?"

Shirel looked up, eyebrows raised. "Slave masters? What slave masters?"

"The Foundation, Shirel. We used to be employees. Now that we're stuck here, it is impossible to quit working for them. That makes us like slaves."

Perturbed by Denver's negativity, I tried to lighten the conversation. "I'm pretty sure Hannah has not asked for permission. She generally does whatever she likes." With a giggle, I added, "she definitely does not consider herself a slave."

Meital said, "I wonder how she has time for extra work."

"She thinks the programming challenge will be psychologically beneficial, a diversion from the drudgery of day-to-day spaceship life."

"That would be nice," Meital mumbled.

My mother changed the subject. "To business. Who is baking challah bread for Sabbath dinner tonight?"

"I baked last week," Meital answered sullenly.

"I'll bake," I said. "Can I use one of my sourdoughs?"

"Sure, Michael." My mother turned to my sister. "Is everything all right, Meital?"

Meital looked up at her. "Sure. Everything's fine," she said, her uncharacteristic sarcastic tone making it clear that everything was not fine.

"Meital, is there –"

"Two of the chickens laid their first eggs."

"That's wonderful news! We should share it with the other ships."

"Yeah, we went and told Captain Becker." Her tone was oddly grim.

"Meital," my mother said encouragingly, "you know that this ends years of discussion about whether chickens would lay eggs in the high-radiation interplanetary environment. *Pioneer Alpha* reported their first eggs laid last week, and now we've duplicated their results."

She nodded apathetically.

"Meital," Denver said softly, "you do not seem happy about the eggs. Why not? I myself have been looking forward to eating an omelet."

She half-turned to him. "Ruby said the same thing. She has been really excited since we began separating the females from the males a couple of days ago."

"And you are not excited?"

"I was excited. For months I've been excited. We've worked hours each day with the birds, feeding, cleaning, examining, all with the hallowed goal of getting eggs. Months of diligent work, and anticipation and yearning! For an omelet."

"But it's great that we'll have eggs now, Meital," I said, trying to be encouraging. "It's important for our nutrition."

"Well, I don't feel that way. After waiting so long, now we have a couple of little eggs, and we put them in the incubator to see if they'll hatch. They probably won't. Super anticlimactic."

Shirel, looking surprised, said, "Certainly they'll hatch. If not the first batch, the next. What about a new generation of chickens? Isn't that exciting?

"More chickens and more eggs. Big deal."

"It is a big deal, Meital," my mother said. "More protein, a more varied diet, a more interesting environment in our future home. Not to mention the next generation of spacefaring birds."

"Mom," Meital said, looking up at her earnestly, "my brain agrees, but my heart feels empty."

I watched my sister closely. Her hair was a mess, half tied behind her head, half falling to her cheeks. The blue Montana lake displayed on the NLED wall sparkled; her brown eyes, gazing at the screen, did not. Meital's face reflected her heart, not her brain.

My sister's disappointment was interrupted by yelling voices. All five of us looked around at each other. Somebody downstairs was quite upset.

"You will end this right now!" It was Captain Becker, yelling again. "I have been requesting nicely for two months now. My patience is finished!"

"Your presumption – *c'est offensant!*" Dr. Claudine's cry was unmistakable.

Shirel hopped from her seat and was almost at the stairwell before my mother reacted, trying to stop her. "Shirel, let's stay out of other families' arguments."

"But it's important, Mom," Shirel said. "I think this is about Dr. Claudine's pregnancy." Turning, though still stepping backward toward the stairs, she added, "You do know she's pregnant, right?"

Dr. Claudine's accented English reverberated up the stairwell. The accent did not hide her livid tone. "You are telling me to murder my own child?"

Shirel's claim now proven – and my own latent suspicions confirmed – I found myself right behind her as she descended the staircase into Mauve Level. Meital and Denver pushed into us from behind.

"Have you no conscience? No morality?" Dr. Claudine yelled, staring furiously at Captain Becker, who stood with his back to us.

Her chest heaved. On the NLED wall behind her, light rain fell on a sandy Riviera beach.

The captain, stunned by the accusation, held up his hands in protest. "Nobody is murdering anybody here, Claudine," he said, his voice softer. "There is no baby yet; it is just a pregnancy. And we cannot have pregnancies in transit."

That was apparently not the captain's best argument under the circumstances, and he seemed to realize it as he turned and saw the audience growing at the edge of the room.

"No baby?" Dr. Claudine shrieked, her face red. She pointed at her belly. "No baby? Shall I take out the ultrasound machine and show you our daughter?" She made a move in our direction, perhaps intending to run upstairs at that very moment to fetch the medical device, but she stopped when she noticed us. Quietly, she added, "My baby daughter has a beautiful face. We have seen it very clearly."

Dr. Jhonathan, attracted by the argument, pushed between us. Dr. Esther followed close behind. Both Dr. Claudine and the captain turned in our direction; they appeared startled that the crowd had grown so large. Then my mother arrived and stepped past us into the room. Before addressing anyone else, she twisted to face my sisters and me, and Denver, and several others who were pressing in from behind. "Kids, go – there's no reason for you to be here!"

Her attempt was futile. Nobody moved.

Preparing to mediate, Dr. Jhonathan sat down at the side of the table and gestured left and right to Dr. Claudine and the captain, inviting them to sit. Dr. Louis, who had been watching silently from the bedroom door, pulled out a chair and sat next to his wife. Dr. Jhonathan caught the captain's eye, then addressed Dr. Claudine. "You knew this day would come, Claudine. You knew the rules and the risks. It is unfortunate that we need to have this discussion."

"We do not need to have this discussion," Dr. Claudine countered emphatically, looking from Dr. Jhonathan to Captain Becker. "The risks are ours alone. Louis and I are as aware as you, and we accept the risks willingly. As to the Foundation's recommendations, they are not relevant now."

"I do not agree, Claudine," said Captain Becker. "The discussion is quite necessary, and long overdue. We all share the risk, and you have put us in danger by maintaining the pregnancy."

Sun

From the side of the room, Dr. Esther interjected, "The discussion may be necessary, but the spectators in the gallery are not. Kids, all of you, please go back upstairs."

Dr. Claudine turned to us. "Perhaps you will join Celina on Yellow Level. She is tutoring Jasmine and Sophie."

It surprised me that Ruby was first to answer for the youth. "With all respect, Mom, and Dr. Claudine, we are as affected as everybody else. I think it is important for us to hear this discussion. If there is a risk to the mission, it is a risk to us too. If a fatal decision is made" – she glanced in the direction of the captain – "we deserve to know how the decision was reached."

The captain replied. "The children ought not hear my recriminations against an adult."

"No, Dietrich," Dr. Claudine said, staring again. "Let the young ones hear if they want to. Let them learn how decisions are made here."

"So be it." He looked around at us, then faced her again. "Claudine, we cannot endure a pregnancy on *Providence*. You know we have no facilities for childbirth, no facilities for postnatal care. Not only that: we know nothing about fetal development in the interplanetary high-radiation environment! The rules are unequivocal. No pregnancies are allowed until we reach Mars. You signed the forms. You agreed to the conditions!

"So what, Dietrich? You will now kill my baby? Because we signed forms?"

"We are not 'killing a baby,' Claudine." He shook his head in exasperation. "We are talking about terminating a pregnancy before there is a baby."

"'Terminating a pregnancy?'" Claudine mimicked. "You talk in silly euphemisms. 'Terminating a pregnancy' means 'killing a baby.'"

Captain Becker shook his hands in frustration. "We are trying to prevent a baby from dying!" He looked at Dr. Claudine imploringly. "If the baby is born, it will surely die. And endanger you in the process! You are my concern here, you along with all the souls on my ship."

"You say my baby will die? Nonsense! We have tracked her development closely. Everything indicates I am carrying a complete and healthy fetus."

"Yes, Claudine, but even if your baby is viable, I am afraid it is not likely to survive. Even if there is no genetic radiation damage – something I doubt greatly – we cannot sustain a baby here. We have no baby formula; we have no diapers." He shrugged his shoulders and threw his hands up. "Heck, we have no mundies for a newborn!" He swept his gaze around the room as if challenging everybody to offer solutions. "How would we dress her?"

Dr. Claudine narrowed her eyes and glared with contempt at Captain Becker. "Everything you say is wrong, completely wrong." She shook her head furiously, struggling to hold back an outburst. Closing her hands into tight fists, she inhaled deeply and exhaled slowly, then answered through clenched teeth. "As regards your radiation, the baby is in the most protected space on board, behind not only twenty centimeters of water, but several more centimeters of dense organic tissue. Me! As regards everything else you said, we will find easy solutions on board. Formula? I nurse my babies! Diapers? We have cloth and safety pins."

"And mundies, Claudine? What will the baby wear? We have no baby mundies!"

Dr. Louis held up a hand and spoke softly. "I have brought along sets of cotton baby clothes. Our baby will be fine and warm."

Captain Becker, an unreadable expression on his face, regarded him for a moment. "Cotton clothes will be 'fine' until an emergency. If we suddenly lose air pressure, what then?"

"G-d forbid, if we have a disaster, we have airtents, Dietrich."

"The airtents are for chickens and parakeets. They are not rated for humans."

"What works for chickens will work for human babies in an emergency. Claudine is correct that we can find solutions for any problem that arises."

Captain Becker took a deep breath and, shaking his head, smiled sadly. "Claudine, it is unfortunate that I must disagree, when you both feel so strongly. Of course, we can put our minds to solving all kinds of problems. But my job, as captain of this craft, is to prevent problems in the first place. We must save our limited resources, and our limited capabilities, and our mental capacity, for the unavoidable problems, if we are to succeed in our mission. This problem, though, is one that is avoidable. Therefore, as captain, I –"

Claudine interrupted. "'Succeed in our mission,' Dietrich? Our mission? Remind me what, exactly, is our mission?"

"Our mission, as we all know" – the captain waved his hand around the room – "is to survive our journey and create a viable human settlement on Mars."

Claudine raised her eyebrows. "'Human settlement!' A settlement of human beings, the pinnacle of creation! A human settlement needs humans, Dietrich, and my baby is a human. Her life, therefore, is essential to the mission."

She leaned back triumphantly and crossed her arms.

"No," countered the captain. "Bearing and raising children on Mars will be essential to our mission. By contrast, this pregnancy, here and now, in transit, is a danger to you and a threat to the mission. It is this pregnancy that we must terminate. You can be pregnant again once we reach Mars. That is my decision, a choice I make gravely but firmly."

Dr. Louis shuddered, and, behind me, Ruby gasped. Dr. Claudine, however, stared silently at the captain. When she finally spoke, her voice was cold and measured. "Dietrich, know that I shall defend my baby with my life. If you are to murder my baby, you will need to murder me first. Perhaps, with this knowledge, you will reconsider" – she paused, then muttered, with harsh contempt in her eyes and in her voice – "your decision."

* * *

Thursday, March 1st, 2029 11:00

Sam's beer was a failure, an absolute disaster. I gagged when I tried to drink it. The rest of Purim, by contrast, was a fantastic success.

It wasn't just Meital who had fallen into melancholy. The drudgery of day-to-day life in an enclosed spacecraft took its toll on all of us. Breaking the routine was essential, and there was nothing like a fun festival to facilitate felicity. Though Purim was a Jewish holiday, its peculiar requirements, established by prophets two and a half millennia earlier, made it possible for us to engage everyone on board. The Jewish prophets had established four *mitzvoth*, mandatory deeds, to commemorate the miraculous salvation of the Jewish nation from a Persian genocide. The first requirement, sending gifts to the indigent, would be unfeasible on board, none of us being physically impoverished. The other three were quite feasible, and each was a joy to perform. The second of the four was to read and hear the biblical Scroll of Esther. We accomplished this by gathering with the Meyers in their living room both Wednesday night and again Thursday morning, for Rabbi Meyer to read the biblical story to us. He read in the original Hebrew, from an actual kosher parchment scroll that his wife had brought along as her artifact.

Requirement number three was to dispatch portions of food to friends, on the morning of the holiday. Preparing said portions had kept us busy much of the preceding night. Ruby and Susan baked sugar pastries, Meital and Shirel made falafel balls for the second time, and Denver helped me prepare a batch of hummus, something we had been getting better at doing.

The ancient Jewish prophets had decreed that each food portion consist of at least two ready-to-eat preparations. Having only one, the hummus, Denver and I traded with Meital and Shirel, giving them half our concoction in exchange for a small plate of falafel balls. I ended up with enough of each to prepare five separate food gifts, each consisting of exactly one falafel ball and two spoonfuls of hummus dip. Finding something to serve them in was difficult, because our own kitchen's dishes had been seized for my mother's salads and the falafel and pastry preparations. I searched up and down the ship, finally appropriating most of Mauve Level's soup bowls from Boris, who seemed amused at my plight.

Thursday morning, as soon as I finished cleaning air filters on Mauve and Green Levels and recharging a carbon-dioxide tank on one of the laundry machines, I grabbed a couple of my falafel-ball bowls and headed upstairs to Pink Level, to present the first one to Sam. Proper performance of Purim gift giving called for an emissary, a go-between who would execute the delivery. I found Susan and silently assigned her the task. I pushed one of the bowls into her hands.

"Can you give this to Sam, please?"

"What about me?" she asked, raising her eyebrows, but by then Sam was standing next to us, and she dutifully handed him the bowl. Sam's reciprocal gift to me, also delivered via Susan, consisted of a covered cup of something and a small boiled bagel. "Save it for the feast," he instructed, pointing at the cup.

Though I had fulfilled the essential requirement through my gift to Sam, I still had four more bowls to share with others. I interrupted Helga, who was in Ruby's and Susan's bedroom analyzing bacterial growth on the walls. "Helga, dear, here is a Purim gift for you. Enjoy!"

"Are you drunk?" she asked, examining me inquisitively as she took the bowl I offered her. "I heard that you all get drunk on this Purim holiday."

"What could I possibly drink to get drunk? The Foundation forbids alcoholic beverages."

Her eyes darted briefly to the cup in my hand before she returned her attention to the walls. "Well, thank you for including me in your holiday," she said diplomatically. "Have fun today, Michael."

Celina was upstairs in the Beckers' living room, sitting with Denver for their Moral Philosophy class, datapads open on the table. I handed her the third bowl, which she placed next to a plate of pastries and salad. "I think I like your Purim more than the other Jewish holidays," she said. "Thank you for the snacks."

"Let me clarify that Michael's bowl is also from me," Denver said.

"That is right," I agreed. "I couldn't have made the hummus without my roommate."

Watching Denver raptly, Celina said, "Thank you both. I am a very lucky girl."

On the way downstairs to retrieve bowl number four for the Bouchet girls, I bumped into Ruby as I exited the stairwell. "Happy Purim, Michael," she said sweetly, looking me directly in the eyes and handing me a plate of pastries and salad, a duplicate of the plate on Celina's table. Taken aback by the intensity of her stare, I froze momentarily before breaking eye contact and accepting her gift. She turned away, her face pink, as I called out "Happy Purim."

Jasmine was jumping rope in her family's Mauve-Level living room. "Look, Michael! I can spin the rope three times under my feet, every time I jump in the air." She faced the sofa and squinted in concentration as she demonstrated her low-gravity rope-jumping prowess.

"Can you do the same facing sideways, toward the kitchen?" I asked.

She stopped and shook her head. "That is a silly thing to suggest. Jumping rope works only in the same direction the spaceship spins."

"Very good! You are a true spaceflight expert," I said, smiling, as I handed her the bowl I had carried down. "This is for you and Sophie to share."

"I am liking this Jewish holiday," she answered, as she placed my gift on the kitchen counter. Several other plates and bowls already waited there. "But *Maman* said we cannot eat the snacks until after we finish lunch."

Back upstairs, I collected my last bowl and set out to look for my mother. I found her with Dr. Esther on Pink Level, preparing the Purim feast that we would enjoy in the afternoon, to fulfill prophetic requirement number four.

"Mom, this is for you," I interrupted, holding out the bowl.

"Michael, that is not necessary," she said, smiling warmly before returning her attention to the stew she was preparing. "Let one of your friends have it."

"Mom, you do everything for us all the time, and we never have a chance to express our appreciation. Please take my falafel ball and hummus – it's all I have to give!"

She put down the stirring spoon and took the bowl from my hands. Watching me, her head tilted, she picked up the single falafel ball, dipped it in the hummus, recited the requisite blessing, and took a bite. Then she kissed me on the cheek. "Thank you, my beloved firstborn. You make my life wonderful."

Not knowing what to reply, I returned the kiss, then turned to join Sam, who was already sitting at the table. There was time for an abbreviated Talmud class before the Purim feast. We had started a new section on folio sixteen, where the Mishna described special obligations one has when paying for damage done by his animal. But then the Talmud launched into a discussion on a series of biblical verses from Jeremiah and Chronicles, an interesting break from the usual legal logical analysis.

The afternoon's feast was a joyful celebration. For the holiday, Dr. Cecylia had permitted a larger vegetable harvest than usual, and my mother and Dr. Esther had worked together to prepare a huge salad, mixing lettuce, tomatoes, carrots, and green and red bell peppers. They garnished the salad with fresh cress and parsley, and dressed it with oil and ground garlic they took from the stash of spices stored in the habitat's attic.

We joined the Meyers at their Pink-Level dining table, having brought along several of our Green-Level chairs. Someone found films of fireworks for the NLED walls, creating a festive flashing effect. Rabbi Meyer began the meal by blessing G-d over a large loaf of bread baked for the occasion. He passed out slices, which we ate with the leftover hummus and the salad. Then it was time for the second course, our mothers' lentil, quinoa and pea stew. As Susan and Shirel went to retrieve the pot from the kitchen, Sam stood and clapped his hands to silence everyone. He turned toward his father, who sat at the head of the table.

"Dad, I have a surprise for you!" A plastic pitcher rested before him. He picked it up and raised it high. Reaching over to pour a cup for his father, he announced, "Beer for Purim, so we can celebrate the right way!"

"Sam, you know alcoholic beverages –"

"Shush, Dad, just taste it."

Rabbi Meyer, suppressing a smile, considered his son for a moment. Then, unexpectedly, he turned to the rest of us and said, "If we are going to do this, then pour cups for everybody. We'll all drink together."

Sam first finished filling his father's cup, then went around the table. As he poured the brew for his mother, she remarked, "I was wondering where that pitcher had disappeared to."

When all who desired were holding cups of the unknown drink, Rabbi Meyer raised his own. "In gratitude to G-d Who redeemed our forefathers in ancient times and Who has kept us safe so far in our journey, and in gratitude to Sam who took upon himself to break the rules…" He took a sip, and everyone else did, too.

And everyone gagged. *Eew!* was the common cry, and the room filled with sour, disgusted faces.

"Sam, I take it that you haven't tasted this yet," his father chided.

"I was waiting for you, Dad," he said, struggling to maintain a straight face. "I wanted to honor you with the first sip of my new beer."

"Such an honor," Rabbi Meyer answered while shaking his head, but his lips curled in an involuntary smile.

In the end, Sam's concoction was the only sour part of an otherwise delightful banquet.

*   *   *

Wednesday, March 7th, 2029 21:45

"Meital, I'm worried about you." I was sitting next to her on her bed. Shirel had gone upstairs to visit with Susan, giving us an opportunity to talk privately.

"And I'm worried about you, too," she answered. "I know you wander around the living room in the middle of the night when you can't sleep."

"Sometimes, but I'm functioning. But you, Meital, seem down all the time."

She turned to me, forced a smile, and pointed at her cheeks. "See? I'm smiling. I'm okay."

"Tell me about the eggs."

"Just because I'm bored with my job doesn't mean I'm not functioning," she retorted, in a non-sequitur manner. Her smile was gone.

"I really do want to know about the eggs."

"None have hatched. We have a dozen in the incubator. We finished putting the hens in separate cages this week, so the eggs they lay will be for food from now on. Captain Becker told us to collect the first batch and save them until we have enough for everyone."

I could not suppress my excitement. "We're getting eggs for breakfast? How soon? How many chickens are there?"

"We have nine hens and eight roosters. Most of the hens are laying eggs daily now, and we've collected almost two dozen already."

"That's enough for everyone."

"I guess so. We can ask the captain for permission to divvy them up –"

She was interrupted, midsentence, by the habitat's high-pitched shrieking buzzer. She grabbed her ears and held her hands over them.

"What is it, another tether break?" I called out to nobody, as I hopped up and ran for the living room. Meital followed me. I noticed that we still had gravity and the room was not spinning, so a tether break seemed unlikely.

The alarm stopped and the captain spoke over the public address system. "The Foundation's heliocentric satellite network has detected a severe coronal mass ejection, and they calculated that we are in its direct path. They estimate that the proton storm will hit us between thirty and one hundred and twenty minutes from now. Prepare for emergency spin-down!"

Meital

Wednesday, March 7th, 2029 22:15

Proton storm! Emergency spin-down!

Meital's expression was of fright and panic, but Denver seemed strangely excited as he came in from the bedroom. "Let's get out the vacuum cleaners and start cleaning before gravity stops," he said.

My mother joined us in the living room and Meital asked her, fear in her eyes, "What's happening?"

"A solar flare. We are about to be bombarded with a wind of charged particles. Denver and Michael, there's no time to vacuum. Stow the table and chairs. Meital, fetch four wall covers from the drawer under my bed and tie them together end-to-end."

Meital did not move. "What for? Is this one of the dangerous ones?"

"We're in the storm's direct path, Meital," Denver answered, "so it could be deadly."

Her eyes widened.

"The habitat is designed to protect us, Meital," my mother said, "if we take proper precautions." She put a hand on her shoulder. "Which is what we are doing. Now, go, get the wall hangings and tie them end to end. We'll demarcate the safe space with them."

"Safe space?" I asked. "You mean the middle of the habitat?" I vaguely recalled a lecture someone had delivered, during our year at Altiplano, about the areas of the habitat that offered the best protection against radiation, and those that were more dangerous. It seemed purely theoretical at the time.

My mother nodded. Meital, still looking worried, hurried into the master bedroom.

Denver and I began folding the chairs. Shirel came bounding down the stairs, face flushed. "What can I do to help?"

"Make sure everything is secure in the kitchen and your bedroom."

Omar was next to pass through. "Cecylia is securing the crops upstairs," he said, and rushed into our level's greenhouse room.

Denver and I were latching the table to the wall in the girls' bedroom when Captain Becker's voice sounded from the NLED wall speakers. "Emergency spin-down commencing. Five minutes to weightlessness."

"Denver, is your guitar stowed?" I asked, as I carried a chair into our bedroom, and checked that we had not left anything lying around.

"Michael, aren't you sprouting kernels?" Shirel reminded me, poking her face through the doorway. "Don't forget to seal the jars."

Meital was back in the living room, a chain of knotted wall hangings in her hands. Ruby called from the stairwell. "Meital, come with me to check the airlock. Did we leave anything unsecured with the birds?"

A slight rumbling from the firing of the reaction control rockets was the only sign that the habitats' rotation was being arrested. Even an emergency five-minute spin-down was slow enough that the deceleration was hard to notice. Denver pointed out that it was like a car traveling sixty-five kilometers per hour taking five minutes to brake to a stop.

"Prepare safe spaces!" Captain Becker's voice declared.

By the time the last chair was stowed against our bedroom wall, we were weightless, and Shirel, not unexpectedly, was upside-down, grinning. "Does anyone know why we usually take half a day to spin up or down, when we can do it in five minutes?"

"Stabilizing the habitats takes less fuel when the process is done slowly," Denver answered, as he floated out the bedroom door. "Isn't that correct, Dr. Dana?"

My mother was busy hooking the knotted wall hangings to the top of the greenhouse doorway's inner doorpost, the one nearer the center of the spacecraft. "Yes, Denver," she answered, not turning her head. "The computers calculate each thruster micro-firing to correct the ship's orientation when accelerating or decelerating the normal way. During fast spin-down, by contrast, many of the firings make the rotation unstable, and every instability needs an extra firing to correct it."

Dr. Cecylia, followed by Celina and Susan, floated down the stairwell carrying vermiculture cabinets. "Shirel," Dr. Cecylia asked, "can you get the other Pink-Level cabinet? We're moving the worms to the airlock for protection."

My mother hooked the chain of wall hangings to the edge of the kitchen wall and pulled it taut. The ersatz barricade tape now split the living room in two, marking the outer third of the room, up to the hull, off-limits.

Dr. Cecylia and Susan returned to remove the vermiculture cabinets from our level's greenhouse room, then disappeared again.

"What else needs to be prepared?" my mother asked nobody in particular. Then, to me, "Michael, where are your sourdough cultures?"

"I have them in the cabinet in my bedroom."

"You don't want the radiation to kill them. If they are at the cabinet's very inner edge, as far from the hull as possible, they should be safe."

I went to check. I Velcroed one jar on each shelf, at the left-hand edge of the cabinet, nearest the center of the ship.

"Make sure everything you'll need is in the safe area," she announced, as Meital, Ruby, Susan and Shirel reappeared from below. Ruby and Susan continued upstairs.

"How long is the storm going to last?" Meital asked. "How long do we need to plan for?"

"I don't know." My mother looked around, thinking. "Bedrolls, everybody! We'll sleep in the living room tonight."

As Denver and I went to retrieve the sleeping bags from our beds, I was thinking about what else I might need. "Prayer tomorrow morning," I mumbled. "What if I have to pray in the living room?"

"Your black boxes," Denver said. "The ones you put on for morning prayer."

"Yeah, thanks," I said, retrieving the phylacteries. I Velcroed them to the cabinet's outside wall. Then, bedrolls in our arms, we exited the bedroom and closed the door behind us.

Dr. Esther floated into our living room and passed under my mother's delineating rope. Her hands were full with a pile of folded white cloths. "Diapers, everyone," she said, pushing half the pile into my hands, before disappearing down the stairwell with the rest.

"Diapers?" Meital asked. "This is worse than I thought."

"The safe space does not include the bathrooms," my mother explained, taking them from me and stuffing them into a black bag, of the type usually used to store sterilized waste. "For the duration of the storm, all we'll have are diapers."

Dr. Claudine was next to appear, several small red pill bottles in her hands. "Everybody needs to take a Thabiodine now. It will help us through the storm, giving twelve hours of protection."

"What's it for?" Shirel asked. "I don't like taking new pills."

"It protects us from radiation," Dr. Claudine answered, handing one of the bottles to my mother.

"I thought the safe space protects us! How does a pill protect from radiation?"

Dr. Claudine looked distracted as she explained. "It will stimulate your body to produce more DNA- and RNA-repairing proteins than usual, and to produce more blood cells to replace damaged ones." She turned and continued upstairs with the remaining bottles.

Dr. Jhonathan's voice sounded from the NLED wall. "Final preparations for the proton storm! You should all have your fleximets and oxypacks ready; place them on your belts. Pick a level and go there now. There will be no movement between levels for the duration of the storm: the stairwells are not in the safe zone. The kitchens are also not safe, so prepare water bottles. Same for the bathrooms: prepare diapers now."

Final preparations were frantic. My mother pulled a container of leftover stew from the kitchen's small refrigerator and Velcroed it to the edge of the kitchen counter. "The outer few centimeters of the kitchen are safe," she said. "I have a schematic somewhere that shows the exact limits." She retrieved a loaf of bread from a cabinet and wedged it between the container and the wall.

"Dr. Dana," Denver said, "do you mind if I go upstairs to the Beckers' level?" He threw me a sideways glance, then turned away.

"You are welcome to ride out the storm with us, or upstairs, as you like," my mother said, her brow furrowed. "But you'll be stuck on the level you choose. I thought you'd want to stay here with Michael."

"Celina and I have studying to do together," he said, and departed, bedroll and datapad under his arms.

Ruby, carrying her sleeping bag, with her fleximet, oxypack and datapad latched on her belt, called from the stairwell. "Meital, how are we going to take care of the chickens if we can't get to them? Don't you think we should go back downstairs so we'll have access to the airlock?"

"Mom," Meital asked, "is Ruby right? Should we spend the storm with the Bouchets, so we can tend to the birds?"

"Yes, that's a responsible idea. I don't mind if you go downstairs." As the girls headed off, she called after them, unnecessarily, "Use your datapad to contact me!"

Shirel glanced around the emptying room and said, "Without Meital this storm is going to be really boring." She noticed my affronted look. "Sorry, Michael. You're not the same as a sister."

"Why don't we invite Susan and Esther to join us here, then?" my mother asked. "We can make it a social event." She called Susan's mother on her datapad.

Apparently, the Meyers liked the idea, as not two minutes passed before Dr. Esther appeared with Susan. Sam followed a minute later, saying "We can study Talmud together instead of wasting the whole time." He clipped his bedroll to a hook on the ceiling.

"What about your father?" I asked. "Has his whole family abandoned him?"

"Jhonathan will be fine," Dr. Esther said merrily. "Boris and Simeon are up there with him, and Omar too. I think they'll enjoy a boys' night out."

"Shutting down electrical systems," Captain Becker's voice sounded from the NLED wall speaker. "This will be my last announcement via the public address system."

A moment later the lights went out. Only a few ceiling LEDs remained lit. The nighttime cityscapes glimmering on the NLED walls disappeared, plunging us into eerie emptiness. The habitat was quieter, too: the air-system fans had been set to their lowest setting.

"Why are the electrical systems shutting down?" Shirel asked. "Does the radiation interfere?"

"No, it's not the radiation," my mother answered. "But we'll be on battery power for the duration of the storm. We need to use as little power as possible so that the batteries don't run out."

"What happened to the sun? Does it stop providing power during a solar storm?"

Dr. Esther shook her head. "No, Shirel. The problem now is too much solar radiation, not too little. We have oriented the habitats in such a way that none of the solar panels face the sun. That means no power generation until we spin back up after the storm."

"I thought the solar panels face all directions," I said. "During our first spacewalk back in September we hung the solar panels all around the ship."

"All directions except up and down," my mother corrected. "You surrounded the sides of the habitat, but not the bottom or the top."

"What about the Mars-Entry stage?" Susan asked. "It also has solar panels."

"It does," her mother answered, "but they face forward and back, not up and down." She made a circle in the air with her hand. "As we rotate, one side faces the sun through part of each circuit, then the other side, as we complete each rotation."

"How is that?" Shirel asked, staring at her hands as she moved them around, trying to picture the habitats in relation to the sun. "Doesn't the sun shine on us all the time as we spin around?"

"We rotate toward the sun," Sam explained. He held out his left arm, clenching his fist. "If this is the sun, then we rotate like this." With his other hand, he made circles in the air, first toward his left hand and then away from it, each circle bringing his hands together and then apart. "As we are here" – his hand was raised above his head – "the solar panels on one side of the habitat and one side of the Mars-Entry stage face the sun." He stretched his hand to the rightmost point. "Here, no panels face the sun." He continued the circuit, right hand downward. "At this point, the other side faces the sun, and the panels generate electricity." He completed the circuit, bringing his hands together again. "Here the bottom of the ship faces the sun, and again no power is generated."

"So, we generate electricity only half the time while spinning," I concluded.

"A bit more than half," said Dr. Esther. "The panels are surprisingly efficient at sharp angles. But yes, essentially, that's correct."

"So why no power now?" said Shirel. "At what position in Sam's circle did we stop spinning?"

"That is a strikingly important question." Dr. Esther watched her in the dim light. "During the storm, we must be perfectly perpendicular to the sun. That's where Sam's hands were closest together, or furthest apart."

"Which? Close together, or far apart?"

"It depends on which habitat. If I am not mistaken, we, *Providence*, stopped with our bottom directly facing the sun. *Mars Hope*, at the far end of the cables, stopped with the tip of its top facing directly toward the sun." She glanced up. "Or, actually, facing us. From *Mars Hope's* point of view, *Providence* blocks out the sun completely."

"How does that help during the storm? What makes it safer to have the bottom or top of the ship facing the sun? Doesn't the water in the tubes" – Shirel pointed at the far end of the living room, where the thick black water tubes we had filled on our second day aboard the habitat were visible against the hull – "protect us from radiation?"

Sam shook his head. "The water surrounding us is not effective against proton radiation. Protons and alpha particles easily pass through twenty centimeters of water. If that were all the protection we had, we'd be in big trouble."

Shirel's eyes widened. "What other protection do we have?"

"Not to worry, Shirel," Dr. Esther said, still watching her. "Our main protection during the storm is the Mars-Entry stage's fuel. The sodium-magnesium solid-fuel alloy at the very bottom of the ship stack is effective at blocking the most dangerous radiation."

"But particle impacts with the metal cause dangerous secondary radiation," Sam commented unhelpfully.

Shirel's expression was frozen as she looked from Sam to Dr. Esther.

Dr. Esther admonished her son with a sharp glare. "The main fuel tanks absorb the secondary radiation. Liquid methane is particularly effective when the ship is oriented exactly vertically, relative to the sun."

"But what if we are not oriented exactly vertically, Mom?" Susan asked.

"Not to worry. We designed the habitat to withstand solar storms. Exact vertical orientation is part of the plan, and the computers are very accurate."

Shirel blurted, "So why the silly rope of wall hangings, Mom?" She pointed to the makeshift partition. "If we are so safe, why did you divide the living room?"

"The Mars-Entry stage shields only the center of the habitat, dear," my mother answered, and reached out to pull Shirel into a hug. "The stage is narrower than the habitat's living space. That's why we're gathered in the inner side of the living room."

"What happens if I float over to the other side of the marker?" she asked, resisting the hug.

Sam offered "Don't do that, Shirel. It could be fatal."

"That's right," my mother said. "Everybody, it's late. Time for bed. Set up your sleeping bags. "G-d willing, the storm will be over by the time we wake up."

Shirel raised her voice. "Mom, how can we sleep in this situation?"

"I agree with Shirel," Susan said, quietly. "What if we float over to that side and wake up dead?"

Dr. Esther answered, "Susy, don't talk like that! Nobody's floating anywhere. You'll hook your sleeping bag to two of the hooks on the ceiling or walls." She pointed to small looping hooks installed at the edges where the bedroom doorposts met the ceiling.

I wondered how I had never noticed those hooks. Or perhaps I had noticed, but not stopped to wonder why they were there.

"What if we become unhooked?" Shirel cried, eyes moist. "What if my sleeping bag tears from the hook while I sleep and I float over there?" She pointed to the side of the living room that was, I surmised, already being burned, invisibly, with lethal ionizing radiation.

"Shirel, that's not –"

"Mom!" she shrieked. "Take me seriously!" Her eyes welled with tears. "We're standing – floating – right next to a place that you say can kill us!" She trembled. "You put up a string of wall hangings?" Looking at my mother incredulously, she shouted, "That's supposed to save us?"

"Dana, I have some Benzodiax with me," Dr. Esther said quietly to my mother, eyeing my increasingly hysterical sister. She reached into a pouch on her belt.

"You are going to drug me?" Shirel screamed lividly. "Because I'm afraid for my life?"

Susan stared at her friend, fear, or concern, or both, in her eyes.

"Please calm down," Dr. Esther said, grabbing Shirel's shoulders. Shirel opened her mouth to yell something, but Dr. Esther raised her own voice imploringly. "Please listen! We designed the habitat for this exact scenario. Let me explain!"

Dr. Esther's datapad, fastened to her waist, started ringing. Everybody's eyes, even Shirel's, turned to look, and Dr. Esther released her shoulders to answer the call. Her husband's face appeared on the screen, dimly, in the muted light of the upstairs living room. "Is everything okay down there?" Dr. Jhonathan asked. "We hear screaming."

"We have the situation under control," Dr. Esther answered, eyes intent on Shirel. "The girls have expressed some concerns, and we're addressing them."

Shirel shouted, "The situation is not under control! We are this close to dying!" She held her thumb a centimeter from her forefinger and sobbed uncontrollably.

Dr. Esther closed the videophone program and refastened the datapad to her waist. "Now, listen to me! Do you remember that I spent a month and a half, in the summer of '27, in Earth orbit aboard the prototype habitat?"

Shirel continued her sobbing and covered her face with her hands. My mother tried again to draw her close.

"One of our many research topics was radiation protection. We kept close measurements of all radiation, both outside and inside the prototype. We tracked the dissolution of the Van Allen belts, which the Foundation had undertaken to remove. We endured several small solar flares and coronal mass ejections, and measured their effects."

Shirel, shaking with fear, was obviously not listening.

"Esther, let's give her the Benzodiax," my mother said, watching Shirel hyperventilate. My sister, lost in her sobbing, had no words and offered no protest as the pill was forced into her mouth, followed by a water bottle's drinking tube. Then my mother held her tight as she continued heaving tearfully.

Helplessly, we watched her cry for several minutes.

"Dr. Esther," I said, after the drug had begun to take effect and my sister relaxed, "you were telling us about your research project. Were you saying that you tested the habitat during solar storms?"

"None so severe as what we are enduring at the moment, but, yes, we did test under varied solar radiation conditions." Susan and Sam gazed in awe at their astronaut mother, whose eyes were still on Shirel.

"What's most important about the work we did," she continued, "is that we simulated this situation and made sure we would have everything we need."

"And did you?" Sam asked. "Did you have everything you needed?

"No, actually." She smiled. "As we laid out our sleeping bags in the protected part of the living room, we realized that in a real situation we would have no gravity."

"Obviously," Susan said. She held Shirel's hand.

"It was not obvious at the time, because we didn't spin down for the solar storm simulation." She looked around. "In particular, I realized we would need to fasten the sleeping bags so that we not float over to the unprotected side of the room."

"You thought about that?" Susan asked.

"Yes, like you, I thought about it." She pointed to the ceiling's edges. "I take credit for inventing the little hooks."

"They were your idea, Mom?"

"Yes," Dr. Esther said, smiling warmly, "they were my idea. Those hooks are my most important contribution to the habitat design. I take great pride in my hooks!" She turned toward Shirel. "A sleeping bag, properly attached, will not inadvertently detach while you sleep." Looking back at the rest of us, she added, "Now, each of you, select two opposite hooks, attach your bedroll, get in bed and sleep tight."

* * *

Thursday, March 8th, 2029 03:15

Voices, agitated voices. I opened my eyes in the muted nightlight and found myself looking down from the living room ceiling. It took a few moments to remember the solar storm, and recall that we were holed up in the safe-space side of our living room. My panicked sister was sedated, and we were all in danger of radiation poisoning.

I heard my mother's voice say something about "Dimenphillax." She was floating below me, by her bedroom door, talking into her datapad. Focusing my eyes, I identified Dr. Claudine's face on the datapad screen.

"We do not have that medicine down here," Dr. Claudine said. "An oversight during preparations. But I do not know if it would stop the vomiting at this point."

"Did Meital move outside the safe space?" my mother asked, her brow furrowed with worry. Her eyes glistened in the dim light.

"I do not think so. She was going back and forth to the airlock with Ruby, but the airlock is supposed to be safe, so I do not know how she was exposed."

I pulled out of my sleeping roll. "Mom, is she saying that Meital is vomiting from radiation poisoning?"

"Michael, go back to sleep. It's okay," she reassured, but her voice shook. Dr. Esther, floating behind my mother, gently held her shoulders.

"It's not okay!" I floated down to position my face in view of my mother's datapad's screen. I spoke into the camera. "Dr. Claudine, what is happening to my sister?"

"She has been vomiting a bit for a couple of hours, but we are taking care of her."

"But you said she needs a medicine." Turning from the screen, I added, "Mom, I'll go upstairs to get it."

Alarmed, she answered, "You will do no such thing! The stairwell is not safe, and we have no indication that the storm is subsiding. You will not expose yourself."

"Dr. Claudine, which medicine do you need me to fetch?"

"Michael, stop!" My mother lowered her voice, seeing Sam and Susan stirring in their sleeping bags, but she spoke stridently.

"Meital is under the direct care of two medical doctors. Both Louis and Claudine are with her. Leave this to them."

Now both of my sisters were in trouble and I could not save them. My stomach twisted. "Mom, we have to help Meital! A few seconds on the staircase won't matter. I'll be okay!" My heart pounding, I pushed off the wall to cross under my mother's improvised barrier.

With surprising rapidity and strength, Dr. Esther grabbed my foot. Action and reaction: I slowed, but my momentum dragged her along with me. Letting her datapad go, my mother grabbed Dr. Esther's arm with one hand and held her bedroll with the other. Forming a human chain, the two pulled me back to the middle of the safe zone. Dr. Claudine's face, glowing on the datapad's screen, spun slowly as the datapad floated toward the ceiling.

"Michael, don't be stupid!" Tears welled in my mother's eyes. "One lost child is too many! Don't endanger yourself, too."

Dr. Esther snatched the floating datapad and looked into its camera. "Claudine, what can we do to help?"

"Nothing, really. One of us will stay awake here to make sure Meital does not dehydrate or choke. You sleep for now. Please." The screen went blank.

"Back in your sleeping bag, Michael," my mother said, eyes moist. "Am I going to have to stay up all night to make sure you don't do something stupid?"

I looked into her eyes and felt tears in my own, as well. "Mom, first Shirel, now Meital! What are we going to do?"

"Shirel will be okay," she said, pointing. "And Meital is in the Bouchets' hands."

"And G-d's."

"And G-d's. Michael, this is a dangerous journey. We're doing all we can. That includes sleeping, now."

Reluctantly, I pulled myself up and into my ceiling-mounted sleeping bag, and my mother kissed me.

*   *   *

Thursday, March 8th, 2029 06:45

Agitated, I dozed off and on for a couple of hours. Opening my eyes after too little sleep, I was again looking down from the living room ceiling. A few more LEDs had lit, so our new battery-powered day was just barely less dim than night had been.

I heard my mother whispering something to Dr. Esther.

"Is the storm over?" I asked.

Dr. Esther's face reflected her datapad's light as she examined its screen. "No, not yet." Her expression was unsettled. "The radiation detectors recorded a drop in radiation during the night, but the levels have picked up again."

"How is Meital?"

"Better," my mother answered. "Dr. Claudine reported that she finally stopped vomiting, and has been drinking water."

"Mom, I need to use the bathroom," Shirel said, emerging drowsily from her sleeping bag.

"Remember – no bathrooms. Take a diaper."

I took one too. It was weird and uncomfortable, but, floating in the privacy of my bedroom – careful to huddle at the end nearest the living room – after a minute of concentration, I was finally able to relieve myself. My mother collected our wet diapers and stuffed them into a second black bag. I wiped my face and hands on a clean cloth, which I had wetted with drops of water from one of the bottles my mother had filled the night before.

I cried as I prayed my morning prayers, beseeching G-d to heal Meital, comfort Shirel, and save us from our predicament. Then, hungrily, we ate a simple breakfast of bread dipped in leftover stew. We devoured all the food my mother had taken out the night before.

Dr. Jhonathan called to instruct us to take another round of Thabiodine pills, despite his reservations. "Such a long storm is rare, and we did not fully plan for it. I'm concerned about the side effects of taking two pills. I've been consulting with Dr. Tavera on *Mars Hope*. Balancing the risks and benefits, on the whole we think it is better to take the second pill now."

"Michael, your eyes are bloodshot," Sam said, looking me over. "You look like you barely slept."

I told him about Meital's overnight vomiting. "I'm losing my sister to radiation poisoning. How could I sleep?"

"Michael, we don't know that yet," my mother said, watching Shirel, who was less groggy as the effects of the Benzodiax wore off. "We'll do medical examinations after the storm. Until then, let's not conjecture."

I glanced at Shirel, who looked back at me with sad eyes and an uncharacteristically pathetic expression. "Okay, no conjecturing," I said brightly. Even to myself my voice sounded forced and false.

"Michael, we need a distraction. Let's learn," Sam suggested. "It's why I came down here last night in the first place." He opened the Talmud application on his datapad, so I opened mine, too.

I scrolled to the current location in our methodical progression through the text. "Look, Sam," I said, noting the break in the text in the middle of the page. "Folio seventeen – we're in the final stretch to finish tractate Bava Kama's first chapter this morning. This should be easy." Of course, it was not easy; proper Talmud learning is never easy. But it was enthralling: in one of the Talmud's characteristic breaks from its regular legal discourse, the page exegeted a series of biblical verses, each extolling the immeasurable benefits of studying Torah. "Everyone who busies himself with Torah learning and acts of kindness earns an inheritance equivalent to two tribal portions," we read, based on a verse in Isaiah. We took the time to look up each of the verses in context, to understand how the Talmud extracted deeper messages based on core meanings of Hebrew verb roots. Finally, late in the morning, we reached the Mishna excerpt that began the second chapter, and called upstairs to Rabbi Meyer to share the news. His face appeared on Sam's datapad.

"Congratulations, Michael and Sam! Nice work. I'll prepare an exam on the material you've learned so far, okay?"

"Dad, maybe that's not necessary. What's with the storm? Shouldn't it be over by now?"

"The sensor on the Mars-Entry stage is still reporting high radiation levels. But not as high as several hours ago. The captain and I are consulting to decide whether to start spinning up now, or if we can afford to wait a bit more."

"If there are still high radiation levels, why rush to spin up? What's a few more hours?"

"The problem, Sam, is that our batteries are running low, and *Mars Hope's* situation is even worse. We need to spin up before no power remains available."

"Even if it means exposing ourselves to ionizing radiation? Instead of just waiting a couple of hours in the dark without power?"

"It's not sitting in the dark that concerns me, Sam, though that might scare the younger children. What the captain and I are worried about are the reaction control rockets. They cannot ignite without electric power. For the pumps and valves."

"We'll be stranded without power?" Shirel asked, pushing between me and Sam. She was anxious again.

"We'll make sure not to become stranded. Regardless of the situation outside, we will spin up if the batteries reach critical levels."

* * *

Thursday, March 8th, 2029 12:30

The batteries did reach critical levels, the sensor was still intermittently reporting spikes in radiation levels, and, Dr. Claudine informed us, Meital was vomiting violently again. It was lunchtime and we were hungry, but we had no food left in the accessible area of the habitat. Shirel had taken another Benzodiax, and Susan was hovering next to her, holding her hand again.

My datapad buzzed. Hannah's face appeared, lit only by the glow of her own datapad screen. "How are you guys managing?" Her voice was soft but strained, her expression severe.

"Not so great. This has been going on too long now and my sisters aren't doing well. We're worried."

"Here, too. My mother thinks the radiation sensor may be malfunctioning."

"Really? Why?"

"She and Captain Ravel, and your captain and first officer –"

"Captain Becker and Dr. Jhonathan Meyer."

"– so they were all talking together, and I heard them saying that the sensor at the bottom of your ship is giving erratic data. No radiation, then radiation, then none again. They don't know if the data is reliable."

"Nobody told us anything about that yet. What are they going to do?"

She lifted her face from the screen, which went completely dark, to ask somebody something.

"My mom says they're going to try to get data from the communications satellite." Her face reappeared. "They shut down the satellite during the storm, and they're trying to restart some of its systems."

"Let's hope it works. Why is it so dark over there?"

"They closed down all electric systems half an hour ago. Even stopped the air circulation. There's only one LED light lit on the whole level."

"You're not reassuring, Hannah."

She shrugged her shoulders. "Neither are you. By the way, thanks for blocking the radiation for us. I have to go – my datapad's battery is low and I have no way to charge it. Watch over your sisters. Bye."

The screen went blank.

We sat in silence. I opened Asimov's *Foundation and Empire* on my datapad and tried to read. I had been making slow progress through the series. I preferred reading on my ebook, for the feel of physical pages in my hands, and because I liked flipping back and forth to reread sections. Its LCD-paper pages were also loaded with *Foundation and Empire*, but the ebook was inaccessible at the moment, as it sat in my night-table cabinet, on the radiation-exposed edge of my bedroom. I wondered if the radiation would erase its pixels.

Dr. Esther's datapad buzzed and her husband's face appeared. "Captain Becker asked me to update you," Dr. Jhonathan said, "while he calls downstairs to the Bouchets. He would have made the announcement on the public address system, but we don't want to start up the systems just yet."

"This way is fine, dear," his wife assured, as we all gathered around.

"We have been getting erratic readings from the Mars-Entry stage's radiation sensor, and suspect a malfunction. We've initiated startup sequences on the communications satellite, to try to get readings from its sensors, but we fear we've run out of time. *Mars Hope's* batteries are depleted, and ours are not far behind, so we've decided to begin spin-up now."

"At the risk of radiation exposure," Dr. Esther said without emotion.

"Yes, that is the risk. The alternative is to be stranded with no power."

"It does not sound like much of a choice," my mother said.

"That's about right. It's unfortunate –"

"I would say so!"

"No, I mean besides the radiation risk, there's another unfortunate factor. We should be using the fact that we've spun down to make a midcourse correction."

"We are not pressed for time. We can spin down in a couple of months and correct then."

"That's what we will need to do, but we'll be running low on reaction control fuel. We've already spun up three times; this will be our fourth. After we spin down for a final course correction, there won't be enough fuel to spin up again."

My mother said, "Then let's hope that a course correction is not necessary. We'll add that to the hope that the solar storm has by now subsided and we're not about to expose ourselves to ionizing radiation."

I added, "And to the hope that Meital does not have lasting effects from radiation sickness."

"And that Dad recovers from his illness," Shirel said.

"We have a lot to hope and pray for," Dr. Jhonathan said, and the datapad screen went blank.

Dr. Esther sighed. "Nobody promised smooth sailing all the way to Mars."

* * *

Thursday, March 8th, 2029 15:45

"Michael, your turn," Ruby called as she passed us on her way up the stairs. I dismounted the cycle and delicately made my way down to Mauve Level, where both Drs. Bouchet were carrying out physical examinations on everybody. Gravity had reached moon strength, I estimated, with the spin-up half-complete. I jumped down the staircase in a single bound. Meital was strapped to the table, with Dr. Claudine methodically pressing fingers into her belly.

"Michael, on the couch," Dr. Louis directed. In his hand was a narrow device, glowing both red and blue from an aperture at one end. He held out the device. "Stick your index finger in here."

I did so, and after thirty seconds the device made a beeping sound, and Dr. Louis pulled it off my finger. He sat down next to me and examined his datapad.

Meital

"Red cell count – normal," he read off the screen. "White blood cell – slightly above normal. That's to be expected after the Thabiodine. How do you feel?"

"How do I feel? Normal, I guess."

"No nausea? Dizziness? Shortness of breath?"

"A little shortness of breath, maybe. But that's not surprising. I just spent forty minutes cycling."

"We're looking for signs of radiation sickness. I don't think you have any."

He looked back at his datapad. "It's been a couple of months since your last official checkup. Let's weigh you."

"How can you weigh me while we're still spinning up to full gravity? Doesn't my weight depend on how fast the habitats spin?"

He opened a dark canvas bag of medical equipment, rummaged through its contents, and extracted a flat electronic scale. "The ship's computer knows how fast we are spinning. It will take that into account."

He laid the scale gently on the floor and we waited for it to calibrate itself. When it displayed zero, I stepped upon it. Numbers flashed and settled on 12.4 kilograms.

"Seventy-three kilos, Michael," Dr. Louis read from his screen. "Earth kilograms. You're down half a kilo since your last checkup." He tapped the screen, apparently recording my weight, then tapped a few more times and read silently. Looking up, he said, "Your wrist, Michael, let's take a look." He reached for my left arm and systematically squeezed each part, all the way down to my hand. "Does that hurt?"

"No, not at all," I answered. Without me noticing, my wrist had healed automatically and I had forgotten the injury. It was funny, I thought, how easy it was to complain when something hurt, yet, after it healed, how difficult it was to notice and be thankful! "*Baruch Rofeh kol basar*," I recited quietly in Hebrew: "May the Healer of all flesh be blessed."

"Great!" Dr. Louis said, tapping again on his datapad. "You are good to go. Put on some weight. Eat more bread."

"Thanks, Dr. Louis."

I looked over at my sister, who was giggling ticklishly but struggling to suppress it. "What about Meital, Dr. Claudine? Is uncontrolled laughing a sign of radiation poisoning? I've been really worried."

Dr. Claudine turned and faced me, her pregnant belly protruding noticeably under a bright yellow summer dress that hung over her mundies. She laughed mirthfully. "Giggling is a sign that the patient is ticklish in the area of the spleen." She unstrapped Meital. "You can get up now." Turning back to me, she said, "Your sister is healthy. Surprisingly so, in fact. It was noble of you to be concerned last night, Michael, but we worried unnecessarily. Whatever it was that made Meital vomit, it does not seem to be related to radiation."

"What was it, then, Dr. Claudine?" Meital swung her legs off the table and sat up.

"We cannot be sure, but Louis suspects you might be allergic to the anti-radiation medicine. You vomited twice –"

"It was way more than twice!" Meital protested, a greenish tinge appearing on her face as she recalled the experience.

"– Two episodes of vomiting, then," Dr. Claudine continued, "each a bit more than an hour after you took the pill. An unusually delayed reaction, but it is our best theory. I'll make a note in your medical record, in case we need to prescribe Thabiodine again."

* * *

Thursday, March 8th, 2029 19:30

"I've prepared a sumptuous meal for a hungry family," my mother announced, as we gathered around the table. Denver was back, and Meital sat next to Shirel, hugging her closely. A large loaf of bread, one of the extras I had baked Monday night, sat in the middle of the table. "I figured after last night you need a mother-cooked meal."

"Captain Becker told us everyone should fill up on protein and iron," Denver said. "He decided it's time to start eating eggs. And that everyone should take an extra vitamin tablet tonight."

"That's why I've cooked eggs for all of you." My mother handed out plates, each containing a single poached egg garnished with boiled barley and chickpeas, thin slices of cucumber, small wedges of a deep red tomato, and a single purplish vitamin tablet. "Meital and Ruby helped Cecylia gather all the unfertilized eggs the chickens laid over the past week. We waited until we had enough for everybody, which happened to coincide with today's special nutritional requirements." She removed her apron and sat down at the end of the table.

After I recited the traditional Jewish blessing over the bread and everyone took a slice, Meital asked, "Can we say the '*Shehecheyanu*' blessing for the first time we are eating eggs?"

"Another blessing?" Denver asked. "How many do you have?"

"It's a special blessing thanking G-d for keeping us alive and providing our needs up 'til now," Meital explained. "We make the blessing when we eat a fruit for the first time in a new season, expressing gratitude that we made it through another year to get to eat the fruit again."

"Having eggs for the first time in six months should count," Denver said.

"Yes, maybe it should," I said, "but Jewish Law stipulates that the blessing be said only for fruits from a tree, or for new clothing, or for certain specific occasions."

"You're not going to get a lot of chances, then," Denver said, shaking his head, "since we have no trees and no new clothing. I think you should bend the rules."

Meital looked at the two of us. "No offense, Denver, but I'll go with my brother on matters of Jewish Law. We can say 'thank you' to G-d without saying the actual blessing." She looked around the table, took a deep breath, then concentrated on the contents of her plate. "Thank you, G-d, for keeping us alive and healthy as we travel across space, and for protecting us during the solar storm, and for keeping the chickens alive, and for making sure Ruby and I did not kill them all by accident, and for making them lay eggs!"

"… and for giving us a mother who knows how to cook them," Shirel added.

"Amen," everyone said.

I sliced my egg and tentatively put a bit into my mouth. I chewed and savored it, enjoying the texture of the moist yolk. Dormant taste buds reawakened to sense what was the first non-vegetable food we had eaten in months.

"Thank you, Mom, for preparing the eggs so deliciously!"

"My pleasure, Michael," she answered, chewing her own with a smile on her face. "Thank you, Meital, for raising the birds so diligently all these months."

"And Ruby," Meital said. "And Dr. Cecylia, and everybody" – she looked at me – "who helped us clean the droppings."

Spring

Monday, March 12th, 2029 21:45

I was lying in bed with my ebook in my hands, reading Robert Heinlein's *Red Planet*, homework for literature class. My father's most recent email called the book's accuracy into question: he assured us that no native three-legged aliens inhabited Mars. Even so, I enjoyed the story, though the homework Dr. Jhonathan had assigned loomed large before me. A critical summary and review were due by the end of the semester, a week and a half away, and I still had fifty ebook pages to read.

We had had our second egg-based supper just four days after the first. Now that nine hens were laying eggs most days, everyone could have three eggs each week. Tonight's had been scrambled, served with rice.

Denver slid the door open and came into the room, saying nothing. His eyes drooped, as did the edges of his lips.

"Denver, are you okay? You seem down, more than usual."

He raised his eyes. "So, you are saying that I'm usually in a bad mood. Thanks, Michael."

"No, I mean that something's up tonight. What's the matter?"

"Why the sudden interest, Michael? It has been a while, I think, since you criticized my mood."

"Not criticizing, Denver. I'm trying to be your friend. You've avoided opening up to me for weeks. Ever since the punishment."

"Thanks for reminding me." He hopped up onto the top bunk, datapad in hand, and sat with his legs hanging over the side.

I Velcroed the ebook to the night table, rolled off my bed, avoided his feet, and stood to face him. "I won't have to remind you, if you can finally forgive me for my part in all that. I've told you again and again that I did not volunteer to testify. I was only trying to help as best I could."

"And I told you again and again that I forgave you."

"But you don't act like it."

"You are confusing forgiveness with trust. I forgive you, but I do not trust you anymore."

That hurt. "You don't trust me? Your loyal friend for more than seven years? After all the things we got away with together at the Red Rock facility during our time in Arizona, that we never told anybody about?" I raised my eyebrows and lowered my voice. "After our unauthorized excursions together from the Altiplano barracks?"

"We did get away with a lot." He looked up and almost smiled. "It's not just you, Michael," he sighed. "I don't feel there is anybody I can count on."

I knew he had trust issues. "I'm not your parents, Denver. Maybe someday you'll make peace with them, from afar, but me you can count on now, right here! Stop holding everything inside. What is it that's bothering you?"

He looked at me appraisingly – a good sign. His mouth opened, then closed, then opened again.

"It's not my parents. It's Celina." He shook his head dejectedly.

"Celina? I thought you two were getting along great. You've spent a lot of time upstairs lately."

"Yes, I have. But we had a fight. It started, I guess, with something I said during the solar storm. She complained about it today. Girls are too sensitive."

"What did you say?"

"Really, she started it, not me. She criticized me for not answering my parents' emails."

"What emails? Have your parents been writing to you?"

"Seems so. Emails started arriving a few weeks ago, mostly from my father. But I do not open them. They all go to the trash folder."

"Why don't you read them?"

"You, too, now? Stop pushing! First Dr. Jhonathan, then Celina, now you. It is my own decision if to ignore my parents. They ignored me until now; why should I not ignore them?"

"Is that what you said to Celina during the storm?"

"Something like that. Maybe with stronger words."

"And she took offense that you want to decide for yourself what to read and what not?"

He looked up at me, nodding. "Maybe I should have said it more the way you said it. She did not respond at the time. But today she said she thinks I am making a mistake, and I told her that Dr. Jhonathan is my therapist, not her, and that maybe she should take care of her own psychological problems."

My eyes widened. "You didn't actually say that."

He sighed. "I actually did."

"It's not surprising she took offense! You should say you're sorry. Especially since I doubt you really think that. Celina's always seemed perfectly stable to me."

"You'd be surprised. There is definitely something going on in that family. Something they hide, something they never talk about."

He dangled his legs back and forth.

"Whether or not that's true, you are going to have to apologize."

"Okay. But then she will bother me again to read the emails."

"Denver, I'm announcing officially: you do not have to read the emails if you don't want to, no matter what anyone says. But if we're discussing the topic, please tell me, why not?"

He gazed at me and stopped swinging his legs.

"Anger, Michael, anger. I am so filled with anger whenever I think about my father. After what he did, abandoning us that way. And before that. The fighting, the violence."

"Violence? I can't imagine him hitting your mom!"

"No, of course not, never!" Denver shook his head vehemently. "He never laid a hand on her."

I was confused. "Then what violence?"

He stared at the floor, looking humiliated. "Me, Michael, me. Whenever he was angry at my mom, he found some excuse to beat me."

"Beat you? Not when we were at Red Rock, though? I remember punishments, but you never said anything about beatings. I would have helped you."

He jumped off his bed and fell in slow motion, Mars-speed, landing gracefully on his feet. "Yes, even at Red Rock. There is nothing you could have done. Only my mother could have protected me, but she was too timid."

He retrieved his toothbrush from the cabinet. At the doorway, he turned and sighed. Shaking his head back and forth, he whispered, "I miss her so much. And that just makes me angrier."

* * *

Wednesday, March 14th, 2029 16:00

"Omar, I need to leave class early for my dental appointment."

We had our heads in the Mauve-Level mushroom cabinet, checking the progress of our portobello mushrooms. We had harvested continually for six weeks and it looked like the harvest cycle would last a couple more. Then it would be time to clean out the cabinet and compost again.

"Go. We'll continue on Sunday."

Upstairs, Captain Becker waited for me, acting in his role as resident dentist, wearing a white cotton robe over his mundies. His Yellow-Level dining table was covered with a mattress and pillows. Helga stood by him, a tray of instruments in one hand, a large cup in the other. Behind her, on the NLED wall screen, a sunlit garden of elms swayed in the wind.

"Onto the table, please."

I climbed up and the captain fastened straps across my waist so I would not roll off. I leaned my head against the pillows, eyes facing upward. The ceiling lights shone more brightly than usual, with every LED light lit for the examination. I squinted.

"It was much easier at your last checkup, six months ago," he commented. "I had a proper examination chair for you to sit in."

"Sacrifices, Pa, sacrifices," Helga interjected with a smirk. "Some things are just a bit more difficult on the way to Mars."

"I wasn't complaining, my dear," he answered in mock defense. "I'm just warning Michael here that he will need to accommodate me. He'd better lift his head, or tilt his head, or whatever I tell him to do, if he does not want to get inadvertently pierced!"

"Whatever you say, Captain Becker," I answered, slightly alarmed. I definitely did not want to get pierced.

He pulled sterile latex gloves over his hands.

"Captain Becker, while you examine me, if you don't mind, can I ask you a question? It's for a project my father suggested."

"Ask me anything now, but then you must stop talking while I work."

"Thanks. Here's the question. Why did you choose to join the expedition? What motivated you to leave everything behind for such a life-changing undertaking?"

"That's quite a big question, Michael."

Helga, smirk gone, watched her father with a strange look on her face.

"We had various reasons, Michael. I'm sure everyone has different reasons." He stuck a dental mirror into my mouth. "Open wide!" He prodded my teeth with a sickle probe.

"Michael, spit in here." Helga held out a cup that substituted for the suction device that a dentist would use in more conventional circumstances. I spat.

"But Captain Becker," I said, "there must be something specific that excited you, or compelled you to set out to colonize Mars. For example, Leon Murke discusses the dangers of climate change on Earth in his treatise. Humanity needs at least two planets."

"Tilt your head this way," he said, continuing his probing. Then he scoffed, "Dangers of climate change? It annoys me that people fear-monger about the weather."

After I spit into the cup again, I said, "But what about the scientific models? The simulations predict rising temperatures, and all kinds of resultant problems, as carbon dioxide levels rise."

"Scientific models?" He resumed the examination, poking my upper teeth as I leaned my head back and opened my mouth wide. "Models are not scientific. Not in the strict sense. Just because someone claims a model is a 'simulation' does not mean it is actually similar to reality, Michael. Not everything people call 'science' is really science, in the strict sense of 'knowledge about the physical nature of the world.'"

Still squinting under the bright lights, I watched him inquisitively.

He continued. "The philosopher Herbert Villenova differentiated three aspects of what we call 'science.' The first and third are rightly called 'science' in his opinion, but the second is not, at least not in the strict sense, though people make that mistake."

"Huh?" I managed to say, as I twisted my head in his direction.

"You want to hear the idea? Some other time perhaps I will explain it fully, but now I can maybe give you the outline."

I nodded as he probed, and he resumed talking. "The first branch of science, which Villenova calls 'Babylonian Science,' involves gathering and classifying evidence. The Babylonians traced the movements of the stars and planets over centuries, recording times and positions in great detail. They did not develop theories to explain the behavior, as far as we know. In other words, they did not look to relate cause and effect. But they observed carefully and recorded their observations carefully. Such observations are, according to Villenova, valid science."

"Spit, Michael," Helga said. I sat up and spat, and she handed me a cup of water to rinse my mouth.

The captain unstrapped me. "You can get up – that's all. Your teeth are healthy, I am happy to say. Especially since I do not like to fill cavities with the limited equipment we have with us here. Keep brushing regularly."

I nodded and stood, and asked, "What are the other two aspects, according to –"

"Herbert Villenova." Checking his datapad, he said, "I see your sister's examination is next, but we have five minutes." He gestured for me to sit with him on the sofa. "Villenova called the second aspect 'Greek-Roman' science. That is when a person recognizes an idea as pleasing, aesthetically or emotionally, and then assumes it is true. Of course, deciding that something is true does not make it so, and is certainly not scientific." He looked at me with narrowed eyes. "You would be surprised how much of what people call 'science' is actually just 'Greek-Roman' in this sense."

"Because people think it is true because it makes sense? So, for example, chemistry, all the details we know about elements and compounds and how they combine, all that is true only because we decide it is?" I pointed at the humming air processors behind the stairwell. "We have machines keeping us alive here based on what we know! Isn't that a better reason to believe chemistry is true?"

"It certainly is. Modern chemistry is not Greek-Roman in Villenova's system; instead, it is a result of experimental science, what he calls 'Judeo-Protestant Science.' That is where our explanations predict behavior, and we are confident in the predictions because abundant experimentation has failed to falsify them."

"Falsify them?"

"'Falsification' is when experiments do not produce the results we predict. It means that we are wrong, and we need to adjust our theories and try again. Knowing that our ideas might be wrong, and having to keep adjusting them to match experimental reality, is very different from just assuming that a pleasing idea is true. The possibility in 'Judeo-Protestant Science' that a theory might be falsified keeps our imagination in check."

"So, if we just believe it, it is Greek-Roman – what I've always assumed to be 'rational' – but if we prove it experimentally, it is Judeo-Protestant – meaning it's religious? That sounds backward! And, if you don't mind me asking, I thought you don't believe in G-d?"

"I guess it can sound a bit backward when you say it that way. I wish we had time for a fuller discussion."

Meital arrived upstairs for her appointment. "Discussion about what, Captain Becker?"

"Michael has me summarizing Herbert Villenova's Philosophy of Science." He turned back to me. "Let's talk about Villenova in more detail some other time. For now, just a few quick responses to what you said, if Meital" – he glanced at my sister – "does not mind waiting a moment."

"Okay with me," she said.

"First, Villenova claims that we can never prove anything experimentally; we can only fail to disprove. We can never be sure we have not overlooked factors that influence our results. Second, Villenova demonstrates that experimental science does not begin until we make several assumptions about the Universe. For example, that behavior we measure here and now is identical to behavior in all other places and at all other times. Otherwise, experimentation would be useless, because it would not tell us anything universal.

But if you think about it, no logical reason compels us to make that assumption. Maybe the Universe does behave differently in other places or at other times. Only religious belief – specifically, Judeo-Protestant belief, according to Villenova – provides a rationale for his assumptions. That is why, he claims, modern science originated in a religious Europe. Third, regarding my religious beliefs, I do not know if G-d exists or not, but I do agree that religious assumptions underlie modern science, and are useful in that sense."

"Michael," Dr. Cecylia called from the kitchen where she was kneading dough, "aren't you late for your next class?"

I checked my datapad and saw that it was already 16:35. "*Oops!* I was supposed to be in Materials Synthesis class five minutes ago!"

I rushed downstairs, realizing that the captain had not fully explained his disdain for climate change models. Also, he had avoided answering my question about his reasons for joining the expedition. I wondered when I would find the opportunity to ask him again.

*　　*　　*

Sunday, March 18th, 2029 19:15

It was sometime after the solar storm that I noticed the temperature fluctuations. All winter long, I recalled, the habitat environment had been held at a steady, comfortable, twenty-one degrees Celsius. In recent days, though, I had felt cold, then warm, then cold again.

"Mom, is it me? Am I sick, or has the temperature been going up and down?"

I was sitting on a chair in our living room, a cotton cloak draped around my neck and shoulders. It was haircut time again, my mother had been reminding me. I finally acquiesced and she wasted no time getting out the scissors.

"You're not sick," she said, pressing her hand to my neck and forehead to make sure. "And you are correct about the temperature. As winter ends, the computer alternates between hot and cold, making small changes compared to the usual."

"Why?" I asked, gazing at the flowerbeds displayed on the NLED wall in front of me. It appeared to be part of a documentary on the flora of some earthly region, but, with the audio silenced, I could not tell where. The scissors snipped and snapped, and my hair fell onto the cape.

"It's based on a hypothesis the Foundation's doctors have been testing. The idea is to stimulate the body's immune system a couple of times a year. They're hoping to induce minor colds in everybody."

"I'm supposed to catch a cold?"

"Well, maybe just sneeze a bit. Shall I do your beard?"

I reached my hand out of the cape and felt my chin. It was fuzzier now than it had been at launch. And my cheeks, too; dark hair had sprouted during the winter in transit. I was reluctant to give it up, but I took too long to answer "no." My mother was already trimming away.

* * *

Thursday, March 22nd, 2029 16:15

"'The uncast slingshot' – I liked that one most of all," Dr. Jhonathan said, eyes on his datapad, as he reviewed my Writing and Composition homework. "That will stick in my mind for the rest of the trip. Every time I think about our two habitats spinning around each other through space."

"Does that mean I've mastered the metaphor?" I asked hopefully. The homework had been particularly difficult.

"You've definitely made progress, Michael. Keep practicing. Maybe go back and edit that journal you've been keeping. You can use what we've been working on to spice it up."

I was not convinced that the story of our ten-month tumble through the void needed more spice, but I nodded.

"Let's cut short today's writing lesson and discuss your schedule for next semester. It starts right after the holidays."

I was thinking more about my final Materials Synthesis class, which was to start ten minutes later, but I nodded again.

"I assume you'll continue the syllabus for each branch of science. If so, I'll sign you up for Living Systems –"

"Not Biochemistry?"

"Living Systems comes after the introductory biology course. For chemistry, though, I'll give you a choice. Mineral Formations, Structural Geology, or Metallurgy?"

"Don't I need all three?"

"Yes, but you can't study them all at the same time. I thought Mineral Formations and Geology might be more interesting for you once we are on Mars. How about Metallurgy? Denver and Celina both chose it."

"Will they want me in class with them?"

Dr. Jhonathan looked at me curiously.

"Okay, yes, Metallurgy."

He nodded and pushed his datapad toward me. "Pick a physics class. Denver said he'll join you in whichever class you choose."

"How about Electrical Engineering?"

"That's a good choice, because several of you are eligible. In fact, it might end up your biggest class, in terms of the number of classmates. I think Sam will join you and Denver. Maybe also Celina and Helga."

"Who's teaching it?"

"I thought I'd let Simeon teach his first class. Now, Mathematics. Applied Differential Equations." He clicked on his datapad. "Computer Science: Neural Networks and Automated Learning. Agriculture –"

"Mycology is a year-long course, isn't it?" I knew Omar expected to cover much more material. In particular, he was planning to spawn several new species after the current harvest ended.

"Correct." He clicked again. "Now, humanities. How about Early Modern European History?"

"Rabbi Meyer, I was wondering –"

"I'm not a rabbi, Michael."

"Sorry. I was wondering if Sam and I might add another hour each day for Talmud learning. We're enjoying it, and I'm getting more and more used to the language and the text, but we're making very slow progress. We're barely a sixth of the way through tractate Bava Kama."

"Progress is not measured in pages, Michael, but in skills and understanding. You've grown plenty in your learning, for a beginning student, and should be very happy."

"Rabbi Meyer," I pleaded – he narrowed his eyes but did not say anything – "I've made a calculation. Sam and I haven't even covered one percent of the Talmud in nearly six months of hard work together. How will we ever finish at our current pace, just an hour and a half a day?"

"Your enthusiasm gladdens me, Michael; it is a prerequisite for true scholarship. Keep in mind that Talmud study is a long-term endeavor. Since it is important to you – as I think it should be – I'm willing to let you try an additional hour each day. If Sam agrees. But it means you'll have a heavy course load."

"Can I drop a couple of courses? Like literature?"

He glared at me for several relentless seconds and I cowered. "English Literature or Hebrew Literature?"

"Both?"

"Was that the real purpose of your request, Michael? To drop literature? I thought your enthusiasm was about learning more, not less."

"Yes, it is; it's about learning more Talmud. But you're right about the heavy course load. How about if I continue English Literature and skip just Hebrew Literature? Can the Talmud itself count as Hebrew literature?"

"The Talmud is about learning, and about learning how to learn, and learning how to think, and learning to grow. It is not a literary study. But yes, I'll let you count extra Talmud hours in place of Hebrew Literature."

* * *

Monday, March 26th, 2029 13:00

Intersession meant a break from studies, but with the Passover and Easter holidays less than a week away, we had no time for recreation. The Jewish Passover in particular required days of preparation, preparation that included, based on the requirements of Jewish Law, eradicating all traces of leavening from the midst of *Providence's* Jewish families. Even just the absorbed flavor of yeast needed to be eliminated. That meant passing every utensil through boiling water, to boil out any lingering remnant. Only then would our utensils be permitted for use during the holiday.

Up in the Pink-Level kitchen, I watched Rabbi Meyer as he stood over a large pot in the induction stove's socket. The pot was three quarters full of roiling, boiling, steaming water. Something about the scene bothered me, something incongruous. Looking again, I realized what it was: Rabbi Meyer was wearing his bulky, insulated spacewalk gloves, normally used only outside the ship.

Shirel had noticed them, too. With a twinkle in her eye, she asked, "Dr. Jhonathan, can I bring you your fleximet, too? Just in case the boiling water splashes?"

He missed the humor. "Just stand back, everybody, and we'll be safe."

He dipped a second pot – one of the smaller ones – sideways into the large pot. Holding it loosely, he rotated it so that all sides and surfaces entered the boiling water. Then he took it out and handed it to Ruby, who was also wearing gloves. She dried the pot and placed it on the dining table, as Sam took the next utensil from a pile on the kitchen counter and handed it to his father.

While the three of them continued this way, Meital and I, at our station on the other side of the table, stacked and sorted the pots, pans, plates, and cutlery, both pre-purified and post-purified.

"What if we were to lose gravity suddenly?" Susan asked. "We're never supposed to have an open pot hot on the stove."

"This is a rare exception," her father answered, not taking his eyes off the water. "Wait a moment." Visible bubbling was required for the koshering procedure to be valid and expunge all taint of leavening. The water cooled a bit each time a vessel was immersed, so Rabbi Meyer waited for it to boil again.

"Susy, it's not as dangerous as would be back home," Sam told his sister. "At habitat air pressure, the water is only seventy degrees Celsius."

She looked at him skeptically. "I don't want to be scalded even by seventy-degree water."

We finished koshering all the utensils. Then Shirel exclaimed, "Wait a minute!" and, brown hair bouncing behind her, bounded downstairs. A minute later she returned, carrying a pile of folded tablecloths, towels and napkins. "Mom said not to forget these, since we will use them at the Passover Seder and all week long, and Passover food will touch them."

"We never boiled the tablecloths before," Meital said. "Why now?"

"Because," I started, recalling discussions with Boris about how our laundering technology worked, "the supercritical carbon dioxide in our in-flight washing machine does not heat clothing when it cleans it. Jewish Law requires heat for koshering. Isn't that right, Rabbi Meyer?"

Pulling out the dripping first towel and immersing the second, he answered without looking up. "Yes, Michael. And, again, I am not a rabbi."

* * *

Tuesday, March 27th, 2029 10:30

"Thanks, everyone, for getting here so promptly," Rabbi Meyer said. "We have a long day ahead."

It was matzo-baking day. Back on Earth we had never baked the special unleavened Passover bread ourselves. Since Jewish Law's requirements were complex, we might have inadvertently produced flatbread unfit for the festival. But here on *Providence* we had no choice. Our local store did not stock matzo.

"We'll make this an assembly line." Rabbi Meyer pointed to the shiny-clean living room table, the scrubbed-down kitchen counters, and the dry, empty pot inserted in the stovetop's socket. "We'll prepare the dough in small batches. Remember, from the moment water touches the flour, we have eighteen minutes – not a second more – to complete its baking. Susan, do you have the stopwatch ready?"

"Yes, Dad."

"I have a question before you start," said Denver. Though he did not plan to celebrate Passover with us, he had offered to help on the matzo production line. His words had been something like, "I have to see this craziness with my own eyes."

"All questions are welcome."

"This eighteen-minute rule, is that in Earth minutes or whatever time unit our computers have us at now? Our days are longer than Earth days now, so our minutes and seconds are longer, too."

"That's right," Susan said. "Isn't this the week we're skipping our first date? No March 31 for us. We'll go straight from the thirtieth into April."

"Right, Susy," Sam said. "And Passover is Thursday night for us, a day early. Back on Earth at the same time it will be Friday night."

"So that's my question, Dr. Jhonathan. What do you mean by eighteen minutes?"

"Eighteen minutes is an upper limit, based on the ancient rabbinic estimate of the time it takes an average person to walk a mile. That's an ancient mile, around a kilometer and a half in today's units."

"A mile on Earth, or a mile on Mars?" Denver chuckled.

"I'll make that an Earth mile," Susan announced, "so Earth time. I've set my datapad timer to Earth-time mode."

"Sounds good, Susan," Rabbi Meyer agreed. "Michael, you're up!"

I poured half a kilo of wheat kernels into my hand mill's grain receptacle. I had disassembled the mill the night before, and scrubbed down and dried every part. Then I had reassembled the mill in gravity mode. That included installing the receptacle in the top position. I started cranking.

Meital took the first cup of flour and poured it into a bowl. "I'm starting the timer," Susan declared when Ruby added the water. Flour and water – that was the full set of ingredients. Meital and Ruby proceeded to knead small balls of dough, handing each, one at a time, to Sam, who rolled them flat at his station at the end of the kitchen counter. Shirel's job was to pierce the flat pieces with tiny holes, to prevent them from rising.

"Ready for the first matzo?" Rabbi Meyer asked enthusiastically, as he pried a piece of dough off the counter and placed it by hand into the dry, heated pot. It baked for two minutes, at which point he flipped it with a spatula. After two more minutes, he hurriedly removed the now-ready matzo, pushed it into Denver's hands, delicately picked up the next piece, and put it in the pot.

He was removing our third matzo when Susan called out, "Time up!"

"Discard all unbaked dough," he instructed. There was not much, because Meital and Ruby had stopped mixing the flour with water, but Sam had been rolling what would have been our fourth matzo if time had not run out. He put it into a bowl designated for non-Passover use.

Swiftly, we washed and scoured everything that had contacted the dough: the dining table, the kitchen counter, the rolling pin, Shirel's fork, our hands. The first cleaning took more than six minutes, but over the next hour we got better at it, eventually managing four or five matzos per eighteen-minute cycle, with three-minute scrub-downs. We reached a pace of fifteen or sixteen Passover breads per hour and had a stack of twenty-four when we broke for lunch, downstairs, at half past twelve.

"Let's get going again," Rabbi Meyer prodded as we finished my mother's pea-and-chickpea stew. "We've really only just begun. There are nine of us celebrating Passover, and we'll be celebrating for eight days. If everyone is going to have just two matzos every day, we need one hundred and twenty more!"

Meital groaned. "That will take us all day and into the night! This is so inefficient."

"We only have one pot, Meital," Sam said, "so we can do only one at a time. Next year on Mars we'll build a big oven to bake much more, much more quickly."

"I'm glad you're so optimistic," his father said, as he placed the washed pot into its socket and reactivated the stove. "I expect that next year at this time we'll still be using the habitat kitchens."

"Won't we be living underground in the trenches by then?" I asked, cranking the mill to grind the next half-kilo of wheat kernels.

"I certainly hope we will, for health reasons. But our kitchens, and life-support, and bathrooms – all that equipment we'll take down from the habitats. Expect the same type of stovetop, at least for the next few Passovers."

Loss

Tuesday, March 27th, 2029 22:30

"Denver, I need a favor."

"I'm reading," he mumbled from the bed above me. "I need to finish *Im Westen Nichts Neues* by next week. Captain Becker assigned it as an intersession project."

"Is it a good book?"

"It's a classic, about a World War at the beginning of the last century. I would enjoy it, except for the report I have to write for Captain Becker." He sat up. "What do you want?"

I stood to face him. "The Passover holiday is the day after tomorrow."

"Yeah, I kind of noticed that, Michael, baking the Jewish bread with all of you today!"

"So, one of the laws is that we are not allowed to own anything that contains leavening. Anything we can't eat we are not allowed to own for the duration of the holiday."

He twisted his face skeptically. "You don't own anything here. Everything belongs to the Foundation."

"Almost everything, Denver. But what about our artifacts? Since we brought them along by choice, they are ours individually. All my sourdough cultures, Denver. They're mine and I need them not to be, before Passover."

"Sourdough is a problem?" He thought for a moment. "Yes, I guess it must be, since it makes leavened bread. So why not give it to your sisters?"

"I can't give my sourdough to my sisters. That won't help. They're Jewish, too. They have the same Passover restrictions!"

"I see," he said, pressing his lips together. "So, I'm your useful, easily-available non-Jewish person. For all the things Jewish people are not allowed to own – you want to give them to me?"

"I'm lucky to have a best friend who can help me celebrate Passover properly." I tilted my head and smiled at him. "Thanks. But no, I'm not giving you the sourdough: I need to sell it to you."

"This keeps getting better. You know I have no money, so I have nothing to pay you with."

"We can trade," I said, looking around the room for something of Denver's not owned by the Murke-Berger Foundation. I found nothing.

"According to your logic," Denver said pensively, "the only thing I have to trade is my guitar. That is my single artifact." He looked me straight in the eye. "No way. There is no way I'm trading my guitar for some sourdough. Especially not after I finally managed to fix it."

"It's only for the week of the holiday. Then you can have it back, and you'll give me back my cultures."

"So, I am renting your sourdough and you are renting my guitar."

"No," I said, smiling but shaking my head. "It has to be a sale. An unconditional sale. I'll probably let you use the guitar all week long, though, and it would be fair of you to assume I'll give it back afterwards."

"Do I trust you? Let me think…"

"Remember our illicit excursions!"

That made him smile. "Okay, I'll trust you. You can have my guitar in exchange for your sourdough. What do we need to do?"

"A simple exchange."

Shaking his head dubiously, he bent down and removed the guitar from the drawer under my bed. I ceremoniously lifted it from his hands, and he in turn picked up each of my sourdough jars, effectively acquiring them for himself.

I checked one more item off my Passover preparation list.

* * *

Wednesday, March 28th, 2029 11:15

Our Mars-transit diet was by now almost complete, but one comestible remained. Vegetables had been on the menu for most of our journey, mushrooms for months, and eggs for several weeks. The only thing left was fresh meat. Today was the day for that: Rabbi Meyer was about to slaughter four of the eight surviving roosters, fowl for Thursday night's Passover Seder and Sunday's Easter celebration.

Sam, reading from folio twenty of Talmud tractate Bava Kama on his datapad, roused me from my reverie. He translated, "A goat saw a turnip resting upon a porcelain cask, and, climbing up to retrieve the turnip, shattered the cask. Rava's court ordered the goat's owner to pay full damages. Why?"

"Good question," I said, focusing. Even though winter semester had ended and summer semester would not start for a week and a half, we had agreed to continue our daily Talmud study. "An owner is not supposed to have to pay the full amount when his animal damages in an unexpected fashion. Goats don't normally break porcelain casks. We would think the owner is exempt and does not have to pay."

Sam continued. "Asks the Talmud: what's different in this case?"

Before he could translate the Talmud's answer, Meital, out of breath, called to us from the stairwell. She was grasping a brown chicken tightly against her stained apron. "Dr. Jhonathan is about to start the slaughtering! Come now if you want to see." She disappeared up the stairs.

I looked at Sam. "With all the excitement of Passover preparations, I'm having trouble concentrating. Should we go upstairs and watch?"

"Skip out on Torah learning? Not a good thing."

"But I've never watched a kosher slaughtering. It's a learning experience."

"I prefer not to see blood," Sam said squeamishly. He shook his head, wrinkled his nose, forced his eyes back to his datapad, and read. "But here the owner ought to have expected his goat to climb on top of the cask to get at the turnip. So –"

Loss

Then Ruby appeared at the stairwell, a gray bird in her arms, tears in her eyes.

Sam looked up, distracted this time by his sister. "Ruby, what's wrong?"

She glanced at the rooster she was clutching. "This guy is one of my favorites. He's special. His name is Don. Now Dad's going to butcher him."

"Can't you swap him with one of the others? I thought you were keeping two of the males for breeding."

"But those two are also my favorites! Dan and Dean."

"What's special about this, uh – Don?" I asked.

Ruby stepped toward me. "Look at the color of his wattle. It's purplish, more than the others. And he has a funny squawk."

Sam stood and held out his arms. "Shall I carry it upstairs for you? You can stay here. Then you won't need to see Dad doing the slaughtering."

"Oh, I don't mind watching him slaughter. Not the others. Just Don."

Sam and I shared a confused look; then, blanking our screens, we silently agreed to follow our sisters upstairs. A small crowd had preceded us and was gathered outside Pink Level's greenhouse room.

Celina, holding Denver's hand, stared wide-eyed. "That was interesting," she said, mostly to herself. "My first time ever seeing an animal killed!" Still staring, she released his hand, stepped away from the doorway, and settled onto the couch.

Rabbi Meyer stood with his back to us, alone in the brightly lit but cramped greenhouse. He held Meital's brown rooster upside-down by its feet, under the cucumber vines. Blood dripped from the severed neck, falling onto the exposed soil – several covers had been removed. Ever the teacher, he explained, "The Torah forbids us to eat blood. It also commands that we cover the blood of birds we slaughter. After I've done all four, we'll take new soil from the vermiculture cabinet for that purpose."

He tied a string around the still-twitching feet and hung the bird from the same wire that held the suspended vines. Then he picked up his knife and examined its edge under the greenhouse room's bright, fully lit, LED lights. The slightest nick in the blade would disqualify it for subsequent slaughtering.

"Who has the next bird for me?" Turning around, he saw Ruby and asked, "What's the matter?"

"I like this guy, Dad. Here, take him. I'll go downstairs to get the next one. I don't want to watch."

"My poor girl! It's always hard to get used to this at first. Let me give you a hug."

"*Ugh!* Your smock is splattered with blood!" She handed him the bird. "Later, Dad." She dashed out of the room.

Twenty minutes later, all four butchered birds hanging among the cucumber vines, Rabbi Meyer recited the blessing over the fulfillment of the Jewish commandment to cover their blood. "You are the Source of blessing, O L-rd, our G-d, King of the Universe, Who sanctified us with his commandments, and commanded regarding covering blood with earth." He poured a pail of rich, dark, spaceship-manufactured soil over the bloodstained dirt.

*   *   *

Thursday, March 29th, 2029 18:30

As millions back on Earth gathered around their tables for the Passover Seder meal, the annual commemoration of the Exodus of the Jewish People from Egypt three thousand three hundred and forty-one years previously, we on *Providence* joined them from afar.

"Really afar, more afar than anyone else ever," I thought aloud. "The most afar anyone has made a Seder in three thousand three hundred and forty-one years of Jewish history."

"Not right, Michael," Meital said, sitting tightly next to me at the corner of the Meyers' dining table. "What about Dad and Uncle Aviel? They had Passover during their trip out two years ago."

"But they had to celebrate separately on different spacecraft. We're celebrating together."

Passover, the fifteenth of the Hebrew month of Nissan, fell on Friday night, March 30 on Earth, but for us, at the same time, it was only Thursday night, March 29. The discrepancy was due to our longer days, as the computer continued to slow our clocks ever so imperceptibly. Each *Providence* day, at this point in our journey, was twenty Earth-minutes longer than a standard earth day. Compared to everyone back on the home planet, we had skipped an entire sleep cycle. As we counted, we had reached only the twenty-ninth of

Loss

March, whereas earthlings were already on the thirtieth. March 30 for us would be the thirty-first on Earth. But then, as April started, we would synchronize our calendars by skipping a date. There would be no March 31 on the six expedition habitats: as midnight of the thirtieth passed, April would begin. It would be April 1 throughout the solar system.

"Everybody, take a Haggadah," my mother said, handing out pamphlets containing the traditional Passover Seder service in both English and the original Hebrew.

Skipping the last day of the month would be a common occurrence for us on Mars. Making the calculation had been a bit of a nerdish pastime for Denver and me during our years of training. The extra thirty-nine and a half Earth-minutes of each Martian sol would add up to a full Earth day every thirty-six and a third sols. Nine or ten of every twelve months, we calculated, would need to be one day shorter on Mars, to keep the planets' respective calendars from diverging wildly.

"Michael, put the *karpas* on the table," Shirel said from behind me, pushing a bowl of small cucumber slices into my hand. Susan followed a moment later, handing me a bowl of salt water, before taking her place next to my sister on the other side of the table.

Unlike dates of the month, we would not synchronize Martian and Earth weekdays. Sunday for Mars might be Thursday on Earth. Mismatched days had already started for us, and the discrepancy would be evident a couple of days later, when April 1, 2029 would be Sunday on Earth but Saturday for us. Quite the April Fool's joke!

Rabbi Meyer called us to order and recited the Kiddush benediction, sanctifying the evening, beginning the Seder ceremony. We lounged comfortably on our chairs as we drank the first of four cups of reconstituted grape juice. Wine was the preferred choice, but grape juice was suitable, especially since we had no wine.

Final preparations for the Seder had been hectic. Rabbi Meyer had examined the innards of all four slaughtered chickens, making sure none had disqualifying internal damage that would render them unkosher. Dr. Esther plucked them, then salted the meat to remove remaining blood. Most of two of the chickens were dispatched downstairs to the Bouchets' small refrigerator, ready for Dr. Claudine to start cooking for Easter a couple of days later. Of the other two, my mother contributed all four wings for Sophie and Jasmine, but she did keep an extra leg in exchange. She roasted nine portions in a kosher-for-Passover pot, garnished with fresh radishes and carrots and one medium-sized potato taken from the very limited crop Denver, Sam, and Celina had grown in their Grains and Vegetables class.

"This is the bread of affliction our forefathers ate in Egypt!" Rabbi Meyer announced, holding up a piece of space-baked Matzo, starting the recitation of the story of Passover. "Let all who are hungry come and eat; may everyone who needs to, join us for the Passover feast."

While my mother had roasted the chicken, Dr. Esther had prepared other kosher-for-Passover dishes, including gathering lots of lettuce – we had avoided harvesting any for a couple of weeks – which would serve as the requisite bitter herb. Wednesday night we had performed the mandatory search for leavening, using flashlights instead of candles – "no open flames in high-oxygen environments!" – to make sure we had not inadvertently left breadcrumbs behind during our rigorous Passover cleaning.

Shirel, youngest at the table, was tasked with reading the famous Four Questions. "Why is this night different from all other nights?" she began. "On all nights we eat leavened or unleavened bread." She looked around as she added, untraditionally, "even on a spaceship!" That brought smiles to all, as she continued, "but on this night, it's all matzo."

I looked around the room at the participants. Faces glowed in simulated candlelight glimmering from both NLED walls. Susan had programmed the walls to display a sequence of images corresponding to the Haggadah story. Passover was holy like the Jewish Sabbath, so computer use was restricted, but graphical sequences programmed in advance, though wildly unconventional, were not prohibited.

"We were slaves to Pharaoh in Egypt," announced Rabbi Meyer, "and G-d took us out from there with a strong hand and outstretched arm. Had the Blessed Holy One not extracted us, we and our children and grandchildren would still be enslaved to Pharaoh in Egypt!"

I gazed across the Seder table from my cramped perch at the corner between Meital and Sam. Nine of us had gathered around the table designed for six; Rabbi Meyer led from the far end. The traditional Seder plate sat before him, remarkably complete. One might have expected to see four of the six traditional foods, those we produced locally: a bone of roasted meat (a chicken leg), a bitter herb (mature lettuce), a hard-boiled egg, and the *karpas* vegetable (cucumber). Less expected was a spoonful of horseradish, reconstituted from the powdered contents of one of a few freeze-dried packs taken along specifically for this night. Least expected was the *charoset* dip Dr. Esther had managed to prepare. The traditional Passover food, designed to recall the mortar the enslaved Israelites were forced to prepare and fashion into bricks, ought to have contained apples, pears, raisins, walnuts, cinnamon sticks, red wine and other similarly sweet and crunchy ingredients. None of those being available on *Providence*, Dr. Esther instead creatively combined carrots and beets, some grated, others boiled and mashed, with a couple of the very first harvested celery sticks. Copious quantities of sugar and cinnamon completed the concoction.

Meital elbowed me, whispering, "Michael, your turn to read." She pointed helpfully at the location on the page. I began, "The Egyptians considered us evil and afflicted us, and placed upon us hard labor."

The excitement of the celebration grew within me as I read to the end of the section. Memories of past Seders melded with the present, the compact venue and low gravity notwithstanding. We might have been at the communal table at Altiplano, or the dining room in our Red Rock apartment, or even back in our old flat in Beer Sheva, where my sisters and I lived our earliest years. Except that my father would have been leading the event. I wondered how he was celebrating tonight.

"How many great qualities the Omnipresent expressed on our behalf!" my mother read, as the group broke into song. "If He had taken us out of Egypt, but not judged them, *dayyenu!*" That alone would have been sufficient reason for appreciation. "If he had judged them, but not destroyed their idols, *dayyenu!*" Another detail for which to give thanks. "If he had brought us to the Land of Israel, even without building the Temple, *dayyenu!*" Endless gratitude would be justified.

"All the more so," read Rabbi Meyer, "double and quadruple must be our gratitude to the Omnipresent, for all He did for us."

"And all He continues to do for us, even now, even here," Ruby interjected.

Then came the passage explaining the significance of the special Passover sacrifice in the ancient holy Temple in Jerusalem. Rabbi Meyer recited it, and the passages about the matzo and the bitter herb, each of which he held high. The time arrived for the second glass of wine – again, reconstituted grape juice – followed by the obligatory matzo-eating.

"This tastes excellent, almost like real matzo," exclaimed Shirel.

Our bitter herb, fresh romaine lettuce, was sweet and tart at the same time. But what made the holiday truly festive was the main course. "Mom," I said with my broadest smile, "this is the best roast chicken I've had in as long as I can remember!"

She smiled back.

Late in the evening, having finished the feast, the Grace-after-Meals blessings, the Haggadah's psalms of gratitude, and the final cups of wine – yet again, reconstituted grape juice – we finally came to the end of the Seder service.

"Next year in Jerusalem!" called out Rabbi Meyer.

"Next year in rebuilt Jerusalem!" we all responded.

"Next year in Jerusalem?" asked Meital brashly, looking around the room at us. Her eyes glistened with unexpected sadness.

I did not understand her reaction. The holiday was a happy occasion and the meal had been joyful. "Meital," I said, "Jerusalem, the holy city, rebuilt! The perfection of humanity, the era of the messiah. It's how we end the Seder every year. What's the matter?"

She stood, her expression an incongruous mix of bewilderment and disillusion. All eyes watched her. "Next year in Jerusalem?" she asked again. "Next year? Jerusalem? On Earth?" She crossed her arms, raised her eyebrows, and frowned.

"Just like we pray every day –" my mother started.

"Mom, are you serious? Do we really mean the words we're saying?"

"Yes, of course. Why wouldn't we, my dear daughter?"

"Then what are we doing here, on a spaceship, millions of kilometers from Jerusalem?" She threw her hands into the air and raised her voice. "On our way to a different planet?" She pointed with an outstretched arm and shouted, "In the wrong direction!"

Loss

I supposed that she herself was pointing in the wrong direction, but I pushed that insensitive thought from my mind.

"What is it you want, Meital?" my mother asked softly, concerned eyes focused on my sister, apparently hoping she would respond to the calm tone.

"Mom, what are we doing here?" Tears welled in her eyes and she sobbed. "Here we are, believing that the Jerusalem Temple will be rebuilt, that history will culminate in the perfection of Earth, and that all this is imminent. Then why have we left? Don't we want to be part of it?"

"Life is more complicated than that –"

She cried out, "What madness overtook us when we decided to join this insane expedition?" Shaking her head, she continued, "You convinced us to come. You convinced me, Mom, and I agreed! Did I lose my mind? Did we all lose our minds?"

"Meital –"

"It's your fault, Mom!" she yelled. "You brought us here!" Utterly defeated, my poor sister fell onto the living room couch, slumped her head on her knees, and, sobbing silently, said softly, "What mother does that to her children?"

We all watched; nobody knew what to say.

"Meital," Rabbi Meyer called imploringly, and she lifted her head. Now her expression was apathetic. Apathetic worried me more than defeated.

"'*Im yihye nidahecha beqsei hashamaim,*'" he quoted from Deuteronomy, and translated. "G-d promises us, 'Even if your dispersed will be at the edge of the heavens, from there the L-rd your G-d will collect you, and from there He will take you, and the L-rd your G-d will bring you to the land your forefathers inherited.'" He nodded encouragingly. "Nobody, not even those of us on Mars, which is way closer to Earth than the 'edge of the heavens,' will be left behind."

Meital shook her head dejectedly and got up and left the room.

* * *

Wednesday, April 12th, 2029 16:25

"Michael, I need you here for a few minutes."

"Mom, I need to wash my hands before Metallurgy class," I protested.

"And your face, too. Look at you! Wash up and meet me in your room."

Celina and I had just finished summer semester's second Mycology class. We had harvested the last flush of mushrooms from the Mauve-Level greenhouse room's mushroom cabinet. In class the following week, Omar had promised, we would learn how to pasteurize the darkened cabinet to destroy pests, before beginning the composting for the next production cycle.

Celina flashed me a wide-eyed "you're in trouble!" look as she headed upstairs. "Try to hurry," she called out. "Dr. Esther starts her classes exactly on time!"

Denver ought to have followed her up to class, but instead he held back, watching me with a curious smirk. "I have to see this. If we're late, I can blame you."

I myself was curious. I found my mother waiting for me as I left the washroom. My face was very clean (I had checked twice in the mirror). In my mother's hands was a black meter-long plastic roll, which I recognized as a bag of sterilized bathroom waste. I had packed quite a few such bags, up to the day that Captain Becker had angrily swapped my spaceship-maintenance task with Denver's.

"It's your turn," my mother said, leading me to my bedroom and pointing to the wall behind my bed. "We need the space to store 'future fertilizer.' Take down the wall hanging."

"It's not so bad, Michael," Denver said, apparently noticing my repulsed expression. "I packed this one myself." He did not hide his glee.

"Anyway," my mother said, "it's time to choose a new wall covering. A change of scenery. Why not pick a different color? There are dozens to choose from in the drawer under my bed."

I unsnapped the corners of the wall hanging, exposing several rows of the water tubes that surrounded the habitat. The tubes were critically important, not just for storing our water supply, but also for protecting us from radiation: the twenty-centimeter-thick wall of water reduced our exposure by half. I noticed, with concern, that the second row above my bed was empty, its tube lying flat. I knew that our water supply dwindled as we electrolyzed it, to extract oxygen for breathing, but I did not want to be the one who suffered increased radiation exposure as a result.

"Mom, I've been unprotected from cosmic rays and I didn't realize it!"

"Just from this morning," she said, handing me the bag, "when I instructed the computer to redirect water out of this particular tank. Michael, I wouldn't put my own son in danger!"

Denver raised his eyebrows. "But someone else's son you would? Like me?"

I watched them both as I knelt on my bed and heaved the bulging bag onto the vacated shelf. It fit snugly. I closed the straps that would hold it in place.

"Of course not, Denver. You are like a son to me." My mother flashed him a wicked smile. "But some of those kids upstairs ...."

*   *   *

Thursday, April 20th, 2029 18:30

Sam and Omar swapped places with my sisters for Thursday afternoon's exercise session. Denver and I pedaled vigorously on the cycles while Omar and Sam rowed. We were watching the second half of the vintage film *2001: A Space Odyssey*. The astronauts were discussing shutting down HAL, the omnipresent computer, and had made every effort to hide their conversation from its ubiquitous ears. Unbeknownst to them, while they plotted in a closed pod shuttle, the computer watched them through a window, reading their lips.

"Monday is a holiday for me," Omar interrupted. "*Eid al-Adha*. The Feast of the Sacrifice. It will be lonely to celebrate by myself."

Sam turned to his roommate. "No way we're going to let you celebrate by yourself, Omar. If you invite us, we'll come."

In the film's next scene, astronaut David Bowman watched his colleague, Frank Poole, on a small video screen. Poole had set out to retrieve a component the computer reported faulty. Wearing his pressure suit and helmet, he exited the shuttle spacecraft.

"Captain Becker would go crazy if we did something like that," Denver remarked. "To go floating, untethered, through the void."

I imagined the captain's reaction. "He might shackle us to a wall."

"Sam, of course you are invited," Omar said. "You two, also. Please join me Monday night – I am planning a feast."

On the NLED wall, Poole's shuttle pod rotated silently, opened its gripping claws, and set out in ominous pursuit.

"We'll be there," Sam promised.

"Us, too," I added.

The movie scene changed. Frank Poole's space-suited body flew across the screen. The stricken astronaut struggled, haplessly, to reconnect his air hose, as Bowman looked on, unable to help.

"I look forward to dining with you," Omar said.

Frank Poole's lifeless body tumbled through space.

*   *   *

Monday, April 24th, 2029 20:00

"What class are you skipping, Michael?" Omar asked.

"European History. I got special permission from the instructor."

"The instructor is Dr. Dana," Denver commented. "His own mother let him skip night class."

"Tell her thanks from me. I am glad not to be alone."

"Thank you for inviting us," Sam said.

The four of us were sitting around the Pink-Level dining table. A documentary about the Hajj in Mecca played silently on the NLED wall beside us. Pilgrims were circling the Kaaba at the Great Mosque, under a sunny blue sky.

"Especially since you are offering the best meal on board," Denver said. "Thanks for inviting us to share the last chicken."

"It is supposed to be a cow, or a camel, or a sheep," Omar said. "We slaughter it in memory of the willingness of the Prophet Ibrahim –"

"That's Abraham to us," Sam unnecessarily interjected for my edification.

"– to sacrifice his son. But he sacrificed a ram instead."

"But a chicken is acceptable?" I asked.

"No, not really. The idea is to slaughter livestock and share the meat with the poor and indigent. And spend the holiday's four days visiting relatives and celebrating with them."

"So why the chicken?"

"Captain Becker insisted. You all had chicken for your holidays, so I got a chicken for mine. I am not complaining; I appreciate the fairness."

That was true: the Beckers and Bouchets had dined on a couple of chickens for their Easter celebration three weeks earlier. A week later, Rabbi Meyer slaughtered a fifth bird for Simeon and Boris, who invited Sophie and Jasmine and their parents to share their Orthodox Easter meal. A sixth rooster, one of the three that remained, was designated for Omar, and Rabbi Meyer had slaughtered it for him that very morning.

Omar changed the subject. "Michael, what is with your sister? She was supposed to start a new Grains and Vegetables class this semester, but has not attended. Can you talk to her?"

"I know that she's been unhappy the past few weeks." That was an understatement; her mood had not improved since the Passover scene. "But I didn't know she was skipping class."

"She spends a lot of time in her bedroom," Denver said.

"I think she's been caring for the chickens as usual," Sam said. "At least Ruby hasn't mentioned anything out of the ordinary."

"I am worried about Meital," Omar said, "and I think you should be, too. See if you can encourage her."

It was not to be.

* * *

Wednesday, April 26th, 2029 10:05

Neither Yellow nor Pink Level had air filters dirty enough to replace or clean Wednesday morning, so I finished my chores early. I had just taken the ebook from my night-table cabinet, thinking I could make some progress through Asimov's *Second Foundation*, when Ruby knocked on the doorpost.

"Michael, I'm glad you're here. I'm alone downstairs this morning. Have you finished your chores? Can you help me clean the chicken coops?"

"Where's Meital?"

"She's your sister. Maybe you know."

"She's your friend."

"Yes, she is, and I'll probably forgive her, again, for leaving me alone to deal with the birds, again." She caught my eye and flashed an exaggerated grin. "Meanwhile, I know I can count on you to fill in for her."

"You don't give me much choice." I followed her bouncing frizzy hair down to Mauve Level, then through the airlock hatch gaping in the living room floor, and down the red rope ladder into the chickens' bay.

"Grab the handheld vacuum cleaner and clean the floor of the main coop."

"What about the eggs the chickens laid?"

"I've already gathered today's batch." She waved vaguely toward the wall behind her. Much of the airlock's round white wall was hidden by cages, but she indicated an exposed section. High hooks held folded airtents, packed Mylar spacewalking suits, and other outdoor equipment. A couple of low shelves held various containers, including, I supposed, one with the recently laid eggs.

I opened the largest cage and reached in to begin vacuuming. Not having to worry about breaking eggs, I did not pay much attention to the task. Instead, I twisted around to search the airlock, and asked, "Isn't there supposed to be an incubator here with fertilized eggs? Is anything hatching?"

Ruby was replacing water bottles in the parakeet and canary cages. The bottles were ingenious devices, designed to deliver drops of water to petite bird beaks, whether in gravity or in weightlessness. Snapping a bottle into place, she answered, "We gave up on those eggs weeks ago. Nothing hatched."

I looked up at her. "That's disappointing."

"Not really. We were doubtful about whether the young hens' eggs would hatch. We'll try to breed the birds in earnest after we've settled into the underground trenches on Mars. If the hens survive the trip." She closed and latched the canary cage.

"And the roosters," I said.

"We don't really need any roosters." She pushed the last empty water bottle into a nylon bag. "Males aren't particularly necessary. They make only a minor contribution to the breeding process, and we bring that 'contribution' along, frozen." She looked at me and giggled, then blushed and looked away.

"Males are useful for vacuuming," I said, finishing the floor of the main coop. "What's next?"

"The parakeet cages."

I got to work cleaning and Ruby distributed feed in each of the cages. She looked at me, then turned away. Then she looked at me again. "Michael, what do you think you'll do once we get to Mars?"

"When we get to Mars?" I raised my head to face her. "I've never given it much thought. Just getting there has always been the challenge. What will I do?" I shrugged. "For starters, I'll give my father a thousand hugs! Then, I guess, I'll get to work with everybody else to build the new settlement. Like the Foundation expects us to."

"The Foundation expects more than that."

When she did not elaborate, I asked, "What do you mean?" I stretched my arm as far as possible into the cage, to suck up the last droppings from the corner. Then I pulled the vacuum out, latched the door shut, and stood up.

Ruby focused on the feed tray she was attaching inside the canary cage. Quietly, she said, "We're supposed to build families." Still looking into the cage, she added, "Do you think you'll marry?"

I thought of Hannah. "Yes, eventually, at some point, I expect I will."

"Why 'eventually?'" She turned and looked directly at me. "What is there to wait for?"

"What about you?" I asked, uncomfortable under her steady gaze.

"I would marry right away if I could." She smiled, a deep, warm smile, her green eyes glowing, but then she blushed a second time and broke eye contact. "Let's take the droppings upstairs to Susy for the worms."

*   *   *

Tuesday, May 2nd, 2029 15:15

Simeon played with his goatee as he explained Ohm's Law again. He had a bunch of equations up on the NLED wall, behind where he was sitting at the head of the Mauve-Level table. He ran a hand through his dark brown hair.

Helga, sitting next to her sister, raised her hand. "I do not see how your explanation matches the equation."

Sam, on the other side of the table, asked, "is there a mistake there?"

"No," Denver said. "It is the resistance that is constant. Is that what you meant, Simeon?"

Somebody wailed upstairs. We all looked up. Loud sobbing followed.

"That's your mother, Michael."

Everybody was suddenly staring at me.

I jumped from my seat, heart pounding in my chest, my vision tunneling. I barely remember leaping up the seven steps to Green Level, but I do remember Dr. Jhonathan catching me as I emerged and pulling me into a tight hug.

"Michael, I'm so sorry. Your father has died."

Doriel

Tuesday, May 2nd, 2029 15:30

I stood frozen in Dr. Jhonathan's embrace. My father? On Mars? The room blurred around me. My heart pounded. My eyes squeezed shut over salty tears.

"Mom?" I heard myself whisper. "What about Mom?" With effort, I opened my eyes and looked over Dr. Jhonathan's shoulder. On the other side of the room stood my mother, in Dr. Esther's embrace, sobbing softly, tears strewn across her cheeks. She looked up and caught my eye. Rising stoically, she dressed her face in a we-are-strong-enough-to-face-this-together demeanor. I pushed away from Dr. Jhonathan and ran to her.

But then I saw Shirel. Standing alone in the corner, frozen in place, shock twisting her face in a heartbreaking, heartbroken expression, my baby sister was lost and alone. I changed direction.

As I reached her and pulled her into my own tight embrace, she moaned, "Michael, how will we settle Mars without Dad?"

All I could push from my lips was "I don't know."

"Why, Michael, why?"

"We knew he was sick...."

"But why, why are we going?"

I wanted to have an answer. I realized I had none. I tried to think.

Somebody grabbed us into a triple hug. "My babies, my beautiful babies," my mother purred soothingly in our ears. She sobbed a forced whisper, "Don't worry; we are not alone. You will never be alone." She held us tightly and did not let go.

I felt very alone.

Again, I tried to think. "The funeral, Mom," I said. "What about the funeral? What will we do?"

"You will not do anything." Dr. Louis's voice was unexpected but firm. He stood behind us, next to Captain Becker, eyes on his datapad. "Stephen and Ofer are taking care of everything."

"Will Dad have a Jewish burial?" Shirel asked, watching my mother as she stepped back.

"I don't know. I think so ... they will try."

"Shirel," Dr. Jhonathan said, "I'm sure they are doing the best they can under the circumstances, but they do not have a ceremonial mikveh pool for the purification."

"But they have lots of room for a cemetery," I heard myself saying, ridiculously.

"Yes, Michael, there is room for all of us, but not, we pray, for a very, very long time.

I tried to focus my thoughts. Thinking was difficult. I asked, "Is Dad the first?"

"What do you mean?"

"I mean, is my father the first human being to be buried on Mars? Is he setting a record?"

"Michael," Captain Becker answered in a voice meant to sound sympathetic, "your father was one of the first twelve people on Mars. He already set a record."

"Where's Meital?" Shirel interjected. "Did anyone tell her?"

A glance around the living room confirmed that Meital was missing. Her bedroom door was tightly shut, so I knocked, but there was no response, which was not unexpected, given that the habitat's folding doors were made of soft material. I slid the door open and looked inside. There she was, crouched on her lower bunk, feet on the floor, head on her knees, an entangled mess of long black hair obscuring everything. She did not move.

"Meital."

She did not move. I sat down next to her.

"Meital."

"Go away."

Shirel and my mother stood in the doorway, but I waved them out. My sister needed her older brother.

"Meital." A third time, louder. "We've had a family tragedy. We've lost our father. You can't do this alone."

"Go away. I am alone. I want to be alone."

I almost gave up. I started to stand, but I stopped myself and settled back onto the bed. I put my arm around her.

She shook off my arm and sat up straight. "Go away!" A third time, louder.

"No."

"No?" She lifted her head and glared at me: her misery was momentarily replaced by astonishment at my impudence. Her cheeks were awash with tears.

"No, Meital, I'm not going away. You once told me you would always be here for me if I needed to talk. Same by me: I'm here for you if you need to talk."

"I don't need to talk." She was crying again, and sobbing, and her head fell back to her knees.

"Yes, you do! You obviously need to talk! Stop avoiding me."

"Avoiding you?" She sat up and glared again (I counted that as progress). "There's nothing to avoid. There's nothing left to say."

"Nothing left to say? Dad has died, and you have nothing to say?"

"Dad died long ago. He died the day he joined the mission. Then we decided to join him. We're dead too. We're all dead."

My Meital, not disposed to craziness, was bewildering me. "I'm not dead," I protested, somewhat unnecessarily.

"Michael," she said, looking straight into my eyes, "we are as good as dead." She exhaled slowly and steadied her breathing. "This mission is slow suicide. We were abject morons, or perhaps just overtaken with excitement-induced madness, to agree to come. Earth is for living people. Space is death. Dad just proved the obvious."

I wanted to argue. I wanted to encourage my beloved sister. I wanted to recall why we had been so enthusiastic, so excited about our pioneering opportunity. I wanted to remind her about our plans for building a future for humanity on Mars. I wanted to console a mourning soul.

What came out was "I wish you were wrong." But she was not wrong. At that moment, as my orphanage commenced, it was clear to me that we had all chosen death.

* * *

Wednesday, May 3rd, 2029 07:30

Mourners in Judaism do not bathe. We do not study. We do not leave the house. We do not shave or cut our hair. We sit on the floor for seven days, reflecting, talking about the life of the deceased, accepting comfort from friends and acquaintances. Even on a spaceship.

I adjusted my position on the thin mattress I had dragged out to the empty living room. Despite the low one-third-Earth gravity, sitting on the floor was uncomfortable, and I said so.

"Perspective, Michael," Sam would tell me sometime later that week. "Losing your father is what's really uncomfortable."

Mourning started, officially, Wednesday morning, when we awakened to the news that my father had been laid to rest. This news came in the form of a video message from Stephen Anders, broadcast indirectly from Mars via Earth relay. My mother put the message up on the NLED wall for all of us to watch. Dad's closest friend on Mars appeared on the screen, sitting in their MiniHab's upper deck, the drab hull visible behind the small couch. His dark hair was cropped, his beard trimmed, but his eyes were dull with sadness.

"Dana, we are so sorry for your loss. Your loss is our loss."

The other habitat mates, Ofer and Ricardo, appeared briefly, nodding their condolences.

"We established the cemetery a few hundred meters from the ships, in a small depression at the edge of the valley. We would have preferred to dig the grave ourselves, but the ground is packed and frozen, too hard for human diggers. It's hard because of its water content, so that's not a bad thing, but we needed to have the mining robots dig the grave. We placed Doriel's body there, dressed in his mundies and his deflated fleximet, covered in his woolen prayer shawl, everything done according to Ofer's instructions. We were all there – all eleven of us; even Taro managed to get out, despite his weakened state. I eulogized Doriel and so did Sonny. We gave him an honorable burial.

"Your husband was a huge asset to our project and will forever be remembered as indispensable to the first founding of human Martian settlement. He worked ceaselessly, even as he suffered more and more from his illness. He insisted on helping oversee the mining robots, making sure we kept pace with water collection and with preparing the tunnels. Most importantly, he kept us sane. We have no other psychologist here and we had no better friend. Who will comfort us until your arrival?

"Dana, keep strong, you and your children, and all your friends on *Providence*. Get here soon: it's lonely without Doriel, and without all of you."

The video cut off. In its place appeared a large green lawn under a dreary, cloudy, drizzly sky. Students hurried across crisscrossing paths. I recognized the location, a quadrangle at Brown University. I supposed that my mother had selected this particular video in my father's honor, to recall the place where they first met. The drizzly wetness clouded my eyes.

The burial complete, our mourning had begun. I dropped onto my uncomfortable mattress on the floor, and cried.

* * *

Thursday, May 4th, 2029 11:30

"Thanks, Boris, for doing my job for me today."

"Michael, of course it is not a problem, given what has happened."

He and Simeon pulled up chairs and sat across from us. Simeon looked like he wanted to speak but did not know what to say.

"You never got the chance to meet my husband, isn't that right?" asked my mother, who sat next to me on the mattress.

"We joined the Foundation only after the Vanguard mission had left Earth," Simeon said.

"Only after they landed on Mars," Boris corrected. "The two of us came straight to Altiplano in the summer of '27."

"You were replacements for my uncle and his group after they were lost," Shirel stated bluntly.

I protested. "Shirel, I don't think it's nice to call Simeon and Boris 'replacements.'"

"It is okay," said Simeon. "We were lucky to get to be replacements."

"Not that we are happy at the circumstances that made it possible," added Boris.

"I cannot believe that both brothers have been lost now," Simeon said. "First Aviel, now Doriel. Everyone always said such good things about both of them."

I imagined Boris and Simeon as younger versions of my father and Uncle Aviel. Similar age differences, similar excitement about space exploration and colonization. Different outcomes, I hoped. I prayed silently, *"G-d, please protect them, and all of us."*

"I do not think it would have been possible for us to join the program and train so quickly if not for your husband's psychology research," Boris said. "The accelerated isolation training – being completely alone for four days straight! – was designed to simulate long-term isolation."

"Designed to induce psychological reactions quickly. Reactions that normally would happen only after many months," Simeon said, shuddering. "That was the hardest part of the training."

"I wish I had the chance to meet him. I was looking forward to asking many, many questions." Boris looked at my mother sympathetically. "Dana, how will manage without him?"

She sighed and smiled sadly. "I guess I'll have to find the strength. Not much choice, is there?"

"We could turn around and go back," Shirel said. I could not tell if she meant it seriously.

My mother looked at my sister appraisingly. "No. That is not what Dad would have wanted. It would be disrespectful if we gave up now. Continuing his work on Mars – that's how we'll overcome his loss and honor his memory."

The Radechov brothers got up to leave as Ruby and Susan appeared and took their places.

"Mom made lunch for you," Ruby said. "A mushroom-chickpea salad served with pita bread. Susy and I baked the bread last night." She caught my eye but looked away quickly. "Not as good as yours, Michael. But I think it came out reasonably okay."

"I can't imagine what it's like to lose your father," Susan said. "I'm so sorry for all of you."

"Susan, what do you remember about Doriel?"

"I remember lots, Dr. Dana." She gazed toward the room's far corner. "There was this day that Shirel and I were trying to bake a cake."

"I remember that," Shirel said. "It was for your tenth birthday."

"We thought it would be boring to bake a cake in the regular apartment oven," Susan continued. "We weren't regular girls; we were space pioneers! We went over to the Red Rock facility's engineering lab to try the new space stovetop." She suppressed a giggle. "Of course, the spinning feature is only for weightlessness, but we didn't know that then."

"It wouldn't have been such a problem if they had finished calibrating the speed," Shirel said.

"Or the temperature. Your father discovered us right in the middle of the baking. The pot was much too hot and spinning way too fast! It was a gigantic mess. He was really angry."

"I don't think we actually broke anything," Shirel said defensively.

"The thing was, he didn't yell, or punish us, or anything. He was nice and calm. I thought we deserved much worse."

"Doriel loved all of you," my mother said. "Not just our own kids – of course he loved you three most of all – but all of the program's children. Susan, you were like a niece to him."

"That's how he always made me feel."

*   *   *

Thursday, May 4th, 2029 15:30

Sam and his father came down to console me.

"Michael, I'm lost without you," Sam said, feigning despair. "You've got to finish this mourning week."

"It's not my fault!"

"I didn't say it was. But learning Talmud alone – I can't do it. I need my learning partner. It's my favorite part of the day."

"Mine too, I guess. Thanks. But you don't need me to review what we've been learning. You can learn with your father."

But that was no longer true for me, I realized with a jolt. I felt a queasy emptiness in my stomach. To hide my tumbling emotions, I continued, stumbling over my words, "I assume you've been utilizing your learning time well without me." My voice sounded artificially stern.

Sam did not seem offended. "Yes, sir! Well utilized! Including the extra hours that we added this semester. I spent three hours today reviewing the past few folios."

"You weren't alone today, though," Rabbi Meyer pointed out.

"The two of you learned together? I'm jealous."

They both smiled; then we sat in silence for a few minutes. I pictured myself working through a Talmud folio with my own father, and I held back my tears.

By custom, one waits for the mourner to speak before responding. Sam and his father waited for me. I sighed and shook my head. "It seems pointless to continue."

"To continue mourning, Michael?" Dr. Jhonathan asked, slowly and sincerely.

"To continue anything. Mourning. The mission. The journey. Studying. Anything."

"I can understand your feelings."

"Can you? Have you ever felt as empty as I feel?" My tears broke through.

He reached out and took my hand. "Michael, I can't compare your emptiness to my own. But I lost my father, too, though I was much older. My father lived to see his grandchildren. But that did not matter much to my feelings. I was still his little boy, and he my dad, even at the very end. I still felt empty, and still feel empty now when I think of him."

"Did your father kill himself, Dr. Jhonathan?"

"No, G-d forfend! Of course not! Why do you ask such a question?"

"Because it's worse for me, knowing that my father did."

Sam and his father looked at each other and Sam asked, in a hushed voice, "Dad, should I go and leave you alone with Michael?"

"No, stay, Sam," I said, sincerely. "I'm sorry if I sound angry. It's not against you."

"Michael," Dr. Jhonathan asked again, calmly, "why do you say that your father killed himself? He died of a disease. He did not choose to get sick."

"Maybe he did not choose to get sick, but he sure brought the illness upon himself! He got onto an unprotected spaceship to head out on a deadly journey. It was his choice to leave us. He subjected himself to the obvious outcome. Meital was right: it's no better than suicide." I looked up earnestly. "Just like Uncle Aviel." I shook my head and my tears streamed. "Just like us."

Dr. Jhonathan paused for a moment. Then, "Are you angry at your father?"

My own hesitation was brief. "Of course, I'm angry at him!" My voice, under control up to that point, broke free of all constraints and I screamed, "I'm furious!" I collapsed onto the mattress, wailing and sobbing, my face in my hands. The Meyers waited patiently.

Then Sam joined me on the mattress and placed his arm around my shoulder. He pulled me upright and I leaned into him. My sobbing slowly subsided. I looked at Dr. Jhonathan through blurry eyes.

He gazed back. "Michael, you have plenty of reasons to be angry. This mission is a result of difficult decisions, many resulting in difficult outcomes. Outcomes that have hurt you. Everything about this journey involved difficult choices, compromises, even gambles. Know, however, that none of us took the choices lightly." He stared sadly into my eyes. "Especially not your father."

"It's one thing for a person to make choices that affect himself. But my father's choices affected his family. His children. He should have taken us into account."

"I think he did take you into account." He paused to consider his next words. "A father's choices always affect his children. Doriel and your mother weighed the opportunities and costs, both for themselves and for you, first when they joined the expedition, and later when Doriel and his brother left on the Vanguard mission."

"Obviously, he made the wrong choice, because I'm affected personally, and it infuriates me."

"It's okay that you do not agree with your father's choices."

"Thanks for the confirmation," I said snidely, but immediately regretted my tone. Dr. Jhonathan was the last person who deserved disrespect.

"But it's also okay that your father made choices you disagree with."

"I don't agree."

"Yes, Michael, that's my point. You don't agree, and perhaps you never will. I hope you can at least understand your father's point of view. Maybe someday you'll even be able to forgive him."

"You think I need to forgive him?"

"Now is a time for mourning. It's too early for you to begin to understand your anger, or the hurt. But yes, I think someday you will need to forgive your father."

I did not understand.

*   *   *

Friday, May 5th, 2029 01:45

Was it that I would never see my father again? Or that I would never see my grandmother, or my cousins, or my earthly friends? Or was the cause of my sleepless misery deeper, more internally personal? I had agreed to this folly! I had chosen to come along. I had even encouraged my sisters. It was all my own fault. An impersonal loss – that I could blame G-d for. But this? I myself had pushed my father to go, and now he was gone. I remembered the discussion clearly. *Dad, I think you and Aviel should volunteer for the water-mining mission. Don't worry: we'll come and join you later.* My bedroll closed in on me. My shame was too great to bear. I wanted to vomit. I pushed away the sheets and rolled out of bed.

Denver stirred. Was he listening? Had he heard my quiet weeping? Did he watch as I skulked out of the tiny room? I was not sure, but he did not say a word.

I stood over the space toilet heaving, but no vomit came. My humiliation crushed me. The stupidity. The childish short-sightedness. I stepped back into the darkened living room. There was nobody there but me, but it was me, myself, whom I could not bear. *Run, flee, escape!* But there was nowhere to run to. I could not run from myself. I pulled at my hair in exasperation. Tears of frustration formed in my eyes. *Go! Get out!* But all exits were sealed.

Seven drilled-in years of training kicked in, again, as before, so many times now! "F-L-I-E-R-S," an inner voice intruded. The Foundation's mnemonic for self-calming, "Freeze, Listen, Inhale …."

After years of cognitive programming, even just three steps triggered an effect. By the time I inhaled, I knew where to go: to the forest, my alone place, my place to commune with the Creator. If not exactly a forest, at least the next best thing, the Green-Level greenhouse room. I stepped inside and quietly slid the door shut behind me. I exhaled slowly, and inhaled again, and exhaled, and waited for my eyes to adjust to the indistinct nightlight.

How our tomato crop had thrived! Bushy vines filled half the room, waist-height to ceiling, tomatoes of all sizes hanging before me. A floor above, I knew, a similar tangle of cucumber vines filled the Pink-Level greenhouse room. The cucumbers appeared in my mind's eye, overlaying the tomatoes. And bell peppers downstairs, red, green, and bright yellow – I had dropped in to take a look one afternoon, just a week earlier. Clearly, the Creator had deigned to join us out here in nowhere. That knowledge, philosophically obvious – of course the Creator of everything is present everywhere – was made palpable by the growing greenery.

Still, I could not bear to face myself. Could I face Him?

"Is it all a mistake?" I asked, Him or myself; I was not sure whom.

No answer came. Or perhaps one came, but I was too distraught to hear. Or too guilty. Or too stupid.

"Was it foolishly rash to join this mission?"

The tomatoes hung silently. Bushy carrot and radish leaves filled the shelves to my right, but they did not answer. They barely rustled in the air processors' airflow.

"Could I have saved Dad?" I asked myself. "Is it my fault he died?" That one was to G-d.

Tears again filled my eyes and I cried silently. It could not all be my fault, I told myself.

"But I could have stopped him," I whispered, sobbing, emptiness spreading through my chest. His death was at least partly my fault. My own father! *Who sends his father away like I had sent mine?*

Was it okay, as Dr. Jhonathan had said, that my father made choices I disagreed with? *But I never told him I disagreed.* "How could he have known?" I whispered to myself. "If I had argued with him, maybe he would have changed his mind and he would still be here." My own words hung there, echoing in the greenhouse, torturing me.

"G-d, how can I live with myself?"

I envied the tomatoes and carrots and radishes growing there, silently in the darkness. They lived carelessly, free of doubt and guilt. Their purpose was clear: grow in the LED-light until ripe, then get eaten. Simple and straightforward. My own purpose was foggy. Fry in the interplanetary radiation, then get swallowed by Mars? Like my father?

I do not know how long I stood there crying, torturing myself, my thoughts wracked and twisted, my eyes moist with tears of anguish, before the door slid slowly open. Somebody came in and draped an arm across my shoulders, pulling me close.

"Michael," Denver said quietly, "you are suffering so much."

"Yeah," I muttered, my voice broken by involuntary shuddering sobs.

"You were missing from your bed and were not in the bathroom. I guessed I might find you here."

"It's green in here," I said, as if that explained my choice of self-torment venue.

He held on to me. "I lost my father, too. In a different way. But he is just as gone."

"It's not the same."

"It is almost the same. Maybe even worse. I will never see or talk to my father again."

"Me neither."

"No," Denver said, twisting to face me in the cramped, shadowy space. His expression was sympathetic. "You can always talk to your father. And you will hear his response in your mind."

What was he getting at? How was that any different? "You can imagine your father, too, Denver," I protested.

"But why would I want to? Talking with my father, for real or imagined – even just the idea of his voice makes me angry. But your father was different. He loved you. Loved us."

"Okay."

"Better than okay, Michael. I feel happy – and I am not even his real son – if I imagine him here, laughing with us. Do you not feel that way, too?"

I shrugged my shoulders. I did not know how I felt.

Denver pulled me close again, as my muddled mind tried to decide if imagining my father made me feel any better.

* * *

Friday, May 5th, 2029 19:45

"Meital, I'm so happy you're here with us," Susan said brightly, an orange spoonful of lentil soup at her lips. "I know you are not feeling great, but it's so much better that you are sitting here with us instead of alone in your room."

Meital gazed at her, silently, and nodded almost imperceptibly. Her expression was morose and her eyes were moist. Behind her, on the NLED wall, Sabbath candlelight shone, flickering atop a gorgeous, golden candelabrum. The Sabbath had temporarily suspended the seven-day mourning period and we had gathered together for the traditional Friday-night dinner. Four Tellers still survived, and we joined the five Meyers, crowding again, just barely, around their Pink-Level dining table.

Meital stared at the cabbage-and-carrot salad on her plate.

"Mom," said Ruby, breaking the silence and saving her friend from scrutiny, "the mushroom-chickpea stew is excellent."

"Thank you," said Dr. Esther with a smile.

Susan was still watching Meital. "Meital, why don't you take out your flute tomorrow night? Maybe playing music will raise your spirits."

Shirel nudged her friend, frowning. "We don't need to raise our spirits artificially. It makes no sense for us to pretend to be happy."

Susan started to protest, but Sam interrupted. "Anyway, it's forbidden," he said, offering a Jewish-Law perspective, "to play music during the year of mourning."

"Not necessarily," Dr. Jhonathan said. "Not if it is needed for one's psychological health."

Meital looked like she wanted to slip down her chair and disappear under the table.

"Maybe she could take up painting," Susan persisted. "Shirel, can you lend Meital your paintbrushes?"

I had forgotten about Shirel's paintbrushes, which she had packed somewhere, for eventual use on Mars. The brushes and some watercolor paints were the personal artifact Shirel had selected for her journey.

"Susan," my mother said sensitively, as she too watched Meital, "you are sweet to be concerned. But I think what Meital needs –

what we all need – is time. Coming to terms with our loss will take time." My mother's eyes, like Meital's, glistened in the artificial candlelight.

Ruby brushed a strand of frizzy hair out of her eyes and turned to her younger sister, looking puzzled. "Susy, how exactly is anybody supposed to use the paintbrushes to paint?"

"What's the problem?" Susan toyed with her sister, a mischievous sparkle in her eyes.

"We have no canvas on board," Ruby said, with a look of stating the obvious. "Or even paper. Brushes seem insufficient given the circumstances."

"I found a new program for the NLED walls," Susan said simply. "According to the developers, it uses the wall's cameras to track paintbrush movement. As you brush the wall, the program simulates painting strokes and applies color."

"That's amazing. I wonder if an artist can really paint that way."

"You can even mix colors as if you are mixing real paints," Susan said. "At least according to the developers' notes. We can download the program after the Sabbath. I can email the Foundation and ask them to buy a license."

*   *   *

Monday, May 8th, 2029 20:00

"All four of you impress me," Omar said, joining my mother and sisters and me on the last evening of our mourning week. "You are brave, beyond what I would expect for myself, to have joined the expedition."

"And you are not, Omar?" my mother asked, eyebrows raised.

"Not so much." He glanced around at us. "Certainly there is a special bravery in spacefaring children. More, even, in a mother who is willing to take her babes and watch over them during such an adventure."

Meital finally spoke, but all she said was, "'Recklessness' is the word you are looking for, Omar, not 'bravery.'"

"No, Meital, I really think you are brave. I do not think the mission is reckless."

An alarm blared, then turned to a very loud continuous buzz. Everyone looked around, startled.

The air suddenly seemed very still. "Have the circulation fans stopped?" Omar asked, loudly, competing with the alarm. My mother stood and rushed to the stairwell to check the air-processing systems.

Boris came running up from downstairs, datapad in his hands, eyes glued to its screen. He tapped the datapad a couple of times to shut off the alarm, then joined my mother at the equipment stack. A row of LEDs glowed bright red. He pressed the "Disengage" switch – apparently unnecessarily – then grasped and pulled out the first of the filters. It was caked black with compacted dust. Shaking his head, he pulled out the second filter. It, too, was filthy. He stared at it for a moment, an incredulous expression on his face, then, apprehensively, pulled out the third. This time he did not look surprised to see the grime. Instead, a look of cold fury appeared in his eyes as he turned and found me standing behind him.

Just then Captain Becker arrived from upstairs. "Boris," he said sternly, "what is going on with your air systems?" He was a captain who expected his crew to take responsibility.

"I am working on figuring that out," Boris answered, suppressing his fury, looking from the captain to me. "First we should get the fans up and running on this level." He tapped his datapad. "I'm diverting half the airflow from Mauve Level."

A second alarm rang out, this time from downstairs. Boris looked back at his datapad and yelled a Russian expletive. "Michael, what have you done?" he asked accusingly.

I recoiled, bewildered. "I didn't d-do anything. I haven't touched the systems in days!"

While the buzzing alarm screeched in the background, both Captain Becker and Boris glared at me. The captain held my eyes while he addressed Boris. "Is cleaning the filters not Michael's task? But he has not 'touched the systems in days!' Have you been checking up on your subordinate, Boris?"

I stood frozen in place, mortified. My face burned.

My mother wrapped her arms around me from behind. "Perhaps there has been a misunderstanding," she said.

"Stop that alarm, Boris," the captain commanded. A few taps on the datapad shut down the noise that had been blaring up the stairwell. With no fans running now on two of four levels, the habitat sounded eerily quiet.

Boris's eyes flicked between me and my mother. "Michael, these filters look like they have not been cleaned in more than a week." His tone was patronizing.

"I cleaned them – I think on Monday of last week," I said nervously.

"And you did not notice that they need to be cleaned again?" He held up the three filters, his hand shaking.

"I thought you were checking them," I muttered. "While we have been in mourning over my father."

Captain Becker's expression was unreadable as he turned to me. "Michael, your father's death is a loss to us all. Do you think it is a reason to endanger the lives of everybody on my ship?"

"No, of course not –"

"But you have neglected your duty, when we all rely on you."

"Boris was helping me –"

Looking at me dubiously, Boris said, "I agreed to do your tasks for you, to check the filters on all four levels, the one day you asked me. You never asked me, and I never agreed, to do your work on other days!"

I wanted to melt into the deck below me. Perhaps only my mother's grip prevented it.

Captain Becker glared. "You may be young, Michael, but you have been assigned a responsibility, and, on my ship, everybody with responsibility is expected to accept that responsibility in an adult fashion. That means checking and double-checking, and not forgetting."

"Yes, sir, but –"

"Our lives depend on you, and you have endangered us all."

My face turned white. In my mind's eye, I was shackled to the living room stockade as Denver had been. But perhaps my transgression was worse? Could I have killed half the ship? Was the stockade punishment enough? Perhaps for me it really would be the airlock! Was Captain Becker going to push me outside with only two hours of air, to die in oblivion? Like my father? I collapsed into my mother's grip.

Mercifully, Captain Becker turned his attention from me to Boris. "Please get the air systems back up and running."

Doriel

"Yes, sir." Boris faced the machinery and began cleaning the filters.

The captain turned back to me and I recoiled under his cold, angry stare. He spoke loudly and slowly. "People will go to sleep soon, Michael. We do not want anyone suffocating in a pocket of carbon dioxide. Or choking on debris that should have been filtered out of the air."

I thought to protest that air pockets and debris were hazards only during weightlessness, not while the ships were rotating for artificial gravity, and that there was no real danger. Seeing the captain's menacing expression, I wisely kept my mouth shut.

"Boris," I said in a meek voice as my mother released me, "I'll head downstairs and start cleaning the Mauve-Level filters."

His only response was a courteous nod.

*   *   *

Wednesday, May 10th, 2029 21:30

It was difficult to be back in school after the week of mourning. How were we supposed to go back to normal life when nothing was normal anymore? I was an orphan. Fatherless. Nothing was the same, and never would be the same. My father would be missing when we finally arrived at our desolate destination.

I barely noticed that European History class had finished. Denver and Helga had been actively engaged, asking lots of questions about Amsterdam's development in the early sixteenth century, or something like that; I had been daydreaming. When Dr. Louis finally addressed me – the others were already getting up to leave – I shook my head embarrassedly.

"I'm sorry, Dr. Louis. I've been distracted."

"That is okay, Michael," he said, placing his hands on my shoulders. "Take your time. It might be a couple of weeks before you get back into things." There was a hint of a smile in his voice as he added, shaking me gently, "but don't skip class!" His fatherly jesting was comforting. Except that he was not my father.

"I have something for you," he said as he released me. "From your father. I did not give it to you until now because I had strict instructions to wait."

"Strict instructions? From whom?"

"From him. He wrote an essay a couple of months ago. He sent it to me, explaining that he wanted to contribute a section to your journal. He wrote, 'Michael is writing only about the journey to Mars, but who will document what we, already here, have been doing?' He hoped you would like his essay and agree to include it."

"Of course! How could I not? But why only now? Why is it you giving it to me? Why didn't he send it to me directly?"

"Actually, your father instructed me *not* to give you the essay. He wanted to give it to you himself, when you arrived. Only if he were to – to die – and not be waiting for you to give it to you in person – only then was I to give it to you."

I did not know what to think about that. I would have loved to arrive on Mars and have my father hug me, and kiss me, and offer to complement my writing with some of his own. But that would never happen. Next best would have been a direct email from him while he still lived. But that had not happened either. Instead, my father had entrusted his essay to someone other than me.

"Sending you the message before you arrived would have been admitting that he was not going to live," Dr. Louis said simply, reading my thoughts. He tapped his datapad a couple of times and my own datapad vibrated, indicating that the file with the essay had transferred successfully.

A final message from my father! My disappointment dissipated, and my heart raced with excited trepidation. I managed to articulate only "thank you, Dr. Louis" before turning to rush upstairs to my room. Settling down on my bed, I focused my watery eyes on my datapad and began to read.

Missive

March 13, 2029

It is early in the morning, early in the summer, and I'm awake in time to see the sunrise, if I do not tarry. I don and seal my fleximet. I grab an oxypack and affix it, and inflate, and run the seal test. I pull on my marsmitts. I descend into the MiniHab's little airlock and seal the hatch above me, quietly, so as not to awaken my tired hab-mates. Crouching, I sweep yesterday's dust toward the outer hatch in the center of the floor. It will spill outside easily when I open the hatch. Not yet, though. First, I must purge the airlock and save its oxygen. And save the nitrogen and argon buffer gases, which are even more precious. Such is routine life on Mars. It's not so different from life on Earth if you ignore the effort required to survive in the scant atmosphere.

As the vacuum fans suck the air from our cramped vestibule and my mundies squeeze down around me, I pull on my Mars parka: first trousers, then jacket. Carbon composite cleats complete the outfit and I'm ready to go outside. I unlatch the hatch and swing it inward. I sweep the dust through the portal, then slide myself down, out into the red murkiness.

The MiniHab sits so low that my head is still inside. I have to duck before I pull the hatch shut, and then I have to slouch my way out into the open air. It's dark on Mars before sunrise, really dark: just the starlight shines, but my eyes have not yet adjusted. Even the MiniHabs emit no glow: no candles shine in windows, there being neither candles nor windows. My fleximet lamp lights up. Now I can see a few meters out in front of me.

I have a favorite spot for watching sunrises, just north of the Foundations. We used to call our locale the "encampment" and, before that, the "landing site," but we look to the future. We envision a happy city here, children playing, parents thriving, humanity spreading joyously, all starting from this fortunate location, the Foundations of our anticipated city. I know I will not live to set my eyes upon anything more than the trenches we've dug or the bricks we've laid. Despite my limited time – or perhaps because of it – I choose to picture the future. I observe the Foundations and imagine the sprawl of the city, and a shivery thrill rises through my heart.

But that's in the daytime. Right now, I look for the only visible landmark I know that will lead me in the direction of my favorite spot: the electric cable to our buried thorium nuclear reactor. I'll follow the cable out to where it disappears underground, then continue along in the same direction, walking in as straight a line as I can manage. I'll reach the rock I like to sit on, if I'm accurate. I'm successful most of my sunrise mornings. On the others I just stand. The sunrise comes anyway.

It's cold out, though not as cold as in midwinter. Before a summer sunrise, the temperature ranges as high as minus seventy-five degrees Celsius. I don't feel the cold much, because the thin atmosphere is more an insulator than a heat conductor, even when a breeze blows. My parka trousers and jacket are almost unnecessary. Not my cleats, though. The ground is bitterly cold, dangerously so, and my feet would freeze if I stepped out of them. I remind myself that I do actually need the parka trousers, because my mundies would freeze, and probably tear, if I sat on the ground without them. I need the jacket, too: if I were to slip and fall, Martian rocks might bruise and frostbite me. In the parka, though, I'm allowed to fall. Like ironclad armor, its weave of Kevlar and Aramid fiber shields me against even the roughest shards and nastiest micro-dust.

There, up ahead, I spot my sunrise rock, vaguely visible in the light from my fleximet lamp. The reflection has a dullish orange tinge. I've reached my rock, so today is already a success, even before the sun rises. The sky to my east begins to glow vaguely bluish, though perhaps I'm just imagining that. It will be bluish without a doubt in a few minutes. I like my rock.

I like my life here. Yes, I can finally write that without reservation. I worked hard to like life here. Maybe anybody anywhere must work hard to like his life, but for me it took a long time on Mars to understand that liking life begins with a choice to do so, and then, like anything of value, requires continuous effort. There is a lot here not to like: the solitude (my eleven fellow residents are wonderful and beloved; my residual loneliness is my fault, not theirs), the barrenness (the valley is beautiful, but its beauty is static and uniform), the diet (healthful but boring), the dust (the struggle against it is continual and endless), the weather (I would have loved to feel a breeze on my face back when I used to jog across the valley), the tilt (our MiniHab landed on a slight incline, and we still have not found a feasible way to boost that third leg to level our floors), the gnawing doubts (will we succeed in our construction project, and will our families arrive safely?), and, eclipsing all else, my illness.

But there is a lot here to like. Does that surprise you? We have endless expanses, room to run, space to grow, endless opportunity. We have purpose: we are establishing the next branch of mankind. Someday there will be millions of people on Mars: living, growing, building a caring community, studying, teaching, giving, inventing, writing, praying. A barren rock in a vast, empty Universe will become a new locus of self-reflection, introspection, gratitude, and communion with its Creator. For eons He has observed this planet but nobody has looked back; He has spoken but nobody has answered; He has prepared but nobody has enjoyed. Now that is changing and I have helped to begin it. G-d granted me the opportunity to be a founder, a provisional patriarch of Martian Man. I like that, and I thank Him.

Enough dreaming. A new Martian day begins and there is lots of hard work to do this sol, if we are going to make it possible for humanity to flourish here. But before all that, the sunrise.

First light! Sunrays reflect on high, sparse, wispy, cirrus clouds. A dome of bluish sky appears over the horizon. G-d created beautiful sunrises and, I can testify, gave their beauty to many planets, not just to Earth. And He mixed up the colors. Red sunrises on the blue planet, but, ironically, blue sunrises on the red planet.

I watch an imagined arching line rise upward and slowly wipe the stars from the sky. Outlines of Red Valley's hills appear ahead of me, in shadowy silhouette, their tops jagged in some places but rounded in others. I listen to my relaxed breathing, but the ever-present drone of the oxypack fan is louder.

The sun pops out and climbs steadily above the hills. Periwinkle sunrays bathe Red Valley. The sun looks smaller here than on Earth, less than half the size, if I were to gaze at it directly, but of course I do not: Martian sunlight is no less blinding than Earthen sunlight. The sunlight *feels warm on my face, through the fleximet mask. Perhaps I'm imagining that, too. In an hour or two our neighborhood will indeed warm up, perhaps reaching zero degrees Celsius, water's melting point at standard pressure. There's nothing standard about "standard pressure" here, and water would boil at zero degrees, but I imagine ice rinks melting into sparkling pools throughout the valley's minor craters, someday after we've tented them.*

Our valley comes into view. It's actually a crater, small by global Martian standards and less pronounced than many of the others, but its roughly circular five-kilometer expanse was deemed satisfactory for human settlement by the Murke-Berger Foundation's imagery survey teams. They guessed correctly about the permafrost water content. We landed near the crater's lowest point, not far from the center, where we expected to find the richest aquifer. We renamed our new home "Red Valley" within days of arrival. As the sols passed, we discovered many other colors: rust orange, clay gray, sparkles of topaz blue, reddish yellow in small patches of fine sand, and the darker browns of the deep regolith the mining robots dig out of the trenches. Maybe we should have called the crater "Reddish Valley," but none of us liked that name.

Goshna's other residents, my hab-mates Stephen, Ofer, and Ric, will be rising soon, and they'll want help preparing for the day's work, so I rise to return to the habitat. With my spare oxypack I still have three hours of air, and I'm plenty warm, so there's no physical constraint in staying, but we are here to do a job and that job is not here on my sunrise rock. The three inhabited MiniHabs rest nearly a kilometer ahead of me, lined up in a row. Though one hundred meters separate each from the next, from my angle they appear to be bunched tightly together. Pink sunlight reflects off the tiny teepee shapes. There should have been four teepees there, but at least these three managed the journey out, and the gravity capture, and the landing. Twelve astronauts landed safely – there should have been sixteen – but we twelve have managed to do the job we came to do. Twelve, it turns out, are enough to prepare the Foundations. I miss my brother Aviel.

Still, I dance a bit on the way back; Aviel would have, too. It's a sunny morning, and my beloved wife Dana and our children are well on their way out here. Only four and a half more months! My mates and I have been waiting here for 629 sols, almost an entire Martian year. 142 sols remain until my family's arrival, and I'm counting down the days. We'll have enough water mined by then for all 139 humans, and for a horde of chickens, and parrots and canaries, and parakeets and finches and pheasants, and ants and beetles and worms. We have plenty of energy: one reactor is buried and on-line, producing a whole megawatt, and a second waits in one of the four cargo vessels that stand in a row behind our teepee-MiniHabs. For backup power we've laid out the MiniHabs' solar sheets on the ground. They provide another sixty kilowatts when the sun shines. That's enough to power our life-support systems in an emergency, if we sweep the dust off them regularly. We have a lot to like.

Red Valley radiates before me. In this area it is mostly flat, though quite rocky, like most of the planet's surface. A few tennis-court-sized craters are noticeable if you look, but they are so old and worn that they could be mistaken for simple low mounds and shallow depressions. Farther afield, approaching the crater walls, our valley becomes hillier and some of the rises offer beautiful views, if one has the urge to jog out a couple of kilometers. Stephen and I made the jaunt a bunch of times during our first months here, and I have the photos to prove it.

As I approach our row of homes, the broken Martian landscape appears. We broke it. Deep trenches run eastward from two of the MiniHabs. Someday there will be four trenches, parallel, each the core of a hemicylindrical tented living environment. For now, we are rushing to dig enough of two trenches to provide temporary underground housing for the soon-to-arrive residents. We twelve made the sacrifice to live on the radiation-exposed surface for this long. It's not been good for our health, as Taro and I gravely attest. Our families ought not suffer so.

I pass piles of desiccated dirt, detritus from the nearest trench, as I reach Goshna. Morning sunlight reflects off the habitat's white windowless hull. Behind it sits our first test MarsTent habitat, a small outdoor greenhouse that we set up just a couple of months ago. The rich black dirt we spread on the tent floor has turned green. The first Martian-grown vegetables – at least the first grown outside in natural sunlight – cover the whole four-meter-diameter surface. Plants grow quickly in a four thousand parts-per-million carbon dioxide atmosphere. The hemispherical tent puffs outward, supported only by air pressure, though a couple of rounded tent poles maintain its shape. I expect that, sometime today or tomorrow, I'll step through the airlock we attached to the tent, to sample the air and water the plants.

"Stephen, I'm outside. Is the airlock flushed?" I ask over my fleximet's radio.

My friend's voice answers almost immediately. "Doriel, good morning! We were worried about you. Yes, the airlock's ready for you. We wish you would stop wandering off alone, especially in your current state."

"I'm a Martian," I answer, "and this is my home, and you know I'm going to wander until the day you have to pump me full of morphine."

"You have such a way with English," Ofer says over the connection.

Crouching under the ship, I rotate the outer handle and shove the hatch up and inward. On Earth this would have been difficult – the hatch would weigh nearly thirty kilograms – but on Mars I push up the eleven-kilo hatch with little more than a deep breath and a sturdy shoulder. On Earth I would have to climb into the airlock using my waning upper-body strength, but here on our lightweight home I just jump, grab a handhold on the airlock ceiling, and swing my legs up and inside. But before I do that, I shake them a bit, trying to get as much dust as possible to fall back out. Then I kick the hatch gently to shut it. I twist the inside handle to lock it in place.

"Pressurize."

The computer hears me, runs a silent seal check, then pumps habitat air into the airlock. My mundies slowly release their grip on my limbs. I have barely removed my parka and cleats when the inner hatch opens and a hand reaches down to help me up.

"I'm okay!" I protest as I climb through. But I'm more out of breath today than I was just a couple of weeks ago, so I quietly accept Stephen's hand.

The bathroom is on the lower deck by the four bed-sized bedrooms. It's home: we all have privacy and almost enough space. And the toilet almost always works. I wash up, pray my morning prayers, then join Ofer, Stephen and Ricardo upstairs in the common room. A Murke Industries MiniHab's upper deck is small, just a bit more than three meters in diameter, but its domed ceiling is high to create the illusion of space. Ricardo is boiling rice on the kitchen-counter stovetop and Ofer is setting the breakfast table. Stephen picks a lone ripe cucumber from one of the vines growing under bright LED lights on the other side of the room. It will garnish our breakfast rice.

"Look how that lettuce's leaves have grown since yesterday!" I say, gazing keenly at the second of the three planters. "We should make a salad tomorrow."

"We're out of olive oil," Ric says without looking up. "Someone needs to make a run to the market."

Cargo Vessel Two – that's the cargo MiniHab that Ric jestingly calls the "market." It's still one-third full with dried grains and legumes and other long-term-storable food supplies such as oil, nuts and spices. Three other cargo ships stand with it in a jagged row, a hundred or so meters behind our living modules. Two of the four are early-model MiniHabs that the Murke-Berger Foundation delivered a couple of years before we got here. The other two are larger, fully-loaded cargo-model ZubHabs. They arrived with us back in '27. We won't need to open their food stores until after our families arrive later in the summer. Another two supply ships should arrive soon thereafter. We're well supplied here.

Back in '27. We had been confined inside the MiniHab for the better part of eight months when we arrived. How good it had been to get outside and run across the Martian surface! Like being released from prison. I won't say that our journey to Mars was easy. I won't complain, either, but I will say that the Murke-Berger Foundation learned quite a lot from our experiences on the ride out. We take credit for pushing them to fix a bunch of deficiencies in the original ZubHab design. Like doubling the width of the water pipes surrounding the vessel to protect from solar particle radiation. Or including all the food storage inside the habitat. My hab-mates and I had to take spacewalks every eight weeks to retrieve bags of food from the Mars-Entry stage's hull storage cells. Getting outside for a breather would not have been so bad in itself, but we needed to spin down the habitats before each spacewalk. And then spin them back up after we finished.

How about having more than one bathroom, for backup? Maybe the Foundation had been planning that all along for the full-sized ZubHabs, but our suggestion surely encouraged them. We made that suggestion every time the toilet broke.

After breakfast my hab-mates and I head out to the mining robots. There are twelve of them on Mars, though only eleven are functional at the moment. We detach them from the charging stations and they roll autonomously toward the far ends of the two trenches. I follow one of them. They'll extend the trenches by forty centimeters today, if all goes well, and if all eleven remain operative until nightfall. Each robot has a grinder at one end, a shovel at the other, and a large bin in the middle. And cameras on both ends for vision. I like watching them work. The one I follow descends a ramp into the north trench. She rolls out toward its far end with me trailing close behind. When she nears the trench wall, she engages her grinder. She pushes the grinding plate up against the regolith and happily grinds away. After a few minutes, sensing she's done enough, she backs up, turns around, drives her shovel end up to the wall, and begins scooping up the newly loosened regolith. She lifts up each shovel-full and dumps it into the bin on her back. Only when the bin is full does she talk: Em-oh-three calls me on the radio, asking for my help, because there are some jobs only a human can do. One of them is closing and sealing her bin cover. I swing it up and around, and lock down all three clasps to seal the chamber.

As Em-oh-three spins herself back around to resume grinding her wall, she turns on her bin heater to begin the process of distilling water out of the ground dirt. There is about four percent water content, by volume, in Red Valley's surface regolith, and the robot intends to recover it all. The heat releases the water from the ground rock, freeing it as steam. The steam rises to the underside of the bin cover, then condenses. The robot grinds away enthusiastically as this happens, but at a certain point she ceases grinding and we begin the trek back out of the trench and up to the surface. By the time we reach the towering pile of dirt that lines the side of the trench, six liters of fresh new water have dripped into the holding tank on the robot's underside.

I unlatch her bin cover, swing it up and around to its open position, and latch it to the side. Now Em-oh-three can dump the bin's contents onto the pile. After that, she heads back down into the trench and mines another bin-full. She'll manage thirteen loads today and add another seventy or eighty liters of water to our frozen reservoir.

I head in a different direction. Back at the lip of the MiniHab end of the trench, next to the pile of dirt, I find Beko and Sanjay – they live in Eagle, the southernmost MiniHab – standing by the second of the two brickmaking machines. They have removed the brick molds and are busy unloading yesterday's batch. Thirty new bricks cooled overnight in the open Martian air. After Beko and Sanjay finish unloading them and piling them next to the ones they unloaded earlier from the first machine, I help shovel half a cubic meter of desiccated dirt into the machine's broad tub. The tub will function as both mixer and kiln. Sanjay closes and seals its heavy cover, preparing to produce today's bricks.

"This one's tank is low on water," Terrence Walker says, reading from his datapad screen as he walks over from the other machine. Terry is a resident of Eternum, the middle MiniHab.

Sonny arrives with an insulated thirty-liter jug. Sonny McDeven is one of Terry's hab-mates, and is – in my opinion – the funniest man on Mars. He seals the hose to the brickmaker and tops up its water tank. The machines are extremely efficient, reclaiming more than ninety percent of the water they use to mix the mortar, but the accumulated ten-percent loss needs to be replaced every few days.

"It kilns me that we have to share our drinking water with this ugly contraption," Sonny declaims as he prepares to remove the hose. I imagine his toothy grin, behind his fleximet mask, as he congratulates himself on his witticism. Funniest person on Mars – but that's a low bar.

The mixer starts mixing, turning Mars dirt into low-grade clay. Two hours from now we'll come back to insert the molds, each a forty-by-twenty-centimeter trapezoidal frame. Once the molds are inserted, the kiln can start its twelve-hour cycle. First it dries the bricks and reclaims the evaporated water. When that finishes, it turns up the real heat to fire the bricks, making them as durable as possible with the technologies available to us on this planet. We'll come back tomorrow to remove them after they've cooled. We manage to add sixty new bricks to our stock every sol, assuming neither machine breaks down.

I grab two of the bricks from yesterday's batch and carry them to the nearest ramp. I make my way back down into the trench. It's my turn to perform our third main duty: bricklaying. We try to lay all sixty new bricks each day, keeping up with the manufacturing pace. At this rate we've been extending the enclosed part of the trench by two meters every week. This has been going on for seventeen or eighteen weeks now, and we already have thirty meters of trench walled and covered. Sometime later this year we'll seal the walls and ceiling with MarsTent, set up an airlock, pump in breathable atmosphere, and have the robots push the piled dirt back atop the brick archways for protection against surface radiation. Then we can move into the vaults.

For now, though, we just lay the bricks. We have no mortar, just Martian gravity and traditional vaulted architecture. The bricks are angled slightly on each end, and the same shape serves both for the walls and for the arched ceiling. For the walls, we lay the bricks out horizontally, alternating the orientation so that the angles cancel each other out. For the ceiling, all bricks are laid narrow-side-down, wide-side-up, so that they form an arch. My favorite part of our construction effort is removing the temporary support superstructure every couple of sols, and watching the arch settle to support its own weight.

No superstructure removal today, however. We have walls to finish first. I climb upon a broken brick that lays on the ground so that I can reach the eleventh row of the newest wall section. That's eleven rows out of thirteen. The ceiling rests on the thirteenth row of each wall, at a height of 260 centimeters. The center of the arch is higher, of course, rising to almost three and a half meters. We'll have to live underground for a time, but at least we'll have high ceilings.

I lay my two new bricks side-by-side, each in its correct orientation, then head back up to get another pair. An hour later, we've exhausted our batch of today's bricks, and each group of hab-dwellers heads back to its respective MiniHab for lunch. At some point early on, Ric, Ofer, Stephen and I learned how to squeeze all four of us into the airlock at the same time, parkas, fleximets, and oxypacks included. It's not easy, but we like avoiding extra pressurization-depressurization cycles if we can.

"Doriel, you look pale," Stephen says, looking closely at my face. "You'll stay inside for the rest of the day."

I don't argue. After lunch on the upper deck – rice with some chickpeas, washed down with Martian water – I descend the ladder to the lower deck, to my private room, to lie down. The outdoor MarsTent greenhouse will have to wait until tomorrow, or perhaps Stephen will take air samples today. I'm too tired.

There is no staircase in our MiniHab, only a ladder. It's amazing what Murke Industries managed to squeeze into a capsule that's only five and a half meters in diameter – and that's at the bottom, the widest point. And that's including the outer PlyShield. We have four separate bedrooms on the lower deck, and a bathroom with shower, and a tiny but lush greenhouse room. I jump from the ladder's lowest rung and land on the airlock hatch. I'm now standing in an enclosed person-sized hexagon. Folding doors form four of the sides: the green door to the greenhouse room, the blue door into the bathroom, the red door into Stephen's room, and the yellow door into Ric's. The ladder is on the fifth side. The sixth opens into a very narrow passageway that ends with two more doors that together form a sharp triangle. I squeeze through the pink door on the right. That's my bedroom. It's comfortable – actually higher than wide, like a closet. My quarters occupy just under a fourth of the lower deck's floorspace. There is enough room to stand by the bed, or to kneel, so I can reach into the storage cells beneath. Or I can sit on the edge of my bed and dangle my legs. They almost reach the floor. Sometimes I like the solitude. Additional cabinets at the head and foot of the bed fill the triangular spaces that result from squeezing a straight bed against a curved wall. If I had more possessions, the cabinets might be full, but I have few possessions, so, oddly, there's plenty of extra room in my tiny space.

"Dinner time!" Ofer calls to me, tapping on the wall outside my room to wake me up. I'm surprised by the late hour: my hab-mates departed the habitat, worked outside all afternoon, and reentered the airlock, all while I slept obliviously. I notice that my afternoon naps have become progressively *longer from week to week. The work I do outside each morning feels refreshing and invigorating at the time, but my afternoon exhaustion belies those feelings. The nap restores my strength, though, and Ofer and I continue our Talmud-learning partnership each evening after dinner. That's what Martian nights are for. The holy Torah, G-d's ancient revealed will, studied on Mars! We learn religiously at least one hour every night, as we have done ever since we launched, two and a half Earth years ago.*

I think G-d intended for humans to settle Mars, and that's why he made Mars's days and nights people-sized, almost like Earth's: a bit more than twenty-four hours each cycle. A bit more time to study each night. Amazingly, Ofer and I have managed to complete four tractates during this expedition. Megilla and Horayot, Zevahim and Hullin – four of the Babylonian Talmud's thirty-seven tractates. Tonight, G-d willing, we'll continue our sojourn through Ketubot, the volume that covers laws of marriage contracts and nuptial financial obligations, and various related areas of Jewish Law. Someday our children will marry on Mars. Someday, I had hoped, I would complete the entire Talmud. Alas, not in this lifetime. I won't even live to see my children marry. But at least Ofer and I never stopped progressing.

Nightfall arrives for me on Mars, and I prepare to sleep. I bless my hab-mates, and my beloved family in transit hither, and the loved ones I've left behind on Earth. May you all be healthy, and happy, and safe, and kind, and live out your days meaningfully.

Dana

Sunday, May 14th, 2029 17:15

"Finally, it worked!" I called out to nobody, as the results of my software program scrolled across the datapad screen. Having finished another lesson in my self-taught Machine Learning course, I got up from my bed and stretched my legs. My deep focus on each programming task was therapeutic: I would forget my miserable, bereft predicament, at least for an hour or two.

I slid the door open and headed for the bathroom. It was common for my mother to be teaching a class in the living room, or for Omar and his students to be huddled at the entrance to our Green-Level greenhouse room, but none of them were present. Instead, unexpectedly, there was Meital, standing in front of the NLED wall, a narrow paintbrush in her hand.

"You took Susy's advice?" I asked, examining the wall. "That's a pretty tree." Dozens of greenish strokes – the tree's crown still in progress – capped a trunk in several shades of brown. The outline of a young girl sat against the trunk. Meital gestured toward a palette, displayed on the side of the wall, and the software – apparently watching her movements closely – selected the darker shade of green she indicated.

"It seemed like something to try."

"Shouldn't you be in class right now? What's your schedule?"

She shot a narrow-eyed glare in my direction and turned back to the treetop. She brushed the wall and strokes of jade appeared. "I can't concentrate anyway. I'm tired of wasting time."

"You're skipping all your classes?"

She picked a shade of purplish-red and began dabbing around the leaves.

"Of course not. Just one or two here or there. I'll catch up if I need to."

"What about Omar's Agriculture class?"

"What about it? I go sometimes."

I stroked my sister's shoulder encouragingly as I stepped into the bathroom; she recoiled from my touch. A few minutes later, having washed up, I stepped back into the living room to check on her progress. I expected to see an even prettier, more complete girl-under-tree scene. Instead, everything was a bloody mess.

"Meital, what are you doing?"

It was a dumb question, as I could see exactly what she was doing: she had taken one of the broader brushes, selected a deep red color, and was now throwing paint – virtually, but the software was really good at interpreting her wild gestures – all across what had been, just a few minutes previously, a nicely developing backyard landscape.

"I'm finishing my painting," she said simply.

"You're ruining the beautiful work you were doing!" I grabbed her arm. "Stop!"

She pulled herself fiercely from my grip and splashed more blood-red cyber-paint, this time all over the girl's silhouette. "Why? What does it matter? Maybe I'll paint another one tomorrow. Who cares?"

"I care!" I reached for the "Undo" button the Paint program displayed at the top of the wall, hoping to reverse the messy red strokes, but my hand was too late: Meital had grabbed her datapad and tapped a few taps. The wall went blank. With a final glance in my direction that might have been nasty, or might have been simply sulky – I could not tell which – she darted into her room and slid the door closed behind her.

*   *   *

Monday, May 15th, 2029 19:30

Denver, last to shower after our afternoon exercise session, stepped from the washroom. He wore a navy-blue cotton tunic over his mundies, the fuzz on his chin was neatly trimmed, and a sharp part divided his freshly combed hair. He watched Shirel dump a handful of forks and knives on the table.

"Dr. Dana, I'm heading upstairs for supper. Is that okay?"

"It's okay, but we like it when you join us."

He smiled, but turned and departed. I was not surprised: our dinners were increasingly despondent, whereas Celina's family, somehow, remained in high spirits. Why should Denver deign to dine with us?

My mother placed a pot of chickpea-and-barley soup on the table and sat down. I added some leftover bread I found in our little refrigerator. Meital tapped her datapad and a stark image of Saturn appeared on one of the NLED walls. A second tap, and Jupiter appeared on the other.

"Meital," Shirel shot at her sister, "can't you find some normal pictures?"

"What's wrong with these? If you don't like planets, Shirel, you're in the wrong place."

Shirel glanced at the pot. "Yeah, I probably am. Chickpeas again."

"I'm sorry, Shirel," my mother said, "but if you wanted something else, you could have asked. Or even helped prepare."

"I did ask. I asked for almonds. You told me to check the Foodstock application to see if any almond rations remained for us."

"And did they? You didn't bring me any."

"According to Foodstock, three packages were left for our family. I didn't find them, so I asked Dr. Cecylia, but she couldn't find them either."

My mother paused, brow furrowed, a spoonful of soup hovering by her mouth. She looked confused. "Did we forget to register a withdrawal?"

"Dr. Cecylia didn't think so. She said she's been having trouble finding several of the rare items. She thinks they may have been misplaced."

My mother's eyes narrowed. "We cataloged everything very carefully when we packed the storage attic. That was before you guys even boarded."

"Well, you probably made a mistake," Shirel said, looking glumly at her soup.

"It's possible," my mother said, shaking her head, "but I don't think so."

"Everybody makes mistakes," Meital said.

"Mom makes mistakes," Shirel spat. She looked at my mother with a derision I had never seen before.

"Yes, that may be." My mother sighed, sadness falling across her face.

"Shirel, it's just a missing bag of almonds," I said. "Not a reason to attack Mom!"

She directed her derision at me. "Not a reason? Do you want a better reason? Like forcing us to come on this cursed trip?"

"We didn't force anyone to come," my mother protested.

"Stop with the hogwash, Mom!" Shirel yelled, adding a few words that one does not expect his sister to know. "You didn't give us a choice!"

"I – we – what?" My mother, momentarily baffled, recovered quickly. She sat up straight in her chair and spoke slowly and deliberately. "Shirel, my beloved daughter. We made sure to get your consent at every stage of our family journey, every step of the way. You, Shirel, you yourself agreed to join the Foundation, to start the training, to move to Altiplano, to launch. You gave explicit consent before we boosted into high Earth orbit, and, again back in early November, you agreed – unambiguously! – for us to depart Earth orbit."

"You just don't stop!" Shirel spoke with contempt. She stared into my mother's eyes and pummeled. "I'm a little girl! I was a tiny child, five years old, when you joined the Foundation! Five-year-olds don't 'choose!' You and Dad just took me along for your moronic adventure."

At first, my mother defended herself adeptly. "You were twelve when you decided, and agreed, that we would go to Mars. A twelve-year-old is supposed to be adult enough to make decisions."

"I decided? I decided that *we* would go to Mars? And, anyway, I wasn't even eleven when Dad left on his suicidal 'Vanguard' mission. Did I decide that, too?"

"I did not say that you decided for Dad. But you decided for yourself." Her defense waned. "And you were excited about space travel, about weightlessness, about pioneering."

"I am just a girl!" Shirel stood, knocking her chair against the wall. "A thirteen-year-old is still just a girl! Kids make mistakes! That's why we have parents. To make sure we make good decisions. To stop us from making stupid ones. To keep us from making mistakes. To protect us! Your job was to protect me, not help me destroy my life!"

"We never stopped protecting you. Your life is not destroyed," my mother said softly. Too softly. She had stopped trying.

"You see it yourself, Mom! I know you see it." Shirel wound up for the knockout punch. "My life is ruined. By my own parents! Parents are supposed to protect their kids, not sacrifice them on idiotic excursions!" She clenched her teeth, then shouted, shaking, "You dragged me along to die with you!"

She stormed into her bedroom. My mother sank into her chair.

* * *

Wednesday, May 17th, 2029 17:50

"The carbon monoxide reduces the hematite ore to iron," Dr. Esther was explaining in Metallurgy class, in her Pink-Level living room. "Why is this process fit for use on Mars?"

Celina unnecessarily raised her hand. "Because we will have lots of carbon monoxide, the waste product of producing oxygen from the Martian atmosphere."

"It's not really a waste product, then, is it?" I asked.

Dr. Esther smiled and adjusted the blue kerchief that covered her hair. "You could say that, Michael. The most efficient processes we use in our fledgling settlement will be those that produce materials we can utilize for other processes. So, yes, we will try not to waste our carbon monoxide. Our oxygen generators will save the carbon monoxide produced by the reverse water-gas shift reaction, and we'll feed that into the miniature vacuum smelting furnace."

She tapped her datapad to display the reaction on the NLED wall:

$$Fe_2O_3 + 3CO \rightarrow 2Fe + 3CO_2$$

"Hematite, heated with carbon monoxide, reacts to form iron and carbon dioxide. We then feed the carbon dioxide into the oxygen generator to get more carbon monoxide, to continue the reaction. Oxygen – for the air we breathe – is a useful byproduct."

"Are we sure we'll find hematite?" Denver asked. "Isn't it concentrated only around ancient Martian streambeds?"

"We would be very lucky to find a streambed near our settlement, and, yes, we would expect to find hematite there. But streambeds are far from the only source of iron on Mars. The Vanguard group have already found hematite beads during their excursions. I expect we'll find lots more as we explore our new home together. Especially with the help of the diggers."

She tapped her pad and the formula on the NLED wall was replaced with a snowy, tree-covered mountainside.

"Okay, your homework assignment. Read the next chapter, on processes for hardening and sintering the iron product."

We stood to depart Pink Level. Denver headed upstairs with Celina, but Dr. Esther stopped me. "Michael, just a minute. I made extra stew for your family." She retrieved a container from the kitchen's small refrigerator. "I wasn't sure if your mother cooked today." She pushed the container into my hands before I could refuse. But I was not planning to refuse, because my mother had not done any cooking since Shirel's outburst, and after two days of drab lettuce sandwiches, a stew – even if it turned out to be just more chickpea stew – was a welcome alternative.

"Thanks, Dr. Esther."

"Oh, and tell your sisters that we are expecting you to join us for all the Shavuot holiday meals, from Friday night through Sunday brunch."

Not being in a holiday mood, I had forgotten the upcoming Feast of Weeks festival, seven weeks after Passover. On Earth it would start Saturday night and continue through Monday, but, for us, as our calendar diverged from Earth's, it would start on Friday night and finish on Sunday.

"Okay; thank you, Dr. Esther."

My sisters and I were now charity cases.

I turned toward the stairwell and almost bumped into Boris. "There you are, Michael." He did not look happy. "Come with me; I need your help." His tone was harsh.

"What happened?"

"You'll see," he said brusquely. He spun around and bounded downstairs without looking back. I followed nervously.

"Do you see what happened here?" He pointed at the Green-Level air-processing unit.

"Uh, let me put this down first." I placed the container on our kitchen counter and turned back to the niche by the stairwell. "What's the matter?"

"Do you see that none of the LED lights are lit?"

He was right. The whole unit was powered down.

"Did somebody turn off the air systems?"

"Your level's air pump shut down by itself. I cannot get it to restart. I tried several times before giving up. Your deck is now receiving air diverted from Pink Level. The Pink-Level pumps are working overtime and I'm afraid they will overheat."

"I cleaned the filters this morning, Boris. Shouldn't that be enough for the pump to work?"

"It would have been enough if you had done your job properly. If you had not let the pumps run on dirty air at the beginning of last week. It seems that the air pump became clogged or burned out. I asked Simeon to disassemble it to try to figure out which part is broken."

"If he finds the broken part, can we replace it?"

"We probably do not have a replacement part, Michael. That is why we try so hard to keep things from breaking." He turned toward me, crossed his arms, and stood, waiting, not saying another word. I squirmed like a misbehaving schoolboy confronted by his teacher.

"What do you want me to do?"

He waited a few more moments, possibly just to make me even more uncomfortable. "How about taking responsibility for your mistake, and for printing the replacement parts? Speak to Simeon, find out what parts need to be replaced, download the design plans, and get them printed."

"I'll talk with Denver. He knows how to use the three-dimensional printer."

Boris did not hear me. He had already darted downstairs.

* * *

Thursday, May 18th, 2029 12:25

"There seem to be so many conditions, Rabbi Meyer." Folio thirty of Talmud tractate Bava Kama was discussing a person's liability if he left his property in a public area and it damaged somebody. "Who the owner of the property is, and if someone else put it in the place where it did the damage, and what kind of damage was done. And even the season of the year!"

"That's right, Michael," Rabbi Meyer said. "And, most importantly, whether the owner should have anticipated that his property might cause damage."

"It's a lot to remember!"

"Relationships are complicated," Rabbi Meyer said. "Multiple minds, multiple expectations, conflicting interests. The Talmud wants to train us to anticipate how our actions will affect others."

"Sam, we'll need to review this page again."

He nodded. "We'll have all night, tomorrow night."

"I'm looking forward to it," I said.

Rabbi Meyer watched us with a smile on his face. "Are you two planning to pull a holiday all-nighter, learning non-stop until morning?"

"Yes, Dad," Sam nodded. "That's how we celebrate the Shavuot holiday every year. You'll join us, won't you?"

Rabbi Meyer considered his son's invitation. "Yes, I think I will. Studying Torah through the night, in commemoration of the giving of the Torah on Mount Sinai – it's an ancient custom."

"I bet you can't make it through the night without falling asleep, though," Sam challenged.

Rabbi Meyer frowned at his impertinent son, but there was a hint of a smile in his eyes. "You doubt your own father?"

"We'll see, Dad."

A few minutes later, I headed downstairs to our kitchen and found Meital standing by a pot in the stove niche. My mother was conspicuously absent.

"What's in the pot?"

"Chickpeas."

"You're making a stew?"

She shot me an "Are you kidding?" look. She said, "If I never have chickpea stew again, I won't miss it."

"Then why are you cooking chickpeas?

"Hummus. I thought hummus sandwiches might be better than lettuce sandwiches tonight."

"I thought Mom was going to cook something more interesting."

"I thought Mom was going to act like a mother the whole trip. Have you seen her today? I don't think she's left her room since morning." She glanced at the closed master-bedroom door. "It's sandwiches tonight, or nothing."

Shirel appeared, her hands filthy with worm-dirt. "What's for lunch?"

"Meital's making hummus," I said.

"Not for lunch. Maybe for dinner."

"I'm hungry. Where's Mom?"

Meital and I glanced at each other. "Don't ask," we said together.

Shirel did not look happy.

"Is there leftover bread in the refrigerator?" I asked.

"There's a whole loaf from Helga," Meital said. "She felt sorry for us."

"I don't want people feeling sorry for us," I said. "But Mom's worrying me." I stepped into the living room and knocked quietly on the wall next to my mother's sliding door. "Mom?" I knocked again. "Are you there?"

There was no answer, so I slid the door open and stepped into the darkened room. My mother was asleep in her bed. She stirred when I called to her a third time.

"Michael, I'm sleeping."

"Are you okay? We're worried. Do you want to eat with us?"

"Go ahead and eat without me." She turned over and waved me away.

* * *

Dana

Tuesday, May 23rd, 2029 15:40

The Feast of Weeks holiday came and went. The Meyers insisted that my sisters and I be their guests at all five festive meals. My mother came, too, but those were the only times she left her bed. The Meyers' food was great, and we sang together between courses, and that raised our spirits. On Sunday at least. About Saturday I was not sure – all my memories of Saturday were a sleepy blur – I kept dozing off throughout the day. Sam and I, and his father – despite Sam's low expectations – had managed to stay awake all Friday night, studying almost non-stop, straight through to morning prayer time. We took breaks only to eat sugary holiday cakes that Ruby and Susan had baked. We also drank a lot of soda. The soda was based on our regular carbon-dioxide-injected water, but Sam had added sugar and grape juice concentrate. He claimed, dubiously, that he had created grape soda. It was nothing like the grape soda I remembered from the home planet, but the novel taste did, somehow, enhance the festive feeling.

I had recovered – mostly – by Monday, and on Tuesday I was wide awake in Electrical Engineering class. Simeon was explaining chapter three of *The Mathematics of Electrical Systems*.

"Simeon, you keep confusing me," Celina complained. "Are we supposed to divide or multiply by the resistance?"

Simeon looked at the formula his datapad was projecting on the NLED wall. "No, this is right ... is it not?"

"What kind of school did you study at?" Helga blurted tactlessly. "Did they teach you physics but skip the math?"

"The formulas are described in the textbook," Simeon said defensively. "Did you read the chapter?"

"I have read chapter three, and chapter four, too. I'm sorry, Simeon, but the book is not enough for me." She shook her head. "I am not a textbook learner. I need a competent teacher to help sort out the details."

"Give him a chance, Helga," Denver said. "This is the first time he's teaching a class."

"I am sorry that I expect more," Helga said, sitting upright, "from a person who says he has a degree in Electrical Engineering from St. Petersburg Polytechnic. What kind of schools do you have in Russia?"

Simeon's cheeks turned pink. "Russia has good schools. Maybe not as exclusive as your oh-so-special aristocratic universities in the Netherlands! Not all of us are so lucky like you, Helga."

She shook her head, sighed, and stared at her lap. "I'm sorry I said anything."

"Let me try explaining again," Simeon said. He looked up at the NLED wall, then down at his datapad; then he took a deep breath and started over from the beginning.

* * *

Friday, May 26th, 2029 15:00

I stayed back after Friday's afternoon Talmud session. "Rabbi Meyer, can I ask you something?"

"Sure, Michael. Can Sam listen in?"

I glanced at my friend uncomfortably and turned back to his father. "Maybe you and I can talk privately?" I looked back at Sam. "I hope you don't mind."

"Why would I mind?"

"We can sit in my room," Rabbi Meyer said, watching me with a little too much concern. We stepped into the master bedroom and slid the door closed.

"What's the matter?" He settled onto the edge of the bed.

"It's my mother. She barely left her room all week."

"Yes, I know that Dana – your mother – has not been feeling well. Esther's been checking up on her and keeping me updated."

"I don't know what to do," I sighed. I sat down next to him and rubbed my forehead.

"I don't know if there is very much you can do, other than loving and supporting her."

"Isn't it supposed to be the other way around? She's my mother! What's a mother for? She should be supporting me. I'm just a kid." I stared at the floor.

He placed an arm around my shoulders. "On Earth I might have agreed with you. Here, I'm not so sure."

That confused me. We sat in silence for a few moments.

"Your mother is suffering a bit of depression. It's not your fault, Michael. She needs you and your sisters to be strong right now."

"My sisters? Strong?" A mocking laugh escaped my throat. "That's a joke."

Now he seemed confused. "What do you mean?"

"Shirel and Meital have given up on the expedition. They think the whole thing is a mistake."

He considered silently, then answered, "I can understand that."

That was not what I wanted to hear from Rabbi Meyer. "Really?" I looked at him. "What is there to understand? They have no right to give up!"

"What about you, Michael? Are you giving up?" He waited patiently, arm still on my shoulders.

"No," I finally said. "I can't give up. None of us has that right. What, just because Dad died?" My own raised voice surprised me.

"Yes, Michael," he said, gently, "because your father died. It's natural for you and your sisters to have doubts about the journey."

"No, I disagree. We are not allowed to have doubts. We're stuck here in this ship, on this trip." Frowning, I turned to look at him. "But let's say I have doubts. What difference does it make now, Rabbi Meyer?"

"Michael, I remind you again. I am not a rabbi."

"Stop telling me that! It doesn't help!"

He nodded. "What can I say that will help? I can't stop you and your sisters from doubting. It's a natural reaction."

"What do natural reactions matter here? This is not a natural situation. We're not natural people anymore."

He removed his arm and turned to face me, frowning. "What kind of people are we?"

"We are unnatural people. We are supermen. We are cold people with a cold job to do on a cold planet. We gave up being normal when we left humanity behind."

"Did we leave humanity behind?" His dark eyes bored into mine. "'Humanity' is an ambiguous word."

"We parted from the human race."

"That's a fair characterization of our situation. But I don't agree that we left humanity behind. Not our humanity. Not your humanity, Michael." He laid his hand on mine. "The anger you are feeling is quite human."

"Anger? I'm not angry. I just think my mother and sisters need to grow up and get a grip. Mom signed up for this. She can take some adult responsibility."

Rabbi Meyer looked at me keenly. "You sound angry to me."

I did not like being accused of a forbidden emotion. "Well, I think you are wrong –"

He did not let me finish. "I would expect nothing less from you. You ought to be angry. Everybody has let you down. Your father left you behind and now he's gone. Your mother has stopped coping. Your sisters, you say, have given up. Why wouldn't you be angry?"

"Thanks for being so encouraging."

He sat up straight. "Do you want false encouragement?"

"No, I don't."

He put his arm around my shoulders again and pulled me close. I dropped all resistance and leaned into him. I let him hold me silently for a few minutes.

"Rabbi Meyer, what should I do?"

"Michael, I am not a Rabbi."

"Stop saying that!" I pulled away and looked up. He looked back at me, patiently. "Why do you keep telling me you are not a rabbi? To me you are a rabbi. Why should that bother you?"

"That is a very, very good question." He sighed. "I imagine that you don't want my answer."

"You imagine wrong. I asked because I want to know."

"Are you prepared to encourage me, Michael? You might find that you are not the only one who needs encouragement."

Now Rabbi Meyer was the one staring at the floor, and that unnerved me. I frowned. "It's not supposed to work that way. How can I encourage you? You're the teacher; you're the adult. I'm the kid here."

"Maybe you have no right to be a kid." He shook his head, still staring at the floor. "You are an eighteen-year-old astronaut." He faced me. "Join the crew!"

"Not eighteen yet. Only in three months."

He shook his head again and flashed me a "what does that matter?" kind of look.

"Okay," I yielded. "I will try to encourage you. Tell me why, even though you are a Talmud scholar, and you teach us the Torah, and ethics, and morality, and Jewish Law, you are not a rabbi."

Rabbi Meyer propped his pillow against the teal wall hanging that covered the water pipes. He adjusted himself and leaned back. He smiled sadly. "A rabbi lives his life according to Jewish Law."

"You follow Jewish Law. Scrupulously. You do everything that you teach us to do."

"Not always, it turns out."

"Okay, so you've made mistakes. Nobody's perfect."

"I'm not talking about mistakes. I'm talking about intentionally ignoring the Law."

Rabbi Meyer? Ignoring Jewish Law? No way! "I don't believe you. What rule did you break?"

"The biggest rule of all. To design one's life according to Torah precepts."

"I don't understand."

"Michael, a wise person does not rely on his own judgment. He consults his teachers for every important decision, large or small. Especially large."

I said only "okay." It was my turn to listen patiently.

"If I were truly a rabbi, I would have asked Rabbi Saxman – my teacher back in California – the most important question in my life, and I would have followed his guidance. But I did not ask."

I turned to him, perplexed. "The most important question? In your life? What question was that?"

Leaning forward, he raised his eyebrows, tilted his head to the side, and paused. "Can't you guess? My life's most important question is kind of obvious. It's the same as yours: whether to leave Earth permanently, go to Mars, and take my family with me."

"Okay, I admit that's an important question." I turned to face him. "Then why didn't you ask? Wouldn't you have wanted your rabbi's blessing?" I tried not to sound judgmental.

"Because I did not want to hear his answer." He shook his head again. "I'm pretty sure that if I had asked Rabbi Saxman, he would have ruled that the expedition – the entire Mars settlement project – is wholly forbidden by Jewish Law."

"Forbidden?" *Just lovely*, I thought to myself. *Eight months into an irreversible voyage, now the person I rely on the most for advice tells me the whole thing is a mistake.* But all I said was, "Why?"

"Oh, for multiple reasons. Foremost is the danger. Except in specific cases of necessity, Jewish Law forbids endangering oneself. Also, for reasons of community, and to ensure a proper education for our children, and for Jewish continuity. Not to mention the requirement, according to many rabbinic opinions, that one dwell in the Land of Israel." He sighed as he added, "That's a place on Earth, not Mars."

"I'm sorry, Rabbi Meyer" – ironically, this time he did not protest – "but you are not making sense. If you already knew that the expedition is forbidden, you did not have to ask your teacher. You knew not to come, all by yourself." I tilted my head. "So, then, why did you come? Why didn't you stop us all?"

"That is a very good question, and I've been thinking about it a lot. Too much, perhaps; it causes me great anguish." He shook his head, but then he nodded. "But I know my answer."

"You do?"

"Do you want to hear it?"

"Definitely." My interest was piqued. "Do you trust me enough to share it with me?"

"I trust you, Michael." He glanced at his datapad. "But it's getting late. The Sabbath will be starting soon. Do you need to finish preparations? Did you bake sourdough challah bread this week?"

"I did, last night, so I have time now. Please tell me, why did you decide to go to Mars, if doing so is forbidden?"

"Michael, this expedition is important – I think you'll agree. Critically important. Perhaps more than any of us imagines." He raised his head and faced me squarely. "Our goal is nothing less than to establish an entire new branch of humanity. We carry immense responsibility." His shoulders sagged as if he were carrying an actual weight.

"Okay, it's important. So why not let other people do it? Most people don't care about Jewish Law. They can be the heroes."

"I imagine that Rabbi Saxman would have said just that."

"But you don't say that, obviously. Is that why you did not want to ask him?"

"Oh, I certainly did want to ask him. I just did not want to hear his answer."

"Right. But, again, why not just let other people found humanity's new branch? The Foundation has plenty of volunteers."

"Because I feel responsible. Personally responsible. Given my particular background and my specific training, I have something special to offer. Special and rare."

I stared at him. Bragging was out of character.

"Michael, the new Martian branch of human society is going to be established, with me or without me. But maybe I can make a difference to the society's core values. I can offer Jewish values. It is crucially important – that's my opinion, at least – that our new society's values be influenced, from the start, by the Torah. I think it would be a tragedy if that does not happen. And, I thought, if not me, then who else will bring that influence?"

I thought, judgmentally, *why would anyone assume such responsibility?* But I kept that thought to myself. Instead, I said, "I agree that Jewish values are important. But doesn't everybody in the expedition – everybody in the whole Murke-Berger Foundation – have good values? Let them influence the new society. What's the great 'tragedy' if nobody pushes a Jewish influence?"

He took a deep breath. "Imagine. What would society be like without the Torah's idea that life is sacred, and the immense importance it places on each individual life? Without Judaism's obligations for giving charity and performing acts of kindness? For caring for the weak? For upholding the rule of law and preventing the capricious rule of the strong and powerful? How would we live without Judaism's rules for social cohesion – preventing unnecessary conflict, prohibiting negative speech? Requiring humility?"

"But those aren't only Jewish ideals, Rabbi Meyer. Everybody shares them nowadays."

"True, Michael; Christianity and Islam took Jewish ideas and spread them around the world. They can spread them to Mars. Maybe there's no need for a Jewish influence."

"If so, Rabbi Saxman was right."

"Maybe. Except that I never asked him, so I don't really know."

"So, tell me: was it a mistake for us to come?"

"Maybe. I don't know. But I'll tell you this: pre-Torah human society, three thousand years ago, was cruel and tragic. The powerful enslaved the weak; human sacrifice – murder for ritual purposes! – was commonplace and accepted; women were at the mercy of their fathers and husbands. Tribes warred continually. For most people, life was short and harsh. It is hard to appreciate how revolutionary Jewish ideas were at the time. How subversive they were."

"How so?"

"For example, in non-Jewish society, no rules governed a king's actions: he was above the law. He was right by definition and could do anything he wanted. He could take whatever he desired, kill whomever he despised. The Torah changed that. It bound the king by the same rules as the peasant. It prohibited the strong from injuring the weak or stealing from them. It obligated the rich to support the poor, not exploit them."

"I don't think we have to worry about rich people on Mars exploiting the poor. The fledgling settlement will be a cohesive community for a long time to come."

Rabbi Meyer nodded. "I hope so. But that introduces the opposite problem. For Judaism, the family unit is the building block of society. The Torah prohibits immoral behavior that threatens marital stability. It teaches that every individual – not just dedicated monks or priests – must learn self-control, in action, speech and thought. Who will guarantee that a tight-knit community, living in a shared space, not deteriorate into a structureless commune? That a charismatic or brutal leader not seize control, enslave men, and force women into immoral servitude?"

"That sounds like dystopian fiction. It's hard to think it could happen in real life. And, anyway, the values you describe, including the importance of family units, are exactly the Murke-Berger values."

"Yes, thankfully so. But Mars is very, very far from the Foundation. Think how easily an isolated society might fall into cruel and barbaric practices! Michael, our base natures are not good. Humans seek expediency, especially in difficult times. We twist good concepts into evil at the first sign of difficulty. We devise ingenious schemes of self-justification. We convince ourselves that our evil thoughts and deeds are necessary and virtuous. Stealing, enslaving, even murder – it's surprisingly easy to fool ourselves, especially in the face of adversity."

"Not me. That sounds farfetched."

"Not you?" He raised his eyebrows. "I hope not. But don't you agree that life on Mars will have its difficulties? Who will guarantee that we remain good when cut off from the rest of humanity? That our local leaders not arrogate special rights for themselves and then explain, arrogantly, why they deserve them? Who will protect our weak from the strong, when even the strong fear for their lives? Who will chastise gossipers who denigrate and embarrass, who spread corrosive bitterness and discontent? Who will encourage people to concede humbly, and censure those who stubbornly sustain conflict?" He held out his hands and shrugged. "Who will make peace?"

I wrinkled my brow. "Maybe nobody?" I rested my hand on his shoulder. "Maybe not even you, Rabbi Meyer? How do you know people will listen to you?"

"I'm pretty sure they won't."

I stared at him, surprised at his admission. "Then it was a mistake to come."

"I did not say that."

"You say your justification for joining the expedition is to influence Martian society with Jewish values, but then you say that nobody will listen. If so, what's the point? Why are you here?" I narrowed my eyes. "Why am I here?"

"To set an example, Michael." He sighed. "Maybe we can influence by our example. We'll behave in a holy manner. Others will see us. Maybe they'll be inspired to behave similarly. Maybe that's the best we can do."

"Maybe Rabbi Saxman would agree, if you explain your reasoning."

He shook his head. "Maybe. Maybe not. I don't know."

"You could send him an email."

He just shook his head again.

Breech

Monday, May 29th, 2029 15:20

"Ready, set, press!" Denver tapped his datapad, showing off his three-dimensional-printing proficiency with great enthusiasm. One of the machine's printing heads slid out to the center of the base plate and began its slow process, extruding the initial layer of metallic material. Denver and I watched through the plastic cover, which he had locked shut after firmly affixing the printer to the Beckers' dining table.

"Is that aluminum?"

"Yes, that is what is needed, according to the plans we downloaded. It's printing the first spring."

"Thanks again for your help, Denver." I meant it. Maybe I would be able to face Boris without feeling humiliated.

Denver looked at me with narrowed eyes and a furrowed brow. "You think I'm doing this for you? We breathe the same air. I want my air to be clean." A smile might have hidden behind his accusing glare – I was not sure.

Behind Denver, the Yellow-Level NLED wall showed a large factory floor where red and black robots were assembling silvery vehicles somewhere back on Earth. The audio was turned off, but the repetitive up-and-down and back-and-forth motion silently mesmerized me. I pulled my eyes from the screen and looked back at the buzzing printing head. "How long will this part take?"

"Maybe twenty minutes. Then we'll start the second spring."

Simeon had managed to diagnose the cause of the air system malfunction a few days earlier. He had disassembled the malfunctioning vane pump and examined every part under a magnifying glass. Eventually he found a crack in one of the vanes. Denver took over from there. First, he identified the broken part's catalog number, then located the part's printing plans in the ship computer's database.

Breaking my reverie, he asked, "Did I tell you how much trouble I had with the Foundation?"

"What trouble?" I watched the printing head rotate in slow circles.

"The onboard plans for the vane require titanium." He shook his head. "We do not carry titanium powder in our stores."

"Are you sure?"

"You know I'm sure. Do you want me to list for you every raw material we have on the ship?"

"No, please don't. Are these different plans? Where did you get them?"

Celina, sitting on the couch behind us, answered. "Denver emailed the Murke-Berger Foundation's engineering department."

"That sounds easy. What was the trouble?"

"They sent back the same program!" Denver said. "I had to ask three times before they located the aluminium-based alternative."

Helga, lounging on the couch next to her sister, looked up from the datapad they were sharing. "That is reassuring! It is not like we rely on the engineering department for, well, everything."

Celina laughed.

We were supposed to have been in Electrical Engineering class at that hour, but Simeon had canceled Wednesday's session so that we could print the replacement part.

"Denver," Celina said, "can we get rid of the factory-floor film? It's distracting."

"I put it up for motivation while we are manufacturing."

"You are manufacturing?" She laughed. "You pushed a button on your datapad! The printer does all the work."

"In all fairness," Helga said, nudging her sister, "in the movie, the robots are doing all the work."

"Still, it is not conducive to reading," Celina said. "Denver, choose a season: spring or winter."

Denver dared not argue with her. "Spring."

She clicked her datapad a couple of times. The factory disappeared, replaced by a now-familiar Dutch backyard. It was, I knew, the Beckers' old home, still Celina's favorite scenery. Stately elms swayed in silent wind. Three little girls, a blonde, a brunette, and an auburn-haired toddler, sat in a circle in the lush grass, playing some childhood game.

"Don't forget to stow the printer in the cabinet above my bed when you finish," Helga said blankly. She turned her attention to the datapad screen and pointed out something to her sister.

* * *

Tuesday, May 30th, 2029 18:05

A heavy knock and a loud "Michael!" interrupted my ebook reading; I was on page seventy of Asimov's *Foundation's Edge*. I put it aside and swung my legs to the floor.

"Come in!"

Helga slid the door open.

"Hi, Helga. What's up?"

"A little German boy told me you are skipping exercise sessions."

"'A little German boy?'" I tried not to giggle.

"Get yourself off the bed! You are already five minutes late."

"I don't feel like exercising this afternoon. Who appointed you enforcer?"

She glared scathingly. "Nobody 'appointed' me anything. I worry for myself. I am not going to live on Mars with a horde of sick, flabby weaklings who need me to take care of them."

"And you, Helga?" I checked the clock on my datapad. "Shouldn't you be upstairs exercising now?"

"Yes, I should be, but that little German boy took my spot. He is up there cycling with my sister and my parents. Unfortunately, I have to be down here with you." She looked around the room and clapped her hands. "Let's go! Where are your sprowers?"

There was no point arguing; she would never give up. I stood and stretched. "In my mother's bedroom."

Helga spun and headed for the door.

"Wait – don't bother my mom. Let me do it."

But my mother's door was open and she was not in the room. Maybe that was a good sign. Maybe she was less depressed today.

Helga busied herself folding the dining table, to make room for the exercise equipment. I retrieved the sprowers and set them up. I mounted one, grasped the handgrip, and started to row.

But Helga did not immediately mount the second sprower. Instead, she stood by my sisters' bedroom door and knocked loudly on the doorpost. "Meital and Shirel!" She knocked again. "Exercise time!"

"Go away!" Meital yelled back, leaving no room for argument.

"If that is what you want…" Helga said under her breath, and tapped something on her datapad. A moment later, Captain Becker's face appeared on the NLED wall, filling the screen from floor to ceiling. This was not the first time the captain had used the wall for a video chat, but never had his image been so intimidatingly huge.

"Family Teller!" he called loudly. "Girls! Meital and Shirel! This is your captain speaking. Report immediately!"

It did not take long for my sisters' door to slide open. The two of them slumped into the living room. "What, Captain Becker?" Shirel sounded annoyed at having been disturbed. But when she noticed his colossal countenance, her eyes widened in surprise.

"Your exercise was scheduled for 18:00. That was ten minutes ago. I do not care whether you want to exercise. We have a schedule to keep, and you will keep it, assiduously."

Undaunted, Meital leaned against the doorpost and tapped her foot impudently. "And what if we don't?"

The captain's expression soured. "Then I will come downstairs and shackle your wrists to the wall." He looked deadly serious.

Both Meital and Shirel gasped. They jumped to retrieve the cycles and, still under the captain's watchful eye, affixed them in their slots in the floor. Only after they had mounted and begun cycling did the captain close the connection.

Helga rowed next to me, pacing herself, staring forward. But after a couple of minutes, she paused and faced me, eyes wide with disbelief. "I have never seen my father talk like that."

"Was he serious?" asked Meital, pedaling lazily. "Or did he just want to scare us?"

I answered, "He was serious. Remember how he punished Denver? Maybe he thinks tough treatment will make us forget about Dad."

"Maybe he's getting tired of leading the mission," Shirel said bitterly. "Maybe he's sick of us."

"I don't think he's sick of you," Helga said. "He is sorry that you lost your father."

Meital rolled her eyes. "If that's how he shows compassion, I'd prefer him to leave us alone."

Helga used her datapad to launch a roller-coaster video. Distracted, we rowed in silence. It felt like gliding up and down one hill after another.

Shirel broke the silence. "Helga, maybe your father should be fixing the ship's real problems, instead of wasting his time forcing us to keep a tyrannical schedule."

Helga stopped rowing and twisted around to stare at Shirel. "My father works hard all the time to make sure we have no problems."

"Oh, really? I don't think so. What about the missing food? Somebody stole all our almonds."

"Oh, that. I did not know anybody else noticed."

"Shirel," I said, between strokes, "we don't know they were actually stolen. Maybe somebody made an innocent mistake."

"Yeah, right, taking all the almond packages without logging them in Foodstock. Really innocent."

"My father knows about the problem and he is working to fix it."

"When, already? When will he get the almonds back for us?"

"Get over it, Shirel," Meital scolded.

"No, Meital, I won't get over it. What am I asking for? Just a few packages of almonds to break the monotony! The regular food is so boring. But, no, some jerk took them all and finished everything off."

"Actually," Helga said, resuming her rowing, "it is not just almonds that are missing. Dr. Esther was looking for hazelnuts and the Bouchets asked for pecans. But there are none left. With two months left to Mars, there should still be packages of all the specialty items." She rowed vigorously and breathed heavily. "Even some of the last chocolate is missing! My father was very annoyed when he heard about that."

"Tell us," Shirel demanded, "who is the thief?"

"My parents are trying to figure that out. They have been paying close attention to everyone who comes upstairs to the storage attic."

Meital asked, "But they still haven't figured out who's taking the stuff?"

"You know, Meital, it is funny: when my parents are watching, everyone is careful to log everything they take." She stopped rowing and dismounted. "Swap with us. It's our turn on the cycles."

Helga and I began what would be twenty-five minutes of cycling, while my sisters started on the sprowers. I asked, "What will your father do if he finds the culprit?"

"I can only imagine," Helga said, looking at me as she built up speed. "Probably worse than what he threatened for Meital."

We pedaled quietly for a few minutes until Helga broke the silence, saying, "I think I know who it is."

Shirel dropped the handgrips on the sprower's cords and turned around. "You do? Who? Did you tell your father?"

"Not yet."

"Why not? Who is it? Tell us!"

"Please, girls, no gossip," I said, trying to silence them. "It's *loshon hora*, forbidden speech."

"What gossip?" Helga protested. "It's just my suspicion. There is no proof yet. But I do not trust the guy."

"Who?" Shirel persisted.

"Simeon, obviously." She stopped pedaling. "I think he's a liar. I stopped believing anything he says."

"Why would you say that?" I protested. "Simeon's a nice person, he's a friend. Someone who always wants to help."

Helga looked at me, uncharacteristically irritated. "He is good at fooling you, Michael. And Boris, too. I think it was them. Nobody else would have taken all those extra rations."

"We shouldn't accuse anybody without proof."

She shook her head hopelessly and resumed pedaling.

A loud voice startled me and I almost fell off the cycle. It was Captain Becker, standing right behind me. "Where is Dana?"

"Don't you see we are exercising, Captain Becker?" Shirel asked defensively. "You don't need to complain to Mom!"

"I have bigger problems than your exercising," he answered harshly, crossing the room to peer into my mother's bedroom. "She must already be downstairs."

"What's happening downstairs?" Meital asked.

Captain Becker ignored her. "Helga, find Ruby. We might need her."

"Ruby?" She stopped pedaling. "What for?" But her father had already bounded down to Mauve Level. She jumped off the cycle and headed for the stairwell. "I'll go look for her."

"Maybe it's something with the chickens," Meital said. "I should go." She stood and stretched.

"You were right there in front of him, Meital," Shirel said. "Wouldn't he have told you if it were the chickens?" Then she looked at me, an accusing glint in her eyes. "Maybe it really is Simeon. Maybe Helga is right, and Captain Becker went downstairs to arrest him."

I looked at my sister dubiously. "Then why would he call for Ruby?" I dismounted. "It must be something medical. Giving up on exercising, we all headed downstairs. Meital halted at the bottom step and held up her hand to silence us. Shirel bumped into me from behind.

"Quiet," Meital whispered. "Let me see what's going on." She leaned around the edge and looked into the room.

But we did not need to see. We could hear Captain Becker's rising voice.

"Dana, this is exactly what I warned against. Claudine should have listened when I told her to end the pregnancy! We cannot risk surgery. We do not have the facilities."

Shirel pushed us into the common area as our mother stepped out of the Bouchets' bedroom.

She slid the bedroom door shut and faced the captain, hands on her hips. "Louis is more than capable of performing a Caesarian." She had not spoken so assertively in weeks.

"Surgery on his own wife? That is ridiculous."

Dr. Louis called loudly from the bedroom. "No, Dietrich, it is not ridiculous. If necessary, I would perform the operation, even on my own wife. But it will not be necessary. Claudine prefers to deliver naturally."

"I will not permit the risk, Louis." The captain faced the closed bedroom door. "A breech birth is dangerous. Not only to the baby, but to Claudine, and to all of us."

My mother shook her head. "Dietrich, we can handle a childbirth, even a challenging one. We have two doctors here besides Claudine – three if we include you – and we have all the equipment we need. I think you are overreacting."

"Yes Dana, we can handle a childbirth, but what if we have a second emergency at the same time?" He raised his voice. "What if somebody else is injured? What if a critical system breaks down?"

"The chances of that are small."

"Small or large, we must be ready at all times!"

Helga arrived with Ruby.

"Captain Becker, you asked for me?"

"Yes, Ruby. As part of your nursing training in Red Rock, did you practice external cephalic version?"

"Cephalic what?"

"Massaging a pregnant belly to turn a breech fetus around?"

"Oh, that." She nodded. "Not at Red Rock, but last year at Altiplano. Dr. Pandya showed me techniques."

"Showed you? Did you have a chance to use them?"

"She made me practice on a medical dummy."

Captain Becker raised his hands hopelessly. "Why did I let it come to this? On my own ship!"

"Captain Becker," Ruby said earnestly, "I can try if somebody guides me using the ultrasound."

"Louis already has the ultrasound set up," my mother said. "Go." She slid the bedroom door open and pushed Ruby inside. Then she turned and noticed us. Eyebrows raised, she scolded, "What are you three doing there eavesdropping?"

Helga giggled as she stepped away from us. "This is your problem, Teller children!"

* * *

Wednesday, June 1st, 2029 03:40

Usually when I tossed and turned in my sleep, it was due to inner turmoil. Tuesday night, by contrast, the turmoil was external. For a while I let the whirring of the air circulation systems drown out the noise, and I tried to stay asleep. But the concerned voices and the cries of pain grew louder and louder. Eventually, I gave up, sat up, and looked at the clock on my datapad. It was nearly four in the morning. While I had slept, Tuesday, May 30 had turned into Wednesday, the first day of June. For the second time, we had skipped a date – the thirty-first of May, this time – to keep our Martian schedule synchronized with planet Earth's.

"Denver, are you awake?"

"Yes."

"What's all the noise?"

"I'm guessing that Dr. Claudine is giving birth."

"That's exciting." I sat up. "Shall we go downstairs to see?"

"We should give Dr. Claudine her privacy," he said, but he had already jumped down from his bunk and was stepping out the bedroom door. I followed him to the stairwell.

"Keep quiet," he whispered.

We headed downstairs toward muffled voices.

The Mauve-Level living room lights were on, brightly lit, but the NLED walls were dark. My mother was sitting at the dining table with the Meyers. As we entered, I noticed that her eyes were red with fatigue.

"You two don't need to be here," she said.

"The crying woke me up, Mom."

Before she could answer, the master bedroom door slid open and Ruby staggered out, her frizzy brown hair a tangled mess. She was weary with exhaustion, but she was smiling and her face beamed as she caught my eye. "We did it!"

"Did what?" I asked. "Did Claudine give birth?"

She shook her head as she slid the door closed behind her. "No, not yet; that's hours away."

"Then what did you do?"

She looked at me and shook her fists triumphantly. "We flipped the baby over!"

Dr. Esther stood to hug her daughter. "Congratulations, Ruby."

"So many hours massaging her belly, trying to push the baby around. We tried everything, but the baby did not want to move. Until just in the last hour. It was like she changed her mind and agreed to change direction."

"It's a girl?"

"I'm not supposed to say." Her face flushed.

Another loud moan escaped the bedroom door. It was Dr. Claudine, crying again.

"Can't we do something for her?" I asked. "She is suffering terribly!"

Ruby laughed. "Michael, it's just contractions for the birthing process. It's normal."

"But –"

"Dr. Claudine is very happy right now. All she wanted was a normal childbirth, and that is what is happening." Ruby jumped for joy, which was hazardous in low gravity; her hair brushed the ceiling. "Because, now, the baby is facing the right direction."

"That is fantastic, Ruby," Dr. Jhonathan said. "I'm proud of you for persevering so many hours, for not giving up." He flashed an approving fatherly smile. "Now go get some sleep. You too, Dana. It may be hours before Claudine gives birth."

"Go, all of you," Dr. Esther said, for some reason looking at me as she turned toward the bedroom door. "We're going to take good care of her, and of her baby."

*   *   *

Wednesday, June 1st, 2029 22:45

I tapped at my datapad, finishing an email to my grandmother to tell her about Dr. Claudine's healthy newborn. We had been corresponding more frequently in the month since my father's passing. More than anyone else, my grandmother understood my confused, erratic feelings. Her grief was greater than mine – losing two sons was more tragic than losing one father – but she never discussed her own feelings, only mine. I had described how Ruby had flipped the baby in utero, and what a crying baby sounded like on a spaceship, and how we were cultivating our second mushroom crop, and what it was like to program my first neural network. I told her about lying in bed in the middle of the night, crying for my father. That was something I dared not share with another soul in the solar system.

I finished the email with an "I love you" and tapped the "send" button. My datapad relayed the message through *Providence's* low-gain antenna, which radioed it to the communications satellite that traveled along with us, always just a few kilometers away. The satellite's high-gain laser antenna, aimed precisely at Earth, would shoot the data bits across the void, to be picked up by the Foundation's deep space network. I had lost track of Earth time, but I knew that, if my grandmother was awake, she would see my message in seven or eight minutes.

Denver's feet dangled from his upper bunk. He strummed dissonant chords on his guitar.

"What are you trying to play?"

"I'm teaching myself a new song, 'Neptunian Moons' by the Olympians."

"I thought I recognized those chords," I lied.

"No, I am quite sure you did not." He leaned over and peered down at me. "But give me some time to practice and I will play the whole song for your listening pleasure."

"I'm envious. Maybe I should have learned to play a musical instrument."

"It is not too late. You type well. You would be good with a piano."

"Remind me to buy one at *Martian Music Megastore* after we land."

He hopped down. After he stowed the guitar in the drawer under my bed, he looked up at me. "You know you have a piano application on your datapad, right?"

"The keyboard is too small."

"Project it on the NLED wall in the living room. You can get a full eighty-eight-key spread."

"It's the wrong orientation. I need keys below my fingers, not in front of them."

He stood and shook his head. "Now you are just making excuses."

"I am. I'm too busy learning other things."

"Fair enough. I make excuses, too." He sat down on my bed and faced me. "Like ignoring my parents' emails for months because 'they do not deserve my attention.'"

I raised my eyebrows. Denver deserved my attention. "Are you saying you've finally read them?"

"Yes, a few. I have started."

"That's excellent!" I pulled him into a hug he clearly did not expect. "What changed your mind?"

"Mostly my talks with Dr. Jhonathan." He gently shoved me away. "It is not so much that I changed my mind. More that I have worked up the courage."

I stared at my friend with awe, envying his maturity. He was confiding in me – I felt honored. "How is your mother? And your father?"

"My mother is okay. She went back to Colorado. My father … I don't know. He got a new research job in Cologne."

"I bet they were thrilled to hear from you."

His eyes dropped. "I haven't written back. Not yet."

"You need more courage?"

"Something like that."

*   *   *

Monday, June 20th, 2029 19:05

As far as we knew, Adele Bouchet – a healthy girl with a full head of curly black hair – was the first human in history not born on Earth. It was on our ship that she breathed her first breath, and we felt truly honored, and happy. G-d breathed new life into Adele, and Adele breathed new life into us. Three weeks after her birth, Denver would not stop smiling and Meital and Shirel forgot all their complaints. The girls would dart downstairs at every opportunity, to hold the baby, or change her diaper, or merely to wait on Dr. Claudine as she sat on her living room sofa, nursing. Even my mother was transformed: perhaps only new life could have healed her depression. We had not forgotten our loss, but Claudine needed help, and the newborn's needs were pressing, and the two of them kept my mother busy day and night. She had little time to think of my father.

We all looked for ways to help. I found my niche not with Adele – I was afraid even just to hold the fragile newborn – but with her sisters. Six-year-old Sophie had lost her most-favored status and acted out her frustration in all the ways one would expect of a child who had been confined inside a spacecraft for the better part of a year. She refused to put away her toys, avoided eating, threw tantrums, and even wet her bed once. Yet, whenever I offered to read her a story, she jumped joyfully onto the sofa next to me, eyes beaming in anticipation. Jasmine, a stoic space traveler, had accepted her baby sister with more maturity, but that maturity was no reason to skip story time.

"And so, Michael Collins waited all alone, for nearly a day, while the other astronauts got all the attention."

I had called the girls for a bedtime story – in English, this time – after finishing my afternoon exercise hour. The girls loved hearing about early space travel and did not seem to mind that I had been sweating.

"Why did they make him be alone?" Sophie asked. "Where was his *maman*? Did he not have children?"

"He had children," I said, checking the encyclopedia article on my datapad. "But there was no room on his ship for them. The whole Apollo spacecraft was not much larger than the sofa we are sitting on right now."

"Why did they not give him a big ship like ours?" she asked.

"Because," Jasmine answered sagely, "the ZubHab was not invented yet."

Dr. Louis poked his head into the living room. "Bedtime, girls. Thanks, Michael."

Meital exited the bathroom as the girls reluctantly got up. She waved and said, "All yours, Michael. Be quick – you'll be late for dinner."

On the way to the bedroom to grab a set of clean clothes, I passed a dense, brown, windy forest – a scene playing on the NLED wall; then I headed for the shower. It was strange, I thought, as I stripped out of my dirty mundies, that I still felt vulnerable without them. Captain Becker's stern words, spoken just after launch back in September, echoed in my mind. In the MiniHab on the way up to our habitat, he had warned, "For the rest of our lives, our dwellings will be surrounded by extreme low-pressure environments." Ever since, day or night, we never removed our mundies trousers or long-sleeved shirts. Except while showering.

The warm stream of water and clean soapy scent cleared my mind and relaxed my shoulders. How great it was to have gravity! Otherwise, I would have been sponging myself with drops of water instead of holding a shower head in my hand, spraying water into my hair and down my back. I paused to listen to the water pattering on the shower walls and to watch the stream fall. The water did not drop straight down, but instead twisted to the side in characteristic Coriolis motion. That was an illusion, I knew; the water was moving in a straight line while the spinning habitat rotated the shower, and the whole bathroom, out from under it. Straight or twisted, either way was fine with me; I was just happy to rinse off sweat and breathe in steam twice a day after vigorous exercise.

I closed the faucet to save water while soaping up. Every drop that went down the drain would be filtered, disinfected and recycled, and all that required energy, electricity from our limited solar supply. We saved water to save energy. I unclipped the bar of soap and rubbed it over my legs, arms, chest, and back. I inhaled the soap's rich, perfumed smell. Absent the sound of spraying water, the whooshing noise of air rushing into the atmosphere-processing intake (the toilet) seemed to grow louder and louder, becoming almost overwhelming. I scrubbed between my toes.

BOOM! A crashing noise, like an explosion, ripped through the hull. I flinched and lost my balance. "Is everything okay?" I asked pointlessly, trying to steady myself, all alone there in the shower.

The ship answered my question with a high-pitched screeching alarm that drowned out even the air processing systems. Then an automated computer voice interrupted the alarm, sounding from the public address speakers present even in the bathroom. "Hull breach! Pressure loss! Don fleximets immediately! Hull breach! Pressure loss! Don fleximets immediately!"

I was naked, and my ears were popping.

Adele

Monday, June 20th, 2029 19:27

"Hull breach! Pressure loss! Don fleximets immediately!"

My fleximet was nowhere nearby. I was not even wearing mundies, and I was covered in soap. My ears were popping. We had suffered another micrometeoroid hit, I guessed, but if so, the breach was minor because I was still breathing. That is what the rational part of my brain told me, but my heart pounded in my chest, and the computerized alarm pounded in my ears.

Rinsing the soap off my body was a luxury for people with air. So was dressing, but I needed my mundies to save my life, so I would indulge myself, even as the klaxon roared. I grabbed my towel and wiped myself down. Dropping the soaked, pungent towel on the floor, I unfolded the clean mundies pants and struggled to pull them onto still-damp legs. Getting my mundies shirt on was no easier; still, not more than ninety seconds passed before I was running, ears still popping as the air pressure continued dropping, through the living room toward my bedroom, to retrieve my fleximet, marsmitts, and socks.

Meital and Shirel, fully suited up, were already checking each other's fleximet seals. My mother was inspecting Denver's. "Michael, hurry up – you'll suffocate!" she yelled, her voice muffled by her own fleximet, but her visor did not hide the panicked look in her eyes.

I dug through a pile of colored cotton shirts in the drawer under my bed. My fleximet was at the very bottom. It had been months since we had practiced donning them – was that our fault or the captain's? I unfolded the rubbery material and pulled it over my head. My ears were aching and I gasped for breath, but I managed to follow the procedure: first I aligned the fleximet's three button holes with the mundies' shoulder fasteners; then I massaged the ziplock seals down all around my neck. Gasping again, I realized I had forgotten the oxypack. I bent down and shuffled again through the drawer's contents, finally finding the oxygen tank buried under a blue smock I had never worn. Frantically, I grabbed it, screwed it into the socket on the side of the fleximet, and turned the activation knob. My ears popped again – this time from increasing air pressure – and I felt a rush of cool air on my cheek. Activating the oxypack had activated the radio, and I heard a cacophony of anxious voices, including my mother's.

"Michael, can you hear me?"

I Velcroed the oxypack to the neck of the fleximet. "I'm in the bedroom." My voice sounded meek.

My mother stood in the bedroom doorway, looking even more alarmed than before. Pointing a shaking hand, she asked, "Where are your socks? And your gloves?"

I dug my mundies socks and marsmitts out of the same drawer. I pulled them on, first the socks, then the gloves. It was lucky that everything had been there. The fleximet, oxypack and marsmitts had not crossed my mind for months, not since our spacewalk back in January, when Sam and I had asked to go outside for a breath of fresh air, so to speak.

I slipped on my plastic sandals and followed my mother back to the living room. The same windy forest still showed on the NLED wall, brown boughs waving, orange and red leaves rustling. Strangely, my mundies had not yet started squeezing my legs and waist and chest and hands. That meant that the leak was slower than my panic justified. Despite what my ears felt, air pressure had not dropped significantly.

Also, the computerized alarms had stopped. Maybe it was a false alarm?

Captain Becker's voice echoed over the public address system, both from the NLED wall speakers and from the fleximet speakers, which were too close to my ears. "Prepare for reclamation depressurization. We want to save as much air as possible. Everyone will confirm that their suits are sealed; then Jhonathan will commence the process."

My mother was fiddling with my mundies shoulders. "Michael, you forgot to twist the fasteners. Your fleximet could pop off at any time!" She fixed them herself, then pressed the oxypack's button to test the seal. My ears popped again.

"Thanks, Mom." I turned to face her. "Do you want me to test your seal?"

"I checked Dr. Dana's seal already," Denver said. He peered at me through our visors. "Where are your sourdough cultures? Do you not want to save them?"

"Yeah, right, thanks." I went to retrieve the open jars from the bedroom closet. I found airtight covers for both of them in the kitchen, and screwed them on tightly.

Over the radio, Captain Becker began a general roll call.

"Cecylia, confirm your seal."

"Confirmed, Dietrich."

"Helga."

"Confirmed, Pa."

He continued down the list of names in order of habitat level, finishing his own Yellow, then starting the Meyers' Pink.

"Omar."

"Confirmed, Captain; my suit is sealed. But what about the vegetables and the mushrooms? They will not survive depressurization."

"There is nothing we can do for them – I am sorry. The nitrogen is a more precious resource."

Omar moaned in quiet grief. The captain ignored his protest and continued through the list.

"Sam?"

"My seal is confirmed."

"Michael."

I looked to my mother, who nodded. "Confirmed," I said nervously.

"Meital."

"I need just a moment – sorry."

"Quickly, Meital. Please do not hold us up. Shirel?"

"I'm ready."

In a quiet voice, almost a whisper – we were all speaking on the same shared radio channel – my mother asked, "Where is Meital?" She turned around, searching the room. Shirel and Denver stood next to me in their sealed suits, but Meital was nowhere to be found, not even in her bedroom.

"Louis," continued the captain, loudly.

"Confirmed, but we are still trying to seal Adele's airtent. It might take a few minutes, Dietrich."

The captain did not respond audibly, but I imagined him saying, "I told you so!"

"*Cette tente est trop grande,*" Dr. Claudine said, barely audible on the shared radio. "How will I hold her?"

"I can find a smaller tent in the airlock," Louis answered. "*Un moment.*"

The captain was impatient. "Louis, we –"

"Who sealed the airlock?" Dr. Louis asked sharply. "Dietrich, why is the airlock door closed?" His alarm surprised me, because the door to the airlock was at the end of his own living room floor. Surely, he would have noticed someone closing it.

Simeon spoke over the radio. "I think Ruby and Meital went down to the airlock."

"Yes, this is Ruby here," Ruby's voice declared unnecessarily. "Simeon is right. Meital and I are down here trying to save as many birds as possible."

"Who asked you to do that?" the captain asked harshly. "Who gave you permission to seal the lock?"

"Nobody asked us!" Meital said. "We are responsible for the birds. We were worried that we were running out of time, so we sealed the airlock."

Ruby added, informatively, "Air pressure is steady here, so the breach must be upstairs."

"Meital," Dr. Louis said, "we need one of the small airtents for the baby. Please open the hatch."

"No, Louis, it is too late to move Adele," Claudine answered, sounding like she was holding back tears. "She is safe now in the large airtent. I sealed it and am watching her through the cover."

"Then we will commence the purge," Captain Becker announced. "Including the airlock. Meital and Ruby, confirm that your fleximets are sealed."

"Yes, they are sealed, but the chickens and the parakeets – we need more time!"

"I'll delay depressurizing the airlock for a couple of minutes." It was Dr. Jhonathan's voice. "Everyone else: commencing depressurization."

We waited silently for our mundies to start contracting around our limbs and torsos, to replace the external pressure that our skin needed.

"This is the first time we've been fully suited up with gravity," Denver observed.

I looked at him. "Other than when we trained in Altiplano."

"But that was almost always in atmosphere, not vacuum. This is strange."

Shirel suddenly spun around, tears in her eyes. "The worms! They're all going to die. Mom, help me save the worms."

"I'm sorry, Shirel. There is no protocol for saving the worms from an emergency vacuum situation." My mother pulled her into a tight hug, fleximet to fleximet.

"It's not fair."

"Keep the shared channel clear!" Captain Becker ordered. "Meital and Ruby, confirm that I can begin purging the airlock."

"But why can't we leave it pressurized? The leak is upstairs, not here," Meital protested.

"What Meital means to say," Ruby said, shushing her friend, "is that we are ready." She added, sadly, "We have saved as many birds as we'll be able to."

That was the moment I felt my mundies start squeezing me. The pressure began on my arms and followed immediately on my calves and thighs. Within a few seconds, my shirt clamped down around my chest and belly. My fleximet ballooned and the transparent visor pulled taut, bringing the living room into sharper focus. Gradually, the sound outside the fleximet became quieter and quieter. For the first time in months, the whooshing of the fans was silenced.

As the air pressure continued to drop, we silently examined each other's suits for bulges. Each bulge, a localized failure in the smart fabric's electroelasticity, had to be fixed immediately. My mother appeared with a patch kit and proceeded to repair several bulges in Shirel's shirt, one on Denver's left sleeve, and a minor, questionable swelling she noticed when she asked me to lift my right foot.

Susan was the first to ask the obvious question, "How are we going to plug the hole in the hull?"

Captain Becker ignored her. "Jhonathan, report on ambient pressure."

"Thirty-seven millibars. Still dropping."

"Continue to twenty millibars."

We waited silently. I listened to my breathing, and to the sound of the fleximet fan, and to the air blowing around my ears.

"Twenty millibars confirmed. Pausing depressurization. One moment."

"What are we waiting for?" Shirel asked.

"Keep the channel clear!" Captain Becker said. "Jhonathan, do we have an estimate of the size of the breach?"

There was a delay before Dr. Jhonathan responded. "Nineteen point five millibars. Pressure is dropping slowly. Based on the drop rate, the computer estimates a four- or five-millimeter breach."

"That is going to be difficult to find."

"I ran an acoustic analysis of the strike recording. The computer thinks we were struck between Yellow Level and the upper storage deck, on the starboard side, relative to spin direction."

I tried to picture where exactly that was on the inner hull, but was distracted by the thought that every direction was "starboard" from our interplanetary point of view.

"The program narrowed down the location to a five-by-five-meter area."

"Still a large area to search," the captain said.

"But there are twenty of us," I whispered, afraid the captain might scold me. I had already taken a step toward the stairwell, intending to get started right away with the search, before I realized I had no idea what to look for.

"We may need to spin down," Jhonathan was saying. "In weightlessness we can spray droplets and follow them on the currents."

Dr. Louis spoke. "A search like that will take hours. We cannot keep everyone suited up that long."

"You are concerned for your baby," Captain Becker said in an unexpectedly sympathetic voice.

"Not just the baby. The children. All of us, really. Recharging everybody's oxypacks every two hours will be burdensome."

"I agree," said the captain reluctantly. "Fixing the breach might take days." He sighed. The channel went silent and stayed that way for more than a minute. We waited. His voice finally returned for a simple subdued announcement: "We will abandon ship."

I shuddered with dread. *Abandon ship? Here, in the middle of nowhere?* I was not alone: multiple gasps sounded on the radio. Susan blurted, "We're ditching our habitat? In interplanetary space? Where are we supposed to go?"

"Children, please!" Captain Becker bellowed impatiently. "Keep the channel clear!"

"But she is right, Pa," Celina said. "Where can we go?"

My heart pounded against my mundies-constrained chest. My panting made me lightheaded.

"*Mars Hope* will be our temporary shelter. I have informed Amit – Captain Ravel – about our breach, and he is preparing to receive us."

Would we climb across the void to the other habitat?

"Shall I initiate spin-down?" Dr. Jhonathan asked. "We cannot traverse the tethers while the habitats are rotating."

"I think we have no choice," said Captain Becker.

"Pardon," Boris said dispassionately, "but I count four times that we have spun up since launch. That is the maximum fuel available in the Mars-Entry stage's reaction control system. If we spin down, we will not be able to spin back up."

"Four?" The captain paused, perhaps counting. "That is right, Boris. It is unfortunate, but within the Foundation's operational procedures."

"You are saying we will have no more gravity for the rest of the journey?" Omar asked.

"Yes," Dr. Jhonathan said. "That is correct. Does anyone see an alternative?"

"Yes, I do – this is Simeon," Boris's brother answered hastily, identifying himself unnecessarily. "The meteor will have left a visible mark in the PlyShield. I will go outside and find it. You say that we already know the general area. I am not afraid to search twenty square meters, even while we are still spinning! I will be tethered at all times."

"Simeon," the captain answered, "I appreciate your enthusiasm, even for a ludicrous idea. I will not, however, permit a spacewalk while the habitat spins."

If Simeon felt slighted, he hid it. "Let us weigh the danger of a challenging half-hour spacewalk by one person against the difficulty and danger to health for everybody, if we are without gravity for six weeks. Jhonathan and Louis, do you not agree that the choice is obvious?"

"Simeon," Louis said gently, "I defer to the captain. The obvious choice is to follow his instructions, especially during an emergency."

I thought I knew what Simeon wanted to answer, but I also knew that he respected Louis and would keep his mouth shut.

"I am linking Amit into the line. Stand by."

I looked silently at the airless living room, and at my mother, and Denver, and Shirel. Was this really happening?

"This is Captain Amit Ravel of *Mars Hope*," Captain Becker's counterpart announced ceremoniously. "Residents of *Providence*, I grant you all permission to board my ship."

"Thank you, Amit. Is your group prepared for an emergency spin-down?"

"We'll need fifteen minutes. I'll make the announcement now." There was a short pause before he added, "Godspeed. We expect to see all of you on board safely, soon."

"Fifteen minutes to emergency spin-down," Captain Becker announced. "Jhonathan, complete the atmosphere purge and begin procedures for abandoning ship."

"Okay, everybody," Dr. Jhonathan answered, taking over. "You heard the captain. Please listen carefully. First, pair up. Everybody should know who his buddy is."

Denver and I glanced at each other.

"Dana, if Louis and Claudine agree, I would like to pair you with Jasmine, so that they can focus on the baby and Sophie."

"Yes, okay," all three answered together.

"Ruby, you should be able to open the airlock hatch now. Please do so."

"Okay, Dad."

"After spin-down, you'll need to clear out the airlock and bring the cages upstairs."

"I'll see to it."

"Next, everybody, prepare the ship for weightlessness. Make sure everything is stowed and secure. Each of you is responsible for your own bedroom. Divide the shared spaces. Then pack duffels, one duffel for each pair. Here's the list of contents – listen carefully. Two sets of mundies per person, two dresses or longshirts, and one bedroll each. No pillows and no shoes. Stow your datapads in the duffel, and secure one extra oxypack to your thigh and a water bottle to your neck. Again: that's two sets of mundies and shirts, one bedroll, your datapad, one extra oxypack, and one water bottle. That is all: leave all other belongings on board."

I shook my head. I would not leave my sourdough cultures behind. Or my religious phylacteries.

Dr. Cecylia broke in. "I will pack an extra duffel with food provisions."

"That's a good idea. Get going, everybody. I will switch the radios to four separate level channels so you can communicate among yourselves. We will announce the commencement of the spin-down on the shared channel."

Again Denver and I glanced at each other, and at Shirel and my mother. Shirel was the first to test the local radio channel. "Mom, where is the vacuum cleaner? We should suck up the dust before it floats into the air."

Apparently the Green-Level channel was working, because I heard my mother and Denver both laugh. "It's too late for vacuuming," she said. "We need atmosphere for that."

I got to work with Denver in our bedroom. He stowed his guitar in the drawer, while I pulled out a duffel and shoved two folded sets of mundies into it. I wrapped my bedroll and a couple of sky-blue cotton shirts protectively around my datapad, and pushed them in with the mundies. Denver did the same with his. Then he looked around the room and said, "Michael, don't forget your sourdoughs. Do not let them die."

"I would not have forgotten." I took the two sealed bottles from the cabinet shelf, stuffed them into the duffel, and zipped it shut. The duffel was not airtight, but the bottles were.

While Shirel and Denver cleaned up the living room and stowed the dining chairs so they not float away, I helped my mother arrange the kitchen. There were dirty plates and plasticware in the sink; we gathered them and stowed them in the cabinets. Then I checked the bathroom. I found the bar of soap and towel I had dropped on the floor after my shower. I snapped the soap into the clips above the sink and took the now-dry towel to my room. My unrinsed arms and legs itched.

We were double-checking the whole of Green Level to make sure nothing was resting free (I even knelt down on the floor and peered through my fleximet to make sure the dining table's legs were fastened properly in their floor sockets) when Dr. Jhonathan made his announcement. "Initiating emergency spin-down."

Only five minutes later we were all floating weightlessly around the table. Meital had appeared by then, puffy face visible behind her fleximet visor. Sobbing, she took Shirel's half-packed duffel back into the bedroom to pack her own belongings. "I just watched dozens of birds suffocate to death," she cried.

Shire followed her. "I thought you went downstairs to save the birds, not to watch them die."

"You think we wanted to watch them die? We were trying to save them all! But there were not enough airtents. Or enough time. We managed to pack five tents. Three of them with hens, the others with parakeets and canaries."

"You saved all the hens?" I asked.

"In three airtents? Are you kidding?" She looked back at me and I could see her eyes glistening behind her mask. "We shoved two hens into each airtent. I hope they don't kill each other. Or die of thirst."

"Or suffocate," Shirel added.

"That's the one thing that does not worry me. We got all the oxypacks working, so at least they have air for now."

"Meital, don't get your hopes up," my mother cautioned. "The Foundation has no protocol for maintaining grown birds in airtents."

"I know, Mom, but we had to try."

I watched Meital, appreciating her quick thinking and her empathy for the fowl.

Then the lights went out. If not for a few remaining nightlight LEDs, the room would have been pitch-black.

"What happened?" Shirel asked, alarmed. "Did we lose electricity?"

As if he had heard her question, Dr. Jhonathan announced over the shared channel, "All unnecessary systems have been shut down while we are on battery power. This is planned. Nothing to worry about."

"I'm sure we have something to worry about," I said, but nobody saw my sardonic frown.

Denver faced the girls. "Shirel, about the electricity. Usually, when we are not spinning for gravity, the habitats rotate slowly around the vertical axis. This is for temperature control, so no part stays in the sun too long and gets too hot, or stays in shadow and gets too cold. This time, though, I suspect we have stopped all rotation completely. Even a slow rotation might fling us off the tethers when we start crossing to the other ship in a few minutes."

"What does that have to do with the electricity?" Meital asked.

"Maybe they stopped us with the bottom of the Mars-Entry stage facing the sun. Like during the solar storm. In that position no sunlight hits the solar panels, so there is nothing to charge the batteries."

Dr. Jhonathan's voice interrupted. "The *Mars Hope* airlock has room for only half of us at a time, so we will need to cross over in two groups. The first group will be the Bouchets, and Dana and her girls and Esther and my girls. Prepare to gather in the airlock with your duffels. You have five minutes. Meanwhile, Boris and Simeon, please stow the birdcages in your room."

"We're in the second group," I said to Denver. He nodded.

"Goodbye, Mom. And bye Shirel and Meital." I ignored the butterflies in my stomach and added, "We'll see you on the other side! Good luck."

"I love you, Michael," my mother said, hugging me. "And you, Denver. No worrying! We'll all be fine."

"I'm worrying," Shirel said. Meital grabbed her hand and they followed my mother, floating across the room toward the stairwell, duffels in tow.

* * *

Adele

Monday, June 20th, 2029 20:50

Dr. Jhonathan reopened the general channel for the traversal operation. On the one hand, that meant that Sam, Denver and I had to avoid speaking to each other, floating there in the living room in the dark, because everybody would hear anything we said and our chattering would disturb the group. On the other hand, we were able to listen in as Meital and Shirel, and my mother and Jasmine, and the other Bouchets, and Sam's mother and sisters, all stepped bravely into the void. I pictured them in my mind, in separate groups, climbing slowly up the ship's hull to where the four tethers held the habitat, then latching themselves to the tethers, then pulling themselves across the hundred-meter gap, each group traveling across one of them.

Dr. Esther took continual roll calls as we listened in. I guessed that for her – an experienced spacewalker – this spacewalk was nothing special, so it made sense that she had taken charge. She spoke clearly over the channel. "Meital?"

"I'm doing okay and so is Shirel. The chickens in my airtent – I don't know; I'm worried."

"I'm sure you are doing all you can. Claudine, what about you?"

"The baby is spitting up again," she answered. I imagined her pulling Adele's bloated airtent through the emptiness, mother's eyes fixed on ailing infant, behind the airtent's transparent cover, a vast handbreadth away. Dr. Claudine could not hold her newborn, nor wipe her lips, nor stroke her cheek, nor comfort her with soft whispers. All she could do was say, in a thin, breaking voice, "Adele is crying again."

In space, no one could hear the baby cry. The airtent, designed for birds, had no microphone.

"Claudine," Louis called, "I am right behind you. Let me help!"

"*Merci, mon cœur*, stay with me while we hurry across. I can already see the end of the tether. Sophie, help your Papa."

Dr. Esther continued the roll call. She had nerves of steel. "Dana?"

"We're making good progress. Jasmine is doing great."

"Yes, I can see you."

How did Dr. Esther see my mother? It took a moment for me to realize that they all could see each other once they had climbed to the top and begun the trek across the gap. The four tethers stretched out in parallel, together holding the two ships. Each was a hundred meters long, but only six meters – a bit less than the diameter of the habitats – separated them. My shipmates would feel like they were crossing the void together.

"Shirel?" Dr. Esther called.

"Fine." My sister's voice trembled, but when she added, "The stars are amazing!" her enthusiasm sounded like it might be real.

"Louis?"

"Sophie is well. I am concerned about Adele."

"Claudine," Dr. Esther called, "how's the baby now?"

"I can see her in her tent. We are moving now from the tether to the top rung."

I pictured Dr. Claudine at the far end of the tether, latching herself to *Mars Hope*, preparing to descend the long ladder down its hull, airtented baby in tow.

"How does she look?"

"I am not sure. She was spitting up." Her voice quavered. "I can see the spittle floating in the tent. Some is stuck in her mouth. I fear she has choked."

"We have the airlock open," an unfamiliar *Mars Hope* voice declared. "We are ready to bring you inside as soon as you reach the hatch."

Louis interrupted. "Claudine, switch places with me. I'll run Adele down the ladder."

"No. Keep with Sophie. I will take Adele down. She is not crying anymore."

*   *   *

Monday, June 20th, 2029 21:35

We listened in silence as, one by one, our sisters and friends announced their entry into the *Mars Hope* airlock. I hovered near Sam and Denver at the edge of the dark and dying Mauve-Level living room.

Dr. Esther completed the final roll call. "Ruby and Susan?"

"Coming through now, Mom. I see you."

"Squeeze yourselves in! That will be everybody. We can close the hatch."

"Welcome aboard, *Providence* fliers," Captain Ravel announced. "As soon as you confirm the seal, we will begin pressurization."

The *Mars Hope* radio channel cut off. Nobody had mentioned Adele.

On our end, Dr. Jhonathan did not waste a moment. "It is our turn to cross over," he said. "Everybody down to the airlock. Careful, though: the outer hatch is open. Don't float outside before you are dressed and harnessed, and keep an eye on all equipment!"

I turned on my fleximet lamp and kicked off the wall, following Sam and Denver. We aimed for the airlock hatch in the living room floor.

We glided past Simeon, who was watching us as he pointed toward his bedroom. "Do not look in there," he said over the radio.

For Denver that was an invitation. He turned and illuminated the forbidden room with his forehead lamp. "That is so sad," he said. "And disgusting! Do not look, Michael."

I looked. Boris and Simeon had latched all the birdcages from the airlock to the walls of their bedroom. My sister and Ruby may have saved a few birds, but dozens of others, now bloated, desiccated carcasses, floated in the dim gloom. I saw dead parakeets and canaries, and, deeper in the room, a cage of dead hens. I turned away as my eyes filled with tears. "I can't take the stench."

"There is no stench, Michael."

"I smell it anyway."

Sam nudged me gently from behind. I pulled down into the airlock and he and Denver followed close behind.

Last came Boris and Simeon, completing our group. "We tried chasing water droplets toward the breach," Boris said, "but the pressure was already too low. The water just hung in place. There were no air currents to follow."

"It was worth a try," Helga said.

Captain Becker waited for us to gather. "Thank goodness, ten of us are now safely aboard *Mars Hope*. It is our turn to join them." He rotated slowly, scrutinizing each of us in turn. Even obscured by his visor, his gaze intimidated me. "We will follow the same safety procedures," he continued. "But first, recharge your oxypacks. We have been breathing suit air for two hours now and your tanks are depleted." He scanned the room again, resting his eyes on Sam. "You, take charge of recharging everyone's packs. Now, everyone, quickly!"

I shut down the oxypack affixed to my right shoulder, released it from its Velcro patch, and unscrewed it. My fleximet was suddenly silent. The quiet was brief, however, lasting only until I pulled the second two-liter tank off my thigh, installed it and twisted its activation knob. I examined my first oxypack, which showed nineteen percent air and thirty-seven percent battery remaining. I handed it to Sam.

Captain Becker continued briefing us while Sam recharged the packs. "We will divide into four groups, each taking one of the tethers. Jhonathan, Sam and Omar, you take red. Denver and Michael, yellow. Boris and Simeon, blue. I will take green, with Cecylia and the girls."

"No," said Simeon. "I disagree!"

"You disagree with the tether color assignments?"

"No, I disagree that we should all go. I and Boris can stay behind to find the break. Are you with me, Boris?"

"Simeon," Captain Becker said, sounding irritated and fatigued, "we need to get to safety. Once again you are making things difficult." He shook his head inside his fleximet. "Please," he sighed, "just this one time, follow my lead."

"But we need to repair our ship!"

"No, we need to get to a pressurized environment where I do not need to worry if everybody's oxypacks and mundies are functioning correctly. That is my priority. We will regroup aboard *Mars Hope*. From there, in an environment where we can breathe freely, we will plan our repair excursions."

"With all respect, Captain Becker," Boris broke in, "this time I agree with my brother. Let us avoid an extra trip across the tethers. The two of us will work together now, locate the breach, and assess the damage. Then we will join you on the other ship. In a day or two, when we come back, we will already know what tools to bring for the repairs."

Sam pulled a couple of refilled oxypacks out of the charging sockets. He plugged in the next set.

"Jhonathan, what do you think of Boris's suggestion?"

Dr. Jhonathan turned to face the captain. "It's not a bad idea for two of us to stay behind for a few more hours. But it should be you and me performing the damage assessment, Dietrich. Vessel damage analysis is the responsibility of the command staff."

"Please stop being ridiculous!" Simeon yelled, annoyed. "We will see you on the other end in a couple of hours."

"My brother is right," Boris said. "You two go join your families. Simeon and I know the ship's design, the physical structure, the stress points, the electrical systems. Let us do what we trained for."

Captain Becker took nearly a minute to answer, seemingly considering all options. Finally, he said, "Okay. You have two hours. Take an extra backup oxypack, each of you."

"That will be six hours of air," Simeon said. "Maybe we should take more, just in case?"

The captain ignored him and turned to his daughters. "Update to the groupings: since Simeon and Boris are staying behind, Helga and Marcelina, you take blue tether."

"Understood," Celina said.

"Next: I need volunteers to take three bundles besides your own duffels. Two of them are fowl airtents the first group left behind. The birds may still be alive. Also, Cecylia packed a duffel with food items."

"I can take one of the airtents," I said, "if Denver can handle the duffel we packed with our clothes."

"No problem for me, Michael," Denver said.

Sam volunteered to take the other airtent and Helga grabbed the bundle of food.

"Let's get suited up," Dr. Jhonathan said. "You still need your Mylar suits, even though the sun is blocked. They will reflect your radiating body heat inward to keep you from freezing. You also need harnesses and cords and carabiners. Omar, please help me hand these out and make sure everybody gets the right number of cords.

I found the spacesuit pack with my name on it in the wall cabinet. I extracted and unfolded the Mylar pants and pulled them over my legs, then pushed my feet into the attached boots. I adjusted the elastic band around my waist, then pulled out the matching Mylar pullover. Like a sweatshirt with an oversized hood, it covered

Red Valley

my arms, torso, fleximet, oxypack and water bottle. Once I was dressed, Omar handed me a belt harness, which I secured between my legs and around my waist. Securing the belt was a challenge, requiring fine motor control. That was difficult in the marsmitts, because they clenched my fingers quite tightly in the vacuum. Even the smallest finger movement required effort, but after a couple of tries I managed to pull the belt tight and fasten its buckle.

"Take these, Michael," Dr. Jhonathan said, handing me three nylon cords, each with hooks at both ends. I latched them to my belt. One cord would secure the airtent, while the other two would keep me continuously attached to ladder rungs or to the tether that spanned the gap to the other habitat.

"Michael, you forgot your insulated gloves." Omar pushed a set into my hands. "If you grab the ladder without these – the rungs will be freezing cold – that would not be good."

"Thanks, Omar."

Sam handed me a recharged oxypack, which I pushed deep into my Mylar pants and Velcroed to my thigh. I double-checked that it was secure and would not float around. That was my backup air, my only chance at staying alive if my main pack ran out or failed. I wondered how much air remained in the oxypack I had been breathing from, so I reached up to my neck and tapped its diagnostic button.

"Seventy-four percent oxygen; eighty-two percent power," a robotic voice echoed in my ears.

"How long will it take to get to *Mars Hope*?" I asked. "I have seventy-four percent air."

"Forty-five minutes or so," Dr. Jhonathan answered. "Seventy-four percent should last twice that." He pushed a fowl airtent toward me. I attached a cord, then flipped the tent over to expose its transparent top. I shined my helmet lamp on the tent and looked inside. Something seemed to be moving. That was a good sign.

First out of the hatch were Helga and Celina. As soon as they exited, Denver called to me. "Michael, let's get going!" I watched his head and shoulders rise through the opening. My heart pounded in my chest. Denver paused and asked, "Which ladder are we supposed to take?"

"Yellow tether ... that is ladder four," the captain answered.

Denver had grabbed the wrong side of the large circular opening, so he pushed across to the other side, spinning himself around nimbly in the process. Holding one of the tethers, he stretched out his arm and latched it to a rung I could not see. He pulled himself out, and I moved to follow him into the void.

Outside was frighteningly dark, unfathomably black. My heart raced. Disorientation and vertigo overwhelmed me. I needed air! I breathed heavily. The sound echoed in my ears, louder even than the humming of the oxypack's fans. But if the fans were humming, I had enough air. Why did I feel so out of breath? I tried to focus, to steady myself, to concentrate on what I had to do next. What I had to do was aim my lamp on a barely-visible ladder rung. I was so dizzy!

"F-L-I-E-R-S." The mnemonic, programmed deep in my brain, popped to the surface. "Freeze." That was easy. "Listen." My helmet resonated with blowing air. "Inhale." I took a slow breath. "Exhale." I released the air steadily.

"Michael? Hey Michael! Are you behind me?"

How long had Denver been calling? "I'm here. I'm okay now." I found the first ladder rung, reached out, and clipped my cord's carabiner to it. "Latched," I announced, embarrassed. I concentrated on pulling the airtent with the hens out through the hatch, trying not to bump them against the hull.

Ahead of me, Denver zipped easily across the base of our habitat, latching and unlatching his carabiners in quick succession. I remembered my main responsibility as Denver's buddy: to make sure he adhered to the safety rules. Completely unnecessarily, my voice unsteady, I called over the radio, "Denver, remember to latch onto the next rung before freeing yourself from each prior one!" Then I concentrated on following those same instructions.

Having relaxed a little, I stopped to look around and let my eyes adjust to the darkness. Only by rotating my whole body could I shine my forehead lamp on the Mars-Entry stage, three meters above. Its white top reflected the lamplight. I turned back around and examined the ladder rungs that spread out ahead of me, bending around the ship's bottom edge. I could see five.

Denver had disappeared around the curve. "It is so dark out here!" he called out. "Which direction is the sun?"

Boris, still inside the habitat, answered over the shared channel. "We are parked with *Mars Hope* facing the sun, so it is directly above us. But *Mars Hope* is shielding us from its light."

"The ship's engine bell must be boiling hot," Sam said.

"My understanding is that the rocket bell is designed to get hot," I said, feeling a small smile break through my tense lips.

"No chatter!" Captain Becker barked. "This is my channel. Keep it clear so I can monitor everybody." He intimidated me, and I could not even see him.

At first, I was cold, even shivering. As I picked up the pace my muscles began warming. Vacuum was a strange environment. I felt like I was moving too slowly, but, since nobody admonished me, I could not have fallen too far behind Denver. Barely a minute or two passed before I, too, climbed around the bottom edge. I began to sweat.

Without the Mars-Entry stage to reflect the dim light from our fleximet lamps, the outside world turned indescribably darker. I kept my lamp focused mostly on the ladder rungs, but I did glance to the left and right from time to time at the long, narrow solar panels that we had unfurled all those months ago, and at a landing leg folded against the hull. Shining my light on one of the panels, I had the silly thought that my lamplight was the only thing charging *Providence's* batteries.

Denver performed his duty, reminding me, again and again, "Michael, latch before unlatching!"

These were my primary tasks: latch one cord to the next rung; unlatch the other cord from the previous rung; try to keep the airtent with the chickens from banging the hull's PlyShield; repeat. Check my buddy and make sure he was following the same protocol. Denver kept turning back to look at me, each time shining his helmet lamp at my visor, unintentionally blinding me with the glare.

First to the top of *Providence* were Celina and Helga, who proudly announced that they were beginning their transit across the blue tether. A minute or so later, Sam and Omar reported that they had reached the red tether.

Then it was Denver's turn. "I see the yellow hook," he said. "What do I do?"

"Latch your free carabiner to the tether, Denver," Captain Becker answered. "Then latch the second one. Then pull yourself across the gap."

Denver was only a couple of meters ahead of me, and barely a minute passed before I, too, reached the base of the yellow tether. In my lamplight I examined the shiny cord closely. It was amazingly narrow, no thicker than my gloved thumb; yet it – together with the other three – had held two enormous ships together, countering the huge centrifugal force generated by their spinning, for months on end. That same cord would lead us through the murky emptiness to safety.

"But the tether is not yellow," I said to myself.

"Michael," Denver answered over the open connection, "the clasp is yellow and so are the rings at both the tether's ends. They give it its yellow name."

I examined the clasp and the thimble. The clasp was the size of my forearm and the thimble larger than my hand. The end of the tether wrapped tightly around the thimble and doubled back, to bind to itself under a ten-centimeter-long steel sleeve. More amazingness – how could these connecting parts be so strong?

And Denver was right – the clasp and thimble were yellow. I was in the right place.

I latched my carabiners to the tether and yanked myself forward, hoping to glide the full 105-meter length in one go. The strategy worked for three or four seconds, but my trajectory was not quite parallel to the tether, and as soon as my nylon cords reached their full extent, I bounced back and lost control. Flailing, I managed to grab the tether with my gloved hands. Considering that the tether and the ships it connected were floating freely in space, the tether was surprisingly taut. On the other hand, did I expect my seventy-kilo mass to have a noticeable effect on 500 tonnes of habitats, water, rockets, and fuel?

I steadied myself and untangled the airtent. Henceforth, prudently, I would pull myself along the length of the tether slowly and meticulously. There were no shortcuts.

While we were busy making our transit, Boris and Simeon had begun their search for the breach. Over the shared channel, Simeon announced, "I am climbing up the starboard side. Boris, where are you now?"

"I am back inside, on my way up to the storage attic."

"Do you have the design plans open on your datapad?"

"*Da.* You tell me the outer coordinates of the damage and I will find the inside location."

Dr. Jhonathan interrupted to take a roll call. "Dietrich?"

"Cecylia and I are making good progress."

"I see you. Helga?"

"We are fine."

"Denver?"

"Okay."

I pulled myself along the tether, hand over hand, half-listening to the roll calls, half caught up in reverie. *Would there be enough room for us on* Mars Hope? *Would we ever have our home back?* The airtent trailed behind me. Try as I might, I could not stop it from repeatedly bumping the tether. *Were any of the chickens still alive? Exposed without the protection of the habitat's water-filled tubes, would the interplanetary radiation kill them? And me?*

"Michael?"

"I'm okay."

My eyes adjusted to the darkness. When I turned from the tether to face the void, my helmet light seemed to disappear: there was nothing to reflect its light. Then the stars started to glow. Hundreds, thousands, millions of them. Colors – blue, orange, yellow: endless galaxies! G-d's beautiful artwork, everywhere, even so far out here. I remembered the words I had uttered months before, on my first morning in space, above Earth, overwhelmed by its vivid beauty. Psalm 104. *"Ma rabu ma'asecha Hashem,"* I uttered again. "How numerous are your creations, O L-rd!" But the psalm continued, "The earth is full of your possessions." There was no Earth out here. We had abandoned her, making ourselves bereft.

My bladder was full, hurting. Billions of stars, but no interplanetary outhouse; even had there been one, I would not have used it, undressing being impossible. A diaper might have helped, but I had none. But then, no diaper was necessary for the protocol we had been taught. The Foundation's instructors had explained that our mundies were designed for this very contingency. The clothes pressing down on my limbs and torso were porous, not only for the sweating that regulated body temperature. The warm liquid would evaporate quickly in the empty vacuum, and later laundering would extract remaining solutes.

I looked across at my colleagues, spread out on the tethers. They were watching me, I imagined, and my muscles clamped down. The ache grew. I reminded myself that divers urinated in their wetsuits, even during group dives. I would be like a diver in a vast waterless ocean. I tried to brush aside my embarrassment and noted to myself that nobody would see the evaporating liquid, as it would stay hidden under the Mylar pants. Finally: a moment of concentration, an effort to relax, brief moist discomfort. I looked ahead and noticed the duffel Denver dragged behind him, thinking longingly of the extra sets of mundies inside.

Simeon was speaking. "Interesting … I see a crack over there in a solar panel. I will try to check."

Denver seemed to be getting farther and farther from me. *Am I too slow? Falling behind?* The tether slipped from my hands. I reached out to grab it, but then it was rebounding, pushing back against me.

"… solar panel definitely damaged," Simeon was saying. "I need to see what is underneath."

The tether was again trying to escape my grip. I felt it pulling me sideways. It passed under me, and I flipped around it, holding on tight; then it was pulling me in the other direction.

"Dr. Jhonathan, there is something wrong with the tether. I'm having trouble holding on."

"Are you okay, Michael? I see you. You look unsteady. Denver, can you take a look?"

Denver answered, "Michael is behind me. He is right about the tether. It seems wacky. Pulling, then pushing, then pulling. Not terrible, but it is an effort to hold steady."

I let go, which was not unsafe, as I was still connected by loose cords. I shined my light on the tether, trying to understand what it was doing. It was definitely moving, at least relative to me. "It seems to be waving sideways, to and fro, every few seconds. Maybe fifteen or twenty centimeters each time."

"A standing wave!" Helga answered, excitedly. "You guys must have pulled too hard in one direction and set off a wave motion."

"Helga, how is that possible?" Celina asked. "The two ships are pulling at each other, stretching the tether."

"Not after spin-down, Celina," her father answered. "The computers release the tension on the lines to keep the spacecraft from bouncing back toward each other. There is room for minor waves." He addressed Denver and me, saying, "Just hold on tight, boys."

Simeon was speaking again. "I'm examining the PlyShield under the panel. I think I found the break. Boris?"

"I hear you."

"I am to the right of ladder six, almost at the top of the solar panel."

"Got it. I am identifying the corresponding inner location," Boris said. "Give me a moment."

"There is an exposed wire here," Simeon said. "I am checking it. I think it is –"

Simeon's voice cut off midsentence. *Did something go wrong? What was the wire?* I waited for Boris to ask if his brother was okay. For anyone to ask! Nobody said a word. *Does nobody care that Simeon just disappeared?*

"Simeon?" I called out. "Are you alright?"

He did not answer.

"Boris?"

Nobody answered.

"Denver? Are you there?" My oxypack's fan whirred loudly in my ears. That was the only sound – there were no voices. "Is anybody out there? Denver, do you see me?" The waving tether again escaped my grip.

Simeon was gone. Denver was gone. My heart raced. I felt faint. My breathing was wild, uncontrolled. I could not catch my breath. I gasped. I tried to grasp the tether. My hands flailed in emptiness. The tether was gone. Everything outside my mask was a blur. I was utterly alone in an endless oblivion.

I tried to look around but saw nobody. My eyes would not focus. Everyone had disappeared! I was faint, hyperventilating, sweating. I heard screaming. Who was it? Who had joined me, screaming hysterically inside my fleximet? Nobody, I realized; I was alone. Somewhere from within the noise and the daze, it dawned on me that I was the one screaming. I willed the screaming to stop, but failed.

Out in empty interplanetary space, somewhere between Venus and Mars, I floated in the darkest darkness, profoundly lost, profoundly panicking, profoundly alone.

* * *

Monday, June 20th, 2029 22:05

Silvery arms wrapped around me. In my terror, I tried to push them away, but they squeezed and trapped me. A body pressed into me from behind. I took a deep breath and tried to understand what was happening. The arms were spinning me around, but I resisted. They tried harder, and my world became a bright blinding light. I could see nothing. I squeezed my eyes shut. The light went out, and I opened my eyes to a helmeted face before me. The face came into focus as my eyes adjusted. The silvery arms refused to release me.

The mouth was moving, saying silent words. I heard only the whirring of my fans, but I recognized Denver's face behind the mask, dimly lit by his fleximet's internal lamp. What was he trying to say? Why did he lose his voice?

He released one of his hands and tapped the side of his fleximet, next to his ear. Ear – hearing – he could not hear me? Then he pulled my head close and pressed his facemask into mine. I heard a strange, tinny facsimile of his voice.

"I think you lost your radio!" he said.

I took a breath. Was that right? Was I not actually alone physically, just cut off from the radio connection's illusion of togetherness?

"Can you hear me?" I asked. My own voice sounded normal, if shaky.

"Yes," answered the thin voice. "As long as our masks are pressed together, they conduct sound waves. What is with you, Michael, are you okay?"

"Yes. No. I don't know. Maybe yes." I took another breath. "I think I was panicking."

"Well, stop. I'm here with you. We are almost at the end of the tether. There is nothing to do for your radio out here. Just follow me in silence. I will watch that you are behind me all the time."

"Okay." I felt profoundly stupid. Panicking just because I lost my radio connection?

"Stay close behind," Denver said. "We are in enough trouble already. We cannot afford to lose someone else." He turned, breaking our makeshift connection, and grabbed the tether and started pulling himself along.

Lose someone else? What did Denver mean? Did I hear him correctly?

With new trepidation, I followed my friend silently toward the end of the tether, trailing the airtent with the chickens behind me. When we reached the top of *Mars Hope*, we latched our tethers to its ladder rungs. Denver paused, turned to me, pointed his arm toward the stars, and shook a gloved finger. I looked in the direction he indicated. That direction, like every other, was filled with myriad multicolor stars and galaxies. But then I noticed what he was pointing at, something special in the sky: a flattened circle – a small ovaloid disk – much smaller than the moon would appear from Earth – but clearly round, and bright red. Mars.

Mars! For the first time, our new home was in sight, clearly visible to the fleximetted eye, indifferently awaiting our arrival.

Mars Hope *Residents*

Amit Ravel .... materials scientist; captain of the ship
Nisha Ravel .... geologist, chemist; Amit's wife
Arjan .... their adult son
Ishana .... their young adult daughter
Kumar .... their young son

Steven Gordon .... dentist, chemist, aquaculturist
Judith (Jean) Gordon .... rocket engineer; first officer; Steven's wife
Hannah .... their teenage daughter; Michael's friend
Seth .... their young son

Julio Tavera .... physician, radiation engineer
Laura Tavera .... construction & nuclear engineer; Julio's wife
Matias, and
   Tomas .... their young sons

Sander Phillipe Spencer .... metallurgist, software engineer
Jeretta Simone Spencer ...... surgeon, biologist; Sander's wife
Jerome David, and
   Alfred Argentine .... their young sons
Shona Sojourner .... their young daughter

Yumei Wang .... physicist, chemist, mathematician
Meiling .... her teenage daughter

Zauna Ngana .... mycologist, agronomist
Anastasia Vailakis .... philosopher

Simeon

Monday, June 20th, 2029 22:35

The loud rush of eager voices sounded strangely distant as I removed my fleximet. Our *Mars Hope* colleagues were greeting us excitedly, calling our names, expressing gleeful relief at our safe arrival. I did not want anyone to call my name. All I wanted was to sink into a hidden corner. That was impossible in the perfectly circular, brightly lit, very crowded airlock, but at least nobody paid me any attention as I crouched by the wall, blankly removing my gloves and folding my fleximet. Everybody else had completed the crossing professionally and enthusiastically. Not me, though. I had lost my way, almost had lost myself. Only with Denver's persistent encouragement had I made my soundless way down *Mars Hope's* ladder rungs, around its lower hull, and into its airlock. I barely noticed when Arjan Ravel closed the portal and pressurized the room. Now, watching the others gather under the open hatchway, waiting their turns to float upstairs into our sister habitat, I held back, ashamed.

A hand grasped my shoulder and spun me around. "Michael, let's go up," Denver said. He looked at me questioningly. "What's with you?"

"I don't know. I'm embarrassed." My head hung low. "What is wrong with me, Denver? Everybody else handles the situation normally, and crosses over without any problem. But I panic and almost get myself killed." I looked at him dolefully.

"You lost your radio and got disoriented. It is not a big deal. That happens during spacewalks. You would have figured it out in a minute or two. And if not, that is why we have a buddy system. Maybe I took too long to notice – sorry if so – but as soon as I realized you were out of communication, I established the physical fleximet-to-fleximet connection they trained us for."

"I forgot our training. I was so far gone. So alone, so oblivious!" I stared at the floor.

"Michael, you were not alone. You have never been alone."

I looked up to see Denver watching me closely. I averted my eyes.

"It felt like everybody else – everything else – just disappeared into the void."

"I heard you praying, before you lost your radio. To your G-d! How can you feel alone, as a religious believer?"

"You'd be surprised. Anyway, thanks, Denver. I owe you one." I peered up at him again and managed a feeble smile. "A thousand. I owe you a thousand."

"I will hold you to that. Remember what you said! You are going to pay me back someday. On Mars. I expect the whole thousand! Now, let's get moving." He gestured around the empty airlock. "Everyone else is already upstairs making greetings." He grabbed my shoulders and looked directly at me. "Hannah is here. She will be ecstatic – she has not seen you since September. Are you so cruel that you would keep her waiting?"

"Go ahead without me." I turned away and blushed. "I'm too embarrassed to face the crowd. What will they say about me, the 'pioneer of Martian society' who panicked and froze and failed?"

"Now you are being an idiot – no insult intended." He laughed. "Nobody cares if you got a little scared!"

"A little scared? I was screaming!"

Denver laughed again and shook his head. "Nobody heard you! Nobody knows anything about that. Even I did not know until you just told me." He shook his head again, pulled me tight against his chest, and whispered loudly in my ear, "Your secret is safe with me." Pushing me toward the ceiling, he added with a chuckle, "Celina, too. I know she is going to make me tell her everything." He gave me another shove and sent me rising through the hatch.

Red Valley

My head rose into *Mars Hope's* lowest level, where I expected to witness a crowded, happy reunion among friends who had not been together, physically at least, since departing Altiplano nine months earlier. We had trained together as a group for years, and would work together building Mars for years to come. These months apart had been the exception. Reunion would be natural, even if six weeks premature.

My feet trailed my body into the first-level living room that belonged to Captain Ravel and his family. The room smelled of freshly baked bread. It was crowded as expected, but apparently the gleeful greetings had concluded. The mood was not at all jubilant: instead, it was strangely subdued. All eyes faced the same direction, all of them filled with pity. I pressed my hands against the ceiling to stop my momentum, then followed the collective gaze toward the kitchen, where Dr. Claudine, wearing only her mundies, hovered between the counters, clutching a wrapped bundle to her chest. Tears flooded her eyes. In weightlessness, the moisture stayed in place; it did not drip or streak. She blinked, wept silently, and blinked again. Dr. Nisha Ravel, wearing a bright orange sari over her mundies, dabbed Dr. Claudine's eyes with a cloth. Next to them, Dr. Louis held Jasmine in one arm and Sophie in the other. His eyes also glistened with tears.

I scanned the room. Captain Becker hovered on the far side, with Captain Ravel. He, too, had his eyes on the kitchen; he, too, had pity in his eyes, but there was something else, something ambiguous; perhaps a hint of despair, a bit of annoyance, maybe a memory of unbearable tragedy. Failure.

"Fellows," Captain Ravel said, turning away from Captain Becker, "perhaps you'll all head upstairs and give Claudine and Louis quiet privacy. We'll stay here with them."

"What happened?" I asked, mostly to myself.

"Shush," Ruby said, waving me in the direction of the stairwell. She kept her eyes on me as she floated backward, her expression severe, and mouthed, "Adele." Then, in a quavering voice: "The baby didn't make it."

My heart dropped. That beautiful baby, the first human to be born away from Earth, the newborn who had brought so much vitality and joy into our world, gone so suddenly, not three weeks old! A pain stabbed through my chest, a shared pain, Dr. Claudine's pain and Dr. Louis's pain. Poor Dr. Claudine: to carry a baby for nine months, to struggle through weightlessness and simulated gravity – and loss of gravity – and cramped spacecraft quarters, and a solar storm, for naught! To suffer the captain's opposition, to clash with him, and quarrel, and triumph – and then lose. I recalled the words the captain had spoken when he protested the pregnancy: "If this baby is born, it will surely die. The airtents are not rated for humans." I imagined him now, opening his mouth and yelling, "I told you so!" vindictively, cruelly.

I blinked away my own tears and followed the compliant crowd of newly-arrived guests as they drifted up the red-striped stairwell. We exited into the second-level living room. The barber-pole stripes that covered the first-level stairwell wall gave way to a complex pattern of gray cotton balls and crimson, indigo and golden flowers. Before I had a chance to wipe my eyes and glance around to see who awaited us, a dark-haired, round-faced, exuberant, beaming, familiar female figure grabbed me and kissed my cheek. "Michael, you're here!" Hannah squealed, pulling me into a tight embrace.

Over her shoulder I saw Ruby staring at me, unexpectedly livid. I blushed and disengaged myself. "Hannah, you know we don't do this: no physical touching before marriage! Those are the Torah's rules."

"'Before marriage?'" she repeated, smiling delightedly. "Michael Reuel Teller, are you asking me to marry you?"

"I – um – no – we haven't even finished high school!" I blushed again, fighting a formidable urge to float up through the ceiling and escape Hannah's gleeful gaze and Ruby's ire. Fear, disorientation, panic, worry, sorrow; then joy; now self-consciousness and embarrassment – my emotions kept changing in a bewildering jumble. I shook my head and searched for salvation.

Hannah looked at me quizzically, glee gone. I needed to be fair to her; I did not want to hurt anyone, especially not Hannah. I concentrated hard to say, "Hannah, it's nice to see you, and you look nice, and I can't wait to catch up. I need a few minutes though. Dr. Claudine lost her baby, and there was something on the spacewalk – something happened to me – no big deal – I can't talk about it now –" I averted my gaze and fought another wave of embarrassment – "I need a few minutes." I looked at her imploringly, and at Ruby behind her. I squeezed my eyes tightly shut before they flooded with more tears. "Where is Dr. Jhonathan?" I sobbed, humiliated, my hidden feelings spilling out for everyone to see.

Sam and Denver came from behind and put their arms around me. Sam said, "I saw my father talking with Hannah's father, Dr. Steven, upstairs. Come with us." Tenderly, my friends pulled me toward the stairwell. I avoided the girls' gaze.

* * *

Monday, June 20th, 2029 23:05

Dr. Jhonathan released his hug, leaned back and watched me intently. "Michael, tell me. What is bothering you?" When I did not answer immediately, he added, "Maybe I don't need to ask. We've been through so much. Thank G-d we are here safely."

I opened my mouth and tried to find words, but instead I recalled Simeon's voice disappearing the moment my radio went dead. "What – what happened to Simeon?"

"Nothing that I know of." Dr. Jhonathan looked surprised. "I haven't heard anything." He turned toward the closed bedroom door and called loudly to the living room. "Steven, have we heard from Boris and Simeon?"

Hannah's father answered from outside the door. "Latest status is that they are still looking for the breach. I expect Captain Ravel will give up and tell them to come in. They've been searching for almost two hours."

"I thought they already found the breach," I said. "During the spacewalk I heard Simeon saying something about exposed wires."

"Yes, he found damage, but it turned out not to be the breach we're looking for. I'd not be surprised if we suffered several micrometeoroid hits over the months. I imagine he found one of those." Then, in a quieter voice, "What was it you needed to talk about, Michael?"

I paused. I wondered whether to open up to him. Or maybe just try to forget.

"Come on now. You look like you need to talk." He creased his forehead expectantly. "Go ahead."

I sighed. "I'm a failure." That summed it up, and there was no need to elaborate.

"That's news to me," he answered, in too bright a voice. "All this time I thought you were a brave, clever, proficient, enthusiastic astronaut!" He shook his head. "How could I have been so wrong?"

"You're making fun of me."

"Sorry. That was not my intention. I'm trying to remind you how well you – and your sisters and all your peers – have managed these past months. Space travel for people so young is unprecedented. You're writing the book on it." He raised his eyebrows and smiled again. "Literally, you're writing the book. How's your composition coming along?"

"The last time I wrote seems so long ago. Probably the night before last."

"You'll sure have a lot more to write about now." He put his hand on my shoulder. "Okay, tell me about your failure." He watched me patiently.

"I panicked. I lost control of the situation out there. And not for the first time."

"You lost your radio. By the way, make sure to get a replacement before we return to *Providence*. I have to tell you, I was a bit nervous, too, when you went silent and stopped answering my roll calls."

"But it wasn't you who panicked, Rabbi Meyer. You probably just looked across the gap to see that I was still on my tether. I, though, I didn't even think to look around. I was totally wrapped up and lost in my own fear."

"Michael, I remind you, I'm not a – oh, forget it. That's right, I did not panic, but then I could still hear everybody else on my radio. And I was not dealing with a waving tether. I imagine that was quite a challenge for you and Denver." He gave my shoulder another squeeze. "Okay, so you panicked. But you recovered."

"Only with Denver's help."

"That's why we're doing this together. There's no such thing as solo space travel."

"Yeah, but how can I rely on myself going forward? How can all of you rely on me? If I can't handle a simple spacewalk, how am I going to be useful building a city on Mars? I'll panic at some point and get myself killed."

Dr. Jhonathan sighed. "Do you think we all don't ask ourselves where we're going to find the courage to build our new home? Do you think I don't ask myself how I'll manage to watch over my wife and children on a new planet? And not just over them; over you, too. As far as I'm concerned, you're all my adopted children. Where will I get the strength?"

"Your own self-doubts don't help me with mine," I said, more acerbically than I had intended.

"I don't mean them to; I'm just being honest. We all doubt ourselves. We've taken upon ourselves a superhuman task. We might not always succeed."

"So, I should keep doubting myself? Just accept my failures? My anxiety? My panic?"

He waited, watching me silently. Then, finally, "What do you think?"

A happy female voice interrupted from outside the room. "They found the breach!" It sounded like Hannah's mother, Dr. Jean, but it had been so long since I had heard her voice that I was not sure, until she slid the door open and peeked inside. "Hi, Michael. You'd asked, Jhonathan, so I wanted to update you on that. Simeon found a broken solar controller, and Boris located the breach, directly beneath it, visible from the inside."

"Thanks, Jean."

"You're looking great," she said, eyeing me. "Your face has filled out." She slipped out and slid the folding door closed.

Dr. Jhonathan repeated his question. "What do you think, Michael?" He resumed his patient watching.

I capitulated. "What do I think? I think ...." I took a breath. Maybe it was the good news about Simeon and Boris, or maybe just talking to Rabbi Meyer relaxed me and gave me confidence, but my thoughts were clearer. "I think that I am going to accept my failures. I know I'm afraid. I'm afraid of all the terrible things that might happen –"

"Not to mention the terrible things that have already happened," Dr. Jhonathan interrupted, looking very serious.

"Right. We've been through a lot." I paused again. "Me personally. Like the fact that my father's not waiting on the other end." I sighed, blinked, and shook my head. "But Mars is waiting, and I'm going to do what I can to continue what he started, to do what we joined this mission for."

"You'll have a lot of people relying on you. A lot of us expect you to grow into a leadership role."

"Leadership? Me?" I laughed at the thought. "Probably ill-advised." I shook my head slowly. "If it's up to me, I'd recommend choosing somebody else."

A smile broke across Dr. Jhonathan's face and a small chuckle escaped his lips. "That's exactly why you'll be a good choice."

I smiled, too. "Thanks for the vote of confidence. I guess my panicky experiences could help me understand what other people are going through."

"That's very true. Don't discount what you can learn from enduring frightening events." He waited, watching me, forehead creased. "And don't discount how much they'll enable you to help and support everybody else."

I noticed his stress on the words "everybody else." I said, "Maybe I've been too focused on myself, on my own inner experience."

Dr. Jhonathan nodded, looking pleased. "I think focusing more on what everybody else is struggling with will help you with your own challenges."

"I don't know if anyone else is really 'struggling.'"

"Why would this journey be easier for them than for you?"

"It just feels that way to me."

He stared at me, half smiling, head tilted.

"Well, it does!" While he stared, I listened again to my own words. "Okay, I'm being obtuse."

"Michael, I admire your honesty."

I laughed. "Thank you, Rabbi." I took a deep breath and exhaled. "For always being available to talk, and for listening, and for helping me understand things better." I hugged him. "Okay. From now on I'll try to focus on everybody else." I thought of Simeon and Boris. "By the way, if the Radechovs are analyzing the breach, can we tap into their cameras and watch their progress?"

"I imagine so. In fact, I'd be surprised if we're not the only ones missing the show." He pointed at the door to the living room, which was conspicuously quiet, given that forty-one people had crowded into a craft designed for twenty-two. Most of the others, it seemed, had their eyes glued to the NLED walls.

*   *   *

Monday, June 20th, 2029 23:35

    Hannah's family's Diamond-Level apartment was nearly identical to the Beckers' Yellow-Level home back on *Providence*. Here, too, the ceiling above the living-room couch curved inward, beginning the dome that topped the spacecraft. A large gap in the ceiling opened into an attic storage room identical to ours. There were two striking differences, though. First, the stairwell wall was not painted a solid color; instead, a gaudy black and white pattern of hearts, spades, diamonds and clovers covered it. The diamonds gave the deck its name. Second, I had never seen so many people crowded into the smallest of a ZubHab's living rooms. More than a dozen of us had gathered to watch the views from Boris's and Simeon's fleximet cameras.

    Across the room, Hannah perched with her parents and her younger brother, Seth. They faced the NLED screen on the wall that separated the master bedroom from the living room. Hannah kept twisting around to look at me, each time smiling wanly before looking away. I had hurt her, in my self-obsession, certainly unintentionally, but we would need to talk. As soon as Simeon and Boris were back safely.

    Closer to me, in the middle of the room – the dining table had been stowed – all five Meyers gathered. They watched the NLED screen on the side wall next to the doorway to the darkened greenhouse room. Dr. Jhonathan had his arms around his daughters. Ruby was also glancing at me periodically, her expression unreadable. Meital and Shirel hovered behind them, but I held back at the end of the room, sitting over the couch with my mother.

    I had joined her so I could hold her hand, but also to have a good view of both NLED walls. One of them showed Boris's view. He was inside *Providence* and everything was dark. The Gordons' floating figures blocked part of the wall, but that mattered little, because the small area illuminated by Boris's fleximet lamp fell on the part of the screen I could still see. Simeon's view, from outside, appeared on the other wall, diagonally to my right. It showed the hull breach under his lamp's light.

    The rest of our *Providence* crewmates had spread out among *Mars Hope's* downstairs levels. Those living rooms would be less crowded, I calculated, with only three or four extra visitors in each. I do not know why so many of us – all nine Meyers and Tellers – had decided to crowd together upstairs with Hannah's family, but I was happy to be surrounded by family and friends. Denver was absent; he had disappeared downstairs somewhere with Celina. Perhaps they had gone to visit with her friend Ishana, Captain Ravel's daughter.

Diamond Level was not large enough for so many of us to sleep in that night, but nobody was thinking of sleep at the moment.

"I'm swapping my oxypack," Boris announced. "It has been two hours, and I am down to twelve percent." Each brother had two extra oxypacks with him, so they could stay out for hours more, but the oxypacks needed to be replaced manually. Boris's lamp flitted from wall to wall as he detached his depleted pack, pulled out one of the full tanks stowed on his thigh inside the Mylar pants, and snapped it into place. We heard the sound of rushing air as the oxypack activated. Then we watched him stow the empty one.

"Captain, mark the breach location," he said. "I'm inside the storage attic. I have cleared away a dozen bags of supplies and reached the hull. I will need to stow the bags in one of the bedrooms downstairs later. The breach" – he shined his light on the hull – "is just above the reaction control rockets' bulge."

We heard Captain Becker speak over the radio connection. "Marked. What about you, Simeon? Confirm that you have also swapped your oxypack."

"Soon, just a minute. I still have ten percent. Look here." We watched him shine his lamp over a spot on the hull just above the top of a solar array. I recalled our group spacewalk, all those months before, still in Earth orbit, when ten of us had gone outside to unfurl and secure the panels. "The solar controller has been damaged." A tangled mess of wires and broken printed circuits appeared on the NLED screen. Whatever had hit us earlier that evening had managed to smash through a hardened electronics module, penetrate the entire thickness of the PlyShield armor, and crack the hull. "I want to bring it in so we can assess the damage and prepare a replacement."

"Not necessary, Simeon," Captain Becker said. "We'll make do with one less solar array."

"Yes, Captain, we might have to, but this far from the sun, our power generation is already down, just barely supplying our needs. I promise I will give up if I cannot get the box out, but I am going to try."

Captain Becker did not protest. Perhaps he had tired of arguing with Simeon.

"I'm unplugging the connections to the hull power outlet." His lamplight focused on the jumbled wires. "I'm pulling out the equipment box –"

We watched Simeon's hands on the screen as he braced his knees against the hull and wrestled the box out of its slot. Being a replaceable item, the box had handles, and Simeon grasped them firmly. He used his whole body as leverage as he pulled and pulled. He appeared to be struggling.

Abruptly, the equipment box rotated out of our view. Simeon's camera shifted direction and pointed down the length of the hull. But a moment later we were looking out at the stars, and Simeon's hands were no longer gripping the box.

"Simeon, have you given up?" Captain Becker asked, surprised. "It is okay if so. We have enough data to prepare the repair. Come in now."

Simeon did not answer.

"And replace your oxypack. You have only a few percent left."

Simeon still did not respond. *Providence's* hull rolled back into view, then disappeared again.

"Simeon, please confirm the radio connection."

Boris broke in. "Simeon, can you hear us?"

Simeon stayed silent. My heart raced. Why was he not answering? And why did his view, projected on the NLED wall, keep changing? The hull kept appearing and disappearing as if Simeon's body was spinning. Had he lost consciousness?

Murmuring filled the room. Meital exclaimed, "Somebody should go check on him!"

"Boris," Captain Becker said in an agitated voice, "get to your brother. Quickly."

"I am already on my way." We listened to Boris's heavy breathing, faithfully reproduced by the wall speakers.

Sam appeared by my side. "Boris is going to have to go all the way downstairs to the airlock, then all the way back up the hull. If

Simeon did not swap his oxypack, he'll be out of air before Boris gets there."

"One of us should go out," I said. "How long will it take to cycle the airlock so we can exit the ship?"

"Boris can get there long before any of us," said Susan, now next to Sam. Her face was flushed. "We would have the same distance to cross, inside and outside the ship, not to mention the extra hundred meters of tether."

Captain Ravel's voice sounded over the speakers. "Arjan," he called to his son, "please get down to the airlock and suit up. We'll cycle the airlock so that you can receive Boris and Simeon. Julio, prepare an operating suite with Jeretta on Triangle Level, in case medical intervention is necessary."

Julio, I knew, was Dr. Tavera, one of *Mars Hope's* resident surgeons. My hands shook nervously as I imagined him cutting deep into Simeon's chest with a sharp scalpel, trying urgently to save his life.

We followed Boris's view tensely as he rushed down the stairwells. Finally reaching the open airlock, he pulled himself outside. We watched him latch, and unlatch, and latch his cords, following all safety protocols. It seemed to take too long, at least until he pulled around the hull's bottom edge and his brother came into view. At that point he began moving very quickly, traversing the hull more efficiently than anyone I had ever seen, though still he did not skip any safety steps. He would connect to a rung ahead of him, spin his body – and his camera view – around backward, disconnect from the rung behind him, spin back forward, and repeat. The back-and-forth movement gave us dizzying views up the hull, then down, then up again. Simeon's Mylar suit flashed intermittently in Boris's reflected lamplight. Each latch-unlatch sequence caused a several-second delay, but Boris would not be able to save his brother if he himself lost control and floated away.

We watched nervously, powerless to help.

Simeon came into clear view with a flash, his Mylar suit brightly reflecting Boris's fleximet lamplight. He was floating a couple of meters above the hull, linked to a rung by his safety cord, which was stretched taut. His arms and legs floated relaxedly, too relaxed, more than they should have been. Boris grabbed his brother's body and shined his lamp into Simeon's visor. The visor was fogged on the inside, blocking his face.

"I'm swapping Simeon's oxypack." We watched Boris pull the depleted oxypack out of its slot and insert another. He pushed the activation button. Simeon's fleximet swelled. Boris pointed his lamp into Simeon's visor again, perhaps hoping the fresh air would clear the fog, but still we saw nothing.

"Boris, do not delay any longer," Captain Becker commanded. "Stow the empty oxypack and bring your brother in. We're readying the airlock."

"The empty oxypack … um, I let it go. I was not thinking."

An oxypack in permanent solar orbit. There was some humor in that, but at that moment I could not find it.

Boris latched a cord to connect his harness to Simeon's and started the long journey across the void, his motionless brother in tow.

* * *

Tuesday, June 21st, 2029 00:20

"I've sealed the airlock and am starting pressurization," Arjan Ravel's gruff voice announced over the intercom. "Boris and Simeon are safely aboard."

Boris's twenty-five-minute trek had been a harrowing experience. For him, certainly, but also for the rest of us, watching the screens tensely, murmuring among ourselves. Was Simeon conscious? Had he lost his radio as I had, or was there a more serious problem? What had happened so suddenly? One minute he was speaking lucidly, working a plan to complete his damage diagnosis. The next minute his camera view was spinning, apparently out of control.

Sam nudged me. "What if Simeon is not breathing when they remove his fleximet?"

"I refuse to consider the possibility."

"He's a good man. Motivated and helpful. G-d protect him."

I nodded. "Amen. He is. G-d forbid anything bad happen."

Hannah's mother rose toward the ceiling and called out to get our attention. "We have a team of surgeons on board, led by Dr. Tavera. They will provide medical attention to Simeon."

Simeon

The general murmuring stopped, not due to discipline but because we all wanted details about Simeon. All eyes were on Dr. Jean.

"The rest of us can only get in the way. It's time for sleep, especially for the kids." At that, the murmuring resumed, so she cleared her throat and raised her voice. "I have been tasked with sleep arrangements. Our adult guests will spread out and sleep in the living rooms. Unfortunately, Triangle Level's living room is off-limits – it's going to be the hospital operating suite, but the other three are available. The visiting teenagers – I count nine of you – will be guests in your friends' bedrooms. See me for your assignments."

Hannah drifted over. Hesitantly, she asked, "Michael, can we talk?" She pushed off in the direction of her bedroom, waving me to follow. Once we were inside, she slid the door closed.

"Are you upset with me for some reason?" she asked in a hurt voice.

"No, not at all." I looked around her room. Like Helga's and Celina's, it was a single bedroom, one of only two in the habitat. Everybody else had a roommate, but the curve of the hull in the topmost level left no room for upper bunks. On *Mars Hope*, Hannah and Seth enjoyed the added privacy.

"Why are you avoiding me? I've missed you. I shouldn't say it, but when I heard you were abandoning ship and coming to shelter over here, I felt a secret thrill! Now I'm not so sure."

"I'm sorry. I didn't mean to avoid you. All the stress of everything that's happened just overwhelmed me." I looked away. "Not to mention a small problem I had on the way over."

"You lost your radio and panicked."

I blushed. "You know about that?"

"I was listening in and you missed the roll call. I myself panicked. Why wouldn't you?"

"It was worse than you make it sound."

"I'm sure it was. I feel like you deserve a hug. It bugs me that you won't let me give you one."

I loved Hannah's honesty.

"But," she said, a naughty smile spreading across her face, "I can invite you to sleep in my room with me."

"Uh," – I stuttered, not knowing what to reply, "um, shall I check with your mother whether those are her arrangements?"

"What, are you crazy?" Hannah raised her eyebrows. "She'd never agree, and we don't have to tell her. Where's your bedroll? Go get it, nonchalantly, and we'll hang you over there." She pointed to the wall across from the closet, next to where six dining room chairs were folded and stowed. "We'll get to talk all night."

"I'm worried about Simeon. And I can't stop thinking about baby Adele. And I really need a sponge bath!" My back and chest, still caked with soap I had not rinsed off, all those hours earlier, were itching again.

Hannah stared at me, grinning broadly and shaking her head. "I am not going to give you a sponge bath."

I blushed again. "That's not what I meant."

Hannah seemed to enjoy my discomfort, but then her mother arrived to save me. Dr. Jean slid the door all the way open, leaned into the room, regarded her daughter admonishingly, and announced, "Michael, you'll be sleeping on Triangle Level with Matias and Tomas. Helga Becker will be sleeping here with you, Hannah." She left the door wide open as she departed.

I called after her, "Which level is 'Triangle?'"

*   *   *

Tuesday, June 21st, 2029 01:20

My bedroll was warm but I could not sleep. Matias Tavera had welcomed me happily to the wall of the bedroom he shared with his younger brother Tomas, and Tomas had squealed with nine-year-old delight. The two of them were sleeping soundly now, but their Triangle-Level apartment had become an impromptu hospital, and only a thin sliding door separated me from the operating suite. I could not avoid listening in as the boys' father tried, with his colleagues' help, to save Simeon.

"Electrodes are almost ready," I heard Dr. Julio say.

"Heartbeat is still stable," Dr. Jeretta Spencer announced in her delightful Alabama drawl. That was good news.

A young Indian-accented voice added, "Breathing is also stable, but still no pupil dilation." I recognized Ishana Ravel's soft, chopped speech. At nineteen, she was no doctor, but she had studied nursing with Ruby back at Altiplano.

"Why has he not awakened?" Boris asked miserably. It sounded like he was standing right outside the bedroom door.

"We don't know yet." That was Dr. Jhonathan. Simeon, I thought to myself, would certainly have no reason to complain about the quality of care he received if he ever woke up. Or about the skill of his medical team. "I have the electroencephalogram application open on my datapad. Ready to start?"

"I have placed the last electrode. Start the analysis."

I waited in my bedroll, anxious, worrying about Simeon. The evening had been like no other. I reached for my datapad to check the time. Not six hours had passed since the explosive whack that had broken our ship and started the process that had, so far, led to the loss of our home, the death of Dr. Claudine's baby, and Simeon's medical emergency. Not to mention my own personal terror, though that seemed trite and petty now. I was done with self-absorption, I told myself.

Unfortunately, nobody wanted my help or attention, so I was left absorbed in my own thoughts. I had tried to help: I had emerged from the Triangle-Level bathroom into the operating suite, half an hour earlier, dressed in fresh mundies, my itching finally ended. Dr. Jeretta, a white smock over her mundies, was busy tightening the last strap that held a motionless Simeon to a mattress atop the dining table. Ishana was holding Simeon's arm as Dr. Jhonathan found a vein and skillfully inserted an intravenous drip line.

"What can I do to help?" I had asked.

"Michael, we have this," Dr. Jhonathan answered without looking up. He affixed the saline fluid bag to the side of the table. Regular drip bags did not work in zero gravity, but this one, made of the same material as our mundies, would squeeze out its contents at the exact required pressure. "Pray for Simeon's recovery. Pray for a miracle. Then try to get some sleep."

Trying to sleep was what I was now doing, completely unsuccessfully. Rather, I was wide awake, listening to the doctors' discussion, trying to make sense of what had happened to Simeon.

"I'm picking up only minimal brain activity," Dr. Jhonathan said. "I'm sorry, Boris."

Boris's quiet sobs penetrated the door. New tears welled in my own eyes.

* * *

Tuesday, June 21st, 2029 06:30

At some point in the night, after Simeon had been stabilized and the medical staff had gone to bed, and nobody was left talking in the living room, I drifted off to sleep. Gentle knocking awakened me.

"*¡Despierten, niños!*" Dr. Laura called to her sons. I pulled myself out of my bedroll, hoping to be first to the bathroom; there were twice as many passengers as usual to compete with. Out in the living room, I observed Simeon, still strapped to the table. He had been groomed: somebody had arranged his hair and combed his goatee. His eyes were closed and there was no way of knowing if he was awake or asleep. Boris dozed in his bedroll, latched to the ceiling directly above his brother.

"*Buenos días*, Michael," Dr. Laura greeted me with a smile after I had washed up. "I hope you slept well."

"Yes; thanks for your hospitality."

"I am going to need your help with breakfast, you know. But first, please help my boys clear out their room. My husband wants to put Simeon in there."

Simeon had been reduced to an object to be "put" somewhere. That sounded warped, but I answered only, "No problem. Where will I be sleeping, then?"

"I am afraid you and the boys will need to sleep out here in the living room. I expect it will be only for a few days. We want to get all of you home as soon as possible."

Meital and Ruby exited the second bedroom, rubbing their eyes. They waved a drowsy "good morning." Fifteen-year-old Meiling Wang, their friend and host, followed them out. She noticed me and looked away.

An hour later, after I had prayed and helped slice several loaves of bread, and Simeon had been evacuated to the bedroom, we hovered together around the dining table, Taveras, Wangs, and Tellers. We ate a simple breakfast of wholewheat bread and oatmeal.

"We should all thank Yumei for baking," Dr. Julio said.

Dr. Yumei Wang, a native of Taipei, shook her head modestly. "Not me," she answered, in a thick Hokkien accent. "As soon as we were hearing last night that you will come, Nisha, Zauna and

Anastasia baked bread, so that there not be a shortage of what to eat. They let me help. We should thank them, not me."

Dr. Yumei and Dr. Zauna Ngana, like my mother, had husbands among the small Vanguard team that had arrived on Mars two Earth years earlier. "Thank you, Dr. Yumei," I joined the others in saying. What courage they had – like my mother – to let their husbands leave for another planet, then follow them, years later! *At least Ming Wang and Beko Ngana were still alive*, I thought with a tinge of bitterness.

Boris exited Simeon's bedroom. "He seems stable. He is letting me leave him for a few minutes to eat breakfast."

"Simeon talked?" Shirel asked tentatively.

"No." Boris shook his head. "But I did ask permission. Otherwise I would not leave him alone."

"I'll sit with Simeon while you eat," I offered.

"Thank you, Michael, but it is okay now for a few minutes. Later perhaps you will visit." He turned to Dr. Julio. "My brother needs to eat too. How will we feed him?"

"If you consent, Jhonathan will insert a nasogastric tube later this morning. We will fill an electroelastic bag with liquified food and program it to pump it out at a proper pace."

"You will be operating, cutting into him?" Boris looked half alarmed, half resigned.

"No, this will be a tube in his nose, through his esophagus, down to his stomach. The procedure is minimally invasive."

"How long will he have the tube?"

Dr. Julio sighed. "I am sorry, Boris. I doubt your brother will be able to eat by himself anytime soon."

Boris stared at him. "You are giving up?"

Dr. Julio shook his head gently. "We will not give up. Simeon will go back with you to *Providence* after repairs are completed. Your doctors will help you care for him." Seeing Boris's expression, he added, "There is a chance that he will improve over time. That he might recognize you eventually. The brain is remarkably elastic."

We finished eating in silence. We had no words to comfort Boris.

After breakfast, I followed Ruby and Meital down to the airlock to check on our surviving chickens. At some point the prior evening, after Boris had brought Simeon in, Hannah and Meiling had overseen an operation to release *Providence's* surviving birds into the *Mars Hope* birdcages, and then move all the cages back downstairs.

I followed as Meital dove head-first through the hatch in Stripe Level's living-room floor. It was my second visit to *Mars Hope's* airlock, but this time the room was full of birdcages. Large and small, they were neatly stacked, latched to the round wall as if they had never been moved. The birds grasped their perches, some standing vertically, others diagonally or upside-down, all in a comic weightless mix. I had expected to smell the usual unpleasant odors, but there were barely any. Perhaps Hannah and Meiling had done a quick, thorough cleaning before the emergency spin-down. Or perhaps exposure to vacuum had eliminated all smells. In any case, they were cleaning again: Hannah held a vacuum in her hand, using it to remove droppings that had stuck to the perching bars.

"Which are ours?" I asked loudly over the noise of the air processing fans and the handheld vacuum. "How many chickens survived?"

"You brought over six hens," Meiling said. "Five were alive when we opened their airtents. They look to be doing well – see?" She pointed to a large cage on the side.

"Where did you put Dolly's body?" Ruby asked glumly. She knew each hen by name.

"I gave it to Anastasia. She said it was fresh enough for cooking."

Ruby looked away and did not respond. She turned to the cage and spoke to her surviving hens, quietly comforting them.

"Most of your parakeets and canaries were fine, too." Meiling pointed to a cage on the other side of the airlock. "I hope you do not mind that we put them with our parrots and finches."

Hannah turned off the vacuum. "Michael, it's crowded down here, and we have work to do. But will you join my family for lunch?"

*   *   *

Tuesday, June 21st, 2029 12:45

Hannah had invited all the *Providence* elder youth upstairs for a bread-and-hummus lunch – whether with her mother's permission or not, I did not know. Ten of us crowded in the Diamond-Level living room. The Gordons had not set up their table, so we had a bit more room, though no place other than our thighs to which to Velcro our bowls.

"It was his fault," Helga was saying.

"I don't think we need to blame anyone for an accident," Meital protested.

"Accident? Papa told him to leave it and come in." Helga shrugged. "He should have listened and given up. Especially after showing us those exposed wires."

"Do you think Simeon got an electric shock?" I asked. "Aren't the gloves insulated?"

"Insulated for heat," Denver said. "But not for a high-voltage static charge."

"What static charge? We shut down all the electric systems."

"We shut down the systems to keep the batteries charged after we rotated to hide the sun. They were nearly fully charged when we left the ship."

I noticed bright light escaping the edges of the greenhouse room's door next to where I floated. "I'm surprised the batteries still have charge. You didn't shut down your systems over here."

"Not true," Seth said. "We shut off a lot of systems last night. Full power was not restored until the ships rotated into sunlight during the night."

"We rotated?" Meital asked.

Denver answered. "We should have, if we followed normal procedures. Since we are not spinning for gravity, the ships instead need to rotate on their vertical axis, very slowly, to keep all sides exposed equally to sunlight. And to charge the solar panels."

"So, about Simeon." Sam dipped his slice of bread into the bowl of hummus on his thigh. "You think a single electric shock did that to him? Destroyed his brain?"

Helga twisted her mouth and shook her head. "Oh, come now. He was without oxygen for, like, ten minutes. Unconscious. The fool should have replaced his oxypack."

Hannah widened her eyes. "You sound like you don't like Simeon very much."

"Not since he started swiping rations that belonged to the rest of us."

"That was never proven," Ruby protested. "We do not know who took the last chocolate. It might have been an innocent mistake."

"Not just chocolate," Helga persisted. "My mother discovered many rare items missing from the storage attic. "Now, at least, we will not have more of them vanishing."

Celina watched her sister gravely. "Helga, I think at this point we should be hoping for Simeon's recovery, not speaking ill of him." She raised her eyebrows. "We talked about this."

Helga sneered at her sister. "You do not think he acted foolishly? Papa told him to swap the oxypack. It is his own fault he did not obey."

"Maybe he should have obeyed, but what does it matter now? I think you are acting foolishly, but does that mean I want you injured?"

Hannah interrupted, very loudly. "Strawberries, anyone?" She looked around before settling her gaze on Helga and Celina. "We harvested some, for the first time, a couple of days ago. We were saving them for a special occasion. Dad said inviting all of you for lunch today qualifies." She waved her hand theatrically and turned her cheeks up in an exaggerated smile. "For a relaxed, happy discussion among friends."

Helga, blushing, seemed to regret her acrimonious comments. "Yes, Hannah, strawberries would be nice."

Omar, who had been quiet throughout the meal, said, "Strawberries – one crop we did not grow on *Providence*." He sighed. "The one crop that has not been lost."

"You think we lost everything?" I asked.

"In a complete vacuum? No doubt." His eyes glistened. "I am afraid even to go back and see what remains."

Given our broken hearts for Adele and Simeon, and our worry over the damaged habitat and our desiccated plantings, and our concern about the crowded, stressed conditions on *Mars Hope*, the half-strawberry Hannah handed each of us was a welcome, sweet diversion.

Return

Wednesday, June 22nd, 2029 15:30

By a day and a half into our forced visit, we had settled into a semblance of a routine. The kitchens were busy most of the time, and we all took turns with food preparation. The bathrooms were also busy, but since we were skipping exercise sessions due to lack of space and time, we were not bathing as often. Or laundering. Our hosts had divvied up our soiled mundies after our arrival Monday night and returned them to us clean Tuesday morning, but since then we had skipped changing clothes.

Not exercising was uncomfortable and I felt agitated. "Mom, can we ask for permission to set up the cycles, even just for half an hour?" She and I were sitting together in the Spencers' second-floor Cotton-Level living room, having remained after lunch. I was reading on my datapad, trying to concentrate on an Electrical Engineering lesson. The flowing fields of flowers playing on the NLED walls failed to calm my restless limbs.

"I understand how you feel, Michael, but look around." She gestured at the crowded room. By the sofa, Drs. Cecylia and Esther and their husbands were reading on their datapads. Closer to us, Denver, Celina, Sam and Omar hovered in quiet conversation. Everyone was waiting to help in the kitchen if Dr. Jeretta, or Dr. Zauna, or Anastasia – all three of whom were busy preparing supper – beckoned for help. There was no room for a cycle or sprower.

Then the Bouchets entered from the stairwell to join our crowd. "Dietrich, we need to discuss arrangements," Dr. Louis said.

Captain Becker turned to them. "For the baby, yes?" He looked back and forth between Drs. Louis and Claudine.

Dr. Claudine looked back defiantly. "I know you disagree. You may criticize us if you want." She narrowed her eyes. "But know that I stand by my decision to bear Adele. I regret only that we did not prepare a better way to protect her in an emergency."

"I bear the same regret," Captain Becker said softly. "I, too, failed to find a mechanism."

"You told us, months ago, that you had no way to protect her. You had no interest."

"Yes, I did warn you, but do not think I did not try to find a way! Both before and after the baby's birth. I researched. I consulted with the Foundation's experts."

Dr. Claudine raised her eyebrows.

"Unfortunately, we found nothing safer than the airtents in case of a loss of air pressure." Captain Becker looked uncharacteristically sorrowful. "And then the worst happened, and the airtent proved insufficient." He sighed and shook his head. "Exactly what I wanted to avoid." He raised his eyes and contemplated Dr. Claudine.

She stared back. "We would like to bury Adele on Mars. We will keep her body aboard the ship until we arrive."

"I am not sure how you can do that –"

Dr. Louis said, "We would hope you support our decision, but the burial will be on Mars regardless."

Dr. Cecylia waved a hand. "Claudine and Louis, Dietrich and I most certainly agree to wait to bury Adele after we arrive. You will want to have a gravesite to visit."

Unexpectedly, the captain nodded in agreement.

"I am surprised by your support," Dr. Louis said, watching him gravely. "I would have appreciated such support while the baby was alive."

Captain Becker looked stunned. "You had our support all along."

"We did? I was not aware."

"My concern was to avoid this! To avoid what has happened, to save you the pain of the loss of a daughter." He sighed again. "We shared your thrill at Adele's birth. We expected to watch her thrive in our new home. We wanted you to be happy parents."

"Saving us from pain was not your choice or responsibility, Dietrich. You are not G-d."

"No, I am not. I am just a man with empathy. I know pain and I have no desire to see others suffer it."

Dr. Claudine frowned. "The pain of the loss of our child is ours alone. You cannot share it."

Dr. Cecylia gazed at her, deep sadness in her sour expression. "Do you imagine my husband and I do not know the pain of losing a daughter?" She dropped her eyes shook her head. "You imagine wrong."

We all stared. The Beckers lost a daughter?

The captain spoke gently. "Losing a child is unbearable, Claudine. The pain lasts a long time. The emptiness, forever. And the guilt – could we have prevented what happened? That you now suffer this loss – that is my failure. I tried to protect you. Perhaps it was not my responsibility, but I could not bear the thought that the worst might happen. That you would bring a baby into an environment where we could not protect it. That you would have to share such grief."

Bewildered, I watched him silently.

"You can never run away from your loss. I have tried; it does not work. The loss accompanies you. We will find a solution for Adele. Perhaps we can seal her body in a bag of soil, bury her now, even before arrival. You will have your gravesite on Mars. That is all I can offer."

*   *   *

Thursday, June 23rd, 2029 11:15

Early Thursday morning, Sander Spencer set out to repair the breach in *Providence's* hull. Arjan, the captain's son, joined him. Their assignment to the repair mission followed quite a bit of arguing Wednesday night, after Captain Ravel announced that it would be members of his own crew, not anyone from *Providence*, who would risk the long trek across the gap and the hours of fleximetted breathing.

"We can repair our own ship by ourselves," Captain Becker protested.

"With all due respect, Dietrich," Captain Ravel answered sharply, "you are aboard my ship, and I am in command. This is my decision."

"Yes, but we are discussing my ship. Its fate is mine to decide."

"Your people are reeling from loss. Your best spacewalker is incapacitated. Let my crew share the burden and danger."

Captain Ravel won that argument.

"My husband and I are the best candidates for this job," Dr. Jeretta Spencer announced, gesturing toward Dr. Sander. "We have hours of experience spacewalking together; we are the best choice for this."

She was not exaggerating. The Spencers had been minor celebrities after arriving at Altiplano during the fifth year of our training. Both had been United States Air Force pilots, then Space Force astronauts, before their recruitment for the Mars expedition.

"One of you can go out," Captain Ravel said. "But not both, not at the same time. It is too risky."

"On the contrary. We work well together," Dr. Sander said. "We know each other's movements. We will be most efficient."

"And if something should go wrong? Think of Jerome and Alfred and Shona! I am not sending both parents together. Nothing more need be said."

Captain Ravel won that argument too, but let the Spencers decide which of them would go. Reluctantly, Dr. Jeretta agreed to let her husband take the job. Dr. Sander chose Arjan, who had spacewalked many times during the journey, to be his partner. Arjan liked the idea and won the argument that ensued with his own father.

As was the custom on Murke-Berger spacecraft, everybody gathered in the living rooms to watch live images from the spacewalkers' fleximet cameras. Hannah insisted I join her upstairs on Diamond Level, and also invited Meital and Ruby. It was not long, after Dr. Jean served freshly baked bread sticks and puffed rice, before Sam, Omar, Denver and Celina joined us.

"Whose camera is that?" Meital asked, pointing at the NLED wall across from the kitchen. Its owner had just rounded the bend at the bottom of *Providence*.

"That's Arjan's view on the side wall," Hannah's father answered. "Sander's is on the other screen."

We watched as Arjan approached the entrance to our airlock and shined his light inside.

"Who left the door open?" Sam asked, smirking. "That's irresponsible. All our stuff is inside!"

Ruby turned to her brother and laughed. "The nearest thief is a hundred million kilometers away."

One hundred million kilometers between us and the rest of humanity? I shuddered at the idea.

"Are you sure? Have you checked the whole neighborhood?"

Hannah pointed at the screens. "The only people in the neighborhood are Dr. Sander and Arjan. We here on *Mars Hope* trust Dr. Sander completely."

"What about Arjan?" Celina asked.

"We all like him a lot," she nodded. "But check his pockets when he gets back."

Arjan had entered *Providence's* airlock and was floating up through the hatch. Lights were on again inside our depressingly desolate home. I took a handful of puffed rice from the bag Hannah handed me.

"We are inside at the breach," Dr. Sander announced a few minutes later. He shined his light on the inner hull, at the end of the tunnel Boris had created by clearing out containers of food and supplies. "Arjan, hand over the adhesives."

Arjan's camera view bounced around, projecting blurred images of various-sized containers, as he reached into the equipment kit that was latched to his harness. He handed two toothpaste-sized tubes to Dr. Sander.

We watched as Dr. Sander squeezed paste from one of the tubes, applying it in a circle around what looked like a small dent. He added a second loop of paste from the other tube.

"Kindly hand me a Mylar patch."

Arjan handed him a silvery patch, which he placed over the adhesive. He rubbed it, pressing down all around with his marsmitt. I realized he was not wearing his insulated gloves. How cold would the inside of the habitat's hull be without air? Apparently not so cold that gloves were necessary.

Dr. Sander applied the adhesives a second time, on the patch and on the hull around it.

"Hand me a carbon patch."

Arjan rummaged through the toolkit and pulled out a thin circle of stiff black material the size of the palm of his hand. Dr. Sander placed it over the smaller first patch and pressed down to affix it. Then he applied the adhesives a third time.

"Kevlar, please."

Arjan found the third patch and handed it to him. This patch was a white square and looked to be ten or twelve centimeters on a side. Dr. Sander applied it and rubbed, pressing hard, on every centimeter of length and breadth.

"That should do it, please G-d, if I did everything properly.

Captain Ravel spoke over the radio. "It looked complete to me, Sander. Come back in."

Our eyes remained glued to the screens as the two prepared to descend through the habitat. They pointed their cameras into each room, checking for anything out of the ordinary. The bedrooms all looked okay, and the kitchens, but when Arjan shined his lamp into the Yellow-Level greenhouse room Omar sighed and sobbed. "We lost everything. All of our work, all the greenery, dried up and gone."

"At least you guys are safe."

"If only that were true, Hannah." He sighed again. "We do not know what will be with Simeon."

Dr. Sander and Arjan stopped on each deck. Now projecting from Pink Level, one of them peered into the second greenhouse room. Shriveled cucumbers hung from withered, cracked vines.

"I cannot go back," Omar said. "I cannot face the loss. All those months of work." He sighed sadly.

"What," Celina asked, "would you stay over here?"

Omar considered for a moment. "Yes, actually, I would, if somebody will swap places with me." He reached for Sam's arm. "Sam, I do not mean to insult you."

Sam faced his roommate. "I'm not insulted. Well, maybe a bit. But I understand you. I guess it depends on who you swap with."

"There are not a lot of choices, Omar," Dr. Jean said. "*Mars Hope* is short on single men. In fact, only Arjan comes to mind. That would mean, Omar, that you would room with his thirteen-year-old brother, Kumar."

"That is okay with me."

Dr. Steven shook his head. "Amit would never let Arjan go. He's his right-hand man."

Hannah glanced at me inscrutably, then turned to her mother. "I have an idea. What if I give Omar my room here? It's a single room – he would not have to worry about a roommate."

"Where would you go?" Sam asked, confused. "We need a man, not a woman, to take Omar's place in my room with me."

"Denver could move in with you."

"… Meaning, you would take Denver's place?"

I stared at Hannah. She had unabashedly intimated sharing my room. "I am very flattered, Hannah," I said, suppressing an embarrassed smile, "but I think that is against Foundation rules."

"The Foundation is very far away."

Dr. Jean cleared her throat, loudly, and said, "But your parents are not."

"Omar," Ruby said pointedly, "we are going to replant everything. We'll need you more than ever!"

"We will be landing, *in sha'All-h*, only six weeks from now. That is barely enough time to grow anything."

"True," Denver said, "but the sooner we start, the sooner we'll have fresh vegetables again after we land. It will be a long time before we plant in outdoor greenhouses."

"We will be moving underground after we land," Omar said. "We will plant new, underground greenhouses. We will have much more space than we have here, even before we set up tents."

"True," said Celina, "and we can move the plants we grow into the new underground greenhouses. Ruby is right: we need you and your expertise. Please do not abandon us!"

*   *   *

Sunday, June 26th, 2029 14:30

Sixty hours of successful air-pressure testing, monitored remotely, confirmed that Dr. Sander and Arjan had repaired *Providence* flawlessly. Before they had left the ship Thursday afternoon, they had closed and sealed the habitat's inner airlock hatch, making it possible for Dr. Claudine to send instructions to the computer to begin releasing air from the tanks. She increased cabin pressure progressively over the weekend until the habitat reached the Foundation's standard 350 millibars. She waited an hour after each increase and checked for any change that might indicate a leak. The computer reported none.

Captain Becker, also working remotely, isolated the damaged solar controller, effectively disconnecting it and its two solar-panel arrays from the habitat's electrical systems. Boris – during a rare break from his brother's bedside – protested, "Those two arrays supply five percent of our electricity. Without them, so far from the sun, we will not have enough power to supply all the habitat's needs."

"We can forgo most horticultural lighting," Omar offered, "until our new plantings sprout in a few weeks." He looked from the captain to Boris. "But after that, Boris is right, if we want the vegetables to grow, we will need the missing power. Let us replace the broken part during our climb back to our craft."

Captain Becker shook his head vehemently. "Nobody is going anywhere near that controller. At least not until after we land on Mars. I will not risk another injury."

My mother also kept busy, remotely testing all of *Providence's* water systems. Happily, none of the pipes or valves had cracked. In our absence, the computer had kept water flowing continuously throughout the system to prevent it from freezing. But we would still need to examine all the water purification system's components once we were back on board. The air purification systems also passed a set of remote tests, though there were some questions about the carbon-dioxide tanks. I wondered if our laundry machines would still work.

We joined Hannah's family for what should have been festive Sabbath meals, Friday night and Saturday noon. Five Meyers, four Tellers and four Gordons crowded together in the Diamond-Level living room. Though it was always more difficult to eat without gravity, if there had been gravity, we would have had to crowd around the table instead of spreading out comfortably in the three-dimensional space. We dined on freshly baked challah bread (a complex operation Friday morning!), pea and barley stew, and a lettuce-and-pepper salad. For dessert, Anastasia brought up a bin of chocolate chip cookies she had baked, using *Mars Hope's* remaining chocolate stock. The time together should have been joyous, but our conversation was subdued. Simeon had shown no improvement all week and nobody wanted to mention what many of us were thinking: while we were busy feasting, he was being force-fed through a tube.

Sam provided a respite Saturday afternoon. "Let's get out the Talmud and do some learning. We shouldn't miss another day."

"Can I join you?" Seth asked. "I'm not supposed to start Talmud for a couple of years, but an introduction would be nice."

"Sure! I can help translate difficult words."

We opened our datapads to folio thirty-one of tractate Bava Kama and began a heated discussion about traffic law. The Talmud discussed a case where two people, both carrying earthenware jars, were walking, and the one in front tripped and fell. The second person crashed into the first and both jars broke.

"Why should the first guy have to pay for the damage?" Seth asked. "The guy behind him should have been watching where he was going."

"Maybe he didn't have time. It's a public thoroughfare."

"The rabbis argue about the reasons," Sam explained. "Rabbi Meir says a person is responsible even for accidental falling. Rabbi Yochanan says that, even if one is not responsible for an accident, he needs to get up and clear the way as quickly as possible."

An impassioned discussion followed. The three of us spent the next hour arguing the different rabbis' opinions, each of us taking a side, then switching off to make sure everyone understood all the different points of view. Seth was impressive: he argued well, not at all intimidated.

"What's the rule if you bump into each other while crossing the tether tomorrow?" Seth asked, smiling slyly. "Is a tether considered a 'public thoroughfare?'"

On Sunday morning, Dr. Jean helped me replace my fleximet's communications radio. The radios were surprisingly small and the habitats, it turned out, had an ample supply of spares. Apparently the Foundation had expected them to fail. Snapping the replacement into its slot above the inner neckline was trivially simple.

Sunday afternoon the time arrived to begin our spacewalk home. I was determined to be a net-positive participant this time.

I found Boris floating by his brother's bed on Triangle Level. "Boris, would you like extra pairs of hands to help bring your brother back to *Providence*? Denver and I can join you."

"Thanks, Michael, I appreciate your concern, but Dietrich is doing the assignments for the transfer."

I looked for someone else I could help, and found Shirel and Susan upstairs with Seth and Matias, bouncing tennis balls weightlessly off the walls of Seth's bedroom. "Shirel, how would you feel about being my buddy on the way back?"

"Yeah, I think that's the plan," she said. "You and me and Meital."

"The plan? I was just thinking you'd appreciate brotherly protection."

She shot me a dubious look. "'Brotherly protection?'"

"Sure! Your older brother should look out for you."

"Okay. Whatever. You can watch out for Meital and me on the way back. The three of us are assigned to the second batch."

"We are? Nobody told me about it."

Susan explained. "My mom was up here a few minutes ago. She said they divided us into new groups."

"Different from the way over?"

"Yes. They want most of the adults to go back first and get things set up. The rest of us will come later."

"Susy's mom didn't say it explicitly," Shirel said, "but I think it's about Simeon." She sighed. "You know, to make sure the ship is clean and ready before he arrives."

"Then why am I in the second group?" I asked. "I should go help with the cleaning."

"Go complain to the captain," Susan said. "Tell him you want to swap with me. Ruby and I are the only kids in the first group – they want us to go over with my mother. I'd be happy to wait 'til later."

"They won't allow you to swap," Shirel said. "Meital and I need Michael to accompany us in the second group. We need a 'grown-up.'" Her expression soured. "We're 'too young' to go by ourselves."

But not too young to go with me. I smiled to myself, feeling very mature. Somebody – the captain, or Dr. Jhonathan, or my mother – had decided they could rely on me.

Return

*   *   *

Sunday, June 26th, 2029 17:30

Denver had been assigned to be my mother's spacewalk buddy in the first group. He promised to call me on his datapad after he got back to Green Level and show me video views of what everything looked like. He bid me farewell and dropped into the airlock. I kissed my mother and wished her a safe crossing.

After the hatch was sealed, I headed back upstairs with Helga, Sam and my sisters for dinner with Hannah and her family. We listened in on the spacewalkers' radio channel, monitoring their progress while dipping freshly-baked pita bread into creamy hummus. We followed the group's climb up the *Mars Hope* side ladders and listened in as they latched and unlatched their tethers. Dr. Esther took periodic roll calls, and soon they were crossing the gap. As we started dessert (tomato-flavored crushed ice), they began to announce, one by one, that they had reached *Providence's* hull.

Omar was first to arrive at the airlock. Everyone else had also entered by the time we finished reciting grace. Soon after that, my mother announced that she was closing *Providence's* airlock hatch and initiating pressurization. They folded and stowed their Mylar suits; then, a few minutes later, they opened the inner hatch and closed the audio connection.

*   *   *

Sunday, June 26th, 2029 23:45

I lay awake in my bedroll, hooked to the ceiling in Triangle Level's living room, waiting for Denver to call me. Hannah had come down to chat, but she left at 23:00, curfew time. Finally, just before midnight, my datapad beeped. I tapped the screen and Denver's face appeared, lit only by his own datapad.

"Sorry to keep you waiting. What an evening we had!"

"What have you been up to?"

"Inspecting, and cleaning, and more inspecting. Your mother had me and Celina examine every pipe and valve on Mauve and Green Levels. Then we vacuumed, everywhere. Cleaning, cleaning and more cleaning."

"What was there to vacuum? The whole atmosphere is filtered, all new air."

"Feathers!" He stared out at me from the screen, wide-eyed, and shook his head in the darkness. "You would not believe how many feathers were floating, everywhere."

I thought of the dead birds we had observed, floating in their cages, as we fled the habitat a week earlier.

"Did you get them all?"

"I doubt it. We hunted in as many corners as possible, but it will not surprise me if we open a kitchen cabinet a few days from now and more feathers pop out."

"Are the birds' bodies still shedding?"

Denver's expression soured and he looked green with nausea. "Ruby and Susy – poor girls – the captain asked them to gather up all the carcasses. He handed them a couple of the black bags and pushed them into Boris's bedroom – that is where they had put the birdcages. The girls came out a minute later crying. It was too much for them alone."

"I can imagine. That wasn't fair. Ruby was emotionally attached to all those chickens and parakeets that died."

"She was a real hero, though. Celina and I went back in with her after we finished the inspections and vacuuming. Omar and Dr. Esther also came down to help. All of us, together, began gathering the bodies. But it was Ruby who took charge. She led the operation. Her mother was really proud."

"Did they stink? What's the smell like over there?"

"The birds? No. There was nothing left to rot. They were all dried out and hard as stone. The habitat smells surprisingly new and clean. Just a barely perceptible odor of machine oil from the air-processing equipment."

"How long did it take to pack up all the carcasses?"

"Almost an hour and a half. The big ones were not so difficult. But imagine dozens of tiny dead parakeets and canaries, all floating around the cages. You cannot just sweep them up! A couple got out – it was horrible – I had to chase them through the living room."

"What's left for the rest of us to do?"

"Not much. You lucked out: you'll be coming home to a clean, functioning ship. But there is one thing you need to do for me: do not forget your sourdough cultures! We have nothing interesting left to eat here. At least the bread should taste good."

*   *   *

Monday, June 27th, 2029 10:00

Hannah pecked a kiss on my cheek before I could stop her. "Keep safe!" she said, looking into my eyes. "We'll see each other in fewer than six weeks." Her smile was tinged with longing and a hint of worry, and she sighed.

"We'll talk on our datapads," I reassured, and dropped through the hatch into the airlock. Helga was already there, fitting Jasmine's fleximet, as were Meital and Shirel, who called to me.

"Michael, help me seal this airtent," Meital said. She had two of them in her hands, each with two hens visible under a clear plastic cover. "Dr. Louis told me that the three of us need to bring not only the chickens but also the worms. Yesterday's group left them all for us."

I took an airtent, closed its seal, affixed an oxypack, and opened the airflow. "Only four hens? What about the surviving parakeets?"

"Not worth the risk," Meital said. "They'll be fine here until we land. But the hens – Dr. Cecylia said that it is important that we have at least some eggs being laid, for our nutrition."

Shirel was attaching an oxypack to a third airtent that appeared to contain loose dirt. "What's that?" I asked, pointing.

"These are the worms," she answered. "Hopefully they'll be enough to restock all four decks."

I counted the airtents and the bulging duffel I had carried down. My extra mundies had gone over with Denver the night before, but the rest of my belongings – phylacteries, datapad, and sealed sourdough jars – I had stuffed into the girls' bag. "How are the three of us going to carry all three airtents and a duffel?"

"Yeah, that's a problem," Meital said, turning around. "Helga, can you and Jasmine take one of these?"

Helga frowned. "I am sorry, Meital. I am responsible for Jasmine and also have to carry over the bag with her stuff and mine. I cannot take an extra bag."

At that moment Boris and Sam entered the airlock, pulling along Simeon's limp, unconscious form. Claudine followed, hugging an overstuffed black bag of the kind usually used to store sterilized waste and worm-manufactured soil. I almost asked her what it contained, but realized just in time: it was Adele's body, sealed hermetically for hygienic reasons, preserved for eventual burial on Mars.

I had never seen a sadder procession.

Jasmine tugged at my sleeve. "Michael, I can take your duffel bag."

I smiled as best I could. "Thank you, but you're too young. It might be too much for you."

Her eyes widened with indignation. "I will soon be ten years old!" She grabbed the duffel from my hand and turned her back to me. Helga caught my eye, smiled, and nodded "okay."

We donned, sealed, and tested our fleximets. Boris and Sam struggled a bit with Simeon's, but when they pressed his oxypack's test button, the green light lit, indicating a good seal.

Dr. Louis, holding Sophie's gloved hand in his, checked that everyone's fleximet was properly inflated and that nobody had forgotten to don their marsmitts. "Everyone set?" he asked over the radio connection. He tapped his datapad to initiate the air-pressure purge. My mundies compressed tightly around my legs and arms, then torso and chest. The familiar discomfort under my arms and around my crotch had become easy to ignore. The whirring of the air fans in my ears was more of a distraction.

"Pausing depressurization," Dr. Louis announced. "Check your buddies' mundies for bulges."

This procedure was also familiar, except that it had always been Denver's body that I checked. Now I was examining my sisters' legs, arms, midsections and chests. Shirel giggled as I spun her body around. I found a bulge on her shoulder.

"Boris, I need a repair here."

He pushed the repair kit into my hands.

"Am I supposed to patch it myself?"

"You trained for this!"

I recoiled at the look on his face. He intimidated me even with two visors separating us.

It had been nearly a year since I had practiced patching mundies, back at Altiplano, but I assured myself that I would remember. First, I extracted one of the kit's small epoxy bottles. I squeezed its contents over the bulge and applied a fine, even layer. Next, I pulled out a circular, six-centimeter patch and smeared it, too, with epoxy, this time from the second bottle. I placed the patch on Shirel's shoulder, carefully, and pressed, hard, all around, to seal it.

Boris saw my work and nodded. "Nice job."

The last item in the patch kit was the activation transmitter. After waiting the required two minutes – I estimated the time by counting slowly – I pressed the box-shaped transmitter's blue button. It was surprisingly gratifying to watch Shirel's fabric contract and the bulge disappear.

"Thanks, Michael," Shirel said, her voice soft and sweet.

After Boris had finished patching a bulge on Simeon's arm and Helga had finished patching one on her own leg, Dr. Louis resumed the air purge. "Don your Mylar suits and gloves," he instructed over the radio. We were all dressed and ready, even Simeon, before the airlock was emptied of air and it was time to open the outer hatch. "Everyone, listen to me," Dr. Louis continued. "When we came over last week we were in darkness, so you did not have to be concerned with sunlight. This time, however, the ships are positioned for generating solar power. Your treks up and down the hulls might be in sunlight or in darkness, depending on which side you go up, but we will all be in sunlight while crossing the tethers. Your visors will adjust automatically, but be careful to avoid looking into the sun."

Sam and Boris were first to exit, carefully guiding Simeon, who was tethered to both of them. Sam was also coping with a duffel that was latched to his waist harness. Helga and Jasmine followed them out but headed across the hull in the opposite direction. Then it was our turn. I watched Meital exit, airtent in tow, and start down a set of ladder rungs in the direction Dr. Louis indicated. Shirel followed close behind, carefully pulling the vermiculture airtent through the opening.

My heart raced as I stuck my head outside. Vertigo threatened. I took a deep breath and released it slowly. *I am a flier and I am not going to panic.* I took another breath as I spun my body around in a full circle, getting a good look at the entire bottom hull. When I finished my rotation, the sun was to my right, but my sisters were climbing along the ladder to my left. I reached out in that direction and latched my cord's carabiner to the first rung.

Beads of sweat formed on my forehead. *Trust G-d*, my inner voice instructed. *Recite the Jewish wayfarer's prayer!* I nodded to myself and began to pray. *May it be your will, my G-d and G-d of my fathers, that you guide us toward peace, and advance us toward peace, and walk us toward peace* – *and float us toward peace!* (I added that to the original) – *and bring us to our desired destination, in life and happiness and peace, and save us from every enemy, every wild animal* (none here, I smiled to myself), *and every type of danger* (I could think of lots of those), *and bless all our actions, and may we find grace and kindness in your eyes and in the eyes of everyone who sees us, and may you hear our prayer, because You are the G-d who hears prayers and supplications. You are the Source of blessing, who hears prayer.*

I latched my second cord's carabiner to the next ladder rung and pulled the airtent behind me, careful not to bang the poor chickens against the hull. I unlatched the first cord from the rung behind me, wondering if the hens were feeling as anxious as I was. *G-d, help me trust you, and not panic, and be the big brother my sisters are relying on.* I took another deep breath and settled into the latch-unlatch-latch-unlatch sequence, progressing quickly to keep up with the girls.

"Look at all the stars," Shirel exclaimed over the shared radio connection. "They're so beautiful!"

We were on the dark side and my eyes had adjusted, so I stopped to look around. The sky opened above me, bursting with stars and galaxies in myriad colors: reds, and oranges, and yellows and cold blues. Would I ever have another opportunity to see the heavens in such glory?

Dr. Louis was calling my name. Another roll call. "Michael?"

"I'm here, making progress, right behind Meital and Shirel."

Somewhere up there among the stars was a special red dot, our destination and soon-to-be home. I paused again to look for it. It would not be directly overhead, I reasoned, but diagonally above, perhaps ahead, perhaps behind. What was our orientation relative to the direction of travel? I realized I had no idea. We were not moving toward Mars, but rather toward a point in space that Mars would reach as it orbited the sun. It did not feel like we were moving at all, there being no stationary points of reference. Space was so empty!

"I've reached the top of the hull and am latching myself to the tether," Meital said, interrupting my reverie. She was just beyond Shirel, both of them farther from me than they should have been.

"We've got the yellow tether," she added, apparently examining the thimble and the clasp that held it. "I'm starting across."

I rushed to catch up. After a couple of latch-unlatch steps, I had closed the distance between Shirel and me enough to pause and search again. I found Mars this time, behind and to my left, hanging patiently in the sky, a dusty red disk! It looked bigger than it had during our flight over to *Mars Hope*. Had that been just a week earlier? Was the disk really bigger now? Perhaps I was just imagining. Again, there were no fixed points of reference. I shook my head and turned back to the ladder rungs.

Some minutes later, as the three of us made our way along the tether through empty space, back in bright sunlight, Shirel cried out. "I'm having trouble holding the cable. It's like it's trying to get away from me!"

She was three or four meters ahead, her vermiculture airtent floating by her side.

"I'm noticing the same thing," Meital said. "What's going wrong?"

I felt it then, too. The tether was not stable: it was tugging me, gently, to and fro. Another standing wave. None of the other groups had mentioned a problem. Apparently, of the four tethers, only ours was moving this way. Unlucky again!

"Meital and Shirel," I said, trying to sound confident and authoritative, "it's nothing to worry about." I let go of the tether and watched it move, slowly, side-to-side. "We can't fall off because we're attached to the tether by our cords. It's moving because there's a standing wave going up and down the whole length of the cable. At any given point it seems like it's vibrating back and forth, but that's just the wave passing by."

"The tether is vibrating like a guitar string?" Meital asked.

An image popped into my mind: a huge hand strumming all four tethers. *If space were full of air, what would our ships sound like?* I laughed. "Something like that. It's going to be annoying, but not dangerous. The tether Denver and I crossed last week was doing the same thing."

"What am I supposed to do to hold onto it?"

"Don't try, Shirel. Relax your grip. Give yourself a pull when you have to, but let inertia move you along. I'll be right behind you."

The motion was most pronounced, and most difficult to negotiate, out in the middle of the gap, but as we neared the top of *Providence* it got easier to grasp the tether and pull ourselves along.

"I'm at the habitat," Meital called out, "and latching to the top rung."

"Me, too," Shirel said, not a minute later, breathing an audible sigh of relief. "Glad to be off that wave."

I touched the top of *Providence* and latched a carabiner to the nearest rung. We had reached home. I followed my sisters down *Providence's* ladder, latching and unlatching as quickly as we could. We came around the bottom hull in what seemed like record time. One by one, we entered our own airlock, making sure not to bump the airtents as we passed through the hatch.

As soon as I entered, Jasmine, who had already arrived with Helga, excitedly handed me the duffel. "See? It was easy for me!"

"Thank you so much, Jasmine. I'm lucky to have a young astronaut as a friend."

After the Bouchets came through the hatch we waited, patiently, for several more minutes, until Sam and Boris arrived with Simeon. After he was safely inside, Dr. Louis closed the outer hatch. The airlock filled with air and my mundies relaxed their tight grip on my limbs as I folded and stowed my Mylar suit. At 350 millibars, the computer chimed that we could doff our fleximets. Sam helped Boris remove Simeon's. Dr. Claudine handed Adele's body bag to Helga and rushed over to examine him. She reassured Boris that his brother's breathing was stable.

Dr. Louis opened the inner hatch. One by one, we rose up into our very familiar Mauve Level, where the others anxiously awaited our arrival. My mother grabbed Shirel and Meital and me, pulling all three of us into a warm family hug.

We had all survived the journey across, even Simeon, though he remained unconscious and unmoving. Dr. Louis and Captain Becker transferred him into his bedroom and latched him to his bed. That was for his own protection, so that he not float into walls or furniture. Dr. Jhonathan reinserted Simeon's nasogastric feeding tube, and Boris resumed his bedside vigil.

Moon

Wednesday, June 29th, 2029 09:45

Simeon died, quietly and unexpectedly, two days later. Poor Helga: she was at his bedside when it happened. She had pleaded with Boris to take a break and get some exercise, reassuring him that she would sit with his brother until he finished cycling and showering. "I have nothing else to do: the vacuum killed all the bacterial films. There are no surfaces to disinfect."

Even though I was a level above, purging air filters, I heard her sudden cry. "Louis! Something is not right!"

Denver looked up from the water tube he was examining. We locked eyes and nodded silently to each other, each knowing what the other was thinking. We might not be able to help, but we were too curious not to go check. We headed down the stairwell.

We arrived at Mauve Level just as Dr. Claudine and her husband were going into Simeon's bedroom, medical kits in their hands. Meital emerged from the airlock hatch, wiping her hands on her smock. She noticed Jasmine and Sophie perched at the edge of the living room, looking afraid, not knowing what to do with themselves. "Come with us," she said, taking the girls' hands. "Michael, keep me updated," she whispered loudly, and the three of them headed upstairs.

I heard the Bouchets speaking in tense voices in the bedroom. They spoke in French and their voices were muffled, but I was able to discern the words *oxygène* and *pouls* and *pupilles dilatées*.

Boris exited the bathroom, hair still wet from the shower. Wheezing nervously, he flew across the room, grabbed the bedroom doorpost, and pulled himself inside, crying, "What happened to my brother?"

It was all over within a few minutes. Through the open door I watched Dr. Louis hug Boris and pat him gently on the back. "There was nothing more we could do for him. I am so sorry."

Boris pushed him away. "Is there no way to revive him? Electric shocks? More oxygen?"

Dr. Jhonathan came from the stairwell and floated over. "I don't think so, Boris." He grabbed his hand and looked into his eyes sympathetically. "Even if there had been a way to revive your brother, his kidneys were too weak. It was a matter of hours, maybe a day or two."

"Sit here with him," Dr. Claudine said. "We will give you time to part." She came into the living room, saw Denver and me and the others who had gathered, and chastised us. "Everybody upstairs! Respect Boris's time with his brother."

* * *

Thursday, July 1st, 2029 10:00

We did not eat the next day, the first of July. (The computer had skipped June 30, as our days now nearly matched Martian days in length.) July 1 corresponded to the Jewish calendar's Seventeenth of Tammuz, a day of mourning and fasting. Judaism's fasts commemorated ancient tragedies; this one also marked a new tragedy for us: Simeon's death.

I was listlessly cleaning air filters on Mauve Level when Captain Becker came downstairs. Boris was crying in the living room, while the Bouchets, the Meyers, and my mother all tried to comfort him.

"Boris," said Captain Becker, "I would like to complete the funeral today."

Boris looked up at him, expression neutral, eyes shining with tears.

"We will give Simeon an honorable 'burial at sea.' That is, we will release him from the airlock."

"I would like to bury my brother on Mars, Dietrich."

Moon

The captain shook his head. "I am sorry. That is not possible. Keeping the body on board is a health hazard."

"With respect," Boris said, straightening himself and approaching the captain, "your decision regarding Adele was different. I request the same accommodation."

Captain Becker sighed and hung his head. "I have failed you. All your lives are in my hands, and two lives have now been lost." He looked around the room at everyone present. "You should know that I will relinquish my leadership role as soon as we arrive on Mars."

Dr. Jhonathan began to protest, "There's no need …" but the captain cut him off.

"Until then, however, I am still responsible, and will do my utmost to protect all who still live."

"Simeon's body," Boris said. "We were discussing how to preserve him for burial."

"Yes, Boris, I wish we could, if only there were a way. Louis and Claudine sealed Adele's body in a soil bag. Unfortunately, the bags are large enough only for a baby. We have no means of sealing an adult corpse and the gasses its decomposition would release."

Boris pleaded, "Are there no large bags?"

Dr. Jhonathan answered. "Nothing strong enough, Boris. I'm sorry. I wish there were. Even if we sealed a bag, it would bloat during the coming weeks and might tear or explode. I don't want to think about the hygienic crisis that would result."

The captain nodded. "Also, there is another consideration: our final course correction. Amit and Jean are running the calculations; we should have them within an hour or two. They are computing solutions for a firing Sunday afternoon. We ought to release the body before then, so that it not share our final trajectory."

"I understand," Boris mumbled, head hanging.

*   *   *

Thursday, July 1st, 2029 16:00

Meital cleared out the airlock for the burial – a much easier task than previously, as she needed to remove only four hens in one birdcage. We gathered on our respective levels and listened in on the wall speakers. Dr. Esther and Dr. Louis entered the airlock with

Simeon's body. Boris had affixed and sealed his brother's fleximet, but without an oxypack, and Dr. Louis had fit his marsmitts.

"Simeon is prepared for space," Dr. Esther announced. "We have dressed him in his Mylar pants and pullover. We are releasing him in an honorable fashion."

Captain Becker spoke. "I have prepared a eulogy that I will send to Simeon's parents. I will read it to you now."

"Beginning airlock purge," Dr. Esther interrupted.

"Simeon was a hero. He always went above and beyond what was required. He wanted only to give, to contribute, even at his own risk. As he lived, so he died. Just as he had volunteered for every spacewalk throughout the journey, so too he volunteered – even argued vehemently with me – to go out, in our most perilous hour, to find the breach that threatened our habitat. He found it, but that was not enough for Simeon: he insisted that he begin the repair so that no one else would need to spacewalk unnecessarily.

"Simeon, with his brother Boris, was a late addition to our expedition. The two arrived for training only a year before departure – six years after most of us had begun preparations – barely speaking English, unfamiliar with the Foundation's technologies, outsiders to the group. How quickly Simeon endeared himself to all of us! He invigorated us with his enthusiasm. Dare I say that we had become complacent over the years, that some of our excitement for the mission had waned after we lost the crew of Vanguard's *Armstrong*? Simeon and Boris arrived, fresh and excited, and encouraged us anew. By the winter before our departure, Simeon was already expert at all spacecraft systems; by springtime, he was completely ready for the mission and a good friend to all."

"I'm opening the outer hatch," Dr. Esther said.

"Simeon, though your body will not reach Mars, your memory and your legacy will be with us, always. Your contribution has been invaluable, and will endure in the settlement and society we will build."

"I have stepped outside," Dr. Esther declared, "and am releasing the body."

"Go in peace, Simeon Radechov," Captain Becker proclaimed. "Rest in peace."

*   *   *

Friday, July 2nd, 2029 09:30

"It feels so empty in here," I said to Meital, looking around the airlock. She had returned the lone birdcage after Simeon's burial, but the other cages were folded and stowed away. Three hens perched on the cage's bars. The fourth fluttered its wings and floated toward the feed dispenser.

"Kind of depressing. There's almost nothing to do here now," Meital answered. "Ten minutes to vacuum the airlock, four minutes to fill the dispensers, and a couple of minutes to hunt down the eggs."

"They are laying eggs? That's good news."

"Three of them are." She turned to me and frowned. "Look how low we've sunk. Three eggs a day is considered good news now."

"I'm grasping at anything that might encourage us," I sighed. "With everything we've lost. Which of the chickens isn't laying eggs?"

"No way to tell. They can't brood in zero gravity, so there's no way to know who an egg belongs to." She snapped the handheld vacuum into its recharger on the wall.

"Where's Ruby?"

"In her bedroom, when I visited her last. She's barely come out all week. Anyway, I haven't needed her help." Meital took a last look around the room and pushed up toward the hatch.

"She's that sick?"

"Dr. Claudine's keeping her full of Dimenphillax to keep her from vomiting. It's making her very tired."

I followed my sister through the opening. "After all these months, she hasn't gotten over her space sickness?" How is she going to make it through the next five weeks?"

"I don't know," Meital said. "Space travel is horrible."

*   *   *

Friday, July 2nd, 2029 12:30

"I'm looking forward to going for a long run when we get to Mars," Sam said as we concluded our Talmud-learning session. The folio had discussed whether people were responsible for damage they caused if, when running, they crashed into each other in a public thoroughfare.

"When you do, remember today's lesson. Don't run on any crowded streets," Rabbi Meyer said, pretending to look serious.

Dr. Esther smiled and looked up from the datapad she was reading.

Sam, observing the crowded room, said, "It will be nice to have enough space that we don't have to worry about bumping into each other."

"To me, the habitat feels kind of empty," I said, "after spending a week doubled-up with everybody in *Mars Hope*. There're so few of us here now."

"Don't let Boris hear you say that," Ruby said, sticking her head out the bedroom door. She looked pale.

"Michael, join us for lunch," Dr. Esther said. "I've prepared a bean spread for the bread you baked last night." She pointed at the NLED wall. "We can watch Arjan's spacewalk together while we eat." She tapped her datapad and the deep-blue undersea fish video, filmed at an aquarium somewhere on Earth, disappeared. It was replaced by a view from Arjan's fleximet camera. At first all we could see was the inside of a darkened airlock, but a moment later the camera exited the hatch. The view spun around and we could see an empty tether spool in his hands.

"Starting to climb the hull," Arjan's gruff voice announced.

Susan came rushing out of the stairwell, followed closely by Shirel. "Dad!"

Dr. Jhonathan, a sandwich in his hand, turned to her. "Something urgent, Susy?"

"Yes," Susan panted. "We got the numbers wrong. We forgot about the tether failure."

We all stared at her.

"What did we forget, dear?" Dr. Esther asked, looking concerned.

"Look at Ruby!" Susan exclaimed. Ruby recoiled as we all turned to look. "She's suffering so much in weightlessness. We have to spin up after the burn."

"I wish we could, Susan," her father said. "But the Mars-Entry stages' reaction control systems are low on fuel. We need to save what remains, for attitude control when we enter the Martian atmosphere."

Susan's hands were black with dirt, and she scrubbed them at the kitchen sink with a large drop of water and a small piece of soap. "No, Dad, that's not right."

Dr. Esther handed out more sandwiches as Dr. Jhonathan counted on his fingers. "The Foundation planned for three spin-up-spin-down cycles, and included reaction-control-system fuel for one extra, for contingency. We were supposed to spin up in Earth orbit, then spin down and back up after Mars-transit injection, then down for a midcourse correction, then back up for the rest of the journey."

"Right," Susan nodded, "plus another course correction, if necessary."

"But what actually happened," her father continued, "were two extra cycles, one when the tether broke, and one when we hunkered down for the solar storm." He looked at her. "Our spin-up after the storm in March was the fourth. When we spun down after the unfortunate breach, we finished off the RCS fuel reserves."

"It's what Simeon said," I recalled, "when he argued with the captain against spinning down." My heart dropped. "He said we would not be able to have gravity for the rest of the trip."

Susan turned to me and shook her head. "He was wrong."

Don't let Boris hear that, I thought to myself.

"Explain," Dr. Esther said, interested.

"It's like I was saying. It's wrong to count the tether break. We didn't spin down after that, not with the RCS rockets."

I thought back to those terrifying twelve seconds that followed January's unplanned tether release. "How did we stop our crazy spinning? Wasn't that the RCS system?"

"Yes, it was, but that was only for a small part of our angular momentum."

"She's right." Her father gazed proudly at his daughter and nodded. "Most of the momentum from the spin was stopped when the Mars-Entry stage's main engine fired."

Sam raised his eyebrows, looking concerned. "Will that have an effect on our Mars Entry burn?"

"No, we have reserves. But it does mean that we did not use as much RCS fuel as we thought." He handed his sandwich to his wife, pulled his datapad off his thigh, and started tapping.

"I've already checked the reserve numbers, Dad," Susan said. "I think I found the right data; if so, the numbers match what we're saying."

He nodded, reading off the screen. "It seems you are right. Our reserves are nine percent higher than would be expected after four full cycles." He shook his head. "But it's still not enough to spin up again."

"Not for a full spin-up. But who says it has to be full?" Susan shrugged and raised her arms. "Why not spin up halfway?"

Arjan had reached the top of *Mars Hope* and began climbing up and down the pinnacle to gather the ends of the four tethers. Captain Becker announced that the clasps that held them on our end were open.

"There is no plan for a partial spin-up. The habitats are designed for Mars-level gravity."

"Then what's the problem?" Sam asked. "The tethers can certainly support half the load, right? That would be like moon gravity. Wouldn't that help Ruby?"

"It would help all of us," I said, thinking about how much easier a bit of gravity would make grinding wheat and kneading dough.

Dr. Jhonathan nodded. "I'll get Dietrich, Amit and Jean on a call. We can ask the Foundation to confirm our calculations and run some simulations."

By the time Arjan had completed his spacewalk, having coiled all four tethers on the spool, the email had been relayed to the Murke-Berger Foundation's engineering team back on Earth. Meanwhile, over on *Mars Hope*, Captain Amit and Dr. Jean reran the calculations for Sunday's course correction, to make sure both ships would remain together in their updated trajectories in case we could retether one more time.

*   *   *

Sunday, July 4th, 2029 15:00

"Still no Mycology class," Omar said, when Celina and I found him in the Yellow-Level greenhouse room. "Maybe next week we can prepare new compost. I doubt we'll be able to inoculate before we land, though."

"Should we use the time to read?"

"Perhaps you would stay and help clean out the dead plants." He handed me a black bag and pointed to the shelves that lined the outer hull. "Uproot those dead cress and lettuce plants. But make sure no dirt gets out."

I squeezed into the dimly lit greenhouse room and examined the contents of the upper shelf. Three dozen dead, shriveled romaine lettuce heads topped stalks that protruded through holes in the soil covers. I tucked the bag into the top of my mundies pants and used both hands to twist and break one of the stalks. I took the head and pushed it into the bag.

"How do I remove the roots without dirt getting out?"

Omar handed me a water bottle. "Get the dirt as wet as possible. Then you can remove one cover at a time."

"Why not wait for gravity?" Celina asked from outside the room. "The Foundation approved spinning up to half gravity and my father and Captain Amit are planning to retether sometime this week."

"Why delay replanting?" Omar cut off a tomato-vine branch with the wrinkled remnants of six tomatoes and stuffed them into his own bag. "We did the other three greenhouses last week without gravity. If we finish in here today, we can plant new lettuce and radishes later this week."

After I cut and removed all the lettuce heads, it took several minutes to squeeze the contents of the water bottle into all thirty-six holes. The water soaked quickly into the dry dirt. While Celina and Omar got to work on the tomato and zucchini bushes behind me, I uprooted the broken lettuce stalks. I removed the soil covers, one at a time, to expose the stems. I dug them out with one hand while using the other to hold the moist soil in place so that no dirt would float away. I promptly replaced each soil cover before moving to the next.

It took just over an hour to finish uprooting everything. Omar took the bags from our hands as we exited the greenhouse room, hands dark with dirt.

"What will you do with the bags' contents?"

Omar opened a mushroom compartment and shoved the bags inside, then turned toward Celina. "Some can go into the mushroom compost. We can feed the rest to the worms."

"Should we do that now?" I asked, eyeing the two vermiculture drawers behind Omar.

Omar straightened and smiled – the first time I had seen him smile in weeks. "The worms are very well fed. We have so few, only the ones we brought back from *Mars Hope*. We spread them among all the levels, but it will be weeks before we have enough to keep up with all our rubbish." He floated across to the kitchen to wash his hands.

Shirel exited the stairwell, followed by Susan, both of them quite excited. "Guys, come downstairs. The course-correction engine firing is starting soon." She stared at my hands with disgust. "But clean yourself up first!"

"What's the excitement?"

"Dancing! We're putting on dance music, like we always do during firings."

"Maybe not this time," I said gravely. "A lot of us are in mourning, Shirel. Not a time for music and dancing and celebration."

Susan said, "Maybe we need something to cheer us up now more than ever."

"I asked Boris," Shirel said. "I told him we all share his loss and asked if he minds if we dance like we always do. He said it's okay. He said 'go ahead.'"

A few minutes later, after Omar and Celina and I had washed up, the *Providence* youth all gathered in our Green-Level living room. I should have been starting work on my neural network software project at that time, but we had all been slow to get back to our regular school schedules. That project could wait another day or two.

"Two minutes to the burn," Captain Becker's voice echoed from the NLED wall, which showed an outside camera view. Not much was visible besides blackness and stars, but Denver pointed at a small white streak, saying it was *Mars Hope*, now positioned a few kilometers away.

The captain counted down, "Five – four – three – two – one – ignition." Shirel tapped her datapad to start the music. As during January's course-correction engine firing, the floor came up very slowly to meet us, the simulated gravity barely perceptible and insufficient for dancing. Still, the girls held hands in a circle and managed to spin around a couple of times before the captain announced the end of the burn.

"Everything completed successfully. The computers report that we, *Mars Hope*, and our communications satellite remain in identical trajectories." Then, after a pause, "The thirteen-second burn gave us the required nine point two meters per second of delta-v. We are on track to encounter the Martian atmosphere in thirty-two days."

*   *   *

Tuesday, July 6th, 2029 07:00

Captains Becker and Ravel wasted no time in the effort to restore gravity. A day and a half of slow maneuvering had moved the two habitats back to their tethering position, pinnacle facing pinnacle, exactly one hundred meters apart, 105 meters from tether clasp to tether clasp. Boris volunteered to perform the spacewalk to receive and attach the tethers that *Mars Hope* would send over, but Captain Becker pointedly refused to let him go. Instead, he appointed Dr. Esther, who accepted the assignment enthusiastically. On *Mars Hope*, too, there had been some argument regarding who would go out. Dr. Jeretta Spencer was selected, Hannah told me in a clandestine call late Monday night, and Arjan was not pleased. He had performed every tethering and untethering throughout the journey, but this time Dr. Jeretta insisted on the assignment, after she had been denied the opportunity to join her husband on the *Providence* repair.

Denver and I pedaled on the exercise cycles and Shirel and Meital rowed on the sprowers. We all watched the NLED wall that projected the view from Dr. Esther's fleximet camera. Dr. Jeretta's view was also being broadcast, on the side wall, but twisting our necks to look in that direction was difficult while we exercised facing forward.

"I have attached the ends of all four tethers to the MMU and am sending it your way," Dr. Jeretta announced.

I twisted to face Denver. "Is that our mini-maneuvering unit or theirs?"

"Ours. We sent it over to them back in January, after the tether break, when you and Sam went outside to throw a ball around."

"We didn't actually take the ball out."

"I know – it would not have ended well. The ball would have been lost and we're going to need it to toss around when we get to Mars!"

We watched Dr. Esther reach for the MMU, which floated into her hands. "I have the tethers," she announced. "I'm latching the MMU to the pinnacle ring."

It took her thirteen more minutes to affix all four tethers to their respective clasps, and another fifteen minutes after that to climb back down the hull, stow the MMU in its compartment at the top of the Mars-Entry stage, and reenter the airlock.

"Nice work, dear," Dr. Jhonathan complimented, sounding relieved to have his wife back on board. Before ending the camera transmissions, he added, "Everyone, get ready for our 'Moonwalk' attraction! We'll have nineteen percent Earth gravity by late tonight, G-d willing."

* * *

Thursday, July 8th, 2029 17:45

"Interplanetary trade arises only when a planet is incapable of producing a particular good," Dr. Jhonathan said, summarizing my essay. "Hence, a self-sufficient planet in Asimov's galaxy would have no trade relations."

I nodded. "That's a fair synopsis. The idea is especially apparent regarding the capital planet, Trantor. Trantor began importing significant quantities of food only after the collapse of its indigenous food industry."

That was the gist of my English Literature term paper, "Isaac Asimov's Outlook on Interplanetary Economics." I had finally completed the *Foundation* series, but only after convincing Dr. Jhonathan to assign it as required reading for summer semester's English Literature class.

"Do you think that's our future, too?" Ruby asked, lifting her eyes from her datapad. Although she had chosen Shakespearean theater for her own assignments, she was always willing to discuss science fiction in class. "That our Martian society will have nothing to supply to Earth, because Earth is already self-sufficient?"

A video of Eugene Cernan raising dust on the moon, driving Ferenc Pavlics's lunar rover across rough terrain, was looping on

Pink Level's NLED wall. I tried not to be distracted. "Yes, it makes sense. Why would Earth import anything from Mars?"

"Esther thinks we'll end up exporting heavy metals to Earth," Dr. Jhonathan said. "Because of Mars's low gravity, primordial iridium, platinum and gold might have remained close to the surface, instead of sinking to the core."

"I think we'll invent new things," Ruby said, brushing a strand of frizzy hair out of her green eyes. "Like new medical procedures, maybe using special gas mixtures or air pressures. Martians will be the experts at gaseous medicine because we're the ones who have to manufacture our own atmosphere."

"That's an interesting idea," I said, noticing that Ruby was looking better, with more color in her face, since gravity had returned. "Maybe we'll invent new agricultural techniques, too, that they can use back on Earth."

"I look forward to watching you guys invent all sorts of things over the coming years," Dr. Jhonathan said. "And nice job on your report, Michael. I'll expect the final draft, taking into account my comments, by class on Sunday."

"Ruby," I said, as we got up from the table, "how are you faring, in terms of health, in the low gravity?"

"Much better!" She smiled. "Susan was right. Even moon gravity seems to be enough for me. I think it's the directional confusion – something like vertigo – that makes me sick in zero-gravity. Even low gravity is enough to create a sense of up and down, and that seems to be all I need to keep my stomach settled."

*   *   *

Wednesday, July 21st, 2029 14:30

It took surprisingly little time to adjust to one-sixth Earth gravity. Any gravity was better than none; it made everything easier. Showering, for example: the water took longer – almost comically longer – to fall from the shower head and spiral into the wall, but at least we were permitted to open the stream. A sponge bath was so much less satisfying. I easily slipped back into my daily routine. I focused on schoolwork, and on the Talmudic discussions Sam and I were studying, and on the tasks necessary for daily life. Our recent tribulations had slipped from my mind.

At least until Wednesday two weeks before our planned arrival. It was Tisha b'Av, Judaism's annual day of mourning over the destruction of the ancient Jewish temples, a fast day, a day of introspection and repentance. It was the day we examined ourselves to identify behaviors that prolonged interpersonal strife, distanced us from G-d, delayed redemption, and generally brought about death and destruction.

"Getting on a spaceship to Mars seems like a great way to bring about death and destruction," I mumbled, while kneading half a kilo of dough on the kitchen counter. The dough would become the bread for our break-fast dinner.

"Michael!" my mother exclaimed, turning from the pot she was stirring on the stovetop. "What a thing to say!"

"Oh, sorry. I was just thinking about Tisha b'Av, introspecting about its message, that we bring tragedy upon ourselves by our own actions." I pounded the dough to flatten it.

"That can certainly be true of detrimental behavior, like harboring baseless hatred, speaking negatively about each other, and neglecting responsibilities. But it does not mean we can't explore and settle new places."

"With all we've lost, Mom, do you still believe that?" I folded the dough, then folded it again, then rolled it into a ball.

She turned to face me. "I do, Michael. I do still believe that." She sighed and leaned back against the sink. "Your father did too, even at the end."

I turned to face her. "Mom, I know you'll say you were aware of the dangers before you joined the expedition, it was a choice you made, everything's fine –"

"Everything's not fine, Michael," she interrupted, shaking her head. "It's most definitely not fine to have lost so many of us, first your uncle and his crew, then your father, now Adele and Simeon. What will be with Boris, alone now? I've become a widow, you and your sisters orphans, all because of the expedition." She shook her head sadly. "It's not fine."

"So it's all a mistake."

"I did not say that." She took my hands in hers and looked deeply into my eyes. "I do not regret, not for a minute, our decision to join this voyage. That would be disrespectful to your father's memory. And it would be disrespectful to myself, and to my own sense of wonder, curiosity, and adventure. Coming to Mars was a family decision that we all agreed to."

"Wasn't it more that the Foundation convinced Dad to go on the Vanguard expedition, and then he convinced you to follow?"

"Not true," my mother said, smiling weakly. "Not at all. I might have needed some reassuring, but I did not need to be convinced. In my heart of hearts I'm an adventurer."

"Even now?"

"Most definitely. There is no turning back, and there is no reason we should want to. This is the quintessential adventure! We're on the odyssey your father started but could not complete. G-d willing, we'll complete it, together as a family. You, me, Meital and Shirel. And Denver, too. Thank G-d we have each other. We'll watch over each other, and He'll watch over us." She pulled me into a tight hug. "It might not be easy, Michael, but it is going to be awesome."

Mars

Thursday, July 29th, 2029 12:15

"So he punched him again! What an evil guy," I said, laughing.

"He must not have liked him very much," Sam said, shaking his head incredulously.

The Talmud was discussing an assailant's obligation to pay for embarrassment he causes, in addition to payments owed for damage, pain, medical bills and lost work.

"Who punched who?" Susan asked, having just entered the room with Shirel. Both had excited looks on their faces.

"It's a story in the Talmud," Sam said, pointing at the text on his datapad screen. "A certain 'Evil Hanan' punched a guy in the ear. The court ruled that he had to pay his victim half a dinar for embarrassment."

"Why did he punch him again?"

"He had only one coin, a full dinar, but it was too worn down to exchange for half-dinars. So he went ahead and punched the guy a second time, obligating himself the rest of the coin's value."

"Was he allowed to do that?" Shirel asked.

I caught my sister's eye and smiled. "I'm pretty sure he wasn't, but maybe he thought the fellow deserved it." I looked from her to Susan. "You two look like you came to tell us something."

"Yes!" Susan answered. "My father said we received messages relayed from Mars. *Pioneer Alpha* and *Pioneer Beta* both landed!"

Sam jumped up. "That's fantastic news! When did they touch down?"

"*Pioneer Alpha* landed overnight and *Pioneer Beta* just a couple of hours ago."

"That puts us next in line," I said. "One week from today. Just one more week to Mars!"

"Are all of them fine?" Sam asked. "What was the landing like?"

Susan shrugged. "I don't know. That's all he told us."

*   *   *

Thursday, July 29th, 2029 19:30

Captains Becker and Ravel made an official announcement Thursday evening at dinnertime. Their faces appeared on the NLED walls, replacing a newsreel from Earth nobody was paying attention to.

"You all heard the news by now," Captain Becker said. "Everybody has been asking for information, and Andreas – Captain Bartok of *Pioneer Alpha* – sent details.

"At 13:05 Red Valley local time – around 01:30 for us – *Pioneer Alpha* touched down within six meters of its target location, on the northern edge of the Foundations. Entry burn, heat-shield deceleration, parachute opening and landing-leg deploy were nominal. Due to undiagnosed factors, the ship's position when the parachutes were released was not nominal, but the computer compensated by lengthening the landing burn, and was able to set the ship down on target."

I took a bite of my peanut butter sandwich – I had ground the peanuts myself a couple of nights before. "We finally have proof that manned ZubHabs are capable of landing on Mars."

Meital, sitting across from me, raised her eyebrows. "That's really reassuring, Michael."

The captain continued. "*Pioneer Beta* touched down, sixteen meters off target, at 21:40 local time, just after 10:00 this morning our time. All phases were nominal, other than touchdown, which was, as I said, off target, and also harder than expected. They are still assessing damage. All injuries were minor."

Meital looked alarmed. "Minor injuries? They must have been terrified! What happened?"

The NLED wall's microphone was muted, so Captain Ravel could not have heard her question, but he answered, "*Pioneer Beta* touched down while still moving almost a meter per second. The landing legs absorbed the momentum as they were designed to do in such a contingency, but they suffered partial collapse. At that speed, the fliers would have experienced quite a jolt." He looked up at the camera, appearing to stare at us. "That's why we lie in prone position for landing!"

I dipped my sandwich in the spicey chickpea-and-barley stew my mother had prepared.

Captain Becker cut in. "Captain Grosby and her team have begun work to diagnose the cause of the fault, to make sure the rest of us do not suffer the same anomaly."

"There is more good news," Captain Ravel continued. "The *Pioneer* pair's communications satellite successfully entered Martian orbit."

"How many is that, now?" I asked.

Denver answered. "That's three of five planned for the global network constellation. The first two were already there from when your father's Vanguard group arrived."

"It's a reason to celebrate!" Celina said. She had been eating with us more frequently since our return home, except for those meals when Denver joined her family upstairs. "How many humans are on Mars now?"

"More than fifty," Denver answered. "Eleven from Vanguard" – he shot an uncomfortable look my way – "and a total of forty-three from the two *Pioneer* ships. So, fifty-four people."

"One last thing," Captain Becker announced before concluding the video conference. "Our preparations for landing begin tomorrow. Final spin-down will happen overnight. Please prepare the ships for weightlessness." His image, and Captain Ravel's, disappeared from the NLED walls.

"Another reason to celebrate," Celina repeated, "since tonight is our last night of gravity. Everyone, come upstairs after we finish cleaning. I will get my parents to agree. Denver, bring your guitar. Meital, you too: bring your flute."

My mother stood and began to clear the table. She looked at us and grinned. "I guess you'll need me to convince Jhonathan to officially cancel tonight's school period."

Dr. Jhonathan did cancel lessons and we enjoyed an evening of crowded fun. First, though, we spent an hour stowing every free object and vacuuming every exposed surface. Then we headed upstairs and gathered in the Yellow-Level living room. We talked for a while and munched on popcorn that Dr. Cecylia prepared; then Denver took up his guitar and started strumming. He had finally mastered the Olympians' "Neptunian Moons," and he played it over and over until Meital and Helga learned their own parts. Meital did great on her flute and Helga on her clarinet. The three of them continued playing, while we all sang, until the captain announced curfew.

* * *

Saturday, August 1st, 2029 22:30

After completing the Havdalah ceremony that marked the end of the last Sabbath of our journey, I headed for my bedroom to make a datapad video call to Hannah.

"Hi, sweetie!" Hannah said, smiling broadly. "I was wondering if we would still have a connection tonight."

I smiled back. "The ships are still nearby each other. We'll move apart only after the burn begins tomorrow."

Arjan had spacewalked Friday afternoon, after the overnight spin-down, to gather the tethers that connected our two habitats. Again, nobody from our side went out: after Arjan climbed to *Mars Hope's* pinnacle and latched the ends of the tethers to his spool, Dr. Jhonathan remotely released *Providence's* clasps. We watched the image from Arjan's fleximet camera as he cranked, round and round, slowly rolling the cords onto the spool. "These will be useful on Mars," he had commented.

"I think you're wrong," Hannah said. "My mother fired the RCS thrusters after Arjan came back in, to separate the ships, to avoid risk of collision. You guys are already kilometers away from us."

"A few kilometers are still 'nearby.' We'll be hundreds of kilometers apart in a couple of days, after the water burn."

She looked at me curiously. "I get the part about expelling excess water before we land, to reduce our weight. But burning water? Remind me how that works."

"Each habitat started with fifty cubic meters of water, which we've used, and recycled, and used again. And which provided protection against radiation."

"That part I know."

"Each habitat has around forty-three cubic meters left at this point. Seven of the original fifty got used up over the course of our journey, electrolyzed to replenish oxygen for breathing. We extracted the oxygen and dumped the hydrogen overboard."

"I know about the water being used up. The water tubes in my bedroom wall got emptied out a few months ago. In their place, I got ugly bags of waste packed into the hull by my bed."

"I also have ugly bags in my bedroom's hull." I grinned and tapped the wall cover behind me. "The waste blocks radiation as well as the water did. But there's still a lot of water, and we need to get rid of it, because it's useless extra weight and would mess up our landing."

"And we won't need it on Mars," Hannah agreed, "because they've mined enough Martian water for us already."

"But we won't expel all the water," I said. "We have to carry some down with us in case of emergency."

"In what kind of emergency would water help us? If we don't survive the landing, we won't need water."

"Like if we land safely, but way off course, far from the settlement. We would need our own water to survive. Though I'm not sure how twenty-one people could survive with only three cubic meters." I shuddered at the thought.

Hannah's eyes widened. "G-d forbid something like that happen. Even if we could manage with so little water, what good would it do if we're completely cut off from other supplies? We'd run out of food."

"I asked my mother the same question. She pointed out that each habitat has several months' extra food, enough to last until more supplies could arrive at our location. The Foundation launched two full cargo vessels after us – they're following behind. If we got stranded, the Foundation would direct one of them to land near us."

"That's not something I want to think about!" She shook her head. "But explain how the water gets burned." She tilted her head and smiled alluringly, obviously enjoying the call.

"We need to make final adjustments to our trajectory to line us up for landing at the settlement. And especially to separate our two ships so we don't land at the same time. Altering the trajectory requires an engine burn. But instead of carrying extra fuel, we use the water."

"As fuel for an engine burn?"

"Actually it's the oxidizer. Water is mostly oxygen. The fuel it will oxidize is a powdered mixture of sodium and magnesium, both of which react exothermically with water."

"It sounds explosive!" she exclaimed.

"Yes, but the burn is very slow, and only a small amount of the water actually burns. The rest becomes very hot steam. Most of the thrust comes from the steam's expansion in the engine's nozzle."

"So, you're saying we use a steam engine to slow us down? Sounds very nineteenth century."

I laughed. "That's one way to describe it. A very slow steam engine. It will take forty hours to use up all forty cubic meters of water. I doubt we'll feel any deceleration."

"Disappointing."

We chatted some more until Denver came into the room and reminded me that it was time for lights-out.

"Good luck, Hannah," I said, waving goodbye. "I'll see you on Thursday, G-d willing."

"On Mars! See you on Mars, Michael." She blew a kiss and the screen went blank.

*   *   *

Monday, August 3rd, 2029 15:00

None of us were in the mood for Electrical Engineering class Monday afternoon. Nobody mentioned Simeon's name, but his absence was palpable. Besides that, the water burn, which had started the previous day, signified the beginning of the countdown to landing. Anguish and excitement clashed in our confused hearts. It was hard to concentrate on anything.

Hovering around the table was more challenging than usual, as we had to keep our feet on the floor but not press down too hard. The weak engine burn created a spacecraft environment unlike anything we had experienced during our nine months en route. Though we felt weightless, anything we released in the air did eventually reach the floor. A plate placed on a kitchen counter bounced at first, but then, after a minute or so, settled back down, if air currents did not blow it sideways into the living room. It was the same for our bodies: if we did not brace ourselves gently against the floor, we would ultimately disappear under the table.

Boris had reluctantly replaced his brother as instructor for the class, but had given up on the day's lesson. Instead, he discussed landing preparations. "I expect all of you to volunteer for tomorrow's spacewalk," he said. "We need ten of us to roll up the solar panels, same as when we installed them."

"Denver and I both volunteer," Celina said. Denver nodded.

"Count me in, too," Helga said. "I want to see what Mars – the whole planet – looks like from close up."

"And me," said Sam.

"What about you, Michael?" Boris asked.

It was hard to grasp that ten months had passed since we had climbed up the hull, still back in Earth orbit, each of us unrolling and installing two panels. We had begun this journey with one spacewalk and would finish it with another. "Sure, I'll join," I said with a smile.

The water pipes clicked and clacked at the far end of the living room. The computer emptied another rubber-tube tank, directing its contents through pipes to the Mars-Entry stage's firing engine.

"Pick your buddies," Boris said.

Celina turned to Denver. "Would you be my spacewalk partner?" she asked brightly.

Denver looked to me, then back at her. "Celina, I would love to be your partner. But loyalty demands: Michael has been my buddy all along. I will not abandon him now."

"Thanks, Denver," I said. "We've been a good team." I had not forgotten how he had grabbed me, embraced me, saved me, when I panicked, after the hull breach, on the way up to *Mars Hope*. "We understand each other."

"Celina, you can stick with me again, then," Helga said.

"Okay," Boris continued. "We are six, seven with Omar. Three more will be easy to arrange – I'll talk with Esther. The water burn will end around noon tomorrow; then we can begin. Everyone, meet me in the airlock right after lunch, at 13:30."

*　　*　　*

Tuesday, August 4th, 2029 13:30

"Are we sure it is safe to go out?"

Ten of us were in the airlock, fleximets sealed and inflated, but Helga hesitated. "What if there is a solar storm we do not know about?" she asked over the shared radio connection.

We had lost all external communications when the water burn started and the ships and the communication satellite went their separate ways. The satellite needed to enter an inclined orbit around Mars, and that required a trajectory very different from our own. Without a nearby satellite, we had no way to broadcast anything more than the most basic telemetry, and no antenna capable of receiving data either from Earth or from Mars. Among the data we could not receive were the space-weather reports the Foundation had sent, continually, since launch.

"I don't think we need to worry much," Dr. Esther said. "The chance of a solar flare in any particular direction at any particular time is negligible."

"Yet we were hit by a solar flare in March," Helga protested. "Just for curiosity's sake, what would happen if another one hits while we are outside?"

Captain Becker placed his gloved hand on his daughter's arm. "Certainly, Helga, it would not be good. And it would matter little if we are outside or inside. We have lost most of our water protection. If we reoriented the ship to place the Mars-Entry stage toward the sun where it would absorb most of the radiation, we might miss our entry burn Thursday morning."

"It is true that this is the riskiest part of the journey," Dr. Esther explained. "The lead-up to landing and the landing itself. Our job is to act professionally. And to pray for success – prayer always helps."

Helga shook her head doubtfully as the airlock fans started up.

My mundies squeezed my body as the room emptied of air. Buddies checked each other for bulges; then we collected our Mylar suits and donned them as the captain opened the outer hatch. We prepared to exit, two by two.

"Take these," Boris said, handing me a couple of empty meter-long canisters, each labeled "Advanced Solar Technologies." I latched both to my belt harness; then Boris pushed me toward the exit. I stuck my head out and looked around. The Mylar-suited fliers who had preceded me were climbing along six different ladders, all extending radially from the hatch.

Boris tapped my leg and said, "Michael, take the ladder to your right."

I reached in the direction he indicated, latched a safety cord to the first rung, and pulled myself out. Denver followed the path to my left and caught up quickly. We reached the gaping nozzle of the landing rocket, at the habitat's edge, and paused to wait for instructions.

"Dana," Boris said over the shared radio connection, "confirm isolation of the habitat's panels."

My mother's voice answered. "Confirming. The habitat's solar collection system has been shut down and disconnected from batteries and electrical systems. You are safe to go."

"Everybody, start by unhooking the panel to your right and begin rolling it up as you climb."

I reached for the bottom of the ten-meter-long solar panel. My gaze followed its length, stretching all the way up the hull. The two bottom corners were latched to small hooks that protruded from the ship's PlyShield covering. I gently detached each corner, then began rolling the panel as I ascended.

Denver and I climbed under the bright sun. Protected by the Mylar suit, I barely felt its warmth. I knew that the ladder rungs had heated to several hundred degrees, but my insulated gloves prevented my hands from burning. The whole way up I did all the latching and unlatching with just my left hand, because I had to use my right hand to roll the panel against the hull. That took most of my attention. I tried to roll the panel up like a carpet, but I kept floating away from the hull. Pulling myself back each time slowed my progress. Nearly fifteen minutes passed before we reached the top of the hull where it began curving inward toward the pinnacle.

"Unplug the electric cord before unhooking the top of the panel," Boris instructed. "Make sure you have a good grip – we do not want to lose any of them!"

Unhooking the top of the panel was the most challenging part of the operation. I needed both hands to hold onto the rolled-up panel, to keep it from escaping my grip and floating away. I used my feet to anchor myself to the hull. Only on my third attempt did I manage to unhook the last corner, and I held the freed panel triumphantly in my hands.

As if on cue, Boris said, "Insert the panel into one of the canisters. Then turn yourselves around and start on the panel to your right."

I paused to look up. The sky was full of stars – besides the sun itself, which I was careful to avoid – but there was no red planet. "Disappointing," I said. "I was hoping to see Mars!"

"Everybody will get to see it," Boris said curtly. "If you cannot see the planet now, it will appear by the time we get back down. That will take at least fifteen more minutes, during which time the habitat will rotate another one hundred and eighty degrees. Meanwhile, please keep the shared radio channel free."

I unplugged and unhooked the second panel and began another slow, challenging trek down the hull, again rolling the panel up with my right hand while managing the tethers with my left. All was silent except for the incessant whir of the fleximet's fan. The sun set slowly behind the ship's edge, but we were not cast into the pitch-black darkness I had expected. Instead, a reddish glow illuminated the hull around me.

"Michael, there it is, Mars!" Denver exclaimed. I was still busy unhooking the bottom edge of my second panel. After I managed to get the panel stowed safely in its canister, I stopped to look back up. Looming large over me was our new home. Two days before our arrival, planet Mars did not yet fill the sky, but it was large enough to need me to stretch out my arms if I were to embrace the whole orb.

"Is that Olympus Mons?" Denver asked, pointing. Wispy clouds and dusty haze covered the white polar caps, but the middle of the planet was clear and I could see a roundish darkened area that I supposed was the caldera of the solar system's largest volcano.

"Yes, Denver, that's likely," Dr. Esther confirmed. "I'm not sure what you're looking at, but I can clearly identify Olympus Mons. Also, part of Valles Marineris is just barely visible."

Boris and the captain let us linger a few minutes to watch Mars, until it disappeared beyond the edge of the slowly rotating habitat. At first I tried to identify other landmarks, but soon I stopped just to stare and enjoy the red planet's beauty. As the red glow faded, Denver and I climbed around the hull and through the airlock hatch, dragging the stowed solar panels behind us. Sam and Omar were the last to lose their view of the red planet, so they were last to come in. They thanked Captain Becker profusely for letting them take their time.

The spacewalk was not yet complete: several tasks remained. After Boris checked that all twenty canisters were stowed and latched, he and Esther recharged their oxypacks and prepared to head back outside.

"While we install the parachutes," Dr. Esther said, "refill your air, all of you."

My oxypack registered enough oxygen for at least another hour, so I let the others go first. I stuck my head out the hatch to watch Boris and Dr. Esther extract four disk-shaped packs from compartments at the top of the Mars-Entry stage. Each pack appeared to be fifty or sixty centimeters in diameter and was covered in a striped pattern. It was too dark to make out the colors, though I thought I saw a flash of red as Dr. Esther rounded the ship's edge in the sunlight direction.

Minutes passed. If we had been inside the habitat, we would have watched views projected from their fleximet cameras. Stuck in the airless airlock, we could only listen in to the shared radio channel. Unfortunately, nobody said very much.

Finally, Dr. Esther spoke. "The first parachute is in position. Dana, please close the yellow clasp to lock it into place." Then, a few seconds later, "Perfect! Yellow parachute is installed."

Boris's turn was next. "Close the red clasp," he said; then he confirmed successful installation.

I pictured them climbing up two of the pinnacle ladders, then back down the other two, to bring parachutes to the remaining clasps. Minutes passed; then they confirmed successful installation, to blue and green clasps, respectively. Those same clasps had held the tethers that connected us to *Mars Hope* for most of our ten-month journey, allowing us to spin for artificial gravity. Now the clasps were prepared for their final function: anchoring the parachutes that would slow the habitat during the two-minute second phase of the landing sequence.

"Nice work," Captain Becker said. "Now the last job: bring in the heat shield tethers."

We waited another forty minutes while Boris and Dr. Esther performed the most dangerous part of the spacewalk: removing the tethers that had held the heat shield – the habitat's radiator – in place during those long months. Until they did so, it would be impossible to rotate the shield into its descent position below the habitat. We listened in as they climbed along each tether to where it connected to the heat shield. After unlatching the far end, they used the freed cord to pull themselves back toward the habitat, coiling it up along the way. They brought the coiled cords into the airlock after they completed their last jaunt.

"What will hold the heat shield in place during the Mars Entry burn?" Celina asked, while her father closed the hatch and initiated repressurization.

"The shield is still connected by the main boom," Captain Becker answered. "It should be okay during the burn, even without the stabilization tethers. The acceleration will be minimal."

All tasks complete, Mylar suits stowed, fleximets folded in our hands, we floated up out of the airlock into the Bouchets' living room. The room was remarkably dim: only a few LED lights were lit. With the habitat's solar panels dismantled, we had only the Mars-Entry stage's panels. The habitat's panels had supplied more than half our power during the months in transit; now, without them, we needed to manage with the little that the Mars-Entry stage could provide.

"I remind you all," Captain Becker said, "essential electric systems only, until we land! Then we will hook up to the settlement's nuclear reactor and we can turn all our lights back on."

* * *

Wednesday, August 5th, 2029 19:30

It was the last dinner of our journey and we invited the Meyers and Omar to join us. I baked a dozen pita breads while Meital and Ruby made hummus. Together with my mother's spicy bean stew, we had a meal as varied and tasty as any since the loss of our fresh vegetables. Because the table had been stowed for landing, we had nowhere to put the dishes other than our laps. We Velcroed our bowls of stew to our thighs in the usual manner, but we held the pita sandwiches in our hands.

"I can't believe landing is tomorrow," Shirel said. "I'm nervous. And I'm restless!"

"We've been waiting ten months," Meital said. "It's about time we finally reach the end."

"I'm a little amazed we managed to get everything packed away," I said. "What's with the chickens? How did you prepare them for landing?"

"Each is in an airtent with food and water," Ruby said. "They sure weren't happy today when Meital and I moved them."

"Wait 'til tomorrow," Meital added. "When we seal their tents just before landing. They're really not going to like that."

"We'll sedate them before we seal the tents," Dr. Jhonathan said. "They won't have much time to complain. It will make the landing easier."

"Anything left to lock down?" Dr. Esther asked, turning to Sam. "What did you guys forget today?"

Sam, looking affronted, answered, "Just the kitchen, Mom. We can wash and stow the remaining dishes in the morning."

"Dr. Esther," I said, "I think we managed to get everything else ready. We checked all the drawers and cabinets in the bedrooms. Everything's in place."

"How about your sourdough cultures?" Denver asked. "Don't forget them."

"Sealed and stowed. They should be fine that way for a day."

"I want everyone to have a good night's sleep," my mother said. "Get to bed early."

"Mom, how are we going to be able to fall asleep tonight?" Shirel protested. "We're all too excited."

"That's exactly my point. If you are in bed by nine, perhaps you'll fall asleep by eleven."

* * *

Thursday, August 6th, 2029 12:05

"Our last dance!" Shirel tapped her datapad to start the music, the aptly named "Dancing on Mars," another of the Olympians' songs. Denver, Sam, and I watched from the side as the six girls joined hands in a circle. The Mars Entry burn was about to commence: the computer would ignite the engine to slow our ship by almost six thousand kilometers per hour. That would prevent us from disintegrating when we slammed into the Martian atmosphere a few hours later. This would be the longest firing – other than the forty-hour water burn – since the Mars-transit injection that had thrown us out of Earth orbit back in November. That burn had accelerated us to send us on our way; this one would decelerate us for arrival.

"Commencing in thirty seconds," Captain Becker announced over the public address speakers.

We counted down. The NLED walls were dark – not enough electricity remained to power them – so we would have no camera view, but the captain had permitted us to blast music from the wall speakers for the duration of the twenty-four-minute burn.

"Five – four – three – two – one – ignition!" we all called out. The walls vibrated; then the floor slowly came up to meet us. The girls began their dancing, spinning round and round excitedly. The acceleration was stronger than it had been during the course correction a month and a half earlier. Since we had expelled most of our water, the ship was lighter, so the same engine force had greater effect. Still, the girls could do little more than shuffle sideways with their knees bent, the gravity being so low – still less than an eighth of Earth's.

The next song in the girls' playlist was the famous twentieth-century ballad "Crocodile Rock." The girls were having too much fun, so I acquiesced and joined in, grabbing my sisters' hands. I was careful not to jump or bounce because I did not want to smash my head into the ceiling. But I danced and we shuffled, song after song. Eventually Denver took Celina's hand, and Sam grabbed Ruby and

Susan, and we laughed and sang, our mood brighter than it had been in months. We were on the seventh or eighth song when the burn ended, gravity ceased, and we all crashed into the walls.

"The engine performed nominally," Captain Becker announced over the NLED walls' speakers. "We are analyzing the resulting trajectory. Stand by for confirmation."

My thoughts raced as I imagined the various disasters that could befall us if we missed our designated path into the atmosphere. We could fly by Mars, like Uncle Aviel's spacecraft had done, or skim the atmosphere and bounce off into permanent solar orbit. We could shoot straight down and impact the surface at dozens of kilometers per second. We might even land successfully, but be off-target by half a planet.

Finally, the captain stated, "The computer confirms, based on starfield analysis, that we are in position for a nominal Martian atmosphere entry in one hundred and fifty-nine minutes."

I sighed in relief.

Celina grasped Denver's hands in hers. "We will be on the Martian surface in three hours! Are you ready?"

Denver grinned. "I'm ready. Totally ready!"

I shook my head. "How can anyone really be ready to land on a new planet? It's too momentous to contemplate."

"I'm ready," Ruby said. "Momentous or not, I want real gravity."

"Me, too," said Meital. "Gravity, room to run, real-life vistas. I only wish Dad were there to greet us."

I nodded. "He's there. We'll visit his grave. At least we'll have that."

"Ten seconds to stage separation," the captain announced.

I counted down. After the engine burn, the Mars-Entry stage was useful only for the electric power that its solar panels supplied. But we could not land while still joined to the stage, so we had no choice but to give it up and rely on the ship's batteries. I expected to see or feel some indication that the stage had been jettisoned, but there was none, other than the captain's quiet confirmation.

"The stage has separated," he said. "We are now flying independently. Restrict all electricity use until further notice – we'll have limited power until after we land. Stand by for landing-engine test firing."

My mind raced again. The last phase of the complex landing sequence was the firing of the habitat's six landing rockets. In the thin Martian atmosphere, the parachutes would slow us only partially, nowhere near enough for a safe landing. If the rockets did not fire at the exact designated time, one minute before landing, we would slam into the ground and smash into thousands of pieces. The landing rockets had last fired on a test stand back on Earth. I hoped nothing had broken!

"Engines prepped for firing. Stand by."

I thought I felt the ship vibrate for a moment, but I might have imagined it. My feet did hit the floor, though, so perhaps we had indeed experienced a brief, miniscule acceleration.

"Test firing complete. The computer reports all six engines ignited, burned for half a second, and produced nominal thrust."

* * *

Thursday, August 6th, 2029 13:20

We listened, tensely, as Captain Becker announced that he had begun rotating the heat shield into its Mars-entry position underneath the habitat. Throughout the journey, the heat shield had been located by the habitat's side. There, it pointed away from the sun most of the time, to radiate the ship's excess heat without itself heating up in sunlight. During landing, by contrast, it had to be positioned directly below us, to shield us from the high temperature of the shock wave we would create as we plummeted through the atmosphere. Otherwise our ship would burn up and disintegrate. The heat shield had not been able to rotate into landing position as long as the Mars-Entry stage was still attached: only after jettisoning that stage could we move it into place. This was all part of a specific sequence of events that had to occur, in proper order, in the final hours before landing. First the entry burn, then stage separation, then the test firing of the engines, then the shield. At that point, if anything went wrong, we would be in deep trouble. Only a last-minute spacewalk might save us.

"Esther and Boris, confirm airlock purge."

"Confirming," Dr. Esther answered. "The airlock is empty of air. We have donned our Mylar suits and are ready to exit if necessary."

They were prepared for the nightmarish scenario in which the seventeen-meter-wide heat shield needed to be rotated or locked into place manually. They were ready to frantically fix anything that might block successful deployment.

"Hatch is open and I can see Mars below us," Boris said. Then, "The shield is rotating."

I sighed in relief, but was again disappointed that the NLED walls showed no camera view.

"The computer reports rotation is complete. Visual confirmation, please, Esther."

"Confirming. The shield appears to be in the correct position."

"Struts should now be locked into place. Please confirm!"

We waited anxiously for Dr. Esther's answer. Finally, she said, "All seems to be fine. We're closing the hatch and repressurizing the airlock."

*   *   *

Thursday, August 6th, 2029 15:15

Not two hours later, we lay on our bunks inside our bedrolls. As usual, the bedrolls were latched to the beds, but, unusually, we all wore our fleximets, sealed and pressurized. This was our landing position: each of us lying prone on a soft mattress. The mattresses were designed not only to offer a good night's sleep, but also to absorb the immense forces of deceleration. We would start feeling those forces as our ship careened, a few minutes later, deep into the Martian atmosphere. Moving at thousands of kilometers per hour, we would hit the atmosphere like a rock hitting water. The sparse atmosphere would slow us so rapidly that we would feel four Earth gravities. Those forces would crush our bones if we were not lying down.

My fleximet's radio was tuned to the shared channel. "Roll call!" Dr. Jhonathan declared. "When I call your name, confirm that your fleximet is sealed and pressurized, and that you are lying prone and secured."

In the terrifying scenario where we lost cabin pressure during entry, our fleximets – if sealed correctly – would keep us breathing, and we might even survive the landing.

"Dietrich."

"Confirmed, both Cecylia and I."

"Helga."

"Confirmed!" she yelled in an inappropriately enthusiastic tone.

He continued down the list.

"Michael!"

"Confirmed," I said, my voice cracking. "I'm in my bunk and my fleximet is pressurized."

"Denver!"

"Confirmed. I'm here with Michael."

Last to be polled were the Bouchets, who verified that Jasmine and Sophie were secured safely between them, the whole family lying together in the master bed on Mauve Level. Everyone was in place.

We would be on the surface of Mars in under fifteen minutes. What would our new lives be like, after so many months confined to the spaceship? How long before we moved into the underground bunkers my father had given his life to build? Certainly not right away: we would need to complete the work he and his colleagues had begun. The trenches had been dug, but hundreds of meters remained to be enclosed.

Dr. Jhonathan announced, "Thirty seconds to atmosphere contact!"

Isolated in my bunk, I counted down the seconds, but stayed silent: I was afraid to disturb the shared connection. Twenty seconds. *G-d, protect us*, I prayed. *Bring us safely through the atmosphere; grant us a successful landing.* Ten seconds. *Bless us so that we can sanctify You and bring holiness to a new planet.*

Dr. Jhonathan counted down the final seconds. "Five – four – three – two – one – contact!"

Nothing happened for a few moments. But then a subtle vibration shook through the ship.

May we all survive this!

The subtle vibration became turbulent shaking. I was no longer weightless.

What would life be like after landing? Would we enjoy the manual labor on the Martian surface? How long would it take to complete the vaults? How difficult, to transfer the life-support systems, the kitchens, the toilets – everything! – from the ships to our temporary underground home?

All my friends on the expedition's other vessels – I looked forward to seeing them after so many months apart. We would work together on the building project, outside, under the sun. *But Simeon will not be with us. And Adele, just born, is already gone.*

The fierce shaking disturbed my reverie. I began feeling very, very heavy, as the force of deceleration pressed me into my mattress. Denver's bunk, above me, rattled threateningly.

Don't fall on me!

Dr. Jhonathan, trying to reassure, called out, "The vibrations are normal and expected."

The g-forces increased inexorably and it took effort to breathe. I imagined the scorching shock wave our heat shield created as it smashed through the Martian air. I touched the empty pipe in the wall next to me; even through my glove I could feel it getting hot. Mars, though, would be cold.

"Two minutes to parachute deploy! Hold on – we're almost through this."

The ship was rocking from side to side, vibrating violently.

Mars is cold and empty. My father was supposed to be there to greet us when we land. Now he is gone. It will be so lonely without him.

"One minute to parachutes!"

So much to develop. A new branch of humanity! A huge weight of responsibility on our shoulders.

"Ten seconds. Brace yourselves!"

I took a breath and counted down. The four parachutes opened and the entire habitat lurched. The vibration ceased but the rocking intensified as the parachutes filled with air.

My friends and I are about to begin building a whole new world! But without my father.

It wasn't supposed to be this way.

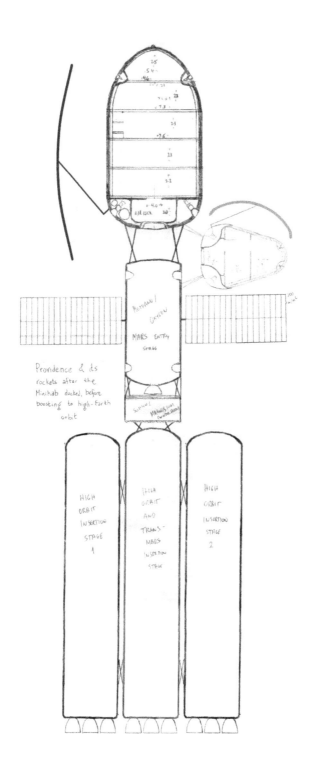

Red Valley

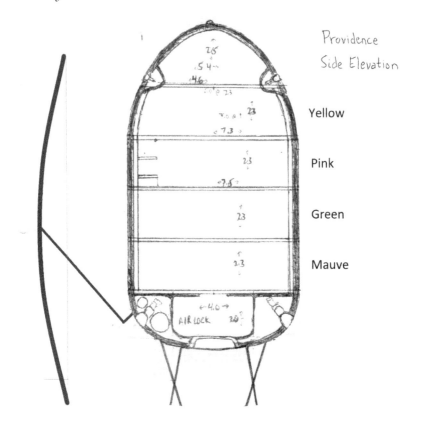

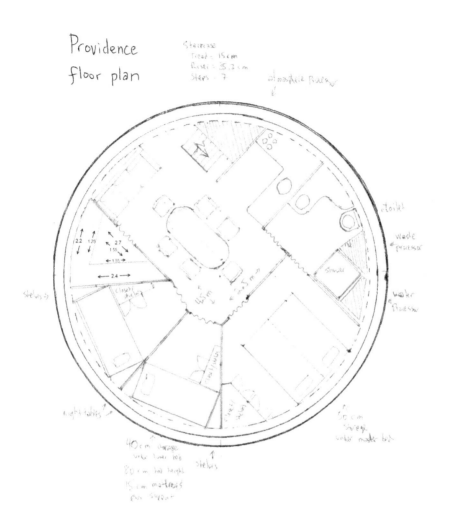

Red Valley

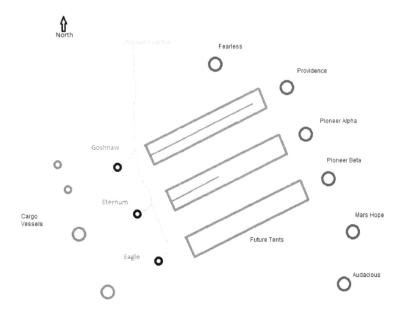

"Red Valley" Site Map

Acknowledgements

These eight years, spent preparing for this endeavor and describing the journey, have been immeasurably challenging, and I owe debts of gratitude to many. To Leon Murke and Jake Berger, for developing all those technologies, and for inspiring my generation and me – there would be no story without their leadership. To Professor James Head of Brown University, whose Interplanetary Geology courses excited so many; and to Robert Zubrin, whose seminal book, *The Case for Mars*, described the "habcraft" that served as the basis for the ZubHab's design. To my Talmud learning partner, who helps me grow, sharpens my mind, and inspired this writing project. To my siblings, always there for me, and to my friends who accompanied me throughout. To my mother, who taught me gratitude, and has never stopped pushing me to grow. To the woman I eventually married – I have no better friend. To my father – I wish he were still alive to see this accomplishment; I know he would be proud. And most of all, to G-d, Who has kept us healthy, and guided our hands, and sustained us; Who continues to bless us, and always awaits our return.

Printed in the USA
CPSIA information can be obtained
at www.ICGtesting.com
CBHW031248280524
9177CB00001B/2

9 789659 305537